RANDOM
HOUSE

LARGE
PRINT

RANDOM
HOUSE
LARGE
PRINT

BLACK
LEOPARD
RED
WOLF

MARLON JAMES

BLACK LEOPARD RED WOLF

RANDOM HOUSE
LARGE PRINT

Copyright © 2019 by Marlon James

Published in the United States of America by Random House Large Print in association with Riverhead Books, an imprint of Penguin Random House LLC, New York.

Cover illustration: Pablo Gerardo Camacho
Cover design: Helen Yentus
Photograph of the author © Mark Seliger
Maps by Marlon James

The Library of Congress has established a Cataloging-in-Publication record for this title.

ISBN: 978-1-9848-8290-5

www.penguinrandomhouse.com/large-print-format-books

FIRST LARGE PRINT EDITION

Printed in the United States of America

10 9 8 7 6 5 4 3 2 1

This Large Print edition published in accord with the standards of the N.A.V.H.

To Jeff, for quartermoon and a million other things

CONTENTS

Contents

THE SAND SEA

UBANGTA RIVER

1

2

FOREST LANDS

5

TWO SISTERS RIVER

6

7

HILLS OF
ENCHANTMENT

3

LAKE ABBAR

4

8

LOWER UBANGTA

THE DARKLANDS

9

10

THE
MWERU

UWOMOWOMOWOMOWO VALLEY

WHITE LAKE

11

RED LAKE

KEGERE RIVER

12

13

THE
BLOOD
SWAMP

N

KEY

1. FASISI
2. MANTHA
3. THE PURPLE CITY
4. JUBA
5. KU
6. GANGATOM
7. LUALA LUALA
8. KONGOR
9. MITU
10. MALAKAL
11. DOLINGO
12. KALINDAR
13. WAKADISHU
14. NIGIKI
15. LISH

THE
NORTH
LANDS

14

15

THOSE WHO APPEAR
IN THIS ACCOUNT

IN JUBA, KU, GANGATOM

KWASH DARA, son of Kwash Netu; King of the North Kingdom, aka the Spider King

TRACKER, hunter known by no other name

HIS FATHER

HIS MOTHER

BELOVED UNCLE, a great chief of the Ku

KU, a river tribe and territory

GANGATOM, a river tribe, territory, and enemy of the Ku

LUALA LUALA, a river tribe and territory north of the Ku

ABOYAMI, a father

AYODELE, his son

WITCHMAN, necromancer of the Ku

ITAKI, a river witch

KAVA/ASANI, boy of the Ku

LEOPARD, shape-shifting hunter known by a few other names

YUMBOES, bush fairies and guardians of children

THE SANGOMA, an antiwitch

THE MINGI, who are:

    Giraffe Boy

    Smoke Girl

    Albino

    Ball Boy

    The joined twins

ASANBOSAM, monstrous eater of human flesh

THE GANGATOM CHIEF

IN MALAKAL

THE AESI, chancellor of Kwash Dara

BUNSHI/POPELE, river jengu, mermaid, shape-shifter

SOGOLON, the Moon Witch

SADOGO, of the Ogos, tall, mighty men who are not giants

AMADU KASAWURA, a slaver

BIBI, his manservant

NSAKA NE VAMPI, a mercenary

NYKA, a mercenary

FUMELI, the Leopard's bowman

BELEKUN THE BIG, a fat elder

ADAGAGI THE WISE, a wise elder

AMAKI THE SLIPPERY, an elder nobody knows

NOOYA, a woman possessed by the lightning bird

THE BULTUNGI, avengers

ZOGBANU, trolls originally from the Blood Swamp

VENIN, a girl raised to be food for the Zogbanu

CHIPFALAMBULA, a great fish

GHOMMIDS, sometimes-nice forest creatures

EWELE, a vicious ghommid

EGBERE, his cousin, vicious when hungry

ANJONU, spirit of the Darklands who reads hearts

THE MAD MONKEY, a deranged primate

IN KONGOR

BASU FUMANGURU, elder of the North Kingdom, murdered

HIS WIFE, murdered

HIS SONS, murdered

THE SEVEN WINGS, mercenaries

KAFUTA, lord of a house

MISS WADADA, owner of a brothel

EKOIYE, a whore who loves civet musk

THE BUFFALO, a very smart buffalo

KONGORI CHIEFTAIN ARMY, local constables

MOSSI OF AZAR, third prefect of the Kongori chieftain army

MAZAMBEZI, a prefect

RED OGO, another Ogo

BLUE OGO, another Ogo

THE MASTER OF ENTERTAINMENTS, the Ogo fight master

LALA, his slave

THE MAWANA WITCHES, dirt mermaids, aka mud jengu

TOKOLOSHE, a small gremlin who makes himself invisible

IN DOLINGO AND THE MWERU

OLD MAN, lord of a hut and southern griot

THE QUEEN OF DOLINGO, as it says

HER CHANCELLOR

DOLINGON SLAVE BOY

THE WHITE SCIENTISTS, darkest of the necromancers
and alchemists

BAD IBEJI, a malformed twin

JAKWU, white guard for King Batuta

IPUNDULU, vampire lightning bird

SASABONSAM, winged brother of Asanbosam

ADZE, vampire and bug swarm

ELOKO, grass troll and cannibal

LISSISOLO OF AKUM, sister of Kwash Dara, nun of the
divine sisterhood

SHADOWINGS, night demons who serve the Aesi

IN MITU

IKEDE, a southern griot

KAMANGU, a son

NIGULI, a son

KOSU, a son

LOEMBE, a son

NKANGA, a son

KHAMSEEN, a daughter

IN THE MALANGIKA AND THE SOUTH KINGDOM

A YOUNG WITCH

A MERCHANT

HIS WIFE

HIS SON

KAMIKWAYO, a white scientist turned monster

1

A DOG, A CAT, A WOLF, AND A FOX

Bi oju ri enu a pamo.

ONE

The child is dead. There is nothing left to know.

I hear there is a queen in the south who kills the man who brings her bad news. So when I give word of the boy's death, do I write my own death with it? Truth eats lies just as the crocodile eats the moon, and yet my witness is the same today as it will be tomorrow. No, I did not kill him. Though I may have wanted him dead. Craved for it the way a glutton craves goat flesh. Oh, to draw a bow and fire it through his black heart and watch it explode black blood, and to watch his eyes for when they stop blinking, when they look but stop seeing, and to listen for his voice croaking and hear his chest heave in a death rattle saying, Look, my wretched spirit leaves this most wretched of bodies, and to smile at such tidings and dance at such a loss. Yes, I glut at the conceit of it. But no, I did not kill him.

Bi oju ri enu a pamo.

Not everything the eye sees should be spoken by the mouth.

This cell is larger than the one before. I smell the dried blood of executed men; I hear their ghosts still screaming. Your bread carries weevils, and your water carries the piss of ten and two guards and the goat they fuck for sport. Shall I give you a story?

I am just a man who some have called a wolf. The child is dead. I know the old woman brings you different news. Call him murderer, she says. Even though my only sorrow is that I did not kill her. The redheaded one said the child's head was infested with devils. If you believe in devils. I believe in bad blood. You look like a man who has never shed blood. And yet blood sticks between your fingers. A boy you circumcised, a young girl too small for your big . . . Look how that thrills you. Look at you.

I will give you a story.

It begins with a Leopard.

And a witch.

Grand Inquisitor.

Fetish priest.

No, you will not call for the guards.

My mouth might say too much before they club it shut.

Regard yourself. A man with two hundred cows who delights in a patch of boy skin and the koo of a girl who should be no man's woman. Because that is what you seek, is it not? A dark little thing that cannot be found in thirty sacks of gold or two hundred cows or two hundred wives. Something that you have lost—no, it was taken from you. That light, you see it and you want it—not light from the sun, or from the thunder god in the night sky, but light with no blemish, light in a boy who has no knowledge of women, a girl you bought for marriage, not because you need a wife, for you have two hundred cows, but a wife you can tear open, because you search for it in holes, black holes, wet holes, undergrown holes for the light that vampires look for, and you will have it, you will dress it up in ceremony, circumcision for the boy, consummation for the girl, and when they shed blood, and spit, and sperm and piss you leave it all on your skin, to go to the iroko tree and use any hole you find.

The child is dead, and so is everyone.

I walked for days, through swarms of flies in the Blood Swamp and skin-slicing rocks in salt plains, through day and night. I walked as far south as Omororo and did not know or care. Men detained me as a beggar, took me for a thief, tortured me as a traitor, and when news of the dead child reached your kingdom, arrested me as a murderer. Did you know there were five men in my cell? Four nights ago. The scarf around my neck belongs to the only man who left on two feet. He might even see from his right eye again one day.

The other four. Make record as I have said it.

Old men say night is a fool. It will not judge, but whatever comes it will not warn. The first came for my bed. I woke up to my own death rattle, and it was a man, crushing my throat. Shorter than an Ogo, but taller than a horse. Smelled like he butchered a goat. Grabbed me by the neck and hoisted me up in the air while the other men kept quiet. I tried to pull his fingers but a devil was in his grip. Kicking his chest was kicking stone. He held me up as if admiring a precious jewel. I kneed him in the jaw so hard his teeth sliced his tongue. He dropped me, and I charged for his balls like a bull. He fell, I grabbed his knife, razor sharp, and cut his throat. The second grabbed for my arms, but I was naked and slippery. The knife—my knife—I rammed it between his ribs and heard his heart pop. The third man danced with his feet and fists, like a night fly, whistling like a mosquito. Made a fist I did, then stuck two fingers out, like rabbit ears. Jabbed his left eye in the quick and pulled the whole thing out. He screamed. Watching him bawl on the floor, searching for his eye, I forgot the other two men. The fat one behind me, he swung, I ducked, he tripped, he fell, I jumped, I grabbed the rock that was my pillow and bashed his head until his face smelled fleshy.

The last man was a boy. He cried. He was too shaken to beg for his life. I told him to be a man in his next life, for he is less than a worm in this one, and flung the knife right into his neck. His blood hit the floor before his knees. I let the half-blind man live because we need stories in order to live, don't we, priest? Inquisitor. I don't know what to call you.

But these are not your men. Good. Then you have no death song to sing to their widows.

You have come for a story and I am moved to talk, so the gods have smiled on both of us.

There was a merchant in the Purple City, who said he lost his wife. She went missing with five gold rings, ten and two pairs of earrings, twenty and two bracelets, and ten and nine anklets. **It is said you have a nose for finding what would rather stay lost,** he said. I was near twenty in years, and long banished from my father's house. The man thought I was some kind of hound, but I said yes, it has been said that I have a nose. He threw me his wife's undergarment. Her trail was so faint it was almost dead. Maybe she knew that one day men would come hunting, for she had a hut in three villages and no one could tell which one she lived in. In each house was a girl who looked exactly like her and even answered to her name. The girl in the third house invited me in and pointed to a stool for me to sit. She asked if I was thirsty and reached for a jug of masuku beer before I said yes. Let me remind you that my eyes are ordinary but it has been said that I have a nose. So when she brought over the mug of beer I had already smelled the poison she put in it, a wife's poison called cobra spit that loses taste once you mix it with water. She gave me the mug and I took it, grabbed her hand, and bent it behind her back. I put the mug to her lips and forced it between her teeth. Her tears ran down and I took away the mug.

She took me to her mistress, who lived in a hut by the river. My husband beat me so hard that my child fell out, the mistress said. I have five gold rings, ten and two pairs of earrings, twenty and two bracelets, and ten and nine anklets, which I will give you, as well as a night in my bed. I took four anklets, and I took her back to her husband because I wanted his money more than her jewelry. Then I told her to have the woman from the third hut make him masuku beer.

The second story.

My father came home one night smelling of a fisher woman. She was on him, and so was the wood of a Bawo board. And the blood of a man not my father. He played a game against a binga, a Bawo master, and lost. The binga demanded his winnings, and my father grabbed the Bawo board and smashed it on the master's forehead. He said he was at an inn far away so that he could drink, tickle women, and play Bawo. My father beat the man until he stopped moving and then left the bar. But no stink of sweat was on him, not much dust, no beer on his breath, nothing. He had not been in a bar but in the den of an opium monk.

So Father came into the house and shouted for me to come from the grain shed I was living in, for by now he had banished me from the house.

"Come, my son. Sit and play Bawo with me," he said.

The board was on the floor, many balls missing. Too many for a good game. But my father was looking to win, not to play.

Surely you know Bawo, priest; if not I must

explain it to you. Four rows of eight holes on the board, each player gets two rows. Thirty and two seeds for each player, but we had fewer than that, I cannot remember how much. Each player puts six seeds in the nyumba hole, but my father placed eight. I would have said, Father, are you playing the game southern style, eight instead of six? But my father never speaks when he can punch, and he has punched me for less. Every time I placed a seed he would say, Capture and take my seeds. But he was hungry for drink and asked for palm wine. My mother brought him water, and he pulled her by the hair, slapped her twice, and said, Your skin will forget these marks by sunset. My mother would not give him the pleasure of her tears, so she left and came back with wine. I smelled for poison, and would have let it be. But while he was beating my mother for using witchcraft to either slow her aging or hurry his, he missed the game. I sowed my seeds, two to a hole right to the end of the board, and captured his seeds. This did not please my father.

"You took the game to mtaji phase," he said.

"No, we are just beginning," I said.

"How dare you speak to me with disrespect? Call me Father when you talk to me," he said.

I said nothing and blocked him on the board.

He had no seeds left in his inner row and could not move.

"You have cheated," he said. "There are more than thirty and two seeds on your board."

I said, "Either you are blind from wine or you cannot count. You sowed seeds, and I captured them. I sowed seeds all along my row and built a wall that you have no seed to break."

He punched me in the mouth before I could say another word. I fell off the stool and he grabbed the Bawo board to hit me the way he hit the binga. But my father was drunk and slow, and I had been watching the Ngolo masters practice their fight craft by the river. He swung the board and seeds went scattering in the sky. I flipped backways three times like I saw them do and crouched down like a waiting cheetah. He looked around for me as if I had vanished.

"Come out, you coward. Coward like your mother," he said. "This is why it brings me joy to disgrace her. First I will beat you, then I will beat her for raising you, then I will leave a mark so that both of you remember that she raised a boy to be a mistress of men," he said.

Fury is a cloud that leaves my mind empty and my heart black. I jumped and kicked my legs out in the air, each time higher.

"Now he hops like an animal," he said.

He charged at me but I was no longer a boy. I charged at him in the small house, dived to the ground with my hands, turned my hands to feet, and flipped up, spun my whole body like a wheel with my legs in the air, spun towards him and locked him with my two feet around his neck and brought him down hard. His head smacked the ground so loud that my mother outside heard the crack. She ran inside and screamed.

"Get away from him, child. You have ruined both of us."

I looked at her and spat. Then I left.

There are two endings to this story. In the first, my legs locked around his neck and broke it when I brought him down to the ground. He died right there on the floor and my mother gave me five cowries and sorghum wrapped in palm leaf and sent me away. I told her that I would leave with nothing he owned, not even clothes.

In the second ending, I do not break his neck, but he still lands on his head, which cracks and bleeds. He wakes up an imbecile. My mother gives me five cowries and a sorghum wrapped in banana leaf and says, Leave this place, your uncles are all worse than he.

My name was my father's possession, so I left it by his gate. He dressed in nice robes, silks from lands he had never seen, sandals from men who owed him money, anything to make him forget that he came from a tribe in the river valley. I left my father's house wanting nothing that reminded me of him. The old ways called out to me before I even left and I wanted to take every piece of garment off. To smell like a man, with funk and stink, not the perfume of city women and eunuchs. People would look at me with the scorn they save for swamp folk. I would step into the city, or the bedchamber, headfirst like a prized beast. The lion needs no robe and neither does the cobra. I would go to Ku, where my father came from, even if I did not know the way.

My name is Tracker. Once I had a name, but have long forgotten it.

The third story.

A queen of a kingdom in the West said she would pay me well to find her King. Her court thought she was mad, for the King was dead, drowned five years now, but I had no problem with finding the dead. I took her down payment and left for where those dead by drowning lived.

I kept walking until I came to an old woman by a river with a tall stick sitting at the banks. Her hair white at the sides, her head bald at the top. Her face had lines like paths in the forest and her yellow teeth meant her breath was foul. The stories say she rises each morning youthful and beautiful, blooms full and comely by midday, ages to a crone by nightfall, and dies at midnight to be born again the next hour. The hump in her back was higher than her head, but her eyes twinkled, so her mind was sharp. Fish swam right up to the point of the stick but never went beyond.

"Why have you come to this place?" she asked.

"This is the way to Monono," I said.

"Why have you come to this place? A living man?"

"Life is love and I have no love left. Love has drained itself from me, and run to a river like this one."

"It's not love you have lost, but blood. I will let you

pass. But when I lay with a man I live without dying for seventy moons."

So I fucked the crone. She lay on her back by the bank, her feet in the river. She was nothing but bones and leather, but I was hard for her and full with vigor. Something was swimming between my legs that felt like fishes. Her hand touched my chest and my white clay stripes turned into waves around my heart. I thrust in and out of her, unnerved by her silence. In the dark I felt she was getting younger even though she was getting older. Flame spread inside me, spread to the tips of my fingers and the tip of me inside her. Air gathered around water, water gathered around air and I yelled, and pulled out, and rained on her belly, her arms, and her breasts. A shudder ran through me five times. She was still a crone, but I was not angry. She scooped my rain off her chest and flicked it off in the river. At once fish leapt up and dived in, leapt up again. This was a night when dark ate the moon, but the fishes had a light within them. The fishes had the head, arms, and breasts of women.

"Follow them," she said.

I followed them through day and night, and day again. Sometimes the river was as low as my ankle. Sometimes the river was as high as my neck. Water washed all the white from my body, leaving just my face. The fishwomen, womenfish, took me down the river for days and days and days until we came to a place I cannot describe. It was either a wall of river, which stood firm even though I could push my hand through it, or the river had bent itself downward and I could still walk, my feet touching the ground, my body standing without falling.

Sometimes the only way forward is through. So I walked through. I was not afraid.

I cannot tell you if I stopped breathing or if I was breathing underwater. But I kept walking. River fish surrounded me as if asking me my business. I kept walking, the water around me waving my hairs loose, rinsing under my arms. Then I came upon something I have never seen in all the kingdoms. A castle in a clear field of grass made of stone, two, three, four, five, six floors high. At each corner, a tower with a dome roof, also in stone. On each floor, windows cut out of the stone, and below the windows, a floor with gold railings called a terrace. And from the building was a hall that connected it to another building and another hall that connected it to another building so that there were four joined castles in a square.

None of the castles were as huge as the first, and the last was a ruin. When the water disappeared and left stone, grass, and sky I cannot tell you. There were trees in a straight line as far as I could see, gardens in squares, and flowers in circles. Not even the gods had a garden like this. It was after the noon and the kingdom was empty. In the evening, which came quick, breezes shifted up and down, and winds went rough past me, like fat men in a hurry. By sunset men and women and beasts were moving in and out of sight, appearing in the shadows, disappearing in the last sunrays, appearing again. I sat on the steps of the largest castle and watched them as sun fled the dark. Men, walking beside women, and children who looked like men, and women who looked like children. And men who were blue, and women who were green, and children who were yellow, with red eyes and gills in the neck. And creatures with grass hair, and horses with six legs, and packs of abadas with zebra legs, a donkey's back, and a rhinoceros's horn on the forehead running with more children.

A yellow child walked up to me and said, "How did you get here?"

"I came through the river."

"And the Itaki let you?"

"I don't know of Itaki, only an old woman who smelled like moss."

The yellow child turned red and his eyes went white. His parents came and fetched him. I got up and climbed the steps twenty feet into the castle, where more men, women, children, and beasts laughed, and talked, and chatted, and gossiped. At the end of the hallway was a wall with panels of wars and warriors cast in bronze, one I recognized as the battle of the midlands where four thousand men were killed, and another from the battle of the half-blind Prince, who led his entire army over a cliff he mistook for a hill. At the bottom of the wall was a bronze throne that made the man in it look as small as a baby.

"Those are not the eyes of a God-fearing man," he said. I knew it was the King, for who else would it be?

"I have come to take you back to the living," I said.

"Even the dead lands have heard of you, Tracker. But you have wasted your time and risked your life for nothing. I see no reason to return, no reason for me, and no reason for you."

"I have no reason for anything. I find what people have lost and your Queen has lost you."

The King laughed.

"Here we are in Monono, you the only living soul, and yet the most dead man in this court," he said.

Inquisitor, I wish people would understand that I have no time for this argument. There is nothing I fight for and nothing I will fight over, so waste none of my time starting fights. Raise your fist and I will break it. Raise your tongue and I will cut it out of your mouth.

The King had no guards in the throne room, so I stepped towards him, watching the crowd watching me. He was neither excited nor afraid, but had the blankness of face that said, These are the things that must happen to you. Four steps led up to the platform where his throne sat. Two lions by his feet, so still I couldn't tell if they were flesh, spirit, or stone. He had a round face with a chin peeking below the chin, big black eyes, a flat nose with two rings, and a thin mouth, as if he had eastern blood. He wore a gold crown over a white scarf that hid his hair, a white coat with silver birds, and a purple bib over the coat trimmed also in gold. I could have picked him up with my finger.

I walked right up to his throne. The lions did not stir. I touched the brass arm, cut like an upturned lion's paw, and thunder rumbled above me, heavy, slow, sounding black and leaving a rotten smell on the wind. Up in the ceiling, nothing. I was still looking up when the King jammed a dagger into my palm so hard that it dug into the chair arm and stuck.

I screamed; he laughed and eased back into his throne.

"You may think the underworld honors its promise, to be the land free from pain and suffering, but that's a promise made to the dead," he said.

Nobody else laughed with him, but they watched.

He watched me with a suspicious eye and stroked his chin, as I grabbed the dagger and pulled it out, the pull making me yell. The King jumped when I grabbed him, but I cut into the tail of his coat and ripped a piece off. He laughed while I wrapped my hand. I punched him full in the face, and only then did the crowd murmur. I heard deathly footsteps coming towards me and turned around. The crowd stopped. No, they were held back. Nothing on their faces, neither anger nor fear. And then the crowd jumped back as one, looking past me to the King, standing, the bloody lion's paw in his hand. The King threw the paw in the air, right up to the ceiling, and the crowd oohed. The paw never came down. Some at the back started to run. Some in the crowd shouted, some screamed. Man trampled woman who trampled child. The King kept laughing. Then a creak, then a rip, then a break, as if gods of the sky were ripping the roof open. Omoluzu, somebody said.

Omoluzu. Roof walkers, night demons from an age before this age.

"They have tasted your blood, Tracker. Omoluzu will never stop following you."

I grabbed his hand and sliced it. He bawled like a river girl while the ceiling started to shift, sounding as if it was cracking and breaking and hissing, but staying still. I held his hand over mine and collected his blood while he slapped and punched like a little boy, trying to pull away. The first shape rose out of the ceiling when I threw the King's blood in the air.

"Now both of our fates are mixed," I said.

His smile vanished, his jaw dropped, and his eyes popped. I dragged him down the steps as the ceiling rumbled and cracked. Men black in body, black in face, black where eyes should be, pulled themselves out of the ceiling like men climbing out of holes. And when they rose they stood on the ceiling the way we stand on the ground. From the Omoluzu came blades of light, sharp like swords and smoking like burning coal. The King ran off screaming, leaving his sword.

They charged. I ran, hearing them bounce off the ceiling. One would hop and not fall to the floor but land back on the ceiling, as if I was the one upside down. I ran for the outer court but two ran ahead of me. They hopped down and swung swords. My spear blocked both blows but the force knocked me over. One came at me with sword craft. I dodged left, missed his blade, and ran my spear right into his chest. The spear moved in slow as if piercing tar. He jumped away, taking my spear with him. I grabbed the King's sword. Two from behind grabbed my ankles and swooped me up to the ceiling, where blackness swirled like the night sea. I sliced the sword through the black, cut their limbs off, and landed on the floor like a cat. Another tried to grab my hand but I grabbed him and pulled him to the ground, where he vanished like smoke. One came at me sideways and I dodged but his blade caught my ear and it burned. I turned and charged at his blade with my own, and sparks popped in the dark. He flinched. My hands and feet moved like a Ngolo master's. I rolled and tumbled, hand over feet over hand, until I found my spear, near the outer chambers. Many torches were lit. I ran to the first and dipped my spear in the oil and flame. Two Omoluzu were right above me. I heard them ready their blades to cut me in two. But I leapt with the burning spear and ran right through them both. Both burst into flames, which spread to the ceiling. The Omoluzu scattered.

I ran through the outer chamber, down the hallway, and out the door. Outside the moon shone faint, like light through cloudy glass. The little fat King did not even run.

"Omoluzu appear where there is a roof. They cannot walk on open sky," he said.

"How your wife will love this tale."

"What do you know of love anyone had for anyone?"

"We go."

I pulled him along, but there was another passage, about fifty paces long. Five steps in, the ceiling began ripping apart. Ten steps in and they were running across the ceiling as fast as we ran on the ground, and the little fat King was falling behind me. Ten and five steps and I ducked to miss a blade swinging for my head that knocked off the King's crown. I lost count after ten and five. Halfway along the passage, I grabbed a torch and threw it up at the ceiling. One of the Omoluzu burst into flame and fell, but vanished into smoke before hitting the ground. We dashed outside again. Far off was the gate, with a stone arch that could not have been wide enough for the Omoluzu to appear. But as we ran under two jumped out of the ceiling and one sliced across my back. Somewhere between running to the river and coming through the wall of water, I lost both the wounds and the memory of where they were. I searched, but my skin bore no mark.

Mark this: The journey to his kingdom was much longer than the journey to his dead lands. Days passed before we met the Itaki at the riverbank, but she was no old woman, only a little girl, skipping in the water, who looked at me in the sly way of women four times her age. When the Queen met her King, she quarreled and cussed and beat him so hard, I knew that it would be mere days before he drowned himself again.

I know the thought that just ran through you. And all stories are true.

Above us is a roof.

TWO

When I left my father's house, some voice, maybe a devil, told me to run. Past houses and inns and hostels for tired travelers, behind mud and stone walls as high as three men. Street led to lane and lane led to music, drinking, and fighting, which led to fighting, drinking, and music. Seller women were closing shops and packing away stalls. Men walked by in the arms of men, women walked by with baskets on their heads, old people sat in door-ways, passing night as they did day. I walked right into another man and he did not curse, but smiled wide with gold teeth. You are as pretty as a girl, he said. I fled along the aqueduct, trying to find the east gate, the way to the forest.

Day riders with spears, in flowing red robes, black armour, and gold crowns topped with feathers, mount horses dressed in the same red. At the gate, seven riders were approaching, and the wind was a wolf. Quarrels done for the day, their horses galloped past me, leaving a cloud of dust. Then the sentries started closing the gate and I ran out, down the Bridge That Has a Name Not Even the Old Know. Nobody noticed.

I walked through open lands that stretched on like the sand sea. That night I walked past a dead town with walls crumbling. The empty hall I slept in had no door and one window. Behind was a hill made from the rubble of many houses. No food, and the water in the jars tasted rank. Sleep came to me on the floor to the sound of mud walls crumbling around the town.

And my eye? What of it?

Oh but it were a mouth, the tales it would tell you, inquisitor. Your lips broke open the first time you saw it blink. Write what you see; be it witchcraft, be it white science, my eye is whatever you think it is. I have no guise. I have no look. My face is a forehead wide and round, like the rest of my head. Brows that hang so far over my eyes they give them shade. A nose sloped like a mountain. Lips that feel as thick as my finger when I rub them with red or yellow dust. One eye that is mine and one that is not. I pierced my ears myself, thinking of how my father wore a turban to hide his. But I have no look. That is what people see.

Ten days after I left my father's house I came to a valley, still wet from rain that fell a moon before. Trees with leaves darker than my skin. Ground that held you for ten paces only to swallow you on your next step. Dens of the slitherers, cobra and viper. I was a fool. I thought you learned the old ways by forgetting the new. Walking through the bush I told myself that though every sound was new, none was frightening. That the tree was not betraying where I tried to hide. The heat under my neck was not fever. The vines were not trying to jump my neck and strangle me until I died. And hunger and what passed for hunger. Pain hitting against my belly from the inside until it was tired of hitting. Looking for berries, looking for young tree bark, looking for monkeys, looking for what monkeys eat. More madness. I tried to eat dirt. I tried to follow snakes following rats through the brush. I felt something big following me. I climbed over a rock and wet leaves hit my face.

I woke up in a hut, cool like the river. Fire burning inside, but the heat was in me.

"The hippopotamus is invisible in water," a voice said.

Either the hut was dark or I was blind; I did not know.

"**Ye waren wupsi yeng ve.** Why did you not heed the warning?" he said.

The hut still loomed dark, but my eye saw a little more.

"The viper has no quarrel with anyone, not even foolish boys. Oba Olushere, the cool and gentle snake, is the most dangerous."

My nose led me into the forest. I saw no viper. Two nights before, when he found me shivering under the crying tree, he was so sure I was near dead that he dug a hole. But then I coughed green juice throughout the night. And there I was lying on a mat in a hut that smelled of violet, dead bush, and burning shit.

"Answer from the heart. What are you doing in the deep bush?"

I wanted to tell him that I had come searching for myself, but those were the words of an idiot. Or like something my father would say, but back then I still thought there was a self to lose, not knowing that one never owns the self. But I've said this before. So I said nothing and hoped that my eyes could speak. Even in the dark I could tell he was staring at me. Me and my wild ideas about the bush where men ran with lions, and ate from the land, and shat by the tree, and had no art among them. He came out of the dark corner and slapped me.

"The only way to inside your head is I cut open and look, or you speak it out."

"I thought—"

"You think men of bush and river grunt and bark like dogs. That we don't wipe the ass when we shit. Maybe we rub it on our skin. I talking to you as man."

You, inquisitor, are a man who collects words. You collect mine. You have verse for a cool morning, verse for the noon of the dead, verse for war. But the setting sun does not need your verse and neither does the running cheetah.

This wise man did not live in the village, but near the river. His hair was white from ash and milk cream.

The only time I witnessed my father undress, I saw dot scars like stars in a circle on his back. This man had a circle of stars on his chest. He lived alone in the hut he built with wild branches for the wall and bush for the roof. He rubbed the walls with black rock dust until they shone, then drew patterns and paintings, one of a white creature with arms and legs tall as trees. I have never seen the like.

"And a good thing that is, for you would not be alive to tell me of it," he said.

I fell asleep, woke up, fell asleep, woke up, and saw a great white python wrapping around a trunk, woke up and saw the snake fade against the wall. Sunlight came in, lit up the walls, and I saw we were in a cave. The walls shaped like candlewax melting on candlewax. In the dimness, parts of it looked like a screaming face, or elephant legs, or a young girl's slit.

The wall, when I rubbed my hand against it, felt like yam skin. Near the opening was soft with shrubs sticking out like loose hairs. I rose and this time did not fall. Wobble I did, like a man soaked in palm wine, but I stepped outside. I staggered and pressed against the rock for balance, but this was not rock. Nothing like stone. Tree bark. But too wide, too big. I looked as high as I could look and walked as far as I could walk. Not only was sun still behind the branches and leaves, but this trunk was without end. By the time I walked around it, I forgot where it began. Only at the top were there branches, stubby like baby fingers and sticking out in a web of twigs and leaves.

Little leaves, thick like skin, and fruit as big as your head. I heard little feet scrambling up and down, a baboon and her child.

"The monkeybread tree was the fairest in the savannah," the witchman said behind me. "This was before the second dawn of the gods. But what a thing—the monkeybread tree knew she was pretty. She demanded all makers of song sing of her beauty. She and her sister prettier than the gods, even prettier than Bikili-Lilis, whose hair became the one hundred winds. This is what came to pass. The gods gave birth to fury. They went down to earth and pulled up every single monkeybread tree, and thrust them back in the ground upside down. It took five hundred ages for the roots to produce leaves and five hundred more to sprout flower and fruit."

In one moon every member of the village came to the tree. I saw how they looked at him while hiding behind branches and leaves. Once, three of the strong men of the village came. They were all tall, broad in shoulder, rippled where fat men had bellies, with legs strong as the bull. The first man dressed himself head to toe in ash, white as the moon. The second marked his body with white stripes like a zebra. The third had no colour but his dark and rich skin. They wore necklaces and chains around their waists that needed no further adornment. I did not know what they came for, but I knew to them I would give it.

"We watch you many times in the bush," the striped one said. "You climb trees and hunt. No skill, no craft, but maybe the gods are pushing you. How old are you in moons?"

"My father never counted moons."

"This tree ate six virgins. Swallowed them whole. You can hear them scream at night but it comes out as a whisper. You think it is wind."

He stared at me for a while, then they laughed.

"You will come with us to the Zareba rite of manhood," the striped one said.

He pointed to the moonlit one.

"A snake killed his partner right before the rains. You will go with him."

I did not say that I was saved from snakebite.

"We meet at the next sun. You should know the way of warriors, not bitchmen," said the moonlit one.

I nodded a yes. He looked at me longer than the others. Somebody had carved a star on his chest. A ring in each ear that I knew he pierced himself. He was taller than the others by a head at least but I only noticed then. Also, these men won't still be boys in Juba.

"You will go with me," I heard him say, though I did not hear him say it.

In the Zareba, the rites of manhood, there are no women. But you must still know of their use to man. The Zareba is in your mind; the Zareba is out in the bush a journey from sunrise to noon. You arrive at the hall of heroes, with clay walls and a thatch roof. And sticks, and spaces for fighting. Boys enter to learn from the strongest fighters in all the villages and all the mountains. You cover yourself in ash so that at night you look as if you've come from the moon. You eat durra porridge. You kill the boy who is you, to become the man who is you, but everything must be learned. I asked the moonlight boy how to learn of women with no women to learn from.

Will you hear more, inquisitor?

One morning I caught the smell of kin following me to the river. A boy who thought I was his uncle's son. I was hunting fish. He came to the bank and hailed me like he knew me, until he saw that he did not know me. I said nothing. His mother must have told him about the Abarra, the demon that comes to you like someone you know, with everything but a tongue. He did not run, but walked away slow from the bank and sat on a rock. Watching me. He could not have been more than eight or nine in years, with a white clay streak from ear to ear and over his nose, and white dots like a leopard's all over his chest. I was a boy of the city and would have no luck catching fish. I dipped my hands in water and waited. Fish swam right into my hands but slipped out every time I tried to grab one. I waited, he watched. I grabbed a big one but it wriggled and frightened me and I tripped and fell into the river. The little boy laughed. I looked at him and laughed as well, but then came a smell in the forest, moving closer and closer. I smelled it—ochre, shea butter, underarm stenches, breast milk—and he smelled it too. We both knew the wind was carrying someone, but he knew who it was.

She came out of the trees as if out of the trees she sprung. A taller woman, an older woman, her face already cut sharp and gruff, her right breast not yet lanky. Her left she wrapped in a cloth slung over her shoulder. A band, red, green, and yellow around her head. Necklaces of every colour but blue piled one on top of the other, like a mountain all the way up to her earlobe. Goatskin skirt with cowries over a belly fat with child. She looked at the boy and pointed behind her. Then she looked at me, and pointed the same way.

On a morning with a lazy sun, the witchman woke me with a slap, then walked out of the hut, saying nothing. He laid beside me spear, sandals, and fabric to wrap around my hips. I rose quick and followed him. Down the river the village opened itself up with huts spread across a field. The first we passed were mounds of dry grass with a peak like a nipple. Then we passed by round huts of clay and dirt, red and brown with a roof of thatch and bush. In the center, the huts got bigger. Round and built in a cluster of five or six huts so that they looked like castles, with walls joining them together saying this is all for one man. The bigger the huts the shinier the walls, from those who could afford to rub the walls with black-stone. But most of the huts were not big. Only a man with many cows could have one hut for grain and another for cooking it.

The man with the biggest huts had six wives and twenty children, none of them a boy. He was looking for a seventh wife to give him a son at last. He was one of the few who came out of their huts to see me. Two boys and a girl, naked with no paint, followed the witchman and me until a woman shouted something in a harsh tongue and they ran to a hut behind us. We were now in the middle of the village, outside this man's cluster. Two women were spreading a fresh layer of clay on the side of a grain keep. Three boys about my age came back from a hunt with a dead bushbuck. I did not see the moon-lit one.

The return of the hunters woke up the town. Man and woman, girl and boy, all came out to see the fruit of the hunt, but stopped when they saw me. The witchman said a name I did not know. The man with six wives came out and walked right up to me. A tall man, with a big belly. A clay hair bun to the back of his head in gray and yellow, with five ostrich feathers on top. The bun for he was a man, each feather for a major kill. Yellow clay lined his cheekbone and victory scars covered his chest and shoulder. This man had killed many men, and lions and one elephant. Maybe even a hippopotamus. Two of his wives came out, one was the woman at the river.

The witchman said to him, "Father who speaks to the crocodile so that he does not eat us during wet season, hear me." Then he said something to the man that I did not understand.

The man looked at me from head to toe, and toe to head. He came in closer and said, "Son of Aboyami, brother of Ayodele, this path is your path, these trees are your trees, this house is your house, and I am your beloved uncle."

I did not know these names. Or maybe these were just names for people who had nothing to do with me. Family was not always family in the bush, and friend was not always friend. Even wife was not always wife.

He took me past the entrance and inside the yard, where children chased chickens. They smelled of clay and pollen and chicken shit underfoot. The house had six halls. Through the window, two wives grinding flour. Beside the grain keep the kitchen let out the sweetness of porridge; beside the kitchen, a wife washed herself under a stream of water pouring through a hole in the wall. Beside that a wall, long and dark, spotted with nipples made of clay. Then an open area under a thatch roof, with stools and rugs, and behind that the longest wall. My uncle's sleeping room, which had a huge butterfly above the sleeping rugs. He saw me looking and said the circles in the center were rippling pools of water, meaning renewal each wet season, or whenever he dips into the wet of his new wife's wiwi. Beside his hall was the room for storage, and for the children to sleep.

"This house is your house, these rugs are your rugs. But those wives are mine," he said, and chuckled. I smiled.

We sat in the open area, me on a rug, him on a chair set back so far that he was lying, not sitting.

Cut with a curve to fit his buttocks, firm in the back with three slats carved to look like three lines of eggs. I remember my father sighing as he rubbed his own back against one like it. A headboard curved like a huge headdress of horns. The big back and chubby legs made it look like a bush buffalo. My uncle lying there changed into a powerful animal.

"Your chair. I have seen the like, beloved uncle," I said.

He sat up. He seemed disturbed that there were two.

"Did your people make this?" I asked.

"The Lobi, wood masters in the city, claimed to have made only one. But city folk lie; that is their nature."

"You know of city streets?"

"I have walked many."

"Why did you return?"

"How do you know I left village for the city and not city for the village?"

I couldn't answer.

"Where did you see this chair?" he asked.

"In my house."

He nodded and laughed. "Blood still behaves like blood even if separated by the sand," he said, and slapped me on the shoulder.

"Bring my blood palm wine and tobacco," he shouted at one of his wives.

———

The people called themselves and their village Ku.
Once they controlled both sides of the river. Then
the enemy, the Gangatom, got bigger and stronger
and many more joined them, and drove the Ku to
the setting-sun side. Ku men had skill with bow and
arrow, leading the cattle to fresh fields, drinking milk,
and sleeping. The women had skill with pulling grass
for thatch roofs, plastering walls with clay or cow shit,
building fences to keep in the goats and the children
chasing after goats, fetching water, washing the milk
skins, milking the cattle, feeding the children, cooking the soup, washing the calabashes, and churning
the butter. The men went out in the nearby fields to
sow and reap their crops. They dug in water. I nearly
fell into a hole dug so deep you heard the old devils,
big as trees, rustle in their sleep at the bottom. The
moonlight boy told me that it was soon time to gather
the durra harvest, for the women to come to the fields
with baskets to take the crop away.

One day I saw nine men who came back to the village, tall and shining from new paint on some, red
ochre and shea butter on others, men who looked like
they were just born as warriors.

At nighttime they sang and danced and fought,
and sang again, and put on Hemba masks that looked
like the chimpanzee but Kava said was in the image
of all the elders gone, to speak to them in the spirit
trees. They sang in Hemba masks to break the curse

of many moons of bad hunting. The drum beat a **kekeke. Bambambam, lakalakalakalaka** under the wind.

The village woke up to a new smell and it was everywhere. New men and new women ripe to burst. I watched them from the man who would be my uncle's house, as he watched his wives and scratched his belly.

"A boy told me he would take me to the rites of manhood," I said.

"A boy promise you the Zareba? Under whose command?"

"By his own hand," I said.

"Is that what he tell you now?" he said.

"Yes. That I will be his new partner as the old one died by snakebite. I speak your tongue now. I know your ways, beloved uncle. I am your blood. I am ready."

"Which boy is this?" my uncle said.

But I did not know where lived this boy. My uncle rubbed his chin and looked at me. "You were born when you were found, and that is not even a moon. Do not rush to die so soon," he said.

I did not tell him that I was a man already.

"You have seen them. Boys running around, smaller than the men who came back to the village."

"What boys?"

"Boys with red tips, the female cut off from the male."

I did not know what he was talking about so he

took me outside. The sky was gray and fat with wait-ing rain. Two boys ran past and he called at the taller one, his face red, white, and yellow, the yellow a line in the middle of his head going all the way down. Remember, my uncle is a very important man, with more cows than the chief, and even some gold. The boy came over, shining from sweat.

"I was chasing a fox," he said to my uncle.

My uncle waved him closer. He laughed, saying the boy knows he has the mark of the end of youth, and wants the village to know. The boy flinched when my uncle grabbed his balls and cock as if to weigh them. Look, he said. The paint almost hid that the skin was gone, cut away, leaving the bold blossom tip. In the beginning we are all born of two, he said. You are man and you are woman, just as girl is woman and she is man. This boy will be a man, now that the fetish priest has cut the woman away, he said.

So stiff was this boy, but he tried to stand proud. My uncle kept talking. "And the girl must have the man deep inside her cut out of her neha for her to be a woman. Just as the first beings was of two." He rubbed the boy's head, sent him away, and went back inside.

Off on a rock men gathered. Tall, strong, black, and shining with spears. I watched them stand still until the sunset made them shadow. My uncle turned to me, almost whispering as if telling me horrible news around strangers.

"Every sixty times the earth flies around the sun, we

celebrate death and rebirth. The very firstborn were twins, but only when the divine male loosed his seed in the earth was there life. This is why the man who is also a woman, and the woman who is also a man, is a danger. It is too late. You have grown too old and will be both man and woman."

He watched me until his words spoke to my mind.

"I will never be a man?"

"You will be a man. But this other is in you and will make you other. Like the men who roam the lands and teach our wives woman secrets. You will know as they know. By the gods, you might lay as they lay."

"Beloved uncle, you cause me great sadness."

I did not tell him that the woman was already raging inside me and I desired her desires, but otherwise did not feel like a woman for I wanted to hunt deer, and run and sport.

"I wish to be cut now," I said.

"Your father should have cut you. Now it is too late. Too late. You will be one always on the line between the two. You will always walk two roads at the same time. You will always feel the strength of one and the pain of the other."

That night the moon did not come, but when he appeared outside the hut, the boy still glowed.

"Come see what new men and women do," he said.

"You must tell me your name," I said.

He said nothing.

We went through the bush to the place where drummers were sending messages to gods of sky, and ancestors in the ground. The moonlight boy walked fast and did not wait. I was still afraid of stepping on a viper. He vanished through a wall of thick leaves and I stopped, not knowing where to go until a white hand pushed through the thick leaves, grabbed mine, and pulled me in.

We came upon a clearing where the drummers drummed, while others beat sticks and others whistled. Two men approached to start the ceremony, and we hid in the bush.

"The bumbangi, the official and provider of food. Also stealer. See him in his mweelu mask of sprouting feathers and a giant hornbill beak. Look beside him, the makala, master of charms and spells," Kava said.

The new men lined up shoulder-to-shoulder. All wore skirts of fine cloths, which I had only seen on my uncle, and all now wore clay buns with ostrich feathers and flowers. Then they jumped, up and down, higher and higher, so high that they stayed in the air before stomping the ground. Stomping the ground so hard the earth shook. And they kept jumping to **bodom, bodom, bodom, bodom.** There were no children. Maybe they were like the moonlight boy and me, hiding in the bush. Then the new women came to the clearing. Two women walked right up to the men and started to jump with them, **bodom, bodom, bodom.** Man and woman jumping closer and closer, moving in until skin touched skin, chest touched chest, nose touched nose. The moonlight boy was still holding my hand. I let him hold it. The people joined in and the clearing was a cloud of dust from jumping and stomping and older women now doing a dance in and out of the crowd, possessed by divine smoke.

The bumbangi sang again and again:

Men with a penis
Women with a vagina
You do not know each other
So build no house yet

The boy pulled me off into thicker, colder bush. I smelled them as soon as he heard them. Sweat funk rising and spreading on wind. The woman squatted down on the man, then up, then down, up and down. I blinked until I had night eyes. Her breasts jiggled. They both made sound. In my father's room only he made sound. The man did not move. In my father's room, only he moved. I saw ten things this woman did for the one thing the man did. The woman hopped up and down, jiggled, whispered, panted, bawled, grunted, screamed, squeezed her own breast, opened and closed herself. The moonlight boy had moved his hand between my legs, pulling my skin back and forth to match her up and down. The spirit struck me, made me spurt and made me shout. The woman screamed and the man jumped up, pushing her away. We ran off.

My father said he left his place of birth because a wise man showed him that he was among backward people who never created anything, never knew how to put words down on paper, and fucked only to breed. But my beloved uncle told me different. Listen to the tree where you live now, for your blood is there. I listened to branch upon branch and leaf upon leaf, and heard nothing from the ancestral fathers. A night later I heard my grandfather's voice outside, mistaking me for his son. I went out and looked up in the branches and saw nothing but dark.

"When will you avenge your father's killer? Restless sleep rules me, it waits for justice," he said. He also said, "With Ayodele slayed, you are eldest son and brother. That defiles the plan of the gods and must be avenged. My heat has not gone cold, my weak son."

"I am not your son," I said.

"Your brother Ayodele, who is eldest, is here with me, also in troubled sleep. We await the sweet smell of enemy blood," Grandfather said, still mistaking who I was.

"No son of yours am I."

Did I look so much as my father? Before I had hair, his was gray, and I have never seen myself in him. Except for stubbornness.

"The quarrel runs fresh."

"I have no quarrel with crocodile, no quarrel with hippopotamus, no quarrel with man."

"The man who killed your brother also killed his goats," my grandfather said.

"My father left because killing was the old way, the way of small people with small gods."

"The man who killed your brother still lives," my grandfather said. "Oh how big the shame when that man in your house left the village. I shall not speak his name. Oh what a shameful way, more weak than the bird, more cowardly than the meerkat. It was the cows who told me first. The day he saw that I would not rest until he took revenge, he left the cows in the bush and fled. The cows took their own way back to the hut. He has forgotten his name, he has forgotten his life, his people, hunting with bow and arrow, guarding the sorghum field against birds, caring for the herds, staying away from mud left by flood for that was where the crocodile sleeps to keep cool. And you. Shall you be the only boy in a hundred moons that the crocodile hates?"

"I am not your son," I said.

"When will you avenge your brother?" he asked.

I went around the back and found my uncle drawing snuff from an antelope horn, like rich men in the city. I wanted to know why he left for the city, like my father, and why he returned, unlike my father. He was coming back from a meeting with a fetish priest, who had just returned from reading the future at the mouth of the river. I couldn't read on his face if the priest foretold more cows, a new wife, or famine and sickness coming from a petty god. I smelled it on him, the dagga he was chewing for second sight, meaning he didn't trust the priest with his news and wanted to make sure for himself. This sounded like something my uncle would do. My father was an intelligent man, but he was never as smart as Uncle. He pointed to the white line on his forehead.

"Powder from lion's heart. The priest mix it with woman's moon blood and mahogany bark, then chew it to tell the future."

"And you wear it?"

"Which would you choose, to eat the lion's heart or to wear it?"

I did not answer.

"Grandfather's ghost is a mad spirit," I said. "He asks, over and over, when shall I kill my brother's killer. I have no brother. He also thinks I am my father."

Uncle laughed. "Your father is not your father," he said.

"What?"

"You are the son of a brave man but the grandson of a coward."

"My father was as old and frail as the elders."

"Your father is your grandfather."

He did not even see how he shook me. Silence grew so thick I could hear the breeze shake leaves.

"When you were only a few years, though we do not count in years, the Gangatom tribe across the river killed your brother. Right after he came back from the Zareba rite of manhood. On a hunt in the free lands, owned by no tribe, he came across a group of Gangatom. It was agreed by all, there should be no killing in the free lands, but they chopped him to death with sharp hatchet and ax. Your true father, my brother, was the most skilled bow and arrow man in the village. A man must know the name of the man on whom he is taking revenge, or he runs the risk of attacking a god. Your father listened to no man, not even his father. He said that the blood that runs in him, a lion's blood, must have come from his mother, who had always cried for revenge. Her cries for revenge drove her out of her husband's house. She stopped painting her face and never groomed her hair again. Some think it foolish to avenge the death of one son with the killing of another son, but it was the time of foolishness. He avenged the death, but they also killed him. Your father took up his bow and six arrows. He set his aim across the river and vowed to kill six living souls he saw. Before noon, he killed two women, three men, and one child, each from a different family. Now six families were against us. Six new families now meant us death. They killed your father in the free lands, when a man living there said the skins he bought from him fell apart after two moons. Your father went to see about the complaint and defend his good name. But the man had betrayed him to three Gangatom warriors two moons before. A boy took aim with his bow and struck him in the back, right through the heart. The story of the bad skins came from the Gangatom, as this man had no art in him to come up with a clever deception. That is what he told me before I cut his throat."

Also this, my uncle told me. My grandfather grew tired of killing and took my mother and me from the village. He was the one who left the cows. This is why from when I was young, my father was old, old as the elders here with humps on their backs. Running made him thin, with skin and bone. He always looked ready to flee. I wanted to run from my uncle to my father. Grandfather. The ground was right now not the ground, and the sky was not the sky, and lie was truth and truth was a shifting, slithering thing. Truth was making me sick.

I knew my uncle had more words to tell me; words that would give my head sense, because it had taken up foolishness and I could not believe my own ancestors. Or maybe I believe everything. I believe an old man who was not my father and a younger woman who was my mother. Maybe she was not my mother. They slept in the same room, in the same bed, and he climbed on top of her like husbands do; I had seen them. Maybe my house was not my house, and maybe my world was not the world.

The spirit in the upper branches of this tree was my father talking to me. Telling me to kill for my own brother. And the village knew. They came to my uncle's house to ask. The old women sent word with the children, When will you avenge your brother? The other boys asked me as they taught me to fish, When will you avenge your brother? Each time someone asked the question, the question had new life. After years of wanting to be nothing like my father, I now wanted to be him. Except he

was my grandfather; I wanted to be like my grandfather. My grandmother had gone mad from her need
for revenge.

"Where does she live?" I asked my uncle.

"A house built then left behind by large birds,"
he said. "Half a day from this village if you stay on the
riverbank."

I sat behind the grain keep.
    I stayed there for days.
    I spoke to no one.
    My uncle knew it was wise to leave me alone. I
thought of my grandfather and my uncle, and tried
to make in my head what my father looked like.
But that always died and left me with my grandfather
and my mother, both naked but not touching. What
does the bearer do with the thing he can't bear, throw
it off? Let it crush him underneath? I was a fool for
they all knew. I was an animal who would kill the
first person to speak of fathers and grandfathers.
I hated my father even more. My grandfather. So
many moons telling myself that I did not need my
father. We came to punches and blows, me and
my father. And now that I have none I want him.
Now that I know he would have made a sister also
an aunt, I wanted to kill him. And my mother. Rage,
maybe rage would lift me up, make me stand, make
me walk, but there I was, still by the grain keep. Still

not moving. Tears came and passed without me even knowing it, and when I knew it I refused to think it was so.

"Fuck the gods, for now I feel like I can skip on air," I said out loud. Blood was boundary, family a rope. I was free, I told myself. And would tell myself all night and all day for three days.

I never went searching for my grandmother. What would she have done but tell me more things I did not want to hear? Things that would make me understand the past but give me more tears and grief. And grief was making me sick. I went to he who was building a fire outside his hut. Why his hut, his grain keep, his fires were all without the company of woman, I did not ask. For a boy who was not yet a man, he was raising himself.

"I will take you to the Zareba, and you will gain manhood. But you must kill the enemy before the next moon, or I will kill you," he said.

"I call you moonlight boy in my head," I said.

"Why?"

"Because your skin was dark-white like the moon, when I first saw you."

"My mother calls me Kava."

"Where is she? Where is your father, sister, brothers?"

"Night sickness, they all die. My sister was last."

"When?"

"The sun circle this world four times since."

"I feel sick from the talk of fathers. And mothers. And grandfathers. All blood."

"Cool that rage like me."

"I wish blood could burn."

"Cool that rage."

"I have them and I lost them and what I have is a lie, but the truth is worse. They left my head on fire."

"You will go to the Zareba with me."

"My uncle says I am not for the Zareba."

"You still take word from your blood then."

"My uncle says I'm not a man. That the woman at the end of this has not been cut away."

"Then pull the skin back."

Behind his hut was not far from the river. We went down to the banks. He had a gourd in his hand. He scooped water in his hand, poured it into the gourd, and waved me over. I stood still and he took some of the wet white clay and painted my face. He marked my neck, my chest, my legs, my calves, and my buttocks. Then he dipped his hand in the water and marked my skin in lines like a snake that tickled. I laughed, but he was stone. He marked lines on my back, down my legs. He grabbed my cock foreskin and pulled it hard and said what to do with this shriveled foro? Words were spoken up in the trees, but I ignored them. Kava said, "I wish I had an enemy to avenge my mother and father. But which man has there been, that has ever killed air?"

THREE

Here are the things I have seen.

Three days and four nights in Kava's house. My uncle made no fuss. He was the man of this house in sun and in moon, and thought I looked at his wives with the same open mouth and loose tongue they looked at me. Truth, my uncle's house was large enough that we could go a quartermoon and never meet. But I could smell out what he hid from his women—expensive rugs from the city under the cheap ones, precious skins from great cats under cheap skins of zebra, gold coins and fetishes in pouches that stunk of the animal whose skin it was cut from. His greed made him squeeze in on himself to hide everything, which made him smaller even with his big belly.

But Kava's hut.

He had cloths and skins on the ground that were garments when I pulled them up. Black dust in a gourd for shining walls fresh. Jars of water, jars for churning butter, a gourd and a knife for drawing cow blood. This was a home still run by a mother. I never asked if his parents were buried right under him, or maybe his father left him with his mother so he learned woman's work, since he never went to hunt.

I did not want to go back to my uncle, and I would not talk to voices in trees, who never gave me anything but now demanded something. So I stayed at Kava's hut.

"How do you live alone?"

"Boy, ask what you want to ask."

"Fuck the gods, then tell me what I want to know."

"You want to know how I live so good without mother and father. Why the gods smile on my hut?"

"No."

"The same breath carrying news of your father tell you he is dead. I cannot—"

"Then don't," I said.

"And your grandfather is a father of lies."

"So."

"Like any other father," he said, and laughed. He said this also: "These elders, they say it and sing with foul mouths that a man is nothing but his blood. Elders are stupid and their beliefs are old. Try a new belief. I try a new one every day."

"What do you mean?"

"Stay with family and blood will betray you. No Gangatom looking for me. But I envy you."

"Fuck the gods, what is there to envy?"

"To know family only after they are gone is better than to watch them go."

He turned in to the dark corner of his hut.

"How did you know the ways of woman and man?" I asked.

He laughed.

"Watching the new men and women in the bush. Luala Luala, the people above the Gangatom, have man who live with man like a wife, and woman who live with woman like a husband, and man and woman with no man or woman, who live as they choose, and in all these things there is no strangeness," he said.

How did he know since he was not yet a man, I did not ask. In the mornings we went to river rocks and painted what sweat washed away in the night. In the night I knew him as he knew me, when he wanted to sleep, his belly touching my back when he breathed. Or face beside face, his hand between my legs scooping my balls. We would wrestle and tumble and grab and jerk each other until lightning struck inside both of us.

You are a man who knows pleasures, inquisitor, though you look selfish with yours. Do you know how it feels, not in the body but in the heart, when you have made a man strike lightning? Or a woman, since I have done so with many. A girl whose inner boy in the fold of her flesh was not cut out is blessed twice by the god of pleasure and plenty.

Here is my belief. The first man was jealous of the first woman. Her lightning was too powerful, her screams and moans loud enough to wake up the dead. That man could never accept that the gods would gift the weaker woman with such riches, so before every girl becomes a woman, man sets up to steal it, cut it away, and throw it in the bush. But the gods put it there, hid it deep so that no man would have business going to find it. Man will pay for this.

I have seen more than these things.

The day was out, but the sun was hiding. Kava said we go into the bush and shall not be back for more than a moon. I thought good, for everything in me was growing sick from the thought of family. Of anything Ku. I thought if I stayed here much longer I would turn myself into a Gangatom, and start killing until there was a hole in the village as big as the hole I see when I close my eyes. A dead thing never lies, cheats, or betrays, and what was a family but a place where all three bloom like moss. "As long as it takes for my uncle to miss me, then," I said.

I hoped it was a hunt. I wanted to kill. But I was still afraid of the viper, and Kava stepped through bowing trees and kneeling plants and dancing flowers as if he knew where to go. Twice I was lost, twice his white hand pushed through thick leaves and grabbed me.

"Keep walking and shed your burden," Kava said.

"What?"

"Your burden. Let nothing stop you and you will shed it like snakeskin."

"The day I heard I have a brother is the day I lost a brother. The day I learned I had a father is the day

I lost a father. The day I heard I had a grandfather was the day I heard he was a coward who fucks my mother. And I hear nothing of her. How do I shed such skin?"

"Keep walking," he said.

We walked through bush, and swamp, and forest, and a huge salt plain with hot cracked white dirt until daylight ran away from us. Every moment in the bush jolted me and I fell asleep and jumped awake all night. The next day, after some long walking, and me complaining about long walking, I heard footsteps above me in the trees and looked up. Kava said he had followed us since we turned south. I did not know we were heading south. Up above us in the tree was a black leopard. We walked and he walked. We stopped and he stopped. I clutched my spear but Kava looked up and whistled. The Leopard jumped down in front of us, stared hard and long, growled, then ran off. I said nothing, for what could be said to someone who had just spoken to a Leopard? We went farther south. The sun moved to the center of the gray sky but the jungle was thick with leaves and bush, and cold. And birds with their **wakakakaka** and **kawkawkawkaw.** We came upon a river, gray like sky and moving slow. New plants popped out of a fallen tree that bridged one side of the river to the other. Halfway across there rose out of the water two ears, eyes, nostrils, and one head as wide as a boat. The hippopotamus followed us with her eyes. Her jaws swung open wide, her head split in two, and she roared. Kava turned around and hissed at her. She sunk back under the river. Sometimes we caught up to the Leopard, and he would run off farther into the forest. He waited for us whenever we fell too far back. Though the bush got colder, I sweated more.

"We climb," I said.

"We climb from before the sun gone west," he said. We are on a mountain.

You only need to be told down is up for down to change. I was not walking south, I was walking up. The mist came down on the ground and floated through the air. Twice I thought it was spirits. Water dripped from leaves and the ground felt damp.

"We are not far," he said, right before I asked.

I thought we were searching for a clearing, but we went deeper in the bush. Branches swung around and hit me in the face, vines wrapped around my legs to pull me down, trees bent over to look at me and each line in their barks was a frown. And Kava started talking to leaves. And cursing. The moonlight boy had gone mad. But he was not talking to leaves but to people hiding underneath them. A man and a woman, skin like Kava's ash, hair like silver earth, but no taller than your elbow to your middle finger. Yumboes, of course. Good fairies of the leaves, but I did not know then. They were walking on branches until Kava grabbed a branch and they climbed his arms up to his shoulders. Both of them had hair on their backs, and eyes that glowed. The male sat on Kava's right shoulder, the female on the left. The man reached into a sack and pulled out a pipe. I stayed behind until my jaw came back up to my mouth, watching tall Kava, two halflings, one leaving a thick trail of pipe smoke.

"A boy?"

"Yes," said the man.

"Is he hungry?"

"We feed him berries, and hog milk. A little blood," said the woman. They both sounded like children.

For a long time walking all I saw was Kava's back. I smelled the baby's dried vomit before he got to him, sitting up on a dead anthill, flower in his mouth, his lips and cheek red. Kava kneeled before the baby, and the little man and woman jumped off his shoulder. Kava took up the baby in his arms and asked for water. Water, he said again, and looked at me. I remembered that I was carrying his waterskins. He poured some in his palm and fed the child. The little man and woman both carried over a gourd with a little hog's milk left. I was over Kava's shoulder when the baby smiled, two top teeth like a mouse's, gums everywhere else.

"Mingi," he said.

"What does that mean?"

He started walking, with the baby, not answering me. Then he stopped.

"The gods had no watchful eye on him," the little man said. "We could not . . ." He did not finish.

I didn't see until we passed the sweet stink of it. Two little feet peeking out of the bush, the bottoms of the feet blue. Flies raising nasty music. The last meal threatened to come up through my mouth. The sweet stink followed us even when we had gone very far. A bad smell, like a good one, can follow you into tomorrow. Then it rained a little and the trees sent the smell of fruit down to us. Kava hid the baby's face with his hand. He spoke before I asked.

"Do you not see his mouth?"

"His mouth is a baby's mouth, like every other baby's mouth."

"Too old to be such a fool," Kava said.

"You don't know my age and neither—"

"Quiet. The boy is mingi, also the dead girl. In his mouth, you saw two teeth. But they were on the top, not bottom; that is why he is mingi. A child whose top teeth come before bottom teeth is a curse and must be destroyed. Or else that curse spreads to the mother, the father, the family and brings drought, famine, and plague to the village. Our elders declared it so."

"The other one. Were his teeth also—"

"There are many mingi."

"This is the talk of old women. Not the talk of cities."

"What is a city?"

"What are the other mingi?"

"We walk now. We walk more."

"Where?"

The Leopard jumped out of the bush and the little people ran behind Kava. He growled, looked behind him, and roared. I thought he wanted Kava to hand him the baby.

The Leopard crouched down on the ground, then rolled on his back, and stretched and shook like he had a sickness. He growled again like a dog hit with a stone. His front legs grew long but the back legs grew longer. His back widened and sucked up his tail. The fur vanished but he was still hairy. He rolled until we saw a man's face, but eyes still yellow and clear like sand struck by lightning. Hair on his head black and wild, going down his temple and his cheek. Kava looked at him as if in the world one always sees these things.

"This is what happens when we move too late," the black Leopard said.

"The baby would still be dead, even if we had run," Kava said.

"I mean late by days; we are two days late. This one's death is on our hands."

"All the more to save this one. Let us move. The green snakes have already caught his scent. The hyenas caught the scent of the other."

"Snakes. Hyenas." The black Leopard laughed. "I will bury that child. I am not following you until I do."

"Bury her with what?" Kava asked.

"I will find something."

"Then we wait," Kava said.

"Do not wait sake of me."

"I do not wait because of you."

"Five days, Asani."

"I come when I come, cat."

"I waited five days."

"You should have waited longer."

The black Leopard growled so loud I thought he would change back.

"Go bury the girl," Kava said.

The black Leopard looked at me. I think that was the first time he noticed I was here. He sniffed, turned his head away, and went back into the bush.

Kava answered a question before I asked it.

"He is just like any other in the bush. The gods made him, but they forget who the gods made first."

But that was not one of the questions I wanted to ask.

"How did you come upon each other?"

Kava still watched where the Leopard left in the bush.

"Before the Zareba. I had to prove that the boy with no mother is worthy of becoming a man, or die the boy. **He must go out past the bush, slip past Gangatom warriors in open fields. He must not come back without the skin of a great cat.** Listen to what come to pass. I was in the yellow bush. I heard a branch crack and a baby cry and I saw that Leopard holding a baby at the neck. With his teeth he's holding him. I draw my spear and he growls and drop the baby. I am thinking I will save this baby, but the baby start bawling and will not quiet until the Leopard pick him up again with his teeth. I throw my spear,

I miss, he is on me and even as I blink I see a man about to punch me. He says, You are just a boy. You will carry the baby. So I carried him. He found me the skin of a dead lion and I took it back to the chief."

"The beast just says carry this mingi child and you carry him?" I asked.

"What was mingi? I didn't know until we came to she," Kava said.

"That is not . . . Who is she?"

"She is who we come to meet."

"And since then you sneak off near the end of every moon and bring mingi children to this she? Your answer leaves more questions."

"Then ask what you want to know."

I was quiet.

We waited until the Leopard came back, in the shape of a man with the frown gone from his face. Now he walked behind us, sometimes so far back that I thought he went off on his own, sometimes so close I could feel him sniff me. On him I smelled the leaves he ran through and the fresh wet of dew, the dead scent of the girl and the fresh musk of the grave dirt under his fingernails. The sun was almost ready to go.

Kava is like most men; he carries two smells. One when the sweat runs down his back and dries, the sweat of hard work. And one that hides under the arms, between the legs, between the buttocks, what you smell when close enough to touch with lips. The black Leopard had only the second smell. Never had I seen it before, a man whose hair was black cotton. On his back and legs when he passed me to take the baby from Kava. His chest, two little mountains, his buttocks big, legs thick. He looked as if he would crush the child in his arms, but licked dust off the baby's forehead. Only birds spoke. There we were, a man white like the moon, a Leopard who stood as a man, a man and a woman tall as a shrub, and a baby bigger than them both. Darkness was spreading herself. The little woman hopped from Kava to the Leopard, and sat on his arm, laughing with the baby.

A voice inside me said they were some sort of blood kin and I was the stranger. Kava told no one who I was.

We came up to a small, wild stream. Large rocks and stones marked the banks, green moss covering them like a rug. The stream cackled and sprayed mist up into the branches, ferns and bamboo stalks hanging over. The Leopard placed the baby on a rock, crouched right by the banks, and lapped the water. Kava filled his waterskins. The little man played with the baby. I was surprised he was awake. I stood by the Leopard but he still took no notice. Kava stood farther down, looking for fish.

"Where are we going?" I asked.

"I told you."

"This is not the mountain. We went around, then down several paces ago."

"We will get there in two more days."

"Where?"

He crouched down, cupped some water, and drank it.

"I want to go back," I said.

"There is no going back," he said.

"I want to go back."

"Then go."

"Who is the Leopard to you?"

Kava looked at me and laughed. A laugh that said, I am not even a man yet, but you give me man problems. Maybe the woman in me was rising. Maybe I should have grabbed my own cock skin and smashed it off with a rock. This is what I should have said. I did not like the man-Leopard. I did not know him to dislike him, but disliked him anyway. He smelled like the crack of an old man's ass. This is what I would have said. Do you talk without speaking? Do you know each other as brothers? Do you sleep with your hand between his legs? Shall I stay awake till the moon is fat and even the night beasts sleep to see if he comes to you—or will you go to the Leopard and lie on top of him, or him on top of you, or maybe he is like one of those my father liked in the city, who put men in their mouths?

The baby, sitting up, laughed at the little man and woman making faces and jumping up and down like monkeys.

"Name him."

I turned around. The Leopard.

"He needs a name," he said.

"I don't even know yours."

"I don't need one. What did your father name you?"

"I don't know my father."

"Even I know my father. He fought a crocodile, and a snake and a hyena only to drive himself mad with man envy. But he chased after the antelope faster than a cheetah. Have you done that? Bit deep with your sharpest teeth so that the warm blood bursts into your mouth and the flesh is still throbbing with life?"

"No."

"You are like Asani then."

"My uncle calls him Kava, and all in the village."

"You burn food, then eat it. You eat ash."

"Will you leave tonight?"

"I shall leave when I feel to. We sleep here tonight. In the morning we take the baby across new lands. I will find food, though it will not be much since all the beasts heard our approach."

I knew I was going to stay awake that night. I saw Kava and the Leopard walk off, the flames rising and blocking my view. I told myself that I was going to stay awake and watch them. And I did. I moved so close to the flame that it nearly singed my brow. I went to the river, now cold enough to shake bone, and threw water on my face. I stared through the dark, followed the white spots of Kava's skin. I curled my fingers into a fist so hard that my nails dug into the palm. Whatever those two would do, I was going to see and I was going to shout, or hiss, or curse. So when the Leopard stirred me awake, I jumped, shocked that I had fallen asleep. Kava threw water on the fire, just as I rose.

"We go," the Leopard said.

"Why?"

"We go," he said, and turned away from me.

He changed to a cat. Kava wrapped the baby in cloth and slung him on the Leopard's back. He did not wait. I rubbed my eyes and opened them again. The little man and woman were back on Kava's shoulder.

"One owl talk to me," the little woman said. "A day behind in the bush. Them say you read wind? No so? He say you have a nose."

"I don't understand."

"Somebody, they following us," she said.

"Who?"

"Asani, he saying you have a nose."

"Who?"

"Asani."

"No, who is following us?"

"They moving by night, not by day," Kava said.

"He said I have a nose?"

"He saying you were a tracker."

Kava was already walking away when he said, We go. Farther off into the darkness, Leopard jumped from tree to tree with a baby strapped on his back. Kava called me over.

"We need to move," he said.

All around was dark, night blue, green, and gray; even the sky had few stars. But then the bush began to make sense. Trees were hands pushing out of the earth and spreading crooked fingers. The curling snake was a path. The fluttering night wings belonged to owls, not devils.

"Follow the Leopard," Kava said.

"I don't know where he went," I said.

"Yes, you do."

He rubbed his right hand across my nose. The Leopard came to life right in my face. I could see him and his trail, ripe as his skin through the bush. I pointed.

Leopard had gone right, then down fifty paces, crossed the stream by jumping from one tree to the next, then went south. Stopped to piss at four trees to confuse whoever was following us. I knew I had the nose, as Kava said, but I never knew that it could follow. Even as the Leopard got far he was still right under my nose. And Kava, and his smells and the little woman, and the rose she rubbed in her folds, and the man, and the nectar he drank, and the bugs he ate, too much of the bitter when he needed the sweet, and the waterskins, and the water inside that still smelled of buffalo, and the stream. And more, and more than that, and even more, enough to drive me to some kind of madness.

"Breathe everything out," Kava said.

"Breathe everything out.

"Breathe everything out."

I exhaled long and slow.

"Now breathe in the Leopard."

He touched my chest and rubbed around the heart.
I wished I could see his eyes in the dark.

"Breathe in the Leopard."

And then I saw him again with my nose. I knew
where he was going. And whoever spooked the Leopard was beginning to spook me. I pointed right.

"We go this way," I said.

We ran all night. Beyond the stream and the
branches bent over it, we ran through trees with grand
roots, roots that rose above the ground and snaked
the lands in tangles and curls. Right before dawn I
mistook one for a sleeping python. Trees taller than
fifty men standing on shoulders, and as soon as the
sky changed, the leaves turned into birds that flew
away. We came up the grasslands, with shrubs and
weeds that reached above our knees, but no trees. We
came upon salt lands in a low valley with white dirt
that blinded us with light and crunched under our
feet, with no animals as far as one could see, which
meant those following us could see us. I said nothing.
The grasslands stretched from last of the night to first
of the day, where everything was gray. That Leopard
scent in front like a line, or a road. Twice we came
close to see him, running on all fours with the baby
tied to his back. Once, three Leopards ran alongside
him, and left us alone. We passed elephants and lions
and scared a few zebras. We passed through a thicket
of trees with few leaves, like the bones of trees, and
their whispers were louder. And still we ran.

Morning peeked as if about to change her mind.

The fourth day since Kava and I set out. The little woman said whoever was following slept by day and hunted at night. So we walked. Past a forest of killed trees the air went wet again, thick as it went down the nose into the chest. The trees had leaves again and the leaves were getting darker, bigger. We came upon a field of trees larger than anything I had ever seen in the world. I would have run out of men to count. They weren't even trees, but the crooked fingers of buried giants sticking out of the ground and covered in grass, branches, and green moss. Giant stalks bursting out of the ground and reaching into the sky, giant stalks curling into the ground like an open fist. I walked past one and beside it I was a mouse. The ground was mounds and little hills; nowhere was level. Everywhere looked as if another giant finger was going to push through the ground, followed by a hand and an arm and a green man taller than five hundred houses. Green and green-brown and dark green, and a green that was blue, and a green that was yellow. A forest of them.

"The trees have gone mad," I said.

"We come close," Kava said.

Mist split the light into blue, green, yellow, orange, red, and a colour I did not know was purple. One hundred or 101 paces down, the trees all bent in one direction, almost braiding together. Trunks growing north and south, east-west, shot up, reached down, twisting into and out of each other, then down on the ground again, like a wild cage to hold something in or keep something out. Kava jumped on one of the trunks, bent so low that it was almost flat with the ground. The branch was as wide as a path, and the dew on the moss made it slippery. We walked all the way on one trunk and jumped down to another bending below it, moving up again, and jumping from trunk to trunk, going up high, then down low, then around so many times that only on the third time did I notice we were upside down but did not fall.

"So these are enchanted woods," I said.

"These are hot-tempered woods, if you don't shut up," he said.

We passed three owls standing on a branch, who nodded at the little woman. My legs burned when we finally broke into sky. The clouds were thin as cold breath and the sun, yellow and hungry. In front of us, it floated on the mist. Truth, it stood on branches but the walls were set against the trunk, and had the same flowers, and moss. A house set in the tree with colours of the mountain. I couldn't tell if they built the tree around the branches or if the branches grew in to protect it. Truth, there were three houses, all wood and clay with thatch roofs. The first was small as a hut, no bigger than a man six heads tall. Children were running around it, and crawling into the little hole in the front. Steps curled around the house and led to the one above it. Not steps. Branches set straight, and forming steps as if the trees played their part.

"These are enchanted woods," I said.

The branch steps led to a second house, larger with a huge opening instead of a door, and a thatch roof. Steps came out of the roof and led to a smaller house with no openings, no doors. In and out of the second house came children, laughing, yelling, crying, screaming, oohing and aahing. Naked and dirty, covered in clay, or wrapped in robes too big for them. At the opening of the second house the Leopard looked out. A naked little boy grabbed his tail and he swung around and snarled, then licked the boy's head. More children ran out to greet Kava. They attacked him all at once, grabbing a leg or an arm, one even climbed up his slippery back. He laughed and stooped to the floor so they could run all over him. A baby crawled over his face, smearing the white clay. I think that was the first time I saw his face.

"A place like this was where the North King kept wives who couldn't breed boys. Every child here is mingi," he said.

"And so would you be if your mother believed in the old ways," she said before I saw her. Her voice loud and coarse, as if in her throat was sand. A few children ran off with the Leopard. I saw her robes next, robes like I haven't seen since the city, yellow and with a pattern of green snakes and flowing, so the snakes looked alive. She came down the steps and into the room, which really was a hall, an open space with a wall to the front and back, and the sides open to the branches, leaves, and sky mist. The robes reached right under her plump breasts and an infant boy was sucking the left one. The red-and-yellow head wrap made her head look to burst in flames. She looked older, but when she came in closer I saw a look I would see more than once, of a woman not aged but ravaged. The boy was sucking hard with its eyes closed. She grabbed my chin and looked at my face, tilted her head and peered into my eyes. I tried to hold her stare, but looked away. She laughed and let go, but still stared at me. Beads upon beads, a valley of necklaces right down to her nipples. A ring hanging from a pierced bottom lip. A double pattern of dot scars from her left cheek curling up to her brow and down the right. I knew the mark.

"You are Gangatom," I said.

"And you don't know who you are," she said. She looked down at my feet all the way up to my head, which was getting wild but not as wild as the Leopard's. She looked at me as if I was answering questions without opening my mouth.

"But what can you know, running around with these two boys?"

She smiled. Both were still playing with children. A baby was on the Leopard's back and Kava was making noises and crossing his eyes for a girl whiter than river clay.

"You have never seen the like," she said.

"An albino? Never."

"But you know the name. City learning," she huffed out.

"I carry some stink from the city?"

"Yours is the place where a child born with no colour is a curse from the gods. Disease comes to the family, and barrenness comes to the women. Better toss her out for the hyena, and pray for another child."

"I'm from no place. Crocodiles on the hunt have more noble hearts than you people of the bush."

"And where do noble hearts live, boy, in the city?"

"Boy is what my father calls me."

"Mother of gods, we have a man among us."

"Nobody delivers a child to the hyena or the vulture. You call the collector of children."

"And what your collector do with them in your precious city? How they make use of a girl like her?" she said, and pointed at the girl, who giggled. "First they send messages with birds in the sky and drums on the ground, maybe even with note on leaf or on paper to those who would read. Saying look we have caught an albino child. Who these people? Talk to me, little boy. Do you know which people?"

I nodded.

"Sorcerers, and merchants that sell to sorcerers. For the whole child, your collector can fetch a good price. But for real fortune he auctions each part to highest bidder. The head for the swamp witch. The right leg for the barren woman. The bones grounded to a grain, so that your grandfather's cock will stay hard for several women. The fingers for amulets, the hair for whatever a witchman tells you. A good collector of babies can make fifty more for her parts than she would by just selling the whole child. And double for the albino. Your collector even cuts the baby into pieces himself. The witches pay more if they know the baby was still alive for part of it. Fear blood sauces their brews. So that the noblewomen of your city can keep your noblemen, and so that your concubines never bear children for their masters. That is what they do with little girls like her in the city where you come from."

"How do you know I come from the city?"

"Your smell. Living with Ku won't mask it."

She did not laugh, though I thought she would. That city was not mine to defend. Those streets and those halls brought nothing but disgust in me. But I did not like her speaking as if she had been waiting for years for a man she could laugh at. It was growing tiresome, men and women looking at me once and thinking they knew my kind, and of my kind there was not much to know.

"Why did Kava bring me here?"

"You think I tell him to bring you?"

"Games are for boys."

"Then leave, little boy."

"Except you told him to bring me here. What do you want, witch?"

"You call me witch?"

"Witch, crone, scar-speckled Gangatom bitch, pick the one you like."

She smiled quick to hide the scowl, but I saw it.
"You care for nothing."

"And a crone with a boy sucking a tit with no milk will not change that."

The smile on her face vanished. Her frown made me bolder; I folded my arms. Like, I like. Dislike, I love. Disgust, I can feel. Loathing, I can grab in the palm of my hand and squeeze. And hatred, I can live in hatred for days. But the smug smile of indifference on someone's face makes me want to hack it off. Both Kava and the Leopard stopped playing and looked at us. I thought she was going to drop the baby, and perhaps slap me. But she kept him close, his eyes still shut, his lips still sucking her nipple. She smiled and turned away. But not before my eyes said, Things are better this way, with understanding between us. You know me, but I know you too. I could smell everything about you before you came down those steps.

"Maybe you brought me here to kill me. Maybe you send for me because I am Ku and you are Gangatom."

"You are nothing," she said, and went back upstairs.

The Leopard ran to the edge of the floor and jumped into the tree. Kava was sitting on the floor, his legs crossed.

For seven days I stayed away from the woman and she stayed away from me. But children will be children and they will not be anything other. I found loose cloth made for children and wrapped my waist in it. Truth, I felt like the city was back in me and

I failed at being a man of the bush. Other times I cursed my fussing and wondered had any man or boy fussed so over cloth. The fifth night I told myself it is neither clothed nor unclothed, but whatever I feel to do or not to do. The seventh night Kava told me of mingi. He pointed to each child and told me why their parents chose to kill them or leave them to die. These were lucky that they were just left to be found. Sometimes the elders demand that you make sure the child is dead, and the mother or father drowns the child in the river. He said this while sitting on the floor of the middle house as the children fell asleep on mats and skins. He pointed to the white-skinned girl.

"She is the colour of demons. Mingi."

A boy with a big head tried to grab a firefly.

"His top teeth grew before the bottom. Mingi."

Another boy was already asleep but his right hand kept reaching out and grabbing air.

"His twin starved to death before we could save both. Mingi."

A lame girl hopping to her spot on the floor, her left foot bent in a wrong way.

"Mingi."

Kava waved his hands, not pointing to anyone.

"And some born to women not in wedlock. Remove the mingi, remove the shame. And you may still marry a man with seven cows."

I looked at the children, most sleeping. Wind slowed and the leaves swayed. I could not tell how much of the moon darkness had eaten, but the glow was bright enough to see Kava's eyes.

"Where do the curses go?" I asked.

"What?"

"These children are all cursed. If you keep them here, you are keeping curse on top of curse. Is the woman a witch? Is she skilled in removing curses, curses that come out of the womb? Or is she just pooling them here?"

I cannot describe the look on his face. But my grandfather looked at me that way all the time, and all day, the day I left.

"Being a fool is a curse too," he said.

FOUR

Kava and Leopard have been saving mingi children for ten and nine moons.

The Leopard did not sleep on the house floor, not even when he was a man. Each evening he climbed farther up the tree, and fell asleep between two branches. He changed to man mid-sleep—I have seen it—and did not fall out. But there were nights when he would go far out searching for food. One night was a full moon—twenty-eight days since I left the Ku. I waited until the Leopard was long gone and followed his scent. I crawled on branches twisting north, rolled down branches twisting south, and ran along branches that stretched flat, east to west, like a road.

When I found him, he had just dragged it up between the branches with his teeth, and his head never looked so powerful. The antelope he killed with that grip still around its neck. The air heavy with fresh kill. He bit the base of the back leg and ripped it away for the softer flesh near the belly. Blood splashed his nose.

The Leopard bit off more flesh, chewed and swallowed quick, like a crocodile. The carcass almost slipped his clutch when he saw me, and we stared at each other so long that I started to think that maybe this was a different leopard. His teeth ripped away red meat, but his eyes stayed on me.

The witch went up to the top hut at night, the house with no doors. I was sure that she entered from a hatch in the roof and I wanted to see for myself. Dawn was coming up. Kava was somewhere under a pile of sleeping children, himself asleep. The Leopard went out to finish what was left of the antelope. The mist came in thicker and I couldn't see the steps at my feet.

"These are the things that must happen to you," said a voice I had not heard before. A little girl.

I jumped, but nobody stood before or behind me.

"You might as well come up," another voice said. The woman.

"You have no door," I said.

"You have no eyes," she said.

I closed my eyes and opened them, but the wall was still the wall.

"Walk," she said.

"But there is no—"

"Walk."

I knew that I was going to hit the wall, and I would curse her and the baby who was probably still sucking her breast, because perhaps he was not a baby at all, but a blood-sucking obayifo with light coming from his armpits and asshole. Eyes closed, I walked. Two steps, three steps, four and no wall hit my forehead. When I opened my eyes, my feet were already in the room. It was much bigger than I thought, but smaller than the hut below. On the wood floor, carved every-where, were marks, incantations, spells, curses; I knew now.

"A witch," I said.

"I am Sangoma."

"Sounds like a witch."

"You know many witches?" she asked.

"I know you smell like a witch woman."

"Kuyi re nize sasayi."

"I am not an orphan in the world."

"But you live the difficult life of a boy no man will claim. I hear your father is dead and your mother is dead to you. What does that make you? As for your grandfather."

"I swear by god."

"Which one?"

"I tire of verbal sport."

"You sport like a boy. You have been here more than one moon. What have you learned?"

I made silence between us. She still had not shown herself. She was in my head, I knew. All this time, the witch was far away and threw her voice to me. Maybe the Leopard had finally eaten his way to the heart of the antelope and promised it to her. Maybe the liver too.

Something gentle hit my head, and someone giggled. A pellet hit my hand and bounced, but I didn't hear it hit the floor. Another hit my arm and bounced again, bounced high with no sound. Too high. The floor looked clear. I caught the third just as it hit my right arm. The child giggled again. I opened my hand and a small clump of goat shit leapt from it, jumped high and did not come down. I looked up.

Somebody had shined that clay ceiling with graphite. The woman was hanging from the ceiling. No, standing on it. No, attached to it looking down on me. But her robe stayed in place even with the gentle wind. Her dress covered the breasts. Truth, she stood on the ceiling the way I was right there standing on the floor. And the children, all the children were lying on the ceiling. Standing on the ceiling. Chasing after each other over and under, around and around, hissing and screaming, jumping but landing back on the ceiling.

And what children? Twin boys, each with his own head, his own hand and leg but joined at the side and sharing a belly. A little girl made of blue smoke chased by a boy with a body as big and round as a ball, but no legs. Another boy with a small shiny head and hair curled up like little dots, a little body but legs as long as a giraffe. And another boy, white as the girl from yesterday but with eyes big and blue as a berry. And a girl with the face of a boy behind her left ear. And three or four children who looked like any mother's children, but they were standing upside down on a ceiling, looking at me.

The witch moved towards me. I could touch the top of her head.

"Mayhaps we stand on the floor and you stand on the ceiling," she said.

As soon as she said it, I broke from the floor and stuck out my hands quick before my head hit the ceiling. My head spun. The smoke child appeared in front of me, but I was not scared or surprised. There was no time to think it, but think I did, that even a ghost child is a child first. My hand went right through her and stirred some of her smoke. She frowned and ran away on air. The joined twins rose from the floor and ran over to me. Play with us, they said, but I said nothing. They stood there looking at me, the one striped loincloth covering both of them. The right child wore a blue necklace; the left one, green. The boy with long legs bent over me, his legs straight, in loose, flowing pants like what my father wore, in that colour I did not know. Like red in deep night. Purple, she said. The long-legged boy spoke to the twins in a tongue I did not know. All three laughed until the witch called them away. I knew who these children were, and that is what I said to her. They were mingi in the full flower of their curse.

"You ever go to the palace of wisdom?" she said, one arm to her side, the other around a child who did not wish for her nipple. I passed this palace every day, and walked in more than one time. Its doors were always open, to say wisdom is open to all, but its lessons I was too young for. But I said, "Where is this palace?"

"Where is the palace? In the city you ran from, boy. Pupils ponder the real nature of the world, not the foolishness of old men. The palace where they build ladders to reach the stars, and create arts that have nothing to do with virtue or sin."

"There is no such palace."

"Even women go to study the wisdom of masters."

"Then as there are gods there is no such place."

"Pity. One day of wisdom would teach you that a child don't carry a curse, not even one spirit-born to die and born again. Curse come from the witch's mouth."

"You a witch?"

"You afraid of witches?"

"No."

"Be afraid of your bad lies. What kind of woman you going to undress with such a salty mouth?"

She looked at me for a very long time.

"How come I miss it before? My eyes going blind from the sight of shoga boys."

"My ears going tired from the words of witches."

"They should be tired of you being a fool."

I made one step towards her and the children stopped and glared at me. All the smiles gone.

"Children cannot help how they are born, they had no choice in it. Choosing to be a fool, though . . ."

The children went back to being children, but I heard her above the noise of play.

"If I were a witch, I would have come to you as a comely boy since that is the way inside you, false? If I were a witch, I would summon a tokoloshe, fool him that you are a girl and have him rape you while invisible each night. If I were a witch, every one of these children would have been killed, cut up, and sold in the Malangika witches market. I am not a witch, fool. I kill witches."

Three nights after the first moon, I woke up to a storm in the hut. But there was no rain and the wind dashed from one part of the room to the other, knocking over jars and water bowls, rattling shelves, whipping through sorghum flour, and disturbing some of the children awake. On the rug, Smoke Girl was shaking out of her own shape. Moaning, her face solid as skin, then fading into smoke, about to vanish. Out of her face popped another face that was all smoke, with terror eyes and a screaming mouth, shaking and grimacing as if forcing herself out of herself.

"Devils trouble her sleep," Sangoma said as she ran over to Smoke Girl.

Two times the Sangoma grabbed her cheeks, only for the skin to turn to smoke. She screamed again, but this time we heard. More children woke up. Sangoma was still trying to grab her cheek, yelling for her to wake up. She started to slap the girl, hoping that she would turn from smoke to skin long enough. Her hand hit her left cheek and the girl woke up and bawled. She ran straight to me and jumped up on my chest, which would have knocked me over were she any heavier than air. I patted her on the back and went right through her, so I patted again, gentle.

Sometimes she was solid enough to feel it. Sometimes I could feel her little hands holding my neck.

The Sangoma nodded at Giraffe Boy, who was also awake, and he stepped over sleeping children to get to the wall, where she had covered something with a white sheet. He grabbed it, she handed me a torch, and we all went outside. The girl was asleep, still gripping my neck. Outside was still deep dark. Giraffe Boy placed the figure on the ground and pulled away the sheet.

It stood there looking at us like a child. Cut from the hardest wood and wrapped in bronze cloth, with a cowrie in its third eye, feathers sticking out of its back, and tens of tens of nails hammered into its neck, shoulders, and chest.

"Nkisi?" I asked.

"Who show you one," the Sangoma said, not as a question.

"In the tree of the witchman. He told me what they were."

"This is nkisi nkondi. It hunts down and punishes evil. The forces of the otherworld are drawn to it instead of me; otherwise I would go mad and plot with devils, like a witch. There is medicine in the head and the belly."

"The girl? She just had troubled sleep," I said.

"Yes. And I have a message for the troubler."

She nodded at Giraffe Boy, who pulled out a nail that had been hammered in the ground. He took a mallet and hammered it into the nkiski's chest.

"Mimi waomba nguvu. Mimi waomba nguvu. Mimi waomba nguvu. Mimi waomba nguvu. Kurudi zawadi mari kumi."

"What did you do?" I asked.

Giraffe Boy covered the nkisi, but we left it outside. I held the girl to put her down and she was solid to the touch. The Sangoma looked at me.

"Do you know why nobody attacks this place? Because nobody can see it. It is like poison vapor. The people who study evil know there is a place for mingi. But they do not know where it is. That does not mean they cannot send magics out on the air."

"What did you do?"

"I returned the gift to the giver. Ten times over."

From then I would wake up in blue smoke, the girl lying on my chest, sliding down my knee to my toes, sitting on my head. She loved sitting on my head when I was trying to walk.

"You are blinding me," I would say.

But she just giggled and it sounded like breeze between leaves. I was annoyed and then I was not and then I just took it as it was, that at nearly all times there was a blue cloud of smoke on my head, or sitting on my shoulders.

Once, me and Smoke Girl went with Giraffe Boy out into the forest. We walked for so long that I did not notice we were no longer in the tree. In truth I was following the boy.

"Where do you go?" I asked.

"To find the flower," he said.

"There are flowers everywhere."

"I go to find the flower," he said, and started skipping.

"A skip for you is a leap for us. Slow, child."

The boy shuffled but I still had to walk swift.

"How long have you lived with the Sangoma?" I asked.

"I do not think long. I used to count days but they are so many," he said.

"Of course. Most mingi are killed just days after birth, or right after the first tooth shows."

"She said you will want to know."

"Who, Sangoma?"

"She said he will want to know how I am mingi but so old."

"And what is your answer?"

He sat down in the grass. I stooped and Smoke Girl scampered off my head like a rat.

"There is it. There is my flower."

He picked up a small yellow thing about the size of his eye.

"Sangoma saved me from a witch."

"A witch? Why would a witch not kill you as a baby?"

"Sangoma says that many would buy my legs for wicked craft. And a boy leg is bigger than a baby leg."

"Of course."

"Did your father sell you?" he said.

"Sell? What? No. He did not sell me. He is dead."

I looked at him. I felt a need to smile at him, but I also felt false doing so.

"All fathers should die as soon as we are born," I said.

He looked at me strange, with eyes like children who heard words parents should not have said.

"Let us name a stone after him, curse it, and bury it," I said. Giraffe Boy smiled.

Say this about a child. In you they will always find a use. Say this as well. They cannot imagine a world where you do not love them, for what else should one do but love them? Ball Boy found out I had a nose. Kept rolling into me, almost knocking me over, and shouting, Find me! then rolling away.

"Keep eye sh—" he shouted, rolling over his mouth before saying **shut.**

I did not use my nose. He left a trail of dust along the dry mud path, and squashed grass in the bush. He also hid behind a tree too narrow for his wide ball of a body. When I jumped behind and said, I see you, he looked at my open eye and burst into crying, and bawling and screaming. And wailing, truly he did wail. I thought the Sangoma would come running with a spell and the Leopard would come running ready to rip me apart. I touched his face, I rubbed his forehead.

"No no no . . . I will . . . you hide again . . . I will give you . . . a fruit, no a bird . . . stop crying . . . stop crying . . . or I . . ."

He heard it in my voice, something like a threat, and cried even louder. So loud that he scared me more than demons. I thought to slap the cry out of his mouth but that would make me my grandfather.

"Please," I said. "Please. I will give you all my porridge."

He stopped crying in the quick.

"All?"

"I will not even taste a dipped finger."

"All?" he asked again.

"Go hide again. I swear this time I shall only use my nose."

He started laughing as quickly as he cried before. He rubbed his forehead against my belly, then he rolled off quick like a lizard on hot clay. I closed my eyes and smelled him out, but walked right past him five times, shouting, Where is this boy? with him giggling as I shouted, I can smell you.

In seven days we would have been living with the Sangoma for two moons. I asked Kava, Will none from Ku come looking for us? He looked at me as if his look was an answer.

Hear now, priest. Three stories about the Leopard.

One. A night fat with heat. Sometimes I woke up when the smell of men from a place I've been got stronger, and I knew they approached, on horse, on foot, or in a pack of jackals. Sometimes I woke up to a scent getting weaker, and I knew they were leaving, fleeing, walking away, or finding somewhere to hide. Kava's scent getting weaker and the Leopard's as well. No moon in the night but some of the weeds lit up a trail in the dark. I ran down the trees and

my foot hit a branch. Hit my ass, hit my head, rolling, tumbling down like a boulder cut loose. Twenty
paces in the bush, there they were under a young
iroko tree. The Leopard, belly flat on the grass. He
was not a man; his skin was black as hair and his
tail whipped the air. He was not Leopard; his hands
grabbed a branch, and thick buttocks slapped against
Kava, who was fucking him with fury.

How much I hated Kava, and whether it was the
hole of the woman at the tip of my manhood that
made me hate, even if between my legs was a tree
branch, and that my hate had nothing to do with the
woman since at the tip of me was not a woman for
that was old wisdom, which was folly, even the witchman said so.

That I wanted to hurt the Leopard and be the Leopard. How I smelled the animal and how that smell got
stronger, and how much people change smell when
they hate, and fuck, and sweat, and run from fear and
how I smell it, even when they try to mask it.

What witchery do you work today, inquisitor?
What shall you know?

Shoga? Of course I knew. Does such a man not
always know? This is the third time I have said the
name and yet you do not know it? As for us shoga
men, we found inside ourselves another woman that
cannot be cut out. No, not a woman, something
that the gods forgot they made, or forgot to tell men,
maybe for the best. Will you hear me, inquisitor, that
whenever he touches it, rubs it hard or soft, or jerks it

when inside me, that I will stay here, and spurt seed on the wall over there. Hit the ceiling. Hit the top of the tree, spray across the river to the other side and hit a Gangatom in the eye.

So you do laugh, inquisitor.

This is not the first you have heard of shoga men. Call them with poetry as we do in the North; men with the first desire. Like the Uzundu warriors who are fierce for they have eyes for only each other. Or call them vulgar as you do in the south, like the Mugawe men who wear women's robes so you do not see the hole you fuck. You look like a basha, a buyer of boys. And why not? Boys are pretty beasts; the gods gave us nipples and holes and it's not the cock or the koo, but the gold in your purse that matters.

Shoga fight your wars, shoga guard your bride before marriage. We teach them the art of wife-being and house making and beauty and how to please a man. We will even teach the man how to please his wife so that she will bear him children, or so that he will rain all over her with his milk every night. Or she will scratch his back and curl her toes. Sometimes we will play tarabu music on kora, djembe, and talking drum, and one of us will lie as woman, and another will lie as man and we show him the 109 positions to please your lover. You have no such tradition? Maybe that is why you like your wives young, for how would they know if you are a dismal lover? Me and Kava only used our hands. I thought it was not strange, maybe because I still carried the woman on the tip. I once asked the witchman to cut it off, after my uncle forbade it. He looked at me with all his wisdom gone, and nothing left but puzzlement, a wrinkle between his brows, and his eyelids squeezing like a man losing vision. He said, "Do you wish for one eye as well, or maybe one leg?"

"It was not the same," I said.

"If the god Oma, who made man, wanted you cut to reveal such flesh he would have revealed it himself," he said. "Maybe what you need to cut away is the foolish wisdom of men who still make walls with cow shit."

Two. The next day Leopard kicked me in the face and woke me up. I opened my eyes and looked at his face, his wild shrub hair and eyes, white with a tiny black dot in the center. I was more afraid of the man than the Leopard. His big head and shoulders a warning that he can still carry up a tree beasts three times as heavy. He stepped on my chest, a bow slung over his right shoulder and a quiver of arrows in his left hand.

"Wake up. Today you will learn how to use a bow," he said.

He took me from the house, down the twisting trunks to another field that felt far away. We passed the little iroko tree where he let Kava fuck him. Beyond that, and beyond the sound of the little river, to another field of trees, so tall they scraped the sky and branches like spider legs all tangled together. Behind him the hair on his head went down to his neck, across his back, and down to a point and disappeared above his buttocks. Hair sprouted back on his thigh and went down to his toes.

"Kava said when he first saw you, he tried to kill you with a spear."

"What a storyteller he is," the Leopard said, and kept walking.

We stopped in a clearing, a tree about fifty paces away from us. The Leopard took off his bow.

"Are you his and is he yours?" I asked.

"What Sangoma says about you is true," he said.

"That woman can go lick between the ass cheeks of a leper."

He laughed.

"You'll be asking of love next," he said.

"Well, do you have love for the man, and does the man love you?"

He looked straight at me. Either he just grew whiskers, or I just saw them.

"Nobody loves no one," he said.

He turned away and nodded at the tree. The tree spread its arms to welcome him and exposed a hole right near where the heart would be, a hole that I could see right through. The Leopard already had the bow in his left hand, the string in his right, an arrow between his fingers. Before I even saw him raise the bow, draw the string, release the arrow that went through the hole in the tree with no sound, he had already drawn and shot another. He drew and shot another, then handed me the bow. I thought it would have been light, but it was about as heavy as the baby in the forest.

"Follow my hand," he said, and held it right to my nose.

He moved left and my eyes followed him. His arm went too far and I turned my neck to see if he was about to slap me, or some other little evil. Then he moved his hand right and I followed him with my eyes until I couldn't see it.

"Hold it with your left hand," he said.

"Your arrow," I said.

"What of it?"

"It shines like iron."

"It is iron."

"All the Ku arrows are bone and quartz."

"The Ku still kill children whose top teeth grow first."

This is how the Leopard taught me to kill with bow and arrow. Hold the bow on the side of the eye you use less. Draw the bow from the side of the eye you use more. Spread your feet until they are shoulder wide. Use three fingers to hold the arrow on the string. Raise and draw the bow, pull the string to your chin, all in the quick. Aim for the target and release the arrow. The first arrow went up into the sky and almost struck an owl. The second struck a branch above the hole. The third, I don't know what it struck but something squealed. The fourth struck the trunk near the ground.

"She is getting annoyed with you," he said. And pointed to the tree. He wanted me to retrieve the arrows. I pulled the first out of the branch and the little hole closed up. I was too scared to pull out the second, but the Leopard growled and I yanked it quick. I turned to run but a branch hit me flat in the face. The branch wasn't there before. Now the Leopard laughed.

"I can't aim," I said.

"You can't see," he said.

I couldn't see without blinking, couldn't draw without shaking, I couldn't point without shifting to the wrong leg. I could release the arrow, but never when he said so and the arrows never hit anywhere I pointed. I thought of aiming for the sky just so it would strike the ground. Truth, I did not know the Leopard could laugh this much. But he would not leave until I shot an arrow through the hole in the tree, and every time I struck the tree, it slapped me with a branch that was either always there or never there. Night sky was heavy before I shot an arrow through the target. He grabbed arrows and started walking, his way of saying we were done. We went down a path that I did not recognize, with rock and sand and stone covered in wet moss.

"This used to be a river," he said.

"What happened to it?"

"It hates the smell of man and flows under the earth whenever we approach."

"Truly?"

"No. It's the end of rainy season."

I was about to say that he has been living with the Sangoma for too long, but didn't. Instead I said, "Are you a Leopard that changes to man or a man that changes to Leopard?"

He walked off, stepping through the mud, climbing the rocks in what used to be a river. Branches and leaves blocked the stars.

"Sometimes I forget to change back."

"To man."

"To Leopard."

"What happens when you forget?"

He turned around and looked at me, then pressed his lips and sighed.

"There's no future in your form. Smaller. Slower, weaker."

I didn't know what to say other than "You look faster, stronger, and wiser to me."

"Compared to whom? You know what a real Leopard would have done? Eaten you by now. Eaten everyone."

He didn't frighten me, nor did he intend to. Everything he stirred was below my waist.

"The witch tells better jokes," I said.

"She told you she was a witch?"

"No."

"Do you know the ways of witches?"

"No."

"So you either speak through your ass or fart through your mouth. Be safe, boy. You would have made a terrible meal. My father changed and forgot how to change back. Spending the rest of his life in the misery of this shape."

"Where is he now?"

"They locked him in a cell for madmen, when a hunter came upon him as a man fucking a cheetah. He escaped, boarded a ship, and sailed east. Or so I heard."

"You heard?"

"Leopards are too cunning, boy. We can only live alone; leave it up to us we'd steal each other's kill. I have not seen my mother since I could kill an antelope myself."

"And you don't kill the children. That is a surprise."

"That would make me one of you. I know where my mother keeps. I have seen my brothers, but where they run is their business and where I run is mine."

"I had no brothers. Then I came to the village to hear I had one but the Gangatom killed him."

"And your father became your grandfather, Asani told me. And your mother?"

"My mother cooked sorghum and kept her legs open."

"You could have a family of one and still drive them apart."

"I don't hate her. I have nothing for her. When she dies I will not mourn, but I will not laugh."

"My mother suckled me for three moons and then fed me meat. That was enough. Then again I'm a beast."

"My grandfather was a coward."

"Your grandfather is the reason you're alive."

"Better to give me something to be proud of instead."

"For you have no pride already. What would the gods say?"

He came up to me, close enough for me to feel his breath on my face.

"Your face has gone sour," he said.

He stared deep into me as if trying to find the lost face.

"You left because your grandfather is a coward."

"I left for other reasons," I said.

He turned away and spread his arms wide as he walked, as if talking to the trees, not me.

"Of course. You left to find purpose. Because waking, eating, shitting, and fucking are all good things, but none of them is a purpose. So you searched for it, and purpose took you to the Ku. But your Ku purpose was to kill people you don't even know. My word stands. There is no future in your form. And here we are. Here you are, and Gangatom women wash their children right across that river. You could go kill a few. Right a wrong. Even please the gods and their vile sense of balance," the Leopard said.

"You blaspheming the gods?"

"Blaspheming means you believe."

"You don't believe in gods?"

"I don't believe in belief. No, that is false. I do believe there will be antelope in the woods and fish in the river and men will always want to fuck, which is the only one of their purposes that pleases me. But we talk of yours. Your purpose is to kill Gangatom. Instead you run to a Gangatom woman's house and play with mingi children. Asani I could read in one day, but you? You are a mystery to me."

"What did you read about Asani?"

"You can walk away from it."

"I have walked away from it."

"But it's still in your heart. Men killed your father and brother and yet it's your own family that makes you angry."

"I so tire of people trying to read me."

"Stop spreading open like a scroll."

"I am alone."

"Thank the gods, or your brother would be your uncle."

"That is not what I mean."

"I know what you mean. You are alone. But it makes your heart sick to be alone. We do not have this in common. Learn not to need people."

I could smell the huts above us.

"Do you like fucking better as man or beast?" I said. He smiled.

"There is salt in that question!"

I nodded.

"I like his chest on my chest, his lips on my neck, looking at him as he enjoys me. He likes when my tail whips his face."

"Is that what you read of him?"

"I read feet that have taken him as far as he can go."

"He has love for you and you for him?"

"Love? I know hunger, fear, and heat. I know when hot blood spills into your mouth when you bite down in the flesh of fresh kill. Asani, he was just a man who walked into my territory that I could just as well kill. But he found me on a night with a red moon."

"I do not understand."

"No you do not. As for territory . . ." He walked from one tree to the next, and the next, marking the ground with piss. He walked up to the tree that took us up and wet the base.

"Hyenas," he said.

I jumped. "Hyenas are coming?"

"Hyenas are here. They watch us from afar. Wouldn't you . . . no, you don't know their smell. They know who lives up this tree. So is that the way with you? Once you know the scent you can follow it anywhere?"

"Yes."

"Me?"

"Yes."

"For how long?"

"I could find my grandfather right now, with my eyes closed, even with him being seven or eight days away. And either of his three mistresses, including one who moved to another city. Sometimes there are too many and my mind skips and goes dark and comes back with everything at once, as if I woke up in the city square and everyone is screaming at me in a language I don't know. When I was young I had to cover my nose, almost killing myself when they got too loud. I still go mad sometimes."

He stared at me for a long time. I looked away at the weeds glowing in the dark and tried to make out shapes. When I turned back to him, he was still looking at me.

"And the smells you don't know?" he said.

"A fart might as well be from a flower."

Third story.
It took the night for me to know we had been with the Sangoma two moons.

"Ten and seven years I studied in the ithwasa, the initiation to become Sangoma," she said.

I went to the top hut this and every morning when I felt her calling me. Smoke Girl ran up my legs and chest and sat on my head. Ball Boy bounced around me. Sangoma was feeling the beads of a necklace she had buried three nights before, and whispering a chant. The boy she used to suckle kept running into the wall, walking backward, running into the wall, again and again, and she did not stop him. The day before she told the Leopard to take me out and teach me archery. All I learned was that I should try something else. Now I throw the hatchet. Even two at the same time.

"Ten and seven years of purity, humbling myself before the ancestors, learning divination and the skill of the master I called Iyanga. I learned to close my eye and find things hidden. Medicine to undo witchcraft. This is a sacred hut. Ancestors live here, ancestors and children, some of them ancestors reborn. Some of them, just children with gifts. Just as you are a child with gifts."

"I am not—"

"Modest, true. That much is plain, boy. You are also neither patient, wise, nor even very strong."

"Yet you had Kava and the Leopard bring this boy of no quality here. Should I leave?" I turned to go.

"No!"

That was louder than she meant, and we both knew it.

"Do as you wish. Go back to your grandfather posing as your father," she said.

"What do you want, wit—Sangoma?"

She nodded at the boy with the long legs. He went to the far end of the room and came back with a bamboo-weaved tray.

"During my ithwasa, my master told me that I would see far. Too far," the Sangoma said.

"Close your eyes, then."

"You need to respect your elders."

"I will, when I meet elders I can respect."

She laughed. "With so much leaving your front hole, no wonder you wish for something to enter the back."

She was not going to see me offended. Or hear me, or smell me. Or give news to the moonlight boy or the Leopard. Not even for the blink of an eye.

"What do you want?"

"Look at the bones. I throwing them every night for a moon and twenty nights, and always they land the same. The hyena bone lands first, meaning that I should expect a hunter. And a thief. Right after the first night you come."

"That knowledge passed me."

"Why be blessed with eyes? I know two who could use them more than you."

"Woman—"

"I never finish. Use the nose the gods gave you, or you will not notice the viper next time."

"You want my nose?"

"I want a boy. Seven nights now he gone. The bones tell me, but I was thinking no boy would run too far from good food."

"Good is not what—"

"Don't cross me, boy. He stop believing like a child, stop believing what I tell him all these moons. Child thief he call me! But such is the way— which child wants to know his own mother leave him to the wild dogs? Child thief he call me, then go off to find his mother. He even struck me when I wouldn't move out the way. My children were too shocked, or they would have killed him for true. He jumped the tree and run south."

I looked around. I knew some of these children could kill me in the quick.

"You will have back the boy."

"The boy can climb into his mother shrivel-up koo and sew the life string to his belly for all I care. But he steal something precious to me."

"A jewel? Proof that you are a woman?"

"Cursed a day it going to be when your mind catch up to your mouth. The gallbladder of the goat they sacrifice at my initiation ceremony. It has been in my hair from then. He left at morning, but took it the night before, while I was sleeping."

"Stole it from your own head."

"I was sleeping, I say."

"I thought enchanted beings slept light."

"What do you know of enchanted beings?"

"That anything wakes them."

"Must be why you go wandering at night."

"I don't—"

"Hope you find what you looking for. Enough. I will have it back. You talk of witches. Without it, witches will know of this place. You may not care for children, but you will care for gold coin."

"No need for gold in the vill—"

"You will never return to that village."

She looked at me, the scar pattern around her eyes making them fierce.

"Take the coins and find the boy," she said.

"Why wouldn't I just ta—"

She slapped me in the face with a loincloth. The funk rushed to my nose before I could breathe.

"Because I know how that nose work, boy. You never going to stop looking for who leave the smell, or it will drive you mad."

She was right. I did not know I could hate her more.

"Take the coins and find the boy."

She sent the Leopard and me. He has a nose too, she said. I thought she was going to send me with Kava. The Leopard looked neither pleased nor displeased. But right before we left, I saw them on the roof of the third hut, Kava waving his hands up and down like a madman, the Leopard looking as he always does. Kava threw a stick and the Leopard jumped him quick as lightning, his hand around Kava's throat. The Leopard released him and walked away. Kava laughed.

"Watch where that fucking cat takes you," Kava said to me when I saw him not long after.

I was filling wineskins with water by the river. This is what happened. After I filled them, I looked for red mud and white clay. When I found clay, I drew a white line and divided my face. Then another right along my brow. Then red lines on my cheeks and tracing my ribs, which I was seeing more, but it did not worry me the way it would have my mother.

"He takes me nowhere. I go to find the boy," I said.

"Watch where that fucking cat takes you," he said again.

I said nothing. I tried to mark behind my knees. Kava came up behind me and scooped up white clay. He rubbed it on my buttocks all the way down to my knees and down to my calves.

"Leopards are cunning. Do you know of their ways? You know why they run alone? Because they will betray even their own kind, and for a kill even the hyenas won't touch."

"Did he betray you?"

Kava looked up at me but said nothing. He was painting my thighs. I wanted him to stop.

"After you two find the boy, he will go on to southern lands. The grasslands are drying up and the prey is foul."

"If he wants."

"He has been a man too long. Hunters will kill him in two nights. The game is wilder, beasts that will rip him in two. Out there the hunters have poison arrows and they kill children. There are beasts bigger than this tree, blades of grass that love blood, beasts that will r—"

"Rip him in two. What do you want him to do?"

Kava washed his hands of clay and started to mark a pattern on my legs.

"He will leave with me, and forget this woman and her cursed children. It was his idea to save them, and lead them here, not mine. Whether they lived or died was the gods' business. Who lives at the top?" he asked.

"I don't—"

"She takes food up there every day. Now she takes you."

"Jealous."

"Of you? My blood is the blood of chiefs!"

"It was not a question."

He laughed. "You want to play with her dark arts, do as you wish. But the Leopard comes with me. We are going back to the village. Between us we kill the people responsible for the death of my mother."

"You said wind killed your kin. You said—"

"I know what I said, I was there when I said it. The Leopard said he will set out once you two find the boy. Tell him that you will not go."

"And then?"

"I will make him see," Kava said.

"There is no future in your form."

"What?"

"Somebody told me that a few days ago," I said.

"Who? Nobody passes this place. You're growing as mad as that bitch. I've seen you, on the roof of that hut, holding up air and playing with it like a child. She infects this place. What news have you of the boy? That he fled because he was ungrateful? Did she call him a thief? Maybe a killer?"

He stood up and looked at me.

"So she did. Do you think as a man, or does she rule all your thoughts? The boy escaped," he said.

"This is no prison."

"Then why he run off?"

"He thinks his mother cries for him at night. That he is not mingi."

"And who says he lies? Sangoma? No child here knows any different. Sangoma living in the trees for years and years, so where are the children who come of age? You and the animal hunt him down to bring him back. What will you do when he says no, I will not come back?"

"I hear you now. You think the Leopard is a fool for her too."

"Leopard is no fool. He does not care. She says go east, he goes east, as long as there is fish and the warthogs are fat. Nothing is in that heart."

"What blazes in yours."

"You two fucked in the forest," he said.

I looked at him.

"He said he taught you archery. The fucking beast was feeding me verse."

I thought about leaving him with the mystery of it, or telling him we did not and never would to give him ease, but also thinking fuck the gods and his need for ease.

"He will never love you," Kava said.

"Nobody loves no one," I said.

He punched me in the face—right on the cheek—and knocked me down in the mud. He jumped me before I got up. Knees on my arms pinning me down, he punched me in the face again. I kneed him in the ribs. He yelled and fell off. But I was coughing, gasping, crying like a boy, and he jumped me again. We rolled and my head hit a rock and the sky went gray and black and the mud was sinking and his spit was hitting my eye but I could not hear him, only see the back of his throat. We rolled into the river and his hands grabbed my neck, pushing me underwater, pulling me up, pushing me under, water rushing into my nose. The Leopard leapt on his back and bit him in the neck. The force knocked them both in the river. I pulled myself up to see the Leopard still on Kava's neck, about to toss him like a doll, and I yelled. The Leopard dropped him but growled. Kava staggered backways into the river and touched his neck. His hand came away with blood. He looked at me, then at the Leopard, who was still walking in circles in the river, still marking that this is where you shall not pass. Kava turned, ran up the banks and into the bush. The noise brought out the Sangoma, who came down with Giraffe Boy and Smoke Girl, who appeared in front of my eyes and vanished again. The Leopard was back to a man and he walked past the Sangoma, back to the hut.

"Don't forget why I sent for you," she said to me.

She threw me a thick cloth when I stepped out of the river. I thought it was to dry myself, but the boy's scent was all over it.

"That boy could be in my nose for moons."

"Then you better make haste and find him," she said.

———

We took one bow, many arrows, two daggers, two hatchets, a gourd tied to my hip with a piece of the cloth inside, and set out before first light.

"Are we finding the boy or killing him?" I said to the Leopard.

"He's seven days ahead. These are if someone finds him first," he said behind me, trusting my nose, even though I did not. The boy's smell was too strong in one spot, too weak in the other, even if his path was set right before me. Two nights later his trail was still ahead of us.

"Why didn't he go north, back to the village? Why go west?" I asked.

I stopped and the Leopard walked past me, turned south, and stopped after ten paces. He stooped down to sniff the grass.

"Who said he was from your village?" he asked.

"He did not go south, if you're trying to pick up the boy."

"He's your charge, not mine. I was sniffing out dinner."

Before I said more, he was on all paws and gone into the thicket. This was a dry area, trees skinny as stalks, as if starving for rain. The ground red and tough with cracked mud. Most of the trees had no leaves, and branches sprouted branches that sprouted branches so thin I thought they were thorns. It looked like water had made an enemy of this place, but a water hole was giving off scent not far away. Near enough that I heard the splash, the snarl, and a hundred hooves stampeding away.

Leopard got to me before I got to the river, still on four paws, a dead antelope in his mouth. That night he watched in disgust as I cooked my portion. He was back on two legs but eating the antelope leg raw, ripping away the skin with his teeth, sinking into the flesh and licking the blood off his lips. I wanted to enjoy flesh the way he enjoyed flesh. My burned and black leg disgusted me as well. He gave me a look that said he could never understand why any animal in these lands would eat prey by burning it first. He had no nose for spices and I had none to put on the meat. A part of the antelope was not cooked and I ate it, chewed it slow, wondering if this was what he ate when he ate flesh, warm and easy to pull apart, and if the feeling of iron spilled in your mouth was a good one. I would never like it. His face was lost in that leg.

"The trees are different," I said.

"Different kind of forest. The trees are selfish here. They share nothing under the earth; their roots send nothing to other roots, no food, no news. They will not live together, so unless rain comes they will die together. The boy?"

"His scent is north. It grows neither strong nor weak."

"Not moving. Asleep?"

"Mayhaps. But if he stays, we find him tomorrow."

"Sooner than I thought. This could be your life if you wish it."

"You wish to go on when we find him?"

He threw down the bone and looked at me. "What else did Asani tell you before he tried to drown you?" he said.

"You will send me back with the boy, but will not return."

"I said I might not return, not will not."

"Which is it?"

"That depends on what I find. Or what finds me. What is it to you?"

"Nothing, nothing at all."

He grinned, stood up, and came over beside me. The fire threw harsh lines on his face and lit up his eyes. "Why do you go back?"

"She wants her bladder."

"Not the cursed Sangoma, the village. Why do you go back to the village?"

"My family is there."

"You have no one there. Asani told me all that awaits you is a vendetta."

"That is still something, is it not?"

"No."

He looked to the fire. His mouth goes sick from the sight of cooking, but he made the fire. From the gourd I pulled the piece of cloth carrying the boy's scent. These were not trees he could sleep in, even if he preferred to sleep off the ground.

"Come with me," he said.

"Where?"

"No. I mean come with me after this. After we find the boy. She has no interest in him; she wants her foul bladder to place in her foul hair. We find him, scare him, send him back. We go west."

"Kava wants—"

"Is Asani lord over anyone here?"

"Something came to pass between you two."

"Nothing came to pass. That is the stick between us. He passes you in years, but in every other way he is the man younger. Gambles with lives, and kills for sport. The disgusting features of your form."

"Then stop changing into it. You raise no cry over the disgusting acts you like."

"Name the like. You think in this kind of moon, you can judge me, little boy? There are lands where men who love men get their cocks cut off, and are left to bleed to death. Besides, I do as gods do. Of all the terrible features of your form, shame is the worst."

I knew he was looking at me. I was staring into the flames but could feel him turn his head. The night wind was sending a fragrance I did not know. Ripeness from fruit, maybe, but nothing was fruitful in this bush. This made me remember something and I was surprised that I only now remembered it.

"What happened to them who were following us?"

"Who?"

"The night we came to the Sangoma. The little woman said somebody was following us."

"She is always fearing something or someone is after her."

"You believed it too."

"I don't believe in fear, but I believe in her belief. Besides, there are at least ten and six enchantments to throw off hunters and wanderers."

"Like vipers?"

"No, those are always real," he said with a wicked smile.

He reached over and grabbed my shoulder.

"Go be with pleasant dreams. Tomorrow we find the boy."

I jumped out of sleep, to my feet, hungry for air. It wasn't air. I darted left and right as if I had lost something, as if somebody stole from me. It woke up the Leopard. I walked left, right, north, and south, covered my nose and breathed in deep, but still nothing. I almost walked into the dying fire before Leopard grabbed my hand.

"I'm nose-blind," I said.

"What?"

"His smell, it is lost to me."

"Do you mean he's—"

"Yes."

He sat in the dirt.

"We should still get her bladder," he said. "Let us continue north."

It took us till dusk to get out of that forest. The

thicket, smelling the fresh funk of us, would not let us go, slapping and whipping us across our chests and feet, sticking out little branches to grab our hair, scattering thorns in the dirt to prick our feet, and signaling to vultures flying overhead to swoop low. We, two animals, fresh meat, did not interest them. We crossed the savannah and neither the antelopes, egrets, nor warthogs took notice. But we headed to another thicket that looked empty. Nobody went in, not even two lions who looked at the Leopard and nodded.

The new thicket was already dark. Tall trees but thin with branches reaching upward, which would break from the Leopard's weight. Trunks peeling skin, showing age. We stepped on bones scattered all over the ground. I jumped when the scent hit me.

"He is here," said the Leopard.

"I don't know his death smell."

"There are other ways to know," he said, and pointed at the ground.

Footprints. Some small like a young man's. Others large but like handprints left in grass and mud. But some of them gone wild as if walking, then running, then running mad. He walked past me for a few steps and stopped. I thought he would change but instead he opened the sack and threw me the hatchets. Then he grabbed an arrow and pulled his bow.

"All this for a stinking gallbladder?"

The Leopard laughed. Truth, he was more pleasant than Kava.

"I'm starting to think Kava speaks true about you," I said.

"Who said he spoke false?"

Truth, I shut my mouth and just stared at him, hoping he would change what he just said.

"The boy was kidnapped. Sangoma took him herself. She stole him from her own sister. Yes there is a story, little boy. Do you know why she has such malice for witches? Her sister was one. Is one. I don't know. Her sister's story is that Sangoma is a child thief who takes babies from their mothers and trains them in wicked arts. Sangoma's story is that her sister is a dirt witch and that is not her boy, since all dirt witches are barren from all the potions they drank for powers. She stole the child and was set to sell his parts in the Malangika, the secret witches market. Many sorceresses would give plenty coin for a baby's heart, cut out that day."

"Which story do you believe?"

"The one where a dead child is not one of my choices. No matter. I'll circle around. He will not escape."

He ran off before I could say I hated this plan. I do have a nose, as people say. But it was useless when I did not know what I smelled.

I stepped over a thick shrub and went in. Few paces in and the ground was drier, like sand and the dirt stuck to my feet. I climbed over a massive skeleton, the tusks telling me it was a young elephant, with four of his ribs crushed. Turn back and let him scare the boy out, my mind told me, but I kept walking. I passed a gathering of bones, like an altar, a stepped mound, and pried two small trees apart to step through. Above nothing stirred, no fowl, no snake, no monkey. Quiet is the opposite of sound, not the absence of it. This was absence.

I looked behind me and could not remember from where I came. I walked around the tree, stepping on shrubs and wild bush, when something cracked behind me. Nothing but smells, pungent and foul. A foulness that came from rot. Man rot. But nothing was in front of me, nothing behind. Yet I felt the boy was here. I wanted to call his name.

A crack again, and I turned around but did not stop walking. A wet thing touched my temple and cheek. A smell, that smell—rot. I touched my cheek and something came away, blood and slime, spit maybe. Entrails hung down like rope, another curled up below the ribs, smelling like man rot and shit. The skin ripped with tears, as if everything below had been cut away by a ragged knife. Some of the skin had peeled away at his side and his ribs poked out. Vines under his arms and around his neck held him up. The Sangoma said to look for a ring of little scars around his right nipple. The boy. Up in the tree were other men, and women, and children, all dead, most missing half their bodies, some their heads, some their hands, and fingers, their entrails all dangling out.

"Sasabonsam, brother from the same mother, he

likes the blood. Asanbosam, that is me, I likes the flesh. Yes, the flesh."

I jumped. A voice that sounded like a stench. I stepped back. This was the lair of one of the old and forgotten gods, back when gods were brutish and unclean. Or a demon. But all around me were dead people. My heart, the drum inside me beat so loud I could hear it. My drum beat out of my chest and my body trembled. The foul voice said, "Gods send us a fat one, yes he is. A fat one they send us."

I likes the flesh
And bone
Sasa like blood
And seed. He send we you.
Ukwau tsu nambu ka takumi ba

I spun. No one. I looked in front, the boy. The boy's eyes open, I did not notice before. Wide open, screaming at nothing, screaming for us being too late. **Ukwau tsu nambu ka takumi ba.** I knew the tongue. **A dead thing does not lack a devourer.** The wind shifted behind me. I spun around. He hung upside down. A huge gray hand grabbed my neck and claws dug into the skin. He squeezed the breath out of me and pulled me up into the tree.

I don't know how long my mind was black. A vine snaked itself across my chest and around the trunk, around my legs and around my forehead, leaving my neck clean and belly open. The boy hung right across, looking at me, his eyes wide open, searching. His mouth still open. I thought it was his death pose, the last scream that did not come out, until I saw something in his mouth, black but also green. The gallbladder.

"Broke a tooth we is, when all we want is a little taste. Little, little taste."

I knew his smell and I knew he was above me, but the scent would not stay. I looked up to see him fall, hand to his side as if he was diving fast, heading for the ground. Gray and purple and black and stink and huge. He dove past a branch but his feet caught it and the branch bounced. His feet, long with scales on the ankles, one claw sticking out of the heel and another jutting instead of toes, curved around the branch like a hook. He let go, dove, and caught another branch, low enough that his face was facing me. His purple hair ran along a strip in the center of his head. Neck and shoulders, muscle packed on top of muscle, like a buffalo. Chest like the crocodile's underbelly. And his face. Scales above his eyes, nose flat, but nostrils wide with purple hair sticking out. Cheekbones high as if he was always hungry, skin gray with warts, two sharp shiny teeth sticking out of the corners of his mouth even when not talking, like a boar.

"We hear in lands where no rain, mother speak we and frighten children. You hear it? Tell we true, delicious, delicious."

And this, his breath, fouler than corpse rot, fouler than the shit of the sick. My eyes followed his chest and the ridges of bones pushing under his skin, three on the left, three on the right. His thighs thick with muscle, tree trunks above skinny knees. He tied me up tight. I heard my grandfather talk of how he would welcome death when he knew it was coming, but right here I knew he was a fool. That was the kind of talk from someone who expected death to meet him in sleep. And I would scream how wrong this was, how unfair to see death coming, and how I will cry in an eternal sadness that he chose to kill me slow, to pierce me and all the while tell me how he delights in it. To chew away at my skin and chop my fingers, and each tear of flesh will be a new tear, and each pain will be a new pain and each fright will be a new fright, and I will watch his pleasure. And I will want to die quick because I suffer so, but I do not want to die. I do not want to die. I do not want to die.

"You no want to die? Young boy, you never hear of we? Soon soon soon soon soon you begging for it," he said.

He took his hand, warts all over, hair on the knuckles, claws at the fingertips, and grabbed my chin. He yanked my jaw open and said, "Pretty teeth. Pretty mouth, boy."

A body above dripped something on me. That was the first time I thought of the Leopard. The Leopard, who said he would go around the bush, but nobody knew the bush was seven moons wide. The shapeshifting son of a sniveling cat bitch will leave here. Asanbosam swung himself up and hopped away.

"He going be angry with us, he will. Angry, angry,

so so angry. Don't touch the flesh until I have my blood, he say. I am the oldest, he say. And he whip us terrible. Terrible. Terrible. But he gone and I hungry. And you know what worse? What worse and worse? He too eat the best flesh, like the head. Is fair? I ask fair?"

When he swung back down to face me, a hand, black skin rotting to green, was in his mouth. He bit the fingers off. He reached for me with his left hand and a claw dug into my forehead and drew blood.

"No fresh flesh in days," he said. His black eyes opened wide, as if pleading with me.

"Many, many days."

He put the arm in his mouth, chewing bit by bit until elbow flesh hung on his lips.

"Need his blood yes he do, so he say and he do. Leave them alive, he say."

He looked at me, his eyes open wide again.

"But he never say leave you whole."

He sucked in the little sliver of dead flesh.

"Cut bit of fle—"

The first arrow burst through his right eye. The second shot right into his scream and burst out the back of his neck. Third bounced off his chest. Fourth shot straight through the left eye. Fifth ran right through his hand as he reached for his eye. The sixth pierced the soft skin at his side.

His claw feet slipped off the branch. I heard him hit the ground. The Leopard jumped up from branch to branch, leaping from a weak one before it broke and landing on a strong one. He sat where the trunk split into branches, and stared at the bodies, his tail wrapping around a bunch of wilted leaves. He changed to man before I could rage at him for taking so long. Instead I bawled. I hated being a boy, my own voice telling me, A child is what you are. He went down for the sack and came back up with a hatchet. I fell into his arms and stayed there, crying. He patted my back and touched my head.

"We should leave. They travel in two, his kind," Leopard said.

"His brother?"

"They live in trees and attack from above, but I have never heard of one this far from the coast. He is Asanbosam, the flesh eater. His brother, Sasabonsam, is the bloodsucker. He is also the smart one. We should leave now."

"The gallbladder."

"I grabbed it."

"Where is it?"

"We should go."

"I never saw you—"

He pushed me.

"Sasabonsam will soon return. He has wings."

FIVE

The Leopard chopped off Asanbosam's head, wrapped it in sukusuku leaves, and shoved it in the sack. We left the way I came, weapons out, ready for whichever beast would show itself that night.

"What will you do with the head?" I asked.

"Stick it on a wall so I can scratch my ass when it itches."

"What?"

He said no more. Four nights we were on foot, around forests that would have been quicker going through, and two-faced animals who would have smelled the Asanbosam's flesh and alerted his brother. At just a morning's distance from Sangoma's huts a smell came to me, and the Leopard too. Smoke, ash, fat, skin. He growled and I shouted, Go. I grabbed the bow, the weapons, and the sack and ran. When I came to the stream, a little boy was floating in it, facedown. The Leopard jumped into the water and fished him out, but an arrow had pierced his heart. We knew the boy. Not one from the top hut, but still mingi. There was no time to bury him, so the Leopard placed him back in the river, faceup, closed his eyes, and let him go.

On the path two bodies blocked the way, a boy and the albino girl, each with a spear stuck in the back. Everywhere was red from the blood of children, and the huts were on fire. The lower hut had caved into a huge mound of ash and smoke, and the middle, weak from burned beams, split in two. One half fell into the rubble of the lower hut. The tree swayed, black and naked, all its leaves burning off. Fire raged in the top hut. Half of the roof was burning, half of the wall black and smoking. I leapt for the first step and it broke under me. Falling, tumbling, I was still rolling when the Leopard jumped up safer steps and ran straight into the hut. He had kicked a hole into the back wall, still safe from flames, and kept kicking till it was big enough. He came out a cat, holding a boy by the neck of his shirt, but the boy did not move. Leopard nodded towards the hut, telling me there were more in there.

Inside the flames were screaming, laughing, jumping leaf to leaf, wood to wood, cloth to cloth. On the floor, the boy with no legs, holding on to the boy with giraffe legs, and screaming for him to move. I pointed to the opening and picked up Giraffe Boy. The boy with no legs rolled through the opening and I looked around for anybody I had missed.

The Sangoma was on the ceiling, still, her eyes wide open, her mouth in a silent scream. A spear went right through her chest, but something pinned her flat to the ceiling as if it was the floor, and it was not the spear. Witchwork. There was only one person I could think of who could do witchwork. Somebody had broken through her enchantments and made it all the way to her floor. Fire hopped on her dress and she burst into flames.

I ran out with the boy.

The twin boys came out of the bushes, their eyes wide open and mouths loose. A look I knew would never leave them, no matter how many moons. The Leopard pulled away a dead boy to see another, an albino, alive and under him. He screamed and tried to run but stumbled and the Leopard grabbed him. I placed Giraffe Boy on the grass when blue Smoke Girl appeared, trembling so hard she was breaking into two, three, four girls. Then she ran off, vanished, reappeared at the edge of the forest. She vanished, and appeared in front of me again, yelling quiet. She ran off again, stopped, ran, vanished, appeared, stopped, and looked at me until I saw that she wanted me to follow.

I heard them before I saw them. Hyenas.

Off behind a fallen tree three of them were fighting over a piece of flesh, scowling, ripping, biting each other to get a grip, and swallowing chunks whole. I shut it out, any thought of what they could be eating. Four more had chased a little boy right up a tree,

snarling and laughing, mocking before the kill. Smoke
Girl appeared right in front of the boy and frightened
the pack. They backed away but not far enough for the
boy to run. I climbed a tree fifty paces away, and
jumped from branch to branch, tree to tree as I saw
the Leopard do. From one branch high I jumped to
one low, then swung back up to a branch on high. I
scrambled down one branch and leapt onto another,
slid down the trunk that split in two like a slingshot,
through leaves slapping me in the face, jumped and
grabbed another branch that bent from my weight
and then threw me up.

The hyenas were cackling, setting up order, de-
ciding who should kill him. And that tree was tall
with thin branches, not in talk with the trees around
it. I jumped from a branch on top, grabbed another,
swung from it, and landed in the tree, breaking all
the branches around me, scraping my legs and left
cheek and swallowing leaves. The four hyenas moved
in closer and Smoke Girl tried to hold the boy. Large
hyenas, the biggest in the pack. Female. I threw a
dagger and missed a paw. One jumped back, right
into my second throw, which struck her head. One
ran off, two stayed and snarled and cackled.

A hatchet in each hand, a knife in my mouth, I
jumped from on high, down right in front of one
of the remaining two, and double-chopped her face
quick, yanking, chopping, yanking, chopping until
blood and flesh splashed my face and blinded me.
She knocked me over and bit into my left hand, tear-

ing at it, crushing it, making me gnash teeth and frightening the boy. The second tried to bite my feet. I stabbed the first hyena in the neck. Pulled out and stabbed again. Stabbed again. Stabbed again. It fell. The hyena snapping at my feet moved in to bite. I swung my good hand and the knife sliced across her face, bursting one eye open. She squealed and ran off. Two other hyenas bit into the little flesh left by the others and took off.

My left hand, bloody and stringing with hanging flesh, went lifeless. The boy was so scared that he backed away from me. Smoke Girl ran to me and beckoned him to come over. Just as he ran, a hyena leapt at him. She landed right on top of the boy, dead with two arrows right through her neck. The boy screamed as I pulled him out. The Leopard shot two more and the rest of them ran away.

The little boy the Leopard pulled out of the hut never woke up. We buried six, then stopped because there were so many and each death was killing us. The four others we found, we wrapped in whatever cloth or skin we could find and set on the water for the river to take them to the underworld. They looked like they were flying to the call of the goddess. After we found berries and cooked meat for the children, and they fell asleep long enough to stop crying and screaming in their sleep, the Leopard led me into the woods.

"Cast blame," he said.

"Why? You know who did this."

"Can you smell him?"

"I can smell all of them."

"There will be more."

"I know."

Smoke Girl would not let me go. She followed me to the edge of the clearing, past what was once protected by enchantments, until I shouted at her to go back. The Leopard had those left alive—the boy we saved from hyenas, the albino boy, Ball Boy, the twins, Giraffe Boy, and her. There were too many bodies to bury and most were burned. The roof of the top hut caved when I turned to leave, and the albino boy started crying. The Leopard did not know what to do. He pawed the boy's face until he climbed up and rested his head on his shoulder.

"I should go," he said.

"You can't track them."

"You can't kill them."

"I will take the hatchet and the knife. And a spear."

"I can follow them now."

"They masked their tracks going through the river. You won't find them."

"You have only one arm."

"I only need one."

He wrapped my arm in aso oke cloth that I knew was Sangoma's head wrap. The men's smells were fading before, but had stayed strong since dusk. Resting for the night. Step for step they had come to the hut on the same trail we had. I could have found them even without my nose. Trinkets tossed all along the way, when they realized the Sangoma's charms were worth nothing. I found them and my uncle before deep night, roasting meat on a spit. The burning-meat smoke had scared all the cats. The half-moon gave dim light. Uncle must have come to prove he could still use a knife. Against children. They were between two marula trees, joking and mocking, one of them spreading his arms, bugging his eyes, sticking out his tongue, and saying something in village tongue about a witch. Another was eating fruit off the ground, walking drunk and calling himself a rhinoceros. Another said the witch had bewitched his belly so he was going off to shit. I followed him past the trees out to where elephant grass reached past his neck. Far enough that he could hear them laugh but they wouldn't hear him strain. The man lifted his loincloth and crouched. I stepped on a rotten twig for him to look up. My spear struck him right through the heart and his eyes went white, his legs buckled and he fell in the bush, making no sound. I pulled the spear out and shouted a curse. The other men scrambled.

At another tree I climbed up and threw my voice again. One of the men came close, feeling his way around the trunk, but not seeing anything in the dim light. His smell I knew. I wrapped my legs around a branch and hung down right above him with the ax as he called for Anikuyo. I swung my arm in swift and chopped him in the temple. His smell I knew but his name I could not remember, and thought about it too long.

A club hit me in the chest and I fell. His hands around my neck, he squeezed. He would do it, he would chase my life out, and boast that he did so himself.

Kava.

I knew his smell, and he knew it was me. The moon's half-light lit up his smile. He said nothing, but pressed into my left arm and laughed when I bit down a scream. Somebody shouted to see if he'd found me, and my right hand slipped from his knee but he didn't notice. He squeezed my neck harder; my head was heavy, then light and all I could see was red. I didn't even know that I'd found the knife on the ground until I grabbed the handle, watched him laugh and say, Did you fuck the Leopard? and jammed it right in his neck, where blood spurted out like hot water from the ground. His eyes popped open. He did not fall, but lowered himself gently on my chest, his warm blood running down my skin.

This is what I wanted to say to the witchman.

That the reason he could not see me in the dark, could not hear me move through the bush, could not smell me on his trail, running after him as he ran away because he knew something had fallen like twisted wind on his men, the reason why he tripped and fell, the reason why none of the stones he found and threw hit me, or the jackal shit he mistook for stones, the reason why, even after binding her with a spell, and killing her on the ceiling, the Sangoma's witchcraft still protected me, was that it was never witchcraft. I wanted to say all that. Instead I jammed the knife in the west of his neck and slashed his throat all the way east.

My uncle shouted at them not to leave, the last two who were near him. He would double their cowries, triple them, so they could pay for other men to fight their blood feuds or gain another wife from a comelier village. He sat down in the dirt, thinking they were watching the bush, but they watched the meat. The one on the right dropped first, my hatchet slicing his nose in two and splitting open his skull. The second ran right into my spear. He fell and was not quick. I ran my spear through his belly and struck the ground, going for his neck. Enough time for my uncle to think there was hope. To run.

My knife struck him in the back of his right thigh. He fell hard, yelling and screaming for the gods.

"Which of the children did you kill first, Uncle?" I said as I stood over him. He groveled, but not to me.

"Blind god of night, hear my prayers."

"Which one? Did you take the knife yourself, or hire men to do it?"

"Gods of earth and sky, I have always given you tribute."

"Did any scream?"

"God of earth and—"

"Did any of them scream?"

He stopped crawling away and sat in the dirt.

"All of them scream. When we lock them in the hut and set it on fire. Then there was no more screaming."

He said that to shake me, and it did. I didn't want to become the kind of man who was never disturbed by such news.

"And you. I knew you were a curse but I never thought you would be hiding mingi."

"Don't ever call—"

"Mingi! You ever see rain, boy? Feel it on your skin? Watch flowers burst open in just one night because the earth is fat with water? What if you never saw the like again? Cows and cats so scrawny their ribs press through skin? All of these you would have seen. You will wonder for moons why the gods have forgotten this land. Dried up the rivers and let women give birth to dead children. That is what you would bring on us? One mingi child is enough to curse a house. But ten and four? Did you not hear us say hunting was bad and getting worse? Bumbangi can wear foolish mask and dance to foolish god; none of them will listen in the presence of mingi. Two more moons and we would be starving. No wonder the elephant and the rhinoceros has fled and only the viper remains. And you, the fool—"

"Kava was the one protecting them, not me."

"Watch how he lie! That is what Kava say you would do. He followed you and some Leopard you lying with. How many abominations can there be in one boy?"

"I would say let Kava prove his word, but he no longer has a throat."

He swallowed. I stepped closer. He limped away.

"I am your beloved uncle. I am the only home you have."

"Then I shall live in trees and shit near rivers."

"You think drums won't hear? People will smell all this blood and blame you. Who is he, the one without family? Who is he, the one without child? Who was the one that Kava returned to the village and spoke of, saying he was working curses on his own people? All these men you have killed, what will their wives sing? You, who chose wicked children, and cursed the land, have now taken their fathers, sons, and brothers. You're a dead man; you might as well take that knife and cut your own throat."

I yawned. "Do you have more? Or will you get to your offer now?"

"The fetish priest—"

"Now you take the word of fetish priests?"

"The fetish priest, he told me something would fall like a storm on us."

"And you thought lightning. If you thought at all."

"You are not lightning. You are plague. Watch me now, how you come to us at night like bad wind, and set flow curses. You were supposed to kill Gangatom. Instead you have done their work. And even they will never turn on their own. Nobody is yours and you will be nobody's."

"You a soothsayer now? Is tomorrow before you? Beloved uncle, I have one question."

He glared at me.

"Gangatom came for my father and my brother,

and caused my grandfather to flee. How is it, beloved uncle, that they never came for you?"

"I am your beloved uncle."

"And when I asked how I know you, the ways of the city, you said you came with your brother, my father—"

"I am your beloved uncle."

"But my father was dead. You fled to the city with my grandfather, did you not? You bought yourselves chairs like bitchmen. My house had two cowards, not one."

"I am your beloved uncle."

"Loved by who?"

I ducked before he threw it, my own knife. It hit the tree behind me and fell. He jumped up and yelled, charging me like a buffalo. The first arrow burst right through the left cheek and right. The second shot into his neck. The third through his ribs. He stared at me as his legs failed, falling to his knees. The fourth also went through his neck. Beloved uncle fell flat on his face. Behind me, the Leopard put down his bow. Behind him were the albino, Ball Boy, the twins, Giraffe Boy, and Smoke Girl.

"This was not for their eyes," I said.

"Yes it was," he said.

At sunrise, we took the children to the only people who would have them, people for whom no child could ever be a curse. The Gangatom villagers drew spears when they saw us approach, but let us through when the Leopard shouted that we brought gifts for the chief. That man, tall, thin, more fighter than ruler, came out from his hut, and eyed us from behind a wall of warriors. He turned his head to the Leopard, but his eyes, set back under his brow and in shadow, stayed on me. He wore a ring in each ear and two beaded necklaces around his neck. His chest, a wall of scars from tens on top of tens of kills. The Leopard opened his sack and threw Asanbosam's head out. Even the warriors jumped back.

The chief stared at it long enough for flies to swarm. He stepped past the warriors, picked it up, and laughed.

"When the flesh eater and the blood drinker brother take my sister they suck just enough blood to keep her alive but feed her so much filth that she become their blood slave. She live under their tree and eat scraps of dead men. She follow them across all lands until even they tired of her. She follow them into rivers, over walls, into a nest of fire ants. One day Sasabonsam grab his brother and fly off a cliff, knowing she going follow."

He held up the head, and laughed again. The people cheered. Then he looked at me and stopped laughing.

"So, Leopard, is it boldness or foolishness you have? You bring a Ku here?"

"He comes bringing gifts too," the Leopard said.

I pulled my uncle's goatskin cape and his head

fell out. His warriors stepped closer. The chief said nothing.

"But are you not his blood?"

"I am nobody's blood."

"I can see it in you, smell it, whether you deny it or not. We kill many men and several women, most from your tribe. But we do not kill our own. What kind of honor do you think this bring you?"

"You just said you killed several women, yet you will talk of honor?"

The chief stared at me again. "I would say you cannot stay here but you did not come to stay."

He looked behind us.

"More gifts?"

We left the children with him. Two women grabbed Giraffe Boy, one by the ass cheek, and took him to their hut. A young man said his father was blind and lonely and would not care that the twins were joined together. That way he never had to worry about losing one. A man with noble feathers in his cap took Ball Boy on a hunt that day. Several boys and girls surrounded the albino, touching and poking him until one of them gave him a bowl of water.

The Leopard and I left before sunset. We walked along the river because I wanted to see even a glimpse of someone Ku, someone I would never see again. But no Ku would have come to the river to meet a Gangatom spear. Leopard turned to go back into deep forest when leaves rustled behind me. Most times she passes like a spirit but if afraid enough, or happy, or angry, she will rustle leaves and knock over bowls. Smoke Girl.

"Tell her she cannot follow," I said to the Leopard.

"I'm not who she follows," he said.

"Go back," I said when I turned around. "Go be the daughter to a mother, or the sister to a brother."

Her face appeared out of the smoke, frowning as if she did not understand me. I pointed to the village, but she did nothing. I waved her off and turned away, but she followed. I thought if I ignored her, and ignored what it did to my heart beating, she would go away, but Smoke Girl followed me to the edge of their village and after.

"Go back!" I said. "Go back, I don't want you."

I started walking and she appeared in front of me again. I was about to shout but she was crying. I turned away and she appeared again. The Leopard started to change and growled, and she jumped.

"Go back before I curse you!" I shouted.

We were at the edge of Gangatom territory going north into free lands and then Luala Luala. I knew she was behind me. I picked up two stones and threw one at her. Went right through her, the stone did, but I knew it would horrify her, the move.

"Go back, you fucking ghost!" I shouted, and threw the second stone. She vanished and I did not see her again. The Leopard had walked off far before I realized I was still in one spot and had not moved. I wouldn't until he growled.

I went with the Leopard to Fasisi, the capital city

of the North, and found many men and women with
lost things and people, who could use my nose. The
Leopard grew tired of walls and left after two moons,
and I was for long moons alone.

When I next saw the Leopard, years had passed and
I was a man. Too many bitter men knew me in
Fasisi, so I moved to Malakal. He was there for four
nights before leaving word with my landlady that
he would see me, which I thought was clear since he
would have no reason to see this city. The Leopard
was still strong in jaw and handsome and came in
man form, tunic and cape, as men in the city would
have killed a beast. His legs thicker, the hair around
his face wilder. He wore whiskers, but this was a city
where men loved men, priests married slaves, and sadness was washed away with palm wine and masuku
beer. I smelled his arrival the night he came to the
city. A night where even the rain, waking up old
smells, could not weaken his funk. He still smelled
like a man who only washed if he happened to cross
a river. We met at Kulikulo Inn, a place where I did
business, a place where the fat innkeeper served soup
and wine, and nobody cared who or what came
through the door. He held a jug of beer and offered
me palm wine that he would not drink himself.

"You look well, so different, a man now," he said.

"You look the same," I said.

"How is your nose?"

"This nose will pay for this wine, since I see no pouch on you."

He laughed and said he came with a proposal.

"I need you to help me find a fly," he said.

2
MALAKIN

Gaba kura baya siyaki.

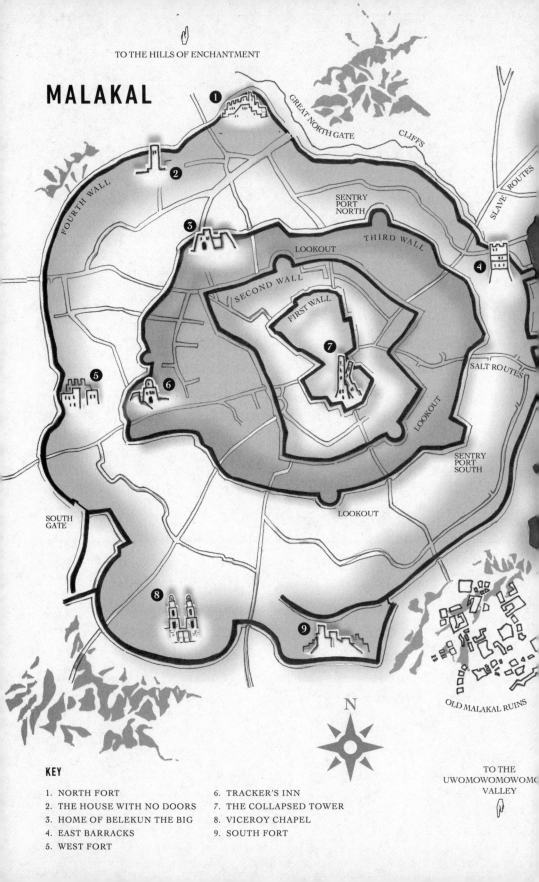

MALAKAL

TO THE HILLS OF ENCHANTMENT

GREAT NORTH GATE

CLIFFS

SLAVE ROUTES

FOURTH WALL

SENTRY PORT NORTH

THIRD WALL

LOOKOUT

SECOND WALL

FIRST WALL

SALT ROUTES

LOOKOUT

SENTRY PORT SOUTH

SOUTH GATE

LOOKOUT

OLD MALAKAL RUINS

N

TO THE UWOMOWOMOWOMO VALLEY

KEY

1. NORTH FORT
2. THE HOUSE WITH NO DOORS
3. HOME OF BELEKUN THE BIG
4. EAST BARRACKS
5. WEST FORT
6. TRACKER'S INN
7. THE COLLAPSED TOWER
8. VICEROY CHAPEL
9. SOUTH FORT

SIX

This.

You wish that I read this.

Check the account for yourself, you say. Make my mark where it says different from what happened. I don't need to read; you write as Ashe wishes. Ashe is the everything, life and death, morning and night, good luck and bad tidings. What you in South think is a god but is where the gods come from.

But do I believe it?

A smart question. Fine, I will read it.

Testimony of the Tracker on this the ninth day. A thousand bows to the elders' pleasure. This testimony is written witness, given appeal to the gods of sky who stand in judgment with lightning and viper venom. And as is the elders' pleasure, the Tracker gives account both wide and far, since great many years and moons have passed from the loss of the child to the death of the same one. This is the middle of the Tracker's many tales,

meaning which be true and which be false I shall leave to the judgment of the elders, alone in the counsel of the gods. The Tracker's account continues to perplex even those of uncommon mind. He travels deep in strange lands, as if telling tales to children at night, or reciting nightmares to the fetish priest for Ifa divination. But such is the pleasure of the elders, that a man should speak free, and a man should speak till the ears of the gods are filled with truth.

He goes into the sight, smell, and taste of one memory, with perfect recall of the smell in the crack of a man's buttocks, or the perfume of Malakal virgins in bedchambers coming out of windows he walked underneath, or the sight of the glorious sunlight marking the slow change of seasons. But of spaces between moons, a year, three years, he says nothing.

This we know: The Tracker in the company of nine, including one more who still lives and one not accounted for, went searching for a boy. Kidnapped, he has alleged. The boy at the time was alleged to be the son or ward of a slaver from Malakal.

This we know: They set out first from Malakal at the beginning of the dry season. The search for the boy took seven moons. A success, the child they found and returned, but four years later he was lost again and the second search, in smaller company, took one year and culminated with the boy's death.

At the request of the elders, the Tracker has spoken in detail of his upbringing, and with clear speech and fair countenance has recounted a few details of the first search. But he will speak only of the end of the second search, and refuses to give testimony of the four years in between, where it is known that he took up residence in the land of Mitu.

This is where I, your inquisitor, set a different bait. He had come, that ninth morning, to talk of the year he reunited with the mercenary called Leopard. Indeed, he had said before that it was the Leopard that came to him with the offer to search for the child. But a lie is a house carefully built on rotten stilts. A liar often forgets the beginning of his tale before he gets to the end, and in this way one will catch him. A lie is a tale carefully told if allowed to be told, and I would seek to break his untruth by asking him to tell a different part of the tale. So I asked him not of the first search or the second, but of the four years in between.

INQUEST: Tell me of the year of our King's death.

TRACKER: Your mad King.

INQUEST: Our King.

TRACKER: But the mad one. Forgive me, they are all mad.

INQUEST: Tell me of the year of our King's death.

TRACKER: He is your king. You tell me.

INQUEST: Tell me of —

TRACKER: It was a year, as years go. There were days, there were nights with nights being the end of day. Moons, seasons, storms, drought. Are you not a fetish priest who gives such news, inquisitor? Your questions grow stranger by the day; this is true talk.

INQUEST: You remember the year?

TRACKER: The Ku don't name years.

INQUEST: Do you remember the year?

TRACKER: It was the year your most excellent King shat his most excellent life out in the most excellent shit pit.

INQUEST: Speaking ill of the King is punishable by death in the South Kingdom.

TRACKER: He's a corpse, not a king.

INQUEST: Enough. Tell me of your year.

TRACKER: The year? My year. I lived it full and left all of it behind when it ended. What more is there to know?

INQUEST: You have nothing else?

TRACKER: I fear that you would find greater tales among those of us dead, inquisitor. Of those years I have nothing to report but steadiness, boredom, and the endless request of angry wives to find their unsatisfied husbands—

INQUEST: Did you not retire those years?

TRACKER: I think I am the best to remember my own years.

INQUEST: Tell me of your four years in Mitu.

TRACKER: I spent no four years in Mitu.

INQUEST: Your testimony on the fourth day said after the first search you left for the village of Gangatom and from there, Mitu. Your testimony on the fifth day began, When he found me in Mitu I was ready to leave. Four years remain unaccounted for. Did you not live it in Mitu?

[Note: The sandglass was a third from being empty when I asked him this question. He looked at me as men do when they contemplate petulance. An arch in his eyebrow, a scowl in his face, then a blankness, a drop in the corner of his lips, and his eyes wet, as if he went from anger at my question to something else at the thought of an answer. The sandglass was empty before he spoke again.]

TRACKER: I know of no place named Mitu.

INQUEST: You? The Tracker who claims to have been to so many kingdoms, to the place of flying beasts, and the land of talking monkeys and lands not on the maps of men, but you have no knowledge of an entire territory?

TRACKER: Take your finger out of my sore.

INQUEST: You forget which of us gives the orders.

TRACKER: I have never set foot in Mitu.

INQUEST: A different answer from I know of no place named Mitu.

TRACKER: Tell me how you wish this story to be told. From the dusk of it to the dawn of it? Or maybe as a lesson, or praise song. Or should my story move as crabs do, from one side to the next?

INQUEST: Tell the elders, who shall take this

writing as your very own speech. What happened, your four years in Mitu?

I will describe his face without impression or judgment. His eyebrows raised higher than before, he opened his mouth but did not speak. It is my impression that he growled or cursed in one of the northern river tongues. Then he jumped from his chair, knocking it over and pushing it away. He leapt at me, yelling and screaming. I barely shouted out for the guard before his hands grabbed my throat. Truly it is my conviction that he would have strangled me until dead. And still he squeezed tighter, pushing me backward on my chair until we both fell to the ground. I daresay his breath was foul. Stab him I did, with writing stick into his hand and at the top of his shoulder, but I can say in testimony that I was indeed leaving this world and doing so with haste. Two guards came from behind and struck him in the back of the head with clubs until he fell on top of me, and even then his grip did not relax, until they struck him a third time.

I must say it was a fair account, though I remember my ribs suffering several kicks from your men, even after they bound me. My back suffering beatings from a yam sack. Also this: my feet meeting so much whipping I am surprised that I walked to this room. My memory cheats—they dragged me here. And that was not even the worst, for the worst was you having them put me in robes meant for slaves—what offense have done I to cause that?

Now look at us. Me in the dark even in daylight, you over there on a stool. Balancing paper and writing stick on your lap while you try not to knock over the ink at your foot. And these iron bars between us. The man beside me calls for the love goddess each night, and I have not heard such sounds since I searched for my father, my grandfather in a whorehouse. Between me and you, I wish she would answer, for his cries get ever louder each night.

So. My father and brother murdered and my uncle slain by my hand. Go back to my grandfather? To give him what tidings? Hail, Father, who I now know as my grandfather though you lie with my mother. I killed your other son. There was no honor in it but you are already a man with no honor. You truly are cunning. A cunning one, inquisitor, to get me so angry I speak to them and not you. What kind of testimony is this?

You have washed since I saw you last. Spring water with precious salts, spices, and fragrant flowers. So many spices I would suspect that your ten-year-old wife was trying to cook you. But Priest, I smell the blister on the right of your back, right where she poured boiling water and scalded you. By all the gods, she did try to cook you. You struck her, of course, hard in the mouth. You've brought her blood with you before.

Where is what happened next? After your guards clubbed me in the back of the head, but before they took me down here. The part where I strangled you till you were near dead. The part where the guards had to slap you like a fool on opium in a spirit monger's den. Don't ask about Mitu again.

One more thing. When did you move me to Nigiki? I ask because these are Nigiki slave robes. Besides, I smell the salt mines every direction I turn. Did you move me at night? What strange potions kept me asleep? People say a cell in Nigiki is more lavish than a palace in Kongor, but such people have never been in this cell. Did you move her as well or just your dear, difficult Tracker?

My last time in this city I was in chains as well.

I will tell you the story.

I let myself be sold to a nobleman in Nigiki, because a slave still had four meals, none by his own purse, and lived in a palace. So why not be a slave? Whenever I felt for freedom I could just kill my master. But this nobleman had the ear of your mad King. I knew because he would tell anyone who would hear. And since I was in a new game—total subservience to another—I was the one to tell. Slaves are not to be resold in the South Kingdom, especially not in Nigiki, but he did so, and that was how he made his fortune. Sometimes the slave was freeborn and stolen.

The master was a coward and a thief. He whipped his wife at night and punched her in the day so that the slaves could see that no man or woman was above him. I said to her once when he was away: If it pleases the mistress, I have five limbs, ten fingers, one tongue, and two holes, all at her pleasure. She said, You smell like a boar but you may be the only man in Nigiki who does not smell of salt. She said, I hear things of you men from the North, that you do things to women with your lips and tongue. I searched through her five robes, found her koo, spread its lips west and east, then flicked my tongue on the little soul deep in the woman that the Ku think is a hidden boy that must be cut out, but is beyond boy or girl. She made noises louder than when whipped, but since I was hidden under her robes, her slaves thought it was the recall of a whipping, or the god of harvest giving her rapture.

She never let me put anything inside her but my tongue, for such is still the way of mistresses.

"How can one lie with a boar?" she would say.

You are waiting to see how this ends. You're waiting to see if I ever did pull apart the seas of her robes and take her without her ever asking such, because that is what you southern lords do. Or you are waiting for that moment when I kill her husband, for do not all my tales end in blood?

Soon I said to the nobleman, It is not yet a moon, yet I am already bored with being your slave. Not even your cruelty is interesting. I said good-bye, made an obscene sign with my lips and tongue to the mistress, and turned to leave.

Yes, in this way I left.

Fine, if you must know, I did strike the nobleman in the back of the head with the flat side of a long sword, bid a slave to shit in his mouth, and tied a rope around his head to keep his jaw shut. Then I left.

The children?

What does it matter?

I tried to see the children. More times than once or twice. One quartermoon after we left them with the Gangatom, I was sneaking along the two sisters river. By then the village would have smelled on wind the bodies of Kava, the witchman, and my beloved uncle. And coming up, on the Gangatom side of the river, a spear could meet my chest at any moment and my killer would not have lied when he said, Here I killed a Ku. I skipped from tree to tree, bush to bush knowing that I should not have gone. It was only a quartermoon. But maybe the albino ran into a boy who would stick him to see if his blood was white, and maybe the women of the village were scared of Smoke Girl's troubled sleep and needed to know that one should not fear her, for how else would they know? And to let her sit on your head if she wants to sit on your head, and maybe my boy who thinks he is a ball rolls into a man because that is the only way he knows to say, Here I am, play with me, I am already a toy. And to never call Giraffe Boy giraffe. Not once.

And the twins, such cunning minds and such joyful hearts, one will call you over the right shoulder saying, Where is east? while the other steals sips from your porridge.

And there was no Leopard to vouch for me; he found work and amusement in Fasisi. But the river runs through both lands, and trees stood far apart. I stopped at one tree, and was about to skip to the next, ten and seven paces ahead, when arrows shot past me. I jumped back and the tree caught the three arrows hitting it. Voices of Ku, men across the river, thinking they'd killed me. I dropped to my belly and scurried away like a lizard.

Two years later I went to see my mingi children. I came from Malakal, taking a different route than used by Ku. Giraffe Boy was now as tall as an actual giraffe, his legs reaching my head; his face, a little older but still young. He saw me first when I entered the Gangatom township. The albino, I did not know was the oldest until I saw that he grew the most, thick in muscle and a little taller in height, and very handsome. I couldn't tell if he really grew up in the quick or had I only now noticed. Even as he ran to me, the women's eyes followed him. The twins were in the bush hunting. The boy with no legs got even more fat and round, and rolled himself everywhere. You will be useful in war, I said to him. Are you all warriors now? The albino nodded while the boy with no legs giggled and rolled right into me, knocking me over. I did not see Smoke Girl.

And then after a moon I went walking with Gi-raffe Boy and said, Smoke Girl, does she hate me still? He did not know how to answer me, because he had never known hate. Every man who comes into her life leaves, he said as we walked back to his home. At the door, the women raising him said, The chief is dying and the man to be the next chief has bad feelings for all Ku, even one who lives with other people in houses of stone.

You don't need their names.

As for the Leopard, five years passed before I met him at Kulikulo Inn. He was at a table, waiting for me.

"I need you to help me find a fly," he said.

"Then consult the spider," I said.

He laughed. The years had changed him, even if he looked the same. His jaw was still strong, his eyes, light pools where you saw yourself. Whiskers and wild hair that made him look more lion than panther. I wondered if he was still as quick. For long I wondered if he aged as a Leopard or as a man. Malakal was a place of civil butchery, and not a city for were-folk. But Kulikulo Inn never judged men by their form or their dress, even if they wore nothing but dust or red ochre spread with cow fat, as long as their coin was strong and flowed like a river. Still, he pulled skins from a sack and wrapped something coarse and hairy about his lap, then draped shiny leathers over his back. This was new. The animal had learned the shame of men, the same man who once said that the Leopard would have been born with skirts if he was supposed to wear any. He asked for wine and strong drink that would have killed a beast.

"No embrace for the man who saved your life more times than a fly blinks?"

"Does the fly blink?"

He laughed again and jumped from his stool. I took his hands, but he pulled away and grabbed me, pulling in tight. I was ready to say this feels like something from boy lovers in the east until I felt myself go soft in his arms, weak, so weak I barely hugged back. I felt like crying, like a boy, and I nodded the feeling out of me. I pulled away first.

"You have changed, Leopard," I said.

"Since I sat down?"

"Since I saw you last."

"Ay, Tracker, wicked times have left their mark. Are your days not wicked?"

"My days are fattening."

He laughed. "But look at you, talking to the cat of change." His mouth was quivering, as if he would say more.

"What?" I asked.

He pointed. "Your eye, you fool. What kind of enchantment is that? Will you not speak of it?"

"I have forgotten," I said.

"You have forgotten there is a jackal's eye in your face."

"Wolf."

He moved in closer and I smelled beer. Now I was looking at him as deep as he was looking at me.

"I am already waiting for the day you finally tell this one to me—lusting for it, I am. Or dreading it."

I missed that laugh.

"Now, Tracker. I found no boys for sport in your city. How do you make do with night hunger?"

"I quench my thirst instead," I said, and he laughed.

It was true that in those years I lived as monks do. Other than when travels took me far and there were comely boys, or not as comely eunuchs, who though not pretty were more skilled in love play. And even women would sometimes do.

"What have you been doing the last few years, Tracker?"

"Too much and too little," I said.

"Tell me."

These are the stories I told the Leopard as I drank wine and he drank masuku beer at Kulikulo Inn.

One year I lived in Malakal, before I moved to Kalindar, the disputed kingdom at the border with the South. Home of great horse lords. Truly, the place was more a set of stables with lodging for men to fuck, sleep, and conspire. No matter which side you came from, the city could only be reached by hard land journey. War-loving people, bitter and vengeful in hate, passionate and vigorous in love, who despised the gods and challenged them often. So of course I made it home.

So in Kalindar was a Prince with no princedom,

who said his daughter was kidnapped by bandits on the trail north. This is what they wanted in ransom: silver, the weight of ten and seven horses. Hear this, the Prince sent his servant to get me, which he tried to, in a way keeping with the Prince's foul manners. I sent him back missing two fingers.

The Prince's second servant bowed and asked me to please the Prince with my appearance. So I went to his palace, which was just five rooms, each stacked on the other, in a courtyard overrun with chickens. But he had gold. He wore it on his teeth and stringed it through his eyebrows and when the privy boy passed by, he carried a shit pot of pure gold.

"You, the man who took my guard's fingers, I have use for you," he said.

"I cannot find a kingdom you have not lost," I said. The Kalindar have no double tongue, so the remark went right back out to sea.

"Kingdom? I don't need kingdom finding. Bandits kidnapped my daughter, your Princess, five days ago. They have demanded a ransom, silver the weight of ten and seven horses."

"Will you pay it?"

The Prince rubbed his bottom lip, still looking in the mirror.

"First I need trustful word that your Princess is still alive. It has been said that you have a nose."

"Indeed. You wish that I find her and bring her back?"

"Listen to the way he speaks to princes! No. I only

wish you find her and give me good report. Then I shall decide."

He nodded to an old woman, who threw a doll at me. I picked it up and smelled her.

"The price is seven times ten gold pieces," I said.

"The price is I spare your life for your insolence," he said.

This Prince with no princedom was as frightening as a baby crying over shitting itself, but I went searching for the Princess, because sometimes, the work is its own pay. Especially when her scent took me not to the north roads, or the bandit towns, or even a shallow grave in the ground, but less than a morning's walk from her father's little palace. In a hut near a place that used to be a busy market for fruit and meat, but is now wild bush. I found her at night. She and her woman-snatchers, one of whom was reeling from a slap to the side of his head.

"Ten and seven horses? Is that all I am to you, ten and seven? And in silver? Was your birth so low that you think this is what I am worth?"

She cussed and snarled for so long that it began to bore me, and still she cussed. I could tell the kidnapper was coming to think mayhaps he should pay the Prince to take her back. I smelled the shape-shifter's gift on him, a cat like the Leopard. A Lion, perhaps, and the other men lying about were his pride and the woman by the fire looking at them both with a scowl was his mate until this princess. All of them squeezed into a room with the Princess yapping like cockatoo. This was the plan: that the Lion and his pride kidnap the Princess and demand a sum. A sum which her father would gladly pay because his daughter is worth more than silver and gold. The ransom, the Princess would use to pay mercenaries to overthrow this Prince, who had no princedom to overthrow. At first I thought she was like those boys and girls kidnapped too young, who in the midst of captivity start to show loyalty to their captors, even love. But then she said, "I should have picked Leopards; at least they have cunning." The head Lion man roared so loud it frightened people in the street.

"I think I know how this story ends," the Leopard said. "Or maybe I just know you. You told the Prince his daughter's plot, then slipped away as quiet as you came."

"Good Leopard, what would be the fun in that? Besides, my days were long and business slow."

"You were bored."

"Like a god waiting for man to surprise him."

He grinned.

"I went back to the Prince and gave good report. I said, Good Prince, I have yet to find the bandits, but on my way, I did pass by a house near the old market, where men were conspiring to take your crown."

"What? Are you sure of it? Which men?" he asked.

"I did not look. Instead I hurried back to you. Now I will go find your daughter," I said.

"What should I do with these men?"

"Have men sneak up to the house like thieves in the night and burn it to the ground."

The Leopard stared at me, ready to pull the story out of my mouth.

"Did he?"

"Who knows? But next moon I saw the daughter at her window, her head a black stump. Then I cursed Kalindar and moved back to Malakal."

"That is your story? Tell me another."

"No. You tell me of your travels. What does a Leopard do in new lands where he cannot hunt?"

"A Leopard finds flesh wherever he can find it. And then there is flesh he eats! But you know how I am. Beasts like us were never made for one place. But nobody traveled as far as I. Boarded a ship I did, eager I was. I went to sea, then boarded another ship and it went farther out to sea for moons and moons."

He climbed up in the chair and stooped on the seat. I knew he would.

"I saw great sea beasts, including one that looked like a fish but could swallow an entire ship. I found my father."

"Leopard! But you thought he was dead."

"So did he! The man was a blacksmith living on an island in the middle of a sea. I forget the name."

"No you did not."

"Fuck the gods, maybe I don't want to remember. He was no longer a blacksmith, just an old man waiting to die. I stayed there with him. Saw him forget to remember, then saw him forget that he forgets. Listen, there was no Leopard in him—he had forgotten it all living with his young wife and family under one roof, which is no Leopard's nature. Curse you and your whiskers, he said to me many times. But some days he would look at me and growl and you should see how startled he was, wondering where the growl came from. I changed in front of him once and he screamed as an old man screams, making no sound. Nobody believed him when he shouted, Look a wildcat, he will eat me!"

"This is a very sad story."

"It gets sadder yet. His children in that house, my brothers and sisters, all had some trace of the cat in them. The youngest had spots all over his back. And none of them liked to wear clothes, even though on this island in the river, men and women covered everything but eyes. When he was dying he kept shifting from man to Leopard to man on his death mat. It scared the children and grieved the mother. In the end it was only me, my youngest brother, and him in the room, since everybody else but the youngest thought it was witchcraft. The youngest looked at his father and finally saw himself. We both became Leopards and I licked my father's face to calm him. In endless sleep, I left him."

"That is a sad story. Yet there is beauty in it."

"You a lover of beauty now?"

"If you saw who left my bed just this morning, you would not ask that question."

I missed his laugh. The entire inn heard when the Leopard laughed.

"A wanderer I became, Tracker. How I moved from land to land, kingdom to kingdom. Kingdoms where people's skin was paler than sand, and every seven days they ate their own god. I have been a farmer, an assassin, I even took a name, Kwesi."

"What does it mean?"

"Fuck the gods if I know. I even became an entertainer of the bawdy arts."

"What?"

"Enough, man. The reason I sought you out—"

"Fuck the gods with your reason, I will hear more of these bawdy arts."

"We don't have much time, Tracker."

"Then be quick about it. But spare no detail."

"Tracker."

"Or I shall rise and leave you with the bill, Kwesi."

He almost winced when I said that.

"Fine. Enough. So I was a soldier."

"This doesn't begin like a bawdy story."

"Fuck the gods, Tracker. Maybe the story begins when a man found an army—"

"North or South?"

"Fucks for both. I say, this man found an army with need for a man with superior archery skills. This man found himself in lands with no food, and no amusement. This man might have been great with killing the enemy, but was not great keeping peace between his fellow soldiers. Though one or two comely ones served their use."

"Ever the Leopard."

"This is how it came to pass. We attacked a village that had no weapons besides stones to cut meat, and burned down their huts with women and children still in them. It happened this way. I said, I do not kill women and children, not even when hungry. The commander's little bitch says, Then kill them with your bow. I say these are not fighters in war and he says you have an order. I walk away because I'm no soldier and this was not a fight worth coin.

"Say this also happened. The little bitch screamed traitor and in the quick his men were upon me; meanwhile soldiers were still setting fire to children trapped in huts. Four soldiers came at me, and I fired four arrows between four sets of eyes. The little bitch tried to scream again but my fifth arrow went right through his throat. So it goes without telling you, Tracker, that I had to leave, under the cover of fire smoke. But then I wandered for days and days before I found that I was in the sand sea where nothing lives. Four days without water or food, I started to see a fat woman walking on clouds and lions walking on two legs, and a caravan that never touched the sand. Men from the caravan picked me up and threw me in the back.

"I woke up when a boy's mother had him throw water in my face. The caravan dumped me at some doorstep in Wakadishu."

"From the sand sea to Wakadishu takes moons, Leopard."

"'Twas a fast caravan."

"So now you're a mercenary," I said.

"Look at this leper accusing another leper of leprosy."

"But I find men, not kill them."

"Of course. It's cow's blood you're always wiping from your helmet. Why do we war over words? Are you happy, Tracker?"

"I am content with much. This world never gives me anything, and yet I have everything I want."

"Fool, not what I asked you."

"Beasts look for happiness now? Be less the man and more the Leopard, if this is the man you are going to be."

"Fuck the gods, Tracker, 'tis a simple question. The longest answer is but one word."

"This affects your offer?"

"No."

"Then there's your answer. I am busy and better busy than bored, is that not so?"

"I'm waiting—"

"For what?"

"For you to say that sadness is not the absence of happiness, but the opposite of it."

"Have I ever said that?"

"You say something close. And who does your heart belong to?"

"You told me once nobody loves no one."

"I may have been young, and in love with my own cock."

"Jakrari mada kairiwoni yoloba mada."

"What use is that tongue to a cat?"

"Your cock is like a camel to you."

I was starting to tell him things just to hear that cat laugh.

"I don't trust people who take voyages without return; it gives them no stakes. I've been, let's say, disappointed by men with nothing to lose," he said.

"Are **you** happy?" I asked.

"You answer a question with a question?"

"Because here we are, whining like first wives of husbands who no longer want us. But then I'm a boy raised by no one and you pretend to be a man when it suits you, but there are many enchanted beasts that can talk. Whatever this offer is of yours, I'm liking it less and less."

"My offer hasn't left my lips, Tracker."

"No, but you are doing some kind of test."

"Forgive me, Tracker, but I have not seen you in moons upon moons."

"And you are the one who sought me out, cat. And now you waste my time. Here's coin for the raw boar. And extra for all the blood they left in for you."

"It does me good to see you."

"I was about to say the same, then you started wondering about my heart."

"Oh brother, your heart I wonder about all the time. Worry too."

"This too is part of it."

"What?"

"Your fucking test."

"Tracker, we are freeborn. I am drinking and eating with another. At least sit if you're never going to eat."

I got up to leave. I was a good few paces away from him when I said, "Send word for me when I have passed whatever test it was you were trying to give me."

"You think you passed?"

"I passed when I came through the door. Or you wouldn't have waited four days to call on me. You ever see a man who doesn't know he's unhappy, Leopard? Look for it in the scars on his woman's face. Or in the excellence of his woodcraft and iron making, or in the masks he makes to wear himself because he forbids the world to see his own face. I am not happy, Leopard. But I am not unhappy that I know."

"I have word of the children."

He knew that would stop me.

"What? How?"

"I still trade with the Gangatom, Tracker."

"Give me this word. Now."

"Not yet. Trust me, your girl is fine, even if she still huffs and puffs and turns to blue smoke when she loses her temper, which is often. Have you seen them?"

"No, not ever."

"Oh."

"What is this oh?"

"A strange look on your face."

"I have no strange look."

"Tracker, you are nothing but strange looks. Nothing is ever hidden from your face, no matter how much you try to mask it. It's how I can judge where your heart is with people. You are the world's worst liar and the only face I trust."

"I will hear of the children."

"Of course. They—"

"Did none say I came to see them? Not one?"

"You just said you have not seen them. Not ever, this is what you said."

"Not ever it might as well be, if they say they have not seen my face."

"More strangeness, Tracker. The children are fat and smiling. The albino will soon be their best warrior."

"And the girl?"

"I just told you about the girl."

"Eat."

"We have other matters to discuss, Tracker. Enough with nostalgia for now."

He took the last chunk of flesh in his mouth and chewed. There was blood on the dish. He looked at it, I looked at it, then he looked at me.

"Oh be a fucking beast, Leopard. Your wanting man's approval troubles me."

He smiled his huge grin, put the plate to his face, and licked it clean.

"Not fresh kill," I said.

"But it will do. Now finally. Why I came to see you."

"Something about a fly?"

"That was me being clever."

"Why did you ask if I was happy?"

"This road I am asking you to come on. Oh, Tracker, the things it will take from you. Best if you have nothing in the first place."

"You just said it was better if I have something to lose."

"I said I've been disappointed by men who have nothing. Some. But the Tracker I know has nothing and cultivates nothing. Has that changed?"

"And if it had?"

"I would ask different questions."

"How do you know I . . ."

Leopard swung around, trying to see what took my words.

"Nothing," I said. "Thought I noticed . . . thought it went and came back. . . . It . . ."

"What?"

"Nothing. A thought loose. Nothing. Come now, cat, I'm losing patience."

The Leopard got off the chair and stretched his legs. He sat back down and faced me.

"He calls him little fly. I find it strange that he does so, especially in that voice of his that sounds like an old woman more than a man, but I think the fly is dear to him."

"Once more. This time with sense."

"I can only tell you what the man told me. He was very clear—Leave instructions to me, he said. Fuck the gods, you men who are not direct. Fucks for you too—I saw that look. Friend, this is what I know. There is a child that went missing. The magistrates said he most likely got swept off in a river, or mayhaps the crocodiles got him, or river folk, since you will eat anything if hungry."

"Thousand fucks for your mother."

"A thousand and one if we're speaking of my mother," he said, and laughed. "This is what I know. The magistrates think this child either drowned or was killed and eaten by a beast. But this man, Amadu Kasawura is the name he goes by, he is a man of wealth and taste. He is convinced that his child, his little fly, is alive, mayhaps, and moving west. There is compelling stuff there, Tracker, in his home, evidence so that you believe his story. Besides, he is a rich man, a very rich man given that none of us come cheap."

"Us?"

"He has commissioned nine, Tracker. Five men, three women, and hopefully you."

"So his purse must be the fattest thing about him. And the child—his own?"

"He says neither yes nor no. He is a slaver, selling black and red slaves to the ships that come from people who follow the eastern light."

"Slavers have nothing but enemies. Maybe somebody killed the child."

"Mayhaps, but he is set in his desire, Tracker. He knows that we might find bones. But then he would at least know, and knowing for certain is better than years of torment. But I skip too much and make the mission—"

"Mission, is it? We're to be priests now?"

"I'm a cat, Tracker. How many fucking words do you think I know?"

This time I laughed.

"I told you what I know. A slaver is paying nine to either find this child alive, or proof of his death, and he does not care what we do to find him. He may be two villages away, he may be in the South Kingdom, he might be bones buried in the Mweru. You have a nose, Tracker. You could find him in days."

"If the hunt is so swift, why does he need nine?"

"Clever Tracker, is it not clear to you? The child didn't leave. He was taken."

"By who?"

"Better if it comes from him. If I explain you might not come."

I stared at him.

"I know that look," he said.

"What look?"

"That look. You are more than interested. You're glutting on the very idea of it."

"You read too much in my face."

"It's not just your face. At the very least come because something will intrigue you and it won't be the coin. Now speaking of desires . . ."

I looked at the man, who not long before the sun left convinced an innkeeper to give him raw meat soaking in its own blood for dinner. Then I smelled something, the same as before, on Leopard yet not on him. When we stepped outside the inn, the smell was stronger, but then it went weak. Strong again, stronger, then weaker. The smell got weaker every time the Leopard turned around.

"Who is he, the boy following us?" I asked.

I spoke loud enough for the boy to hear. He shifted from dark to dark, from the black shadow cast by post to the red light cast by a torch. He slipped into the doorway of a shut house, less than twenty paces from us.

"What I would like to know, Leopard, is would you let me throw a hatchet and split his head in two before you tell me he is yours?"

"He is not mine, and by the gods I'm not his."

"And yet I smelled him the whole time we were at the inn."

"A nuisance he is," the Leopard said, watching the boy slip out of the doorway, too timid to look. Not tall, but skinny enough to come across so. Skin as dark as shadow, a red robe tied at his neck that reached his thigh, red bands above his elbow, gold bracelets at his wrists, a striped skirt around his waist. He was carrying the Leopard's bow and arrows.

"Saved him from pirates on either the third or fourth voyage. Now he refuses to leave me alone. I swear it's the wind that keeps blowing him my way."

"Truly, Leopard, when I said I keep smelling him, I meant smelling him on you."

The Leopard laughed, but a tiny laugh, like a child caught right as he is about to do mischief.

"He has my bow when I lose arms and always finds me no matter where I go. Who knows but the gods? He might tell great stories of me when I am gone. I pissed on him to mark him as mine."

"What?"

"A joke, Tracker."

"A joke doesn't mean false."

"I'm not an animal."

"Since when?"

I stopped myself from asking if this is not the fifth boy or sixth you are leading astray, him waiting without hope for something you will never give him, because that is what you give, is it not, your eyes upon his eyes, your ears for whatever he says, your lips for his lips, all things you can give and take away, and nothing that he wants. Or is he your tenth? Instead I said, "Where is this slaver?"

The slaver was from the North, trading illegally with Nigiki, but he and his caravans, full with fresh slaves, had set up camp in the Uwomowomowomowo valley, not even a quarter day's ride from Malakal and quicker by just going down the hill. I asked Leopard if the man had no fear of bandits.

"A pack of thieves tried to rob him near the Dark-lands once. They put a knife to his throat, laughed that he had only three guards that they easily killed and how is it that he had no weapon himself, with such cargo? The thieves fled on horseback, but the slaver sent a message by talking drum that reached where the thieves were going before they approached the gate. By the time the slaver reached the gate the three robbers were nailed to it, their belly skin flayed open, their guts hanging out for all to see. Now he only travels with four men to feed the slaves on the journey to the coast."

"I have great love for him already," I said.

When we reached my lodgings, I tiptoed past the innkeeper, who told me two days ago that I was one moon behind in rent, and while scooping her huge breasts in her hands, said there were other ways to pay. In my room I grabbed a goatskin cape, two waterskins, some nuts in a pouch, and two knives. I left through the window.

The Leopard and I went by foot. From my inn we would leave through the third city wall, going under the lookout to the fourth and outer wall, which went around the whole mountain and was as thick as a man lying flat. Then from the South fort gate, out to the rocky hills and right down into the valley. The Leopard would never travel on the back of another animal, and I have never owned a horse, though I have stolen a few. At the gates, I noticed the boy walking behind us, still jumping from tree shadow to tree shadow and the ruined stumps of the old towers that stood long before Malakal was Malakal. I slept here once. The spirits were welcoming, or maybe they did not care. The ruins were from people who discovered the secret of metals and could cut black stone. Walls

with no mortar, just brick on top of brick, sometimes
curving into a dome. A man from the sand sea who
counted ages would have said old Malakal was from
six ages ago, maybe more. Surely at a time when men
needed a wall as much to keep in as to keep out. De-
fense, wealth, power. In that one night I could read
the old city; rotten wood doorways, steps, alleys,
passages, ducts for water foul and fresh, all within
walls seventy paces high and twenty paces thick. And
then one day, all the people of old Malakal vanished.
Died, fled, no griot remembers or knows. Now blocks
crumbed to rubble that twisted direction here and
there, and around, and back and down what used to
be an alley, halted at a dead end with no choice but
to go back, but back to where? A maze. The boy held
back so far behind us he was at this point lost.

"Truth, you can rip a man's head off in one bite
and yet he's more afraid of me. What is his name?"

The Leopard, as always, walked off ahead. "I never
bothered to ask," he said, and laughed.

"Fuck the gods, if you are not the worst of the
cats," I said.

I held back a few paces, until I too lost myself in
shadow. I saw the boy trying to go from stump to
stump, ruin to ruin, crumbling wall to crumbling
wall. Truth, I could have watched him for as long as
it was dark. He fell deep in the ruins that were not
that deep, and tried to walk himself out of them. As
he began to run, his smell changed a little—it always
does when fear or ecstasy takes over. He tripped over

my foot and landed in the dirt. Perhaps my foot was waiting for him.

"What is your name?" I asked.

"No business it be for you to know," he said, and stood up. He puffed his chest up and looked past me. He looked older than before, one of those who might be ten and five years, but were still ten in the mind. I looked at him, wondered what would be left when the Leopard no longer had use for him.

"I could leave you in these ruins and you will be lost until daylight. And where will your precious Leopard be then, tell me?"

"Is just brick and shit nobody want."

"Careful. The ancestors will hear you, and then you will never leave."

"All him friends fool as you?"

The first one I saw, I picked up and threw at him. He caught it in the quick. Good. But he dropped it as soon as he saw it was a skull.

"He don't need you."

I turned away, back to where I knew the gate would be.

"Where you going?"

"Back to drink some good soup from a bad woman. Tell your, whatever you call him, that you said he didn't need me, so I left. That is if you can find your way out of the ruins."

"Wait!"

I turned around.

"How I get out of this place?"

I walked past him, not waiting on him to follow. I stepped in cold ash, the fire long gone out. Sticking out of the dirt were pieces of white cloth, candle-wax, rotten fruit, and green beads that might have been a necklace. Someone tried to reach an ancestor or the gods more than a moon ago. We made it out of the ruins and the last of the trees to the edge of the valley. Another night with no moon.

"What do they call you?" I asked.

"Fumeli," he said to the ground.

"Guard your heart, Fumeli."

"What that mean?"

I sat down on the rock. Foolishness it would be to try to go down to the valley in this dark, though I could smell the Leopard was halfway down already.

"We sleep till first light."

"But he—"

"Will be right down there fast asleep until we wake him tomorrow."

Two thoughts while I slept that night.

The Leopard says too many things that slip off him like water does oil, but sticks to me like a stain. Truth, there are times I feel like I should wash him out. I am always happy to see him, but never sad when he is gone. He asked me if I was happy and I still didn't understand either the question or what knowledge he would get from an answer. Nobody smiles more than the Leopard but he speaks the same in happiness and sadness. I think both are faces he puts on before matters that strike deep, first in the heart. Happiness? Who needs happy when there is masuku beer? And spicy meat, good coin, and warm bodies to lie with? Besides, to be a man in my family is to let go of happiness, which depends on too many things one cannot control.

Something to fight for, or nothing to lose, which makes you a finer warrior? I have no answer.

I thought of the children more than I believed I would. Soon it was something I felt like a slight pound in the head, or a quickening of the heart, that even when I told myself it was gone, there was no worry, and I have done good by those children, or at least the best I could do, the feeling came that I had not. A dark evening becomes darker. I wondered if it was yet another one of the things the Sangoma left as a stain on me, or maybe it was a mild madness.

I woke up to the boy bent over me.

"Your other eye shine in the dark, like a dog," he said. I would slap him but a new cut above his right eye glimmered with blood.

"How slippery the rocks are in the morning. Especially if you don't know the way."

The boy hissed. He picked up the Leopard's bow and quiver. I wondered if any person ever made me shiver like the Leopard did this boy.

"And I do not snore," I said, but he was already running down into the valley, until he stopped.

He walked, he sat on a rock and pondered, he waited until I was just paces behind him, and set off again. But not very far, for he didn't know where to go.

"Rub his belly," I said. "It pleases him. Great pleasure."

"How do you know that? You must rub all sorts of men."

"He is a cat. A cat loves that you rub his belly. Just like a dog. Is there nothing up in that head of yours?"

The ground turned red and damp, and green shrubs popped up like bumps. The farther down we walked, the larger the valley looked. It went straight to the end of the sky and beyond that. The wise ones said that the valley was once just a little river, a goddess that had forgotten she was a god. That little river snaked through the valley, washed away ground, dirt after dirt, stone after stone, deeper and deeper until by the time of this age of man, she had left valleys that dug so deep that man started to see the opposite, that it was not land lying so low, but mountain reaching so high. Looking up as we went down, and looking across the sky and the mist, we saw mountains pressed beside mountains, each one bigger than cities. So high that they took the colour of sky, not bush. It was enough to keep your eye to the sky and not the ground. The dirt as it reddened, the shrubs as they gave way to trees, the river clear like glass, and in it, fat nymphs, with broad heads and wide mouths, not hiding in the day, and knowing that they were not the prey this caravan hunts for.

The boy, whose name I already forgot, dashed after the Leopard as soon as we came down the mountain. Truth, I knew he was not his Leopard, and I knew the boy would make this cat very angry. He grabbed the Leopard's tail, and he swung around and roared, crouched, and leapt at the boy. Another roar came from near the first caravan and the Leopard, pinning the boy, trotted away. The boy jumped up, brushed himself off before anyone noticed, and ran after his Leopard, sitting as a man on the grass, looking out to the river. He turned to me and smiled, but said nothing to the boy.

"Your bow and quiver. I bring it," the boy said.

The Leopard nodded, looked at me, and said, "Shall we meet the slaver?"

The slaver had a tent at the front of his caravan. And the caravan, as long as a street in Malakal. Four wagons that I have seen only along the border of kingdoms north of the sand sea, among people who wander and never sow root. Horses pulled the first two, oxen pulled the last two. Purple and pink and green and blue, as if the most childish of goddesses painted them all. Behind the wagons, carts open and slatted together from wood. On the carts, women, thick to thin, some red from ochre, some shiny from shea butter and fat. Some wore only trinkets, some wore necklaces and goatskins in yellow and red, some in full robes, but most were naked. All captured and sold, or kidnapped from the river lands. None with the scars of the Ku or the Gangatom. Or the shaved teeth. Men from the East did not find those things beautiful. Behind these carts, men and boys, tall and thin like messengers, with no fat under the chin, just skin and muscle, long in arms, long in legs, many beautiful, and darker than the noon of the dead. Fit like warriors, for most were warriors who had lost in small wars, and would now do what soldiers who lose wars do. All wore irons locked around the neck and the feet, each man chained to the man in front of and behind him. There were fewer men with weapons than I thought I'd see. Seven, maybe eight men with swords and knives, only two carrying a bow, and four women with cutlasses and axes.

"In time. He's holding court and judging the wicked," the Leopard said with a smile that made me think it was a joke.

But past the caravans and in front of a large white tent with a dome top and flowing cloths sat the slaver. To his right a man knelt on the ground, holding a slender smoking pipe, with a folded rug in his lap. To his right, another man, shirtless like the kneeling man, with a gold bowl in his hand and a rag, as if he was about to wash the slaver's face. Right behind him stood another, black in the shadow of the parasol he was holding to keep his master in shade. Another had a bowl of dates, ready to feed him. He did not look at us. But I looked at him sitting there, like the prince he probably was. Kalindar was famous for them, but princes with no kingdoms infested Malakal as well, it was said, because the Kwash Dara was stingy with his favors. His men had draped a long robe over his left shoulder with the right shoulder bare, as is the custom with princes. A white robe, the inner one to hide his royal orb and stick, peeked out underneath. Gold bracelets wrapped around his arms like two snakes in a killing curl. Leather sandals on dirty feet, a woven cap with silk tongues covering his ears over a broad face, and cheeks so fat they hid his eyes when he laughed. He did not look at us.

A man and woman kneeled before him, both kicked to their knees by the two women guards behind them. The man crying, the woman silent like stone. The woman, a red slave and not dark like the men at the back, a slave white in teeth and eyes and with no blemish. Beautiful. She would be a concubine to another master, mayhaps even a master in the East, where a concubine could possess her own palace. A woman captured from Luala Luala or even farther north, straight in nose and thin in lips. The man was darker, and shiny from sweat, not the body oils they rub on slave skin to fetch a bigger price. The man naked, the woman in a robe.

"Tell me true, tell me quick, tell me now," said the slaver. His voice was higher than I expected. Like a young child's, or a ragged witch's. "Man live to plunder, guest attack host, but you was a man under chain. A man **ira wewe.** Chained to one and twenty men with heavy iron that break the leg bone. You can't go unless they go, you can't come unless they come, you can't sit unless they sit, so how you find yourself up the pupu of this future princess?"

The man said nothing. I don't think he knew the midlands tongues. He looked like the men who lived along the two sisters river, kingless and strong, but strong from farming soil, not from hunting or fighting among armies and warriors.

The guard behind the woman said that it was the woman that seek him out, or so go whispers bouncing off their backs. That she lie with him while the other men stay quiet, hoping that she will lie with them too. And she did with one or two but this man most of all.

The woman laughed.

"Tell me true, tell me quick, tell me now. What will I do with a red slave carrying baby for a black slave? No merchant going want you, nobody going one day make you their wife and queen. You're worth less than the robes you wear. Take them off."

The guards grabbed her from behind and pulled the robes off. The red slave looked at the slaver, spat, and laughed.

"The robes I can wash and put on another. But you . . ."

The man feeding him dates bent to his ear and whispered something. "You are worth less than my sickest oxen. Make peace with the river goddess for you shall be with her soon."

"Better you chop my neck off or burn me in flames."

"You choose how you will die?"

"I choose not to be slave to you."

I saw the truth in her before the slaver did. She went and had a child with the black slave because she wanted to. The smile on her face said all. She

knew he would kill her. Better to be with the ancestors than to live bonded to somebody else, who might
be kind, who might be cruel, who might even make
you master to many slaves of your own, but was still
master over you.

"Men who follow the eastern light would have
been good to you. You never hear of the red slave who
become empress?"

"No, but I hear of the fat slaver who smelled like ox
shit, who will one day choke on his own breath. By
the god of justice and revenge I curse you."

The slaver lost his face. "Kill this bitch now," he
said.

The guard took her away as she laughed. Even
gone I could still hear her. The slaver looked at the
man and said, "I tell you true, tell you quick, tell you
now. Only one thing the northern masters love even
more than unblemished woman. Unblemished eunuch. Take him away and make it so."

Two guards took the man. He was weak and bawling, so each grabbed a chain and pulled him away.

The slaver looked at me as if I was the first of the
day's business. He stared at my eye, as everybody else
did, and I had long passed speaking of it.

"You must be the one with the nose," he said.

SEVEN

They took the woman away to drown her, and the man to cut all manhood off.

"This is what you took me here to see?" I said to the Leopard.

"The world isn't always night and day, Tracker. Still haven't learned."

"I know everything I need to know about slavers. Did I ever tell you of the time I tricked a slaver into selling himself into slavery? Took him three years to convince his master he was a master as well, after the master cut out his tongue."

"You speak too loud."

"Loud enough."

The man had so many rugs thrown on the dirt, rugs on top of rugs, rugs clearly from the East, and others with colours for which there were no names, that you would think him a rug seller, not a man seller. He made walls out of rugs, black rugs with red flowers and writing in foreign tongues. It was so dark that two lamps were always burning. The slaver sat on a stool while one man took off his sandals and the other brought over a bowl of dates. He may have been a prince, or at least a very rich man, but his feet stank. The man who held the umbrellas tried to take his hat off but the slaver slapped him, not hard, but playful, too playful. I decided many moons ago to stop reading into the little actions of men. The man with the umbrella turned to us and said, "His most excellent Amadu Kasawura, lion of the lower mountain and master of men, will see you before sunset."

The Leopard turned to leave, but I said, "He will see us now."

The umbrella bearer caught his dropping jaw. The dates bearer turned around as if to say, Now we shall have words. I think he smiled. That was the first time the slaver looked at us.

"I think you not understand our language."

"I think I understand it fine."

"His most excellent—"

"His Most Excellency seems to have forgotten how to talk to the freeborn."

"Tracker."

"No, Leopard."

The Leopard rolled his eyes. Kasawura started to laugh.

"I will be at the Kulikulo Inn."

"Nobody leave without notice," the slaver said.

I turned to leave, and almost made it to the

entrance when three guards appeared, hands on weapons not drawn.

"The guards will mistake you for a runaway. Deal with you first, ask questions later," Kasawura said. The guards clutched their weapons, and I pulled the two hatchets from my back strap.

"Who is first?" I asked.

Kasawura laughed louder. "This is the man who you said time cooled his heat?"

The Leopard sighed loud. I knew this was a test, but I didn't like being tested.

"My name speaks for itself, so make your decision quick and don't waste my time."

Also, I hate slavers.

"Bring him food and drink. A raw goat shank for Kwesi. Make sure is fresh kill, or would you like a live one to kill yourself? Sit down, gentlemen," he said.

Now the umbrella bearer raised his eyebrows and mashed his lips together. He handed the slaver a gold goblet, which he handed to me.

"It's—"

"Masuku beer," I said.

"It has been said you have a nose."

I took a drink. This was the best beer I have ever tasted.

"You are a man of wealth and taste," I said.

The slaver waved it off. He stood up but nodded at us to stay seated. Even he was getting annoyed at the servants fussing over every move. He clapped twice and they all left.

"You don't waste time so waste it I will not. Three years now a child they take, a boy. He was just starting to walk and could say nana. Somebody take him one night. They leave nothing and nobody ever demand ransom, not through note, not through drums, not even through witchcraft. I know the thinking, which you now think. Maybe they sell him in Malangika, a young child would bring much money to witches. But my caravan get protection from a Sangoma, just as one still binds you with protection even after her death. But you knew this, didn't you, Tracker? The Leopard think iron arrows bounce away from you because they are scared."

"There are still things to tell you," I said to the Leopard with a look.

"This child we trust to a housekeeper in Kongor. Then one night somebody cut the throat of everybody in the house but steal the child. Eleven in the house, all murdered."

"Three years ago? Not only are they far ahead in the game, they might have already won."

"Is not a game," he said.

"The mouse never thinks so, but the cat does. You have not finished your tale and it already sounds impossible. But finish."

"Thank you. We heard reports of several men, mayhaps a woman and a child taking a room at an inn near the Hills of Enchantment. They all took one room, which is why one of the guests remembered. We know this news because they find the innkeeper a day after they leave. Listen to me—dead like stone, pale from all the blood gone from him."

"They killed him."

"Who knows? But then we get news of two more ten days later. Two houses all the way down in Lish where we hear of them next, four men, and the child. And everything dead after they leave."

"But from those hills to the blood takes at least two moons, maybe two and a half by foot."

"Tell me something we don't ponder. But the killings the same, everybody dead like stone. Near one moon later people in Luala Luala run from their huts and wouldn't go back, talking about night demons."

"He travels with a band of murderers, but they haven't murdered him? What is his quality? A boy free-born of a slaver? Is he your own?"

"He is precious to me."

"That is no answer." I rose. "Right now, your story has meat where you will not talk, bone where you do. Why is he precious to you?" I asked.

"Do you need to know, to work for me? Talk a true talk."

"No, he does not," the Leopard said.

"No, I do not. But you seek a child missing three years. He could be beyond the sand sea, or long shat out of a crocodile's ass in the Blood Swamp, or lost in the Mweru for all we know. Even if he is still alive, he will be nothing like the child gone. He might be under another house, calling another man father. Or four."

"I am not his father."

"So you say. Maybe he is now a slave."

He sat down in front of me. "You want us to be out with it. Tell me true. You wish to throw words at me."

"About what?"

"Every man here is unlucky in war. Every woman here will be bought into a better life. After all, if their lives were so good, they would not be on a bonds-man's cart."

"He didn't say anything, excellent Amadu, that is just his way," the Leopard said.

"Don't speak for him, Leopard."

"Yes, Leopard, don't speak for me."

"You were a slave, no?" said excellent Amadu.

"I don't have to dip my nose in shit to know it stinks."

"Fair. And yet who are you that I should present my life as just to you? You who would search, and find, and return a wife even though her eyes had been cut out by her husband. Every man in this room has a price, good Tracker. And yours might even be cheap."

"What of him do you have?"

"No, not so quickly. I only need to know that the offer tickling you. We have met, we have drank beer, we will make decisions. This you should know. I have made the offer to more as well. Eight, perhaps nine in number. Some will work with you, some will not. Some will try to find him first. You have not asked how much coin I will pay."

"I don't have to. Given how precious he is to you."

The Leopard was raising a fuss. He didn't know some would be searching for the child on their own. It was my time to hush him.

"Tracker, are you not offended by this?" he said.

"Offended? I'm not even surprised."

"Our good friend the Leopard still doesn't know that there is no black in man, only shades and shades of gray. My mother was not a kind woman and she was not a good woman. But she did say to me, Amadu, pray to the gods but bolt your door. The child has been gone three years."

"Leopard, think. When we find him, we split coin two ways, not nine."

The slaver clapped and the three men rushed in again, doing exactly as before, rubbing his feet, feeding him dates, and looking at me as if I would change into a Leopard too.

"I give you four nights to decide. This not going be no easy journey. There are forces, Tracker. There are forces, Leopard. They come in on wind at morning or sometimes in the highest sun, the hour of the blinding light of witches. Just as I wish him to be found, surely there are those who wish him to stay hidden. Nobody ever send word for ransom, and yet I know he is alive, even before the fetish priest consult the older gods who tell him this is so. But there are forces, you two. Ill wind rolling through the cities in the hot season, and taking what is not for them. Day robber, night thief, I can't tell you what you will find. But we talking too much. I give you four nights. If yes be your answer, meet me at the collapsed tower at the end the street of bandits. You know this place?"

"Yes."

"Meet me there after sunset and let that be your yes."

He turned his back to us. Our business was done with him for the time. They came back to me just then, the woman he killed and the man he made a eunuch.

"Silly Tracker, surely you know how eunuchs are made? That man will surely die," the Leopard said.

I asked the landlady to allow the Leopard stay in a room I knew was empty. I wore nothing when I spoke to her, so she said yes, of course, but now the rent is double, or you will return from one of your trips to find nothing in your room. But I have nothing, I said. The Leopard took the room after I told him that should he find some tree to sleep in as a beast, somebody would take a perfect shot from a bow and arrow and get him right through the ribs. And all the prey in the city belonged to one man or another, so one could not roam about and hunt them. And even if you did kill somebody's goat or chicken, do not bring it back to the room. And even if you did bring it back to the room, do not spill even a drop of blood.

This annoyed the Leopard but he saw there was wisdom in it. I knew he would be in there pacing and pacing, knowing he could not growl. Trying to sleep in the window but knowing he could not, and smelling blood quicken under the flesh of prey down below in the animal pens. So he brought the boy up to his room. The third day he came up to my room, grinning and rubbing his belly.

"You look like you sneaked an impala into your room."

"Quiet as it's kept. I might have been the glutton lately."

"The whole inn knows of your appetites."

"You must be the one nun in the whorehouse. Fantastic beasts, fantastic urges, Tracker. Where go you today? I shall see your city."

"You already saw the city."

"I want it through your eyes, or rather your nose. I know there is something in this city waiting for us."

I looked at him straight. "Go whoring on your own time, cat."

"Tracker, who's to say we can't do both?"

"As you wish. Go wash."

He poked out his tongue, long as a young snake, and licked both his arms.

"Done," he said, and grinned. "Who shall we see? A man owing you coin, whose legs we shall break? To us each a leg!"

They say Malakal is a city built by thieves. Malakal is mountains and mountains are Malakal. The one place that was never conquered because it was the one city nobody ever dared to try. Just the trip up to the mountains would exhaust men and horses. Nearly every man here is warrior born and most of the women too. This was the King's last stand against

your Massykin people of the South, and that from
here we turned back the war and beat you southern-
ers back like the bitches you are. Truce was your idea,
not ours. Nearly every city spreads wide, but Malakal
reaches up to the sky instead, house on top of house,
tower on top of tower, some towers so thin and high
that they forgot steps, leaving you to get to the top by
rope. The towers themselves stacked so close that they
seemed to have collapsed on each other, and to the
south of the first wall was one that did, but was still in
use. Four walls enclosed the city, built each inside the
other, four rings built around the mountains that rose
out of each other. Men built the first wall over four
hundred years ago, after old Malakal went to ruin.
The fourth and last wall was still being built. Come
to it straight and Malakal looks like four forts, each
rising out of the one below it, and towers set on top
of towers. But take the view of birds and you see great
walls like spirals and within them roads shooting out
like spider legs from mountain peak to flat land, with
lookouts for warriors, and arrow slits for archers, and
homes and inns, and workhouses, and trade houses,
and poorhouses, and dark lanes for necromancers,
thieves, and men seeking pleasures and boys and
women giving them. From our windows you can see
the Hills of Enchantment, where many Sangoma live,
but they were too far away. The citizens came to wisdom early how to use space for yards with chickens
to get fat, and fences to keep out dogs and mountain beasts. Down from the mountains is the quickest

way to the slave routes in the valley and the gold and salt routes to the sea. Malakal produces nothing but gold, trades everything that can be enslaved, and demands tribute from all who pass through, for if you are in the North it is the only way to the sea.

Of course I speak of nine years ago. Malakal is nothing like that now.

"I cannot tell you if these are good times or bad times to be in the city because the King is coming," I said to the Leopard as we went out.

His caravan was seen two days out and all of Malakal was expected to celebrate his tenth jubilee as Kwash Dara, the North King, the son of Kwash Netu, the great conqueror of Wakadishu and Kalindar. Of course he celebrates in the city most responsible for saving his royal backside so that he could still have his royal shit wiped away by servants. But the griots were already singing, Praise the King for saving the city of mountains. Men from Malakal weren't even in his army; they were mercenaries who would have fought for the Massykin had they come with good coin first. But fuck the gods if the city was not going to put on great fabrics and feast. The black-and-gold flag of Kwash Dara was on everything. Even children were painting their faces gold and black. The women painted gold for the left breast, black for the right, both in the sign of the rhinoceros. Weavers made cloths, and men wore robes, and women wrapped their heads into large flower arrangements, all of it black and gold.

"Your city is putting on her good face," he said.

"An elder told me that peace is a rumor, and we will be back at war with the South in less than a year."

"So in war or peace, wives will want to know who fucks their husbands."

"That is one of your better points, Leopard."

I lived in town, which was a new thing for me. I have always been an edge man, always on the coast, always by the boundary. That way nobody knows if I have just come or was turning to leave. I kept only as much as I could pack in a sack and leave with in less than a time-glass flip. But in a place like here, where people are always coming and going, you could stay in the center that never moves and still vanish. Which is convenient for a man that men hate. My inn was far west, at the edge of the third wall. People within the third wall other people thought were rich, but that is not true. Most of those people lived within the second wall. Warriors and soldiers and traders bedding for the night stayed within the fourth, in forts at all four points of the city that kept the enemy out. I'm telling you this, inquisitor, because you have never been there and a man of your sort never will.

I took the Leopard down streets that climbed up and rolled down, twisting and turning, winding to the last tower at the peak of the mountain range. I looked around and turned back to see him looking at me.

"He does not follow," he said.

"Who, your little lover?"

"Call him anything but that."

"He'll follow you into a crocodile's mouth."

"Not until the swelling is gone," I say.

"Swelling?"

"Tried to rub my belly last night. Fuck the gods, I would never believe it. Who would rub a cat's belly?"

"Mistook you for a dog."

"Do I bark? Do I sniff men's balls?"

"Well . . ."

"Quiet yourself right now."

I could hold the laugh no longer.

The Leopard frowned, then laughed. We walked downhill. Not many people were about, and whoever came out darted back indoors as soon as they saw us. I would think they were afraid, but nobody is afraid in Malakal. They knew something was afoot and wanted no part in it.

"Darkness comes quickly down this street," Leopard said.

We went to the door of a man who owed me money but tried to pay in stories. He let us in, offered us plum juice and palm wine, but I said no, the Leopard said yes, and I said he means no, ignoring him glaring at me. The man was in the middle of another story about how the money was on the way from a city near the Darklands, and who knows what has happened, but it could be bandits, though his own brother carried the money, and sweets baked by his mother, of which he will give me as much as I could eat. The sweets from his mother was the only new part of this story.

"Is it me or are the trade routes now less safe than they were during the war?" he said to me.

I thought of which finger to break. I threatened to break one last time and to not do so would make me a man who did not keep his promises, and one could not have word like that get out in the cities. But he looked at me just then and his eyes popped open so wide that I thought I had said all that out loud. The man ran to his room and came back with a pouch heavy with silver. I prefer gold, I tell my customers before even going out looking, but this pouch was twice as heavy as the one he owed me.

"Take all of it," he said.

"You overpay, I'm sure."

"Take all of it."

"Did your brother just come through the back door?"

"My house is none of your business. Take it and go."

"If this is not enough I—"

"It is more than enough. Leave so my wife never knows two dirty men come to her house."

I took his money and left, the man mystifying me. Meanwhile the Leopard couldn't stop laughing.

"A joke between you and the gods or do you plan to share it?"

"Your debtor. Your man. Shit himself in the other room he did."

"So strange. I was going to break a finger like I said I would. But he looked at me like he saw the god of vengeance himself."

"He wasn't looking at you."

Just as the question was about to leave my mouth the answer came in my head.

"You . . ."

"I started changing right behind you. Wet his front with piss, frightened he was. Did you smell it?"

"Maybe he was marking territory."

"Some thanks for the man who just fattened your pouch."

"Thanks."

"Say it with sweetness."

"You try my patience, cat."

He came with me to a woman who wanted to send a message to her daughter in the underworld. I told her that I found the missing and she wasn't missing. Another who wanted me to find where a man who was his friend but stole his money had died, for wherever that corpse lay, beneath him would be bags and bags of gold. He said, Tracker, I will give you ten gold coins from the first bag. I said, You give me the first two bags and I will let you keep what is left, for your friend is alive. But what if there are only three bags? he said. I said, You should have said that before you let me smell the sweat, piss, and cum of his bed robes. The Leopard laughed and said, You are more entertaining than two Kampara actors pretending to fuck with wooden cocks. I didn't notice the sun was gone until he skipped a few steps ahead and vanished into the dark. His eyes flashed like green light in the black.

"Is there no sport in your city?" he said.

"Took you long to get to this. Be warned, the pleasure women in this city gave up on being boys a long time ago. Nothing there but the scars of a eunuch."

"Ugh, eunuchs. Better an abuka with no holes, no eyes, no mouth than a eunuch. I thought one became this to swear off fucking, but curse the gods, there they are, infesting every whorehouse, making the blood boil of every man who just wants to lie on his back for a change. I wish we could find the child right now."

"I know who we could find right now."

"What, who?"

"The slaver."

"Gone to the coast to sell his new slaves."

"He is not even four hundred paces from here and only one of his men travels with him."

"Fuck the gods. Well it's been said that you have—"

"Do not say it."

We dipped into an alley and took two small torches.

He followed me past a tower with seven floors and a thatch roof, one with three floors and another four floors high. We passed a small hut where lived a witch, for nobody wanted to live above or below a witch; three houses painted in the grid patterns of the rich; and another building of mysterious use. We had left roads and gone northwest, right at the edge of the fourth wall, and not far from the North fort. I was a savannah dog, picking up too much flesh, living and dead, and burned by lightning.

"Here."

We stopped at a house four floors high, the taller buildings beside it throwing moon shadow. No door stood in front and the lowest window was as high as three men foot-to-shoulder. One window near the top and in the center, dark with what looked like flickering light. I pointed to the house, then the window.

"He is here."

"Tracker, a problem you have," he said and pointed up. "Are you now crow to my Leopard?"

"All the birds in the ten and three kingdoms and a crow is what you call me?"

"Fine, a dove, a hawk—how about an owl? You better fly quick because this place has no door."

"There is a door."

The Leopard looked at me hard, then walked as far around the house as he could.

"No, you have no door."

"No, you have no eyes."

"Ha, 'you have no eyes.' I listen to you and hear her."

"Who?"

"The Sangoma. Your words fall just like hers. You think like her too, that you're clever. Her witchcraft is still protecting you."

"If it were witchcraft it wouldn't be protecting me. She threw something on me that binds craft; this I was told by a witchman who tried to kill me with metals. It's not as if one feels it on the skin or in the bones. Something that remains even after her death, which again makes it not witchcraft, for a witch's spells all die with her."

I walked right up to the wall as if to kiss it, then whispered an incantation low enough that not even his Leopard ears could hear.

"If it were witchcraft," I said.

I shuddered and stepped back. This always made me feel the way I do when I drink juice of the coffee bean—like thorns were under my skin pushing through, and forces in the night were out to get me. I whispered to the wall, This house has a door and I with the wolf eye will open it. I stepped back and without my torch the wall caught fire. White flame raced to four corners in the shape of a door, consumed the shape, crackled and burned, then put itself out, leaving a plain wooden door untouched by scorch.

"Whoever is here is working witch science," I said.

Mortar and clay steps took us up to the first floor. A room empty of man smell, with an archway setting itself off in the dark. Blue moonlight came through the windows. I knew stealth, but the cat was so quiet I looked behind me twice.

People were talking harshly above us. The next floor up had a room with a locked door, but I smelled no people behind it. Halfway up the steps the smells came down on us: scorched flesh, dried urine, shit, the stinking carcasses of beasts and birds. Near the top of the steps sounds came down on us—whispers, growls, a man, a woman, two women, two men, an animal—and I wished my ears were as good as my nose. Blue light flashed from the room, then flickered down to dark. No way we could climb the last steps without being seen or heard, so we stayed halfway. We could see in the room anyway. And we saw what flickered blue light.

A woman, an iron collar and chain around her neck, her hair almost white but looking blue as light flickered through the room. She screamed, yanked at the chain around her neck, and blue light burst within her, coursing along the tree underneath her skin that one sees when you cut parts of a man open. Instead of blood, blue light ran through her. Then she went dark again. The light was the only way we could make out the slaver in dark robes, the man who fed him dates, and somebody else, with a smell I both remembered and couldn't recognize.

Then somebody else touched a stick and it burst into flame like a torch. The chained woman jumped back and scrambled against the wall.

A woman held the torch. I had never seen her before, was sure of it even in the dark, but she smelled familiar, so familiar. Taller than everybody else in the room, with hair big and wild like some women above the sand sea. She pointed the torch to the ground, to the stinking half carcass of a dog.

"Tell me true," the slaver said. "How did you get a dog up into this room?"

The chained woman hissed. She was naked and so dirty that she looked white.

"Move in close and I tell you true," she said.

The slaver moved in close, she spread her legs, her finger spreading her kehkeh, and shot a streak of piss that wet his sandals before he could pull away. She started to laugh but he cracked his knuckles and punched the cackle out of her mouth. The Leopard jumped and I grabbed his arm. It sounded as if she was laughing until the tall woman's torch shined on her again as tears pooled in her eyes. She said, "You you you you you all go. You all must go. Go now, run run run run run because Father coming, he coming on the wind don't you hear the horse go go go you he won't kiss the head of you unclean boys, go wash wash wash wash wash wash wash—"

The slaver nodded and the tall woman shoved the torch right up to her face. She jumped back again and snarled.

"Nobody comes! Nobody comes! Nobody comes! Who are you?" the woman said.

The slaver moved in to strike her. The chained woman flinched and hid her face, begging him not to strike her anymore. Too many men striking her and they strike her all the time and she just want to hold her boys, the first and the third and the fourth, but not the second, for he does not like when people hold him, not even his mother. I still held on to the Leopard's arm and could feel his muscles shift and his hair grow under my fingers.

"Enough with that," the tall woman said.

"This is how you get her to talk," the slaver said.

"You must think she is one of your wives," she said.

The Leopard's arm stopped twitching. She wore a black gown from the northern lands that touched the floor, but cut close to show she was thin. She stooped down to the woman in chains, who still hid her face. I couldn't see it but knew the chained woman was trembling. The chains clanged when she shook.

"These are the days that never should have happened to you. Tell me about her," the tall woman said.

The slaver nodded to his date feeder and the date feeder cleared his throat and began.

"This woman, her story, very strange and sad. It is I who am talking and I will—"

"Not a performance, donkey. Just the story."

I wish I could have seen his scowl but his face was lost to the dark.

"We don't know her name, and her neighbors, she scared them all away."

"No she did not. Your master here paid them to leave. Stop wasting my time."

"As if I give two shakes of a rat's ass about your time."

She paused. I could tell nobody expected that to come out of his mouth.

"This always his ways?" she said to the slaver. "Maybe you tell me the story, slave monger, and maybe I cut his tongue out."

The date feeder pulled a knife from under his sleeve and flipped the handle to her.

"How this for sport? I give you the knife and you try," he said.

She did not take it. The woman in chains was still hiding her face in the corner. The Leopard was still. The tall woman looked at the date feeder, with a curious smile.

"He has chat, this one. Fine, out with your story. I will hear it."

"Her neighbor, the washerwoman, say her name is Nooya. And nobody knows her or claims her so Nooya be her name, but she don't answer to it. She answer to him. Nobody living to tell the story but she, and she not telling. But this is what we know. She live in Nigiki with her husband and five children. Saduk, Makhang, Fula—"

"The shorter version, date feeder."

The tall woman pointed at him. She did not take her eye off the woman in chains.

"One day when the sun past the noon and was going down, a child knock on her door. A boy child, who look like he was five and four years in age."

"We have one word for that in the North. We call it nine," the tall woman said.

She smiled; the date feeder scowled and said, "A boy child knocking on the door raprapraprap like he going to knock it down. They after me, they coming for me, save this boy child! he say. Save this boy child, save him, he said. Save me!"

The chained woman darted a look. "Sssssssssssssss-save the chhhhhhhhhhhhhhhh," she said.

"The little boy screaming and screaming, what could a mother do? A mother with four boys of her own. She open the door and the boy run in. He run right into a wall and fall back and wouldn't stop moving till she close the door. Who is after you? Nooya ask. Is it your father you run from? Nooya ask. Your mother? Yes, mothers can be strict and fathers can be wicked, but the look in his eye, the fear in his eye was not for strong word or the switch. She reach to touch him and he stagger back so quick his head hit the side of a cupboard and he fall.

"The boy wouldn't nod, the boy wouldn't talk, only cry and eat and watch the door. Her four sons including Makhang and Saduk say, Who is the strange boy, Mother, and where did you find him? The boy will not play with them so they leave him alone. All he do is cry and eat. Nooya's husband was working the salt pits and would not be back till morning. She finally get him to stop crying by promising him millet porridge in the morning with extra honey. That night, Makhang was asleep, Saduk was asleep, the other two boys were asleep, even Nooya was asleep, and she never sleeps until all her boys was under the one roof. Hear this now. One of them was not asleep. One of them get up from the mat, and answer the door though nobody knock. The boy. The boy go to the door that nobody was knocking. The boy open the door and he come in. A handsome man he was, long neck, hair black and white. The night hide his eyes. Thick lips and square jaw and white skin, like kaolin. Too tall for the room. He wrap himself in a white-and-black cloak. The boy point to rooms deep in the house. The handsome man go to room of boys first and kill the first son to the third son and the floor was wet from blood. The little boy watch. The handsome man wake the mother by strangling her throat. He lift her up above his head. The boy watch. He throw her to the ground, and she is crippled with pain and she whimpering and screaming and coughing and nobody hear. She watch when he bring out the fourth son, the smallest boy, the little dormouse, holding his sleepy head up. The mother trying to scream no, no, no, no, but the handsome man laugh and cut his throat. She screaming, and screaming and he drop the fourth son and move in for her. The boy watch.

"The father come home when the sun far up in the sky. He come home tired and hungry and know he have to go out again before the sun go down. He put down his hoe, put down his spear, take off his tunic, and leave his loincloth. Where is my food, woman? he say. Dinner should be here and breakfast too. The mother come out of her room. The mother naked. Her hair wild. The room air feel wet and the father say it smell like it going rain soon. He hear her coming to him and want to know where is breakfast and where are the children. She right behind him. The room go dark and light flashing in the room and

he say, A storm coming? It was just bright with
sun. He turns around and his wife is the one with the
lightning flashing through her like it do now. He look
down and see the fourth son dead on the floor. Her
husband jump back and look up and she grab his
head with both hands and break his neck. When
the lightning fade inside, her head come back and she
look around her house and see all of them dead,
the four sons and the husband and she forget the boy
and the handsome man because they both gone. Just
she and the dead bodies and she think she kill them,
and nothing prove her otherwise and the lightning
flash up in her head and she go mad. She kill two
men and break the legs of one before they catch her.
And they lock her up in a dungeon for seven murders.
Even though nobody believe that she could break the
neck of a big man who work in the fields alone. In
her cell, she try to kill herself every time she remember what really happen, because she rather believe
she kill them herself than it was the little boy she let
in that kill them all. But most times she don't remember and just growl like a cheetah in a trap."

"That was a long story," the tall woman said. "Who
was the man?"

"Who?"

"The tall white man. Who was he?"

"His name not remember by any griot."

"What kind of magic did he leave in her why this
happen?"

Light was starting to glow in the woman again. She shook every time it happened, as if she had fits.

"Nobody know," the date feeder said.

"Somebody knows, just not you."

She looked at the slaver.

"How did you get her out of prison?" she asked.

"It was not difficult," the slaver said. "They been waiting long days to get rid of her. She scare even the men. Every day as soon as she wake she would say the master going east or west or south and run in that direction, right into the wall, or the iron gate—two time she break out a tooth. Then she will remember her family and go mad all over again. They sold me her for just one coin when I said I will sell her to a mistress. I have her here for when she going to have use."

"Use? You've been standing in her shit, and the maggots of the dead dog she been eating."

"You don't understand a thing. The white man. He didn't kill her, and what he do, he do it to others. Many a woman like her running loose in these lands and many a man too. Even some children and I hear a eunuch. From women he take everything so they have nothing, but nothing is something too big for any one woman to bear, so she search and she run and she look. Look at her. Even now she want to be with him, she will be near him and want nothing else, she will let him eat her, she will never let him go. She will never stop following. He be her opium now. Look at her."

"I am looking."

"If he shift south she run south to that window. If he change west, she switch and run until the chain pull her back by the neck."

"He who?"

"Him."

"This story of yours growing long in the teeth. And the boy?"

"What of the boy?"

"You know what I am asking, Your Excellence."

The slaver said nothing. The tall woman looked at the chained woman again as she raised her head from filthy arms. It looked like the tall woman was smiling at her. The chained woman spat on her cheek. The tall woman struck her face so hard and so quick, the chained woman's head slammed against the wall. The chain links clicked and clanged from being pulled hard then let loose.

"If this tale had wings it would have flown to the east by now," she said. "You want to follow the trail of a lost boy? Start with those child-raping elders in Fasisi."

"I want you to follow this boy, the one this woman see in the company of a white man. It's him."

"An old tale mothers use to scare children," the tall woman said.

"Tell me true—why you doubt? You never see women like her before?"

"I have even killed a few."

"People from Nigiki all the way to the Purple City talk about seeing a man white as clay, and a boy. And others as well. There are many accounts of them entering city gates, but nobody witness their departure," the date feeder said. "We have—"

"Nothing. From a madwoman missing her dormouse. It is late," the tall woman said.

I grabbed the Leopard's hand, still hairy, still about to change, and nodded to the lower floor. We snuck down and hid in the empty room, looking out in the dark. We looked out as the tall woman went down the steps. Halfway she stopped and looked over to us, but the dark was so thick you could feel it on your skin.

"We will let you know what we decide tomorrow," she said to the others.

The door closed behind her. The slaver and his date feeder followed soon after.

We should leave," I said.

The Leopard turned to go upstairs.

"Cat!"

I grabbed his hand.

"I will free this poor woman."

"The same woman with lightning coursing through her? The woman eating from dog carcass?"

"That is no animal."

"Fuck the gods, cat, you wish to quarrel now? Cut this notion loose. Ask the slaver about the woman when we see him. Besides, you were fine with chains on women only a night ago."

"That is different. Those were slaves. This is a prisoner."

"All slaves are prisoners. We go."

"Free her I will, and you will not stop me."

"I am not stopping you."

"Who calls?" she said.

The woman had heard us.

"Could these be my boys? My lovely noise of boys? You gone so long, and still I didn't make any millet porridge."

The Leopard made a step and I grabbed his hand again. He pushed me away. She saw him and ran back to her corner.

"Peace. Peace be with you. Peace," the Leopard said over and over.

She darted at him, then at me, then back at him, choking on the end of her chain. I stayed back, not wanting her to think we were closing in. She hid her face and started crying again.

The Leopard turned and looked at me. His face was near lost in the dark but I saw his eyebrows raised, pleading. He felt too much. He always did. But it was all sensation to him. Fast heartbeat, lustful swell, sweat down the neck. We stepped over some stones, climbing up the last few steps.

"Leopard, she cannot take care of herself. Le—"

"They want my boys. Everybody took my boys," she said.

Leopard went back down the stairs and returned with a loose brick. Over by the wall, and away from her, he hammered at the chain's end, built into the mortar. First she tried to run, but he hushed her with a **shh.** She looked away as Leopard hammered at the chain. The chain clanged and clanged, it wouldn't break but the wall did, cracked and cracked until he pulled the peg out.

The chain dropped to the floor. In the dark I saw her stand up and heard her feet shuffle. The Leopard was right in front of her when she stopped shaking and looked up. The little light coming in touched her wet eyes. The Leopard touched the shackle around her neck and she flinched, but he pointed to the crack in the wall and nodded. She did not nod, but held her head down. I saw the Leopard's eyes, though the room had been too dark moments before to see them. The light flickering in his eyes came from her.

Lightning flashed from her head and went down her limbs. The Leopard jumped but she grabbed him by the neck, heaved him off the floor, and flung him against the wall. Her eyes blue, her eyes white, her eyes crackling like lightning. I ran at her, a charging buffalo. She kicked me straight in the chest, and I fell back and hit my head; the Leopard was rolling over beside me. She grabbed him by the crook of his arm and sent him flying into the wall on the other side. She was lightning, burning the air. She grabbed his left leg and pulled him back, squeezing the ankle, making him howl. He tried to change but couldn't. Lightning ran through her body and came out of her holes, making her yell and cackle. She kicked him and kicked him and kicked him, and I jumped up and she looked at me. Then she looked away quick like somebody called her. Then back at me, then away again. The Leopard, I knew him, I knew he would be angry, he leapt at her, hitting her in the back and knocking her down, but she turned over and kicked him off. The woman jumped back, blue light inside her a thunderstorm. She tried to run at me but Leopard grabbed the chain and pulled her back so hard she fell again. But she rolled and jumped back up and made for the Leopard. The woman screamed again and raised her hands, but then an arrow burst right through her shoulder. I thought she would scream louder, but she said nothing. The Leopard's boy, Fumeli, was behind me. He shot her again, the second arrow almost in line with the arrow in her shoulder, and she howled. The lightning coursed through her and the whole room glowed blue. She growled at him but the boy drew a new arrow and looked right down the shaft at her. He could aim for her heart and hit. She stepped back as if she knew. Lightning woman leapt for the window, missed, grabbed the sill, digging her nails in the wall, pulled herself up, punched out the window bars, and jumped.

The Leopard ran past Fumeli and me and down the steps.

"Did he teach you how to—"

"No," he said, and went down after him.

Outside, the Leopard and Fumeli were already many paces ahead of me, down a narrow alley with no lantern light coming from any window. They had slowed to a walk when I caught them.

"Do you have her? In your nose? Do you have her?" the Leopard said.

"Not this way," I said, and turned down a lane running south. This street boasted beggars, so many lying in the alley that we stepped on a few, who shouted and groaned. She was running like a madwoman, I could tell from her trail. We turned right, down another alley, this one pocked with potholes full of stinking water and a guard on the ground, shaking and foaming at the mouth. We knew this was her doing, so none of us said it. We followed her scent. She ran ahead of us, upending carts and knocking over mules trying to sleep.

"Down here," I said.

We caught up with her at a fork, the road on the right going back into town, the left heading to the north gate. No sentry at that gate held a club or spear that could stop her. I have never seen a soul run that fast who was not lifted by devils. Two sentries with shield and spear saw her and stepped forward, raised their spears above their heads. Before either could throw she jumped high, as if running on steps of air, and slammed into the city wall. She dug into the mortar before falling, scrambled up to the top of the wall, and jumped off before more guards could get to her. The sentries kept their spears ready to throw at the sight of us.

"Good men, we are not enemies of Malakal," I said.

"Not friends neither. Who else coming to bother us near the noon of the dead?" said the first guard, bigger, fatter, iron armour no longer shiny.

"You saw her too, do not deny it," the Leopard said.

"We seeing nothing. We seeing nothing but three witchmen working night magic."

"You must give us leave," I said.

"Shit we must give you. Leave before we send you somewhere you won't like," said the other guard—shorter, skinnier.

"We are not witchmen," I say.

"All prey gone to sleep. So starve. Or go find whatever entertainment keeping a man up."

"You will deny what you have just seen?"

"I seeing nothing."

"You saw nothing. Fuck the—"

I cut the Leopard off. "That is fine with us, guard. You saw nothing."

I took a bracelet off my hand and threw it at him. It was three snakes, each eating another's tail, the sign of the Chief of Malakal, and a gift for finding something even the gods told him was lost.

"And I serve your chief, but that is nothing. And I have two hatchets and he has bow and arrow, but that is nothing. And that nothing ran by two men as if they were boys and jumped over a city wall as it were a river stone. Open your locks and give us three leave, and we will make sure the nothing that you didn't see never comes back."

This was the north wall. Outside was all rocks and about two hundred paces to the cliff, where the drop-off was sharpest. She stood about a hundred paces away, scurrying left, then right, then left again. It looked like she was sniffing. Then she dropped to the ground and sniffed the rocks.

"Nooya!" the Leopard said.

She turned like somebody who heard a noise, not something she knew was hers, and ran again. As she ran the lightning struck inside her and she screamed. Fumeli, still running, drew the bow and arrow, but the Leopard growled. We ran along the side of the cliff towards its point. We were closing on her, for though she was far faster than us she would not run straight. She ran right to the edge of the cliff and without stopping leapt off.

EIGHT

The boy became air three years ago. On the way to the collapsed tower, I wondered how much one could change in three years. A boy at ten and six is so changed from a boy at ten and three that they may be different people. Many times I have seen it. A mother who never stopped crying or looking, giving me coin to find a stolen child. That is never a problem; it is the easiest of things, finding a stolen child. The problem is that the child is never as he was when taken. For his taker, often a great love. For his mother, not even curiosity. The mother gets the child back, but his bed will remain empty. The kidnapper loses the child but lives on in that child's longing. This is true word from a child lost and then found: None can douse it, the love I have for the mother who chose me, and nothing can bring love for the woman whose kehkeh I dropped out. The world is strange and people keep making it stranger.

Neither I nor the Leopard spoke about the woman.

All I said that night was, "Show the boy some gratitude."

"What?"

"Thanks. Give the boy thanks for saving your life."

I walked back to the gates. Knowing he wouldn't, I said my thanks to the boy as I passed him.

"I didn't do it for you," he said.

So.

Now we were walking to the collapsed tower. Together, but we did not speak. The Leopard ahead, me behind, and the boy between us, carrying his bow and quiver. Since we had not spoken we had not agreed, and I was still half of the mind to say no. Because the Leopard did speak true in this, that it's one thing if you are unlucky in war, of lower birth, or slave born, but chaining a woman as prisoner is something else, even if she was clearly possessed by some kind of lightning devil. But we did not speak of the woman; we did not speak of anything. And I wanted to slap the boy for walking ahead of me.

The collapsed tower stood to the south of the first wall. Nobody on these streets, or paths, or alleys looked like they knew the King was coming. In all my years in Malakal I had never been down this street. I never saw reason to go to the old towers, past the peak, and down below the reach of most of the sun. Or up, as the climb was first so steep that the clay street turned into a narrow lane, then steps. Going down was steep again, where we passed the windows of houses long gone from use. Another two on both sides of the lane that looked like it housed wicked acts, for it was covered in markings and paintings of all kinds of fucking with all kinds of beasts. Even going down, we stood high enough to see all of the city and the flat land beyond it. I heard once that the first builders of this city, back when this was not yet a city, and them not yet fully men, were just trying to build towers tall enough to get back to the kingdom of sky and start a war in the land of gods.

"We are here," the Leopard said.

The collapsed tower.

That itself is a misspeak. The tower is not collapsed, but it has been collapsing for four hundred years. This is what the old people say, that back then men built two towers apart from the rest of Malakal. The building masters went wrong from the day they built on a road going down instead of coming up the mountains. Two towers, one fat and one thin, built to house slaves before ships came from the East to take them away. And the thin tower would be the tallest in all the lands, tall enough, some say, to see the horizon of the South. Eight floors for both but the taller one would reach even farther upward, like a lighthouse for giants. Some say the master builder had a vision, others say he was a madman who fucked chickens and then chopped their heads off.

But what everybody saw was this. The day they set the last stone—after four years of slaves killed by mishap, iron, and fire—was one of celebration. The warlord of the fort, for Malakal was only a fort, came with his wives. Also there, Prince Moki, the oldest son of King Kwash Liongo. The master builder chicken-fucker was about to splash chicken blood at the base and invoke the blessing of the gods, when just like so, the taller, thinner tower rocked and cracked, hissing dust and swaying. It rocked back and forth, west then east, swinging so wide that two slaves on the unfinished roof fell off. The thin tower tilted, tipped, and even bent a little until it ran into the fat tower, like lovers rushing to a hard kiss. This kiss shook and clapped like thunder. The tower looked like it would crumble but it never did. The two towers now squashed together into one tower, but neither gave way, neither fell. And after ten years, when it was seen that neither tower would give way, people even took to living there. Then it was an inn for weary travelers, then a fort for slavers and their slaves, and then as three floors in the thin tower collapsed on each other, it was nothing. None of this explained why this slaver wanted to meet there. On the three top floors, many steps had broken away. The boy stayed outside. Something rumbled a few floors down, like a foundation about to give.

"This tower will finally come down with all of us in it," I said.

We stepped up to a floor like I have never seen, in a pattern like on kente cloth, but black and white circles and arrowpoints, and spinning even though everything was still. Ahead of us, a doorway with no door.

"Three eyes, look they shining in the dark. The Leopard and the half wolf. Is that how you gained the nose? Do you relish blood like the cat?" the slaver said.

"No."

"Come in and talk," the slaver said.

I was about to say something to the Leopard but he changed and trotted in on all fours. Inside, torches shot light up into a white ceiling and dark blue walls. It looked like the river at night. Cushions on the floor but nobody sat on them. Instead an old woman sat on the floor with her legs crossed, her brown leather dress smelling like the calf it came from. She had shaved all around her head but left the top in braids, long and white. Silver circle earrings big as lip plates hung off her ears and rested on her shoulders. Around her neck, several necklaces of red, yellow, white, and black beads. Her mouth moved but she said nothing; she looked at neither me nor the cat, who was trotting around the room as if looking for food.

"My spotted beast," the slaver said. "In the inner room."

The Leopard ran off.

I recognized the date feeder. Right beside his master and ready to stuff his mouth. Another man so tall that until he shifted to his left leg, I thought he was a column holding up the ceiling, carved to look like a man. He looked like one who could stomp and make this tower finally collapse. His skin was dark but not as dark as mine, more like mud before it dries. And shiny even in the little light. I could see the beautiful dots of scars on his forehead, one line curling down his nose and out to his cheeks. No tunic or robe, but many necklaces on his bare chest. A skirt around the waist that looked purple and two boar tusks by his ears. No sandals or shoes or boots, but nobody would have made such things for a man with his feet.

"Never have I seen an Ogo this far west," I said. He nodded, so I at least knew he was an Ogo, a giant of the mountain lands. But he said nothing.

"We call him Sadogo," the slaver said.

The Ogo said nothing. He was more interested in moths flying into the lamp at the center of the room. The floor trembled whenever he stepped.

Sitting on a stool in a corner by a closed window was the tall, thin woman from that night. Her hair, still out and wild, as if no mother or man had told her to tame it. Her gown, still black but with white running a ring around her neck and then down between her breasts. A bowl of plums rested in her hand. She looked like she was about to yawn. She looked at me and said to the slaver, "You did not tell me he was a river man."

"I was raised in the city of Juba, not some river," I said.

"You carry the ways of the Ku."

"I am from Juba."

"You dress like a Ku."

"This is fabric I found here."

"Steal like a Ku. You even carry their smell. Now I feel like I'm passing through the swamp."

"The way you know us, maybe the swamp has passed through you," I said.

Now the slaver laughed. She bit into a plum.

"Are you Ku, or trying to be? Give us a wise river saying, something like one who follows the track of the elephant never gets wet from the dew. So we can say that river boy he even shits wisdom."

"Our wisdom is foolishness to the foolish."

"Indeed. I wouldn't be so bold with it, if I were you," she said, and bit into another plum.

"My wit?" I asked.

"Your smell."

She rose and walked over to me.

She was tall, taller than most men, taller than even the lionskin roamers of the savannah who jump to the sky. Her dress reached the ground and spread so that it looked like she glided over. And this—beautiful. Dark skin, without blemish and smelling of shea butter. Darker lips as if fed tobacco as a child, eyes so deep they were black, a strong face as chipped out of stone, but smooth as if done by a master. And the hair, wild and sprouting in every direction as if fleeing her head. Shea butter, which I already said, but something else, something I knew from that night, something that hid itself from me. Something I know. I wondered where the Leopard went.

The date feeder handed the slaver a staff. He struck the ground and we looked up. Well, not the Ogo; there was no up left for him to look. The Leopard came back in smelling of goat flesh.

The slaver said, "I tell you true and I tell you wise. Is three years ago a child was taken, a boy. He was just starting to walk and could say maybe nana. Taken from his home right here in the night. Nobody left nothing, and nobody called for ransom, not through note, not through drums, not even through witchcraft. Maybe he was sold to the secret witches market, a young child would bring much money to witches. This child was living with his aunt, in the city of Kongor. Then one night the child was stolen and the aunt's husband's throat cut. Her family of eleven children, all murdered. We can leave for the house at first light. There will be horses for those who ride, but you must go around the White Lake and around the Darklands and through Mitu. And when you come to Kongor—"

"What is this house to you?" the Leopard said.

I did not see him change and sit on the floor near the old woman, who still did not speak, though she opened her eyes, looked left, right, then closed them again. She moved her hands in the air, like the old men forming poses down by the river.

"It is the house where they last saw the boy. You don't plan to start the journey from the first step?" the slaver said.

"That would be from the house that gave the child away in the first place," I said.

"Who is they that last saw the boy? You are in the business of slaving lost boys, not finding them," said the Leopard. Funny how willing he was to question our employer when his belly was full.

The slaver laughed. I stared at him, hoping my stare would say, What game are you playing?

"Who is he and what is he to you?" the Leopard asked.

"The boy? He is the son of a friend who is dead," the slaver said.

"And so most likely is the boy. Why do you need to find him?"

"My reasons are my own, Leopard. I pay you to find him, not investigate me."

The Leopard rose. I knew the look on his face.

"Who is this aunt? Why was the child with her and not his mother?"

"I was going to tell you. His mother and father died, from river sickness. The elders said the father fished in the wrong river, took fish meant for the water lords, and the Bisimbi nymphs who swam underwater and stood guard struck him with illness. He spread it to the boy's mother. The father was my old friend and a partner in this business. His fortune is the boy's."

"A slave rich as you, catching his own fish?" I said.

The slaver paused. I said, "Do you know how to tell a good lie, master Amadu? I know how to tell a bad one. When people talk false, their words are muddy where they should be clear, clear where they should be muddy. Something that sounds like it might be true. But it's always the wrong thing. Everything you just said, you said different before."

"Truth don't change," he said.

"Truth changed between one man saying the same

thing twice. I believe there is a boy. And I believe a boy is missing, and if he's missing many years, dead. But four days ago, the boy child was living with a housekeeper. Today you say aunt. By the time we get to Kongor it will be a eunuch monkey."

"Tracker," the Leopard said.

"No."

"Let him finish."

"Good, good, wonderful, fine," the slaver said, and held his hand up.

"But stop lying," the Leopard said. "He can smell when you do."

"Is three years ago a child was taken. A boy, he was just starting to walk and could say maybe papa."

"Late for a child, even a boy," I said.

"I tell you true and I tell you wise. From his home right here in the night. Nobody leave nothing, and nobody send notice for ransom. Maybe—"

I pulled the two hatchets from my back. The Leopard's eyes were going white and his whiskers grew longer. The tall woman stood up and moved to the slaver.

"You heard him?" I said to the Leopard.

"Yes. The same story, almost right down to the word. Almost. But he forgets. Fuck the gods, slaver, you have rehearsed this and still you forget. You must be the worst liar or the echo of a bad one. If this is an ambush I will rip your throat out before he splits your head in two," the Leopard said.

Leopard and I stood side by side. The Ogo saw me and the Leopard on one side of the room and the slaver and tall woman on the other, and stood still, his eyes hiding under the wild bush of his brow. The old woman opened her eyes.

"One room too small for so many fools," she said. But she did not move from the mat.

She must have been a witch. She had the air and the smell of witches—lemongrass and fish, blood from a girl's koo, and funk from not washing her arms or feet.

"Messenger is what he is, all he is," she said.

"The first time, his message was a pig. This time it's a sheep," I said.

"Sangoma," the old woman said.

"What?"

"You talk in riddles, like a Sangoma. Did you live with one? Who teach you?"

"I don't know her name and she taught me nothing. The Sangoma from the Hills of Enchantment. The one who saved mingi children."

"Also the one who give you that eye," she said.

"My eye is none of your business. This some plot against us?" I asked.

"But you be nothing. Why would anyone plot against you?" the old woman said. "You wish to find the child or no? Answer the question plain, or maybe . . ."

"Maybe what?"

"Maybe the woman is still part of the man. No man has cut you. No wonder you so flighty."

"Should I be like you then, a credit to your kind?"

She smiled. She was enjoying this. And there it was, a smell again, stronger this time, stronger mayhaps because of the discord in this room, but also outside it. I could not describe it, but I knew it. No, the smell knew me.

"What do you know of the men who took the boy?" I asked.

"What makes you think they were men?" the tall woman said.

"What is your name?"

"Nsaka Ne Vampi."

"Nsaka," I said.

"Nsaka Ne Vampi."

"As you wish."

"I tell you true, we know nothing," she said. "Night is when they came. Few, maybe four, maybe five, maybe six, but they were men of strange and terrible looks. I can read the—"

"I can also read."

"Then go to the Kongor great hall of records and seek it yourself. Nobody saw them enter. Nobody saw them leave."

"Did no one scream?" said the Leopard. "Had they no windows or doors?"

"Neighbors saw nothing. The women over-charged for her millet porridge and flatbreads, so why would they listen twice what noises come from her house?"

"Why this boy, of all the boys in Kongor?" I asked. "Truly, Kongor is so steadfast in breeding warriors that finding a girl would be a bigger mystery. One boy in Kongor is the same as any other. Why him?"

"That is all we will say until Kongor," the slaver
said.

"Not enough. Not enough by half."

"The slaver said his piece," said Nsaka Ne Vampi.
"You have the choice, yes or no, so make it quick. We
ride in the morning. Even with fast horses it will take
ten and two days to get to Kongor."

"Tracker, we leave," the Leopard said.

He turned to go. I watched the Ogo watch him as
he stepped past.

"Wait," I said.

"Why?"

"Have you not yet finished making marks?"

"What? Make sense, Tracker."

"Not you. Her."

I pointed to the old woman still crouched on the
ground. She looked at me, her face blank.

"You have been drawing runes since we came into
this room. Writing on air, so nobody here would
know. But they are there. All around you."

The old woman smiled.

"Tracker?" the Leopard whispered. I knew how he
was when he understood nothing. He would change,
ready for a fight.

"The old crone's a witch," I said, and the Leopard's
hair went wild across his back. I touched behind his
neck and he stayed.

"You are writing runes either to let someone in or
keep someone out," I said.

I stepped forward and looked around the room.

"Show yourself," I said. "Your stench was with this room from the moment I entered it."

In the doorway, liquid coursing down the wall pooled on the floor. Dark and shiny, like oil, and spreading slow like blood. But the smell, something like sulfur, filled the room. "Look," I said to the Leopard, and pulled a dagger from my waist. I clutched the blade, chucked it at the puddle, and the puddle swallowed it with a suck. In a blink, the knife shot out from the puddle. The Leopard caught it right before it hit my left eye.

"Work of devils," he said.

"I have seen this devil before," I said.

The Leopard watched the puddle move. I wanted to see how the others reacted. The Ogo stooped down, but was still taller than everybody else. He bent even lower. He had never seen the like before. The old woman stopped writing runes in air. She was expecting this. Nsaka Ne Vampi stood fast, but moved backward, one slow step, then another. Then she stopped, but something else made her step back again. She was here for this, but perhaps this was not what she was waiting for. Some beasts can walk through a door. Some must be conjured from ground, and some must be evoked from sky, like spirits. The slaver looked away.

And this puddle. It stopped spreading and reversed, closed in on itself and started to rise, like dough being kneaded by invisible hands. The black shiny dough rose and twisted, and squeezed in, and spread out, even as it grew taller and wider. It twisted on itself, getting so thin in the middle that it would break in two. And still it grew. Little pieces popped away like droplets, then flew back and joined the mass. The Leopard snarled but did not move. The slaver still did not look. The black mass was whispering something I did not understand, not to me but on the air. At the top of the mass a face pushed itself out and sucked itself back in. The face pushed through the middle and vanished again. Two branches sprouted from the top of the mass and turned into limbs. The bottom split and twisted and spun into legs and toes. The form shaped itself, sculpted itself, curved herself into wide hips, plump breasts, the legs of a runner and the shoulders of a thrower, and a head with no hair and bright white eyes, and when she smiled, bright white teeth. She seemed to hiss. As she walked she left droplets of black, but the droplets followed her. Some separated from her head but followed her as well. Truly, she moved as if underwater, as if our air was water, as if all movement was dance. She grabbed a cloak near the slaver and dressed herself. The slaver still did not look at her.

"Leopard, the torch," I said. "The torch right there."

I pointed at the wall. The black woman saw the Leopard and smiled.

"I am not the one you think," she said. Her voice was clear, but vanished on air. She would not raise her voice to make herself heard.

"I think you are exactly as I think," I said. I took the torch from the Leopard. "And I would guess there is as much hate between you and flame as there was with them."

"Who is she, Tracker?" the Leopard said.

"Who am I, Wolf Eye? Tell him."

She turned to me, but said to the Leopard, "The wolf fears that by saying them he will invoke them. Say I lie, if I lie, Tracker."

"Who?" said the Leopard.

"I fear nothing, Omoluzu," I said.

"I rose from the floor while they fall from the ceiling. I speak while they say nothing. Yet you call me Omoluzu?"

"Every beast has its comelier version."

"I am Bunshi, in the North. The people in the West call me Popele."

"You must be one of the lower gods. A godlet. A bush spirit. Maybe even an imp," I said.

"News of your nose I have heard, but nobody said anything about your mouth."

"How he keeps putting his foot in it?" Nsaka Ne Vampi said.

"You know of me?"

"Everybody knows of you. A great friend of cheated wives and an enemy to cheating husbands. How loudly your mother must boast of you," Bunshi said.

"And what are you, God's piss? God's spit, or maybe God's semen?"

Around me the air got thick and thicker. Every

animal knows there is water in the air even without rain. But something was clotting around my nose and it was hard to breathe. The air got denser and wetter and surrounded my head. I thought it was the room but it was only my head, a ball of water forming and trying to force itself up my nostrils even without me breathing. Drowning me. I fell to the floor. The Leopard changed and jumped at the woman. She fell to the ground as a puddle and rose up on the other side of the room, right into the squashing hand of the Ogo around her neck. She tried slipping out but couldn't change. Something about his touch. He nodded towards me, holding her up like a doll, and the water broke away into air. I coughed. The Ogo dropped the woman.

"Leopard, stay if you wish. I go," I said.

The old woman spoke.

"Tracker. I am Sogolon, daughter of Kiluya from the third sister empire of Nigiki, and yes you speak true. There is more to this story. Will you hear it?" the old woman said.

"Tracker?" said the Leopard.

"Fine, I will," I said to her, and stood ground.

"Then speak it, goddess," Sogolon said to Bunshi.

Bunshi turned to the slaver and said, "Leave us."

"If your story is the same as his, or even more dull, I will sit with this knife and carve nasty scenes on the floor," I said.

"What do you know of your King?" she said.

"I know he's not my King," the Leopard said.

"Nor mine," I said. "But of every coin I make the Malakal chief wants half so he can give the King quarter, so yes he is my King."

Bunshi sat in the slaver's chair as men do, leaning to one side, her left leg over the arm. Nsaka was at the doorway, looking out. The Ogo stood still, and the old woman Sogolon stopped writing runes in the air. I felt like I was around children waiting on the grandfather to tell them a new story about old Nan-si, the spider demon who was a man once. It reminded me to never take the story of any god or spirit or magical being to be all true. If the gods created everything, was truth not just another creation?

"This was long past that Kwash Dara, when he was still a prince, had many friends for sporting, and wenching, and drinking, and fighting, like any boy of his own age. One friend most of all could out-sport him, out-wench him, out-drink him, and out-fight him, and yet even with all those things they moved like brothers. Friends even when the old King took sick and went to the ancestors.

"Basu Fumanguru became known as the man who whispers to the Prince. At the time the council of elders also had a death. Kwash Dara hated the council from when he was a child. Why do they always take young girls? he would ask his nana. And I heard they fuck into their hands and take the seed across to the river islands to give to some god, he said. The King when he was a prince studied at the palace of wisdom and glutted on knowledge, and science, and things being weighed and measured, not just believed. So did Basu Fumanguru. Kwash Dara knew Basu as a man like him in all ways and loved him for it. He said, Basu, you are like me in all ways. And just as I ascend the throne I wish for you to ascend the seat of the elders. Basu said he did not want this seat, for the elders sat in Malakal, five to six days' ride from Fasisi, where he was born, where lived, all that he knew. Also, he was still young, and to be an elder meant to renounce many things. The Prince became King and said, You are too old for lovers, and we are too old for sport. It is time to set all that aside and do good for the kingdom. Basu objected, and objected until the King threw down his royal staff and said, By the gods I am Kwash Dara and that is my decree. So Basu Fumanguru took his seat with the elders in Malakal, to report as an ear to the King.

"But then the strangest of turns happened. Basu fell in love with his seat. He became devout and pious and took a wife, handsome and pure. They had many children. The King had put him there to make sure the wisdom of the elders lined up with the desire of the royal house. Instead, Basu demanded that the desires of the royal house line up with the wisdom of the elders. Everything was fight, fight, fight. He challenged the King through dissent sent through the drums, he challenged him with letters and many writs, delivered by men on foot and on horse. He challenged him in visits to court and even in the privacy of the King's chambers. When the King said it is so because I am King, Basu Fumanguru took his case to the streets of Malakal, which spread faster than infection to the streets of Juba, the paths of Luala Luala, and the great roads of Fasisi itself. Basu would say, You are King but you are not divine until you join the ancestors like your father.

"So one day Kwash Dara demanded grain tax from the lands of the elders, which no king had done before. The elders refused to pay. The King sent decree to lock them all up in prison until the tax was paid. But two nights after they locked them away, rain broke all over the North Kingdom and did not stop until all the rivers flooded and killed many, and not just Ku and Gangatom living by the great water. In some places water rose so high that entire towns vanished, and fat bodies floated everywhere. The rain did not stop until the King released Basu Fumanguru. And still things got worse.

"Learn this. In the early years, when the elders clashed with the King, the will of the people was with the elders, for the King was arrogant. It did not make the King weak, for he conquered many nations in war. But in his own country people were starting to ask, Do we have one king or two? I tell you true. Some people were more afraid of Fumanguru than the King, and he was fearsome in all his ways. And righteous in them too. But everything changes. The elders, already fat, got fatter. They got so used to having their will that when people defied them, or were too late with rent, or failed to give proper tribute, they started to take justice themselves instead of leaving such things to the King's magistrates. They captured highway robbers and chopped their hands off. They hung whoever trespassed and ate the fruit of their lands. They stopped seeking the gods and instead met with witches to work spells and curses. They got fat from taxes that never reached the King.

"Listen here now. Some people hated the King, but soon everybody hated all elders but Basu. One man would say, The elders took my cattle saying this is tax for the King, but the tax collector came seven days ago. This elder would say, Give me what you will earn from your crops now and we will make sure the gods double your yield come harvest. But instead of harvest, blight killed the crops. Another man will say, When will they stop coming for our girls? They are taking them younger and younger, and no man will marry them. They were the law in Malakal and all lands below Fasisi, and when they did not meet in council, they spread to their cities and infected each with its corruption. But it was a decree by the King himself that the elders can only be judged by the gods, never men.

"Basu would not sit with any of this. He was never the chief elder—the King never made good on the promise—but they respected him as once a warrior, and he clashed against his own brothers who had gone corrupt. People say, Go to Basu if that elder took your crops, Go to Basu if a witch spun a curse, Go to Basu for he is the one with reason. People say this. One time an elder had seen a girl in the fourth wall and decided he would have her. She was ten and one in years. He told her father, Send your child to serve as maid to the water goddess, or no wind or sun will prevent your sorghum fields from blight. You and your wife and your many sons will starve. The elder did not wait for the girl to be sent; he came and took her himself. This is what happened. Basu was gathering items for a retreat to a holy place in the bush to seek the word of the gods, when he heard the screams of the girl as the elder was on top of her. A rage went up his head and Basu was no longer Basu. He grabbed a gold Ifa bowl, used to divine the will of the spirits, and struck the elder in the head. And struck him, and struck him, and struck him until he was dead. Basu was in new waters after that. His brothers hated him and he was hated by the King and everyone at court. He should have known there were numbers to his days. Fumanguru and his family fled to Kongor.

"Then one night they came. Tracker, you know of who I speak. It was the Night of the Skulls, a powerful omen."

"Your brothers?"

"We are not blood."

"You have no blood."

She looked away from me. The Leopard, his eyes wide open, was listening like a child left in a bush of ghosts. She continued, "There are many ways to summon them. If you have someone's blood, speak a curse and throw it up to the ceiling. But first you would

need to be under a witch's enchantment, or they
will appear and kill you. Or you could call a witch
to do it for you. They appear on the ceiling, people
call them the roof walkers, and whether a witch
summons them or they are lured by your blood,
the hunger in them grows so big that they will
hunt you like starving dogs. And the spell will never
leave you. Nobody can escape them, and even if you
do they will appear anytime you are under a roof,
even for a blink. Many man, many woman, many
young boy and girl sleep under stars because they will
never be rid of Omoluzu.

"You were wondering, Tracker, how come they
never followed you here? How long before you slept
under a roof?"

"Near a year," I said.

"Omoluzu cannot follow you out of the underworld if that is where they found you. And had they
found you here, they cannot follow you there. But if
I were you, I would not throw blood."

"What did the Omoluzu do?" the Leopard said.

Bunshi stood up. Her robes billowed even though
no wind blew. Outside a crash, some shouts, and
some screams. People drunk on drink and sport,
people drunk on the excitement of the coming King.
Kwash Dara, the same king in her story.

"As I said before. They came on the Night of the
Skulls. Fumanguru's seven sons were long asleep and
time was reaching deep night, the noon of the dead.
All of them asleep, even the youngest, also called Basu.

Asleep were the ground and garden slaves, but awake were the cooks milling grain, Basu's youngest and oldest wives, and Basu, in his study, reading volumes from the **Palace of Wisdom.** This is what happened. An elder with friends at court sent a witch to speak a dark enchantment on the house, then paid a slave to gather the youngest wife's menstrual blood. Omoluzu hunger is monstrous—it is the smell of blood that lures them, not the taste. This slave found her blood cloths, bundled them together, and in the dark when the other slaves were asleep, threw her mistress's blood cloths up to the ceiling. The witch never told her to run, so she went to sleep. In the dark the rumble on the ceiling must have sounded like thunder far away. Thunder that even the light sleeper sleeps through.

"The Tracker can tell who they be. They fall from the ceiling the way I rise from the ground. They run on the ceiling as if tethered to sky. When they leap, they almost touch the floor, but land back on the ceiling so hard that you wonder if it not they who are on the ground and you who are in the air. And they have blades made of nothing on this earth. They rose and formed, and chopped up nearly every living slave save one. She ran out screaming that the dark has come to kill us. Tracker is right that I am like them. But I am not them. And yet I felt them, I felt them coming and knew they were near, but did not know which house until I heard Basu himself shout. Omoluzu chased the slave, who ran to Basu's wife. The wife grabbed a torch, thinking of the great legends where light defeats darkness, but they surrounded them and chopped both their heads off.

"Omoluzu appeared in the grain room and killed the cooking slaves. They appeared in the children's room and cut them up before any of them even woke. They were merciful with no one. When I climbed into the house it was too late, and still there was killing. I stepped into a hallway thick with blood. A man ran to me holding a baby, Basu holding young Basu. He looked like a man who knew death was chasing him. I could hear death rumble on the ceiling like thunder, like mortar was breaking apart. Black racing across the ceiling like darkness and coming after him. I say, Give me your child if you want him to live. I am his father, he says. I say, I cannot save both of you and fight them, and he says, You are just like them. But we share neither mother nor father, I say. I did not have time to convince him I was good or evil. I saw the darkness behind him take shape into three, then four, then six Omoluzu. Give me the boy, I said. He stared at his child long, then handed him to me. The baby was only one year born, I could tell. We were both holding him and he could not let him go.

"They are coming," he said.

"They are here," I said.

"He looked at me and said, This was the work of the King. Kwash Dara. This was the work of the court, this was the work of the elders, and my son is witness that this happened.

"Your son will not remember, I said.

"But the King will, he said.

"I flicked up my second finger and it became a blade. I pushed below my rib right here and cut it open. The father was afraid but I told him he need not fear, I make a womb for the boy. I cut my womb open the way midwives sometimes do when the baby is unborn and the mother is already dead. I pushed the baby through and my skin sealed him inside. The father was in terror, but seeing my belly big, as if with child, gave him some peace. Will he die in you? he said, and I said no. Were you a mother? this man Basu asked me, but I did not answer. I tell you true, there was a heaviness in me. I have never carried children. But maybe every woman is a mother."

"You are not a woman," I said.

"Quiet," said the Leopard.

"The Sangoma said you had a mouth on you," she said.

I didn't ask how she knew.

"The Omoluzu had blades. I had blades too."

"Of course you did."

"Tracker, enough," said the Leopard.

"One came for me, swung his one blade, but I had two."

"That's a scene for the griots, a pregnant-looking woman fighting shadow devils with two blades."

"A scene indeed," said the Leopard. I was starting to wonder about him. He was feeding on her story like someone starving, or like someone glutting, I could not tell.

"He swung at me and I ducked. I jumped up to the ceiling, their floor, and chopped his head off with my two blades. But I could not fight them all. Basu Fumanguru was brave. He pulled out a knife, but a blade came for him from the back and stabbed right through his belly. But their bloodlust was not satisfied. They could smell the family's blood on the boy even with him inside me. One swung and cut me in the shoulder, but I swung around and cut his chest open. I ran and jumped through the same window I came through."

"Not anywhere have I heard such a story. Not from the hawk, not even from the rhinoceros," the Leopard said.

"It is a very good story. There were even monsters. None of it makes me want to help you," I said.

She laughed. "If I was looking for noble men with the heart to help a child, I would never have called you. I really don't care what you want. It is a task for which you will be paid four times more than the highest you have ever charged. In gold. What you like or want, whatever it is in your head means nothing to me."

"I . . ." I had nothing to say.

"What of the child—after, I mean?" the Leopard said.

"I did not take him to his aunt. Omoluzu smells blood upon blood and would have, should whoever commanded them willed it, gone after any family. I took him to a blind woman in Mitu, who used to be loyal to the old gods. Without sight she would not know who the child was, or try to find out. She was with a child so could suckle him also, and keep him for a year."

"Used to be loyal?"

"She sold him at the slave market in the Purple City, near Lake Abbar. A baby fetches great coin outside of Kongor, especially a male. She told me this as I started to slit her throat with this finger."

"What wise choices in people you make."

I knew from across the room, Nsaka Ne Vampi rolled her eyes. I did not look, but I knew.

"I tracked the child to a perfume and silver merchant who was going to take him to the East. It took me a moon and it was too late. He was late with his silver and merchants in Mitu sent mercenaries to find him. You know where they found him? At the border of Mitu. They found flies but no stench of death. Somebody ransacked the caravan and killed everyone. Nobody touched the civet, or silver, or myrrh. Never found the boy; they took him."

"The King?" I asked.

"The King would have had him killed."

"So he is gone? Why not leave him gone?"

"You would have a child walking with murderers?" the old woman said.

"Because a child in the company of witches would fare much better," I said. "What use is the boy to murderers?"

"They found use," Bunshi said.

I remember what the date feeder said to the slaver in the lightning woman's tower. About the little boy knocking on the woman's door, crying that he was running from monsters, only to let them in as soon as her family fell asleep. I nodded at the Leopard, hoping he caught what they were not saying.

I couldn't decide whether to sit down, stand up, or leave.

"A little boy survives roof walkers only to be sold into slavery, where he was kidnapped by who, witchmen? Devils? A society of boy-lover spirits starting out the child early? What will happen next, maybe Ninki Nanka the swamp dragon will smell them as they go through the bush and eat them all?"

"You don't believe in such creatures?" Bunshi said. "Despite all you have seen and heard and fought with? Despite the animal beside you?"

"You don't need belief in evil creatures when men flay their own wives," I said. I turned and looked at the Leopard, who was still drinking in this story.

"But you do believe speaking clever is wise. Good. I am not paying for your belief. I am paying for your nose. Bring me back the boy."

"Or proof of his corpse?"

"He is alive."

"And when we find him, what then? You are asking us to go against the King?"

"I'm paying you to expose the King."

"Proof that the King is behind a murder."

"There is more to the story of the King than you know. And if you knew you could not bear."

"Of course."

"She's not paying you to ask or to think. She's paying you to smell," said Nsaka Ne Vampi.

"How do you know they have not killed the child?"

"We know," Bunshi said.

I almost said I know too, but looked at the Leopard. He glanced at me and nodded.

A door opened and shut. I thought it was Fumeli but it was not his smell. Nsaka Ne Vampi walked over to the doorway and looked out. She said, "In two days we ride for Kongor. Come or don't come, it makes no difference to me. She's the one that wants you."

She pointed to Bunshi, but I kept looking past her. I didn't even hear what she said after, because of the scent coming up the stairs. The scent I caught earlier, which I thought was Bunshi, but I had never met her and she was right, she did not smell like Omoluzu. This scent was coming closer, someone carrying it, and I knew I hated it, more than I have hated anything in years, more than I have hated men I have known but killed anyway. He was coming up the stairs, coming closer, I could hear the patter of his feet and with each step my fury was bursting into flames.

"You are late," Nsaka Ne Vampi blurted. "Everyone is—"

I cut her words off with the hatchet that I flung straight past her face to lodge in the door.

"God's fuck! You barely missed me, friend," he said, stepping into the doorway.

"I wasn't trying to miss," I said, and threw the second one straight for his face. He dodged but it grazed his ear.

"Tracker, what the—"

I ran and jumped on him; we fell back on the stairs and rolled down the steps. My hands around his neck and squeezing until either his neck snapped or his breath died. Rolling down the steps, skin bruising, blood shedding, his, mine, the steps, the loose mortar. Me losing earth, him losing voice, rolling and rolling and hitting the floor below, the force of the fall and him kicking me in the chest. I fell back and he was upon me. I kicked him off and pulled a knife, but he knocked it out of my hand and punched me in the belly, then the face, then the cheek, then my chest but I blocked his hand, pushed away the knuckle, punched him under the chin, again across the left eye. The Leopard ran down as Leopard and changed maybe, I didn't see, I kept my eyes on him. He ran, and jumped, and kicked, I dodged and swung up my elbow and hit him square in the face and he was down, head hit the ground first. I jumped on him and punched his left cheek then right, then left, and he hit me in the ribs twice and I fell off, but rolled out of the way of his knife as he stabbed the floor. I kicked his kick, and kicked his kick again and scrambled up as he scrambled up, and the Leopard knew better than to pull me back or stop me, and looking at the

Leopard I didn't see him come up behind and swing for the back of my head and hit and it got wet and I fell to my knees, and he swung his hand back to hit me again and I kicked his feet and he fell. I got on him again and swung my hand back to punch him again, his face running blood, looking like a dark juicy fruit bruised open, and a blade pushed itself against my throat.

"I will cut your head off and feed it to crows," Nsaka Ne Vampi said.

"I smell him all over you," I said.

"Take your hands off his neck. Now," she said.

"No—"

The arrow shot straight through her hair. The Leopard's boy was a floor below, another arrow in the bow, pulled tight and ready. Nsaka Ne Vampi raised her hands. A wild gust of blue wind hit the floor and blew us away from each other in the quick. The Leopard and I hit the wall hard and Nsaka Ne Vampi rolled away.

Nyka laughed on top of it, as he tried to pull himself up. He spat at the wind, which howled louder, pinning me against the wall. Her voice was on top of it, the old woman's. A spell set loose on the floor. The wind died as soon as it came, and we were separated from each other, across the room. Bunshi came down the steps, but the old woman stayed above.

"Them you expect to find this boy?" Sogolon said.

"You two know each other," Bunshi said.

"Black mistress, have you not heard? We are old

friends. Better than lovers since I shared his bed for six moons. And yet nothing came to pass, eh, Tracker? Did I ever tell you I was disappointed?"

"Who is this man?" Leopard asked me.

"But he told me so much about you, Leopard. He never gave any word about me?"

"This son of a leprous jackal bitch is nothing, but some call him Nyka. I swore to every fucking god that would hear me that when I saw you next, if that day ever came, I would kill you," I said.

"That day is not today," Nsaka Ne Vampi said. She had two daggers out.

"I hope for your sake you make him pull out when he fucks you. Even his seed is poison," I said.

"This reunion does not move well, I think. There is thunder under your brow," Nyka said.

"Tracker, let's—"

"Let's what, cat?"

"Whatever you are looking for, today is not the day to find it," he said.

I was so furious, all I could feel was heat, and all I could see was red.

"You didn't even do it for gold. Not even silver," I said.

"Still such a fool. Some tasks are their own reward. Nothing means nothing and nobody loves no one, isn't that what you love to say? Yet you are the one with all this feeling, and you trust it above everything else, even your nose. Fool for love, fool for hate. Still think I did it for money?"

"Leave now, or I swear I won't care who I kill to get to you," I said.

"You leave instead," the old woman said. "But stay, Leopard."

"Where he goes, I go," the Leopard said.

"Then both of you leave," the old woman said.

Nsaka Ne Vampi took Nyka upstairs, her eyes on me the whole time.

"Get out," Bunshi said.

"I was never in," I said.

Deep in the night, I woke up to my room still dark. I thought I was rising from troubled sleep but she had gone into my dream to wake me up.

"You knew you would follow me," she said.

The thickness of her form trickled down the windowsill. She rose into a mound, stretched as high as the ceiling, then shaped herself into a woman again. Bunshi stood by the window, sitting in the frame.

"So you are a god," I said.

"Tell me why you wish him dead."

"Will you grant me the wish?"

She stared at me.

"I don't wish him dead," I said.

"Oh?"

"I wish to kill him."

"I will have the tale."

"Oh you will, will you. Very well. This is what passed between me and Nyka."

Nyka was like a man coming back from things I was yet to go through. It was two years since I last saw the Leopard, and I was living in Fasisi, taking any work I could find, even finding dogs for stupid children who thought they could keep dogs, and who cried when I brought the animal's just-buried carcass back to the father who killed it. Indeed, a roof over my head was the only reason I bedded women, since they were more agreeable to me staying the night than men, especially when I was searching for their husbands.

A noblewoman who lived for the day when she would finally be called to court, but who in the meantime fucked one man for every seven women she smelled on her husband's breath, said this to me as I came at her from behind in the marriage bed and thought of Uwomowomowomowo valley boys smooth in skin: It has been said you have a nose. Both man and wife spilled perfume on the rugs to hide the smell of others they brought to bed. Later she looked at me and I said, Do not worry, I will please myself. What do you wish from my nose? I asked. My husband has seven mistresses. I do not complain for he is a painful, terrible lover. But he has gone stranger of late, and he was already very strange. I feel he has taken an eighth mistress, and that mistress is either a man or a beast. Twice has he come home with a smell that I did not recognize. Something rich, like a burning flower.

I did not ask how she heard of me, or what were

her wishes when I found him, only how much she would pay.

"A boy's weight in silver," she said.

I said, This sounds like a good offer. What would I know of good or bad offers? I was young. Give me something of his, for I have never seen your husband, I said. She grabbed what looked like a white rug and said, This is what he wears under his garment. Are you married to a man or a mountain? I said. The cloth was twice as wide as the span of my arm and still carried the trace of his sweat, shit, and piss. I did not tell her there were two different shits in this cloth, one from him and another from him pleasuring someone's ass. As soon as I smelled him I knew where he was. But I knew where he was when she said burning flower.

"Be careful. Many mistake him for Ogo," she said.

Only one thing smelled of burning flower. Only one thing smelled like something rich burned away.

Opium.

It came from the merchants in the East. Now there were secret dens in every city. Nobody I knew who had taken it had a tomorrow. Or a yesterday. Just a now, in a den with smoke, which made me wonder if this man was opium's seller or slave or a thief of men under opium.

The smell of the husband and the opium led me to the street for artists and masters of craft. Fasisi streets had no plan. A wide street twisted into a narrow lane, burped into a river with just a rope bridge, then another lane again. Most of the houses had thatch roofs and walls built of clay. On the highest hill in the delta, the royal compound sat behind thick walls guarded by sentries. I tell you, it was a mystery why this, the least magnificent of the northern cities, was the capital of the empire. Nyka said this is the city that reminded the King of where we came from and to never go back, but he does not yet enter this story. Fasisi smiths are the masters of iron, if not manners. And iron is what made this backward town conquer the North two hundred years ago.

I stopped at an inn whose name meant "Light from a Woman's Buttocks" in my language. They locked the windows shut but left the door open. Inside, many men lay wherever there was floor, on their backs, their eyes here but gone, their mouths leaking drool, their owners uncaring as the remnants of embers tipped from pipe bowls and burned out on their robes. A woman in the corner stood over a large pot that smelled of soup missing peppers and spices. Truth, it smelled more like the hot water used to skin an animal. Some of the men moaned, but most kept quiet, as if in sleep.

I passed a man smoking tobacco under a torch. He sat on a stool and leaned his back against the wall. Thin face, two large earrings, strong chin, though that might have been the light. The front half of his head he shaved, leaving the back to grow long. Goatskin cape. He did not look at me. From another room came music, which was odd, since nobody in this hall would notice. I stepped over men who did not move, men who could see me but had eyes only for the pipe. The burning-flower smell of opium was so thick that I held my breath. One never knew. Upstairs a boy screamed and a man cursed. I ran upstairs.

For someone not an Ogo this husband was as huge as one. He stood there, taller than the doorway, taller than the tallest cavalry horse. Naked, and raping a boy. I could only see his legs dangling, lifeless. But he was bawling. His two giant hands grabbed the boy's buttocks while he forced himself. The wife did not want him dead, I thought, but said nothing about wanting him whole.

I pulled two throwing daggers, little ones, and flung them at his back. One cut across his shoulder. The husband yelled, dropped the boy, and turned around. The boy landed on his back and didn't move. I watched him, waited too long. The husband was upon me, all muscle and skin, his shoulders massive like an ape's, his hand grabbing my entire head. He picked me up like a doll and threw me across the room. He growled as he had while raping. The boy rolled over and grabbed one of the rugs. The man, like a buffalo, charged at me. I dodged and he ran right into the wall, cracking it and almost bursting right through. I grabbed a hatchet to chop his heel, but he reached back and kicked me all the way to the wall on the other side. It slammed the breath out of my mouth and I fell. The boy scrambled, stepping on my legs as he ran out. The man pulled his head out of the wall. His skin dark, wet from sweat, hairy like a beast's. He batted away a line of spears leaning on the wall. Truly I knew men who were big and men who were fast but no man who was both. I pulled myself up and tried to run but his hand was around my neck again. He cut my breath off, and that wasn't enough. He would crush my bone. I couldn't reach knife or hatchet. I punched, thumped, scratched his arms, but he laughed as if I was the boy he was raping. He glared at me and I saw his black eyes. My sight was going dark and my spit ran down his hand. He even had me off the floor. Blood was ready to burst out of my eyes. I barely saw the man from downstairs break a clay jar on the man's back. The husband swung around and the man threw something yellow and rank in his eyes. The not-Ogo dropped me and fell to his knees, screaming and rubbing his eyes as if about to scratch them out. Air rushed into me and made me fall to my knees as well. The man grabbed my arm.

"Is he blind?" I asked.

"Maybe for the next few blinks, maybe for a quartermoon, maybe forever, you can never tell with bat piss."

"Bat piss? Did you s—"

"A giant is just as dangerous blind, young boy."

"I'm not a boy, I'm a man."

"Die as a man, then," he said, and ran out. I ran after him. He laughed all the way out the door.

He said his name was Nyka. No family name, no

house of origin, no place he called home, and no home he was running from. Just Nyka.

We hunted together for a year. I was good at finding everything but business. He was good at finding everything but people. I should have known but he was right, I was a boy. He made me wear robes, which I did not like, for they made fighting difficult, but people in some cities took me for his slave when I wore only a wrap. Most towns we went to, nobody knew of this Nyka. But everywhere we went where somebody knew him, they wanted to kill him. In a bar in the Uwomowomowomowo valley I saw a woman walk right up to him and slap him twice. She would a third time, but he caught her hand. She pulled a knife with the other and grazed his chest. Later that night my hand was between my legs as I heard them fuck across the room.

Once we searched for a dead girl who was not dead. Her kidnapper kept her in a burial urn in the ground behind his house, and took her out whenever he wanted amusement. He gagged her mouth and bound her hands and feet. When we found him he had just put his children to sleep and left his wife to go around the back to do things to this girl. He pulled away loose plants and scooped away dirt, and took out the hollow stick that he stuck in the top of the urn so that she could breathe. But this night it was not her in the urn, but Nyka. He stabbed the man in the side and he staggered back yelling. I kicked him in the back and he fell. I took a club and knocked him out. He woke up tied to the tree near where he buried the girl. She was weak and could not stand. I put my hand on her mouth, telling her to stay quiet, and gave her a knife. We steadied her hand as she pushed the knife down into his belly, then chest, then belly again over and over. He screamed into the gag until he would scream no more. I would have the girl get satisfaction. The knife fell out of her hand and she lay next to the dead man, crying. Something changed in Nyka after that. We were liars and thieves but we were not killers.

I tell you all this because I want you to see him as I saw him. Before.

Business was drying up in Fasisi. I grew tired of the place and wives missing husbands every seven days. We were at the same inn we always went to split our profits. And drink palm wine or masuku beer or liquor the colour of amber, which set fire in the chest and made the floor slippery. The fat innkeeper with a frown line right above the wart above her brow came over.

"Pour us both the bottled fire," Nyka said.

She produced two mugs and filled both halfway. She said nothing, not even when Nyka slapped her buttocks as she went back to the counter.

"Good fortune awaits in the city of Malakal, or the Uwomowomowomowo valley below," I said.

"Good fortune you thinking? What if I am hungry for adventure?"

"North?"

"I think I shall see my mother," he said.

"You said before, the second-greatest thing you two gave each other was distance. You have also said you have no mother."

He laughed. "That is still true."

"Which?"

"How much bottled fire did you drink?"

"Which mug is yours?"

"You drank from it?" he asked. "Good. When last we talked of fathers, you said you fought yours. One day my father, he comes in from a day of not working, only scheming and plotting and going nowhere. Hitting us was sport. One time he hit my brother in the back of the head with the walking stick and my brother was simple after that. My mother made sorghum bread. He beat her too. One time he whipped her with the walking stick, and she hopped on one foot for two moons and limped after that. So yes, let us say that this was a night he comes home from drink and swings the cane and hits me in the back of the head. Then he kicks and beats me on the ground, knocks another tooth loose, shouting for me to get up and take more. One day we shall talk just of fathers, Tracker. So yes, let us say he swings the stick at my head, but he's too slow, and I too fast, and I catch it. Then I grab the stick from him and swing it to his head. He falls, just like that, on the floor. I take the stick and beat him and beat him, and he holds up his hand, and I break all his fingers, and he holds up his arms, and I break his arms, and he holds up his head and I break his head till I heard crack, crack, crack and still I beat, and then I hear crunch, and then sloosh, slosh, and my mother screams, You killed my husband, you killed your brothers' father. How will we eat? I burned him behind our hut. Nobody asked for him, because nobody liked him, and everybody rejoiced at the smell of his burning flesh."

"And your mother?"

"I know my mother. She is right where I left her. And yet I will see her, Tracker. I leave in two days. Then we can go on whatever adventure you like."

"You are the one always seeking adventure. Meet me in Malakal."

"Meet me where you smell my scent. A lazy night this is, and we have fucked out the entire quarter. Drink some more."

I drank and he drank until we tamed that fire in the chest, and then we drank more. And he said, Let us forget talk of fathers, friend. Then he kissed me on the mouth. This was nothing; Nyka kissed all and everyone, in greeting or parting.

"I shall find you in ten days," I said to him.

"Eight is the better number," he said. "More than seven days with my mother and all I can do is try not to kill her. Drink some more."

A warmth, first on my forehead, ran down my neck. I opened my eyes and the piss hit my face and blinded me. I rubbed my eyes without thinking, and my right hand pulled my left. A shackle on my right hand, a chain, a shackle on my left. In front of me, a leg raised and piss spurting on me. Off in the dark, loud laughter. I lashed out but the chain stopped me. I tried to stand, I tried to scream, the women in the dark laughed louder. The animal, the beast, the dog pissed on me like I was the trunk of a tree. First I thought Nyka just left me drunk in an alley to be pissed on by dogs. Or someone, a madman or a slaver—they infested these alleys—or a husband who did not want me to find him now found me. My mind went wild, thinking three men or four, or five had found me in the alley and said, Here is the man who took the comfort from our lives. But men did not laugh like women. The dog lowered his foot and trotted away. The floor was dirt and I could make out walls. My mind went wild again. I would ask, Who are you men that I shall soon kill, but something gagged my mouth.

Popping out of the dark first, two red eyes. Then teeth, long and white and ready. Light was above me when I looked up, light peeking through branches hiding this hole. A trap I fell into. A trap long forgotten, so that even the trapper would not know that I shall die here. But who put a gag in my mouth? Was it so that I could not scream while it bit into me and tore chunks apart? And yet before I saw the face, when it was just eyes and teeth, the piss told me everything. The hyena backed up in the dark, then charged straight at me. Another jumped out of the dark from the side and knocked her in the ribs, and they both rolled into the dark, scowling, growling, barking. Then they stopped and started laughing again.

"Men in the West call us the Bultungi. You have unfinished business with us," she said in the dark.

I would have said I have no business with spotted devils, or that nothing glorious springs from deceiving scavengers, but I had a gag in my mouth. And hyenas, from what I knew, had no qualm with live flesh.

The three came out of the dark: a girl; a woman older, perhaps her mother; and a still older woman, thin, with her back straight. The girl and the old woman wore nothing. The girl, her breasts like large plums, hips spread wide; her nana, a sprout of black-haired bush. The old woman, her face mostly cheekbones, her arms and frame thin, and her breasts lanky. The middle woman, her hair in braids, wore a red boubou tunic with rips and smudges. Wine, or dirt, or blood, or shit, I didn't know; I could smell all of them. Also this. I looked into the dark for the male who pissed on me, but no man came. But the two naked women came in the little light, and I saw it on both of them. Long cocks, or what looked like cocks between their legs, thick and swinging quick.

"Behold, it looks at us," the middle one said.

"Look at hyena womankind, longer and harder than you," the young one said.

"Shall we eat it now? Take him in? Limb by limb?" the old one said.

"Will you raise much fuss, man? Living or dead flesh makes no difference to us," the middle one said.

"Come, come no fuss, rend the flesh, juice the blood, eat it, us," the old one said.

"I say we kill him now," the young one said.

"No, no, eat him slow, start with the feet, precious meat," the old woman said.

"Now."

"Later."

"Now!"

"Later!"

"Quiet!" the middle one shouted, then swung her arms wide and struck both.

The young one changed first, in a blink. Her nose and mouth and chin shot out of her face and her eyes went white. The muscles on her shoulder pumped and popped up, and those in her arms raised from arm to fingertip as if snakes ran under the skin. On the old woman her chest spread as if new flesh was tearing out of the old, all under her rough skin. Her face went the same. Her fingers, now black claws, the tips like iron. All this happened far quicker than I describe it. The old woman growled, and the young girl did the heh-heh-heh laugh that was not a laugh. The old woman charged the middle one but she swatted her away like a fly. The old woman pawed the ground, thinking to charge again.

"It took your ribs five moons to heal last time," the middle one said.

"Take the gag out and let him give us sport,"

the old one said. The young one changed back to girl. She came to me and indeed her smell was foul. Whatever she last ate, she ate days ago and chunks of it rotted somewhere on her body. She ran her hands around the back of my head and I thought of banging my head against the wall, anything, even the slightest thing to resist. She laughed and her foul breath ran past my nose. She pulled the gag and I coughed up vomit. They all laughed. She came in close to my face as if about to lick the vomit off, or kiss it.

"A comely bitch, this one be," she said.

"As man goes, he will not be the worst to go down my stomach," the old one said.

"Long in leg, thin in muscle, lean in fat, he will not be much of a meal," said the old one.

"Salt him with his brains, and add some hog fat to his flesh," said the young one.

"I give him this," said the middle one. "In the only matter that counts with man, he impresses me. How do you run with it swinging so low?"

I coughed until my throat was raw.

"Maybe he will have water," the old one said.

"I have in me some strong water," the young one said, and laughed. She hiked up her left leg and grabbed her dangling cock, then laughed instead of pissed. The old one laughed as well.

The middle one stepped forward. She said, "We are the Bultungi, and you have unfinished business with us."

"Unfinished business I will finish with my hatchet," I coughed. They all laughed.

"Chop it off, place it in another room, and boom! Man still acting like he swinging," said the old one.

"Old bitch, not even me understand that," said the young one.

The middle one stood right before me. "Do you not remember us?" she said.

"The hyena has never been a memorable beast."

"Make me give him something to remember," the young one said.

"Truly who remembers the hyena? You look like the head of a dog pushing out of the asshole of cat walking backwards."

The old and middle women laughed, but the young one flipped to fury. She changed. Still on two legs, she charged for me. Middle one kicked her leg out and tripped her. Young one landed hard on her chin and slid a little. She crouched and growled at the middle one, then started to circle her as if about to fight over fresh kill. She growled again, but the middle one, still in the form of woman, let loose a snarl louder than a roar. Maybe the room shook or maybe the young one, but even I felt something shift. She whimpered heh-heh-hehs under her breath.

"How long since you saw our sisters?"

I coughed again.

"I stay away from half-dead hogs and rotting antelope, so I would never see your sisters."

I only noticed now, with her close, that her eyes were all white as well. The old one went off in the dark but her eyes popped out of the black.

"And what sisters? You boy-beasts who change to women, what are you?"

They all laughed.

"Surely you know us. We are the beasts where the woman do the tasking and the men do the tasks. And since men have made it that the biggest cock rules ground and sky, does it not make sense that woman should have the biggest cock?" said the middle one.

"This is a world where men rule."

"And what good has come of your rule?" the old one said.

"There is game, there is bush, there are rivers without poison, and no child starves because of the gluttony of his father, since we put men in their place, and the gods willed it," said the middle one.

"He don't remember any of them. Maybe we cry. Maybe we make him cry," the young one said.

"I would tell you how many moons have passed, but we do not fear gray in the hair, nor the crook in back, so we do not count moons. Do you not remember the Hills of Enchantment? A boy with two axes jumped a pack of us, killing three and maiming one. Who could no longer hunt, became prey."

The other two groaned.

"Women doing what they do. Protecting their young. Nurturing, providing—"

"Feeding them whatever young child you were too glutted to feed yourself."

"That is the way of the bush."

"And should you come across me with half of your cub in my mouth, would you tell yourself that too is the way of the bush? Fuck the gods, if you are not the shiftiest of creatures. If you are in the bush, and of the bush, why do I smell your fucking stink in the city? You roll in the street and grovel like a mangy bitch to the women whose children you snatch at night."

"You have no honor."

"You bitches have me down in a hole full of man bones, and the smell of children you murder. A group of you killed ten and seven women and babies over twenty nights in Lajani until hunters killed them. Until I passed through and asked why does everywhere reek of hyena piss, they thought they were hunting wild dogs. I see your ways. You shift form to move among children, do you not? Then drag them away to kill. Not even the lowest shape-shifter kind sinks so low. Honor. There's more honor to the worm."

"He keeps calling us dogs," the young one said.

"We followed you for a year," the middle one said.

"Why grab me now?"

"I told you time is nothing to us, nor is haste. It's your friend who took a year."

"Awhoa! Sister, look at his face. Look how it falls when you speak of the friend. Did you not yet see in your mind-eye that he betrayed you?"

"Nyka. That is his name. Was there strong love between you? You thought he would never sell you for
silver or gold, and yet how do we know his name?"

"He is my friend."

"Nobody ever gets betrayed by their enemy."

"Nothing, he says. Now he says nothing. Watch
the face. It's drooping longer. No sting like betrayal's
sting. Watch the face," the young one said.

"It turns into a . . . a . . . scowl? Is it a scowl, sisters?" the old one asked.

"Come out of the dark so you can see clear."

"I think the boy shall cry."

"Take heart, boy. He sold you to us a year ago. In that
time I think he might have even grown to like you."

"He just like gold coin more."

"Do you wish that we kill him?" the middle one
said as she stooped in front of me.

I lunged at her as far as the chains would let me,
but she did not even flinch.

"I can do this for you. A final wish," she said.

"I have a wish," I said.

"Sisters, the man has a wish. Should one of us at-
tend to it or all three?"

"All three of you."

"Give us this wish, we shall hear it," said the old
one.

I looked at them. The middle one smiling as if she
was the healer woman come to touch my forehead,
the old one cupping her ear as she looked at me, the
younger one spitting and looking away.

"I wish you would stay in hyena form, for though you are a hideous animal and your breath always stinks of rotting corpse, at least I didn't have to bear you in the mockery form of women. Women who make me ask what kind of woman smells as if she shits from the mouth."

The old and young ones howled and changed form again, but I knew the middle one would not allow them to touch me. Yet.

"I wish to see the view of the gods, when I kill each of you."

The middle one threw herself at me as if to kiss. Indeed she grabbed my head as if to kiss and parted her lips. Sisters, she said, and both ran to me as women, and grabbed my arms. Strong, strong women, they held me down no matter how hard I struggled. She moved in to kiss my mouth, but moved her lips upward, touching my nose, brushing my cheek, and stopping at my left eye. I closed it before she licked it. She took her fingers and pried it open. She covered it with her mouth and licked the eye. I yelled and struggled, jerked my chest up and tried to nod my head out of her grip. I screamed before I knew what she was doing. Then she stopped licking. And started sucking. She pressed her lips around the eye and sucked, and sucked, and I could feel myself pulling out of my own head, sucked into her mouth. I screamed and screamed but that made the other two laugh and laugh. She sucked and sucked and all around my eye was dark and hot. It was leaving me. It was leaving me. It was forgetting where it should be and leaving for her mouth. My eye, she sucked it until the whole thing plopped out of my lids and into her mouth. She pulled it slow. She licked around it once, twice, three times and I think I said no. Please. No. Then she bit it off.

I woke up in total dark. They raised my arms up and my face rested on the right. I could not touch my face, even though surely that had been a dream? I did not want to do it. I could not touch my left eye, so I closed the right. Everything went black. I opened again and there was the light on the ground. I closed again and everything was black. The tears ran down my cheeks before I even thought to cry. I tried to bring my knees up and my foot stepped on it, slippery and soft. They left it there for me to see. The goddess who hears man's cry and returns the same cry mocked me.

I woke up, feeling cloth on my face, wrapped around my eye.

"Will you now say that you will kill us, we mockery of women?" the middle one said. "I wish to hear of your rage, or your savage talk. It entertains me."

I had nothing to say. I wanted to say nothing. Not to spite her, since I didn't want that either. I wanted nothing. That was the first day.

Day two, the old one woke me with a slap.

"Look how little we feed you and yet you still piss and shit yourself," she said.

She threw me a piece of meat with the fur still on

it. Be glad it's fresh kill, she said. But I still could not eat raw flesh. Eat it and think of him, she said, then went back into the dark. She changed slow and it sounded like bones cracking and joints popping. She threw another piece at me. The side of a warthog's head.

Day three, the young one ran in as if somebody was chasing her. She of the three liked changing to woman the least. She came right up to me and licked my shoulder and I flinched. I knew the **heh-heh-heh** was not a laugh, but it felt like mockery. She made a sound I never heard before, like a whine, like a child saying EEEEEEEE. She opened her mouth, flattened her ears, and tilted her head to one side. She bared her teeth. Out of the dark came another hyena, smaller, the spots on the skin larger. She EEEEEEEE'd again and the other one came in closer. The hyena sniffed my toes, then trotted away. The young one changed to woman and yelled at the dark. I laughed but it came out like a sick man's laugh. She punched me quick in the left cheek, and again and again, until my head went dark again.

Day four, two of them argued in the dark. Present him to the clan, the old one said, for now I knew her voice. Present him to the clan and let them judge him. Every woman in the clan deserves a bite of his flesh. Every woman is not my sister, said the middle one. Every woman did not raise her cubs like my own, she said. Revenge is true, but not just for you, the old woman said. But I shall have it, the middle one said. No other woman has longed for this day, no other. The old one then said, Why not kill him, then, kill him now? You should hand him to the clan, I say this again.

In the night when the hole was all dark, I could smell the middle one.

"Do you miss your eye?" she said.

I said nothing.

"Do you miss home?"

I said nothing.

"I miss my sister. We were wanderers. My sister was everything that is home. The only thing that is home. Did you know that she could change, but chose not to? Only twice, the first when we were still cubs. Both of us, daughters of the highest in our clan. The other women who were of one form hated us, and fought us all the time even though we were stronger and had more craft. But my sister did not want to be smarter or sharper, she just wanted to be any beast moving east to west. She wanted to vanish in the pack. She would have walked on all fours forever, had she a choice. Is that strange, Tracker? We women of the clan are born to be special, and yet all she wanted was to be like everyone else. No higher, no lower. Are they among your kind, people who work hard to be nothing, to vanish in a group of your own? The one-bloods hated us, hated her, but she wanted them to love her. I never wanted their love but I remember wanting to want it. She wanted them to lick her skin, and tell her which male to growl at, and call her sister. And yet she wanted no name, not even sister. I called her a name that she would not answer to, so I called her that name over and over until she changed only to say stop calling me that or we will never be sisters again. She never became woman again. I forget the name.

"She died as she would have wanted to, fighting in the pack. Fighting for the pack. Not fighting with me. You took her from me."

Day five, they threw me raw meat. I grabbed it up with both hands and ate it. Afterward I screamed all night. I never used my birth name but until then, I still remembered it.

Day six, they woke me again with piss. The young and the old woman, both naked, and pissing on me again. I thought they did it to see if they could get me to shout or scream or curse, for indeed I heard the young one in the night say, He speaks no longer, this bothering me more than when he yap-yap-yap-yap. They pissed on me but not in my face. They pissed on my belly and my legs and I did not care. I did not even care for an early death. Whatever sport it was from this day to the next and the one after that I did not care. But the hyena from three days ago came out of the dark. He inched back.

"Make it quick, little fool. You are only the first," the young one said.

"Maybe we help them," the old one said, and grinned.

The young one cackled. She grabbed my left foot and the old one grabbed my right, pulled them up and spread them wide. I was so weak. I screamed, and screamed again, but they howled each time to drown me out. The hyena came out of the dark. Male. He came right up to me and sniffed their piss. The hyena jumped between my legs and tried to push himself into me. They laughed and the old one said, You be soft and they be quick. The hyena kept shifting until his wet stinking body was in me. The boy the not-Ogo raped told me that the worst was when the gods gave you new sight so you see yourself and say this is the thing that is happening to you. The hyena kept shifting and thrusting, and forcing it past my screams, loving everything coming out of my mouth, pushing in more. Then he jumped off me. The young one laughed and the old one said, You be soft and they be quick. Another came in when he was done. And one after that. And another one.

Day seven, I saw that I was still a boy. There were men stronger, and women too. There were men wiser, and women too. There were men quicker, and women too. There was always someone or some two or some three who will grab me like a stick and break me, grab me like wet cloth, and wring everything out of me. And that was just the way of the world. That was the way of everybody's world. I who thought he had his hatchets and his cunning, will one day be grabbed and tossed and thrown in with shit, and beaten and destroyed. I am the one who will need saving, and it's not that someone will come and save me, or that nobody will, but that I will need saving, and walking forth in the world in the shape and step of a man meant nothing. The strong female piss made them all take me for female. The smell faded when the last one was still in me. He lunged at my throat but they kicked him away.

Somebody was in the hole. Coming at me in the dark. I could see myself as the gods see me, cowering and cringing, but still unable to stop myself. Somebody dragged something along the ground. It was still day and some light came down from above. The middle one came into the light pulling the hind leg of a dead thing. In the light the wet skin glimmered. Half still beast, a hind leg on the left, a woman's foot on the right. A belly of spotty fur, dead hands spread out, the right one still a paw, the left one claws, not fingernails. The nose and mouth still pushed out of the young one's face. Still holding her hind leg, the middle one dragged her back into the dark.

Day eight or nine or ten, I lost count of days, and ways to mark them. They let me out in open savannah. I could not remember them letting me out, just being out. The savannah grass was tall but already brown for dry season. Then I saw the old one and the middle one far off, but I knew it was them. I heard the rest, rumbling through the bush and then charging. The whole clan. I ran. With every step my mind said, Stop. This is the end of you. Any end is a good end. Even this. They strangled prey before ripping them apart. They gave themselves a thrill tearing flesh while the animal was still alive. I didn't know which was true or false, which might be why I ran. The rumble of them as they came closer and closer, while I burned and bled down my legs, and my legs forgot how to run. Three of them, male, jumped out of the bush and knocked me down. Their growls in my ears, their spit burned my eyes, their bites cut into my legs. Many more jumped in, blocking the sky with dark, and then I woke up.

I woke up in sand. The sun was already halfway across the sky and everything was white. No hole, no bush, no bones all about, and no smell of hyena nearby. Sand all around. I did not know what to do, so I started to walk away from the sun. How did I get here and why did they let me go? I have never learned why. I thought I was in a dream, or perhaps the last few days were a dream, until I touched my left eye and felt cloth. Then I thought they never wanted to kill me, only leave me lame, for there was dignity in a kill and shame in not being worth even that. The sun burned my back. She was angry at me turning my back to her? Then kill me already. I was tired of it all, man and beast threatening to kill me, sucking my want to live, but never killing me. I walked until there was nothing to do but walk. I walked through day and night. Cold swept across the sand and I fell asleep. I woke up in the back of a cart of pigs and chickens. Fasisi we go, said an old man as he whipped his two donkeys. Maybe the man was kind, maybe he planned to sell me into slavery. Whatever the reason for his kindness, I jumped from the cart as we rode over rough, uneven road, and watched him continue, not aware that I was gone.

I knew Nyka was not in Fasisi. His scent was already out of town, many days away, in Malakal, perhaps. But he left my room as it was, which surprised me. Did not even take the money. I took what I needed and left everything else.

The closer I got to Malakal the stronger it was, his scent, though I told myself I was not looking for him, and I would not kill him when I found him. I would do much worse. I would search for his mother, whom he claims to hate but always speaks of, and kill her, and switch her head with an antelope's, sewing them to each other's bodies. Or I would do something so evil and vengeful it was beyond me being able to think of it. Or I would leave him alone, and go away for years, and let him go fat in the thought of me long dead, and then strike. But as soon as I was walking streets he walked, and stopping at places he stopped, I knew he was in Malakal. In a day I knew the street. Before the sun went down I knew the house. Before night, the room.

I waited until I was stronger. The rest came from hate. He paid his innkeeper to lie for him and had taught him how to make poisons. So when I came

into the innkeeper's kitchen, he tried to act as if he
was not startled. I did not ask for Nyka. I said to
him, I am going upstairs to kill him. And I will kill
you before you can reach the poison in your cabinet.
He laughed and said, Do what you want, I care not
for him. But he pulled a dart out of his hair and
threw it at me. I dodged; it hit the wall behind me
and started to smoke. He ran but I grabbed him
by the same hair and pulled him back. Here is how
you will not reach, I said, and placed his right hand
on the counter and chopped it off. He screamed
and ran off. The innkeeper made it to the door,
even opened it halfway, before my hatchet struck
the back of his head. I left him there in the doorway and went upstairs. His smell was everywhere,
but he refused to show himself. Nyka might have
been a thief and a liar and a betrayer of men but he
was no coward. The scent was strongest in the cupboard and it was not a dead smell. I opened the
cupboard and all of Nyka was hanging on a hook.
His skin. But just his skin, what was left of it. Nyka
shed his skin. I have seen men, women, and beasts
with strange gifts but never one who could shed like
a snake. And with the skin gone, he left the scent
behind too. Somehow he is a new man now.

"Then how did you know it was him coming up
the steps?" Bunshi asked.

"He always chewed khat. Keeps him alive, he used
to say. You might ask if I ever wondered why the hyenas let me go. I have not. Because to wonder is to

think of them, and I have not thought of them until you came through my window. He did not even notice my eye. My eye, he did not even notice."

"Forward is the hyena, backward is a fox," Bunshi said.

"A better friend, the hyena."

"And yet he was the one who said, Only Tracker can find this boy. To find the boy, you must find the Tracker. I will not insult you by throwing more coin at your feet. But I need you to find this boy; agents for the King are already on the hunt because somebody told him the boy might still be alive. And they only need proof of death."

"Three years is too late. Whoever took him he answers to."

"Name your price. I know it is not in coin."

"Oh, but it is in coin. Four times the four times you offered to pay."

"Your tone makes me ask: What else?"

"His head. Cut off and shoved so hard on a stake that the tip bursts through the top."

She looked at me in the dark and nodded once.

NINE

But everybody knows of your mad King, inquisitor. I say better a mad king than a weak one, and better a weak king than a bad one. What is evil anyway, a sad soul infected with devils who take his will, or a man thinking that of all his mother's children he loves himself the best? You wish to know how I've come by two eyes when I just said I lost one. Here I thought your ears would have been pricked by our glorious Kwash Dara entering the story.

Do you know Bunshi? She never lies, but her truth is as slippery as her skin, and she twists it, shapes it, and lines it up straight beside you, like a snake does when she decides it is you she should eat. To tell true, I did not believe that the King had an elder's family murdered. I wanted to go back to my room and ask the innkeeper if she had ever heard of the Night of the Skulls, and what happened to Basu Fumanguru, but I still owed her rent and, as I said, she had way too many notions on how I could pay other than in coin.

And yet what Bunshi said about the King lined up with the little I knew, and heard. That he increased taxes on both the local and the foreign, on sorghum and millet and the transport of gold, tripled the tax on ivory, but also of the import of cotton, silk, glass, and instruments of science and mathematics. Even the horse lords he taxed for every sixth horse, and hay came at a cost. But it was the aieyori, the land tax, that made men grimace and women fret. Not because it would be high, for it always was. But because these northern kings have a way that never changes, where each decision tells the keen observer what decision will come next. A king used an aieyori for only one reason, and that is to pay for war. Things that seem like water and oil were in truth something that was a mix of the two. The King demanding a war tax, in truth a tax to pay for mercenaries, and his chief opponent, maybe even enemy, the one who could turn the will of the people against him, now dead. Killed three years ago and vanished perhaps from the books of men. Certainly no griot have sung of the Night of the Skulls.

You look at me as if I know the answer to the question you have yet to ask. Why would our King want war, especially when it is your own, the shit eater of the South, who last started it? A smarter man could answer that question. Listen to me now.

That morning, after Bunshi left, I set out on my own, to the northwest of the third wall. I did not tell the Leopard. When I was walking away, the sun was just rising, and I saw Fumeli sitting in the window. I neither knew nor cared if he saw me. In the northwest slept many elders, and I was looking for one I knew. Belekun the Big. These elders were fond of describing themselves as if locked out of their own joke. There was Adagagi the Wise, whose stupidity was profound, and Amaki the Slippery, but who knew what that meant? Belekun the Big stood so tall that he lowered his head before walking through every door, though to tell truth, the doors were high enough. His hair was white and grained, and stiff like a head plate, with small flowers he liked to wear on top. He came to me three years ago, saying, Tracker, I have a girl you must find for me. She has stolen much coin from the elders' treasury, after we showed her kindness by taking her in one rainy night. I knew he lied, and not because it had not rained in Malakal for nearly a year. I knew of the elders' ways with young girls before Bunshi told me. I found the girl in a hut near the Red Lake, and told her to move to one of the cities of the midlands with no allegiance to North or South, maybe Mitu or Dolingo, where the order of elders had no eyes in the street. Then I went back to Belekun the Big and told him that hyenas got to the girl, and vultures left only this bone, an ape's leg bone I threw at him. He leapt out of the way like a dancing girl.

So. I remembered where he lived. He tried to hide that he was annoyed to see me, but I saw the change in his face, quick as a blink, before he smiled.

"Day has not yet decided what kind of day it seeks

to be, but here is the Tracker, who has decided to come to my house. As it is, as it should be, as it—"

"Save the greeting for a more worthy guest, Belekun."

"We will have manners, boy bitch. I have not yet decided if I should let you pass this door."

"Good thing I won't bother to wait," I said, and walked past him.

"Your nose leads you to my house this morning, what a thing. Just another way you were always more like a dog than a man. Don't sit your smelly self on my good rugs and rub your stinking skin on it and— milk a god's nipple and what evil is that in your eye?"

"You talk too much, Belekun the Big."

Belekun the Big was indeed large, with a massive waist and flabby thighs, but very thin calves. This too was known of him: Violence, the hint of it, the talk of it, even the slightest flash of rancor made him flush. He almost refused to pay me when I came back without a living girl, but did so when I grabbed those little balls through his robes and pressed my blade against them until he promised me triple. This made him a master of double-talk; my guess was it made him think himself not responsible for what-ever nasty business he paid people to do. The King, it has been said, has no eye for riches, something the elders more than made up for. In Belekun's welcome room he kept three chairs with backs that looked like thrones, cushions of every pattern and stripe, and rugs in all the colours of the rain serpent, with green walls covered in patterns and marks and columns that went all the way to the ceiling. Belekun dressed himself like his walls, in a dark green and shiny agbada outer robe with a white pattern on the chest that looked like a lion. He wore nothing underneath, for I smelled his ass sweat on the seat of his robes. He wore beaded sandals on his feet. Belekun threw himself down on some cushions and rugs, waking up a pink dust. He still did not invite me to sit. Laid out on a plate beside him were goat cheese and miracle berry, and a brass goblet.

"You truly are a hound now."

He chuckled, then laughed, then laughed into a brutal cough.

"Have you had miracle berry before lime wine? It makes the whole thing so sweet, it is as if a flower virgin spurted in your mouth," Belekun said.

"Tell me about your brass goblet. Not from Malakal?"

He licked his lips. Belekun the Big was a performer, and this show was for me.

"Of course not, little Tracker. Malakal went from stone to iron. No time for the fineries of brass. The chairs are from lands above the sand sea. And those drapes, only precious silks bought from eastern light traders. I am not confessing to you, but they cost me as much as two beautiful slave boys," he said.

"Your beautiful boys who didn't know they were slaves before you sold them."

He frowned. Somebody once warned me about

loving to grab fruit low to the ground. He wiped his hand on the robe. Shiny, but not silk, for were it silk he would have told me.

"I seek news of one of you, Basu Fumanguru," I said.

"News of the elders be only for the gods. What be they to you that you should know? Fumanguru is—"

"Fumanguru **is**? I heard he **was**."

"News of the elders be only for the gods."

"Well you need to tell the gods he is dead, for news on the drum did not reach the sky. You, though, Belekun . . ."

"Who seeks to know of Fumanguru? Not you, I remember you as just a carrier."

"I think you remember more than that, Belekun the Big," I said, and brushed my bulge on the way to grabbing my bracelet.

"Who is it that will know of Fumanguru?"

"Relations near the city. It seems he has some. They will hear what became of him."

"Oh? Family? Farmer folk?"

"Yes, they are folk."

He looked up at me, his left eyebrow raised too high, goat cheese lodged in the corner of his mouth.

"Where is this family?"

"They are where they should be. Where they have always been."

"Which is?"

"Surely you know, Belekun."

"Farming lands are to the west, not Uwomowomowomowo, for there are too many bandits. Do they farm the slopes?"

"What is their livelihood to you, elder?"

"I only ask so that we may send them tribute."

"So he is dead."

"I never said he was alive. I said he is. We are all is, in the plan of the gods, Tracker. Death is neither end nor beginning, nor is it even the first death. I forget which gods you believe in."

"Because I don't believe in any, elder. But I will send them your very best wishes. Meanwhile they wish for answers. Buried? Burned? Where is he and his family?"

"With the ancestors. We should all share their good fate. That is not what you wish to know. But yes, all of them, dead. Yes they are."

He bit into some more cheese and some miracle fruit.

"This cheese and miracle fruit, Tracker, it is like sucking a goat's teat and sweet spices come out."

"All of them are dead? How did this happen, and why do people not know?"

"Blood plague, but the people do know. After all, it was Fumanguru who angered the Bisimbi in some way—he must have, yes he did, of course he did—and they cursed him with infectious disease. Oh we found the source, who was also already dead, but nobody goes near the house for fear of the spirits of disease—they walk on air, you know. Yes they do, of course they do. How could we have told the city that their beloved elder or anyone died of blood plague? Panic in the streets! Women knocking down and trampling their own babies just to get out of the city. No, no, no, it was the wisdom of the gods. Besides, no one else had contracted the plague."

"Or the death, it seems."

"It seems. But what is this? Elders have no obligation to speak of the fate of elders. Not even to family, not even to the King. We tell them of death only as a courtesy. A family should regard an elder as dead as soon as he joins the glorious brotherhood."

"Maybe you, Big Belekun, but he had a wife and children. They all came to Kongor with him. Fled, I heard."

"No story is so simple, Tracker."

"Yes, every story is. No story resists me cutting it down to one line, or even one word."

"I am lost. What are we talking about now?"

"Basu Fumanguru. He used to be a favorite of the King."

"I would not know."

"Until he angered the King."

"I would not know. But it is foolish to anger the King."

"I thought that was what elders do. Anger the King— I mean, defend the people. There are marks on the streets, in gold, arrows that point where the King shall stop. One lies outside your door."

"Wind can blow a river off course."

"Wind blows shit right back to the source. You and the King are friends now."

"All are friends of the King. None are friends of the King. You might as well say you are friends with a god."

"Fine, you are friendly with the King."

"Why should any man be an enemy of the King?"

"Did I ever tell you of my curse, Big Belekun?"

"We have no friendship, you and I. We were never—"

"Blood is the root. Like it is with so many things, and we are talking about family."

"My supper calls me."

"Yes it does. Of course it does. Eat some cheese."

"My servants—"

"Blood. My blood. Don't ask me how it would get there but should I grab my hand"—I pulled my dagger—"and cut my wrist here, not enough that life runs out, but enough to fill my palm, and—"

He looked up at the ceiling, even before I could point in that direction.

"And yours is very high. But it is my curse. That is, if I throw my own blood up in the ceiling, it breeds black."

"What does that mean, breed black?"

"Men from darkest darkness—at least, they look like men. The ceiling gets unruly and spawns them. They stand on the ceiling as if it is floor. You know when the roof sounds like it is cracking."

"Roof—"

"What?"

"Nothing. I said nothing."

Belekun choked on a berry. He gulped down lime wine and cleared his throat.

"This, this Omoluzu sounds like a tale your mother told you. Sometimes the monsters in your mind burst through your head skin at night. But they are still in your mind. Yes."

"So you have never seen one?"

"There is no Omoluzu to be seen."

"Strange. Strange, Belekun the Big. This whole thing is strange."

I walked over to him; the knife, I put back in the sheath. He tried to roll himself up to a seat but fell back down harder on his elbow. He grimaced, trying to turn it into a smile.

"You looked up before I said ceiling. I never said Omoluzu, but you did."

"Interesting talk always makes me forget my hunger. I just remembered I am hungry." Belekun stretched his fat hand out to a cushion with a brass bell on top, and rang it three times.

"Bisimbi, you say?"

"Yes, those little devil bitches of the flowing waters. Maybe he went to the river on the wrong night for a divination and annoyed one or two, or three. They must have followed him home. And the rest, they say, is the rest."

"Bisimbi. You are sure?"

"As sure as I am that you annoy me like a scratch on the inside of my asshole."

"Because Bisimbi are lake spirits. They hate rivers; the flowing water confuses them, makes them drift too far when they fall asleep. And there's no lake in Malakal or Kongor. Also this. The Omoluzu attacked his house. His youngest son—"

"Yes, that poor child. He was of age to bull-jump his way to a man."

"Too young for a bull jump, is this not so?"

"A child of ten and five years is more than old enough."

"The child was not long born."

"Fumanguru has no child not long born. His last was ten and five years ago."

"How many bodies were found?"

"Ten and one—"

"How many were family?"

"They found as many bodies as there should have been in that house."

"How are you so certain?"

"Because I counted them."

"Nine of the same blood?"

"Eight."

"Of course. Eight."

"And the servants all accounted for?"

"We wouldn't want to still be paying for a corpse."

He rang the bell hard. Five times.

"You seem unsettled, Belekun the Big. Here let me help you u—"

As I bent over to grab his arm, air zipped past the back of my neck twice. I dropped to the floor and looked up. The third spear shot through, quick as the first two, and pierced the wall beside the other two. Belekun tried to scramble away, his feet slipping, and I grabbed his right foot. He kicked me in the face and crawled across the floor. I jumped up to a squat as the first guard ran at me from an inner room. Hair in three plaits and red as his skirt, he charged at me with a dagger. I pulled my hatchet before he got twenty paces and flung it straight between his eyes. Two throwing daggers passed over him, and I ducked to the ground again as another guard charged me. Belekun was trying to crawl to his door, but violence made even his fingers stiff, and he could barely move, like a tired fish too long out of water. My eyes on Belekun, I let the other guard get close to me, and as he swung a large ax I rolled to miss, before it hit the ground and sparked little lightnings. He swung it over his head and brought it down again, almost chopping my foot. Like a devil, this man. I pushed myself up on my elbows and jumped back right as he swung the ax to my face. He swung it right above me again, but I pulled my second hatchet, ducked under his swing, and chopped into his left shin. He screamed and the ax fell. He went down hard. I grabbed his ax and swung a chop to his temple. My blink blocked blood before it splashed my eye.

Belekun the Big pulled himself up. Somehow he found a sword. Just holding it made him tremble.

"I give you this, Belekun, for I give charity to all elders. You may deliver the first blow. First parry. Stab me. Chop if that is what the gods tell you," I said. He blubbered something. I smelled piss.

Belekun trembled so hard his necklaces and bracelets all rattled.

"Raise your sword," I said. Sweat ran from his forehead to his chins. He raised the sword and pointed it at me. It dipped from his hands and I stopped it with my foot, lifted it up until it pointed at me.

"I give you one more charity, Belekun the Big. I'll fall on it for you."

I threw myself on the sword. Belekun screamed. Then he looked at me, still in the air, his sword below me, both of us suspended as if we were the backsides of magnets.

"A sword cannot kill you?" he said.

"A sword cannot touch me," I said. The sword flew out of his hand and I fell. Belekun rolled himself up and ran for the door, screaming, "Aesi, lord of hosts! Aesi, lord of hosts!"

I yanked a spear from the wall, took three steps, and threw it. The iron tip burst through his neck, shot through his mouth, and lodged in the door.

Six days after Leopard and I met at Kulikulo Inn, we were in the Uwomowomowomowo valley. No Bunshi, but the slaver was there trying to show the boy Fumeli how to ride a horse. He gripped the reins too tight, told the horse clashing messages, so of course she jumped up on two legs and threw him off. Three other horses stood off near a tree, grazing, all dressed in the floral cotton quilt saddles of the northern horse lords. Two horses, harnessed to a chariot, red with gold trim, stood waiting off in the distance, their tails whisking away flies. I had not seen a chariot since I tracked a pack of stolen horses far north of the sand sea. The horse threw Fumeli off again. I laughed out loud, hoping he heard. The Leopard saw me and changed, trotting off as I waved to him. I thought I would feel nothing when I saw Nyka coming out of the bush, Nsaka Ne Vampi beside him, both in long blue djellaba, dark as black skin in the night. His hair plaited tight into one braid, and curved out and up at the back like a horn. She covering her hair in a wrap. His bottom lip red and swollen, and a soiled white linen strip above his brow. The slaver kept one caravan, the prettiest one left behind, and from it came Sogolon the witch. She looked angry that sunlight was in her eyes, but that might have been how her face always looked.

"Wolf Eye, you look younger in the daylight," Nyka said. He smiled and winced as he touched his bottom lip.

I said nothing. Nsaka Ne Vampi looked at me. I thought she would nod but she just looked.

"Where is the Ogo?" I said to the slaver.

"By the river."

"Oh. Ogo are not known as bathers."

"Who said he bathes?"

The slaver ran to Fumeli, who was trying to jump back on the horse.

"Young fool, stop. One horse kick, you go down and down you shall remain. I tell you true," he said.

The slaver waved us over. The man who fed him dates came out of the caravan with a sack slung over his shoulder and a silver tray carrying several leather pouches. The slaver grabbed them one by one and threw them to us. I felt the texture of silver coins, heard them clink.

"This not your reward. This is what my book-keepers have portioned out for your expenses, each according to your ability, which means you all received the same. Nothing is cheap in Kongor, especially information."

His date feeder opened a sack, pulled out scrolls, and handed them to us. Nyka refused and so did Nsaka Ne Vampi. I wondered if she refused because he did. She talked much those nights ago, but said nothing now. Fumeli took one for the Leopard, who was still a Leopard, though he was listening.

"That is a map of the city drawn to the best recollection, since I have not been there in years. Beware of Kongor. Roads seem straight, and lanes promise to take you where they say they go, but they twist and snake you, and bend into places you will not want to go, places of no return. Listen to me good, I tell you true. There are two ways to get to Kongor. Tracker, you know of what I speak. Some of you will not. When you head west and get to the White Lake, you can go around it, which will add two days to your journey, or cross, which will take a day, for the lake is narrow. That is your choice, not mine. Then you can choose to ride around the Darklands, which will add three days to your journey, or ride through, but it is the Darklands," the slaver said.

"What is the Darklands?" the boy Fumeli said.

The slaver grinned, then lost his grin. "Nothing that you can conceive in your head. Who here has been through the Darklands?"

Both Nyka and I nodded. We went through it together many years past, and neither of us would talk of it here. I already knew I was going around it, no matter what the others thought. Then Sogolon nodded.

"Again. Your choice, not mine. Three days' ride to go around the Darklands, but one day to go through. And with either, it would still be three more days before Kongor. If you go around, you will head through nameless lands not claimed by any king. If you go through you will also travel through Mitu, where men have put down arms to ponder the great questions of earth and sky. A tiresome land and a tiresome race, you might find them worse than anything awaiting you in the Darklands. It will take you a day's ride just to get out. But this again is your choice. Bibi here shall come with you."

"Him? What shall he do? Feed us what we can reach for with our own hands?" Nyka said.

"I go for protection," he said.

I was surprised at his voice, more commanding, like a warrior's, not like someone who was trying to sing like a griot. This was the first time I really looked at him. Skinny as Fumeli and wearing a white djellaba gown past the knee, with a belt tied around the waist. From the belt hung a sword, which was not there the last two times I saw him. He saw me looking at it and approached me.

"I have never seen a takouba this far from the East," I said.

"The owner should have never come west then," he said, and smiled. "My name is Bibi."

"Was that the name he gave you?" I asked.

"If that 'he' is my father, then yes."

"Every slave I know, the master forced on him a new name."

"And were I a slave, a new name I would have. You think me a slave because I feed him dates? He has me playing his deceits. People say much to a man who is less than a wall."

I turned away from him, but that meant facing Nyka. He walked off a few paces, expecting me to follow.

"Tracker, you and me, we both left something in the Darklands, eh?" he said.

I stared at him.

"He should have left his woman tip," Nsaka Ne

Vampi said, and I was furious that he was telling her things about me. Betraying me still. They walked off, even though the slaver opened his mouth to say more.

"Of course, to tell you true, there are rumors. The last place eyes have seen him was not even Kongor, but not only eyes see. I told you before. You can follow the trail of the dead, who was found dead and quickly buried, sucked out like juice from a berry. There was word of a boy and four others in Nigiki, one time long ago in Kongor. But find him and bring him back to me in Malakal where—"

"You no longer ask for proof of his death?" I asked.

"I will be at the collapsed tower. This is all I have to say. Sogolon, I will speak to you alone," he said.

Sogolon, who had not said a word up to this point, went off with him to the caravan.

"I know you need no help to get to Kongor," Nyka said.

I was already looking west, but I turned around to see his face. Always a handsome man, even now with white hair peeking under his chin and brushing across the top of his plait. And his swollen lip.

"Here is a question only you are fit to answer. Though you never was one for words, which is why you used to need me. If you take the way through the Darklands, how many of you will make it to the other side, hmm? The Leopard? Cunning as a cat but too hot as a man, his temper makes him foolish. Like a young you, no? The crone talking to master slaver? She going to drop dead before you even get to the

lake. So, that little boy over there, who fucks him,
you or the cat? He will not even mount a horse, much
less ride it. That leaves you with the slave—"

"He is not a slave."

"No?"

"He said so."

"I did not hear."

"You did not listen."

"So the man who is not a slave and the Ogo, and
you know how much trust one can put in an Ogo."

"More than one can put in you."

"Hmm." He laughed. Nsaka Ne Vampi stayed
back. She noticed that I noticed. I also noticed he
said you, not us.

"You have made other plans," I said.

"You know me better than I know myself."

"Must be some kind of curse, knowing you."

"No man has known me better."

"Then no man has known you at all."

"So you wish to settle this now, hmm? How about
it? Right here. Or maybe down by the lake. Or shall
I expect you to come quick in the night like a lover?
Sometimes I wish you did love me, Tracker. How can
I give you peace?"

"I wish nothing from you. Not even peace."

He laughed again, and walked away. Then he
stopped, laughed yet again, and walked over to a
huge, filthy tapestry that was covering something.
Nsaka Ne Vampi climbed the chariot and grabbed the
reins. Nyka pulled off the tapestry, revealing a cage,

inside of which was the lightning woman. The Leopard saw her too. He trotted right up to the cage and growled. The woman scrambled to the farther side, though there was nowhere to go. She looked like a woman now. Her eyes were wide as if fright stuck itself on her face, like those children who were born in war. Nyka pulled the lock. The woman pushed back even farther and the cage shifted with her. The Leopard trotted away and lay in the dirt, but still he watched her. She sniffed around, looked around, then sprang out of the cage. She spun one way and then the next, looking at the caravan, the trees, the Leopard, the man and woman in the same blue, then jerked her head north, as if somebody just called her. Then she ran, barely on her two legs, hopped over a mound, leapt as high as a tree, and was gone. Nyka jumped on the chariot, just as Nsaka Ne Vampi whipped the reins, and the horses galloped away. North.

"The lake, not west?" Bibi, the date feeder, said.

I did not answer.

This boy was going to scare his horse into galloping, throwing him and breaking his neck. I wasn't about to teach him. The Leopard was no use since he stayed the cat, spoke to no one, and ran off as far as he could get from us while still hearing us. Sogolon would need help mounting a horse, I thought. Or she would attach some cot or cart to carry herself and whatever it was witches carry, maybe the leg of a baby, shit from a virgin, the hide of an entire buffalo stored in salt, or whatever she needed for conjuring. But she

strapped a deerskin bag over her shoulder, grabbed
the saddle horn with her left hand, and swung herself
up, right into the saddle. Even the Ogo noticed. He
of course would squash ten horses just by sitting on
them, so he ran. For a man of such height and weight
he made almost no sound and shook no ground.
I wondered if he had bought a gift of stealth from
a Sangoma, a witchman, a witch, or a devil. These
were strong horses, but only good for a day's ride at a
time, so two days to the White Lake. I tied the second
supplies horse to mine. Sogolon had gone ahead of
us, but the Ogo waited. I think he was afraid of her.
Bibi jumped off his horse and tied a sisal rope from
his saddle to the bridle of one of the horses carrying
supplies and told Fumeli to mount it.

We had set off. Bunshi did not travel with us. Sogolon wore a vial around her neck the colour of Bunshi's skin. I noticed it when she rode past me. When
we were so close our horses nearly touched she leaned
in and said, "That boy. What is his use?"

"Ask the one who uses him," I said.

She laughed and galloped off into the savannah,
leaving a scent trail that I couldn't identify. I was in
no hurry to reach Kongor since the missing boy was
doubtless dead and in no danger of getting more
dead. And they were all annoying me—the Leopard
with his silence; Fumeli with his petulance, which
I wanted to slap out of his sullen cheeks; this date
feeder Bibi, who was trying to appear as something
more than a man who stuffs food into another man's

mouth; and Sogolon, who had already decided that no man was smarter than she. The only other choice was to think of Belekun the Big, who tried to kill me when I asked about the missing boy's father. He knew of Omoluzu and he knew Omoluzu killed the boy's father, though he might not have known that one has to summon them with serious malcontent. He called to someone as lord of hosts. They never grow less stupid, men who believe in belief. We had not yet set out and there were people who I longed to see less.

That left the Ogo. The larger the being, the less they needed words, or knew them, I have always found. I slowed my horse, waiting for him to catch up. He really did smell fresh as if he was bathing in the river before, even under his arms, which on the wrong giant could knock down a cow.

"I think we will make it to the White Lake in two days," I said. He kept walking.

"We will make it in two days," I shouted. He turned around and grunted. Oh, this was going to be the most wonderful trip.

Not that I even cared for company. Certainly not these people. But I spend most of my days alone, and my nights with people I never wish to see in the morning. I will admit, at least to my darkest soul, that there was nothing worse to be than in the middle of many souls, even souls you might know, and still be lonely. I have spoken of this before. Men I have met and women too, surrounded by what they think is love and yet are the loneliest in all the ten and three worlds.

"Ogo. You are Ogo, are you not?"

He slowed his walking and my horse strode beside him. He grunted and nodded again.

"I saw you around the back after your bath, you kneeled before some rocks. A shrine?"

"A shrine to who?"

"The gods, some god."

"I do not know of any gods," he said.

"Then why build a shrine?"

He looked at me blank, as if he had no answer.

"Are you here for the slaver, the demigod, or the witch?" I said.

He kept walking, but looked at me and said, "Slaver, demigod, or witch? Which is which, I say to you, which is which. Are you sure the black one is a demigod and not a god? I have seen more of her kind—one was a man, at least he shaped like a man, but are made by the gods. People in the South say that a demigod is a man changed by the gods but not through death, and death is the thing, the fearful thing. I don't like the dead, I don't like noon of the dead, I don't like eaters of the dead and I have seen them, old men in black coats that sweep the ground and white fur around the neck as if they wear the skin of vulture. But she is of a strange kind, whatever you call the animal that is half elephant, half fish, or half man and half horse, that is where you should put her, but the slaver is why I am here, he came to me and said, Sadogo I have work for you, and he knew I did not have work, for in the West what work is there for an Ogo? Yes I was out of work, and at my home, which I left open day and night for who would be foolish to rob from an Ogo, did they not hear we are terrible beasts? But at my home, rather my hut, was the slaver who said I have a job for you, great giant, and I said I am not a giant, giants are twice my height, have nothing between their ears but meat, and rape horses because they think all animals with long hair must be womenfolk and a kick from a horse means there will be much sport in the fucking, so he said again I have work, I need you to find some men who are evil to me, and I said what should I do with these men when I find them, and he said kill them all except for one who is not a man but a boy and to not disturb a hair on his head unless he is no longer a boy. He says to me, Ogo, what he might have changed into will not be man, but something else, something that even the gods spit upon as abomination, and then he said more but I did not understand a thing after he said abomination, and then I said where is this boy that you would have me find, and he said I will have men join you, and women too for this is not as easy as it is to say, and I said that it sounds simple enough and I will be back before I miss my house and my crops start to fail, but then I thought of the last man I killed and how his family will soon miss his cruelty and search for him, and when they come with a mob, I will leave many wives widows and boys orphans, so then I thought, let this mission take us for as long as it will take us for I have nothing to return to, and he said then you have that in common with all the others, that none of you have anything to return to, but I do not know if that is true, I do not know any of you, but I have heard of Sogolon the witch of the moon, do you know of her? How did you know she was writing runes? She is three hundred, ten and five years in age, she said this to me and other things too, for people always think the Ogo are simple in the head so one can tell them anything, and this she did; here is what she said: They call me Sogolon, and I had never answered to any other name. They used to call me Sogolon the ugly, until all who called me so died by the same choke in the throat. Sogolon the Moon Witch, who always made craft in the dark, others say. She said she is from the West, but I come from the West and to me she smells like the people of the Southwest who smell sour but the good sour that mixes with sweet, and sparkles life, which you also know because I heard that you have a nose. Does she write runes always? Her hands are never steady, never still. A woman as old as she was expert in the keeping of secrets, so I assumed she had some other reason that she would not say, since coin could not have meant much to her. Then she spoke in riddles and rhyme but there was no art to it. All this time there was no wrath in her, but no mirth either, or pleasantness. I have guessed that she vanishes and returns, as is her way. And that is what I know. You must forgive Ogo. So few people speak to him that when they do he always has too much to say. And . . ."

And like this Sadogo the Ogo talked through the night. Through our stopping and tying off the horses to a tree. Through us building a fire, and cooking porridge, and losing the star that pointed us west, through trying to sleep, failing to sleep, listening for lions moving through the night, waiting for the fire to burn out, and finally falling into the kind of sleep where he spoke through dreams. I could not tell if it was the sun or his voice that woke me up. Fumeli fell asleep. Bibi, lying beside me, was awake and frowning. The Ogo's voice went lower, with silence eating off the end of his lines.

"From now on I shall be quiet," he said.

I stared at him for a long time. Bibi laughed and went off in the bush to piss. I rolled myself to a sit and yawned.

"No, please go on, good Ogo. Sadogo. I will have your words. You make a long trip short. You know Nyka?"

His glare was worth it. "I met him a moon before I met you," he said.

"And he gives you gossip of other people already."

"When the slaver came to me, both Nyka and Nsaka Ne Vampi rode with him."

"This is indeed news. What did he say of me?"

"The slaver?"

"No, Nyka."

"That you can trust the Tracker with your life, if he thinks you have honor."

"That is what he said?"

"Is it false?"

"I am not the person to answer that."

"Why is it not? I have never lied but I see that to lie may have purpose."

"And betrayal? Does betrayal have a purpose other than what it is?"

"I don't know what you mean."

"No worry. It is dead, the thought."

"This one was in the cart too," he said, pointing to Bibi walking back.

We saddled the horses and set off. I turned to Bibi. "Tell me this. Your master lied to us about the boy. The truth is he has no stake in the child. But he has much in pleasing Bunshi.

"He is worried by the silence of the gods," Bibi said. "He thinks he's displeased them when the gods' silence has fallen on every house."

"He should worry more about the silence of all the slaves plotting against him," I said.

"Ha, Tracker, I saw your face. Few days ago. Much enjoyment I got from it, your disgust. I think you are too hard on the noble trade."

"What?"

"Tracker, or whatever your name is. Were it not for slaves, every man from the East would be a virgin at marriage. I met one once, this is a true word. He thought woman bred child by sticking her breasts into a man's mouth. Were it not for slaves, good Malakal would be left with nothing but false gold, and cheap salt. I justify it not. But I do know why it is here."

"So you approve of the ways of your master," I said.

"I approve of the coin he gives me to feed my children. From the look of you I know you have none. But yes, I stuff his face because every other work he gives to slaves."

"Is he who you wish to be? When you are a man?"

"Unlike the bitch boy I am now? Here is more truth. If my master as you call him were any more dumb I would have to prune and water him three times a quartermoon," Bibi said, and chuckled.

"Then leave."

"Leave? Just like that. Speak to me of this Leopard. What kind of man, with such ease, walks away as he pleases?"

"One who belongs to no one."

"Or no one belongs to you."

"Nobody loves no one," I said.

"The son of a bitch who taught you that hates you. So, as my master would say, tell me true, tell me plain, tell me quick. Is it you with the boy behind me, or the spotted one?"

"Why does every mis-bred soul ask me about this mis-bred boy?"

"Because the cat isn't talking. The other servers of the King—they are slaves, mind you—were all casting bets. Who is the rod, who is the staff, and who takes it up the shithole."

I laughed. "What did you guess?" I asked.

"Well, since you are the one they both hate, they say you are being fucked by both."

I laughed again. "And you?"

"You don't walk like someone who gets fucked often up the ass," he said.

"Maybe you don't know me."

"Didn't say you weren't fucked in the ass. I said you weren't fucked often."

I turned and stared at him. He stared at me. I laughed first. Then we couldn't stop laughing. Then Fumeli said something about not sticking the horse hard enough and we both nearly fell off our horses.

Except for Sogolon, Bibi looked the oldest among us. Certainly the only one so far to mention children. It made me think of the mingi children of the Sangoma who we left with the Gangatom to raise. The Leopard was to give me word of what has happened to them since, but has not.

"How did you come by that sword?" I asked.

"This?" Bibi withdrew it. "I told you, from a mountain man east who made the mistake of going west."

"Mountain men never go west. Let us speak true, date feeder."

He laughed. "How old are you in years? Twenty, seven and one?"

"Twenty and five. Do I look so old?"

"I would guess older but did not want to be rude to so new a friend." He smiled. "I have been twenty twice. And five more years."

"Fuck the gods. I have never known men to live that long who were not rich, or powerful, or just fat. That means you were old enough to see the last war."

"I was old enough to fight in it."

He glanced past me, at the savannah grass, shorter than before, and the sky, cloudier than before, though we could feel the sun. It was cooler as well. We had long left the valley for lands no man has ever tried to live in.

"I know no man who has seen war that will speak of it," Bibi said.

"Were you a soldier?"

He laughed short. "Soldiers are fools not paid enough to be fools. I was a mercenary."

"Tell me about the war."

"All one hundred years of it? Which war are we speaking?"

"Which one did you fight?"

"The Areri Dulla war. Who knows what those buffalo-fuckers of the South called it, though I heard they called it the War of Northern Belligerence, which is hilarious, given that they threw spears first. You were born three years after the last truce. That was the war that caused it. Such a curious family. With all the inbreeding producing mad kings you would think one day a king would say, Let us find some fresh blood to save the line, but no. So we have war upon war. This truth. I cannot say if Kwash Netu was a rare good king or if the new and mad Massykin King was just madder than the last, but he was brilliant at war. He had an art for it, the way some have an art for pottery or poetry."

Bibi halted his horse and I did mine. I could tell

Fumeli looked up, annoyed. The air was wet with the rain that was not going to come.

"We need to move now," Fumeli said.

"Rest easy, child. The Leopard will be just as hard when you finally get to sit on him," Bibi said.

This I turned around for. Fumeli's face was as horrified as I knew it would be. I turned back to Bibi.

"My father never spoke of the war. He never fought in any," I said.

"Too old?"

"Maybe. He was also my grandfather. But you were talking of war."

"What? You . . . Yes, the war. I was ten and seven years and staying in Luala Luala with my mother and father. The mad Massykin King invaded Kalindar, a moon and a half's march to Malakal, but still too close. Too close to Kwash Netu. My mother said, One day men will come to our house and say we have chosen you for war. I said, Maybe if I fight in war it will finally bring back the glory to our house that Father squandered with wine and women. With what will you bring glory, for you have no honor, she said. She was right, of course. I was between killings, and people have less need for private battles when all are caught up in war. And just as she said, great warriors came to the house and said, You, you are young and strong, at least you look it. Time to send that Omororo Bitch King back to his barrenlands with his tail between his legs. And what should I fight for? I asked, and they were offended. You should fight for the glorious Kwash Netu and for the empire. I spat and opened my robe to show him my necklace. I am of the Seven Wings, I said. Warriors of the coin."

"Who are the Seven Wings?"

"Mercenaries, kidnapped from drunkard fathers with debts they cannot pay. Skilled in weapons and masters of iron. We travel quick and vanish like an afterthought. Our masters test us with scorpions so we know no fear," Bibi said.

"How?"

"They sting us to see who lives. In battle, we make the formation of the bull. We are the horns, the most ferocious; we attack first. And we cost more than most kings can pay. But our Kwash Netu was quite wise in the art of war. I heard this from the mad King: One ruler cannot be in two places at once or three, for he is only one. He sits in Fasisi, so let us attack Mitu. So the Massykin attacked Mitu, and Mitu was his. He thought it was victory, and it is not an unwise thought that since the King cannot be in two places at once, he let us attack a place he cannot be. This was his mistake, Tracker. Hear this, that was no weakness. The southern armies played into the very greatness of Kwash Netu, being in many places at once."

"Witchcraft?"

"Not everything comes from the womb of witches, Tracker. Your King's father knew how to move armies faster than any king before or since. Movements that would take even the Kongori seven days, his army could cross in two. He chose wise where to fight, and

where he could not, he bought the best, and most
brutally taxed his people to do it. The best were the
Seven Wings. Take this as truth as well. The mad King
was a flighty fool who screamed at the sight of blood,
and did not know the name of his own generals—
while Kwash Netu had his own men to lead in the
territories, strong men, who could run a city, or a
state when he was gone to war in another. Did you
hear of the war of women?"

"No. Tell me."

"After his generals said to the mad King, Most Divine, we must retreat from Kalindar, our four sisters
are in jeopardy, the King agreed. But then that night
at the camp, for he demanded to be with his men in
war, he heard two cats fucking and thought it was a
night devil calling him a coward for retreating. So he
demanded they advance again into Kalindar, only to
be beaten by women and children hurling rocks and
shit from their mud-brick towers. Meanwhile, Kwash
Netu took Wakadishu. The final stand at Malakal
was not even much of a stand. It was the dregs of
an army fleeing stone-throwing women. The war was
already won."

"Hmm. That is not what they teach in Malakal."

"I have heard the songs and read leaves of paper
bound in leather-skin, how Malakal was the last stand
between the light of Kwash Netu Empire and the
darkness of the Massykin. Songs of fools. Only those
who have not fought in war fail to see they were both

dark. Alas, a mercenary without a war is a mercenary without work."

"You know much about war, generals, and court. How ended you here, stuffing a fat pig dates for a living?"

"Work is work, Tracker."

"And horseshit is horseshit."

"Sooner than later the darkness of war shades every man who fought it. My needs are simple. Feeding my children as they too become men is one. Pride is not."

"I don't believe you. And after all you just said, I believe you even less. There is craft in your ways. Do you plan to kill him? I know, a rival hired you to get closer to him than a lover."

"If I wanted to kill him I could have four years ago. He knows what I can do. I think it pleases him that people think I'm a silly girl-boy who likes to play with his mouth. He thinks it means I can sift through his enemies and deal with them."

"So you are his spy. To spy on us?"

"Fool, he has Sogolon for that. I am here for whatever surprises the gods have in store for you."

"I would hear more about what these great wars have done to you."

"And I would say no more about it. War is war. Think of the worst that you have seen. Now think of seeing that every three steps for one quartermoon's walk."

We were now in deep grassland, greener and wetter

than the brown bush of the valley, with the horses'
hooves sinking deeper in the dirt. Ahead, maybe
another half a day's ride, trees stood up and spread.
Mountains hung back all around us. On the side,
going west from Malakal, the mountains and the forest both looked blue. Along the grass and the wetness,
bamboo giants of the grass sprouted, one, then two,
then a clump, then a forest of them that blocked the
late-afternoon sun. Other trees reached tall into
the sky and ferns hid the dirt. I smelled a fresh brook
before I heard or saw it. Ferns and bulbs sprouted out
of fallen trees. We followed what looked like a track
until I smelled that both the Leopard and Sogolon
had gone that way. On my right hand, through the
tall leaves, a waterfall rushed down rocks.

"Where they gone?" Fumeli asked.

"Fuck the gods, boy," I said. "Your cat is but a—"

"Not him. Where are the beasts? No pangolin, no
mandrill, not even a butterfly. Can your nose only
smell what is here, and not what is gone?"

I did not want to talk to Fumeli. I would punch
whatever rudeness came from his mouth.

"I will call him Red Wolf now—that is what he
told me," Bibi said.

"Who?"

"Nyka."

"He mocks the red ochre I used to rub on my skin,
saying only Ku women wear red," I said.

"Truth for your ears? I have never seen a man in
that colour," Bibi said.

Bibi stopped, his brow furrowed, and looked at me as if trying to catch something he missed, then shook it out.

"And wolf?" he asked.

"You have not seen my eye?"

I knew his look. It said, There is a little that you are not telling me, but I care not enough to press it.

"What is that smell on the witch? I cannot place it," I said.

He shrugged.

"Tell me something else, Sadogo," I said to the Ogo. This is true: The Ogo did not stop talking until evening caught us. And then he talked about the night catching us. I forgot about Fumeli until he hissed, and paid no attention until he hissed a third time. We came to a fork in the trail, a path left and a path right.

"We go left," I said.

"Why left? This is the trail Kwesi take?"

"This is the trail I take," I said. "Go your own way if you wish, just untie your horse from Bibi." I heard the dull clump of hooves on mud and branches cracking.

I did not wait for him to say anything. The trail was narrow but there was a path and the sun was almost gone.

"No bat, no owl, no chirping beast," Fumeli said.

"What twig is up your asshole now?"

"The boy is right, Tracker. No living thing moves through this forest," Bibi said. One hand on the bridle, the other gripped his sword.

"Where is your great nose now?" Fumeli said.

I set it down in my mind right there. Never again would this boy be correct on anything. But both of them were right. I knew many of the animal smells of the montane grasslands, and none passed by my nose. And the scents of the forest that I did smell— gorilla, kingfisher, viper-skin—were too far away. No living thing but trees conspiring in circles and river water rushing down rocks. The Ogo was still talking.

"Sadogo, quiet."

"Huh?"

"Hush. Movement in the bush."

"Who?"

"None. That is what I say, there is no movement in the bush."

"I was the one to say it first," said Fumeli.

Was he worth me turning around so he could see my scowl? No.

"Many people say you have a nose, not I. What does your precious nose smell now?"

A neck as thin as his, thin as a girl's, I could snap with no effort. Or I could let the Ogo break him in many pieces. But when I took in a deep breath, smells did come at me. Two that I knew, one I had not come across in many years.

"Grab your bow and draw an arrow, boy," Bibi said.

"Why?"

"Do it now," he said, trying to whisper harshly. "And dismount."

We left the horses by a brook. The Ogo dipped into

his bag and pulled out two shiny gauntlets, which I have only seen on the King's knights. His fingers were now shiny black scales and his knuckles, five spikes. Bibi pulled his sword.

"I smell an open fire, wood, and fat," I said. Bibi covered his mouth, pointed at us, then pointed at his mouth.

I said nothing else, now that I knew what we would find, judging from the smell. The sour stink of hair, the saltiness of the flesh. Soon we could see the fire and the light slipping through the forest. There it was, stuck on a spit, cooking above the fire while the fat dripped into the flames and burst. A boy's leg. Farther off, hanging from a tree, was the boy looking at his leg, a rope tied around the stump. They had cut off his right leg all the way to the thigh and his left leg to the knee. His left arm was cut off at the shoulder. They hung him in the tree by rope. They also hung a girl, who seemed to have all four limbs. Three of them sat a good distance from the fire, a fourth off in the bush, but not far, crouched to shit.

We rushed them before we could see them, before they could see us. Hatchets out, I aimed for the first one's head, but it bounced off. Fumeli shot four arrows; three bounced off, one struck the second one's cheek. The Ogo punched the third straight into the tree. Then he punched a hole through his chest and the tree. Bibi swung his sword and struck the third in the neck but it lodged there. He pushed him off the blade with his foot, then stabbed him in the belly. The first one charged straight at me, holding nothing in his hands. I dipped out of his reach and something knocked him over. On the ground I jumped on him and hacked straight into the soft flesh of the face. The nose. I chopped again and again until his flesh splashed on me. The thing that knocked him over growled before changing back to a man.

"Kwesi!" Fumeli shouted, and ran to him, then stopped. Fumeli touched him on the shoulder. I wanted to say, Go behind the tree and fuck if you wish. None of us remembered the last of them shitting in the bush until the girl tied up in the tree screamed. He came at us waving his arms, his claws shining in the firelight. He roared louder than a lion, but something cut the roar. Even he was confused that his own mouth closed up on him, until he looked down to his chest and saw a spear bursting right through it. He whimpered his last and fell facedown.

Sogolon stepped over his body and approached us. I lit a dry stick and waved it over the beast nearest the fire. A snap. Ogo had broken the one-limb boy's neck. It was for the best that he died quick, and nobody said different. The girl, as soon as we lowered her down, started screaming and screaming until Sogolon slapped her twice. She was covered in white streaks but I knew all the marks of the river tribes and these were none of them.

"We are offerings. You should not have come," she said.

"You are what?" the Leopard said.

I was very happy to see him as a man again and not sure why. It still irritated me to talk to him.

"We are the glorious offerings to the Zogbanu. They leave alone our villages that are on their lands and let us plant crops. I was raised for this—"

"No woman is raised for man to use," said Sogolon.

I pulled the spear out of the last one and rolled him over with my foot. Horns large, curved, and pointed to a sharp tip like a rhinoceros's sprouted all over his head and neck, with smaller horns on his shoulders. They pointed in all directions, these horns, like a beggar with locks thickened by dirt. Horns wide as a child's head and long as a tusk, horns short and stumpy, horns like a hair, gray and white like his skin. Both brows grew into horns and his eyes had no pupils. Nose wide and flat with hair sticking out of the nostrils like bush. Thick lips as wide as the face and teeth like a dog's. Scars all over his chest, maybe for all his kills. A belt holding up a loincloth on which hung child skulls.

"What kind of devil is this?" I asked.

Bibi crouched and turned its head. "Zogbanu. Trolls from the Blood Swamp. I saw many during the war. Your last King even used some as berserkers. Each one worse than the one before."

"This is no swamp."

"They are roving. The girl is not from here either. Girl, where do they go?"

"I am the glorious offering to the Yeh—"

Sogolon slapped her.

"Bingoyi yi kase nan," the girl said.

"They eat man flesh," Sogolon said.

That's when we all looked at the leg cooking on the spit. Sadogo kicked it over.

"They are traveling?" I asked.

"Yes," Bibi said.

"But she just said she was a sacrifice so that they would share their land," I said.

"Not nomads," the Leopard said.

He walked right up to me, but looked at Bibi. "And they are not traveling, they are hunting. Somebody told them a bounty of flesh would be coming through these woods. Us."

The girl screamed. No, it was not a scream, there was no fear in it. It was a call.

"Get the horses!" the Leopard shouted at us. "And cover that girl's mouth!"

You could hear the shuffle through the bushes even as we ran. The rustle coming from all corners and all sides moving ever closer. I slapped Fumeli's horse and she took off. Sogolon appeared with her horse and galloped away. I followed, kneeing my horse sharp in the ribs. Bibi, riding beside me, said something or laughed, when a Zogbanu leapt out of the dark bush with a club and knocked him off. I did not stop and neither did his horse. I looked back only once to see Zogbanus, many of them, pile on top of him until the pile became a hill. He did not stop shouting until they stopped him. I caught up with Sogolon, but they caught up with us. One leapt for me and missed, his horns slicing the rump of my horse. She leapt up and nearly threw me. Two came out of the bush and started pawing at her. Arrows went into the first one's back, and more went into the other's chest and face. The Leopard, now on the same horse as Fumeli, shouted for us to follow him. Behind us more Zogbanus than eyes could count, growling and snarling, sometimes their horns tangling and causing a few to fall. They ran almost as fast as the horses through the thick brush. One came of the brush, his face running right into my hatchet. I wished I had a sword. Sogolon had one, riding and slashing and cutting as if clearing away wild bush. Bibi's horse fell back without a rider to push him. The Zogbanu jumped him, all as one, the way I see lions do a young buffalo. I kneed my poor horse harder; many still chased us. Then I heard the **zip-zip-zip-zip** past us. Throwing daggers. The beasts had weapons. One struck Sogolon in her left shoulder. She grunted, but kept slashing with her right hand. Ahead I could see the Leopard and ahead of him a clearing and the glimmer of water. We were coming out when in the quick a Zogbanu jumped my horse right behind me and knocked me off. We rolled in the grass. He grabbed my throat and dug into my neck. They liked their meat fresh, so I knew he was not going to kill me. But he was trying to make me quick-sleep. His breath blew foul and left a white cloud. Smaller horns than the others, a young one out to prove himself. I fumbled for the daggers and plunged one into his right ribs and another into the ribs on his left again, and again, and again, until he fell on me and I could not breathe. The Leopard pulled him off me and shouted for me to run. He changed and growled. I don't know if that scared them. But by the time I got to the lake, everyone had already boarded a wide raft, including the girl and my horse. I staggered on just as the Leopard jumped past me. Zogbanu swarmed the shore, maybe ten and five, maybe twenty, so close they looked like one wide beast of horns and thorns.

Without anyone pushing it, the raft set off. At the front, sitting as praying in her quiet little chamber, unaware of the world as it fucking burned, was Bunshi.

"Night bitch, you were testing us," I said.

"She do no such thing," said Sogolon.

"This was not a question!"

Sogolon said nothing, but sat there as if praying, when I knew she was not.

"We should go back for Bibi."

"He's dead," Bunshi said.

"He is not. They take their victims alive so they can eat the flesh fresh."

She stood up and turned to face me.

"Not telling you nothing you do not know. It's care that you lack," I said.

"He is a slave. He was born to die servin—"

"And you could be your mother's own sister. His birth was more noble than yours."

"You speak against the water—"

Bunshi waved her hand and Sogolon stayed quiet.

"There are bigger things than—"

"Than what? A slave? A man? A woman? Everybody on this raft thinking, At least I am better than that slave. They will take days to kill him, you know this. They will cut him up and burn each wound so he will not die from sickness. You know how man-eaters work. And yet there are bigger things."

"Tracker."

"He is not a slave."

I dived into the water.

The next morning I woke up in thin brown bush with a hand on my chest. The girl from the night before, some of her clay washed off, cupping and feeling it, as if weighing iron because she had only seen brass. I pushed her off. She scrambled back to the other side of the raft, right to the feet of Sogolon, who stood like a captain, holding her spear like a staff. The sun had been up for some time, it seemed, for my skin was hot. Then I jumped.

"Where's Bibi?"

"Do you not remember?" Sogolon said.

And as she said it, I remembered. Swimming back in water that felt like black slick, the shore moving farther and farther away, but me using rage to get there. The Zogbanu were gone, back into the bush. I had no hatchets and only one knife. The Zogbanu's skin had felt like tree bark, but by his ribs felt soft, and as with all beasts, one could throw a spear right through. Someone grabbed my hand with old fingers. Fingers black as night.

"Bunshi," I said.

"Your friend is dead," she said.

"He is not dead just because you say he is dead."

"Tracker, they were on the hunt for food and we took away their last meal. They will not eat the boy whose neck we broke."

"I am still going."

"Even if it means your death?"

"What is that to you?"

"You are still a man of great use. These beasts will certainly kill you, and what would be the use of two dead bodies?"

"I shall go."

"At least do not be seen."

"Will you cast a masking spell?"

"Am I a witch?"

I looked around and thought she was gone until wetness seeped between my toes. The lake getting pulled to the shore by the moon, I was sure of it. Then the water rose to my ankles but did not return to the lake. There was no lake water at all, just something black, cool, and wet crawling up my legs. I caught fright, but only for a blink, and let her cover me. Bunshi stretched her skin up past my calves to my knee, around and above it, covered my thighs and belly, going onto every bit of skin. Truth, I did not like this at all. She was cold, colder than the lake, and yet looking down I wanted to go to the lake just to see myself looking like her. She reached my neck and gripped it so tight that I slapped her.

"Stop trying to kill me," I said.

She relaxed her grip, covered my lips, face, then head.

"Zogbanu see bad in the dark. But they smell and hear and feel your heat."

I thought she was going to lead me but she was still. We did not get very far.

The fire was already raging in the sky. One of the Zogbanu grabbed Bibi's head and pulled him up. He held half of Bibi in the air. His chest was already cut open to remove the guts, his ribs spread out like a cow killed for a feast. They threw him on the spit and the fire rose to meet him.

I snapped myself back from the dream and vomited. I stood up. It wasn't the dream that made me want to vomit, but the raft. And what raft was this? A huge mound of bone dirt and grass that looked like a small island, not something made by man. The Leopard sat on the other side, his legs up. He looked at me and I looked at him. Neither of us nodded. Fumeli sat down beside him, but did not look at me. Only one of the supply horses survived, cutting our meals in half. The painted girl kneeled down beside the standing Sogolon. The raft island sunk a little underneath the Ogo. What is it, this thing we sail on? I wanted to ask, but knew his answer would take us into night. Sogolon, standing there as if seeing lands we could not see, was without doubt steering this with magic. The painted girl looked at me, wrapping herself in leather-skin.

"Are you a beast, like him?" she asked, pointing at the Leopard.

"You mean this?" I said, pointing to my eye. "This is of the dog, not of the cat. And I am not an animal, I am a man."

"What is man, and what is woman?" the girl said.

"Bingoyi yi kase nan," I said.

"She said that to me three times in the night, even in sleep," she said, pointing at Sogolon.

"A girl is a hunted animal," I said.

"I am the glorious offering of—"

"Of course you are."

Everyone was so quiet that I could hear water gurgle under the raft. The Ogo turned around. He said, "What is man and what is woman? Well that is a simple question with a simple answer, except for when—"

"Sadogo, not now," I said.

"Your name? What do they call you?" I asked.

"The higher ones call me Venin. They call all chosen ones Venin. He is Venin and she is Venin. The great mothers and fathers chose me from before birth to be a sacrifice to the Zogbanu. I have been in prayer from birth till now and I am still in prayer."

"Why are they this far north?"

"I am the chosen one to sacrifice to the horned gods. This is how it was with my mother and the mother of my mother."

"Mother and mother of moth . . . Then how are you here? Someone remind me, why did we take this one?" I said.

"Maybe stop asking questions where you know the answer," the Leopard said.

"Is that it? Where would I be without the wise Leopard? What is this answer that I already know?"

"They would have eaten down to girl and boy bones by now. They were waiting for us."

"Your slaver told them we were coming," I said to the Leopard.

"He's not my slaver," he said.

"You both fool. Why send we on a mission then stop we from doing it?" Sogolon asked.

"He changed his mind," I said.

She frowned. I was not going to say, Sogolon, what you say here is true. The Leopard nodded.

"Nothing point to no betrayal from the slaver," she said.

"Of course. The Zogbanu was just following shifting winds. Maybe it was someone on this raft. Or off it."

The sun was right above us and the lake had gone deeper blue. Bunshi was in the water, I saw her low down in the blue; her skin, which looked black in the night, now looked indigo. She darted like a fish, up above the water, then down, the east far off and west far off, then back, right beside the raft. She was like water creatures I have seen in rivers. A fin right down the back of her head and neck, shoulders and breasts and belly like a woman's, but from the hip down the long swishy tail of a great fish.

"What is she doing?" I said to Sogolon, who up till now hadn't bothered to look at me. The view ahead was nothing but the line separating sea from sky, but she fixed her eyes on it.

"You have never seen a fish?"

"She is not a fish."

"She is speaking to Chipfalambula. Asking her for one more traveling mercy to take us to the other side. We are not here by permission, after all."

"Not where?"

"You fool," she said, and looked down.

"This?" I said, and kicked up dirt.

Her standing there, looking like a leader, annoyed me. I walked past her to the front of the raft and sat down. Here the mound sloped down into the river. I could see the rest of the raft under the water. It was not a raft, it was a floating island controlled by wind or magic. Two fishes, maybe as tall as I am, swam in front.

What I saw next I was sure I did not see. The island below the sea opened a slit right at the front where I sat and swallowed the first fish. Half of the second stuck out, but the opening chomped it down. Below my right heel I saw Chipfalambula's eyes looking up at me. I jumped. Her gills opened and closed. Farther down her enormous fins, each wider than a boat, paddled slow in the lake, the half below the water a morning blue, the half above the colour of sand and dust.

"Popele asks permission of the Chipfalambula the toll taker to take us to the other side. She has not yet given an answer," Sogolon said.

"We are long gone from land. Is that not her answer?"

Sogolon laughed. Bunshi leapt fully out of the water and dived, right in front of it, whatever it was.

"Chipfalambula does not take you into deep water to carry you to the other side. She takes you out to eat you."

Sogolon was serious. Nobody felt the thing moving but we all felt when it stopped. Bunshi swam right up to its mouth and I thought it would swallow her. She dove under and came up by the side of her right fin. It swatted her as one would a wasp and she flew into the sky and landed far off into the water. She swam back in a blink and climbed back on top of the big fish. She walked past us to stand with Sogolon. The great fish started moving again.

"Fat cow, cantankerousness growing in her old age," she said.

I went over to the Leopard. He still sat with Fumeli, both of them with knees drawn up to chest.

"I will have words with you," I said.

He stood up, as did Fumeli. Both wore leather skirts, but the Leopard was not as uneasy with it as he was back at Kulikulo Inn.

"You only," I said.

Fumeli refused to sit, until the Leopard turned around and nodded.

"Wearing sandals next?"

"What is this about?" Leopard asked.

"You have something else pressing you? Another meeting on the back of this fish?"

"What is this about?"

"I went to see an elder about Basu Fumanguru. Just to see if these stories would turn true. He told me that the Fumanguru house fell to sickness, caught from a river demon. But when I said something about cutting my hand and throwing blood, he looked up to the ceiling before I even said it. He knows. And he lied. Bisimbi is not a river demon. They have no love for rivers."

"So that is where you went?"

"Yes, that is where I went."

"Where is this elder now?"

"With his ancestors. He tried to kill me when I told him he was lying. Here is the thing. I do not think he knew of the child."

"So?"

"A chief elder and not know about his own? He said the youngest boy was ten and five."

"It's still riddles, what you say," the Leopard said.

"I say this. The boy was not Fumanguru's son, no matter what Bunshi or the slaver or anyone says. I am sure the elder knew Fumanguru was going to be murdered, might have ordered it himself. But he counted eight bodies, which is what he expected to count."

"He knows of the murder, but does not know of the child?"

"Because the child was no son of Fumanguru. Or ward, or kin or even guest. The elder tried to kill me because he saw I knew he knew about the murder. But he did not know there was another boy. Whoever is behind the killing told him nothing," I said.

"And the boy is not Fumanguru's son?"

"Why would he have a secret son?"

"Why does Bunshi call him a son?"

"I don't know."

"Forget money or goods. People trade only lies in these parts." He said this looking straight at me.

"Or people only tell you what they think you need to know," I said.

He looked around for a while, at everybody on the fish, for a good while at the Ogo, who went back to sleep, then back at me.

"Is that all?"

"Is that not enough?"

"If you think so."

"Fuck the gods, cat. Something has curdled between us."

"This is what you think."

"This is what I know. And it has happened in the quick. But I think it's your Fumeli. He was but a joke to you only days ago. Now you two pull closer and I am your enemy."

"Me pulling him closer, as you say, makes you my enemy."

"That is not what I said."

"It is what you meant."

"Not that either. You don't sound like yourself."

"I sound like—"

"Him."

He laughed and sat back down beside Fumeli, drawing up his legs to his chest as the boy did.

Daylight ran away from us. I watched it go. Venin was by Sogolon, watching her, sometimes watching the river, sometimes drawing her feet together when she saw she sat on skin, not ground. Everybody else slept, stared into the river, watched sky, or minded their own business.

We came to the shore in the evening. How much time was left for sun, I did not know. The Ogo woke up. Sogolon left the fish first, walking with her horse. The girl, right behind her, grabbed Sogolon's robe tight, afraid to be even arm's length away, maybe more because of the oncoming dark. The Ogo wobbled off, still sleepy. The Leopard said something at which Fumeli laughed. He swung his head left and right, then rubbed the boy's cheek with his forehead. He grabbed the reins of the boy's horse and walked right past me. Following him, Fumeli said, "Looking out for the date feeder?"

I squeezed my knuckles and let him pass. The girl Venin walked right beside Sogolon as did Bunshi, the fins in the back of her head disappearing. Only a hundred paces from us there it was, rising out of mist so heavy it rested on the ground, with trees tall as mountains and long branches splayed like broken fingers.

Huddled together, sharing secrets. So dark green it was blue.

The Darklands.

I have been here before.

We stood and looked at the forest. The Darklands was something mothers told children; a bush of ghosts and monsters, both lie and truth. A day stood between us and Mitu. To go around the Darklands took three or four days and had its own dangers. The forest had something I could never describe, not to them about to go in. Woodpeckers tapped out a beat, telling birds far away that we approach. One tree pushed past the others as if to catch sun. It looked surrounded. Fewer leaves than the other trees, exposing branches spread out wide like a fan, though the trunk was thin. The Darklands was already infecting me.

"Stinkwood," Sogolon said. "Stinkwood, yellow-wood, ironwood, woodpecker, stinkwood, yellowwood, ironwood, woodpecker, stinkwood, yellowwood—"

Sogolon fell back. Her head jerked left like some-body slapped her, then right. I heard the slap. Everyone heard the slap. Sogolon fell and shook, then stopped, then shook, then shook again, then grabbed her belly and snarled something in a language that I have heard in the Darklands. The girl holding her robe fell with her. She looked at me, her eyes wide open, about to scream. Sogolon stood up but air slapped her down again. I drew my hatchets, the Ogo squeezed his knuckles, the Leopard changed, and Fumeli drew his bow. The Leopard's bow. The Sangoma's enchantment was still on me, and I could feel it the way one feels the sharp cold on the air of a coming storm. Sogolon staggered away, almost falling twice. Bunshi went after her.

"Madness has taken her," the Leopard said.

"Cannot bind these and cover those," Sogolon said in a whisper, but we heard her.

"She is old. Madness take her and gone away," said Fumeli.

"If she is a madwoman, then you are dim-witted and young," I said.

Bunshi tried to grab her but she pushed her away. Sogolon fell to her knees. She grabbed a stick and started drawing runes in the sand. In between what looked like someone punching her and slapping her she scratched them in the dirt. The Ogo had enough. He pulled on his iron gloves and stomped to her, but Bunshi stopped him, saying his fists cannot help us here. Sogolon marked, and scratched, and dug, and brushed dirt with her fingers, making runes in the dirt and falling back and cursing until she made a circle around her. She stood up and dropped the stick. Something moved through the air and dashed at her. We couldn't see it, only hear the wind. Also this, the sound of something hitting, like sacks thrown against a wall, one, then three, then ten, then a rain of hits. Hitting against a wall of nothing all around Sogolon. Then nothing.

"Darklands," Sogolon said. "Is the Darklands. All of them feeling stronger here. Taking liberties like they get passage from the underworld."

"Who?" I asked.

Sogolon was about to speak, but Bunshi raised her hand.

"Dead spirits who never liked death. Spirits who think Sogolon can help them. They surround her with requests, and become furious when she says no. The dead should stay dead."

"And they were all lying in wait at the mouth of the Darklands?" I asked.

"Many things lie in wait here," Sogolon said. Not many people hold her stare, but I was not many people.

"You are lying," I said.

"They are dead, that's no lie."

"I've been around those desperate for help, living and dead. They may grab you, hold you, and force you to look, may even pull you down to where they died, but none slap you around like a husband."

"They are dead and that's no lie."

"But the witch is responsible and that's no lie either."

"Zogbanu is hunting you. There are more."

"But these spirits on this shore are hunting her."

"Think you know me. You know nothing," Sogolon said.

"I know the next time you forget to write runes on

sky or in dirt they will knock you off your horse or push you off a cliff. I know you do it every night. I wonder how you sleep. **Tana kasa tano dabo.**"

Both Bunshi and Sogolon stared at me. I looked at the others and said, "If it is ground, it is magic."

"Enough. Nowhere is where this is taking us. You need to get to Mitu, then Kongor," Bunshi said.

Sogolon grabbed her horse's bridle, mounted, then pulled the girl up. "We go around the forest," she said.

"That will take three days, four if the wind is against you," the Leopard said.

"Still, we gone."

"No one is stopping you," Fumeli said.

I wanted nothing in the world as much as I wanted to slap this boy. But I did not want to go into the Darklands either.

"She is right," I said. "There are things in the Darklands that will find us, even if we are not looking for them. They will be looking for—"

"It is less than a day through this silly bush," the Leopard said.

"It is never less anything in there. You have never been."

"There you go again, Tracker, thinking whatever has beaten you shall beat me," the Leopard said.

"We go around," I said, and turned for my horse. The Leopard mumbled something.

"What?"

"I said, Some men think they have become lord over me."

"Why would I seek to be your lord? Why would anybody, cat?"

"We go through the forest. It is only trees and bush."

"What is this ill spirit in you all of a sudden? I said I have been to the Darklands. It's a place of bad enchantments. You stop being yourself. You won't even know what that self is."

"Self is what men tell themselves they are. I am just a cat."

His rudeness made no sense and I have seen him at his most brash. It was too quick, like some boil hidden for years that just burst. Then the boil opened his mouth.

"Through the Darklands in one day. Around the lands is three days. Any man with sense would make the choice," Fumeli said.

"Well, man and boy, choose whatever you want. We go round," I said.

"The only way forward is through, Tracker."

He grabbed the horse and started walking. Fumeli followed.

"Everyone finds what they are looking for in the Darklands. Unless you are what they are looking for," I said.

But they were no longer looking. Then the Ogo started to follow them.

"Sadogo, why?" I asked.

"Maybe he thinking he tired of your fat verse," Fumeli said. **"Everyone finds what they are looking**

for in the Darklands. You sound like those men with white hair and shriveled skin, who think they talking wise when they just talking old."

The Ogo turned to answer but I cut him off, although I should have let him explain for days. At least that would have kept him from following them.

"Never mind. Do what you have to," I said.

"Seems like the boy finds his use," Sogolon said, then rode off with the girl.

I mounted my horse and followed her. The painted girl held on to Sogolon's sides, her right cheek resting on her back. Evening was running after us, and doing it in the quick. Sogolon stopped.

"Your men, any of them ever travel through the Darklands?"

"The Leopard said it's only bush."

"None of them ever go before, not even the giant?"

"The Ogo. Ogos do not like to be called giant."

"His small brain is all that is saving him."

"Make your meaning clear, woman."

"I clear as river water. They not going to reach the other side."

"They will if they stay on the path."

"You already forget. That is what the forest hoping you do."

"They will have much to tell us on the other side."

"They not going to reach the other side."

"What is this bush?" the painted girl said.

"Do you not have a name?"

"Venin, I told you."

"You going back for your friends?" Sogolon asked.

"They are not my friends."

I looked at her and Venin, and the sky.

"Where is Bunshi?"

Sogolon laughed. "How long you going take to find the missing if you take this long to notice the gone?"

"I don't track the goings and comings of witches."

"Will you go for them?"

"None would show me gratitude for it."

"Gratitude is what you seeking? You come cheap."

She grabbed the reins.

"You wish to save them, save them. Or don't. What a band of fellows this turn into. Bunshi and her fellowship of men, which is why it fail before it even begin. Cannot make fellowship with men. A man alive is just a man in the way. Maybe we meet again in Mitu, if not Kongor."

"You say that as if I am going back."

"I will see you or I will not. Trust the gods."

Sogolon rode off in a gallop. I did not follow.

TEN

The witch was right. I turned off into the bush before I got to the path. The horse pulled up. I rubbed his neck. We stepped through the bush. I thought there would be cool mist but wet heat swept in and pushed sweat out of my skin. White flowers opened and closed. Trees stretched far into sky with foreign plants bursting out of the trunks. Some vines hung loose, others swung back up into the trees, where leaves blocked most of the sky, and the sky that could be seen already looked like night. Nothing swung or swayed, but sounds bounced in the bush. Water drizzled on me, but was too warm to be rain. Off in the distance three elephants blared and startled the horse. You could never trust the animals in the Darklands.

Above me a woodpecker pecked slow, tapping out a message above the beat and under it. **Men walk through the bush. Men walking through the bush. Men they walk now through the bush.**

Above me swung ten and nine monkeys, quiet, not
meaning harm, curious perhaps. But they followed
us. The elephants blared again. I did not notice we
were on the path until they were right in front of
us. An army. They blared, they swung their trunks,
they raised and stomped, then charged at us. They
stomped louder than thunder but the ground did not
shake. I leaned into the horse's neck and covered her
eyes. This startled her again, made her shift, but the
elephants would have been worse. They passed beside
us and right through us. The ghosts of elephants—
or the memory of elephants, or somewhere a god
dreaming of elephants. You could never tell in the
Darklands what was flesh and what was spirit. Above
us was total night but light came through the leaves as
if from small moons. Farther off on the left, in what
looked like cleared bush but was not, apes stood,
three or four in front, pushing away large leaves. Five
in the clearing hit with light. More stood behind,
some jumping down from branches. One of the apes
opened his mouth, bared his flesh-tearing teeth, long
and sharp, two atop and two at the bottom. I never
learned the tongue of apes, but I knew if I stopped
they would charge us and run away, then charge us
again, closer and closer each time until they grabbed
me and the horse, beating us both to death. Not the
ghosts of apes or the dream of apes, but real apes,
who liked living among the dead. My head brushed
some leaves and they opened up to reveal bunches of
berries bold and bloodlike. Eat just one and I would

sleep for a quartermoon. Eat three more and I would never wake up. This god-forgotten forest where even the living things played with death and sleep. Above, more birds cawed and cackled and trilled and yapped, and mimicked and screeched and screamed. Running past us, two giraffes as small as house cats, running from a warthog as big as a rhinoceros.

I should not have come here. **No you should not have,** a voice said inside and outside my head. I did not look around. **Whatever you are looking for in the Darklands, you will always find it.** In front of me hung threads of thin silk, hundred and tens of hundreds reaching the ground.

A little closer and I saw it was not silk. Above me, sleeping upside down like bats, were creatures I have never seen, small like ghommids and black like them, but hanging upside down, their feet claws clutching branches. The silk came from their gaping mouths. Drool. Thick enough for my knife to cut them away as I rode through. Truth, there were swarms of them, hanging from every tree. As I passed one hanging low his eyes popped open. White, then yellow, then red, then black.

It was time to leave the trail anyway, and my horse was thirsty. **Leave now or stay,** a voice said, soft inside my head. The pond, as she drank, became clear as day. When I looked up in the sky it was still night. I pulled her away from the water. The blue in it did not mirror sky. This was the air from somewhere else, and not a kingdom underwater, which I would have sensed. This was a mirror to a dream, a place where I was the dream. I crouched and leaned so far I almost fell in. A floor in patterns like stars, white and black and green shiny stones, pillars rising out of the floor and so tall they went beyond the pond. A great hall, a hall for a man of great wealth, more wealth than chief or prince. I saw what glimmered like stars. Gold trim in the floor grout, gold swirling around the pillars, gold leaves in the drapes swaying in the wind.

A man entered the room, his hair short and red like a berry. The man wore a black agbada that swept the floor and a cape that woke up the wind. It was gone before I could see it full, black wings that appeared on his back and then vanished. He looked up, as if he saw something behind me. He started to walk towards me. Then he looked straight at my face, eye into eye. His robes spread wide like the wings before, and his look turned into a stare. He shouted something I could not hear, seized a guard's spear, and stepped back, ready to hurl it. I jumped back from the pond and fell on my back.

And now the Leopard's words walked through my head: **The only way forward is through.** But it was not the Leopard's voice. I turned east. At least my heart told me it was east; there was no way I could know. East was getting darker, but I could still see. My last time in the Darklands that spirit announced himself clear, like the killer with the victim bound who says what he will do as he does it. The forest was too thick, the branches hanging too low for me to stay on the horse, so I jumped down and walked her. I smelled their burn stink before I heard them, and I knew they were following me.

"Neither him nor the big one fit, we say."

"A piece of the big one? A piece is a pass."

"He going run she going run, they all going run, we say."

"Not if we make them go through the dead brook. Bad air riding the night wind. Bad air straight through the nose."

"He he he he. But what we do with the what left? Eat we fill and leave them still, and they going spoil and rot and vultures going glut, till they fat and when hunger come for we again the meat going gone."

These two had forgotten that I had met them before. Ewele, red and hairy, whose black eyes were small as seeds, and who hopped like a frog. The loud one, bursting with rage and wickedness, and so much plotting that would come to something were he not as smart as a stunned goat. Egbere, the quiet one, raised no more than a whimper, crying over all the poor people he ate, for he was so very sorry, he told any god who would listen, until he was again hungry. Then he was more vicious than his cousin. Egbere, blue when the light hit him but black otherwise. Hairless and shiny where his cousin was hairy. Both sounded like jackals growling in a violent fuck. And they fussed, and fought so much that by the time they remembered to eat me, I had rolled out of their trap, a net made from the web of a giant spider.

The Sangoma never taught the spell to me, but I watched her as she did it, and learned every word. Such a waste of time it was to use the spell on them, but I would lose much more waiting on them to plot. I whispered into the sky her incantation. The two little ghommids quarreled still, even as they hopped from branch to branch above me. And then:

"Where he gone? Where he go? Where he went?"

"Whowhowho?"

"Himhimhim! Look look look!"

"Where him gone?"

"So I say already, fool."

"Him gone."

"And shit stink and piss rank and fool is fool, just like you."

"He gone, he gone. But he horse. He still there."

"He be a she."

"She who?"

"The horse."

"The horse, the horse, let we take the horse."

They hopped down from the tree. Neither carried weapons, but both opened mouths wide as a slit cut from ear to ear, with teeth, long, pointed, and numerous. Egbere charged at the horse to leap for her rump but ran into my kicking feet, my heel smashing his nose. He fell back and screamed.

"Why you kick me, son of a whoring half cat?"

"Me behind you, you fool. How me to kick you in the—"

I swung the hatchet right for Egbere's forehead and

chopped in deep, pulled it out, and chopped into his neck. I swung again and again until his head came off. Ewele screamed and screamed that the wind is killing his brother, the wind is killing his brother.

"I thought he was your cousin," I said.

"Who is it, who is demon of sky that killed my brother?"

I know the ghommids. Once upset they are out of control. He would never stop crying.

"You kill my brother!"

"Shut your face. His head will grow back in seven days. Unless it gets infected, then he will just grow back one big ball of pus."

"Show yourself! I am hungry to kill you."

"You kill my time, troll."

You have no time, someone said in my head. I heard him this time. It was a him and he spoke to me like I knew him, with the warmth of an old friend but only in sound, for it felt colder than the lower regions of lands of the dead, which I have been to in a dream. The voice took me out of the spell and Ewele jumped me. He screamed and his mouth opened wide, his sharp teeth grew, he became all mouth and teeth like the great fishes I have seen in the deep sea. And he got stronger as he got madder. My hand pushed him away from my face but his hair was slippery. He snapped and snapped and snapped and flew straight up in the air and vanished. My horse had kicked him away. I mounted her and rode off.

Why did you come back? he said.

"I did not come back. I am passing through."

Passing through. But you are on the road.

"The horse cannot ride for long in the bush."

I knew you would.

"Fuck the gods for all you know."

I knew you would come back.

"Fuck the gods."

What kind of a story would the griots tell of you? You are no story. A man of use to no one. A man no one depends on, no one trusts. You drift like spirits and devils and even their drift is with purpose.

"Is that all people are? Their purpose? Their use?"

You have no purpose. You are a man loved by no one. When you die, who will grieve you? Your father forgot you before you were even born. They raised you in a house where people murdered memory. What kind of hero are you?

"That what you want? A hero?"

I have word from your father and your brother.

I stopped the horse.

"Are they disappointed again? Do they hang their heads in shame in the underworld? They never seem to change, my father and brother."

I have word of your sister.

"I have no sister."

Much has come to pass since you took yourself from your mother's house.

"I have no sister."

And she has no brother. But she has a father,

who is also her grandfather. And a mother who is also a sister.

"And you say I am the one bringing shame to his family?"

What do you want?

"I want you to either kill me or shut up."

What kind of man has no quality?

"For a spirit, it staggers me how much you care about what ordinary men think. You talk about purpose like the gods shat it out of a divine ass, then gave it to man as if they would know the difference. I had a purpose, given to me by my blood, my father and my grandfather. I had a purpose and I told them to go fuck themselves with it. You use that word purpose like there is something noble to it, something of the best gods. Purpose is the gods saying what kings say to men they want to rule. Well a thousand rapes for your purpose. You want to know what's my purpose? To kill the men who killed my brother and father, leaving a grandfather fucking my own mother. To kill the men who killed my brother, because they killed him because he killed one of theirs. Who killed one of his, who killed one of theirs, and on and on while even gods die. My purpose is to avenge my blood so that one day they can come and seek vengeance on me. So no, I don't want purpose and I don't want children born in blood. You want to know what I want? I want to kill this bloodline. This sickness. End this poison. My name ends with me."

I am your—

"You are an Anjonu and you bore me."

Something like a scream came through the bush. The same leaves brushed past my arms, the same smells slipped past me. I came to a clearing I had just walked through. Trees were deceitful in these parts.

You close your mind the way a furious child closes his fists.

We came upon another clearing, where the grass was low and the air was evening. Or early morning. The Darklands was always dark, but it was never night. Not deep night, never a noon of the dead. In the clearing, built around the base of an assegai tree, stood a hut, plastered in cow dung. Dry, but carrying a fresh stink. Behind the hut, flat on his back with his legs spread wide, was the Ogo.

"Sadogo?"

He was dead.

"Sadogo?"

He was asleep.

"Sadogo."

He groaned, but still slept.

"Sadogo."

He groaned again.

"The mad monkey, the mad monkey," he said.

"Wake up, Sadogo."

"Not, not, asleep . . . not . . . I do not sleep."

Truth, I thought this was sleep making him sound mad. Or maybe the worst dream, where he did not know he was asleep.

"The mad monkey . . ."

"The mad monkey, what did he do?"

"The . . . mad . . . the . . . mad . . . he blew bone dust."

Bone dust. The Anjonu tried to make himself my master with that once, but the Sangoma's protection was on me, even in this forest. He then studied more wickedness, trying to uncover what the Sangoma's enchantment did not cover. He says he speaks to your head, even to your spirit, but he is just a lower demon who despises his form and who works an Ogudu spell on whoever is cursed to cross his path. He blows the bone dust and the body goes to sleep, though the mind is awake and in terror.

"Sadogo, can you sit?"

He tried to get up but fell back down. He lifted his chest again and fell back on his elbows. He paused and his head fell back like a sleepy child's until he snapped himself awake.

"Roll over and push yourself up," I said.

If bone dust did this to an Ogo, left him drunk, then the other two must be sleeping deeper than the dead. Sadogo tried to push himself up.

"Slow . . . slow . . . great giant."

"I'm not a giant. I am an Ogo," he said.

I knew that would rile him. He pushed himself up to a sit, but his head started to swing.

"Giant is what they call you. Giant!"

"Not a giant," he tried to shout, but his mumble ate the words.

"You are not anything, drooling on the floor."

He stood up and wobbled so low that he grabbed the tree. We would not make it out of this forest if we had to run. He shook his head. A drunkard he would have to be, then. If anything he could fall on our enemy and that would be no joke.

"The mad monkey . . . bone dust . . . inside . . . put them . . . insi—"

"The others are inside."

"Huh."

"Inside the hut?"

"I already said."

"Don't get testy with me, giant."

"Not a giant!"

That made him straighten right up. Then slouch again. I went over and grabbed his arm. He looked down, swung his face around as if the strangest thing had landed on his arm.

"Bone dust is a favorite trick of the Anjonu, but you will be as new in five flips of an hourglass. You must have been under its wickedness for some time now."

"Bone dust, the mad monkey . . ."

"You keep saying that, Sadogo. The Anjonu is a wicked, ugly spirit, but he is no monkey."

The thought jumped in my head. The Anjonu likes to torment, but he torments with blood, with family. Why would he bewitch the Ogo, the Leopard, even the boy? The Darklands have the dead, the never born, the spirit-like, and those let loose from the underworld. But because I have not seen many, I

forgot that it is also infested with every vicious creature born wrong. Worse than the bat men sleeping
and drooling.

"Can you fit inside?"

"Yes. I tried to leave before but fell . . . fell . . .
fell—"

"It will not be long, Ogo."

Inside the hut smelled not like cow dung, but like
meat saved in salt. Inside the hut, brightness like day
came through, but from nowhere, and it lit up one
red rug in the center, and a wall of knives, saws, arrowheads, and cutlasses. The Leopard, facedown on
the rug, his back covered in spots and the back of his
arms bristling fur. Trying to change but the Ogudu
gripped too strong. His teeth had grown long and
stuck out from his lips. Fumeli lay on his back in the
dirt floor. I stooped down beside the Leopard and
touched the back of his head.

"Cat, I know you hear me. I know you want to
move but cannot."

I saw him in my mind, trying to move, trying
to turn his chin, trying just to move his eye. The
Ogo, still wobbling, came through the door and hit
his head.

"A dung hut with a door?" he said.

"I know."

"Behold, anoth . . . nother."

Another door in line with the first on the other side
of the hut. The Ogo leaned too far and stumbled. He
braced himself against the wall.

"Who locked this door? Who infested it . . . with so many locks?"

The door looked stolen from the hut of someone else. Locks and bolts went all the way down to one side, from the top of the door right down into the earth.

That is—

"That is what?"

"Wha . . . what is what?"

"Not you, Sadogo."

"Then wh . . . my head keeps rolling out to sea."

You know this door.

"Stop speaking to me."

"I'm not . . . talking to you . . ."

"Not you, Sadogo."

There are only ten and nine such doors in all the lands, and one in this forest you call the Darklands.

"Sadogo, can you carry the Leopard?"

"Can I—"

"Sadogo!"

"Yes, yes, yes, yes, yes."

"I'll carry the boy."

The ten and nine doors, surely you have heard of them.

"Another trick."

"Who do you talk to?" Sadogo said.

"A minor demon who will not be quiet."

"I worked for slavers once," Sadogo said.

"Not now, Sadogo."

"I . . . do not know why . . . my head keeps rolling out to sea. But I have seen many days working for a slaver. I stopped a slave revolt once all by my own, with these hands you see here. They said I could

kill five and not affect their profits so I killed five. I don't know why I did it. I know why I killed them but . . . my head goes out to sea, I do not know why I was in a slaver's employ. . . . Did you know there are no female Ogos . . . or I have found none in all the lands I have seen. . . . Know this, Tracker . . . why do I wish to tell you, why do I wish to tell you so? I have never . . . ever . . . never been with a woman, for who can the Ogo mate with that he does not kill . . . and if this does not kill her . . ."

He lifted up his skirt. Long and thick like my entire arm.

"And if this does not kill her, giving birth to an Ogo surely will. I do not know my mother, just as no Ogo knows. The King of the South tried to breed a race of Ogo to fight in the last war. He kidnapped girls . . . some very young . . . some not childbearing age . . . wickedness, witchcraft, noon magic. Not a single Ogo he produced, but monsters now roam. We are not a race . . . we are a mishap."

"Grab the Leopard, Sadogo," I said.

The Ogo stooped, still wobbly, scooped the Leopard by the waist, and slung him over his right shoulder. Fumeli, as light as I thought he would be, I slung over my right and picked up his bow. The Ogo went to the door and stopped.

"The mad monkey . . ."

"Sadogo, there is no mad monkey. The Anjonu was trying to trick you."

Kafin ka ga biri, biri ya ganka.

"The mad monkey . . ."

"Sadogo, do—"

"The mad monkey . . . outside."

Before you see the monkey, the monkey has seen you.

The scream again. A long **EEEEEEEEEE** that screeched through the leaves. I went to the door. The creature was maybe two hundred paces away and moving very fast. Faster than a galloping horse and coming to the door. His arms flailing about, his legs hopping long leaps, his knees almost hitting his chin. Sometimes he stopped and pushed his nose in the air, catching a smell on the wind, then looked our way and dashed again, gnashing and spitting. His thick tail swishing, whipping away. Skin like a man's, but also green like rot. He ran headfirst, two eyes popping, the right small, the left bigger and smoking. He screamed again and the ghost of birds flew off. Too fast. Ripped cloth flapped all over him.

"The door, Sadogo, the door!"

Sadogo threw off the Leopard, slammed the door, and dropped the three bolts across it. A bang hit the door like a lightning bolt. Sadogo jumped. The creature EEEEEEEEEE'd again, threatening to deafen every soul close.

"Shit," I said.

The walls of the hut were stick leaves and dry shit. The creature would punch a hole right through it as soon as he saw that he could. It banged and banged and the old wood started to crack. He EEEEEEEEEEE'd again and again. Sadogo picked up the Leopard.

"The door," he said.

I thought he was pointing to the front door, but he nodded at the back. The creature punched a hole through the front door and pushed his face against it. Face shaped like that of a man bred with a devil. His left eye really did smoke. Nose punched in like an ape's and long, rotten teeth. He snarled and spat through the hole, then pulled away. I could hear his feet, his footsteps quicker and louder, running, right into the door. The hinges broke, but did not break off. His face pushed through the hole again. **EEEEEEEEEEE.** He ran off to charge again.

Sadogo grabbed each lock and ripped them off the back door. The mad monkey rammed into the wood and his whole head burst through. He tried to pull himself but was stuck. Now he looked up at us and yelled and screamed and snarled and I could hear his tail whip against the hut. We turned to the back door and all the locks Sadogo had ripped out appeared again.

"He will get through the door the third time," I said.

"What kind of magic is this . . . what kind of magic?" Sadogo said.

I stood next to Sadogo and studied this door. There

was magic, but my nose was no help in unraveling its making. I whispered an incantation I never remembered hearing before. Nothing. Nothing like the house back in Malakal. Something from the Sangoma's tongue, not mine. I whispered it again so close my lips kissed the wood. A flame sparked at the top right corner and spread around the entire frame. When the flames vanished, so had the locks.

Sadogo went past me and pushed it open. A white light shot through. The mad monkey EEEEEEEEEEE'd. I wanted to stay and fight him but I had two asleep and one about to fall down in a blink.

"Tracker," Sadogo said.

The light lit the whole room white. I picked up Fumeli. The Ogo took the Leopard and stepped through first, then I hobbled behind. A crash behind us caused me to turn just as the front door broke off. The mad monkey charged in screaming, but as his chipped fangs reached for the back door, it slammed itself shut, leaving us in darkness and quiet.

"What is this place?" Sadogo asked.

"The forest. We are in the for—"

I went back to the door behind us. What could it be but a mistake to do so, but I opened it anyway, just a little, and looked inside. A dusty room, with stone tiles, and from floor to wall stood books, scrolls, papers, and parchments. No broken door. No mad monkey. At the end of this new room, another door that Sadogo pushed open.

Sun. Children ran and stole, market women yelled

and sold. Traders eyed a good deal, slavers squeezed red slave flesh, buildings squat and fat, buildings skinny and looming, and far off a great tower I knew.

"Are we in Mitu?" Sadogo said.

"No, my friend. Kongor."

3

ONE CHILD
MORE THAN
SIX

Ngase ana garkusa ura a dan
garkusa inshamu ni.

KONGOR

KEY

1. MISS WADADA'S HOUSE OF PLEASURABLE GOOD AND SERVICES
2. BASU FUMANGURU'S HOUSE
3. ALLEY OF THE PERFUME MERCHANTS
4. TOWER OF THE BLACK SPARROW HAWK
5. THE OLD LORD'S HOUSE
6. KONGORI CHIEFTAIN ARMY FORT
7. GREAT HALL OF RECORDS
8. SINKING OLD HOUSE
9. NIMBE CANAL

TAROBE

NYEMBE

BORDER ROAD

BORDER ROAD

BORDER ROAD

BORDER ROAD

NIMBE

IMPERIAL DOCKS

OLD TAROBE (FLOODED)

GALLUNKOBE/MATYUBE

N

"eave the dead to the dead. That is what I tell him."

"Before or after we went in the Darklands?"

"Before, after, dead is dead. The gods tell me to wait. And look—you alive and unspoiled. Trust the gods."

Sogolon looked at me with neither smile nor sneer. The only way she could care less would be to try.

"The gods had to tell you to wait?"

I woke up when the sun sailed to the middle of the sky and forced shadows underfoot. Flies buzzed about the room. I slept and woke three times before the Leopard and Fumeli woke once, and the Ogo could cast off the sluggishness of the Ogudu. The room, dim and plain, walls the brown-green colour of fresh chicken dung, with sacks packed on top of each other all the way to the ceiling. Tall statues leaning against each other, sharing secrets about me. The floor smelled of grain, dust, perfume bottles lost in the dark, and rat shit. On the two side walls facing each other, tapestries ran to the ground, blue Ukuru cloth with white patterns of lovers and trees. I lay on the floor, above and under blankets and rugs of many colours. Sogolon stood by the window, in that brown leather dress she always wore, looking out.

"You leave your whole mind back in the forest."

"My mind is right here."

"Your mind not here yet. Three times now I say to you that journey around the Darklands take three days, and we take four."

"Only one night passed in the forest."

Sogolon laughed like a wheeze.

"So we come three days late," I said.

"You lost in that forest for twenty and nine days."

"What?"

"A whole moon come and go since you gone into bush."

And perhaps this, like the last two times she said it, was where I threw myself back down on the rugs, stunned. Everything not dead had twenty-nine days—a whole moon—to grow, including truth and lies. People on voyages have long returned. Creatures born got old, others died, and those dead withered to dust in that time. I have heard of great beasts who go to sleep for cold seasons, and men who fall ill and never rise, but this felt like someone stole my days and whoever I should have been in them. My life, my breath, my walk, it came to me why I hate witchcraft and all magic.

"I have been in the Darklands before. Time never stopped then."

"Who was keeping time for you?"

I knew what she meant behind the witch double-speak. What she said, not out loud, the word inside the word, was who in the world would care for me that they would count my days gone? She looked at me as if she wanted an answer. Or at least a half-wit answer she could reply to with a full-wit mockery. But I stared at her until she looked away.

"A whole moon come and go since you gone into the bush," she said again, but soft as if not to me. She looked out the window.

"Trust for the gods be the only reason why I here for a moon in Kongor. If it was my will over the gods, this whole place and every man in it would burn. Can't trust no man in Kongor."

"Can't trust any man, anywhere," I said. She flinched when she saw I heard.

"My gratitude for waiting in a city that does you ill," I said.

"Not for you I do it. Not even for the goddess."

"Should I ask who?"

"Too many children in Kongor don't have an end to they story. That older than two hundred years, that older than when I was a child. So let this be the one child who story have an ending, no matter how grim, and not be another one that wash up with no head when the floodwater roll back."

"You lost a child? Or were you the child?"

"I should have make distance between me and this city. Make distance four nights after you didn't show. Last time I walk these roads a man of good breeding pay five man to steal me so he can show me what an ugly woman was for. Right there in Torobe. Couldn't beat him wife because she from royal blood, so he bond me for that."

"Kongori masters have always been cruel."

"Low-wit donkey, the man was not my master, he was my kidnapper. A man would know the difference."

"You could have run to a prefect."

"A man."

"A magistrate."

"A man."

"An elder with a kind ear, an inquisitor, a seer."

"Man. Man. Man."

"Justice could have come for your kidnapper."

"Justice did come. When I learn a spell and the wife pregnancy devour her from the inside. Something else go up inside the man."

"A spell."

"My knife."

"When you last pass through Kongor?"

"Amadu debt to me doubling just by me coming back."

"When last, Sogolon?"

"I already tell you."

Noise bounced up to the window, but it had order,

and rhythm, beat and shuffle, the clap of sandals and boots, the trot of hooves on hard dirt, and people who oohed to other people's aahs. I joined her by the window and looked out.

"Coming from all corners of the North and some from the South border. The border men wear a red scarf on the left arm. Do you see them?"

The street stretched behind the house, several floors below. Like most of Kongor, it was built of mud and stone, mortar to stop the rains from beating the walls away, though the side wall looked like the face of man who suffered pox. Six floors high, ten and two windows across, some with wood shutters, some open, some with a platform outside for plants but not people to stand, though children stood and sat on many. Indeed the whole house looked like a large honeycomb. Like all buildings in Kongor, this looked finished by hand. Smoothed by palms and fingers, measured by the old science of trusting the god of skill and creation to measure what is good weight and what is good height. Some of the windows were not in line, but up and down like a pattern, and some were taller than others, and not perfect in shape, but smooth, and done with either the care of a master or the crack of a master's whip.

"This house belong to a man from the Nyembe quarter. He be in my debt for many things and many lives."

I followed Sogolon's eyes as she looked down from the window. In the winding snake of a street, men approached. Groups of three and four walking so in step it looked like marching. Coming from the east, men on white and black horses with red reins, the horses not covered head to tail like the stallions of Juba. Two men passed below us, side by side. The one closer to the street wore a helmet of lion hair, and a black coat trimmed in gold with splits to the sides, with a white robe underneath. He carried a longsword in his belt. The second man kept his head bald. A black shawl draped his shoulders, covering a loose black tunic and white trousers, and a shiny red sheath for a scimitar. Three men on horseback went back up the snake street, all three in black wraps to hide their faces, chain mail, black robes over legs in armour, with a lance in one hand and the bridle in the other.

"Whose army assembles?"

"No army. Not King's men."

"Mercenaries?"

"Yes."

"Who? I spend little time in Kongor."

"These be the warriors of the Seven Wings. Black garments on the outer, white on the inner, like their symbol the black sparrow hawk."

"Why do they assemble? There is no war, or rumor of war."

She looked away. "None in the Darklands," she said.

Still looking at the mercenaries gathering, I said, "We came out of the forest."

"The forest don't lead into the city. The forest don't even lead to Mitu."

"There are doors, and there are doors, witch."

"These sound like doors I know."

"Wise woman, do you not know everything? What kind of door closes on itself and is no more?"

"One of the ten and nine doors. You talk of it in your sleep. I didn't know of a door in the Darklands. You smell it out?"

"And now you have mirth too."

"How you know there be a door in the Darklands?"

"I just knew."

She whispered something.

"What?" I said.

"Sangoma. It must be the Sangoma's craft on you why you can see even when you eyes blind. Nobody know how the ten and nine doors come to pass. Though old griots say each make by the gods. And even the elder of elders will look at you and say, Fool, nothing never go so in all the worlds above and below sky. Other people—"

"You speak of witches?"

"Other people will say that it is the roads of the gods when they travel this world. Step through one and you in Malakal. Step through one in the Darklands and look: You in Kongor. Step through another and you even in a South kingdom like Omororo, or out in the sea or mayhaps a kingdom not of this world. Some men spend till they gray just to find one door, and all you do is sniff one out."

"Bibi was of Seven Wings," I said.

"He was just an escort. You smelling a game that nobody playing."

"Seven Wings works for whoever pays, but nobody pays more than our great King. And here they assemble outside this lookout."

"You tracking small matters, Tracker. Leave the big things to the big people of the world."

"If this is why I woke myself I will go back to sleep. How are the Leopard and the Ogo?"

"Gods give them good fortune, but they recover slow. Who is this mad monkey? He rape them?"

"Strange how I never thought to ask that. Maybe he was going to suck their souls, and lick their feelings."

"Ba! Your sour mouth tire me out. The Ogo of course stand because he never fall."

"That is my Ogo. Does the girl still ride with you?"

"Yes. Two days I slap out this foolishness about running back to Zogbanu."

"She is dead weight. Leave her in this city."

"What a day when a man tell me what to do. Will you not speak of the child?"

"Who?"

"The reason we come to Kongor."

"Oh. In these twenty and nine days gone, what news have you of the house?"

"We did not go."

This "we" I left for another day. "I do not believe you," I said.

"What a day when I care what a man believe."

"What a day when these days come. But I am tired, and the Darklands took my fight. Did you go to the house or no?"

"I bring peace to a girl that monsters breed to make breakfast of her flesh. Then I wait for usefulness to return to you. The boy not more missing."

"Then we should go."

"Soon."

I wanted to say that nobody seemed too earnest in completing our mission and finding this boy, nobody meaning her, but she went to the doorway and I noticed there was no door, only a curtain.

"Who owns this house? Is it an inn? A tavern?"

"I say again. A man with too much money, and too many favors he owes me. He meet us soon. Now he running around like a headless chicken, trying to build another room, or floor, or window, or cage."

She was already beyond the curtain when she looked back.

"This day is already given. And Kongor is a different city at night. See to your cat and giant," she said. Only then did my head remember that she was saying she was over three hundred years old. Nothing said old more than an old woman thinking she was even older.

The Ogo sat on the floor, trying on his iron gloves, punching his left palm so hard that little lightning sparked in his hands. It was all over his face, blankness. Then as he punched his hand, he worked up into a rage that made him snort through his teeth.

Then he went blank again. Standing in front of him as he sat there was the first time our eyes met on the same line. Sun was running from noon, but inside his room dimmed to evening. Things were stored in this room as well. I smelled kola nuts, civet musk, lead, and two or three floors below, dried fish.

"Sadogo, you sit there like a soldier itching for battle."

"I itch to kill," he said, and struck his palm again.

"This might happen soon."

"When do we go back to the Darklands?"

"When? Never, good Ogo. The Leopard you should have never followed."

"We would have slept there still, if not for you."

"Or be meat for the mad monkey."

Sadogo roared lion like, and punched the floor. The room shook.

"I shall rip his tail from his shit-smeared ass, and watch him eat it."

I touched his shoulder. He flinched for a blink, then rested.

"Of course. Of course. As you say, it will be done, Ogo. Will you still go with us? To the house. To find the boy, wherever it takes us?"

"Yes of course, why would I not?"

"The Darklands leave many changed."

"I am changed. Do you see that? That on the wall."

He pointed to a blade, long and thick, iron brown with rust. The grip wide for two hands, a thick straight blade right down to halfway, where it curved to a crescent like a bitten-out moon.

"Do you know it?" Sadogo said.

"Never seen the like."

"Ngombe ngulu. First I grab the slave. The master bred red slaves. One ran away. The gods demanded a sacrifice. He struck the master. So I set him before the execution floor. Three bamboo stalks sticking out of the ground. I push him down, force him to sit up, lean him against the stalks, and tie both hands back. Two small stalks, I drive in right by the feet and bind the ankles. Two small stalks I drive in right by the knees, and tie the knees to them. He's stiff, putting on bravery, but he's not brave. I take a branch from the tree and strip it of leaves and pull it down so it bends tight like a bow. The branch is angry, it wishes to be straight again not bound, but bind it I do, bind it to grass rope, then I tie it around the head of the slave. My ngulu is sharp, so sharp that looking at it will make your eyes bleed. My blade catches sunlight and flashes like lightning. Now the slave starts to scream. Now he calls for ancestors. Now he begs. They all beg, do you know? Men all talk of how they rejoice the day of meeting the ancestors but nobody has joy when it comes, only crying and pissing and shitting. I swing back my arm with the sword, then I scream and I swing and I chop off the head right at the neck, and the branch breaks free with the head and flings it away. And my master is happy. I killed one hundred, seventy and one, including several chiefs and lords. And some of them were women too."

"Why did you tell me this?"

"I do not know. The bush. Something about the bush."

Then I saw the Leopard. In his room, lying on rags bunched up as if he'd slept as a cat. Fumeli not there, or gone, or whatever. I had not thought of him, had not, I just realized, even asked Sogolon of him. The Leopard tried to turn behind him, craning his neck.

"There are holes in the ground, baked clay and hollow like bamboos."

"Leopard."

"They take your piss and shit away when you pour water from the urn in the hole after."

"Kongor is unlike other cities in what she does with piss and shit. And bodies as—"

"Who put us in this place?" he said, pulling himself up to his elbows, frowning at being watched.

"Take that up with Sogolon. This lord seems to owe her many favors."

"I wish to leave."

"As you wish."

"Tonight."

"We cannot go tonight."

"I never said we."

"Leave? You can't even stand. Change form and a half-blind bowman could kill you. Find your strength, then go where you wish. I will tell Sogolon—"

"Don't speak for me, Tracker."

"Then let Fumeli speak for you. What does he not do for you?"

"Speak again and—"

"And what, Leopard? What poison has come over you? Everybody sees you and that little bitch of a boy."

This made him angrier. He rose from the rugs but stumbled.

"What makes you laugh so? Nothing is funny."

"Nobody loves no one. Remember? Verse I learned from you. I have heard of warriors, mystics, eunuchs, princes, chiefs and their sons, all wither from futile love for the Leopard. And who is it, that finally clips your balls? This little clump, who wouldn't be worth saving if he was the only man on the boat. Hark, everyone in this house. Hark how your bitch turns the great Leopard into an alley cat."

"And yet watch this alley cat find the boy on his own."

"Another great plan. How went the last one? And yet it is I, the man whose love you have forgotten, who rode in to save you. And the little bitch. And lost all our horses doing so. Maybe I saved the wrong animal."

"You want thanks?"

"I have truth. Join Nyka and his woman, or make trails with your bitch."

"Call him that one more . . . By the gods I will . . ."

"Find your strength and go. Or stay. Your malcontent is no mystery to me anymore. You are always the

Leopard. But maybe you stay out of bushes you don't know. I won't be there to save you next time."

Fumeli stood in the doorway. He carried bow and quiver and straightened, trying to puff his chest out. Whether to laugh or slap him I could not decide. So I passed him close enough to knock him out of the way. The Ogudu was still in him, a weak trace, but he stumbled and fell. He yelled for Kwesi and the Leopard jumped to a crouch and wobbled.

"Deal with him," Fumeli said.

"Yes, deal with me, Leopard."

I scowled at the boy.

"Either he's marking the room as his, or he can't even rise to go piss somewhere else," I said.

In the hallway the girl walked up to me. She had found white clay and covered her body in patterns underneath a red-and-yellow sheath. A headdress hung on her head, little ropes with cowries, and iron loops, with two ivory tusks down each temple. Something wicked came upon me to say something about man- and woman-eaters. But she was just looking through clothes and tusks and scents to find herself. The thought was a wild animal.

Night in Kongor. This city with a most brazen love for war and blood, where people gathered to see man and animal rip flesh, still shuddered to see anyone bare it. Some say this was the influence of the East, but Kongor was far west and these people believed in nothing. Except modesty, a new thing, a thing that I hope never reached the inner kingdoms, or at least the Ku and Gangatom. I grabbed a long strip of Ukuru cloth lying in a bundle on the floor of my room, wrapped it around my waist and then over my shoulder, like a woman's pagne, then tied it with a belt. I lost my hatchets in the Darklands, but still had my knives, and strapped them to each thigh. Nobody saw me leave, so nobody knew where I was going.

The city, almost surrounded by the great river, never needed a wall, only sentries along the banks. Along with fishermen, trade ships, and cargo boats coming from north and south to the imperial docks. Leaving by anything that will take them. During the wet season, in the middle of the year, rain floods the river so high that Kongor becomes an island for four moons. The city rises higher than the river, but some roads in the South were so low that you traveled by foot in the dry season and by boat in the wet. They ate the crocodile here, something that would make the Ku scream in fear and Gangatom spit in disgust.

Down the steps and out the building I looked at this lord's house. The children had left and nobody stood by any window. None of the Seven Wings gathered in the street. He lived in the south of the Nyembe quarter. The matanti winds flew up and rolled through the roads, leaving a dusty haze all over the city.

I took the cloth on my shoulder and wrapped it over my head, like a hood.

Kongor split itself in four. Quarters not equal in size and divided by professions and livelihood and

wealth. Northwest lay the wide, empty streets of the
nobles of the Tarobe quarter. Beside them, for one
served the other, was the Nyembe quarter—artists
and artisans who made crafts for the homes of the
nobles—all that was beautiful. And metalworkers,
leatherworkers, and blacksmiths who made all that
was useful. Southwest was the Gallunkobe/Matyube
quarter, free people and slaves both laboring for masters. Southwest was the Nimbe quarter, with streets
for administrators, scribes, and keepers of logs and
records, with the great hall of records standing tall
in the center.

I went down a wide street. A butcher shop on
the left tried to trap me with carcass smells, antelope, goat, and lamb, but dead flesh all smells the
same. A woman went into her house when she saw
me approach and yelled at her son to come inside
right now lest she call his father to fetch him. He
stared at me as I passed, then ran in. I forgot that even
the poorest house in Kongor had two floors. Packed
close together, leaving a sense of space for the courtyard behind their walls. Also this, each house had its
own entrance door, made by the finest artisans your
pocket could afford, with two large columns and a
cover to shield from sun. The two columns reached
past the ground floor all the way to the roof, with
a little window right above the entrance canopy. A
line of five or ten toron sticks jutting out of the wall
above that. Turrets on the roof like a line of arrows.
It was not yet night, not even late evening, but barely

anyone walked the streets. And yet music and noise came from everywhere.

"Where go the people?" I asked a boy, who did not stop walking.

"Bingingun."

"Oh?"

"To the masquerade," he said, shaking his head at speaking to such an imbecile. The curse of all so young. I didn't ask him where, since he walked, skipped, then ran south.

This too about Kongor. Everything will be as you last left it.

The temple to one of the supreme gods was still there, though now dark and empty, with the doors open as if still hoping someone would come in. The ornaments along the roof in bronze, the python, the white snail, the woodpecker—robbers stole long ago. Not even ten paces from the temple was another place.

"Come, pretty boy boy, how you get it up? How I goin' know which one you like when you wearing some grandmother death shroud?" she said as men lit wall torches behind her.

Still tall as the doorway, still fat from crocodile meat and ugali porridge. Still wearing a long wrap around her waist to squeeze her breasts to almost pop out, but showing her meaty shoulders and back. Still leaving her head bald and bare, a thing not liked by the

Kongori. Still smelling like expensive incense because "Us girls must have one thing out of the reach of other girls," she said every time I told her she smelled like she just bathed in a goddess's river.

"I can just tell you who I want, Miss Wadada."

"Oh. No, boy boy boy. Prefer the other way when your big Tracker just stiff up and point up to the one he like. I don't know why you in that curtain. I feeling all the offense you should be feeling for yourself."

Miss Wadada's House of Pleasurable Goods and Services was not for people who were not themselves. Illusion was for who smoked opium. She let a shapeshifter fuck one of her girls as a lion once, until he swatted her in a fit of ecstasy and snapped her neck. I left my curtain on the floor and went upstairs with the one she said came from the land of the eastern light, which means an emissary raped a girl and left her with child to go back to his wife and concubines. The girl left the child with Miss Wadada, who looked at his skin and bathed him every quartermoon in cream and sheep butter. She forbade him to do any work so that his muscles would stay thin, his cheeks high and hips much wider than his waist. Miss Wadada made him the most exquisite of all creatures, who had all the best stories of all the worst people, but preferred that you fucked each tale out and paid him a fee on top of Miss Wadada's for being the best information hound in all Kongor.

"Look, it is the wolf eye," he said. "No man has made a woman of me since you."

His room smelled like the room I just left. I never asked if saying "him" brought offense since I only called him Ekoiye or "you."

"I can't tell if you live with a civet or have its musk all over you."

Ekoiye rolled his eyes and laughed. "We must have nice things, man-wolf. Besides, what man wants to enter a room where he can smell the man who just left?"

He laughed again. I liked that he only needed himself to laugh at his jokes. I saw it in people who had to endure other people. With Ekoiye it mattered not if you were a fine or a foul lover, or if you were a man of much or little sport. He took pleasure for himself first. Whether you shared in it was your business. He crowded his little room with terra-cotta statues, even more than I remember last. And this, a cage with a black pigeon I mistook for a crow.

"I change every man into one before he leaves this room," he said, and pulled a comb from his hair. Curly hair fell down like little snakes.

"Indeed. Your shows deserve an audience. Or at least a griot."

"Man-wolf, don't you know the verses about me?"

He pointed to a stool with a back like a throne. A birthing chair, I remembered.

"Where is your friend? What name did they give him, Nayko?"

"Nyka."

"I miss him. He was a man of great light and noise."

"Noise?"

"He made the greatest noise, something like a loud cat's purr, or the coo of a rameron pigeon, when I put him in my mouth."

His hand grabbed me as he said that.

"You little liar. Nyka was never one for the company of boys."

"Good wolf, you know I can be whatever you want me, even the girl you've never had . . . under certain wine and in a certain light."

His robes fell down all around him, and he stepped out of the pile on the floor. He straddled me and winced as he lowered himself and I rose up inside him. This is how he always played. Sinking down on me until his ass sat on my thighs, then, without climbing off, turning around so that his back was to me. I told him once that only men who tell lies to their wives need to fuck from behind; he still did it this way. He asked what he always asked: Do you want me to fuck you? And I said what I always said: Yes. Miss Wadada always asked if he'd injured me when I left.

"Fuck the gods," I said in a hiss, and curled my toes so tight they cracked like knuckles.

I pushed him down on the floor and jumped on top. After, with me out of him, but him straddled on top of me, he said, "You follow the eastern light now?"

"No."

"Ghost walkers of the West?"

"Ekoiye, the questions you ask."

"Because, Tracker, all men under the sky, men who love to think they are different from each other, perhaps to make sense of when they war, are all the same. They think whatever troubles them here"— he pointed to his head—"they can fuck it out into me. This is foreign thinking, that I did not expect from a man from these lands. Maybe you wander too much. You'll be praying to only one god next."

"I have nothing in my head to fuck out."

"Then what does the Tracker want?"

"Who needs more after this?" I said, and slapped his ass. The move felt hollow and we both knew so. He laughed, then leaned until his back was on my chest. I wrapped my arms around him. I dripped sweat. Ekoiye was ever dry.

"Tracker, I lied. Men from the eastern light never fuck anything out. They always want to get sticked in the ass. So again, what does the Tracker want?"

"I seek old news."

"How old?"

"Three years and many moons."

"Three years, three moons, three blinks are all flat to me."

"I ask about one of Kwash Dara's elders. Basu Fumanguru is his name."

Ekoiye rolled away from me, stood up, and went to the birthing chair. He stared at me.

"Everyone knows of Basu Fumanguru."

"What does everyone say?"

"Nothing. I said they knew, not that they would talk. They should have burned that house down, to kill the plague, but none will step near it. It is a—"

"You think the house fell to disease."

"Or a curse from a river demon."

"I see. How powerful is he, the man who pays you to say such?"

He laughed. "You paid Miss Wadada to fuck."

"And I pay you far above your sum to talk. You saw my pouch and you know what is in it. Now talk."

He stared at me again, then. He looked around, as if more were in the room, then wrapped himself in a sheet. "Come with me."

He pushed away a pile of chests and opened a hatch door no higher than my thigh.

"You will not be coming back to this room," he said.

He crawled in first. Dark and hot, crumbly with dust, then hard from wood, then harder from mud and plaster, always too black to see. Hear much I did. From every room came men shouting and fucking in all ways and manners, but girls and boys who all moaned the same, saying fuck me with your big, your hard, your Ninki Nanka battering ram, and on and on. Training from Miss Wadada. Twice the idea ran through me that this was a trap, Ekoiye coming out first being a sign to kill the man who crawls out after. There might have been a man with a ngulu sword waiting for my neck, though Ekoiye did not hesitate. For we crawled even longer, long enough to make me wonder who built this, who traveled this long for Ekoiye's bed. Ahead of him, the dark twinkled with stars.

"Where are you taking us?" I asked.

"To your executioner," he said, then laughed. We came to a flight of steps, which led to the roof of a place I did not know. No smell of civet, no smell of Miss Wadada, no scent or stench of the whorehouse.

"No, there is no smell of Miss Wadada," he said.

"Are you hearing my words unsaid?"

"If you think them so loud, Tracker."

"Is this how you know the secrets of men?"

"What I hear is no secret. All the girls can hear them too."

Laughter burst out of me. Who else would be expert at reading the minds of men?

"You are on the roof of a gold merchant from the Nyembe quarter."

"I smell Miss Wadada's perfume south of us."

Ekoiye nodded. "Some say it was murder, some say it was monsters."

"Who? What do you speak of now?"

"What happened to your friend, Basu Fumanguru. Have you seen the men who gather now, in our city?"

"The Seven Wings."

"Yes, that is what they are called. Men in black. The woman who lives beside Fumanguru said that she saw many men in black in Fumanguru's house. Through the window she saw them."

"Seven Wings are mercenaries, not assassins. Not like them to kill just one man and his family. Not even in war."

"I didn't call them Seven Wings, she did. Maybe they were demons."

"Omoluzu."

"Who?"

"Omoluzu."

"I do not know him."

He went over to the edge of the roof and I followed him. We were three floors up. A man rolled in the road, palm wine smell coming of his skin. Other than him, the street was empty.

"Such a swarm of men, who want this man dead. Some say Seven Wings, some say demons, some say the chieftain army."

"Because they share a love for black?"

"You the one seeking answers, wolf. This is known. Somebody entered the house of Basu Fumanguru and killed everyone. Nobody see no bodies and there were no burial rites. Imagine an elder of the city of Kongor dead with no tribute, no funeral, no procession of lords with a man of royal blood leading it, nobody even declaring him dead. Meanwhile thornbush sprung wild around the house overnight."

"What do your elders say?"

"None come to me. Do you know he was killed on the Night of the Skulls?"

"I do not believe you."

"That it was the Night of the Skulls?"

"That none of those chatty child-fuckers have seen you since."

"I think the Seven Wings assemble for the King."

"I think you dance away from the question."

"Not how you think."

"Lowly people all seem to know the ways of kings these days."

He grinned. "I know this, though. People visit that house, including one or two of the elders. And maybe one or two Seven Wings. One not from here, they call him Belekun the Big, because that is how men around here joke. He was one who could not keep any of his holes shut, his mouth the worst. He came here with another elder."

"How do you remember after three years?"

"It was last year. As they both took turns fucking a deaf girl, Miss Wadada heard also. Them saying that they need to find it. They need to find it now, or it will be the execution sword for them."

"Find what?"

"Basu Fumanguru wrote a long writ against the King, they said."

"Where is this writ?"

"People keep breaking in his house and not finding anything, so not there mayhaps?"

"You think the King killed him over a writ?"

"I think nothing. The King is coming here. His chancellor is in the city."

"His chancellor visits Miss Wadada?"

"No, stupid Tracker. I have seen him, though.

Kinglike but not the King, skin blacker than you and hair red like a new wound."

"Maybe he will come sample your famous services."

"Too pious. Holiness itself. As soon as I saw him I forgot when I first saw him and it was as if I was always seeing him. Do I sound like the fool?"

A dark man with red hair. **A dark man with red hair.**

"Tracker, you look gone."

"I am here."

"As I say, nobody can think of a time when he was not chancellor, but nobody can remember when he became so, or what he was before."

"He was not chancellor yesterday, but has been chancellor forever. Did they kill all in Fumanguru's house?"

"Maybe you should ask a prefect."

"Maybe I will."

He turned to look down in the street and wrapped the cloth over his head.

"One more thing. Come closer, one-eyed wolf."

He pointed down into the street. I came up beside him as the clothes fell from him. He arched his back, his body was saying I could have him again right there. I turned to face him and he smiled a smile, all black. He blew it all in my face, black dust. Kohl dust, a large cloud in my eyes, nose, and mouth. Kohl dust mixed with viper poison, I could smell it. He looked at me deep, not with any malice, just with great interest, like he was told what would happen next. I punched him in the neck bump, then grabbed his throat and squeezed.

"They must have given you the antidote," I said, "or you would have been dead by now."

He coughed and groaned. I squeezed until his eyes bulged.

"Who sent you? Who gave you kohl dust?"

I pushed him hard. He fell back from the edge of the roof screaming and I caught his ankle. He kept flailing and yelling and almost slipped from me.

"By the gods, Tracker! By the gods! Mercy!"

"Mercifully release you?"

I eased my grip and he slipped. Ekoiye screamed.

"Who knew I would come to you?"

"No one!"

I let his ankle slip again.

"I don't know! It's an enchantment, I swear it. It must have been."

"Who paid you to kill me?"

"It was not to kill you, I swear."

"There is venom in this kohl. An ingenious thing like you must know of enchantments, so learn this. Nothing born of metal can harm me."

"It was for anybody who ask. He never said kill you."

"Who?"

"I don't know! A man in veils, more veils than a Kongori nun. He come in Obora Dikka moon, in the Basa star. I swear it. He said blow kohl breath in the face of anyone who asks of Basu Fumanguru."

"Why would anyone ask you of Basu Fumanguru?"

"Nobody ask until you."

"Tell me more of this man. What colour his robes?"

"B-black. No blue. Dark blue, his fingers blue. No, blue in the fingernails like he dyes great cloths."

"Are you sure he was not in black?"

"It was blue. By the gods, blue."

"And what was to happen next, Ekoiye?"

"They said men would come."

"You said he before."

"He!"

"How would he know?"

"I was to go back to my room and release the pigeon in the window."

"This story grows more legs and wings by the blink. What else?"

"Nothing else. Am I a spy? Listen, I swear by the—"

"Gods, I know. But I do not believe in gods, Ekoiye."

"This was not to kill you."

"Listen, Ekoiye. It is not that you lie, but that you don't know truth. There was enough venom spewing from your mouth to kill nine buffalo."

"Mercy," he said, weeping.

Sweat made him slippery in my hand.

"The ever-dry Ekoiye breaks into sweat."

"Mercy!"

"I am confused, Ekoiye. Let me retell this in a way that adds up to sense, for me and perhaps you. Even though Basu Fumanguru has been dead three years, a man in blue robes hiding his face still approached you, little more than a moon past. And he said, Should anyone speak of Basu Fumanguru, a man you would have no reason to know, take this antidote, then blow viper-soaked kohl dust in his face and kill him, then send word for me to pick up the body. Or not kill him, just put him to sleep as we can collect him as garbage mongers do for a fee. Is that all?"

He nodded, over and over.

"Two things, Ekoiye. Either you were not supposed to kill me, only leave me helpless so they can squeeze fact from me themselves. Or you were supposed to kill me but ask deeper questions before."

"I don't know. I don't know. I don—"

"You don't know. You don't know anything. You don't even know if the antidote, the poison killer, kills the poison. Here I thought you were a wise boy trapped in an unwise life. No antidote ever kills the poison, Ekoiye, it only delays it. The most you live is eight years, maybe ten, pretty one. Nobody told you? Maybe there is not too much venom in you, and you live ten and four years. I still don't understand why they came to you."

Now he laughed. Loud and long.

"Because everybody comes to the pleasure monger later or sooner, Tracker. You cannot help yourselves. Husbands, chiefs, lords, tax collectors, even you. Like a pack of hungry dogs. Later or sooner you all come back to who you are. Like you pushing me down and fucking the little he-whore rough because you were a dog even before that eye. You know what I wish, man-fucker? I wish I had venom to kill the whole world."

When I let him go he screamed all the way down. He would not be dead—the fall was not high enough. But he would break something, maybe a leg, maybe an arm, maybe a neck. I went back the way we came, passed under the same sounds of men fucking every last coin into wet rugs, and bolted the hatch behind me. The pigeon that he kept in a bamboo cage by the small window I took out and held gentle. The note wrapped around her left foot I removed. At the window I let it loose.

The note. Glyphs, the like I had seen before, but could not remember it. I pushed the birthing chair into the darkest corner of the room and waited. The window looked large enough. The door would mean that others knew about this arrangement, among them, Miss Wadada. I thought on this hard. Nothing could have happened under Miss Wadada's roof without her knowing of such. But this too is so of the Kongori. If I did kill Ekoiye tonight, she would still welcome me tomorrow with a **Take off those robes so I can see you, big stiff prince,** and then send me off with her newest girl-boy.

Even as night grew deep the heat still crawled around, leaving my back sticking to the seat. I peeled off the wood and almost missed it, the kick of feet on the wall. Climbing without ropes, a man perhaps under enchantment, where whatever the foot touched became floor. Hands at the windowsill first, knuckles ashy. Hands pulled up the elbows, which pulled up the head. Black head wrap around the forehead and the mouth. Eyes, an opium-lover red, sweeping the room, locking with my eyes, but not seeing me. Shoulder robes in blue, a leather sash over the left shoulder. One leg in, and at the bottom of the sash, two sheaths for two swords and a dagger dangling. I waited until all of him was in and his long blue robes swept the floor.

"Hail."

He jumped. He grabbed for his sword. My first dagger cut his neck, my second plunged under his chin, killing his head before his legs knew he was dead. He fell, his head slamming into the floor right at my foot. Undressing him felt more like unwrapping him. Scars on his chest, a bird, lightning, an insect with many legs, glyphs that looked in the style of the note. Top joints of both index fingers missing. He was not Seven Wings. And he had the knotty, violent crotch scar of a eunuch. I knew I did not have much time, for whoever sent him was either awaiting his return or followed him here. He had no fragrance other than sweat of the horse he rode on whatever journey led him to be lying dead on Miss Wadada's floor. I turned him over and traced the glyphs on his back to remember. Two thoughts came to me, one just gone and one now come. Now come: that there was no blood, though where the knife stabbed him, blood usually bursts forth like a hot spring. Just gone: that the man really had no smell. The only scent coming from him was his horse, and the white clay from the wall he'd climbed.

I rolled him over again. Two glyphs on his chest matched the note. A crescent moon with a coiled serpent, the skeleton of a leaf on its side, and a star. Then his chest rumbled, but it was not the rattle of the dead. Something hitting against each bone of his ribs, pumping up his chest and his heart, making his eyes pop open. Then his mouth, but not like he was opening it, but as if someone was pulling his jaws apart, wider and wider until the corners of his lip began to tear. The rumble shook him all the way to his legs, which hammered into the floor. I jumped back and stood up. Ripples rose from his thighs, moved up to his belly, rolled under his chest, and then escaped through his mouth as a black cloud that stank of flesh much longer dead than the man. It swirled like a dust devil, getting wider and wider, so wide that it knocked over some of Ekoiye's statues. The spinner closed in tight on itself and turned to the window. In the spin of cloud and dust it formed and then broke apart back into dust, the bones of two black wings. It might have been a trick of poor light, or the sign of a witch. The spinning cloud left through the window. Back on the ground the man's skin turned gray, withering like a tree trunk. I stooped. He still had no scent. I touched his chest with one finger and it caved in, then his belly, legs, and head crumbled into dust.

Here is truth. In all the worlds I have never seen such craft or science. Whoever sent the assassin would

certainly be coming now. The man, or spirit, or creature, or god behind such a thing would not be stopped
by two daggers, or two hatchets.

His name, Basu Fumanguru, walked into my
thoughts right then. Not only did they kill him, but
they that did so wanted him to remain dead. I had
questions, and Bunshi would be the one to answer
them. She left the child with an enemy of the King,
but many men challenge the King in great halls and
in notices and writs, and they are not killed for it.
And if the child was marked for death, why not kill
him before? I have heard nothing that would push
anyone to get rid of Fumanguru that would not have
done so before, certainly no King. As a man he was
no more than a chafe on the inside of the leg. Then
the thought you knew you would be left with, but
denied because one would never wish to be left with
such a thought, announced itself. This Bunshi said
the Omoluzu came to kill Fumanguru and she saved
his child as his dying wish. But it was not his child.
Somebody told Ekoiye to send word as soon as someone came asking of Fumanguru, because somebody
knew one day a man would come to ask. Somebody has
been waiting for this, for me, for someone like me all
along. They were not after Fumanguru.

They were after the child.

TWELVE

lying outside my window was the flag of the black sparrow hawk. My return to Kongor disturbed no one, my waking earlier than the sun caught nobody, so I went outside. The flag flew two hundred, maybe three hundred paces away, at the top of a tower in the center of the Nyembe quarter, flapping wild, as if the wind was furious with it. Black sparrow hawk. Seven Wings. The sun was hiding behind clouds fat with rain. It was near the season. So I went outside.

In the courtyard, pulling up the few shrubs from the dirt, stood a buffalo. Male, brown-black, body longer than one and a half of me lying flat, his horns already fused into a crown and dipping downward to curve back upward like a grand hairstyle. Except I have seen a buffalo kill three hunters and rip a lion in two. So I gave this buffalo wide space as I walked to the archway. He looked up and moved right into my way. I remembered again I needed new hatchets, not that either hatchet or knife could win against him. I did not smell urine; I was not stepping into his boundary. The buffalo did not snort and did not kick his hooves in the dirt, but he stared at me, from my feet all the way up to my neck, then down, then up, then down, then up and slowly annoying me. Buffalos cannot laugh but I would swear to the gods that he did. Then he shook his head. More than a nod, a rough swing left then right, then right and left again. I stepped aside and walked but he stepped right in my way. I moved to the other side and so did he. He looked up and down again and again and I would again swear to the gods, demons, and river spirits that he laughed. He came in closer, and stepped back once. If he wanted to kill me I would have been walking with the ancestors already. He came closer, hooked his horn in the curtain I wore, and pulled it off, making me spin and fall. I cursed the buffalo, but did not grab the curtain. Besides, it was early morning—who would see me? And if anyone did see me, I could claim that I was robbed by bandits as I bathed in the river. Ten paces past the arch I looked back and saw that the buffalo followed me.

Here is truth: The Buffalo was the greatest of companions. In Kongor even old women slept late, so the only souls on the street were those who never slept. Palm wine drunkards and masuku beer fools, falling down more than they got up. My eye jumped over to their side each time we passed one of them, looking at them looking at a near-naked man walking alongside a buffalo not the way some walked with dogs, but how men walked with men. A man flat on his back in the road turned, saw us, jumped up, and ran right into a wall.

The river had flooded the banks four nights before we came, and Kongor was an island again for four moons. I marked my chest and legs with river clay, and the buffalo, lying in the grass and grazing, nodded up and down. I painted around my left eye, up to my hair and down to the cheekbone.

"Where are you from, good buffalo?"

He turned his head west and pointed with his horns up and down.

"West? By the Buki River?"

He shook his head.

"Beyond? In the savannah? Is there good water to be had there, buffalo?"

He shook his head.

"Is that why you roam? Or is there another reason?"

He nodded yes.

"Were you called upon by that fucking witch?"

He shook his head.

"Were you called upon by Sogolon?"

He nodded yes.

"When we were dead—"

He looked up and snorted.

"By dead I mean not dead, I mean when Sogolon was of a mind we were dead. She must have found others. Are you one of her others?"

He nodded yes.

"And already you have sharp thoughts about how I dress. I must say you are a particular buffalo."

He went off in the bush, his tail whipping flies. I heard a man's heavy footsteps through the grass fifty paces away and sat by the banks, my feet in the river. He moved closer; I pulled my dagger but did not turn around. The cold iron of a blade touched my right shoulder.

"Nasty boy, how you deh manage the things?" he asked.

"Deh managing them fine," I said, mocking his tongue.

"You lost? You look like is so."

"That be how me look?"

"Well, partner, you trotting round here, no robes on your person, like you mad or you a boy-lover, or a father-fucker or what?"

"I just washing my foot in the river."

"So you looking for the boy-lovers quarter."

"Just washing my foot in the river."

"For the boy-lovers quarter, that be, it be where now? Hold that bridle. We has no boy-lovers quarter round here."

"Eh? You sure you talking true? 'Cause last time me in the boy-lovers quarter, my eyes peep your father, and your grandfather."

He slapped the side of my head with his club. "Get up," he said. At least he wasn't about to slay me without a fight. On his back he strapped two axes.

Shorter than me by almost a head, but in the white bottom and black top of a Seven Wing. My first thought was to ignore his anger and ask why the Seven Wings assemble, since not even the wise Sogolon knows. He then said something to me in a thicker voice than before.

"Dats what we going do with men laka you?" this wing said.

"What?"

"Who you want me to send your head to, boy-fucker?"

"You wrong."

"How me wrong?"

"About me being the boy-fucker. Most time is the boys who fuck me. Hark, but there was this one, best in many a moon, so tight believe you me I has to stuff a corncob up to ease the hole. Then I ate the corn."

"Me chop off your bolo first, and then your head, then throw the rest of you in the river. How you liking that? And when you parts flow down de river, people going say luku laka pon the boy-fucker shoga rolling down in the river, don't drink from the river lest you become boy-fucker too."

"Chop me with those axes? I have been looking for iron as fine as such. Forged by a Wakadishu black-smith or did you steal them from a butcher's wife?"

"Drop the knife."

I looked at this man, not much taller than a boy, confusing stout with muscular and dashing shit on my quiet morning. I dropped the dagger in my hand and the one strapped to my leg.

"I would love to greet this sun and bid it good-bye without killing a man," I said. "There are some people above the sand sea who have a feast every year where they leave a space empty for a ghost, a man who was once alive."

He laughed, pointing the club at me with his left hand, and pulling an ax with his right. Then he dropped the club and pulled out the left ax.

"Maybe me should be doing the killing for you mad tongue, and not you perverse ways."

He waved his axes in front of me, swinging and swirling them, but I did not move. The mercenary stepped forward just as a wad of something hit the back of his neck.

"Aunt of a donkey!"

He swung around just as the buffalo snorted again, and nose juice hit the warrior in the face. Eye-to-eye with the buffalo, he jumped. Before he could swing an ax, the buffalo scooped up the warrior with his horns and threw him off far into the grass. One ax landed in the field. The other came straight at me but bounced off. I cursed the buffalo. It was some time before the warrior sat up, shook his head, rose to his feet, and staggered off when the buffalo rushed him again.

"You took your time. I could have made bread."

He trotted off and slapped me with his tail as he passed. I laughed and picked up my new axes.

The house had woken up by the time I got back.
The buffalo stooped in the grass and sunk his head
on the ground. I said he was as lazy as an old grandmother and he swished his tail at me. In a corner near
the center doorway sat Sogolon, and a man I assumed
was the lord of the house. Bisabol blew out of him,
expensive perfume from lands above the sand sea. A
white wrap around his head and under his chin, thin
enough that I could see his skin. A white gown with
a pattern of the millet plant, and over that a coat,
coffee dark.

"Where is the girl?" I asked.

"Down some street, annoying some woman, because clothes remain something that fascinates her.
Truly, old friend, she never ever seen the like," Sogolon said.

The man nodded before I realized she was not
speaking to me. He took a puff of his pipe, then
handed it to her. The smoke from her mouth I would
have taken for a cloud, it was so thick. She had drawn
six runes in the dirt with a stick and was scratching a
seventh.

"And how is the Tracker managing Kongor?" he
asked, though he still did not look at me. I thought
he was speaking to Sogolon in that rude way men
who are rich and powerful can speak about you right
in front of you. Too early in the day to make men test
you, I said to myself.

"He not one for the Kongori custom to cover his
snake," Sogolon said.

"Indeed. They whipped a woman . . . seven days ago? No, eight, it was. They found her leaving the house of a man not her husband without her outer robes."

"What did they do with the man?" I said.

"What?"

"The man, was he whipped as well?"

The man looked at me as if I had just spoken in one of the river tongues even I don't know.

"When do we go to the house?" I said to Sogolon.

"You didn't go last night?"

"Not to Fumanguru's."

She turned away from me, but I would not be flashed off by these two.

"This grand peace is walking on a crocodile's back, Sogolon. Is not just Kongor and is not just Seven Wings. Men who don't fight since the Prince was just born are getting word that they must reach for armour and weapon, and assemble. Seven Wings assemble in Mitu as well, and other warriors under other names. The Malakal you left, and the Uwomowomowomowo valley, both now gleam from the iron and gold of armour, spear, and sword," the man said.

"And ambassadors roam each city. Sweat not from heat but from worry," she said.

"This I know. Five days ago four men from Weme Witu come for talks, for all come to Kongor to settle disputes. Nobody see them since."

"What they disputing?"

"What they dispute? Not like you to get deaf ears to the movement of people."

She laughed.

"Here is a true thing. Years before this skinny boy's mother spread her koo to piss him out, right before they mark the peace on paper and iron, the South retreat back to the South."

"Yes, yes, yes. They retreat south, but not full south," Sogolon said.

"The old Kwash Netu give them back a bone. Wakadishu after conquering it."

"I was just in Kalindar and Wakadishu."

"But Wakadishu never liked that arrangement, not at all. They say Kwash Netu betray them, he sell them back to slavery under the southern King. They been bawling for years upon years and this new King—"

"Kwash Dara looking like he hear," she said.

"And all this movement up north making the South rumble. Sogolon, word be that the mad King's head is again infected with devils."

This was annoying me more and more. Both were saying things the other already knew. Not even discussing, or reasoning or arguing or repeating, but finishing each other's thoughts, like they were talking to each other but still not to me.

"Earth and sky already hear enough," Sogolon said.

"You talk of kings and wars and rumors of war as if anybody cares. You're just a witch, here to find a boy. As is everybody, except him," I said, pointing to the lord. "Does he even know why we're under his roof? See, I too can talk around a man as if he's not there."

"You said he have a nose, not a mouth," the lord said.

"We waste time talking about politics," I said, and walked past them inside.

"No one speaks to you," Sogolon said, but I did not turn back.

Upstairs one floor, the Leopard came towards me. I couldn't read his face, but this was a long time coming. So let us have it out, with words or fists or knives and claws, and whoever is left let him have at the boy, you to fuck him, me to beat him with a shit stick, and send him right back to whatever thing shat him out. Yes, let us have this. The Leopard ran up, almost knocking over two of the dozen statues and carvings in the hallway, and embraced me.

"Good Tracker, I feel I have not seen you in days."

"It has been days. You couldn't pull yourself out of sleep."

"This is a true word. I feel as if I was sleeping for years. And I wake to such dismal rooms. Come now, what sport is there in this city?"

"Kongor? In a city pious as this even the mistresses seek marriage."

"I already love it. Yet is there not some other reason we are here? We hunt a boy, do we not?"

"You don't remember?"

"I remember and I do not."

"You remember the Darklands?"

"We went through the Darklands?"

"You were one for harsh words."

"Harsh? To whom? Fumeli? You know he likes when we spar. Are you not hungry? I saw a buffalo outside and thought to kill it, or at least bite off the tail, but he seems an ingenious buffalo."

"This is very strange, Leopard."

"Tell me at the table. What happened these few days since we left the valley?"

I told him we were gone a moon. He said that was madness and refused to hear any more.

"I hear the gap in my belly. It growls obscene," he said.

This table was in a great hall, with plate after plate of scenes covering all the walls in the room. I got to the tenth plate before I saw that these works of the grand bronze masters all showed scenes of fucking.

"This is strange," I said again.

"I know. I keep looking for one where the cock goes in the mouth hole or the boo hole but I couldn't find any. But I hear this is a town of no shoga. How could that be tru—"

"No. It's strange that you remember nothing. The Ogo remembers everything."

The Leopard, being a Leopard, ignored the chairs and jumped up on the table, not making a sound. He grabbed the bird leg from a silver tray, crouched on his heels, and bit into it. I could tell he did not like it. Leopards eat all things, but there was no rush of blood, hot and rich, spilling into his mouth and over his lips as he bit into it, which always made him frown.

"You are the one strange, Tracker, with your riddles and half meanings. Sit, eat porridge while I eat—what is this, ostrich? I've never had ostrich, could never catch one. You said the Ogo is remembering?"

"Yes."

"What does he remember? Being in the enchanted bush? I remember that."

"What else?"

"A great slumber. Traveling but not moving. A long scream. What does the Ogo remember?"

"Everything, it seems. His whole life came back to him. Do you remember when we set out? You had a problem with me."

"We must have solved it, for I do not remember it."

"If you heard yourself, you would not have thought so."

"You are confusing, Tracker. I sit and eat with you, and there is love between us that until now was the kind we never had to declare. So stop living in a squabble so little that I cannot remember it, even with you prompting me. When do we go to the boy's house? Shall we go now?"

"Yesterday you wer—"

"Kwesi!" his arrow boy shouted, and dropped the basket he was carrying. Maybe I did forget his name out of spite. He came over to the table, not looking or even nodding at me.

"You are not well enough to be eating strange things," he said to the Leopard.

"Here is meat and here is bone. Nothing is strange."

"Go back to the room."

"I am well."

"You are not."

"Are you deaf?" I said. "He said he is well."

Fumeli tried to glare at me and fuss over the Leopard with the same face, but it came out as him fussing a little over me and glaring a little at the Leopard. Even when it was not funny, this boy provoked me to laugh. He stomped off, grabbing his basket on the way out. One of his little parcels fell out. Cured pig, I could smell it. Supplies. The Leopard sat down on the table and crossed his legs.

"I should lose him soon."

"You should have lost him moons ago," I mumbled.

"What?"

"Nothing, Leopard. There are things I must tell you. Not here. I do not trust these walls. Truly there are some strange things here."

"You've said this four times now. Why is everything strange, friend?"

"The black puddle woman."

"It's these statues that bother me. I feel like an army is going to watch me fuck at night."

He grabbed one of the statues by the neck, and grinned that wide smile I couldn't remember when last I saw.

"This one the most," he said.

"Grab your bird," I said.

We wrapped our waists in cloths and walked south

to Gallunkobe/Matyube. The freemen and slave quarter, also the poorest, except for vulgar houses that spread wide instead of tall for freemen with much coin, but no noble air. Most of the houses were one room or hall, and packed so tight that they shared the same roof. Not even a rat could squeeze between each wall. The towers and roofs of the Nyembe quarter made it look like a huge fort or a castle, but no towers rose in this quarter. Freemen and slaves had no need to watch anyone, but everyone needed to watch them. And despite having the most men and women sleeping there at night, by day it was the emptiest quarter, freemen and slaves at work in the other three.

"When did Bunshi tell you such a story?"

"When? Good cat, you were there."

"I was? I don't . . . yes I do remember . . . memory comes forth, then slips away."

"Memory must be one of them who heard what you do in bed."

He chuckled.

"But, Tracker, I remember it as if somebody told me, not as if I was there. I have no smell of it. So strange."

"Yes, strange. Whatever that Fumeli makes you smoke, stop smoking such."

I was happy to talk to the Leopard, as I always am, and I did not want to bring up the sourness of the days past—one moon past, a fact that staggered him every time I said it. I think I know why. Time is flat to all animals; they measure it in when to eat, when to sleep, when to breed, so missed time to him feels a board with a huge hole punched out.

"The slaver said the boy was his partner's son, now an orphan. Men kidnapped the boy from his housekeeper and murdered all others in that house. Then he said the house belonged to his aunt, not his housekeeper. Then we saw him and Nsaka Ne Vampi try to pry information out of the lightning girl, who we set free but then she jumped off a cliff and landed in Nyka's cage."

"You tell me things I know. Everything but this lightning woman in the cage. And I remember thinking for sure this slaver lies, but not about what."

"Leopard, that was when Bunshi poured herself down the wall and said the boy was not that boy, but another who was the son of Basu Fumanguru, who was an elder, and on the Night of the Skulls the Omoluzu attacked the house and killed everyone but the boy who was then a baby and who Bunshi hid in her womb to save him, but then she took him to a blind woman in Mitu who she thought she could trust, but the blind woman sold him to a slave market where a merchant bought him, perhaps for his barren wife, but then they were attacked by men of malicious means. A hunter took the boy and now none can find him."

"Slow, good friend. None of this I remember."

"And that is not all, Leopard, for I found another elder, who called himself Belekun the Big, who said the family died of river sickness, which was false, but the family was eight, which was true, and of it six were sons and none were just born."

"What are you saying, Tracker?"

"Do you not remember when I told you this on the lake?"

The Leopard shook his head.

"Belekun was always liar and I had to kill him, especially when he tried to kill me. But he had no reason to lie about this, so Bunshi must have. Yes, Omoluzu killed Basu Fumanguru's family, and yes, many know this including her, but that the boy we seek was not his son as he had no young sons."

The Leopard still looked confused. But he raised his brow as if a truth suddenly struck him.

"But, Leopard," I continued, "I have done some looking and some digging and somebody here in this city also asks of Fumanguru, meaning they asked to be told if somebody asks, which means the closed matter of the dead elder is not so closed, because one thing remains open, this missing boy who is not his son, and though he may not be his son, he is the reason why others search for him and why we search for him and given that Fumanguru was an annoyance but not a real enemy of the King, whoever sent roof walkers to his house was not there to kill the family but was there for the boy, who Fumanguru must have been protecting. They too know he is alive."

I told the Leopard all this and this is truth, I was more confused by the telling than he was by listening. Only when he repeated all that I said did I understand it. We were still ankle deep in the water when he said, "You know this buffalo stands behind us as we speak."

"I know."

"Can we trust him?"

"He looks like a trustworthy beast."

"If he lies, I will bring him down with my jaws and make supper out of him."

The buffalo snorted and started kicking up his right front leg in the water.

"He jests," I said to the buffalo.

"A little," the Leopard said. "To this man's house with us. These robes make my balls itch."

Sadogo sat on the floor in his room, punching his left palm with his right hand and setting off sparks. I stepped into the doorway and stayed there. He saw me.

"There he was. I grabbed his neck and squeezed until his head popped off. And her, her too, I swung this hand, this I hold up right here and slapped her so hard that I broke her neck. Soon the masters would gather seats and men and women who paid cowrie, and corn, and cows to watch me execute women, and children, and men with my hands. Soon they built seats in a circle and charged money and cast bets. Not for who would best me, for no man can ever best an Ogo. But for who would last longest. The children their necks I breaked quick so they would not suffer.

This made them mad—who would watch, for they must have it, don't you see? Don't you see, they must have show. Curse the gods and fuck them all in the ears and ass, they will have a show, that is what I tell you."

I knew what would happen. I left the Ogo. He would be talking all night, no matter the misery such talk caused him. Part of me wanted to give him ears, for there was depth there, things he had done that he buried wherever Ogos bury their dead. The Leopard was already grabbing his crotch when he went in the room with Fumeli. Sogolon was gone, and so was the girl and the lord of the house. I wanted to go to Fumanguru's home, but did not want to go alone.

There was nothing to do but wait on the Leopard. Down the stairs, night crept up without me even seeing it. Kongor plays as a righteous city under sunlight, but turns into what all righteous cities turn into under the dark. Fires lit up patches of the sky, from the Bingingun far off. Drums at times jumped over roofs, and above the road, and shook our windows, while lutes, flute, and horns sneaked in under. I did not see a single man in Bingingun all day. I went out the window and sat in the sill, looking across to rooms with flickering lights, few, and rooms already dark, many. Fumeli, wearing a rug, walked past me carrying a lamp. He returned shortly after, passing me again carrying a wineskin. I followed him, ten and two or so paces behind. He left the door open.

"Grab your bow, or at least a good sword. No, make it daggers, we go with daggers," I said.

The Leopard rolled around in the bed. On his back he snatched the wineskin from Fumeli, who did not look at me.

"You drink palm wine now?"

"I'll drink blood if I wish," he said.

"Leopard, time is not something we have to lose. Kwesi."

"Fumeli, tell me this. Is it ill wind blowing under that window, or is it you speaking in a tone that sours me?"

Fumeli laughed quiet.

"Leopard, what is this?"

"What is this indeed? What is this? What is this, Tracker? What. Is. This?"

"This is about the house of the boy. The house that we are going to visit. The house that might tell us where he went."

"We know where he's gone. Nyka and that bitch of his already found him."

"How do you know? Some drums told you? Or a little whore whispered something before sunset?"

A growl, but from Fumeli, not him.

"I go to only one place, Tracker. I go to sleep."

"You plan to find him in dreams? Or maybe you plan to send your little maiden here."

"Get out," Fumeli said.

"No no no. You do not speak to me. And I only speak to him."

"And if the him is me, then I say, you don't speak to him or me," the Leopard said.

"Leopard, are you mad or is this some game to you? Are there two children in this room?"

"I'm not a chil—"

"Shut up, boy, by all the gods I'll—"

The Leopard jumped up. "By all the gods you will . . . what?"

"What is this relapse? First you are hot then you are cold, you are one thing, and then you are another. Is this little bitch bewitching you? I don't care. We go now and argue later."

"We leave tomorrow."

The Leopard walked over to the window. Fumeli sat up in the bed, stealing looks at me.

"Oh. So we are in these waters again," I said.

"How funny you talk," Fumeli said. In my mind my hands were at his throat.

"Yes. In those waters, as you've said. We go our own way to find the boy tomorrow. Or we don't. Either way we leave here," the Leopard said.

"I told you about the boy. Why we need to find—"

"You tell me many things, Tracker. Not much of it any use. Now please go where you came from."

"No. I will find what is this madness."

"Madness, Tracker, is you thinking I would ever work with you. I can't even stand drinking with you. Your envy stinks, did you know it stinks? It stinks as much as your hate."

"Hate?"

"It confused me once."

"You're confused."

"But then I realized that you are full from head to toe with nothing but malcontent. You cannot help yourself. You even fight it, sometimes well. Enough for me to let you lead me astray."

"Fuck the gods, cat, we are working together."

"You work with no one. You had plans—"

"To what, take the money?"

"You said it, not I. Did you hear him say it, Fumeli?"

"Yes."

"Shut that fucking ass mouth, boy."

"Leave us," said the Leopard.

"What did you do to him?" I said to Fumeli. "What did you do?"

"Other than open my eyes? I don't think Fumeli seeks credit. He's not you, Tracker."

"You don't even sound—"

"Like myself?"

"No. You don't even sound like a man. You're a boy whose toys Father took away."

"There's no mirror in this room."

"What?"

"Leave, Tracker."

"Fuck the gods and fuck this little shit."

I jumped at Fumeli. Leapt onto the bed and grabbed his neck. He slapped at me, the little bitch in him too weak to do anything else, and I squeezed. "I knew you consulted with witches," I said. A big, black hairy mess knocked me down and I hit my head hard. The Leopard, full black and one with the dark, scratched my face with his paw. I grabbed at his neck skin, and we rolled over and over on the floor. I punched at him and missed. He ducked right down to my head and clamped his jaws on my neck. I couldn't breathe. He clamped and swung his head, to break my neck.

"Kwesi!"

The Leopard dropped me. I wheezed air and coughed up spit.

The Leopard growled at me, then roared, almost as loud as a lion. It was a "get out" kind of roar. Get out and don't come back.

I headed for the door, wiping my wet neck. Spit and a little blood.

"Don't be here tomorrow," I said. "Neither of you."

"We don't take orders from you," Fumeli said. The Leopard paced by the window, still a Leopard.

"Don't be here tomorrow," I said again.

I went to the Ogo's room.

Bingingun. This is what I learned from the Kongori and why they hate nakedness. To wear only skin is to wear the mind of a child, the mind of the mad, or even the mind of the man with no role in society, even lower than usurers and trinket sellers, for even such as they have their use. Bingingun is how people of the North set a place for the dead among the living. Bingingun is the masquerade, drummers and dancers and singers of great oriki. They wear the aso oke cloth underneath, and this cloth is white with indigo stripes, and looks like that with which we clothe

the dead. They wear net on the face and hands, for now they will be masquerade, not men with names. When the Bingingun spins and makes a whirlwind the ancestors possess them. They jump high as roofs.

He who makes the costume is an amewa, a knower of beauty, for if you know the Kongori they view everything through the eye of what is beautiful. Not ugly, for that has no value, especially ugliness of character. And not too beautiful, for that is a skeleton in disguise. Bingingun is made from the best of fabrics, red, and pink, and gold, and blue, and silver, all trimmed in cowries and coins, for there is power in the beauty. In patterns, braids, sequins, tassels, and amulets with medicine. Bingingun in dance, Bingingun in march, make for transformation into the ancestors. All this I learned on my travels, for Juba has masquerade, but they are not Bingingun.

I said all this to the Ogo because we followed a procession on the way to the house so that a man as tall as he would not look strange in the torchlight. He still looked strange. Five drummers in front setting the dance—three beating barrel drums, a fourth beating a double-skin bata, and the fifth beating four small bata tied together to make a sound pitched high like a crow call. Following the drummers came the Bingingun, among them the Ancestor King in royal robes and a cowrie veil, and the Trickster, whose robes turned inside out to another robe, and yet another robe, as the Bingingun all swirled and stomped to the drum, **boom-boom-bakalak-bakalaka, bakalakalakalaka-**

boom-boom-boom. Ten and five of this clan shuffled to the left then stomped, then shuffled to the right and hopped. I said all this to the Ogo so that he would not start talking again of whom he had killed with his hands and how there is nothing in this world or the next like the sound of the crushing of skull. Sadogo's face was lost to me in the dark, and as he stood taller than the torches, he waved his hands in the air with the Bingingun, marched when they marched, and stopped when they stopped.

Here is truth. I did not know which house was Fumanguru's, other than that it was in the Tarobe quarter, north of the Nimbe boundary, and that it would be almost hidden by massive growths of thornbush. I said, "Good Ogo, let us look. Let us walk street to street, and stop by which house burns no light and hides in branches that will prick and cut us."

Outside the fourth house Sadogo grabbed a torch from the wall. At the ninth house I smelled it, the fire stink of sulfur, still fresh in its scent after so many years. Most of the houses on this street stacked themselves tight beside each other, but this stood apart, now an island of thornbush. Larger than the other houses, from how it looked in the dark, the bush had grown wide and tall, reaching all the way up the front door.

We went around the back. The Ogo was still quiet. He wore his gloves, not listening when I said they were no use against the dead. Look at how they failed to save you from Ogudu, I thought, but did not say.

He tore away the branches until it was safe to climb. We jumped the back wall and landed in a thick blanket of grass. Wild grass left to grow tall, some of it to my waist. Omoluzu had without a doubt been here. Only plants that grew off the dead grew here.

We stood in the courtyard, right beside the grain keep, with millet and sorghum gone sour from getting wet from many rains, caked with rat shit and fresh with rat pups. The house, a cluster of dwellings, five points like a star, was not what I expected in Kongor. Fumanguru was no Kongori. Sadogo placed the torch in the dirt and lit up the whole courtyard.

"Spoiled meat, fresh shit, dead dog? I can't tell," the Ogo said.

"All three, perhaps," I said.

I pointed to the first dwelling on the right. Sadogo nodded and followed. This first dwelling told me how I would find the rest. Everything left the way Omoluzu left it. Stools broken, jars crushed, tapestry ripped down, rugs and clothes torn and thrown about. I grabbed a blanket. Hidden in the smell of dirt and rain two boys, the youngest, perhaps, but the smell went as far as the wall and died. All the dead smell the same, but sometimes their living smell can take you to the point where they died.

"Sadogo, how do the Kongori bury their dead?"

"Not in the earth. In urns, too big for this room."

"If they had a choice. Fumanguru's family might have been dumped somewhere, appalling the gods. Maybe burned?"

"Not the Kongori," he said. "They believe burning a body frees into air what killed him."

"How do you know?"

"I killed a few. This was how it went. I—"

"Not now, Sadogo."

We went to the next room, which, judging by the Mojave wood bed, must have been Fumanguru's. His wall was all scenes—hunting, mostly—carved into the wood. Shattered statues and books on the floor, and loose paper as well, probably torn out of the books. Omoluzu would not have cared, but the third, fourth, and fifth person to visit this room would have, including Sogolon, whom I smelled since we stepped into the master room, but I did not tell the Ogo. I wondered if, unlike the others who had been here, she found what she was looking for.

"Word was that Basu Fumanguru wrote many writs against the King. Twenty or thirty articles in total, some with testimony to his wrongdoing from subjects, and nobles, and princes he wronged. There was a man who I had words with. He said that people searched for the writs, and that is why he was killed. But what little I know of Fumanguru tells me he is no fool. Also surely he would wish his words to not die with him," I said.

"These writs are not here?"

"No. Not only that, good Ogo, but I don't think that is what people were looking for. Remember the boy? Bunshi said she saved him."

A sword glimmered on the floor. I hated swords

now. Too bulky, too much force against wind when it should be working with her, but I took it up anyway. It was halfway in its sheath. I would need to come back under sunlight, for I had nothing now to guide me but my nose. A man was all over this room, Fumanguru perhaps, and a woman too, but their smells ended in this room, meaning they were dead. Outside, I turned to the room beside another dwelling for servants and the youngest children. I could tell that whoever buried the family either did not see or did not care that a servant was under the broken wood and torn rugs. All that was left lying there was her bones, still together, but flesh all eaten away. I stepped in and the Ogo followed me. His head scraped the ceiling. I grinned, tripped over an overturned urn, and fell hard. Fuck the gods, I said, even though a pile of cloths broke my fall. Robes. Even in the dark I could tell their luxury. Gold trim, but thin fabric, so the wife's. This must be where the servant kept clothes dried after a wash. But there was fragrance in the thin robe that no wash could wash out. Frankincense. It took me out of this room and back into the master's room and then out into the middle of the courtyard and back into the large room beside the grain keep.

"They're in there, Sadogo."

"Under earth?"

"No. In urns."

With no windows, this room was the darkest, but thank the gods for the strength of the Ogo. He pulled the lid off the largest, which I assumed was

Basu, but the frankincense still there told me it was the wife.

"Sadogo, your torch."

He stood up and fetched it. In the urn, there she was, body curled wrong, with her back touching the soles of her feet. Her skull rested in her hair, her bones peeking out of the fabric.

"They broke her back?" Sadogo said.

"No, they cut her in two."

The second urn, smaller but bigger than the others, housed Fumanguru. All his bones collected but broken apart. Deep blue robes like a king's. Whoever buried them stole nothing, for surely they would have taken so luxurious a robe, even off a man diseased. His face bones were smashed, which happened when Omoluzu ripped off a face to wear it. Another large urn housed two children, a small urn housed one. The small child's bones in the small urn now almost powder, except for his arms and ribs. Like the others, he smelled of long-passed death and fading fragrance. Nothing to preserve or mummify the bodies, which meant the story of infection had spread. I nodded at Sadogo to cover the last urn when just a little thing winked at me.

"The torch again, Sadogo."

I looked up, just as the Ogo wiped a tear from his cheek. He was thinking of killed children, but not this one.

"What is that he's holding?" I asked.

"Parchment? A piece of clay?"

I grabbed it. Cloth, simple as aso oke fabric, but not. I pulled at it, but the boy would not let go. He died with this, his last show of defiance, the poor, brave child. I halted the thought before it went further. One more pull and it was free. A piece of blue cloth torn from something bigger. The boy was wrapped in white. I put the cloth to my nose and one year of sun, night, thunder, and rain, hundreds of days of walks, dozens of hills, valleys, sands, seas, houses, cities, plains. Smell so strong it became sigh, and hearing and touch. I could reach out and touch the boy, grab him in my mind and reel from him being so far away. Too far away, my head rushing and jumping and sinking below sea then flying higher and higher and higher and smelling air free of smoke. Smell pushing me, pulling me, dragging me through jungles, tunnels, birds, ripped flesh, flesh-eater insects, shit, piss, and blood. Blood rushed into me. So much blood my eyes went red, then black.

So gone I thought you would never return," Sadogo said.

I rolled on my side and sat up.

"How long?"

"Not long but deep like in sleep. Your eye was milk white. I thought demons were in your head, but no froth came to your mouth."

"It happens only when I am not expecting it. I smell something and someone's life comes to me all in a rush. It is a madness, even now when I have learned to master it. But, Ogo, there is something."

"Another dead body?"

"No, the boy."

He looked in the urn.

"No, the boy we seek. He is alive. And I know where he is."

THIRTEEN

Truly, it was foolish to say I found the boy. I found that he was far away. The Ogo, on hearing my news, grabbed his torch and dashed off to his left, then right, then went into the children's dwelling, and yanked up so many rugs that a cloud of dust rose up and made itself known, even in the dark.

"The boy is nearly three moons away," I said.

"What does that mean?" he said. He was still lifting rugs and waving his torch.

"About as far as the East from the West."

He threw down the rugs and the gust blew out the torch.

"Well at least coming all this way served a purpose," he said.

"I wonder what purpose it served Sogolon," I mumbled.

"What?"

I forgot that Ogos had sharp ears. She was here before and not that long ago, perhaps even last night.

Back in Fumanguru's room, among the fallen books and ripped papers, her smell came on most strong. I made one step into the room and stopped. The smell came to me at once, and from every side. Shea butter mixed with charcoal, used on the face and skin to become one with the dark.

"We go out, Sadogo."

He turned to head to the back wall.

"No, through the front door. It's already open."

We cut through the bush and walked right into a group of armed men. Sadogo pulled back, surprised, but I was not. They wore skin dye to blend with night black. I heard the crunch and scrape of the Ogo squeezing his iron knuckles. Ten and five of them standing in a half-moon, lake-blue turbans on their heads, lake-blue veils covering all but eye and nose. A sash the same blue across chest and back, black tunic and breeches underneath. And with spear, bow, spear, bow, spear, bow, and on and on, till the last one, carrying a sword on his left, sheathed, like mine. I held on to my sword but did not pull it out. Sadogo stepped once and knocked an archer out of his way, sending him and the arrow flying. The men turned to him in a blink, pulling back bows and ready to hurl spears. The man with the sword was not dressed as they. He wore a red cape over his right shoulder and under his left, flapping in the wind and slapping the ground. A tunic with the chest open that stopped right above his thighs and tied at the waist with a leather belt that held his sword. He waved them down, but watched me the whole time. Sadogo stood in position, waiting for a fight.

"You look certain we're not going to kill you," the swordsman said.

"Mine is not the death I worry about," I said.

The swordsman glared at us. "I am Mossi, third prefect of the Kongori chieftain army."

"We took nothing," I said.

"Such a sword could not be yours. Not when I saw it three nights before."

"You waiting for anyone, or just us?"

"Leave questions to me and answers to yourself."

He came in closer until he was right in front of me. He was tall but shorter than me, his eyes almost reached mine, and his face was hidden in black dye. Gourd helmet with an iron stitch running in the middle, though the sun was gone and it was cool. A thin silver necklace, lost in chest bush. Head shaped sharp like an arrowpoint, nose hawk-like, thick lips that curved up as if he was smiling, and eyes so clear I could see them in the dark. Rings in both ears.

"Tell me when you see something that pleases you," he said.

"That sword is not Kongori," I said.

"No. It belonged to a slaver from the land of the eastern light. Caught him kidnapping free women to sell as slaves. Wouldn't part with it without parting with his hand, so . . ."

"You are the second sword thief I have met."

"Steal from a thief and the gods smile. What is your name?"

"Tracker."

"Not your mother's favorite, then."

He was close enough for me to feel his breath.

"There's a devil living in your eye," he said.

He reached for it with his finger and I flinched.

"Or did he punch you one night?" He pointed at Sadogo.

"Not a devil. A wolf," I said.

"So when the moon bares herself do you howl at it?"

I said nothing, but watched his men. He pointed at Sadogo, who still tensed his arms, waiting to strike.

"Is he an Ogo?"

"Try to kill him and find out."

"Nevertheless, this conversation continues at the fort. That way." He pointed east.

"Is that the fort no prisoner leaves? What if we choose not to go?"

"Then this talk between us, sweet and easy, becomes difficult."

"We'll kill at least seven of your men."

"And my men are very generous with their spears. I can lose seven. Can you lose one? This is not an arrest. I prefer talk where streets don't listen. Do we understand each other?"

The fort was in the Nimbe quarter near the east bank of the river, with a view of the imperial docks. We went down steps into a room made out of stone and mortar. Two chairs and a table. Candles on the table, which surprised me—candles were not cheap anywhere. I was sitting long enough for a cramp to shock my left leg. I stood up when the Prefect came in. He had washed his face. Black hair that when long would be loose and curly, but thin like the hair of a horse. Hair I have not seen since I was lost in the sand sea. And skin light as dried clay. Men who followed the eastern light looked like this, or men who bought slaves, gold, and civet, but slaves the most. His eyes made sense to me now, and his lips, which looked thicker now but still thinner than anybody else's in these lands. I could already think of how Ku women and Gangatom women would be horrified at a man looking like this. They would have tied him down and baked him until his skin was the right dark. Legs like the Leopard's, thick with muscle, as if he fought in a war. Kongori sun made his legs darker. I could tell when he pulled his tunic up higher, past where they were before, high enough to show how light the rest of his legs were and how black his loincloth. He pulled the fabric out of his belt and it fell this time below his knee.

"Expecting a jinn to seat you?" He sat on the table.

"Did a pigeon tell you I was coming?" I asked.

"No."

"Did you—"

"I am the one to ask the questions."

"So I am the one to be charged with robbery."

"That mouth again, 'tis like a loose bowel. I can plug it."

I glared at him quiet. He smiled.

"Brilliant answer," he said.

"I said nothing."

"Your best answer yet. But no. No robbery, since you would be the thief's fool. But murder is untaken."

"Kongori jokes. Still the worst in the empire."

"As I'm not Kongori you should be of more laughter. As for these murders."

"You cannot kill the dead."

"Your friend the Ogo already confessed to killing twenty in just as many lands, and shows no sign he will stop."

I sighed loud. "He was an executioner. He knows not what he speaks," I said.

"He certainly knows much about killing."

He looked older than he did in the dark. Or maybe bigger. I really wanted to see his sword.

"Why did you come to Fumanguru's house tonight?" I asked.

"Perhaps I am heedless. People with blood on their hands tend to wash it where they shed it."

"That is the most foolish thing I have ever heard."

"You cast a foolish hand, moving in masquerade and climbing over thornbush yet expecting none to take note."

"I track lost people."

"We found them all."

"You did not find one."

"Fumanguru had one wife and six boys. They are all accounted for. I counted them. Then we sent for an elder who has since moved to Malakal. Belekun was his name. He confirmed all eight were blood."

"How soon after did he move?" I asked.

"One, two moons."

"Did he find the writ?"

"The what?"

"Something he was looking for."

"How do you know the elder was looking for anything?"

"You are not the only one with big, fat friends, prefect."

"Do you itch, Tracker?"

"What?"

"Itch. You scratched your chest seven times now. I would guess you are those river types who shun clothes. Luala Luala, or Gangatom?"

"Ku."

"Even worse. Yet you say writ as if you know what it is. You might have even been looking for it."

He sat back down on the stool, looked at me, and laughed. I could not remember anyone, man, woman, beast, or spirit who irritated me so. Not even Leopard's boy.

"Basu Fumanguru. How many enemies had he in this city?" I asked.

"You forget I am the one to ask questions."

"Not any wise ones. I think you should jump to

that time of the night when you torture me for the answers you want."

"Sit down. Now."

"I could—"

"You could, had you your little weapons. I will not ask again."

I sat back down.

He walked around me five times before he stopped and sat down again, pulling his stool next to me.

"Let us not talk of murder. Do you even know which part of the city you were in? You would have been detained merely for casting strange looks. So what took you to the house? A three-year-old murder or something you knew would still be there, untouched, even unspoilt? I will tell you what I know of Basu Fumanguru. He was loved by the people. Every man knows of his clashes with the King. Every woman knows of his clashes with his fellow elders. They killed him for some other reason."

"They?" I asked.

"What happened to those bodies could not have been by one man, if done by man at all, and not some beast bewitched."

He looked at me so long and so quiet that I opened my mouth, not to speak, just to look as if I was going to.

"I have something to show you," he said.

He left the room. I heard flies. I wondered how they questioned the Ogo, or if they just left him alone to unspool how many he has killed in as many years.

And what about me? Was all this the Ogudu, or did the forest itself leave something in me, waiting to strike? Something other than a reminder of my loneliness? Also this. What a strange thought to be had right here, when a prefect is trying to trap me into whatever charge he long thought to make up.

He walked back in and threw something at me so quick that I caught it before I knew what it was. Black and stuffed soft with feathers, wrapped in the same aso oke cloth that I had shoved into this curtain I was wearing. I was ready this time when it came, everything that came with a smell I now knew.

"A doll," he said.

"I know what it is."

"We found it three years ago near the body of the youngest boy."

"A boy can play with dolls."

"No child in Kongor would have been given one. Kongori think it's training children in the way of worshipping idols—a terrible sin."

"And yet every house has statues."

"They just like statues. But this doll belonged to no one in that house."

"Fumanguru was not Kongori."

"An elder would have respected their traditions."

"Maybe the doll belonged to the killer."

"The killer is one year old?"

"What are you saying?"

"I am saying there was one more child in that

house. Maybe whoever killed the family came for the child. Or something else, much more wild," he said.

"That does sound wild. The child, a poor relation?"

"We spoke to all family."

"So did Belekun the Big. Maybe you asked questions together?"

"Are you saying the elders are doing their own investigation?"

"I say you and I are not the only ones who went messing around dead Fumanguru's house. Whatever they sought, I don't think they found it. This is not feeling like an interrogation anymore, prefect."

"It stopped being so when we entered the room, Tracker. And I told you my name is Mossi. Now do you want to tell me how you just appeared in this city? There's no record of your entry, and Kongor is nothing if not a place of records."

"I came through a door."

He stared at me, then laughed. "I will remember to ask next time I see you."

"You will see me again?"

"Time is but a boy, sir Tracker. You are free to go."

I walked to the door.

"The Ogo as well. We have run out of words to describe his killings."

He smiled. He had rolled up his tunic right above his thigh—better for running, and battle.

"I have a question," I said.

"Only one now?"

I wish he were not so eager to show me he is quick-witted. Few things I hated more than to have a sentence cut off by somebody throwing wit. Again, something about him, not offensive but more irritating than a cut underfoot.

"Why do Seven Wings assemble? Here. Now," I asked.

"Because they cannot be seen in Fasisi."

"What?"

"Because they would raise suspicion in Fasisi."

"That is not an answer."

"Not the answer you want, so here is another. They await instructions from the King."

"Why?"

"Wherever you came from, have they no news there?"

"Not what you are about to tell me."

"You seem sure I'm about to tell you. There is no news. But rumors of war, there have been for moons now. No, not war, occupation. Have you not heard this, Tracker? The mad King in the South has gone mad again. After ten and five years of sense, his head is again taken by devils. Last moon he sent four thousand men to the borders of Kalindar and Wakadishu. The South King mobilizes an army, the North King mobilizes mercenaries. As we say in Kongor: We cannot find the body, but we smell the stench. But alas, war or no, people still steal. People still lie. People still kill. And my work is never done. Go get your Ogo.

Until we meet again. You can give me the story of your single dim eye."

I left this man to go irritate someone else.

I did not want to confront the Leopard. Nor did I want to see Sogolon before I could unravel whatever secret she was weaving. I looked at the Ogo and thought of a time, perhaps soon, when I would need a person to hear me pull the darkness out of my own heart. Besides, neither of us knew the way back to the man's place and there were too many homes in this city that smelled like his. The Ogo's mouth was still trembling with killings to confess, words to say, a curse to rinse from his skin. The route had many trees and only two houses, one with faint flickering light. I saw a rock up ahead and, when we got to it, sat down.

"Ogo, tell me of your killings," I said.

He spoke, shouted, whispered, yelled, screamed, laughed, and cried all night. The next morning, when there was light to see our walk home, the Leopard and Fumeli were gone.

FOURTEEN

The Ogo told me of all his killings, one hundred,
seventy and one.

Know this, no mother survives the birth of an
Ogo. The griot tells stories of mad love, of women
falling for giants, but these are the stories we tell each
other under masuku beer. An Ogo birth comes like
hail. Nobody can tell when or how and no divination or science can tell it. Most Ogo are killed at the
only time they can be killed, just after birth, for even
a young Ogo can rip the breast off the poor woman
he suckles, and crush the finger that he grips. Some
raise them in secret, and feed them buffalo milk,
and raise them for the work of ten plows. But something in the head snaps at ten and five years and the
Ogo becomes the monster the gods fated him to
become.

But not always.

So when Sadogo came out of his mother and killed
her, the father cursed the son, saying he must have

been the product of adultery. He cursed the mother's body to a mound outside the village, leaving her to vulture and crow, and would have killed the child or left him exposed in the hollow of an ako tree had word not spread that an Ogo was among them born in the village. A man came two days later, when the man's hut still stunk of afterbirth, shit, and blood, and bought the baby for seven pieces of gold and ten and five goats. He gave the Ogo a name so in that way he would be regarded as a man and not a beast, but Sadogo had forgotten it. When he was ten and two in years, Sadogo slew a lion who had developed a taste for man flesh. Killed him with one punch straight into the skull, and this was before a smith forged him gloves made out of iron.

When Sadogo killed another lion, who was a shape-shifter, the man said, "A killer you surely are, a killer you surely must be. There is no stopping what the gods make you, there is no reshaping how the gods shape you. You must swing the ax, you must draw the bow, but decide who you kill."

The man had many to kill in those years and Sadogo grew strong and fearsome, letting his hair grow—for who would tell him to cut it?—and not washing, for who would tell him to wash? And the man who fed him and gave him leathers to wear and taught him killing science would point to a man working his lands and say, Look at this man. He had every chance to be strong, yet chooses to be weak. In that way he shames the gods. The future of his lands and his cows is with me, so send him to his ancestors. In this way he raised the Ogo. Beyond good or evil, beyond just and unjust, only desiring his master's desire. And he raised himself that way, to think of only what he wanted, what he desired, and who stood in the way, slumping, seething, whining, bawling, begging to be killed.

Sadogo killed everyone as directed by the master. Family, friend turned foe, rivals, men who would not sell land, for the master saw himself a chief. He killed, and killed, and killed again, and the day when he went into the hut of a stubborn man who sold his millet instead of giving it as tribute, and broke the necks of his entire family, including three children, he saw himself in the shiny iron shield on the wall, the last little girl dangling like a limp doll from his hands. So tall that his head was above the shield and it was his monstrous arms and that little girl. And he was not a man, but a beast wearing beast skin, doing something that not even beasts do. Not a man who had heard the griots speak poetry to the master's wife and wished that he could sing himself. Not the man who would let the butterfly and the moth land on his hair and leave them there, sometimes to die, and in his hair they would still remain, like bright yellow jewels. He was lower than a butterfly, he was the killer of children.

Back at the master's house the master's wife came to him and said, He beats me every night. If you kill him you can have some of his coin and seven goats.

And he said, This man is my master. And she said, There is no master and no slave, only what you want, what you desire, and what stands in your way. And when he wavered, she said, Look at how I am still comely, and she did not lie with him for that would be madness, for not only was he already big, but he had a young man's vitality, ten times over, for he was a giant in every way, but she took him with the hands until he yelled, and burst a spray of man milk that hit her in the face and knocked her back four steps. He entered their chamber that night, when the master was on top of the wife, grabbed the back of his head and ripped it off, and the wife screamed, Murderer! Rapist of women! Help me! And he jumped through the window, for the master had many guards.

Second story.

Years grew old, years died, and the Ogo was executioner for the King of Weme Witu in the richest of the South Kingdoms, and who was in truth just a chief who answered to the King of all the South, who was not yet mad. He was called Executioner. There came a time when the King grew tired of wife number ten and four, and spread many lies about her loins spreading for many, like a stream split in two directions, and that she lay with many a lord, many a chief, many a servant, maybe a beggar, and had even been witnessed sitting on the flitting tongue of a eunuch. In this way the story ended. When many gave case against her, including two water maids who claimed to see her take a man in every hole one night, the night itself they could not remember, the court of elders and mystics, all of whom had new horses, and litters, and chariots provided by the King, condemned her to death. A quick death, at Sadogo the executioner's sword, for the gods smiled on mercy.

The King who was but a chief said, Take her to the square of the city so all may learn from her death, that the woman shall never make a fool of the man. The Queen, before she sat in the execution chair, touched Sadogo on the elbow, the softest touch, like fatty cream touching his lips, and said, In me there is no malice to you. My neck is beautiful, unsmeared, untouched. She took off her gold necklace and wrapped it around his machete hand, a machete made for an Ogo, wider at its widest point than a man's chest. By the mercy of the gods make it quick, she said.

Three bamboo stalks stuck out of the dirt. The guards pushed her to the ground, forced her to sit up, and tied her to stalks stuck in the ground. She lifted her chin, but tears ran down her cheek. Sadogo took a branch stripped of leaves and pulled it down till it bent tight like a bow. The branch is angry, it wishes to be straight again not bound, but bind it he did, bind it to grass rope, then he tied it around the head of the wife. She flinched, tried to brace against the branch's hard pull. The branch squeezed around her neck and she cried in pain, and all he could do was look at her and hope his look said, I shall make this quick. His ngulu was sharp, so sharp that even looking at it would make one's eyes bleed. His blade caught light and flashed like lightning. Now the wife bawled. Now the wife wailed. Now the wife screamed. Now she called for ancestors. Now she begged. They all beg, did you know? Every day they talk of how they will rejoice the day of meeting the ancestors but nobody has joy, only crying and pissing and shitting.

He swung back his arm with the sword, then yelled, and swung, and chopped straight into the neck, but the head did not chop off. The city and the people, they watch an execution for a quick cut that makes them laugh. But the blade lodged in the middle of her neck and her eyes popped open and her mouth spat blood and she make a groan like ohhhhhhhhhhhhhhh-ahhhhuck, and the people screamed, the people looked away, the people smelled disgust at people looking at killing, and the guard yelled make it quick. Before he could swing the blade again the impatient branch tore the rest of her head off her neck and flung it away.

Here are some true words. Every road an Ogo takes lands him in Kalindar. The Kalindar that stands between the Red Lake and the sea, and which the King of the North and the King of the South both claim as theirs, is only half of the territory. The rest of the land snakes in forgotten grounds outside the citadel's walls, and in those grounds, men make bets on dark arts and blood sports. There comes a time when the Ogo thinks, If killing is all I do, then killing is all I shall do. And he will hear on warm winds and on secret drums of where there shall be sport, for those who want to play and those who want to watch, in the arena's underground, where the walls are splashed with blood and guts are swept up and fed to dogs. They called it the Entertainments.

Soon Sadogo found himself in this city. Two guards who sat out by Kalindar's gates saw him and said, Walk one hundred man paces, turn left, walk enough paces until you pass a blind man on a red stool, then go south until you come upon a hole in the ground with steps that take you down.

You look ready to die, the Entertainments master said when he saw Sadogo. The man let him into a vast underground courtyard and pointed to a cell.

"You fight two nights hence. And there you shall sleep. You shall not sleep well, all the better you wake with a temper," he said.

But Sadogo was not ill-tempered, but weighed by melancholy. During training the Entertainments master had him whipped with sticks, but all the sticks broke and all the men fell from exhaustion before Sadogo even rose from the floor.

As for Ogos, know this. Most will never feel joy, or melancholy. The Ogos have little understanding and tempers that swing from cold to hot in a blink. Two Ogos who will say, If you kill him you kill my brother, will still smash the head of that brother right down to the stump. Nobody trains an Ogo. Nobody needs to. One only makes him mad, or hungry. And Sadogo is friends with no Ogo, and none are friends with him, and one is taller than trees and built bigger than elephants, and one is short but wide and thick like a rock, and one has muscles in his back and shoulders that rise above his head and people say that one is an ape. And one who paints himself blue, and one who will eat meat raw.

And the master says, Look, I have no chains on you. I am no master of men. You come when you come, you go when you go, and whatever I bet for you, you get half and whatever I bet against you, you get a third and if you win, those who come to watch will shower you with cowrie and coin, of which I only keep a fifth. **Ko kare da ranar sa.** What do you wish for money to do, my melancholy Ogo?

"Enough money to sail on a dhow that can hold me."

"Sail to where?"

"It does not matter. I sail from, not to."

The night of the first fight, seven Ogos and Sadogo marched to the killing ground. It was nothing but a hole deep in the ground, the remains of a well that went down perhaps two hundred arm lengths, maybe more. With rocks pushing out of ragged dirt, and ledges at uneven heights all the way around where men, nobles and chiefs, stood, along with a few women. They had cast their bets for each fight, four for the night. At the bottom of the well, a dry mound rose out of water.

The master put Sadogo in the second bout, saying, This one, he new, he fresh, we call him Sadface. Sadogo came down wearing a red macawii around his waist, and stood before the master. May gods of thunder and food give him strength, because look, here be coming another, the master said, and dashed off into the water, where he pulled himself up on a ledge. The men shouted, cheered, and fussed. A woman in a bucket was lowered to collect all the bets. The master said, Oho, what now, here he come, the backbreaker, and men on the lowest ledge scrambled to higher ground.

Backbreaker was the nastiest, for he ate flesh raw from the beast he killed. Tusks grew out of his mouth. Somebody painted his huge body in red ochre. The master said, Make your bets, dignified gentlemen. But before he finished, Backbreaker swung a punch and knocked Sadogo into the water. The girl screamed, Pull up the bucket! For the red Ogo eyed it as soon as he came in. Backbreaker faced the crowd and bellowed. Sadogo rose from the water and knocked him down, and grabbed a rock to bash in his head, but his grip was wet and Backbreaker slipped out, rolled over, and punched him straight in the chin. Sadogo spat blood. The red Ogo grabbed his club with spikes and swung it at Sadogo's feet. Sadogo dodged and jumped up to a lower ledge. Backbreaker swung his club but Sadogo ducked and kicked him in the balls. The red Ogo dropped to his knees and his own spiked club slammed into his left eye. Sadogo took the club to Backbreaker's head and smashed and smashed. And then he lifted the headless body and threw it at the men on the lowest ledge.

Six took him on, six he killed with that club.

And so his fame spread throughout Kalindar, and

so more and more men came to see, and bet. And since the well was small and could never hold all, they placed more wood beams across the top so more men could see, and the master charged three times, four times, five times, then battle by battle even if they paid before, for the chance to see and bet on the sorrowful Ogo.

"Look upon him, look how his face never changes," they would say.

He faced them all, he killed them all, and soon the lands were running out of Ogos. But the girl in the bucket who collected the bets, she was a slave with eyes sad as his. She brought food though many Ogos tried to rape her. One grabbed her one night and said, Watch how it grows, and pushed her down, and as he climbed on top, Sadogo's hand grabbed his ankle, yanked him out of his cell, swung him like a club, and slammed him into the ground over and over and over until there was no sound from this Ogo. Through all this the girl said nothing, but the master said, "Curse you to the gods, sad one, surely that giant was worth more than that foolish little girl."

Sadogo turned to him. "Do not call us giants," he said.

The girl would come and sit by his cell. She sang verse but not to him. That last one is from lands north, then east, she said.

"We should go there," she said.

———

No man is bound to me and I am bound to no man," the master said when Sadogo said he would soon leave. "Killing has made you rich. But where shall you go? Where is there home for the Ogo? And if there is a home, good Ogo, do you not think someone here would have left for it?"

That evening she came to him and said, I have spoken my fill of verses. Give me new words. He walked to the bars that were not locked and said:

Bring words to voice and
Meat to this verse
Coal and ash
Flicker a flame
Brilliant

She stared at him through the bars.

"What I tell you is a true word, Ogo, you have an awful voice, and that is terrible verse. The griots do get their gifts from the gods." Then she laughed. "Give me this word. What they call you?"

"I am called nothing."

"What does your father call you?"

"A curse from the demons who fucked my whore of a wife and killed her."

She laughed again.

"I laugh, but it makes me very sad," she said. "I come here because you are not like the rest."

"I am worse. Three times as many I have killed, compared to the bravest fighter."

"Yes, but you are the only one who does not look at me like I am next."

He walked right up to the bar and pushed at it, opened it a little. She shifted a little, tried not to look as if she jumped.

"Truly, I will kill anything. Cut past my skin to find my heart and it will be white. White like nothingness."

She looked at him. He was almost three times her height.

"If you were for true heartless, you would not have known it. Lala is my name."

When he told the master that he wished to leave, he did not tell him that he wanted to go north, then east, for whoever speaks such verses that the girl recites will not care that he towers over the biggest of men. He did not ask to buy Lala, but he did plan to take her. But the master learned that this new thinking was the doing of his bet collector. For sure they are not lovers, for not even the hugest of women can take an Ogo, and she is small as a child and frail as a stick. This Ogo was growing close to her head and speaking like her.

The next morning Sadogo woke up to see the blue Ogo, in the middle of the courtyard, pull himself out of her body, leaving her smashed, ripped, and wrecked in a full moon of her own blood. Sadogo did not run to her, he did not cry, he did not leave his cell, he did not speak of it to the master.

"I will pit you against him finally so you can avenge her," he said.

Later that night, another slave girl came to his cell

and said, Look at me, I am now the wagers maid. They will lower me in the bucket.

"Tell the old men it would be foolish to bet against me."

"They have already betted."

"What?"

"They have already cast bets, most for you, some against you."

"What do you mean?"

"The word was you were the smart Ogo."

"Speak plain and true, slave."

"The Master of Entertainments, he send bets, by slave, by messenger, and by pigeon, from seven days before, saying you will be pit against the blue one in a fight to the death."

Before the fight, noise from the well rose loud and thick and bounced off dirt and rock. Noblemen in noble gowns, and gold-streaked slippers, and because this was a special night of special entertainment, they brought several noblewomen with heads wrapped like tall flowers pointing up to the sky. They were impatient, even though many battles left men with broken limbs, smashed heads, and a neck yanked out like from a chicken. Some men started cursing and some women too. Bring the sad-faced one, they chanted. Sad Ogo, sad Ogo, sad Ogo, they said, and shouted, Sad.

Ogo.

Sadogo.

Sadogo.

The blue Ogo threw off a black hood and leapt

from a high ledge to the mound. He puffed his chest out. The women hissed and called for Sadogo. I will ram an iroko branch up his ass till it bursts through his mouth and cook him on a spit, the blue Ogo said.

Sadogo came in from the west, a tunnel no man had used before. He had wrapped his knuckles in straps of iron. The master followed him and began to shout.

"Lightning strike and thunder roll, even the gods stealing a look on this right now. Mark it, good gentlemen. Mark it, good wives and virgins. This day not going to be a day anyone soon forget. Who didn't bet, bet now! Who bet, bet again!"

The new slave girl came down in the bucket and men threw satchels and coins and cowries at her. Some fell in the bucket, some hit her face.

Sadogo saw the new slave girl, lowered to the lowest ledge, then raised from ledge to ledge and swung around to take the bets. Just then it came to him, poetry sung by the girl in a language he did not understand. A language that might have said, Look at us, we speak of melancholy, and melancholy no matter the tongue is always the same word. The blue Ogo's fist clobbered him right on the cheek and he spat the thought out. He fell back down in the water, which rushed into his nose and made him choke.

The blue Ogo waved into the crowd as some cheered and some hissed, clear when Sadogo's ears rose out of the water, murky when he fell back in. The blue Ogo stomped around the mound, shoved his crotch out, and fucked the air. He looked down on Sadogo and laughed so loud that he coughed. Sadogo thought of lying there, hoping the water would rise, perhaps in a tide, and swallow him. The blue Ogo backed up and lowered his head like a bull. He ran three steps and leapt high. He clasped his hands together to bring them down on Sadogo's head. Sadogo jammed his elbow into the mud and pulled himself into a right-hand swing, which punched right through the blue Ogo's chest and burst through his back. Blue Ogo's eyes popped wide. The crowd fell quiet. Blue Ogo fell, and rolled, pulling Sadogo up. Blue Ogo's eyes still popped wide. Sadogo bellowed into the walls, pulled his hand and tore Blue Ogo's heart out. Blue Ogo stared at him quick, spat blood, fell dead. Sadogo stood up, threw the heart at the middle ledge, and all the men dodged.

The Master of Entertainments ran out and addressed the crowd.

"Was ever a champion so, so melancholy, my brothers? When will he be beaten? When will he be stopped? Who shall stop him? And whose death—I said whose death, my brothers—will make him smi—"

The people right in front of the master saw it. Iron knuckles as they burst out of the master's chest. The master's eye flipping up into white. The Ogo's hand pulling back in the quick and wrenching out his backbone. The master crumpled like fabric. The slave looked down from her bucket. The whole well fell quiet until one woman screamed. Sadogo dashed to the first ledge, punched away the wood brace supporting it, and screaming men slid right into his punching fist. First, second, third. The fourth tried to run through the water, but he grabbed her leg and swung her into another ledge full of men, knocking them all off. Men and women screamed to the gods and scrambled up ladders. More men scrambled on people scrambling up ladders. But Sadogo pulled away another brace and two ledges fell, and in one blow, one punch, one rip, one bludgeon, bodies piled on bodies. A man he punched flew into the mud and was swallowed by it. Another he stomped into the water until it went red. And so he pulled down ladder after ladder and ledge after ledge. He leapt onto one of the few ledges left, slamming, jamming, and knocking men off, and jumped from one to another, then another till he was so high that to kill, he just threw people off. He jumped to the top of the well and caught two as they ran, grabbed them both by the head and slammed them into each other. A boy climbed up and ran into him. A boy nowhere near a man, a boy dressed in rich robes like his father, a boy who looked at him more curious than afraid. He touched the boy's face with both hands, gentle, soft, like silk, then grabbed him and threw him down the well. Then he roared like the beast. The slave girl in the bucket was still hanging above. She said nothing.

Sadogo almost skipped all the way to this lord's dwelling. Then he went to his room and fell to snoring in a blink. The buffalo was in the courtyard eating grass, which must have been foul tasting but he seemed to like it. He looked up and saw me wearing the curtain and snorted. I hissed and tugged at it, pretending that I could not take it off. Again, he did something that sounded like a laugh, but none of these horned animals can laugh, although who knew which god was working mischief through him.

"Good buffalo, has anyone come around to this man's place? Any dressed in black or blue?"

He shook his head.

"Any in the colour of blood?"

He snorted. I knew he could not see the colour of blood, but something in this bull made me want to have sport with him.

"Alas, I think we might be watched."

He turned around, then turned back on me and grunted long.

"If any man shows up in black and blue, or in a black cape, raise alarm. But do what you wish with him."

He nodded up and down and gargled.

"Buffalo, before the sun goes we shall go back to the riverside for better bush."

He gargled and swished his tail.

Inside the Leopard's room was only a trace. If I wanted to, I could smell deep into the rugs, past the shit and sperm and sweat of him and the boy, and know where they went and would go. But here is truth: I did not care. All that was left in the room was what they did, nothing of theirs. Here is another truth. I did have some trace of care, enough to know they were going southwest.

"They leave before day burst," said the lord of the house behind me. He wore a white caftan that did not hide that he wore nothing underneath. Old shoga? That was a question I did not wish to ask.

He followed me as I walked to Sogolon's room. He did not try to stop me.

"What is your name, sir?" I asked.

"What? My name? Sogolon said there would be no names. . . . Kafuta. Kafuta it is."

"Great thanks for the room you give us and the food, Lord Kafuta."

"I am no lord," he said, looking past me.

"You are the lord of this magnificent house," I said.

He smiled but it quit his face quick. I would have said, Take me to her room, this is still your house, if I thought to enter her room was what he wished. He was not afraid of her; instead they seemed like brother and sister or sharers of old secrets.

"I shall go in," I said. He looked at me, then past me, then at me, pressing his lips to appear unconcerned. I headed for her door.

"Will you follow?" I asked as I turned around to see him gone.

Sogolon did not lock her door. Not that any of the doors had locks, but I would have thought so of hers.

Maybe every man believes that all an old woman has is secrets, and that was the second time I thought of secrets when I thought of her.

The smells in the room hit me first. Some I knew that took me out of the room, some I have never smelled the like. In the center of the room, a black-and-red rug with the curved patterns of textiles from the eastern kingdoms, and a wood headrest. But on the walls, painted, scrawled, scratched, and written, were runes. Some as small as a fingertip. Some taller than Sogolon herself. From them came the smells, some in coal, some in wood dye, some in shit, and some in blood. I saw the rug and the headrest and paid no attention to the floor. That was covered in runes as well, the freshest ones in blood. The room was so covered in marks that I hesitated to look at the ceiling, for I knew what I would see. Runes but also a series of circles, each wider than the one before. Truth, had I the third eye, I would have seen runes written in air.

One smell in the room, fresher than the rest, moved on the wind and grew stronger.

"You scare the lord of the house," I said.

"He is no lord to me," Bunshi said as she poured herself down from the ceiling to the floor.

I stood still and stiff; there was no way a black mass moving down from the ceiling was going to trouble me.

"I don't think I want to know who are your lords," I said. "Maybe you are a lord yourself that nobody worships anymore."

"And yet you are so gentle with the giant," she said.

"Call him Ogo, not giant."

"That was a noble thing, hearing a man as he empties the whole world of his conscience."

"Have you been spying on us, river witch?"

"Is every woman a witch to you, Wolf Eye?"

"And what of it?" I said.

"All you know of women is your mother jumping up and down your grandfather's cock, yet you blame all of womandom for it. The day your father died was the first day of freedom your mother ever saw until your grandfather enslaved her again. All you ever did was watch woman suffer and blame her for it."

I walked to the door. I would not hear any more of this.

"These are protection runes," I said.

"How do you know? The Sangoma. Of course."

"She covered the tree trunks with them, carved some, branded some, left some hanging in air and on clouds and on the ground. But she was Sangoma. To live as her is to know that evil forces rise day and night to come for you. Or wronged spirits."

"Who did the Sangoma do wrong?"

"I mean Sogolon, not her."

"What a story you have made of her."

I went by the window and touched the marks all around the frame. "These are not runes."

"They are glyphs," Bunshi said.

I knew they were glyphs. Like the brands on that

attacker who came in the whore's window. Like the note wrapped around the pigeon leg. But not the same marks exactly; I could not tell for sure.

"Have you seen them before?" she said.

"No. She writes runes to keep spirits from coming in. For what does she need glyphs?"

"You ask too many questions."

"I need no answer. But I leave today, before the sun goes."

"This day? Do you need me to tell you that is too soon?"

"Too soon? It has been a moon and several days. A moon already wasted in a forest that nobody should have gone into. Me and the Ogo leave this evening. And anyone else who cares to. Maybe the buffalo."

"No, Wolf Eye. There are more things to learn here. More things to—"

"To what? I am here to find a child, collect my gold, and go find the next lost husband who is not lost."

"There are things you don't even know that you don't know."

"I know where goes the child."

"You keep this secret?"

"I tell who I feel needs to know. Maybe you sent us on a mission expecting us to fail. Good . . . whatever you are, for truly I know not . . . how stands your fellowship now? Nyka and his woman—"

"She has a name."

"Fuck the gods if I care to remember it. Besides,

they took off first, before we even left the valley. The Leopard is gone, and so is Fumeli, not that the boy had much use, and now your Sogolon is gone to wherever. Here is truth. I saw no reason for a group to find one child anyway. Nor did any of us. Not Nyka, not that cat, and not your witch."

"Think like a man and not a child, Tracker, this is no task for one, or two."

"And yet two is what you have. If Sogolon returns and is willing then we will be three."

"One, three, or four might as well be none. If all I needed was someone to find the child, Tracker, I could have hired two hundred trackers and their dogs. Two questions, you can choose which to answer first. Do you think his abductor will hand him to you just because you say, I am here, hand me the boy?"

"They will—"

"Is the tracker such a fool to think I am the only one looking for this child?"

"Who else seeks him?"

"The one who visits you in dreams. Skin like tar, hair red, when you see him you hear the flutter of black wings."

"I don't know this man."

"He knows you. They call him the Aesi. He answers to the North King."

"Why would he visit my dreams?"

"They are your dreams, not mine. You have something he wants. He too might know that you have found the child."

"Tell me more of this man."

"Necromancer. Witchman. He is the King's adviser. From an old line of monks who started working secret science and invoking devils and were thrown out of the order. The King consults him on all things, even which direction to spit. Do you know why they call Kwash Dara the Spider King? Because in everything he moves with four arms and four legs, except two of each belong to the Aesi."

"Why does he want the boy?"

"We have spoken on this. The boy is proof of the killings."

"Are bodies not proof enough? Or do they think the wife cut her own self in two? Who is the boy?"

"The boy is the last son of the last honest man in the ten and three kingdoms. I will save him if that is the last thing I do in this world or another."

"I will not ask a third time."

"How dare you ask me anything! Who are you that demands that I make things clear to you? Are you master over me now, is that how you will have it?"

Her eyes bulged and the fin grew out of the back of her head.

"No. I will have nothing but rest. I am tired from this." I turned and walked out. "I leave in two days."

"Not today?"

"Not today. It seems there is more I need to know."

"Where is the child? How many moons away is he?" she asked.

"Don't speak of my mother again," I said.

That night I was again in a dream jungle. A new kind of dream where I wondered why I was in it, and why a dream of trees and bushes and bitter raindrops. And moving but not walking, and knowing something would reveal itself in a clearing, or in the mirror of a puddle, or in the lonely cry of a lonely ghost bird. Reveal something that I already knew. The Sangoma once told me that the dream jungle is where you find things that are hidden in the waking world. And that hidden thing might be a lust. The knowledge is in leaves, and dirt, and mist, and heat thick like a ghost, and it is a jungle because the jungle is the only place where anything can wait behind the cover of a large leaf. The jungle finds you, you cannot seek it, which is why everyone in the jungle seeks why they are there. But looking for meaning will drive you mad, the Sangoma also said.

So I did not ask for meaning when Smoke Girl was the first to run to me, then run past me, not ignoring me but so used to my presence. And in the jungle was a man I only saw by hair on his hands and legs. He touched my shoulder, and chest, and belly, leaned his forehead to touch mine, then grabbed two spears and walked away. And Giraffe Boy stood with his legs wide open, the boy with no legs curled into a ball and rolled right between them, and the patch of sand in the middle of the bush blinked, then smiled, and the albino rose out of the sand as if he came from it and was not just hiding in it. Then he grabbed a spear and went to find the man I had no name for, but still felt warm at the thought that I do know his name. I had stopped walking but I was still walking and Smoke Girl sat down on my head and said, Tell me a story with an ant, a cheetah, and a magic bird, and I heard every word she said.

FIFTEEN

A ghost knows who to scare. As the sun glides to noon, men and women grab their children and run home, close windows, and draw curtains, for in Kongor it is noon that is the witching hour, the hour of the beast, when heat cracks the earth open to release seven thousand devils. I have no fear of devils. I went south, then turned west along the border road to the Nimbe quarter. Then I turned south down a crooked street, west down an alley, then south again until I came upon the Great Hall of Records.

Kongor was the record keeper for all the North Kingdom and most of the free states, and the Hall of Records was open to anyone who stated his purpose. But nobody came to these large rooms, five tall floors of scrolls stacked on shelves, stacked on top of each other, as tall as any palace in Kongor. The hall of records was like the palace of clouds in the sky—people were satisfied that it existed without ever entering, ever reading book or paper, or even coming close.

On the way there I was hoping to meet a demon, or a spirit of someone who would feed the hunger of my two new axes. I truly wanted a fight.

Nobody was here but an old man with a hunch in his back.

"I seek the records of the great elders. Tax records as well," I said to the old man. He did not look up from the large maps he stood over.

"Them young people, too hot in the neck, too full in the balls. So this great King who is only great in the echo of his voice, which is to say not great at all, conquers a land and says this land is now mine, re-draw the maps, and you young men with papyrus and ink redraw the old map for the new and forget entire lands as if the gods of the underworld tore open a hole in the earth and sucked in the entire territory. Fool, look. Look!"

The library master blew map dust in my face.

"Truth, I know not what I look at."

He frowned. I could not tell if his hair was white from age or from dust.

"Look in the center. Do you not see it? Are you blind?"

"Not if I see you."

"Be not rude in this great hall and shame whoever you came out of."

I tried not to smile. On the table stood five thick candles, one tall and past his head, another so down to the stub that it would set things afire if left alone. Behind him towers and towers of papers, of papyrus, of scrolls and books bound in leather and piled one on top of the other, reaching the ceiling. I was tempted to ask what if he desired a book in the middle. Between the towers were bundles of scrolls and loose papers that fell flat. Dust settled like a cloud right above his head and cats fat on rats scrambled.

"Alert the gods, he is now deaf as well as blind," the library master said. "Mitu! This master of map arts, which I am sure he calls himself, has forgotten Mitu, the city at the center of the world."

I looked at the map again. "This map is in a tongue I cannot read."

"Some of these parchments are older than the children of the gods. Word is divine wish, they say. Word is invisible to all but the gods. So when woman or man write words, they dare to look at the divine. Oh, what power."

"The tax and household records of the great elders, I seek. Where are—"

He looked at me like a father accepting the disappointment of his son.

"Which great elder do you seek?"

"Fumanguru."

"Oh? Great is what they call him now?"

"Who says he is not, old man?"

"Not I. I am indifferent to all elders and their supposed wisdom. Wisdom is here." The library master pointed behind himself without looking.

"That sounds like heresy."

"It **is** heresy, young fool. But who will hear it? You are my first visitor in seven moons."

This old bastard was becoming my favorite person in Kongor who was not a buffalo. Maybe because he was one of the few who did not point to my eye and say, How that? A leather-bound book, on its own pedestal and large as half a man, opened up and from it burst lights and drums. Not now, he shouted, and the book slapped itself back shut.

"The records of the elders are back there. Walk left, go south past the drum of scrolls to the end. Fumanguru will bear the white bird of the elders and the green mark of his name."

The corridor smelled of dust, paper rot, and cat. I found Fumanguru's tax records. In the hall, I sat on a stack of books and placed the candle on the floor.

He paid much in tax, and after checking the records of others, including Belekun the Big, I saw he paid more than he needed to. His death wish that his lands be given to his children was written on loose papyrus. And there were many little books bound in smooth leather and hairy cowskin. His journals, his records, or his logs, or perhaps all three. A line here that said keeping cows made no sense in tsetse fly country. Another saying what should we do with our glorious King? And this:

I fear I shall not be here for my children and I shall not be here soon. My head resides in the

house of Olambula the goddess who protects all men of noble character. But am I noble?

Here I was wishing I could slap a dead man. The old man had gone silent. But Fumanguru:

Day of Abdula Dura
So Ebekua the elder took me aside and said Fumanguru, I have news from the lands of sky and the chambers of the underworld that made me shiver. The gods have made peace, and so have spirits of nurture and plenty with devils and there is unity in all heavens. I said I do not believe this for it demands of the gods what they are not capable of. Look, the gods cannot end themselves, even the mighty Sagon, when he tried to take his own life only transformed it. For the gods there is nothing to discover, nothing new. Gods are without the gift of surprising themselves, which even we who crawl in the dirt have in abundance. What are our children but people who continue to surprise and disappoint us? Ebekua said to me, Basu I do not know by how this entered your head, but bid it farewell and let us never speak on such things again.

A smaller book, bound in alligator skin, opens with this:

Day of Basa Dura
Oh I should know the will of Kwash Dara?
Is that what he thinks? Did he not know
that even when we were boys I was my own
man?

Five pages more:

Bufa Moon

And nothing until so far down the edge of the page
the words nearly fell off:

Tax the elders? A grain tax? Something as es-
sential as air?
Obora Gudda Moon
Day of Maganatti Jarra to Maganatti Britti
He set us free today. The rains would not
stop. Work of the gods.

I threw down that book and picked up another,
this one in hairy black-and-white cowskin, not shiny
leather. The pages were bound in brilliant red thread,
which meant this was the most new, even though it
was in the middle of the stack. He put it in the middle, surely. He scrambled the order so that no one
could build the story of his life too easy, of this I was
certain. A cat dashed past me. A flutter over my head
and I looked up. Two pigeons flew out a window high
up over me.

What are we in, but a year of mad lords?
    Sadassaa Moon
    Day of Bita Kara
    There are men that I have lost all love for,
and there are the words I will write in a message I will never send, or in a tongue that they
will never read.

Day of Lumasa
    What is love for child, if not mania? I look
at the magic of my smallest boy and cry, and
I look at the muscle and might of the oldest, and grin with a pride that we are warned
should be only of the gods. And for them and
the four in between, I have a love that scares
me. I look at them and I know it, I know it,
I know it. I would kill the one who comes
to harm my sons. I would kill that one with
no mercy and no thought. I would search for
that one's heart and rip the thing out and
shove it in their mouth, even if that one is
their own mother.

Six sons.
Six sons.

Guraandhala Moon
    Day of Garda Duma
    The same night Belekun left me alone. All
night I wrote. Then these I heard, a whimper,

a gruff reply, a scream slapped short, and another gruff reply. Outside my door, four doors down. I pushed it open and there was Amaki the Slippery. His back wet with sweat. I would say too it was the god of iron but it was my own rage that went up in my own head. His Ifa bowl was right there on the floor at his feet. I brought it down on his head. Again and again. He fell on top of the girl, covering her totally.

They will come for me soon. Afuom and Duku said to me, do not worry young brother, we have made arrangements. We shall come for your wife and boys and people will think they vanished like a loose memory.

He was hiding in Kongor.
Six sons.
Between this book and the one below lay a piece of papyrus. I could tell it once had a strong fragrance, like a note sent to a mistress. His own handwriting, but not as rough and rushed as his journal. It said:

A man will suffer misery to get to the bottom of truth, but he will not suffer boredom.

Basu Fumanguru is a man who had been north of the sand sea. I am guessing because of their love for riddles, games, and double-talk, sometimes at the border of a wicked city, where if you guessed wrong they would kill you on sight. Who was this for? Himself or whoever read it? But Fumanguru knew someone would one day. He knew forces were coming for him and had all this moved from before. Nobody took anything from the hall of records, not even the King. Somebody would come looking, maybe for the writs, which nobody could find and that might not even exist. All this talk about writs against the King, as if nobody has ever written in protest of the King. And yet below these journals were no writs, just pages and pages of tallies for tax, how many more cows he'd gained over the year before. Tallies of crop yield in Malakal. And his father's lands, and a dowry he helped pay for his cousin's daughter.

Until I came up upon a page, in old papyrus, with lines and boxes and names. The candlelight glowed brighter, which meant outside was darker. No sound came from the keeper, which made me wonder if he had left.

The candle burned slow. At the top of the paper and written very large was **Kwash Moki.** The King's great-grandfather's father. Moki had four sons and two daughters. The oldest son was Kwash Liongo the celebrated King, and under his name, four sons and five daughters. Under Liongo's name, his third son, Kwash Aduware, who became king, and under him, Kwash Netu. Under Netu are two sons and one daughter. The oldest son is Kwash Dara, our King now. I don't think I ever knew the King's sister's name, before seeing it written there. Lissisolo. She gave her life to serving a goddess, which one I do not know, but a server of the goddess loses her old name for a new one. My landlady said once that the gossip was that she was not a nun but a madwoman. Because her little head could not handle doing a big terrible thing. What this terrible thing was, she did not know. But it was terrible. They sent her to live in a fortress in the mountains with no way in or out so the women who serve her would be also locked away forever. I put the family map aside, still bothered by Fumanguru's riddle.

Below his map of kings was his handwriting. More tallies, and logs, and other people's tallies, and other people's logs, and inventory of the food supplies of all elders, and a list of visits, and more of his journals, some dating years before the ones that were on top. And even two small books on his advice on love, which looks like he wrote it back when he and the King were looking for anything but such. And books empty of words, and pages carrying smells, and drawings of ships, and buildings, and towers taller than Malakal, and a book marking a tale of the forbidden trip to the Mweru, which I opened, only to see glyphs, but not like what I had seen before.

And also these, book after book and page after page on the wisdom and instruction of the elders. Proverbs he heard or created himself, I did not know. And logs of the meeting of the elders, some not even written by him. I cursed him outright and long until wisdom fell on me.

I was suffering through boredom.

Just as he wrote I would, so I did. Then the whole brilliance of his ways hit me like sudden wind blowing a flower in my face. Suffer through boredom to get to truth. No, suffer through boredom to get to the bottom of truth. To get to truth at the bottom.

I grabbed two stacks of books and papers, both as high as my chin, and put them aside, leaving one on the floor. Red leather binding and tied with a knot, which set fire to my curiosity. The pages were empty. I cursed again and almost flung it across the room, until the last page flew up. **Where birds come in,** it read. I looked up, at the window. Of course. There, in the windowsill, two planks of wood that came loose. I climbed up and moved them aside. Under the wood, a satchel in red leather, all the pages inside, large and loose. I blew the dust off the first page, which read:

Being a writ in the presence of the King
By his most humble servant, Basu Fuman-
guru.

I looked at this thing that some people have already been killed over. This thing that caused men to scheme and plot; these loose, dirty, and smelly pages that have so far changed the course of many a man's life. Some demanded punishment in fines and the end to torture for minor offenses. One asked for the property of a dead man to go to his first wife. But one declared this:

That all free men of the lands, those born so, and those who have been given freedom be never enslaved, or enslaved again, nor are their lives commandeered for war without payment to the scale of what they are worth. And this freedom shall also be for their children and their children's children.

I didn't know if the king would have killed him over this, but I know many who would. And still there was this:

Every just man who feels he has a case against the king shall be protected by law and no harm should come to him or his kin. And should the case against the king be dismissed, no harm should come to him. And should the case go in the man's favor, no harm should come to him or his kin.

Truly Fumanguru was either most wise or most foolish of dreamers. Or he was counting on the king's better nature. Some writs were just a breath away from treason. The one most bold and most foolish came at the end:

That the house of kings return to the ways that had been decreed by the gods, and not this course which has corrupted the ways of kings for six generations. This is what we demand:

that the king follow the natural order set by gods of sky and gods below the earth. Return to the purity of the line as set in the words of long-dead griots and forgotten tongues. That until the kings of the North return to the clean path, they go against the will of all that is right and good, and nothing shall stop this house from falling or be conquered by another.

He called the royal house corrupted. And for a return to the real line of kings, wrong for six generations, or the gods would make sure the house of Akum fell. Fumanguru had written his own death note, words that guaranteed execution before it even reached the king, but had hidden it in secret. For who to find it?

So I read most of his journals and looked through all, including that one he was writing very close to his death. This I know: The last entry was the day before he was murdered, and yet here was the book in this hall of books. But only he could have added to his own stack; no one else would have been allowed. Who am I to put reasoning into unreasonable? There is no farewell here, no final instruction, not even any of that sauce of bitterness when one knows death is coming but does not like his fate.

But something here did not go right. He made no mention of the boy. Nothing at all. Something must have come from this boy—a fragrance of something bigger, deeper, more important, as sure as what I smelled on the doll, but bigger so—if this boy was the reason he and his family were hunted and killed by Omoluzu. But there was nothing here of the boy's worth, nothing here of the boy's kin, nothing here even of the boy's use. Fumanguru was keeping him a secret even from his own records. In his way, keeping him secret even from himself. And among smells was something sour coming from the pages. Something spilled and dried, but from an animal, not from the ground or of the palm or the vine. Milk. Vanished from sight now, but still there. I remembered a woman suckling a baby who sent me in a most curious way a message to save her from her husband and captor. I reached for the candle.

"Bigger fires have started from smaller flames," he said.

I jumped and reached for my axes, but his sword was already at my neck. I had smelled myrrh but thought it was an old bottle the library master had behind him.

The prefect.

"Did you follow me or have me followed?" I asked.

"Do you mean will you need to kill one man or two?"

"I never—"

"You still wear that curtain? Even after two days?"

"By the gods, if one more man says I wear a curtain . . ."

"That is a pattern on the drapes of rich men. Are you not river folk? Why not just wear ochre and butter?"

"Because you Kongori think strange about dress and undress."

"I am not Kongori."

"Your sword is at my neck. Answer my question."

"I followed you myself. But grew tired when I saw the giant would cry to you the entire night. His stories were amusing, but his crying was insufferable. That is not how we mourn in the East."

"You're not in the East."

"And you are not among the Ku. Now why were you about to burn that note?"

"Take your blade away from my neck."

"Why would I do that?"

"Because there is a blade between my big toes. Kill me and I might just fall and die before you. Or I could kick and you become a eunuch."

"Put that down."

"You think I have come all this way to burn this?" I said.

"I don't think anything."

"Not a new thing for a prefect."

He pushed the blade harder against my neck.

"The paper. Down."

I put the paper down and looked up at him. "Look at me," I said. "I shall hold this paper over this flame, for I feel it will reveal something to me. I do not know you, nor do I know how stupid you are, but I cannot make what I say any simpler."

He withdrew the sword.

"How do I know this?" he said.

"You will have to trust me."

"Trust you? I don't even like you."

We stared at each other for a long time. I grabbed a sheet, the one most sour.

"You and your curtain for a dress," he said.

"Will you not stop until I am off with my clothes?"

I waited for a sharp reply, but it never came. I would have gone there, trying to figure out why the sharp reply never came, or try to catch him before he hid it from his face, but I did not.

"What are you—"

"Please, be quiet. Or at least watch for the keeper."

He stopped talking and shook his head. Fuman-guru had written these writs in red ink, bright in col-our but light in tone. I pulled the candle closer to me, then held the sheet right over the flame.

"'Tis Mossi."

"What?"

"My name. The name you have forgotten. It is Mossi."

I lowered the flame so that I could see the flicker through the paper and feel the warmth on my fin-ger. Figures took shape. Glyphs, letters moving left to right or right to left, I did not know. Glyphs written in milk so they would be hidden until now. My nose led me to four more pages smelling of milk. I ran them over the fire until glyphs appeared, line after line, row after row. I smiled and looked up at the prefect.

"What are those?" he asked.

"You said you are from the East?"

"No, my skin went pale when all the colour washed off."

I stared at him blankly until he said something else.

"North, then east," he said.

I handed the first paper to him.

"These are coastal glyphs. Cruel letters, the people call them. Can you read them?"

"No," I said.

"I can read some of it."

"What . . . do . . . they . . ."

"I'm no master of ancient marks. You think Fumanguru made these?"

"Yes, and—"

"For what purpose?" he asked.

"So that even if the wrong man came this close to the water, he would never be able to drink."

"That I understood you makes me very sad."

"Glyphs are supposed to be the language of the gods."

"If the gods are too old and stupid to know the words and numbers of modern men."

"You sound like you stopped believing in the gods."

"I am just amused by all of yours."

It bothered me to look at him and see him looking at me.

"My belief is nothing. He believed that the gods were speaking to him. What draws you to Fumanguru?" Mossi said.

And I thought, for a blink, What should I construct now, and how much will I have to build on it? The thought alone made me tired. I told myself that I was just tired of believing there was a secret to protect from some unknown enemy, when the truth was I was tired of not having someone to tell it to. Here is truth: At this point I would have told anyone. Truth is truth, and I do not own it. It should make no difference to me who hears it, since him hearing the truth does not change it. I wished the Leopard was here.

"I could ask you the same thing. His family died from sickness," I said.

"No sickness cuts a woman in two. The prefect of prefects declared this matter closed, and recommended that to the chiefs, who recommended that to the King."

"Yet here you are, in front of me, because you didn't swallow that story."

He leaned his sword against a stack of books and sat on the floor. His tunic slipped off his knees and he wore no underclothes. I am Ku and it is nothing new to see the man in men, I said to myself three times. Without looking at me, he pulled the tail of his garment up between his legs. He hunched over the papers and read.

"Look," he said, and I leaned over.

"Either his mind went slightly mad, or it is his intent to confuse you. Look at this, the vulture, the chick, and the foot all pointed west. This is northern writing. Some make one sound, like the vulture's sound, which is **mmmm.** Some make a whole word or carry an idea. But look at this down here, the fourth line. Do you see how it differs? This is the coast. Go to the coast of the South Kingdom, or even that place, I forget its name. That island to the east, what is the name . . . ?"

"Lish."

"You can still find this writing in Lish. Each one is a sound, all sounds make—"

"I know what a word is, prefect. What is he saying?"

"Patience, Tracker. 'God . . . gods of sky. They no longer speak to spirits of the ground. The voice of kings is becoming the new voice of the gods. Break the silence of the gods. Mark the god butcher, for he marks the killer of kings.' Is this sounding wise to you? For it is foolishness to me. 'The god butcher in black wings.'"

"Black wings?"

"This is what he says. None of this moves like a wave. I think he meant it so. A king is king by a queen, not a king. But the boy—"

"Wait. Stay, do not move," I said.

He looked up and nodded. His thighs, lighter in skin than the rest of him, sprouted hairs too straight. I went right to the library master's table, but he was still gone. I guessed he kept behind him the logbooks and records of kings and royal subjects. I climbed two steps up a ladder and looked around until I saw the mark of the rhinoceros head in gold. I flipped from the back page and dust rushed into my nose, making me cough. A few pages in was the house of

Kwash Liongo, almost the same as what Fumanguru had scratched out on paper. On the page before was a Liongo, his brothers and sisters, and the King before him, Kwash Moki, who became King at twenty and ruled until he was forty and five.

"What news on black wings?"

I knew I jumped. I knew he saw me.

"Nothing," I said.

I grabbed the batch of papers and placed them on the table. The candles threw colour on them like weak sunlight.

"This is the house of Akum," I said. "Rulers for over five hundred years, right up to Kwash Dara. His father is Netu, here. Above him, here, is Aduware the Cheetah King, who was third in line, when the crown prince died, and his brother banished. Then above him is Liongo the great, who ruled nearly seventy years. Who doesn't know the great King Liongo? Then over here on this leaf, Liongo again and above him, Moki, his father, the boy King."

"Turn the page."

"I did. There's nothing before."

"You didn't—"

"Look," I said, pointing at the blank page. "Nothing is there."

"But Moki is not the first Akum King, that would make the line about two hundred and fifty years old."

"Two hundred and seventy."

"Keep flipping," Mossi said.

"Family map. Fasisi Kwash Dara. Akum. His seat of rule, his praise name, his king name, and his family."

Three pages up, another family map someone drew in a darker blue. At the top of the page was Akum. At the bottom was Kwash Kagar, Moki's father. But above him something curious, and above that even more curious.

"Is this a new line? An old one, I mean," the prefect said.

"House of Akum up to Moki's father. What do you notice?"

"Above Kagar is a line pointing to Tiefulu? That's a woman's name. His mother."

"Beside hers."

"Kwash Kong."

"Now look above Kong."

"Another woman, another sister. Tracker, no king is the son of a king."

"Until Moki."

"There are many kingdoms that follow the wife's line, or the sister."

"Not the North Kingdom. From Moki down, every king is the king's oldest son, not his sister's son. Grab these."

I went back to the glyphs. He followed me over, looking at the maps, not at me.

"What did you say about kings and gods?" I said.

"I said nothing about kings and—"

"You tiresome in all your ways?"

He dropped the papers at my feet and grabbed the writs.

"A king is king by a queen, not a king," he said.

"Give me that. Look at this writ."

He bent over me. This was not the time to think of myrrh. He read, "'That the house of kings return to the ways that had been decreed by the gods, and not this course which has corrupted the ways of kings for six generations. This is what we demand: that the king follow the natural order set by gods of sky and gods below the earth. Return to the purity of the line as set in the words of long-dead griots and forgotten tongues.' This is what he wrote."

"So the northern line of kings changed from king's sister's son to king's son, six generations ago. These are facts for any that would look. No reason to murder an elder. And these writs, sure they call for a return to the old order, which some might say is mad, some might say is treason, but most will never go so far back in the line of kings to check," I said.

"And what do you think will happen if they do?"

"Outrage maybe."

He laughed. Such irritation.

"The times are the times, and people are people. Something so long ago? People will shrug it off like a smelly blanket," he said.

"Something here is missing or—"

"What do you not tell me?" he said. His eyes narrowed in a wicked frown.

"You have seen what I see. I have told you what I know," I said.

"What do you think?"

"I have no duty to tell you what I think."

"Tell me anyway."

He stooped down next to me and the papers. Those eyes of his. Popping bright in the near-dark.

"I think this is connected to that child. The one from Fumanguru's house."

"The one you think the murderers took with them?"

"They were not the ones who took the child. Before you ask how I know, just know I know. Someone I know claims she saved the child that night. Whoever sent assassins to Fumanguru must know somebody saved the child."

"They wish to wash the world clean of him and mask their tracks."

"That is what I thought. But too much has happened. There is no reason to kill Fumanguru, none other than they were after the child in the first place. It would be why so many people are still interested in such an old murder. I asked one who would know two days ago if he picked up any word on any man like Fumanguru. He told me two elders fucking a deaf girl said they had to find the writs, or it would be the death of someone. Maybe them. One was Belekun the Big. You should know I killed him," I said.

"Oh?"

"Not before he tried to kill me. In Malakal. Had his men try to kill me as well."

"A more stupid man has not been born, clearly. Continue, Tracker."

"Anyway, the other was a whore named Ekoiye. He said let us talk in another place, so we went by tunnel to a roof. First he told me that many still go to the Fumanguru house. Including some of you."

"Of course."

"And others in your uniform."

"I only went there twice. Alone."

"There were others."

"Not without my order."

"He said—"

"You trust the good word of a prostitute over a man of justice?"

"You're a man of order, not justice," I said.

"Continue with your story."

"No surprise you confuse the two."

"Continue, I say."

"He told me all who still go by the Fumanguru house—looking for what, he didn't know. Then he tried to cast a spell on me with kohl dust dried in viper venom," I said.

"And you live? One breath could have killed a horse. Or made you a zombi."

"I know. I threw him off the roof."

"The gods, Tracker. Is he dead too?"

"No. But you are right. He tried to make me a

zombi, to drag me back to his room. Then he would release a pigeon to let someone know he has me. I released the pigeon myself. Trust me, prefect, it was not long before a man came to the room, with weapons, but I think he came to take me, not kill me."

"Take you where? To who?"

"I killed him before I could find out. He was dressed as a prefect."

"The trail of bodies you are leaving behind, Tracker. Soon the whole city will stink because of you."

"I said he was dressed as a—"

"I heard what you said."

"He didn't leave a body. I will tell you more of that later. But this. When he died I saw something like black wings leave him."

"Of course. What is a story without beautiful black wings? What has any of this to do with the boy?"

"I seek the boy. That is why I am here. A slaver hired me and some others, strangers to your city, to search for the boy. Together at first, but most have gone their own way. But others seek the boy. No, not hired by the slaver. I cannot tell if they follow us or are one step ahead of us. They have tried to kill us before."

"Well you do not slack when it comes to killing, Tracker."

"We were sent here for a reason. To see from where he was taken, yes, but more to see where they went."

"Oh. There is still much you are not telling me. Like who is this they? Were there people who came to kill him, and people who came to save him? And if the people who came to save him then took him, what is that to you? Would he not be safer with them than with you?"

"The people who saved him lost him."

"Of course. Maybe the same people sold him to witches."

"No, but they trusted the wrong people. But there is this. I think I know who he is, this b——"

"This still follows no sense. I have a different idea."

"You do."

"Yes, I do."

"The world awaits."

"Your trusted Fumanguru was a part of the illicit arts, or trades. Makes no difference; both result in innocents sold, raped, or killed. He dug a hole for himself so deep and wide that he fell into it. It was a clean kill, a complete kill, all but the boy. As long as the boy is alive, all accounts are not settled. Those are the people after your boy."

"A good argument. Except most do not know of the boy. Not even you until I told you."

"What, then?"

"He was protecting the boy. Hiding him. He would have been but a baby back then. You should know that I know who this boy is. I have no proof, but when I do, he will be who I think he is. Until I do, what is this?"

I handed him the paper strip I took from the pigeon. He brought it right to his nose, then held it away from his face. "This is in the same style as the glyphs on the writ. It says, News of the boy, come now."

"The prefect who tried to kill me had these things branded on his chest."

"This?"

"Clearly not this. But characters in this style."

"Do you—"

"No, I don't remember. But Fumanguru uses their tongue."

"Such a puzzle, Tracker. The more you tell me, the less I know."

"Was that all? All of what Fumanguru wrote?"

He looked through the papers again. Two more smelled of soured milk. He traced each mark with his hand as I read them.

"It is instructions," he said. "'Take him to Mitu, to the guided hand of the one-eyed one, walk through Mweru and let it eat your trail.' This is what it says."

"No man comes back from the Mweru."

"Is that true? Or what old wives say? This last of this text is unreadable to me."

"Why would he send him there? He will be a man too," I said.

"Who will be a man?"

"I was talking to myself."

"No mothers taught you this was rude? You said you knew who he is, this child. Who is he?"

I looked at him.

"Then tell me who gives him chase and why."

"That would be to tell you who he is."

"Tracker, I cannot help you this way."

"Who asked for your help?"

"Of course, the gods must smile at how far you have come on your own."

"Listen. There have been three who hired me to find this child. A slaver, a river spirit, and a witch. Between them, they have told me five stories so far of who this child is."

"Five lies to find him or save him?"

"Both. Neither."

"They wish that you save him, but do not wish that you know who you save. Are you one to betray him?"

"I wondered how a prefect felt about men for hire."

"No, you wondered how I feel about you."

He started walking around the stacks, behind a wall of them. I could hear the slight drag of one foot, a limp that he masked well.

"But this is the hall of records, is it not?" he said.

"'Tis your city."

"Who records the lives of kings?"

I turned and pointed behind the keeper's desk. He would not return tonight, that was sure. The book was also leaves, sewn rough and uneven, and bound in a leather sleeve, dustier than the others. An account of Kwash Dara, up until that day. His name, in a line with his two brothers, and one sister. One brother married the daughter of the Queen of Dolingo, to build an alliance. One married the widow of a chieftain with little land, but great wealth in the grasslands.

The oldest sister is listed first among the women, and here it said only that she gave over her life to serving Wapa, the goddess of earth, fertility, and women, after her husband, a prince from Juba, died at his own hand, taking also their children. The story says nothing of where she went, nothing of a mountain fortress.

"What of older kings? Kings of the ages before this one?" said Mossi.

"The griots. Even with the written word, the true mark of a king would have been men committing their story to memory, to recite it as in poetry, or when the people gather to hear praise of famous men. Here is my guess. Written accounts of kings began only with Kwash Netu's age. The rest belong only in the voices of the griots. And there is the problem. The men who sing about the deeds of all kings are in the King's employ."

"Oh."

"There are others. Griots whose record of the kings the King does not know. Men who wrote secret verses, men with songs that would get them executed, and the songs forbidden."

"Who would they sing them to?"

"To themselves. Some men think truth only needs to be in service to truth."

"Alas, dead men then."

"Most. But there are two, maybe three whose songs go back a thousand years."

"Do they claim to go back a thousand years as well?"

"Why do you limp?"

"What?"

"Nothing."

"Oh, boy of such wayward fate. You know, Tracker, you have ventured very far in this, and not once have you even given things a whisper."

"What things?"

"You speaking intrigue on who is still your King. Or that as prefect I am his servant."

Much time had slipped since I looked at his sword. Engage the enemy first, that is how he would have it. But he turned his back to me and stood looking at a stack.

"Fumanguru produces this whatever you call it against the King, and because he was murdered, you figure him blameless. Cast your eyes on the world as we prefects do. You are about to ask what I mean. I mean thus. More times than not, whenever some deed most foul comes to a man's door, it's because he invited him in."

"So every death comes to the victim who deserves it. You truly are a prefect."

"What a wife you will make someone one day."

I did not even bother to glare.

"So do as your superiors do and call the matter shut. Hear this. Since this is an open space where any may enter, and since I am not connected to any crime, be a good member of the Kongori chieftain army and be gone."

"Now hold—"

"Is our business not done, prefect? There is a child you do not believe lives, a writ you think means nothing, about a king whom you serve and believe blameless, and not connected to a series of events that did not happen, or even if they did happen, meant nothing. All surrounding a man whose entire family was murdered because of some snake he took to his home thinking it a pet, only to have it bite him. Is that about all of it, prefect? It surprises me you're still here. Make distance between us. Go ahead."

"I will not be dismissed by you."

"Oh fuck the gods! Then stay. I will leave."

"You forget who has authority in this room," he said, drawing his sword.

"You have authority over your own kind. Where are they, your black-and-blue zombi?"

He held his sword out straight and came at me. The **zup** sound shot between us and we jumped back as the spear lodged itself in the floor. Black with blue marks.

"One of yours," I said.

"Shut your mouth!"

A quick light shone from above us, and only when the arrow lodged into a tower of books did we see the light was flame. A shadow in the window had shot a flaming arrow down at us. The fire rose from the floor and flicked a tail. It twisted left, then right, then left like a lizard seeing too many things to eat. The flame jumped on a stack, and fire burst from each book, one then another, then another, up and up.

Three more arrows came through the windows. The fire halted me, tricked me into stopping to wonder how come an entire wall was raging in flames. A hand grabbed mine and pulled me out of the spell.

"Tracker! This way."

Smoke burned my eyes and made me cough. I couldn't remember if the Sangoma protected me from fire. Mossi pulled me along, cursing that I wasn't moving faster. We dashed through an arch of flames right before they collapsed, and burning paper hit my heel. He jumped over a stack of books, went through a wall of smoke, and vanished. I looked back, almost slowed down to think of the fire's speed, and jumped through the smoke. And landed almost on top of him.

"Stay to the ground. Less smoke. And they will see less of us when we come out."

"They?"

"You think this is one man?"

This section of the hall had only smoke, but the fire was running out of food and hungrier than ever. It jumped from stack to stack, and ate through papyrus and leather. A tower fell and shot flames through the smoke wall at us. We scrambled. I could not remember where to find the door. He grabbed my robe and pulled me again. We ran right, between two walls of books, then left, then right, and then what felt like north but I did not know. Mossi's hand still gripped my robe. The heat was close enough that the hair on my skin burned. We reached the door. Mossi swung it open and jumped back before four arrows hit the floor.

"How far can you throw those?"

I grabbed the ax. "Far enough."

"Good. Judging from how these arrows lean, they are on the roof to the right."

He ran back into the smoke and came out with two books burning. He nodded to window, then pointed at the door. Don't give them a chance to grab new arrows. He threw the books out the window and four arrows cut through the wind, two hitting the window. I ran, dropped, and rolled out the door, then jumped up, ax in hand, and threw it. As the ax spun towards the archers it curved, slicing one man's throat and lodging in the other's temple. I jumped into the dark and out of the path of two arrows. More arrows kept coming, some with flame, some with poison, like rainfall until it stopped.

The hall burned in every wall, every chamber, and a crowd started to gather in the street. No more archers waited on the roof. I slipped away from the crowd and ran around to the back of the building. Up on the roof Mossi wiped his sword on the skirt of a dead man and sheathed it. How he passed me I don't know. Also this: On the roof lay four bodies, not two.

"I know what you will say. Don't sa—"

"These men are prefects."

He walked to the ledge and watched the blaze. "Two of them are dead," he said.

"Are they not all dead?"

"Yes, but two were dead before we killed them. The fat one is Biza, the tall one Thwoko. Both have been missing for over ten and three moons, but nobody knew what happened to them. They—"

I heard them in the dark and knew what was happening. The dead men's mouths tearing open. The rumbling and rattling from toes to head as if death came in fits. Even in the dark the ripples rose from their thighs, to belly, to chest and then flew out the mouth in a cloud inky as night, a cloud we could barely see, which swirled and then vanished in the air. Too many shadows to see, but I knew on the spin of cloud and dust formed wings, for we both heard the flutter. We both stood there, looking at each other, neither wanting to say anything first, anything that spoke of what we just saw.

"They will crumble to dust if you touch them," I said.

"Then best not to touch them," a man said, and I jumped. Mossi smiled.

"Mazambezi, was it the flames that drew you or you missed the smell of me?"

"Indeed, one lives with shit, one gets used to the perfume of it."

Two more prefects climbed up on the roof, neither saying anything to Mossi, but both looking over at the fire and covering their mouths at the smoke that started drifting our way.

"What do we do when we watch our history burn?" Mazambezi said.

"Your words speak of such loss, Mazambezi. We shall fill a new hall," Mossi said.

"How did it start, do you know?"

"Don't you know? Your men—"

"Some men dressed as chieftain army," Mossi said, interrupting me. "I saw them myself, fire arrows into the great hall. Maybe they are usurpers. Hurting us where it would hurt the most."

"This too will need a record. And where shall we store them?" Mazambezi laughed.

"You must take a look at these men, Mazambezi, their whole bodies are racked by dark craft," Mossi said, and looked at the bodies again. It flashed, catching the light of the fire, and I yelled.

"Mossi!"

He ducked just as Mazambezi's sword sliced through the air right above his head. The duck made him stumble. One of the men drew a small bow and aimed at me. I dropped beside the body that had caught my ax in the skull. I tore it out as an arrow flew in and replaced it. I jumped up and flung my ax, which spun and blurred and struck him in the middle of his chest. Mazambezi and a prefect both fought Mossi with swords. Mazambezi charged at him, sword out straight like a spear. Mossi dodged and kicked him in the chest with his knees. Mazambezi elbowed him in the side; Mossi fell and spun out of the other prefect's strike, which sparked lights on the ground. The prefect raised his sword again but Mossi swung from the ground and chopped off his foot. The prefect fell, screaming. Mossi jumped up and drove his sword down into the prefect's chest. He paused, panting, and Mazambezi sliced right across his back. I jumped between them and swung my ax. His blade met my blade and the force knocked him clear across the floor. He rose, shocked, confused, Mossi jumped in between us.

"Enough with this madness, Mazambezi, you called yourself incorruptible."

"You call yourself handsome, and yet I can't see what the women see in you."

Mossi held his sword up, as did Mazambezi, and circled as if to clash again. I jumped in between them.

"Tracker! He will—"

Mazambezi swung his sword a hair's length from my face, and I caught the blade. It shocked the prefect. He pulled his sword to cut my fingers but drew no blood. Mazambezi stood there, stunned. Two swords went straight through his back and came out through his belly. Mossi yanked his swords back, and the prefect fell.

"I would ask how, but do I—"

"A Sangoma. An enchantment. He would have killed me with a wooden sword," I said.

Mossi nodded, not accepting the answer, but not wanting to push for another one.

"More of them will come," I said.

"Mazambezi was not like the others. He spoke."

"He only possesses some. He pays the others."

Mossi turned back to watch the crowd, all lit up by firelight. He cursed and ran past me. I followed him down the rear staircase, jumping three steps like he did. He dashed into the crowd. I ran after him but the crowd surged forward and pulled back like waves. Someone cried that Kongor is lost, for how can we have a future without our past? The crowd confused me, made me deaf and blind until I remembered that I could now smell the library master. Mossi slapped him in the dark, slapped him until I grabbed his hand. The bookkeeper cowered on the ground.

"Mossi."

"This whoreson will not talk."

"Mossi."

"They murder my books, they murder my books," the library master said.

"Let me speak for you. A man came to you and said, Send word if any man comes by asking for records of Fumanguru. I come in, I say where are the records for Fumanguru, and you sent word by pigeon."

He nodded yes.

"Who?" Mossi shouted.

"One of yours," I said to him.

"Stick your falsehoods up your asshole, Tracker."

"The only thing lying to you are your own eyes."

"Why they murder my books? Why they murder my books?" the library master wailed.

"We will see what he knows and does not know."

I went right up to Mossi.

"Listen to me. He is no different from Ekoiye. Told only what he could be trusted to know, which is nothing. Told by just a messenger, not the man sending the message. Maybe chieftain army, maybe not. Somebody is both one step ahead of us, waiting for us to come, and one step behind us, waiting for us to move so that he can follow. Somewhere in the course of the last hour we were being watched, and that person heard enough."

"Tracker."

"Listen to me."

"Tracker."

"What?"

"The keeper."

I cursed. The keeper was gone.

"That old man could not have gone far," Mossi said, just as some women screamed and a man shouted, No, old man, no.

"He didn't plan to," I said.

Right then the library roof caved in and killed some of the flames, but the whole square was hot and bright.

"Distance between us and this place, we need now," I said.

Mossi nodded. We turned down an empty alley that had puddles even though the rains were long gone, and where wild dogs tore through whatever people threw out. A dog looking almost like a hyena made me shudder. Sogolon was nowhere eyes could see and neither was the girl. All I knew of Sogolon's smell was lemongrass and fish, which could have been any of hundreds of women. I've never smelled her skin on the girl's and the Ogo did not have much of a smell. I never thought to make mark of the lord of the house, or the buffalo.

"We should head east," I said.

"This is south."

"You lead, then."

He turned right at the nearest alley, also deserted.

"We Kongori must lack entertainment if a little fire can pull us away."

"There was nothing little about that fire," I said.

He turned to me. "And they will think it the work of a foreigner first."

"Except it was members of your own force."

He tapped my chest. "You need to cut that thought loose."

"And you need to look at what is loose all around you."

"Those were not my men."

"Those men wore your uniform."

"But they were not my men."

"You recognized two."

"Did you not hear me?"

"Oh, I hear you."

"Don't give me that look."

"You can't see my look."

"I know you have it."

"What look, third prefect of the Kongori chieftain army?"

"That one. The one saying he's a fool, or he's slow, or he denies what he sees."

"Look, we can leave or we can have words, but we cannot do both."

"Since your ways of seeing are so superior to mine, look behind you and say if he is friend or foe."

He walked slow as if with his own business. We stopped. He stopped, perhaps two hundred paces behind us, not in the alley but where it crossed the lane going north. This could not be the first time I am noticing that it was dark, I thought. Mossi was beside me, breathing fast.

His hair short and red. Earplugs glimmered in both ears. The same man I saw back in the pool in the Darklands. This man Bunshi called the Aesi. In a black cape that flapped open like wings, waking up the wind and whipping up the dust. Mossi drew his sword; I did not draw my knives. The dust around him would not settle, rising and falling and swirling and shifting into lizard-like beasts as high as the walls, then swirling again into dust, then into four figures as huge as the Ogo, then falling to the ground as dust, then rising again and flapping like wings. The prefect grabbed my shoulder.

"Tracker!"

Mossi ran off and I followed. He ran to the end of the alley and dashed right. Truth, he ran faster than the Leopard. I turned back once and saw the Aesi still standing there, wind and dust unsettled around him. We had run into a street that had some people. They all walked in the same direction and slow as if coming from the fire. He would notice us running faster than everyone else. Mossi, as if he heard me, slowed. But they—women, some children, mostly men—were moving too slow, taking for granted that bed would be as they left it. We were passing them, looking back at times, but the Aesi was not following us. A woman in a white gown pulled her son along, the son looking back and trying to pull away from her. The child looked up and stared at me. I thought his mother would pull him away, but she had stopped too. She stared at me like the boy did, like the blank stare of a dead man. Mossi spun around and saw it too. Every man, woman, and child in the street was looking at us. But they stood still as if made of wood. No limb moved, not even a finger. Only their necks moved, to turn and look at us. We kept walking slow, they kept standing still, and their eyes kept following us. "Tracker," Mossi said, but so under his breath that I barely heard it. Their eyes kept following us. An old man who was walking the other way turned so much, with his feet planted on the ground, that I thought his backbone would snap. Mossi still gripped his sword.

"He's possessing them," I said.

"Why is he not possessing us?"

"I don't—"

The mother dropped her child's hand and charged at me, screaming. I dodged out of her way and swung my foot for her to trip. Her son leapt onto my back, biting into it until Mossi pulled him off. The child hissed and the hiss woke the people. They all charged after us. We ran, I elbowed an old man in the face and knocked him over, and Mossi swatted another with the flat side of his sword.

"Don't kill them," I said.

"I know."

I heard a hum. A man hit me in the back with a rock. Mossi punched him away. I kicked two down, leapt onto the shoulder of another, and jumped over them. Mossi slapped away two children and their mothers who came charging after. Two young boys jumped me and we fell flat in the mud. Mossi grabbed one by the collar, pulled him off, and threw him against the wall. God forgive me, or punish me, I said before I punched the other and knocked him out. And still more came. Some of the men had swords, spears, and daggers, but none used them. They all tried to grab us and push us down in the dirt. We had run only halfway. But from the end of the street came a rumble, and the screams of women and men flying into the air, left, right, then left, then right, then again. Many ran away. Too many ran straight to the buffalo, who charged through them, knocking them away with head and horns. Behind him, each on a horse, Sogolon and the girl. The buffalo plowed down a path for us and snorted when he saw me.

"He will possess all who pass by this alley," Sogolon said as she rode up to us.

"I know."

"Who are these people?" Mossi said, but jumped back when the buffalo grunted at him.

"No time to explain, we should leave. They will not stay down, Mossi."

He looked behind him. Some of the people were waking up. Two swung around and stared at us.

"I don't need saving from them."

"No, but with that sword, they will soon need saving from you," Sogolon said, and pointed him to the girl's horse. Sogolon jumped off her own. Many of the men and women had risen, and the children were already up.

"Sogolon, we leave," I said, mounting her horse and grabbing the reins.

The people were gathering strong, huddling, becoming one shadow in the dark. She stooped and started drawing runes in the dirt. Fuck the gods, we have no time for this, I thought. Instead I looked at Mossi, holding on to the girl, who said nothing, looking grim, looking calm, playing at both. The crowd as one ran towards us. Sogolon drew another rune in the dirt, not even looking up. The crowd was coming in close, maybe eighty paces. She stood up and looked at us, the crowd now close enough that we could see their eyes lost and faces without feeling even though they shouted. She stomped in the dirt; a gust rose and blew them down whom it did not blow away. It knocked men to the ground and women in robes up into the sky and barreled children away. The storm swept the alley all the way down to the end.

Sogolon got back on her horse and we galloped through the quarter, riding as if many were chasing us, though no one did. She gripped the reins, and I gripped her waist. I knew where we were when we came to the border road. The house was northeast, but we did not ride to the house. Instead we stayed on the border road between Nyembe and Gallunkobe/ Matyube until it took us to the flooded river. Sogolon did not stop.

"Witch, you plan to drown us?"

Sogolon laughed. "This is where the river is most shallow," she said. The buffalo ran at her side, the girl with Mossi behind her.

"We will not leave Sadogo behind."

"He awaits us."

I did not ask where. We crossed the river into what I knew would be Mitu. Mitu was fertile grasslands, a gathering of farmers, land lords, and owners of cattle, not a city. Sogolon led us to a dirt path lit only by moonlight. We rode under trees, the buffalo leading, the prefect quiet. He surprised me.

At the first cross paths, Sogolon said to dismount. Sadogo came out from behind a tree shorter than him and stood up.

"How is the night keeping you, Sadogo?" I asked.

He shrugged and smiled. He opened his mouth to say something but stopped. Even he knew that if he started talking it would be dawn before he stopped. He looked over at the girl and frowned when he saw Mossi dismount.

"His name is Mossi. I will tell you in the morning. Should we make a fire?"

"Who said we staying here? In a crossroad?" Sogolon said.

"I thought you witches had special love for crossroads," I said.

"Follow me," she said.

We stood right in the middle of the two roads. I looked over at Sadogo, helping the girl down from the horse, making sure he was between her and the prefect.

"I know I do not have to tell you of the ten and nine doors," Sogolon said.

"That is how we came to Kongor."

"There is one right here."

"Old woman, that is what all old women think about where roads cross. If not a door then some other kind of night magic."

"This look like a night for your foolishness?"

"You are afraid of him. I do not think I have ever seen fear on you. Let me gaze upon your face. Here is truth, Sogolon. I cannot tell if your mood is sour or if that is how you always look. I know who he is. The boy."

"Aje o ma pa ita yi onyin auhe."

"The hen doesn't even know when she will be cooked so perhaps she should listen to the egg," I said, and winked at Sogolon, who scowled.

"So who is he?" she asked.

"Somebody this Aesi is trying with all his might to find before you do. To kill him maybe, to steal him maybe, but he wants to find this boy as badly as you do. And it all points to the King."

"Would you have believe it if it was me who tell you?"

"No."

"The King want to erase the Night of the Skulls, that child—"

"That child is who he was after all along. Maybe the Aesi searches on his behalf, maybe the redhead devil acts alone. I have read Fumanguru's writs."

"There are no writs."

"You're too old for games."

"Nobody could find them."

"And yet I've read them. There are more treacherous words in the games of little girls."

"This is not the place."

"But it is the time. All your witchery and you never read the line on top of the lines."

"Talk plain, fool."

"He wrote notes on top of the words in milk. He said to take the child to the Mweru. You stare at me. So quiet you are. Walk through Mweru and let it eat your trail, that is what he said."

"Yes. Yes. No man ever map the Mweru, and no god either. The child would be safe."

"Might as well say he will be safe in hell."

"There is a door here, Tracker."

"We have already spoken on that. Open it."

"I cannot, and never could. Only those of the Sangoma have the words that open doors. You have used it twice, do not lie."

"The first one was just a door that witches hide. Nothing like the door to Kongor. Who is the boy?"

"You said you know. You don't know. But you brand a guess on you. Open this door and I will tell you what you read in that library. Open the door."

I stepped away from her and looked back at them all watching me. I clasped my hands below my mouth as if catching water to drink, and whispered the word taught to me by the Sangoma. I blew, half thinking the uncaring night would leave me standing here a fool, half thinking that right in front of me fire would form in the shape of a door. A spark formed as high above me as a tree, a spark as if striking two swords together. From the top the flame spread in two directions, curving like a circle until both ends struck the road. Then the flame died out.

"There it is, witch, the flame died and there is no door. Because we are in the crossroads, where there would be no door in the first place. I know you are from lower folk, but even up to a few days ago you must have seen what we call a door."

"Will he shut up soon?" Mossi said to the girl. She laughed. It enraged me. More than I expected anything from him to do. Furious and having no way to show it, I just started walking. Ten and five paces in, I saw the road was not dirt but stone. The dark turned brighter, like silver from moonlight, and the air felt cold and thin. The trees taller and farther apart than Mitu, and far off and above clouds, black mountains.

The others followed. I could not see Mossi's face but knew how shocked he would be.

"Even a sangomin, when he's not whining like an unfed bitch, can do mighty feats. Or just this," she said as she mounted her horse and rode past me.

The buffalo passed me, then the girl. Mossi was staring at me, but other than his eyes, I could not read his face. I ran and caught up with Sogolon. She waited for me to climb on behind her. The air got colder the farther we went, so much that I tried to spread the curtain to cover more of me.

"Do not sleep tonight," she whispered.

"But sleep is already claiming me."

"The Aesi will jump in your dream looking for you."

"Shall I never wake up?"

"You will wake, but he will see morning through you."

"I do not recognize this air," I said.

"You in Dolingo, four days' ride from the citadel," she said, and we continued up the hill.

"The last door took me right into the city."

"The door is not here to obey you."

"I know who your boy is," I whispered.

"You think you know. Who is he then?"

SIXTEEN

L et the girl switch with you or here is where we stop riding," Sogolon said.

"Here I thought you would welcome a young man so near your bottom."

"This the kind of bottom you would be near now? What you selling us now, Wolf Eye?"

She made me so quickly furious that I jumped off.

"You. The witch rather you ride with her," I said to the girl, who hopped down.

"Want to ride or be ridden?" Mossi said to me.

"All but sky shits on me tonight."

He gave me his hand and pulled me up. I tried to brace my hands against the horse's hind instead of holding him, by my hands kept slipping. Mossi reached behind with his hand, grabbed my right, and placed it on his side. Then reached back with his other hand and did the same with my left.

"Wearing myrrh part of being a prefect?"

"Wearing myrrh is part of everything, Tracker."

"Fancy prefect. Coin must be good in Kongor."

"Look, you gods, a man wearing a curtain complains of me being fancy."

The road smelled of wetlands. The horses sometimes stepped as if they were stuck. I grew tired, and felt all the cuts and scrapes from Kongor, one on my forearm feeling the most deep. I opened my eyes to feel two of his fingers on my forehead, pushing me off his shoulder. All I could think was fuck the gods if I had drooled on him.

"He must not sleep, is what she said. Why must you not sleep?" Mossi asked.

"The old witch and her old witch stories. She fears the Aesi will jump in my dreams."

"Is this one more thing I should know?"

"Only if you believe it. She thinks he will visit me in dreams, and take my mind from me."

"You do not believe?"

"I feel if the Aesi wants to take hold of your mind, part of you must have wanted to give it."

"A high regard you all have for each other," he said.

"Oh we are to each other like the snake is to the hawk. But look what love for your prefects has got you."

He said nothing after that. I had the feeling that I hurt him, which bothered me. Everything my father said bothered me, but none so much that I would sit back and think of it. My grandfather, I mean.

We stopped as soon as the ground felt more dry. A clearing surrounded by thin savannah trees. Sogolon took a long twig and scratched runes in a circle around us, then ordered me and the prefect to find wood for the fire. Off in the thick of the trees, I saw her talking to Sadogo and pointing into the sky. Mossi broke two branches off a tree. He turned around, saw me, and walked over till he was not far from my face.

"The old woman, is she your mother?"

"Fuck the gods, prefect. Is it not clear I despise her?"

"That is why I asked."

I shoved my branches on top of his and walked away. She was still scratching runes when I stood behind her. Are these just for you, I thought, but did not say. Sadogo grabbed a tree trunk, ripped it out of the earth, and laid it on its side for the girl to sit. Mossi tried to pet the buffalo, but he snorted at him and the prefect jumped back.

"Sogolon. We will have words, witch. Which lie do you wish to start with first? That the boy was Fumanguru's blood? Or that the Omoluzu were after Fumanguru?" I said.

She threw away the stick, stooped in the circle, and blew a soft whisper.

"We will have words, Sogolon."

"That day is no closer, Tracker."

"That day?"

"The day when you are master over me."

"Sogolon, you—"

A gust hit me in the chest, spun me in the air, and hurled me across the clearing before I saw her even blow. The Ogo ran over and pulled me up. He tried to dust me off, but each brush felt like a punch. I told him I was clean now and sat down by the fire Mossi had started. The girl looked at me awhile before she opened her mouth.

"Annoy her again and she done destroy you," she said.

"And how will she find her boy?"

"She is Sogolon, master of the ten and nine doors. You seen it."

"And yet she needs me to pass through them."

"She don't need you, this I know."

"Then why am I still here? What do you know? Only days ago you were happy to be Zogbanu meat."

The night stayed cold. Sadogo's tree trunk was small enough for me to rest my head on. The fire blazed in the sky and warmed the ground, yet it looked as if it was getting weaker until it went black, though it still crackled and popped.

The slap scorched my cheek and shocked my eyes open. I grabbed my ax to swing when I saw the girl over me.

"No sleep till you come to Dolingo citadel. That is what she say."

I boxed the buffalo's ears until he whipped me with his tail. I asked the Ogo every question I could think of that would make him talk till morning, but he tried to swat me away. Then he yawned and fell asleep. And then the girl climbed on top of him and rested on his chest. There would be nothing of her if he rolled over, but she looked like she had done this before. Sogolon curled like an infant in her circle of runes and snored.

"Walk with me. I hear a river," Mossi said.

"What if I have no wish—"

"Must you be the crabby husband in everything? Come with me or keep your place, either way I go."

I caught up to him in a patch of thin trees with branches that scratched like thorns. He was still in front of me, stepping over dead trunks and chopping away branches and bush.

"And you can sense the boy?" he said, as if we were talking before.

"In a way. It has been said I have a nose."

"By whom?" he asked.

"Whom indeed. If I get the smell of a man, or woman, or child, my nose follows him wherever he goes, no matter how far, until he dies."

"Even to other lands?"

"Sometimes."

"I do not believe you."

"Are there no fantastic beasts in your land?"

"So you call yourself a beast?"

"And every question you reply with a question."

"By my life 'tis as if you've always known me." Mossi grinned. He tripped and I grabbed his arm before he fell. He nodded his thanks and continued. "Where is he now?"

"South. In Dolingo perhaps."

"We are already in Dolingo."

"Maybe the citadel. I don't know. Sometimes his smell is so strong that I think he is where you are, then days later he would vanish as if his scent was something I woke up from. It never goes from strong to weak or weak to strong, just all here sometimes for a few days, then all gone."

"Fantastic beast indeed."

"I am a man."

"I can see that, Tracker."

He stopped and pressed in my chest. "Viper," he said.

"Do people say you have an ear?"

"That was not very funny."

The night hid my smile and I was glad for it. I walked around where he pointed. I heard no river, nor did I smell any river smells.

"Who is this Omoluzu that was after Fumanguru?"

"Would you believe me if I told you?"

"Half a day ago I was in my chambers drinking tea with beer in it. Now I am in Dolingo. Ten days' ride that took less than one night. I have seen one man possess many and something like dust rise out of dead men."

"You Kongori do not believe in magic and spirits."

"I am not Kongori, but you speak true, I do not believe. Some people believe the goddess speaks to leaves so they grow, and whisper in a spell to coax a flower to open wide. Others believe that if they just feed it sun and water, both will make them grow. There are only two things, Tracker: that which men of wisdom can explain, and that which they will explain. Of course you do not agree."

"Just like all you men of learning. Everything in the world cooks down to two. Either-or, if-then, yes-no, night-day, good-bad. You all believe in twos so much I wonder if any of you can count to three."

"Harsh. But you are no believer either."

"Maybe I have no love for sides."

"Maybe you have no love for commitment."

"Do we still speak of Omoluzu?"

He laughed too much, I thought. At nearly everything. We came out of the bush. He stretched his hand out to hold me from stepping farther. A cliff, though the drop was not far. The cloud gathered thick in this part of the sky. It made me think of gods of sky walking the nine worlds, causing thunder, but I could not remember when last I heard thunder from the sky.

"There is your river," he said.

We watched the water below us, still and deep, though you could hear it lash against rocks farther up.

"Omoluzu are roof walkers. Summoned by witches or anyone in a pact with witches. But to summon them is not enough; you must throw the blood of woman or man against the ceiling. Wet or dry. It awakens them, they hunger for it, and they will kill and drink from whoever has it. Many witches have died because they think Omoluzu seeks only the person whose blood is shed. But Omoluzu hunger is monstrous—it is the smell of blood that lures them, not the taste. And once summoned they run along the ceiling the way we run along road, and kill everything not called Omoluzu. I have fought them."

"What? Where?"

"Another place your wise people would say does not exist. Once they've tasted your blood they will never stop following you until you are in the next world. Or the reverse. And you can never live under a roof, or shed, or even pass under a bridge again. They are black like night and thick like tar and when they appear on your ceiling it sounds like thunder and sea. One thing about them. They do not need blood, if your witchcraft is strong, but you would have to be a witch among witches, the greatest necromancer, or at least one of them. One more thing. They never touch the floor, even when they jump; the ceiling pulls them back as surely as this ground pulls us."

"And these Omoluzu killed elder Fumanguru and his wife and all his sons? Even his servants?" he asked.

"Who else could cleave a woman in two with a single chop?"

"Come, Tracker, we seem to both be men of learning rather than faith. So rest, if you don't believe her."

"We both saw this Aesi, and what he can do."

"Ill wind mixed with dust."

I yawned.

"Belief or no belief, Tracker, you are losing this fight with night."

Mossi pulled at his two belts and the scabbard

dropped to the ground. Then he stooped, unstrapped both sandals, unwrapped the blue sashes on his tunic, then grabbed his tunic at the neck, pulled the whole thing right off his head, and threw it away as if he would never wear them again. He stood before me, his chest two barrels, his belly waves of muscle, and below that, a patch that drew shadow before anyone could see lower, and ran back from the edge to give himself a start. Before I could say what a mad idea this was, he ran past me and jumped off, yelling all the way till the splash cut him off.

"Fuck all your gods, this is cold! Tracker! Why are you still up there?"

"Because the moon has not made me mad."

"The moon, precious sister, thinks you are the mad one. A sky with open arms yet you will not fly. A river, her legs spread open, yet you will not dive."

I could see him splashing and diving in the silver water. Sometimes he was like shadow, but when he floated he was as light as the moon. Two moons when he flipped himself up in a dive.

"Tracker. Forsake me not in this river. Regard it, I am attacked by river demons. I shall die of sickness right here. Or will it be a water witch who drowns me so that I can become her husband. Tracker, I shall not stop shouting your name until you do. Tracker, do you not wish to stay awake? Tracker! Tracker!"

Now I wanted to jump, just to land on his head. But sleep came at me like a mistress.

"Tracker. Do not even think of jumping into this river wearing that stupid curtain. You act as if clothes are second nature to the Ku, when we all know."

You have been trying to get me out my robes for two days now, I thought but did not say. My splash was so loud I thought it was somebody else's until I sunk under the water. The cold hit so hard and sharp that I sucked in water and broke the surface coughing. The prefect laughed until he coughed as well.

"At least you can swim. One never knows with men from the North."

"You think we can't swim."

"I think you are so obsessed with water spirits you never go in the river."

He flipped over, dived under, and his feet splashed me.

He was still swimming, and diving, and splashing, and laughing, and shouting at me to get back in the water when I sat on the banks. My clothes were back on the cliff and I needed to get them, but not because it was cold. He stepped out of the water, shaking off the glisten of his wet skin, and sat down beside me.

"Ten years I lived in that place. Kongor, I mean," he said.

I looked out at the river.

"Ten years I lived in that city, ten years among its people. 'Tis a funny thing, Tracker, to live in the same place for ten years with people who are by far the most open yet the least friendly people I have yet to meet. My neighbor would not smile when I said,

Good morning and be safe from ruin, brother. But he will say, My mother is dead, how I hated her in life and will now hate her in death. And he might leave fruits at my door if he has too much, but will never knock on my door for me to greet him and say my thanks, or worse, invite him in. 'Tis a coarse love."

"Or maybe he is no friend of prefects."

I could tell without looking that he was frowning.

"Where do you go with this?" I asked.

"I feel you were about to ask how I felt to have killed men dear to me. And they were, in a way, dear. The truth is I feel remorse at not feeling remorse. I say to myself, How do I feel grief for people who kept their love at arm's length from me always? This bores you. It bores me. Do you still wish for sleep?"

"More talk like this and I will."

He nodded.

"We could talk through the night, or I could point out mighty hunters and wild beasts in the stars. You could also say, Fuck the witch and her old beliefs, I am a man of science and mathematics."

"Mockery is cheap."

"Fear is cheap. Courage costs."

"So I am now the coward for not sleeping. What say you?"

"A strange night this is. Are we near the noon of the dead?"

"It has come and passed, I think."

"Oh."

He was quiet for a while.

"You men from the eastern light worship only one god," I said.

"What is meant by 'eastern light'? The light which falls on that place falls on this also. There is only one god. Vengeful in humor, merciful too," he said.

"How do you know you picked the right god?"

"I don't know what you mean."

"If you can only have one, how did you make the right choice?"

He laughed. "Choosing a lord would be like choosing wind. He chose to make us."

"All gods make. No reason to worship them. My mother and father made me. I don't owe them worship for it."

"So you raised yourself?"

"Yes."

"Really."

"Yes."

"Hard for a child to grow with no parents, East or West."

"They are not dead."

"Oh."

"How do you know your god is even good?"

"Because he is. He says he is," Mossi said.

"So the only proof you have that he is good is his own word for it. Have I told you? I am the mother of twenty and nine children. And I am sixty years old."

"You make no sense."

"I make too much sense. If he says, I am good, there is no proof, only that he said so."

"Maybe you should sleep."

"Sleep if you wish," I said.

"So that you can watch me in slumber?"

I shook my head. "If we are in Dolingo, you are ten days' ride from Kongor."

"There is nothing to ride back to, in Kongor."

"No wife, no children, no sisters or brothers you traveled with? No home with two trees and your own little granary with millet and sorghum to return to?"

"No, no, no, no, no, and no. A few of those I fled to come here. And what do I go back to? A room that I owe in rent. A city where people grabbed at my hair so much that I cut it off. Brothers in the chieftain army I have killed. Brothers who now want to kill me."

"There is nothing to ride forward to in Dolingo."

"There is adventure. There is this boy you search for. There are uses for my skilled sword yet. And there is your back, which clearly needs watching, since nobody else does such."

I did not laugh long.

"When I was young, my mother said that we sleep because the shy moon did not like when we watched her undress," I said.

"Don't close your eyes."

"They are not closed. Yours are, right now."

"But I never sleep."

"Never?"

"A little, sometimes never. Night comes and goes like a flash and I may have slept for two flips of a sandglass. Since I never tire in the morning, I assume I slept according to need."

"What do you see at night?"

"Stars. In my lands night is where people do the evil to enemies they call friends in the day. It's when sihrs and jinns come play, and people scheme and plot. Children grow to fear it because they think there be monsters. They build a whole thing about it, about night and dark and even the colour black, which is not even a colour here. Not here. Here evil has no qualm with striking at noon. But it leaves night beautiful in look and cool of feel."

"That was almost verse."

"I am a poet among prefects."

I thought to say something about wind rippling on the river.

"This boy, what is his name?" he whispered.

"I don't know. I don't think anyone bothered to name him. He is Boy. Precious to many."

"And yet nobody named him? Not his mother? Who has him now?"

I told him the story up to the perfume and silver merchant. He raised himself up on his elbows.

"Not this Omoluzu?"

"No. It wasn't the boy's blood they followed. These were different. The merchant, his two wives and three sons all had their lives sucked out of them. Just like Fumanguru. You saw the bodies. Whoever they are, they leave you worse alive than dead. Did not believe it until I saw a woman like a zombi with light-

ning coursing through her like blood. I came to Kongor to find the boy's scent."

"I see why you need me."

I knew he smirked, even if I didn't see it.

"All you have is a nose," he said. "I have an entire
head. You want to find this child. I will find him in a
quartermoon, before the man with wings finds him."

"Seven nights? You sound like a man I used to
know. Do you care what we do when we find him?"

"Pursuit, Tracker. I leave capture to others."

He stretched out on the grass and I looked at my
toes. Then I looked at the moon. Then I looked at the
clouds, white and shiny on top, silver in the middle,
and black underneath as if pregnant with rain. I tried
to think of why I never think of this boy, not what
he might look like, or sound like, even though he was
the reason we were here. I mean, I thought of him
when I tracked all that happened, but I was more
taken with Fumanguru, and the lies of Belekun the
Big, and the game both Sogolon and Bunshi were
playing with information; taken by all who sought
this boy more than the boy himself. I thought of a
room of women all about to fight over a dull lover.
Even this Aesi wanting the boy sparked something
brighter in me than the boy himself. Though I was
sure that it was the King himself who wanted him
dead. This King of the North, this Spider King with
four arms and four legs. My King. Mossi uttered
something, somewhere between a sigh and a moan,
and I looked over. His face was to me but his eyes

closed and the moonlight moved up and down his face.

Before first light something floated on the breeze, a smell of animals far off, and I thought of Leopard. Anger burned in me, but then it left in the quick, leaving sadness and many words that I could have said. His laugh would have bounced all over that cliff. I did not want to miss him. I had gone years without seeing him before we met at that inn, but until then I always felt that he was the one soul who if I ever needed him would appear without me even asking. The detestable Fumeli crowded my thoughts and made me want to spit. Still, I wondered where he was. His smell was not unknown to me; I could have used the memory of it to find him, but did not.

We set out before sunrise. The buffalo kept nodding to his back until I climbed on, lay down, and went fast to sleep. I woke up to my cheek rubbing against the coarse chest hair of the Ogo.

"The buffalo, he grew tired of carrying you," Sadogo said, his massive right hand cradling my back, his left in the hook of my knees.

Ahead, Sogolon rode with the girl and Mossi rode alone. The sun, almost gone, left the sky yellow, orange, and gray, with no clouds. Mountains far off on both sides, but the land was flat and grassy. I didn't want to be cradled like a child, but I didn't want to ride with Mossi either, and I would have slowed everyone down on foot. I pretended to yawn and closed my eyes. But then he ran across my nose and I jumped. The boy. I almost slipped from Sado-go's hand but he caught me and put me down. South, but heading north, just as sure as we were north heading south.

"The boy?" Mossi said. I didn't see him dismount, or that everybody had stopped.

"South. I can't say how far. Maybe a day, maybe two days. He's heading north, Sogolon."

"And we are heading south. We will meet in Dolingo."

"You seem very sure," Mossi said.

"I sure now. Not so sure ten days ago until I go and do my own work, just as the Tracker go and do his work."

"Here is good trade. You tell me how you come by your knowledge, and I will tell you how I come by mine," I said.

"Yes, the boy run hot, then it run cold. Hot for one day and then cold just like that. Never fades, no? Not like a boy who run too far, he scent just vanish, like he dip himself in the river to throw off wild dogs. This not a riddle, Tracker, surely you know why."

"No."

"A house with a man who owe me many things up ahead. We stop there. And . . . house of a man . . ."

Wind knocked her off the horse, kicked her high in the air, and dropped her flat on her back. Breath burst out of her mouth. The girl jumped off the

horse, ran to her, but a nothing in the air slapped her.
I heard the slap, the sound of wet skin on skin, but
nothing to see, the girl's face twisting left then right.
Sogolon raising a hand to block her face, as if somebody came at her with an ax. Mossi jumped off his
horse and ran to her but wind knocked him back as
well. Sogolon fell to her knees and clutched her belly,
then screamed, then yelled, then said something in
a language I didn't know. All of this I saw before,
right before the Darklands. Sogolon stood up but air
slapped her down again. I drew my axes but knew
they were no use. Mossi ran to her again and the wind
knocked him down. On the wisp of air came voices,
a scream one blink, a laugh the next. Whatever it was
disturbed the Sangoma's enchantment, and I could
feel something on me and within me trying to flee.
Sogolon shouted something in that language again,
as the wind gripped her neck and pushed her down in
the dirt. The girl searched around for a stick, found a
stone, and started drawing runes in the sand. The girl
marked, and scratched, and dug, and brushed dirt
with her fingers, making runes in the dirt until she
made a circle around Sogolon. The air howled until
it was just wind, then nothing.

Sogolon rose, still trying to catch her breath. Mossi
ran over to help her up, but the girl jumped between
them and swatted away his hand.

"She not to be touch by no man," she said.

Which was the first time I was hearing such news.
But she let the Ogo lift her up on her horse.

"These the same spirits from outside the Dark-lands?" I shouted at her.

"Is the man with the black wings," Sogolon said. "Is this—"

I heard it too, along the path, on both sides, a cracking as if earth was breaking apart. The buffalo stopped and swung around. The girl, standing by So-golon, grabbed her staff and pulled it apart to show the tip of a lance. The earth kept cracking, and the girl grabbed Sogolon to help her back on her horse. The buffalo started to trot and Sadogo was about to pick me up and put me on his shoulders. From the cracking earth came heat and sulfur, which made us cough. And the cackle of old women, louder and louder until it turned into a hum.

"We should run," Mossi said.

"Wise counsel," I said, and we both ran to the horse.

Sadogo put on his knuckles. The cracking and the cackling grew louder, until something burst out, right in the middle of the path, with a scream. A column, a tower that bent, and cracked, and split pieces off. Three others burst through the ground on the right, like obelisks. Sogolon was too weak to rein the horse, so the girl pressed her knees into him. The horse tried to gallop but the shifting, cracking column unfolded it-self, shaped itself, and it was a woman, larger than the horse, below the waist dark and scaly and still rising from the earth as if the rest of her body was a snake. She rose as tall as two trees, and spooked Sogolon's horse, which jumped up on her hind legs and threw both of them off. Her skin looked like the moon, but it was white dust floating in the air like clouds. On the two sides of the path rose four more, with thin rib bones pressing against their skin, and breasts plump, faces with dark eyes and wild locks that rose high like flame. The creatures on the right covered themselves in dust, the creatures on the left covered themselves in blood. Also this, the flutter of wings, though none of them had any wings. One swooped in and knocked Mossi down. She raised her hand and her claws grew. She would slice him to nothing before he turned over. I jumped in front of him and swung my ax at her hand, chopping it at the wrist. She screamed and backed away.

"Mawana witches," Sogolon said. "Mawana witches, he . . . controlling them."

One of them grabbed Mossi's horse. Sadogo ran to her and punched her but she still held on to the horse, which was too big for her to eat, but small enough to take down in the hole with her. Sadogo ran, jumped, and landed on her shoulder, his legs wrapped around her neck. She swung up and down and around, trying to throw him off, but he hammered into her forehead until we heard a crack, and she dropped the horse. The Mawana witch grabbed Sadogo and flung him away. He rolled in the dirt until he stopped, on his feet. He was mad now. A bloodied witch grabbed the buffalo's horns to pull him away, but nothing would move this bull. He backed away, pulling her. I jumped up on his back and swung my ax at her, but she dodged and backed away, almost cowered. Sadogo leapt on the back of a dusty one, all of him about the size of the witch aboveground. She swung and slashed and tried to strike but he was on her back. She shot up, swung down, shook her skin rapidly like a wet dog, but Sadogo held on. He wrapped his arm around her neck and squeezed until she choked. She could not get a grip, so she rose and fell and shook, until his legs swung, then she cut into his right thigh with her claws. Yet he would not let go. He gripped her around the neck until she fell. Two more rose, and went after Sogolon and the girl. As I ran to them, jumping over Mossi and shouting for the buffalo to come with me, the girl raised her lance to ram right through the witch's stomping hand. She shrieked and I jumped on the buffalo's horns for him to throw me high at her. My two axes out, I swung both to her neck and chopped her head off. It hung on, swinging on skin. The other witch backed away. Mossi looked at me. The witch was coming up behind him. I threw an ax to him, he caught it and swung his whole body around, throwing force behind the ax and slashing right through her throat. His throat. This one had a long beard. The last two, one dusty, one bloody, rose so high in the air that they looked like they would pull themselves out of the ground and fly away. But both dove back down. I ran towards them and both broke away and dove into the earth as birds dive into the sea.

"I never knew witch would attack witch," I said.

Sogolon, still on the ground said, "They would not attack you."

"What? I fought them all, woman."

"Don't tell me that you never see them all backing away from you," she said.

"It is because I'm still covered by the Sangoma."

"They is flesh, not irons or magic."

"Maybe they afraid of a man-born Ku," I said.

"You did sleep last night?"

"What you think, witch?"

"Don't bother with what I think. You did sleep?"

"And as I said, what do you think?"

The girl grabbed her lance and raised it above her shoulder.

"You was awake all of last night?"

I looked straight at the girl. "Woman-child, what is this you doing? Sogolon teach you two lessons and you think you can throw a lance at me? Let's see if your lance can pierce my skin before my ax splits your face."

"He was awake all night, Sogolon. I was there with him," Mossi said.

"You don't have to vouch for me."

"And you don't have to keep making malice with people right beside you," he said.

He shook his head as he walked past me. The girl helped Sogolon up. Sadogo came back holding his hands out as if he lost something.

"Your horse, she broke two legs," he said. "Nothing to do but—"

"If the Aesi don't jump in your dream, then he find some other way to follow we," Sogolon said.

"Unless you mean the daydream of me between an Omororo prince and his comelier cousin, I will say no."

"What about the prefect?"

"What about me?" Mossi said.

"He attacked you first, Sogolon," I said.

"And he never attack you at all."

"Maybe my runes work better than your runes."

"You the one who can hound the boy. He might need you."

We walked through thick forest bush until we came to see stars dancing across open savannah, where not far away was the house of a man who Sogolon said owed her. Mossi walked beside me but he winced often. Both of his knees were bruised, as was my elbow.

"I don't know why you would know," Mossi said to me.

"What would I know?"

"Why the boy's trail goes hot, then in a blink goes cold, then hot again."

Behind me walked the buffalo, and behind him, Sadogo.

"They are using the ten and nine doors," I said.

SEVENTEEN

Divide the Kongor lord's house by six. A house that is but a room, with an arch door, and walls of clay and mortar. Now put another room on top of that one, then another, then another, and another, then one more and one more on top of that, with a roof that curves like when the moon cuts herself in half. That was this man's house, a house that looked like just one column was cut off and sent to the Dolingo mountain roads. This lord waited outside his hut, chewing khat, and was not surprised when we approached. It was three nights since we left Kongor. Sogolon nearly fell off the horse trying to dismount. The man pointed inside and the girl helped Sogolon in. Then he sat back down on his stoop and chewed.

"Look up inna the sky, **woi lolo.** You be seeing it? You be seeing the things?"

Mossi and I both looked up, him as unclear as me.

"You not be seeing the divine crocodile eat the moon?"

Mossi took my arm and said, "Dost you know anyone not mad?"

I did not answer him, and he would not have known had I asked, but I wondered if I was the only one who noticed that this man looked exactly like the house lord back in Kongor. Leopard would have noticed. He would have said so.

"Do you have a brother north of here?" I asked.

"Brother? Ha, my mother, she going tell you that one boy was one too many. She still living too, my mother, still testing me to die first. But he lick her hard, don't he do? He lick her down hard. Harder than all her blood spirit them."

"Blood spirit?"

"He lick her down, that mean he close, that mean he right back of you. You know who I speak?"

"Who are the blood spirits?"

"Never in this world or any of the other world I mention him name. The one with the black wings." Then he laughed.

That morning, the girl painted runes on Sogolon's door with white clay.

"Did she teach you this when you were both gone?" I asked of her, but she said nothing.

I wanted to tell her that she was wasting her contempt on me, but kept quiet. She saw me coming to the door and blocked me. Her lips shut tight, her eyes narrowing in a stare, she looked like a child told to watch over the younger children.

"Woman-child. Neither might nor craft will stop me from entering this room."

She grabbed her knife but I slapped it out of her hand. She reached for another and I looked at her and said, "Try to stab me with it." She stared at me for a long time. I watched her lips quiver and her brow frown. She stabbed at me, suddenly, but her hand shot past my chest. She stabbed again and the knife in her hand bounced back at her. She stabbed and stabbed, aiming for my chest and neck, but her knife wouldn't touch me. She aimed for my eye and the knife shot over my head. I caught it. She tried to knee me in the balls but I caught her knee and pushed her through the door. She staggered backways and almost fell.

"The two of you have too much time," Sogolon said from the window.

I stepped inside to see one pigeon fly from her hands. She reached in a cage and pulled out another. Something red was wrapped around its foot.

"A message for the Queen of Dolingo to expect us. They don't show kind to people who come with no announcement."

"Two pigeons?"

"There are hawks in these skies."

"How go you today?"

"I go good. Thank you for the concern."

"If you were a Sangoma and not a witch, you

wouldn't need to draw runes everywhere you go, and suffer attack if you forget one. The things you have to keep in your mind all at once."

"Such is the mind of all womenfolk. I forget how big it be, Dolingo. All you can see from here is the mountain pass. It will take another day to be among its trees—"

"A hundred fucks for Dolingo. We shall have words, woman."

"What you speaking to me about now?"

"We speaking about many things, but how we start with this boy? If the Aesi is after him and the Aesi stands behind the King, so is the King."

"That is why they call him the Spider King. I tell you this over a moon ago."

"You told me nothing. Bunshi did. Everything about the boy was in the writs."

"Nothing about this boy in no writs."

"Then what did I find in the library before they burned it down, witch?"

"You and the pretty prefect?" Sogolon said.

"If you say he is."

"And yet you still to escape. Either you too hard to kill, or he not trying hard to kill you."

She looked at me, then went back to the window.

"This is between us two," I said.

"Too late for that," Mossi said, and walked in the room.

Mossi. Sogolon's back was to us but I saw her shoulders tighten. She tried to smile.

"I don't know what people call you, other than prefect."

"Those who call me friend call me Mossi."

"Prefect, this not your move. Best thing for you is you turn around and go back for—"

"As I said. Too late for that."

"If one more man interrupt me, before I finish what I say. This is no mission to find drunk fathers, or lost child and send them home, prefect. Go home."

"Sun's set on that thanks to all of you. What home is there for the prefect? The chieftain army will think all on the roof were killed with my blade. You don't know them as I do. They've already burned down my house."

"Nobody ask you to push up youself."

He stepped right in and sat down on the floor, his legs spread wide apart, and pulled his scabbard around so it rested between them. Scabs on both knees.

"And yet plenty is upon me, whether you asked or not. Who do you have good with a sword? I was doing what I was paid to. That I no longer have that calling is your fault. But I bear no malice. And man should never turn down great sport or great adventure, I think. Besides, you need me more than I need you. I'm not as aloof as the Ogo, or simple as the girl. You never know, old woman. If this mission of yours excites me, I may do it for free."

Mossi pulled out of his satchel a bunch of papyrus leaves folded small. I knew from the smell before I saw what they were.

"You took the writs?" I said.

"Something about them had the air of importance. Or maybe just sour milk."

He smiled but neither I nor Sogolon laughed.

"No laughter to you people below the desert. So, who is this boy you seek? Who presently has him? And how shall he be found?"

He unfolded the papers, and Sogolon turned around. She moved in closer, but not so close it would look like she was trying to read them.

"The papers look burn," she said.

"But they fold and unfold like papers untouched," Mossi said.

"Those are not burns, they are glyphs," I said. "Northern-style in the first two lines, coastal below. He wrote them down in sheep milk. But you knew this," I said.

"No. Never know."

"There were glyphs of this kind all over your room in Kongor."

She glared at me quick, but her face smoothed. "I don't write none of them. Is Bunshi you must ask."

"Who?" Mossi said.

"Later," I said, and he nodded.

"I don't read North or coastal mark," Sogolon said.

"Well fuck the gods, there is something you cannot do." I pointed at Mossi with my chin. "He can."

The room had a bed, though I was sure Sogolon never slept on one. The girl went beside her, they whispered, then she went back to the door.

"The writ the prefect holding be just one. Fumanguru make five, and one come across where I stay. He
say the monarchy need go forward by going back,
so that make me want to know more. You read the
whole writ?"

"No."

"Don't have to. Boring once he stop talking about
the King. Then he just turn into one more man telling woman what to do. But for what he say about the
King, I find him one night."

"Why would anything about the elder and the King
concern you?" I said.

"It never was for me. Why you think no man can
touch me, Tracker?"

"I—"

"Don't bother with the smart tongue. I didn't call
on him for me, but for somebody else."

"Bunshi."

She laughed. "I find Fumanguru because I serve
the sister of the King. From what he write, he sound
like the one man who understand. The one who
could look past his own fattening belly to see what
wrong with the empire, the kingdom, how the North
Kingdom being plagued by evil and misfortune and
malcontent for as long as a child know the kingdom.
Your eyes pass the part where he talk about the history of kings? The line of kings, this I know. That
who succeed the King change when Moki become
King. He not supposed to be King. Every King before
him was the oldest son of the King's oldest sister. So it

was written for hundreds of years. Until now we have Kwash Moki."

"How did he become King?" Mossi said.

"He murdered his sister and all under her roof," I said.

"And when the time come Moki send his oldest daughter to the ancient sisterhood where no girl can become a mother. That way his oldest son, Liongo, become King. And so it go for year after year, age after age that when we come to Kwash Aduware, everybody forget how one become King and who can become King, so that even the faraway griots start singing that so always be the way. This land curse ever since," Sogolon said.

"But all the griots' songs sing of winning wars and conquering new lands. When exactly did a curse happen?"

"Look behind the palace wall. The records show all the children who live. You think it going show all the children who die? Too many dead sons mean the royal blood weak. Records, do they tell you of the three wives Kwash Netu have before he find one that would give him a prince? Kwash Dara lose his first brother to plague. And have three slow sisters because his father breeding concubines. And one uncle as mad as a southern king, and death strike nearly every wife who don't give him a son. In which book all of that write? Rot run through the whole family. Here is a question and answer it true. When you last see rain in Fasisi?"

"And yet there are trees."

"Defeat is not the problem. Victory is."

Even Mossi leaned in when he heard that. Sogolon finally turned around, and sat in the windowsill. I almost expected Bunshi to come seeping down the wall.

"Yes, the great kings of the North make war and win plenty, but they always want more. Free lands, lands in fuss. Those cities, and towns that not take a side. They cannot help themself, man raise by man, not woman. Woman not like man, they don't know gluttony. Each kingdom, spread wider, each king get worse. The South kings get madder and madder because they keep making incest with one another. The North kings get a different kind of mad. Evil curse them, because they whole line come out of the worst kind of evil, for what kind of evil kill he own blood?"

"More interested in questions where the answer is the boy," I said.

"You said you know him? Tell me what you know," Sogolon said.

I turned to Mossi, who was looking at us, back and forth, like somebody who had not yet decided who to believe, who to follow. He rubbed his young beard, longer and redder than I remembered it, and looked at the papers he held in his hand.

"Mossi, read it."

"Gods of sky—no, lords of sky. They no longer speak to spirits of the ground. The voice of kings is becoming the new voice of the gods. Break the silence of the gods. Mark the god butcher, for

he marks the killer of kings. The god butcher in black wings. And the rest?"

"Please."

"Take him to Mitu, to the guided hand of the one-eyed one, walk through Mweru and let it eat your trail. Take no rest till Go."

Sogolon shook her head. She had never read or heard this before, and knew that I knew it.

"So Fumanguru say take the boy to the one-eyed one in Mitu, walk through the Mweru, and then head to Go, a city that only live in dreams. And the Aesi is the butcher of gods? Maybe I choose a wrong man in Basu," Sogolon said.

"You dare say that now? It was your choosing that led to his death," I said.

"Watch your tongue," said the girl.

"Did I hold a knife to his neck and say, Fumanguru, do this? No."

"Mark the god butcher, for he marks the killer of kings," I said.

"And?"

"Leave playing the fool to the girl, Sogolon. The god butcher is the Aesi. The killer of kings is the boy."

Sogolon laughed, soft like a grin at first, then a loud howl.

"They are prophecies, are they not? Of some child—"

"What kind of prophecy rest hope on a child? Which prophet so fool? Witch bitches from the Ku? On a little thing that not going live ten years? Your pretty prefect come from a place where people never stop with the talk of magic children. Children of fate, people put all hope in them. All hope in a thing that stick a finger in he nose and eat what he pull out."

"And yet that prophecy makes more sense than the horseshit you and the fish keep selling," I said. "I took this road with you because I thought it would go somewhere. This boy is as much proof the King killed Fumanguru as a cut on a donkey's ass. You still clutch it in the breast, the truth. I know what you put in my way to not find, Sogolon, including that you were at Fumanguru's house and tried to use a spell to hide it. That you have been looking for ways to find the boy yourself so that you would not need me. You even had one whole moon to do it, and yet here we are. You are right, Bunshi is not your master. But she is not used to lying to men. She nearly went mad when I caught her double-tongue. And what is this girl anyway? You go off in some secret door and make her play with spears and knives and now she calls herself warrior? Is this another person who will die while you watch? I see that too, witch, for that you can also blame the Sangoma. She's more powerful dead than alive."

"I tell only truth."

"So either you are a liar or you have been lied to. I sniffed you out every step of the way, Sogolon. The night Bunshi told me Fumanguru ran afoul of his own elders, I went to see an elder. Then I killed him when he tried to kill me. He also wanted to know about the writs. He even knew about Omoluzu. Your fish told me the boy was Fumanguru's son, but he had six sons, none of them the boy. The day before we met you, the Leopard and I followed the slaver to a tower in Malakal, where he kept a woman with the lightning sickness inside her. Bibi was there too, and Nsaka Ne Vampi. So either you were dropping nuts like a trail for the bird to pick and follow, or your mask of control is just that, and you control nothing."

"Watch your mouth. Do you think I need a man? I need you is what you thinking? I know the ten and nine doors."

"And you still couldn't find him."

Mossi went to stand behind me. Sogolon stared, frowned for a blink, then smiled.

"What is his use, you said to me when you saw the Leopard's boy. A woman like you keeps the grains and burns the chaff," I said.

"Give me the meat and not the fat, then."

"You need me. Or you would have been rid of me a moon ago. Not only do you need me, you waited a whole moon for me. Because I can find this boy; your door only makes it more quick."

"He is with you?"

"Mossi is his own man. We have come a long way, Sogolon. Longer than I would have ever gone on half-truths and lies, but something about this story . . . no, that's not it. Something about you and the fish shaping this story, controlling so hard how each of us reads it, that turned into the only reason I came. Now it will be the only reason I leave."

I turned to walk away. Mossi paused for a second, looking at Sogolon, then turned.

"It right there. Read it. Everything right there. Now you waiting on me to put it together for you like your name is child."

"Be a mother, then."

"Pretty prefect, read that line again."

Mossi pulled the papers out of his pouch again.

"Lords of sky. They no longer speak to—"

"Jump over that."

"As you wish. **Mark the god butcher, for he marks the killer of kings.**"

"Stop."

Sogolon looked at me as if she'd just made everything plain. I almost nodded, thinking I must be a fool to still not see it. I would have left it there too.

"Your little boy is a prophesied assassin who will kill the King?" Mossi said before I could say it. "You want us to find the boy fated by some fool to commit the worst crime one could ever commit. Even this talk right now is treason."

He was still a man following his uniform, even now.

"No. That would take least ten more years, if it was true. A bad slave and terrible mistress? Why you think it say take him to the Mweru, where no man come back from alive? And to Go, which no people ever see? Killer of kings mean killer of the depraved line, rejected by the gods, or else why would the Spider King join so close to the god butcher? The boy not here to kill no King. He is the King."

Both Mossi and I stood silent, the prefect more stunned than me. I said to Sogolon, "You trusted this prince to a woman who sold him as soon as she had the chance."

Sogolon turned back to the window.

"People are deceitful above all things. What can one do?"

"Give us word on this boy. We will have it."

This is what Sogolon told us in the room. The girl was standing at the door, as if guarding it. And then the old man was in the room, though neither I nor Mossi remembered when he stepped past the girl. Sogolon told this story:

When the ewe drummer want to send you tidings good or bad, he pull the drum strings tight to the body and pitch the voice high or pitch the voice low. Through the pluck, through the pitch, through the beat, lie the message that only you can hear if it meant for you. So when Basu Fumanguru write the writ, and decide he going to send the first to the marketplace, the second to the palace of wisdom, the third to the hall of grand elders, and the fourth to the King, he fashion a fifth, to send to who? Nobody know. But nobody even get send the writs and nobody know what they say. Not even those he tell he was going to write. All we know is that we the sisters who serve the King sister was going to the western hall to pour libation to the earth gods since where we live was in the earth, and the gods of sky was deaf to we. And coming up to us was the sound of the drum.

Mantha. The mountain seven days west of Fasisi and north of Juba. From afar, to the eye of warriors, and travelers, and land pirates, Mantha be a mountain and that is all it be. It rise high like a mountain, have rocks like a mountain, and wild bush like a mountain. Cliff, and rock, and bush, and stone, and dirt, all with no plan. You have to go behind the mountain, and to get behind the mountain take one more day, climb for another half day to see the eight hundred and eight steps, cut out of the rock as if gods make them for the gods to walk. In a time older than now, Mantha be the fortress from where the army could see enemy coming close without the enemy knowing they being watched. That way nobody ever take the lands by surprise and nobody ever invade. Over nine hundred years Mantha gone from being the place to watch enemies, to the place to hide one. Kwash Likud, of the old house Nehu, before the house of this King, would send an old wife to Mantha as soon as he married a new one, or if she produce no boy child, or if the children ugly. Right before the Akum dynasty, the King, once they crown him, would banish all brother and man cousin there, a royal prison where they would die, or become the new King if the King die first. Then come the Akum dynasty, and kings who do as the father do before. And Kwash Dara no different from Kwash Netu. And Netu no different from his great-grandfather, who made it a royal decree that the firstborn sister must join the divine sisterhood, in service of the goddess of security and plenty. And so it be again, that kings all follow the way of Kwash Moki, and violate the true line of kings and give the crown to the son.

So it come that the King sister, before he become King and before she reach ten and seven, she to give herself over to the divine sisterhood, but this sister not go. Let ugly woman who no man want become divine sister, she say. Why would I push away great meats and soups and breads to eat millet and drink water with bitter, wrinkled dogs, and wear white for the rest of my days? Indeed no man answer her and among them her father. This princess forget that she be princess and start to walk like prince. Crown prince. She ride horse, and strike and parry with sword, and string the bow, and play the lute, and amuse her father and scare her mother, for she grow up to see what happen to woman with will of her own. Even a princess. Father, send me to join the women warriors in Wakadishu, or send me to be hostage in a court in the East, and I will be your spy, she say to him. What I should do is send you to a prince who will beat your thick head down soft, he say to her and she say, But, great King, are you ready for the war that will break when I kill this prince? And he say, I have no wish to send you to Wakadishu or the eastern land, and she say, I know, good Father, but why let that stop you? She quick of wit, something man in the North think is a gift that only come to man, and the King say to her more than once, How much more like a son you are to me than this one.

For here is truth. Before he was Kwash Dara, he flighty, and vengeful, and carry great malice over small things. But he was no fool. It was Lissisolo who say, Consider returning Wakadishu to the southern King, Father, after the elders said in open court it was wise that a king, after war, keep all spoils and spare none to the enemy, for he will think him weak. It is nothing to us, she said. No good fruit, pure silver, or strong slave comes from there, it is near all swamp. Besides, there is sown so many seeds of rebellion that he will lose it without us lifting a finger. The King nodded at such good wisdom and said, How much like a son you are to me, more than this one. Meanwhile Kwash Dara spend day and nights rejecting the fifty women who say yes, so he can rape and kill the one girl who say no. Or whip any friend and any prince who beat him in horse racing, and demanding they cook the horse. Or say to his father at court, The gods whisper it in my ear, but tell me true, Father, will you die soon? And he say these things because there was many to tell him that he is the most beautiful and wise of men.

Then the King change the rule. What a thing that be! He could not bear to see the kingdom without his daughter so he say, You, my darling Lissisolo, shall never have to join the divine sisterhood. But you must find a husband. A lord, or a prince, but not a chief. So she find a prince, one of the plenty in Kalindar, with no princedom. But the seed strong in him and she make four children in seven years, and still take her place at the King side, while Kwash Dara go to follow warriors three days after battle to hiss that slow horses make him again miss the fighting.

Let us make the story quick. The King dead, choke on chicken bone, they say. Kwash Dara, he take the crown off the head of he father, right there in the battle camp, and say, I am King. Regard your King, and worship me. And when the King's general said, But you are worshipped only on your death, when you become a god, Most Excellent One, Kwash Dara scream at him, but do nothing in front of the other generals. That general dead in one moon. Poison. Not even a year pass by when the people of the empire start to wonder, is it the southern King who mad, or this new King in the North? I not yet serve her, so I not know how it start, first the rumor, then the accuse. But the rumor fly around and land in whispers days before the King, at the assembly of court, rise from the throne, turn, and point straight at he sister, saying, You, dearest Lissisolo, on this my first anniversary, your plot has been found out. Did you think that you could slip it past a King and a god? Lissisolo always laugh at her brother as sport and she laugh as he speak, for how in all the gods this be anything but joke?

And when he walk right up to her and say, The divine

King has ears everywhere, sister, she say, Which King he talking about, Lissisolo don't know since the divine King is their father, who was now with the ancestors. Lissisolo laugh at him and say, You still the little boy in the royal bed, saying what is mine is mine, and what is yours is mine. Even the lords and chiefs who hate him know that was disrespect to Kwash Dara. The King is the throne, and the throne is the King. Mock one and mock the other. He slap her straight across her face and she stagger back on the throne platform, and almost fall off.

"And here comes your Prince consort, from who cares which territory," he say to the Kalindar prince, who step once, think about what a next step going to mean, and hold back.

"You think I don't know you were Father's favorite? You think I don't know he would cut off my own cock and bind it to you by precious sorcery, just to make you the one thing he want me to be? You think I don't know, dearest sister, all the witchcraft you worked on him to convince this greatest and strongest of kings not to send you to the divine sisterhood, and as such violate the sacred tradition of the gods we all serve, even you? If even I, your King, your Kwash Dara, has to bow to the will of the gods, why not you?" he say to his sister.

"I serve who deserve serving," she say.

"Did you hear, excellent people of the court, did you hear? Seems all kings and gods must make themselves worthy of Princess Lissisolo's service."

Lissisolo, she just stare at her brother. Never was smart, this boy, but somebody had been giving him smart counsel.

"Only the gods know my heart."

"So we agree. For I certainly know yours, sister. But enough talk, now we eat. Bring sweet wines, and strong meats, and honey and milk with a little cow's blood like river folk, and beer."

This is what people say happen, people in the exile in the South. That at the great table right before the throne, womanservants and manservants bring out all sort of meat, and all sort of salad and fruit, and drink, in gold cup and silver, glass, and leather. And at the royal table and every table in the great hall was much eating, and drinking, and making merry. No cup of honey wine or beer go empty or a slave would be flogged. On the tables, mutton, raw and cook both, beef the same, and chicken, and vulture, and stuffed doves. Bread, butter, and honey. The air spice up with garlic, onion, mustard, and pepper.

The King step down from the throne and sit at the head of the royal table with his elder warriors and advisers, noblemen and noblewomen. Lissisolo, she about to sit on his right, three places down, where she always sit, when he say, "Sister. Sit at the foot of the table, for we are one flesh. And who else would I want to see when I look up from my meat?"

Everybody at every table wait until the King wave, and they all set to eat. Grabbing meat, grabbing fruits, grabbing raised bread, grabbing flatbread, calling for

honey wine and daro beer, while griots play kora
and drum and sing of how the great Kwash Dara is
even greater one year in the reign. The King grab a
chicken leg, but he not eating it, he watching his sister. Then he clap and two men, thick in arms and
legs, come around the table carrying a large basket
cover in cloth. Then the King turn to the people near
to him, and speak soft as if he sharing a joke for few
ears only.

"Listen to me now. I brought in a special delicacy,
both of them from the noble houses in the South."

He raise he voice when he say, "For you, sister. So
there is no malice between us and we are again equal."

The two men remove the cloth, upturn the baskets,
and two bloody head fall out and land in the table.
People jump back, many women scream, Lissisolo
jump, but not as much as the King did hope, then
just sit there, looking at two lords from the South
Kingdom, one an elder, the other a chief and adviser
to the King, two head cut off and rolling on the table
in front of her. The women still screaming and two
lords get up.

"Sit down, beautiful men and women. Sit down!"

The whole hall go quiet. Kwash Dara stand up and
walk right over to his sister. He grab one of the heads
by the hair and lift up to his face. The eyes still open,
the brown skin almost blue, the hair thick and bushy
and the beard patchy as if he scratch it out.

"Now this one, this boy lover. Is he a boy lover?
He must be a boy lover to think that my sister, a

princess, can become a king. What kind of witchcraft they must work on him, to scheme and plot, and remember, eh, sister? Take some wise words from your wise King. As you drag a man into a plot, so you should also drag the wife, or she will think it a plot against her. Next time you get this plotting sickness, try not to infect anybody else with it, sister. Play a game of Bawo."

He drop the head on the table and Lissisolo jump.

"Remove her from me," he say.

Now here is a true thing. The King still afraid to kill his sister for if divine blood run in his rivers then it must also run in hers too, and who would be the one to kill she born of a god?

He lock her away in a dungeon with rats big like cats. Lissisolo don't scream or weep. She in there for day upon day and they feed her scraps from the royal table so that though she only get bone and dregs, she would know where the dregs come from. The guards take to sporting with her but not touching her. One day they bring her a bowl of water, and say it come with a special seasoning most excellent, and as they place it down she could see a rat floating in it. She turn and say, My bowl has special seasoning too, and dash her piss at them. Two guards rush to the bars, and she say, "Get to it then, be the one to dare touch divine flesh."

Lissisolo don't know it but ten and four day pass her in the dungeon. Her brother come to see her, wearing red robes and a white turban that he place a crown on. No chair in the cell, and the guard hesitate when Kwash Dara point at him to go down be on four, like the donkey, so the King can sit on his back.

"I miss you, sister," he say.

"I miss me too," she say. Always too clever but not clever enough to know when to blow out that wick so she don't shine too bright around a man, even if the man be her brother.

He say to her, "Differences we have and will have, sister. That is just the ways of blood, but when trouble comes, when ill fortune comes, when just bad tidings come, surely I must stand by my blood. Even if she betrayed me, my sorrow is her sorrow."

"You have no proof that I betrayed you."

"All truth rests with the gods, and the King is the godhead."

"When he dies, if the gods wish his company."

"Now, and the gods are bound by their own law."

"Who is your latest coward hiding behind shadows?"

. He come out of the dark into the light of the torch. Skin black like ink, eye so white they glow, and hair red like a fireball flower. She know him name before he say it.

"You are the Aesi," she say. Like every woman, every man, every child in the lands, when she see him, it was as if the Aesi was always behind the King, but nobody can remember when he take that place. Like air and the gods, there was no beginning and no end, only Aesi.

"We come bearing news, sister. It is not good."

The King rock himself on the soldier back. The Aesi approach the bars.

"Your husband and your children all fell from air sickness for it is the season, and they went where malevolent airs were prominent. They will be buried tomorrow, in ceremonies fit for princes, of course. But not near the royal enclosure, for they may still carry disease. You will—"

"You think you sit like a king when you are the speck of shit on donkey's backside that the tail can't wick off. What did you come down here for? A scream? A plea for my children? I fall on the floor so you can laugh? Come to the bars and put your ears here so I can give you a scream."

"I will leave you to grieve, sister. Then I will come back."

"For what? What do you want? Your wife hear you call my name when you fuck her yet, or do you let this one do it?"

The King, he jump up and throw his staff at the cell. Then he turn to leave. The Aesi turn to her and say, "Tomorrow you are to leave to join the divine sisterhood, as was your fate set by the gods. All of the realm will grieve for you and wish you abiding peace."

"Come earlier and I have given you peace I just leave in that bucket."

"We leave you to grieve, sister."

"Grieve? I shall never grieve. I reject it, grief. I

replace it with rage. My rage at you walk higher and wider than any grief."

"I will kill you too, sister."

"Too? Truly, you are an imbecile's idea of an imbecile. The sun has not even set on their deaths and you have confessed to the murder already. Secret griots said you slipped out of Mother and dropped on your head. They are wrong. Mother must have dropped you on purpose. Yes leave, get out, you coward, men should have come and clip you the way they do girls in the river valley. Mark it, brother. From this day I will curse you and your children's names every day."

A curse from blood frighten even Kwash Dara, he leave in the quick, but the Aesi stay to look at her.

"You can still be someone's wife," he say.

"You can still be something other than the King's shit pan," she say.

As soon as the guard close the door she fall to the ground, and wail so hard it turn into a sickness. The morning when they send her to the fortress of Mantha to join the divine sisterhood, anger and grief gone.

Let us make this quick. The water goddess see all and know all. I am a priestess serving in a temple in Wakadishu when I go down the steps that lead to the river, and up jump Bunshi. No fear come from me, though I see she have a fishtail black like pitch. She send me to Mantha with nothing but my leather dress, one sandal, and a mark from the house at Wakadishu. The princess Lissisolo take to her room, and play the kora at sunset and talk to no one. In the divine sisterhood no one have power or class, or rank, so her royal blood don't mean nothing. But all the sisters see her need to be alone. Word was that she walk the lands at night under moonlight to whisper to the goddess of justice and girl children how much she hate her.

After a year, as I walk to the sacred hall to pour libations, she point at me and say, "What is your use?"

"To bring you into your royal purpose, princess."

"Nothing about my purpose is royal and I am no princess," she say.

Two moons, and she move me to her side. Women as equal but knowing she is the royal. Two moons after that, I telling her that the water goddess have greater purpose for her. Three moons more and she believe me, after I summon dew to lift me off the ground and above her head. No, not believe me, she believe that something more be to her life than a childless widow saying prayers to a goddess she hate. No, not belief, for she say, belief will get people around her killed. I say to her, No, my mistress, only belief in love do that. Accept it, return it, cherish it, but never believe love can do anything other than love. The year didn't finish before Bunshi appear to her on the last hot night of the year, when nearly all the women, one hundred and twenty and nine, went to bathe in the waterfall with nymphs, to tell her the truth about her line, and why she will be the one to restore it. We will send a man, it has all been arranged, Bunshi said.

"Look at my life. All of it around a hole owned, ordered, and arranged by men. Now I must take that

from womankind too? You know nothing of sisterhood, you're just a pale echo of men. The true King
will be a bastard? Did this water sprite also fall on her
head at birth?"

"No, Your Most Excellent. We have found a prince
in—"

"Kalindar. Another one? They seem to be everywhere, like lice, these kingdomless princes of Kalindar."

"A marriage to a prince make your child legitimate.
And when the true line of kings return he can claim
before all lords."

"Fuck all lords. All these kings also come from the
womb of woman. What is to stop this man-child from
doing just as all other man has done? Kill all men."

"Then rule them, princess. Rule them through
him. And leave this place."

"What if I like this place? In Fasisi even the winds
conspire against you."

"If it is your wish to stay, then stay, mistress. But as
long as your brother is King, plagues above the earth
and below will visit even this place."

"No plague has visited so far. When is this pesti-
lence taking place? Why not now?"

"Maybe the gods give you time to prevent it, Your
Excellence."

"Your tongue is too smooth. I do not fully trust it.
Let me see this man, at least."

"He will come to you disguised as eunuch. If he
pleases you then we will find an elder who cares for
our cause."

"An elder? So we are doomed to be betrayed, then," she say.

"No, mistress," I say.

I bring the prince from Kalindar. No man put down foot in Mantha for one hundred years, but many eunuchs. None of the women would ask the eunuch to lift he robes for the scars show horrendous knife craft. But at the great entrance stand the big guard, daughter from a line of the tallest women in Fasisi, who grab the crotch and squeeze. Before, I tell this prince, this is what you do, forget you great discomfort and do not betray your unease or they will kill you at the gate and not care that they kill a prince. Take your balls and feel for each, then push them out of the sac up into your bush. Take your kongkong and pull it hard between your legs until it touch near your bottom hole. The guard will feel you ball skin, hangin' on both sides of the kongkong, and think you are a woman. She will not even look at your face. The Prince make it all the way to Lissisolo chamber before he remove veil and robe. Tall, dark, thick in hair, brown in eyes, thick and dark in lips, pattern scars above the brows and down both arms, and many year younger in age. All he know was that this is a crown princess and he will see title.

"He will do," Lissisolo say.

I did not have to go find the elder. Seven moon, and the elder find me. Fumanguru finish the writs, then send a message under the ewe drum that only devout women could hear, for he play it like a devotional, saying he have words for the princess and tidings that may be good, may be bad, but will certainly be wise. I ride horse seven days to meet him, and tell him that his wish, his prophecy, it real, but her son cannot be born a bastard. We ride back in another seven days, me, the elder Basu Fumanguru, and the Prince from Kalindar. Some of the sisters know, some do not. Some know that whatever be taking place was of great importance. Others think new people come and violate the sacred hymen of Mantha, despite that for years upon years the fort was a place for men. I ask some not to speak of what was happening, and I threaten others. But as soon as that boy is born I know he not safe. The only place safe for him is the Mweru, I tell the princess, who would not lose a child again. Keep him here and you most certainly will lose him again, for a sister done betray us, I tell her. And indeed it play true. This sister, she leave at night, not to travel what would be ten and five days by foot, but she go far enough to release a pigeon. She set the pigeon free before I reach her, but I get out of her that she send them back to a master in Fasisi. Then I slit her throat. I go back and say to the princess, No time leave. A message already on the way to court. We take him to Fumanguru that night, knowing it would take seven days, and the princess we leave with another sect of wisewomen loyal to the Queen of Dolingo. The boy stay with Fumanguru three moons and live like him own. You know how the rest go.

We sat there in the morning room feeling the quiet. Mossi, behind me, his breathing grew slow. I wondered where the Ogo was, and how much of the morning was gone. Sogolon was looking out the window so long that I went beside her to see what she was looking at. That is why the boy ran by my nose one blink and vanished the next. Also why sometimes he was a quartermoon, sometimes five moons away.

"I know they are using the ten and nine doors," I said.

"I know you know," she said.

"Who is this they?" said Mossi.

"I know of only one by name, and only because of who he leave behind him, most of them womenfolk. The people in the Hills of Enchantment call him Ipundulu."

"Lightning bird," whispered the old man. A harsh whisper, a curse under his breath. Sogolon nodded at him and turned back to the window. I looked outside and saw nothing but noon coming to pass. I was about to say, Old woman, to what do you look, when the old man said, "Lightning bird, lightning bird, woman beware of the lightning bird."

Sogolon turned around and said, "You about to give us song, brother."

He frowned. "I talking 'bout the lightning bird. Talk is just talk."

"That is a story you should tell them," she said.

"The Ipundulu is—"

"In the way of your ancestors. In the way you raise to do."

"Singer men don't sing songs no more, woman."

"Lie you speaking. Southern griots they still be. Few and in secret but they still be. I tell them about you. How you keep to memory what the world tell you to forget."

"The world have him father name."

"Many a man sing."

"Many don't sing at all."

"We will have verse."

"You the ruler over me now? You giving me orders?"

"No, my friend, I giving you a wish. The southern griots—"

"There is no southern griots."

"Southern griots speak against the King."

"Southern griots speak the truth!"

"Old man, you just say there be no southern griots," Sogolon said.

The old man walked over to a pile of robes and pulled them away. Underneath was a kora.

"Your King, he find six of we. Your King, he kill them all, and not one he kill quick. Do you remember Babuta, Sogolon? He come to six of we, among them Ikede, who you know, and say, Enough with hiding in caves for no reason, we sing the true story of kings! We don't own truth. Truth is truth and nothing you can do about it even if you hide it, or kill it, or even tell it. It was truth before you open your mouth and say, That there is a true thing. Truth is truth even after them who rule send poison griots to spread lie till they take root in every man's heart. Babuta say he know a man in the court of the King who serve the King, but loyal to the truth. The man say the King come into knowledge of you since he have belly walkers on the ground and pigeons in the sky. So gather your griots and let a caravan take them to Kongor, for they can live safe among the books of the house of records. For the age of the voice is over and we in the age of the written mark. The word on stone, the word on parchment, the word on cloth, the word that is even greater than the glyph for the word provoke a sound in the mouth. And once in Kongor, let men of writing save words from lips and in that way they may kill the griot but can never kill the word. And Babuta say, back in the red caves stinking with sulfur, that this be a good thing, my brothers. This sound like we should take the man for his word. But Babuta is from the time when word fall like waterfall in a room and even smell like truth. And the man say, When the pigeon land at the mouth of this cave, in the evening two days from now, take the note from its right foot and follow the instructions of the glyphs, for it will tell you where to go. Do you know of the way of the pigeon? It flies in one direction, only to where is home. Unless they are bound by witchcraft, to think home is an otherwhere place. Babuta say to the man, Watch me now, no man here ever wished to read, and the man say, You will know when you see the glyphs, for the glyphs talk like the world. And Babuta approach the others, and Babuta approach me, and say this is a good thing, we must no longer live like dogs. And so instead we go to the hall of books and live like rats, I say. There is nobody in the King's court any half imbecile should trust. And he say, Go suck a hyena's teat for calling me a fool, and I leave the cave for I know it marked and I start to wander. Babuta and five man wait by the cave, day and night. And it come to pass three night hence that the pigeon land at the cave mouth. No drum ever beat. No drums ever tell where Babuta and the five go. But nobody ever see them again. So there be no southern griots. There be me."

"That was a long story," Sogolon said. "If not verse then no verse. Tell them about the lightning bird. And who travel with him."

"You see how they work."

"So have you."

"One of you stop staring at the shit and tell us the story," Mossi said. And it was going to be the first time he didn't irritate me, had he not smiled at me when he said it.

The man sat down on the bed that Sogolon never sleeps in and said, "A wicked word come from the West, ten and four nights previous. A village right by the Red Lake. A woman say to her neighbor, Is one quartermoon now we don't see anybody from that house, three hut down the left. But they is quiet folk who keep their own company, another woman say. But not even the spirit of the breeze this quiet, another say and they go to the hut to look see. All around the hut death be stinking, but the foul coming from dead beasts, from cows and goats slaughtered not for food but for blood and sport. The fisherman, his first wife and second wife, and three sons dead but they did not smell. How to describe a sight strange even to the gods? They were all gathered around like worship fetishes, piled up as if about to burn. They have skin like tree bark. Like the blood, the flesh, the humors, the rivers of life, something suck it all out. The first and second wife, both of them chest cut open and they heart rip out. But not before he bite them all over the neck and rape them, leaving his dead seed to grow rot in they womb. You already call him name."

"Ipundulu. Who is his witch? He roaming loose like he not under command anymore?" Sogolon asked.

"He not. The witch who control him die before she could pass ownership to she daughter, so Ipundulu change back into the lightning bird and grab the daughter with him claws, and fly with her high and high and high, then let her go. She hit the ground and smash to juice. This is how you know he seed was in the two wife. For little drops of lightning was falling out of they kehkeh even after they start rot. The Ipundulu he the handsomest of men, he skin white like clay, whiter than this one, but pretty like him too."

He pointed at Mossi.

"Ayet bu ajijiyat kanon," Mossi said, and surprised everyone.

"Yes, prefect, he is a white bird. But he not good. He evil as people think. Worser. Ipundulu because he handsome and he in a gown white like he skin, think woman come to him free, but he infect they mind as soon as he enter the room. And he open he gown which is not no gown but his wings and he not wearing no robes, and he rape them, one then two, and most he kill and some he make live, but they not living, they living dead with lightning running through they body where blood used to run. I hear rumors that he change man too. And watch if you step to the lightning bird and he know for he change into something big and furious and when he flap him wing he let loose thunder which shake the ground and deaf the ear and knock down a whole house and lightning that shock your blood and burn you to a black husk.

"This is how it happen in a house in Nigiki. A hot night. See a man and a woman in a room, and a cloud of flies above a bed mat. He a handsome man, neck long, hair black, eyes bright, lips thick. Too tall for the room. He grin at the cloud of flies. He nod at the woman and she, naked, bleeding from the shoulder, walk over. Her eyes, they gone up in her skull and her lips, just quivering. She covered in wetness. She walking to him, her hands stiff at the side, stepping over her own clothes and scattered sorghum from a bowl that shatter. She comes closer, her blood still in his mouth.

"He grab her neck with one hand and feel her belly for sign of the child with the other. Dog teeth grow out of his mouth and past his chin. His fingers roughing between her legs, but she still. Ipundulu point a finger at the woman's breast and a claw pop through the middle finger. He press deep into her chest and blood pump up, as he cut her chest open for the heart. The cloud of flies swarming and buzzing, and fattening up with blood. Flies pull away for a blink and is a boy on the mat, covered in pox holes like chigger. From the pox holes worm burrow out, ten, dozens, hundreds, pop out of the boy's skin, unfold wings and flying off. The boy's eyes wide open, his blood dripping onto the bed mat also cover in flies. Bite, burrow, suck. Him mouth crack open and a groan come out. The boy is a wasp nest."

"Adze? They working together?" Sogolon said.

"Not them two alone. Others. Ipundulu and Adze, they two suck the body life out but they don't drain it to a husk. That be the grass troll, Eloko. He only hunt alone or with his kind, but since the King burn down his forest to plant tobacco and millet, they join anyone. A lightning woman, this be her story. This is what happen when Ipundulu suck out all the blood but stop before he suck out the lifeblood, and breed lightning into her and leave her mad too. A southern griot pull all of this out of her mouth, but he never make no verse out of it. There be those three and two more, and another one. This is what I telling you. They working together. But Ipundulu leading them. And the boy."

"What of the boy?" Sogolon asked.

"You know the story yourself. They use the boy to get into woman the house."

"They force the boy."

"Same thing," he said. "Also this. Another one following them three or four days later, for by then the rotting body and the stinking humors is a pleasing scent to him. He cut them open with he claws and drink the stinking rot juice, then eat the flesh till he full. He used to have a brother till somebody kill him in the Hills of Enchantment."

I looked at them as plain as one could.

"They using the boy, Sogolon," the man said.

"I say nobody ask about—"

"They turn the boy."

"Look here."

"They make the boy into—"

A gust, thick like a storm, blew up from the floor and kicked everybody against the wall. The angry wind hissed, then flew out the window.

"Nobody make the boy into nothing. We find the boy, and—"

"And what?" I said. "What does this man say to displease you?"

"Don't you hear it, Tracker? How long has the boy been missing?" Mossi said.

"Three years."

"He's saying the boy is one of them. If not a blood drinker, then under necromancy."

"Don't provoke her. She will blow the roof off next," the old man said.

Mossi gave me a look that said, This little old woman? I nodded.

"Tracker right. They are using the ten and nine doors," Sogolon said.

"And how many doors have you been through?" Mossi asked.

"One. It is not good for one such as me to go through that door. I get my calling from the green world and that travel violate the green world."

"A very long way to say that gates are bad for witches," I said. "You need me and my Sangoma craft to open them for you. And even passing through each door weakens you."

"What a man, he know me more than I know myself. Write my song for me then, Tracker."

"Sarcasm always masks something else," Mossi said.

"How quickly the Leopard get replace."

"Shut your face, Sogolon."

"Ha, now my loose tongue will be a river."

"Woman, we lose time," the old man said to her, and she quieted herself. He stepped over to the chest and took out a huge parchment.

Mossi said, "Old man, is this what I think it is? I thought these were uncharted lands."

"What do you two speak of?" I asked.

The old man unrolled the scroll. A big drawing, in brown, blue, and the colour of bone. I have also seen the like; there were three in the palace of wisdom, but I did not know what they were or what was their use.

"A map? Is this a map of our lands? Who did such a thing? Such masterful craft, such detail, even of the eastern seas. Was this from a merchant in the East?" Mossi said.

"Men and women in these lands have mastered crafts too, foreigner," Sogolon said.

"Of course."

"You think we run with lions and shit with zebra so we cannot draw the land or paint the buffalo?"

"That is not what I meant."

Sogolon let him go with a huff. But this map thing made him grin like a child who stole a kola nut. The man dragged it to the center of the room and placed two pots and two stones at the corners. The blue pulled me in. Light like the sky, and swirls of dark blue like the sea itself. The sea but not like the sea, more like the sea of dream. Bobbing out of the sea, as if leaping on land, were creatures great and small, grand fishes, and a beast with eight tails gobbling a dhow boat.

"I have been waiting to show this to you, the sand sea before it was sand," the old man said to Sogolon.

Which waters are these? I said to myself.

"A map is just a drawing of the land, of what a man sees so that we too may see it. And plot where to go," Mossi said.

"Thank the gods for this man to tell us what we already know," Sogolon said. Mossi kept quiet.

"You mark them in red? Based on what wisdom?" Sogolon asked.

"The wisdom of mathematics and black arts. Nobody travel four moons in one flip of a sandglass, unless they move like the gods, or they using the ten and nine doors."

"And this is them," I said.

"All of them."

Sogolon kneeled and Mossi stooped down, the man excited, the woman silent and with a frown.

"Where you last hear anything about them?" she said.

"The Hills of Enchantment. Twenty and four nights ago."

"You draw an arrow from the Hills of Enchantment to . . . where does this point, to Lish?" Mossi said.

"No, from the Hills to Nigiki."

"This one points from Dolingo to Mitu, but not far from Kongor," I said.

"Yes."

"But we came from Mitu to Dolingo, and before that the Darklands to Kongor."

"Yes."

"I don't understand. You said they are using the ten and nine doors."

"Of course. Once you go through a door, you can only go in one direction until you go through all doors. You can never go back until you done."

"What happens when you try?" I say.

"You who kiss a door and flame burns away the mask of it, you should know. The door consume you in flames and burn you up, something that would scare the Ipundulu. They must be using them for two years now, Sogolon. That is why they so hard to find and impossible to track. They stay on the course of doors until they complete the journey, then they go back ways. That's why I draw each line with an arrow at the two ends. That way they kill at night, kill only one house, maybe two maybe four, all the killing they can do in seven or eight days, then vanish before they leave any real mark."

I walked over, pointed, and said, "If I was going from the Darklands to Kongor, then here, not far from Mitu to Dolingo, then I would have to ride through Wakadishu to get to the next door, at Nigiki. If they travel in reverse, then already they have come through the Nigiki door. Now they walk through Wakadishu, to get to—"

"Dolingo," Mossi said.

He pressed his finger into the map, at a star between mountains right below the center.

"Dolingo."

4

WHITE SCIENCE AND BLACK MATH

Se peto ndwabwe pat urfo.

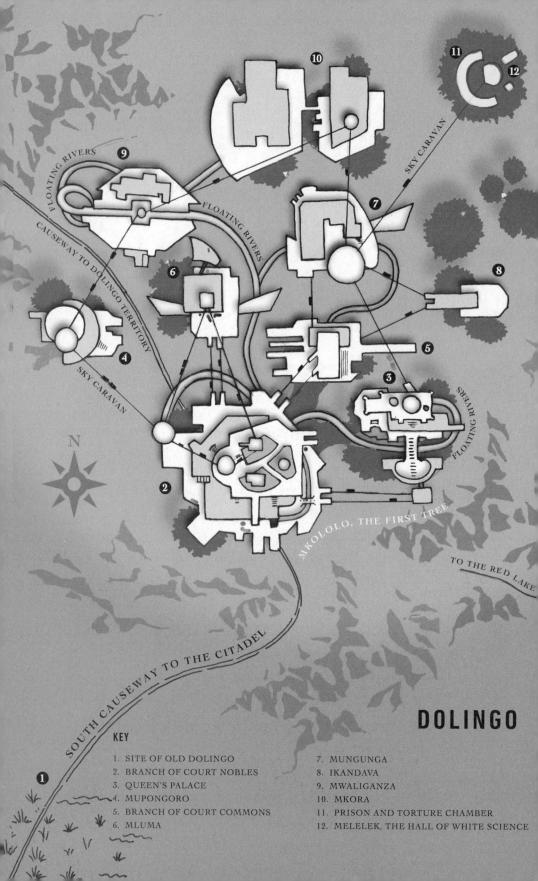

DOLINGO

KEY

1. SITE OF OLD DOLINGO
2. BRANCH OF COURT NOBLES
3. QUEEN'S PALACE
4. MUPONGORO
5. BRANCH OF COURT COMMONS
6. MLUMA
7. MUNGUNGA
8. IKANDAVA
9. MWALIGANZA
10. MKORA
11. PRISON AND TORTURE CHAMBER
12. MELELEK, THE HALL OF WHITE SCIENCE

FLOATING RIVERS

FLOATING RIVERS

FLOATING RIVERS

SKY CARAVAN

SKY CARAVAN

CAUSEWAY TO DOLINGO TERRITORY

MKOLOLO, THE FIRST TREE

TO THE RED LAKE

SOUTH CAUSEWAY TO THE CITADEL

N

EIGHTEEN

We are in the great gourd of the world, where the God Mother holds everything in her hands, so that which is at the bottom of the round never falls away. And yet the world is also flat on paper, with lands that shape themselves like blots of blood seeping through linen, of uneven shape, that sometimes look like the skulls of ill-born men.

I traced the rivers of the map until my finger took me to Ku, which lit nothing in me. I wondered about it, that once I wanted more than anything to be Ku, but now I don't even remember why. My finger took me across the river to Gangatom, and as soon as I touched that symbol of their huts I heard a giggle from my memory. No, not a memory but that thing where I cannot tell what I remember from what I dream. The giggle had no sound, but was blue and smoky.

The day was going, and we were setting to leave at

night. I went to the other window. Outside, the prefect ran up to a mound, making himself black against
the sunset. He pulled off a long djellaba I had never
seen him wear, and stood on a rock in a loincloth. He
bent down and took up two swords. He squeezed the
handles in his hands, looked at one, then the other,
rolled them around his fingers, until he had a firm
grip. He raised his left hand, holding the sword in
blocking position, dropped on one knee, and swung
the right so swift it was if he was swinging light. He
let the swing throw him up in the air, where he spun
and sliced and landed on his left knee. He jumped up
again and charged with the right and blocked with
the left, sliced his left sword to the right side and right
to left, stabbed both in the ground and flipped over,
landing in a crouch like a cat. Then he went back up
on the rock. He stopped and looked this way. I could
see his chest heaving. He could not have seen me.

The old man shuffled again. He took out a kora, larger
than I thought it would look. The base a round, fat half
of a gourd that he steadied between his legs. The great
neck tall as a young boy, and strings to the right and
to the left. He took it by the bulukalos, the two horns,
and sat by the window. From his pocket he pulled what
looked like a large silver tongue rimmed with earrings.

"Great musicians from the midlands, they stick
the nyenyemo to the bridge so the music leaps buildings and pierces through walls, but who needs house
jumper and wall piercer in open sky?"

He tossed the nyenyemo to the ground.

Eleven strings to the left hand, ten strings to the right, he plucked on and it hummed deep into the floor. I have not been this close to music such as this in many years. Like a harp in the many notes rising at once, but not a harp. Like a lute, but not sharp with melody like a lute, and not so quiet.

Outside Sogolon and the girl, she on a horse, the girl on the buffalo, rode out west. Footsteps shaking the floor above us meant the Ogo was moving around. I could feel the floor shake under him until I heard a door slam open. The roof, maybe. I went back to the maps. The old man built a rhythm with his right fingers and a melody with his left. He cleared his throat. His voice came out higher than when he spoke. High like a cried alarm, still higher, with the top of his tongue clicking the top of his mouth to make rhythm.

I it is who is speaking
I am a southern griot
We now few we was once all
Hide in dark I come out of
The wilderness, I come out of
The cave, I come out and see

I was looking for
A lover
I want get
A lover
I did lose

Another
I want get

Time make every man a widow
And every woman too
Inside him
Black like him
Black that suck through the hole in the world

And the biggest hole in the world
Be the hole of loneliness
The man lose him soul give it 'way

For he was looking for
A lover
He want get
A lover
He did lose
Another
He want get

A man when he eat like glutton
Look like a man when he starve
Tell me can you tell one from two
You glutting by day
Then you starving by night, yeah
Look at you, fooling you

You want find
A lover

You want get
A lover
You did lose
Another
You did lose
A lover
You did lose
A lover
You did lose
Another
You did lose

Then he plucked the strings and let the kora alone speak, and I left before he sang more. I ran outside because I was a man, and string and song should never affect me so. Outside, where nothing could suck all the air out of one place. And where I could say it was wind that made my eyes wet, truth it was wind. Out on the rock the prefect stood, wind running past him, whipping his hair. The kora was still playing, riding air, sending sadness all the way down the trail we came. I hated this place, I hated that music, and I hated this wind, and I hated thinking about mingi children, for what were children to me and what use was I to children? And that was not it, that was not it at all, for I never think of children, and they never think of me, but why would they forget me and why would I care that they forget? For what good it be that they remember and why did I remember, and why did I remember now? And I tried to stop it. I felt it coming up, and I said, No, I will not think of my brother who is dead, and my father who is dead and my father who was my grandfather, and why should anybody want anybody? Just have nothing, just need nothing. Fuck the gods of all things. And I wanted day to go and night to come, and day to come again new and cut off from everything before, like a shit stain on cotton that comes out in the wash. Mossi was still standing there. Still not looking at me.

Sadogo, you go to sleep? The sun is not even done with the day."

He smiled. On the roof, he made a space, with rugs and rags and cloths, with several cushions for a pillow. "I witness only nightmares these few days," he said. "Best I lie here and not punch a hole through a wall and bring the house down." I nodded.

"The nights grow cold in these lands, Ogo."

"The old man found me rugs and rags, besides I feel little of it. What do you think of Venin?"

"Venin?"

"The girl. She rides with Sogolon."

"I know who she is. I think we found the boy."

"What? Where is he? Your nose—"

"Not through my nose. Not yet. There is much distance between us and him. Right now he is too far away for me to guess. They might be in Nigiki, on the way to Wakadishu."

"Both are half a moon away. And it will take days to get from one to the next. I may not be smart as Sogolon, but even I know."

"Who questions your mind, Ogo?"

"Venin called me simple."

"That little girl who was never more proud when she was Zogbanu meat?"

"She is different. Different from only three days ago. Before she never spoke, now she grunts like a jackal and is always sour. And she listens not to Sogolon. Have you seen it?"

"No. And you are not simple."

I went over beside him and crouched down.

"Deep in skill he is," the Ogo said.

"Who?" I asked.

"The prefect. I watch him train. He is master of some art."

"Master at arresting people and harassing beggars, yes."

"You do not like him."

"I have no feelings for him, like or dislike."

"Oh."

"Sadogo, I wish you to know what was spoken. The boy, he is with men not of this place, or any place of good men."

He looked at me, his eyebrows raised but his eyes blank.

"Men who are not men, but not demons, though they may be monsters. One is the lightning bird."

"Ipundulu."

"You know him?"

"He is not a real him," he said.

"How do you know?"

"This Ipundulu, long years ago, he tried to cut my heart out. I worked for a woman in Kongor. Seven nights he spent, seven nights seducing her."

"So you have lived in Kongor. You never told me."

"It was ten and four days' work. But Ipundulu. Those days plenty joy he found in taking slow. He had her every night, but this night I heard only sounds from him. When I walked in he already killed her, and was eating her heart. This is what he says—What a bigger meal you shall be—so he flies and jumps on me, and takes his claw and cuts through my skin. But my skin is thick, Tracker, his claw got stuck. I grab his neck. Squeeze, I did, until it started to crack. Indeed I would pop his head off, but his witch was outside the window. She threw a spell and it blinded me for ten and six blinks. Then she helped him escape. I saw him off in the sky, his wings white, his hanging neck loose, but still carrying her."

"He is no longer bound to that witch, or any witch. She left no heir, so now he is his own master."

"Tracker, this is no good thing. He would rip out a child's throat and that was when he was under her. What will he do now?"

"The boy is still alive."

"Not even I myself am that simple."

"If he is using the boy, then the boy is alive. You

saw the ones with lightning blood. They could never hide it. And they have gone mad."

"You speak a true thing."

"There is more. He moves with others, four or five. We've heard accounts. All of them bloodsuckers, it seems they go to houses with many children. The boy knocks first, saying he ran away from monsters, and they let him in. Then deep in the night he lets them in to feed on everyone."

"But the boy is not one of them?"

"No, but you know the Ipundulu, he must have bewitched the boy."

"We in these lands know of him bewitching girls, but never a boy. His head I will smash myself, before he can whip his wings. Those wings bring thunder, do you know?"

"What do you mean?"

"He flaps his wings and a storm blows with lightning and thunder, harder and wickeder than the wind Sogolon makes with magic."

"Then we shall clip his wings. I will tell you of the others later."

"And of wings, what of the man with black wings?"

"The Aesi? He also seeks for the child, and he will not rest till he finds him. But he knows neither where we are, who has the boy, nor of the ten and nine doors, or he would have used them. This is simple. We save the child and hand him back to his mother, who lives in a mountain fortress."

"Why?"

"She is the sister of the King."

"Confusing, is what this is."

"I make it simple."

"Like me?"

"No. No, Sadogo. You are not simple. Listen to me, this is not about being simple. There are things I have been told that I have no words how to tell you, that is all. But know, this child is part of a bigger thing. A truly bigger thing, and when we find him, if we keep him safe, it will echo through all the kingdoms. But we must find him before these men do kill him. And we must find him before the Aesi, for he too will kill him."

"You said it was foolish to believe in magic boys. I remember."

"And I still believe it to be foolish."

I stood up and looked over the wall. The prefect was gone.

"Sadogo, I like simple. I like knowing this is what I will eat, this is what I will earn, this is where I shall go, and this is who I shall fuck. And that is still how I choose to move in this world. But this boy. It is not even that I care so much as it is we are in so deep. Let us finish it."

"Is that all that drives you?"

"Should there be more?"

"I don't know. But I am tired of my hands called to fight when I don't know what to fight for. The Ogo is not the elephant, or the rhinoceros."

"I don't know what to tell you. There is the money. And there is something I suspect, that this child, this boy, has something to do with what is right in this world. And as much as I don't care for this boy or even this world, yet still I move in it."

"You care for nothing in this world?"

"No, I do not. Yes, I do. I do not know. My heart jumps and skips and plays with me. Shall I tell you something, dear Ogo?"

He nodded.

"I am no father and yet I have children. I have no child here, yet they are around me. And I know them less than I know you, but I see them in dreams and I miss them. There is one, a girl, I know she hates me, and it bothers me, because I see with her eyes and she is right."

"Children?"

"They live with the Gangatom, one of the river tribes, at war with my own."

"You have this girl and others?"

"Yes, others, one as tall as a giraffe."

"You have them live with the Gangatom, though you are Ku and they war with the Ku. The Ku will kill you."

"As you say it, yes."

"You make me think, this 'man is simple' is no bad thing."

I laughed.

"You may be speaking truth there, dear Ogo."

"You said the boy might be in Nigiki or Wakadishu."

"They use the same doors we used to escape the Darklands, but they use them in reverse. We had word of an attack on a household at the foot of the Hills of Enchantment that beat even their sacred magics. Twenty and four days ago, almost a moon. They spend seven to eight days in one place, killing and feeding, which means they have used the door to Nigiki. From Nigiki they kill and go to Wakadishu."

"They're almost there."

"They are there already. It takes five days to get to Wakadishu on foot, maybe six, and they are on foot. My guess is that no beast can stomach the filth of them, so no horses. If they are in Wakadishu they will only be there for another two days, maybe three. Then they walk to the next door, the one we came through on the way to Dolingo."

"Shall we not meet them there?"

"They will go through the citadel. They will want to feed, and who can resist such noble stock as the Dolingon? Besides, Sadogo, our numbers are few. We might need help."

"So we cut them off?"

"Yes, we cut them off."

He clapped his hands and it echoed across the sky. Then he spread them and I walked right to him as if to embrace. He flinched a little, not sure what I was doing. I wrapped my arms around him, my head in his armpit, and inhaled deep and long.

"What are you doing?" he said.

"Trying to remember you," I said.

Sadogo then asked me if I thought the girl was pretty.

"Venin, I told you her name," he said.

"She is pretty as girls go, I think, but her lips are too thin as is her hair, and she is only a little darker than the prefect, whose skin is hideous. Do you think her pretty?"

"I feel like half of an Ogo. My mother died when she had me, which is fine for she would have lived to curse me and my birth. But I feel like not the Ogo in many things."

"You are right and you are true, dear Ogo. And yes she is pretty."

The rest of my words I left to my own head, which might have been a crude joke. He nodded and pressed his lips together, satisfied with my answer, and lowered his head on his rugs.

Downstairs, I passed the room with the prefect. "It is yet early, but good night, Tracker," he said as I walked by.

"Night," was all that came out of my mouth.

I only then noticed the old man had stopped playing and was in the room, staring at darkness, maybe. I went down to the ground floor and waited for Sogolon.

Your old man, he was singing."

The girl had come in first, huffing and panting. Sogolon grabbed her hand and the girl pushed her away and pinned her against the wall. I jumped up but the girl let go, growled, and started up the stairs. Sogolon closed the door.

"Venin," she said.

The girl cursed back in that language I did not know. Sogolon replied in the same tongue. I knew that Sogolon tone: I am here to speak and you are here to listen. I imagined the girl wishing her a thousand fucks from a man covered in warts, or something just as vicious. She cursed all the way up two flights and slammed the door shut.

"Nobody in this house know what night is for," Sogolon said.

"Fucking? Or working witch magic? Sleep is for the old gods and who follow him, Sogolon. Your old man was singing."

"A lie."

"No great stake in lying to you, old woman."

"But great sport, maybe. You was right there in the room when only today he refuse to sing. The songs stay inside him mouth and none come out since Kwash Netu was King."

"I know what I heard."

"He don't sing in thirty years, maybe more, but he sing in front of you?"

"Truth, his back was to me."

"A silent griot don't just open him mouth."

"Maybe he was biding time for you to leave."

"Your sting already duller than a moon ago. Maybe somebody giving him something new to sing about."

"He was not singing about me."

"How you know that?"

"Because I am nothing. Do you not agree?"

"I speaking to him when he wake."

"Maybe he sung about himself? Ask him that."

"He not answering that."

"You didn't ask."

"A griot never going explain a song, only repeat it, maybe with something new, otherwise he would give the explaining not the song. Nothing about the King?"

"No."

"Or the boy?"

"No."

"Then for what else he be singing?"

"Maybe what all men sing about. Love."

She laughed.

"Maybe some people in this world still need it."

"Do you?" she said.

"Nobody loves no one."

"The King before this one, Kwash Netu, was never one for learning. Why he would need to? This be something most people don't know about kings and queens. Even back in many an age, learning was for something. I learn the black arts to use for and against. You learn from the palace of wisdom, so that you rest in a better place than your father. You learn a weapon to protect yourself. You learn a map so that you is master of the journey. In everything, learning is to take from where you be to where you like to go.

But a king already there. That be why the King and
the Queen can be the most ignorant in the kingdom.
And this King mind as blank as sky until somebody
told him that some griots sing songs older than when
he was a boy. Can you think it? He never believe that
any man would put to memory anything that happen
before he born, for that is how kings raise their boys.

"But this King didn't know there was griots who
sing songs of King before him. Who they be. What
they do. Everything from the wicked work of Kwash
Moki. The King didn't even hear a song. The man at
him side say, Most Excellent Majesty, there is a song
that can rise against you. Then they round up nearly
every man of song with verse from before Kwash
Moki's time and kill them. And who they couldn't
find to kill, they kill wife and son and daughter. Kill
them and burn down they house and order all to
forget that any song sing that way. Kill everyone in
this man family, they do. He escape but even now he
wondering why they didn't kill him. They could have
silence him without killing nine people to do it. But
such is the way with these kings of North. I speak to
him when he wake, that I know."

Sobs woke me up before sun. First I thought it was
wind, or something hanging on from a dream, but
there he was across from the bed I slept in, the Ogo
crouched in a corner by the south window, crying.

"Sadogo, what is—"

"It is like he thought if he walk on it he could ride it. That is how he looked. Could he ride it? Why didn't he ride it?"

"Ride what, dear Ogo? And who?"

"The griot. Why didn't he ride it?"

"Ride what?"

"The wind."

I ran to my north window, looked out for a blink, then ran to the south window, which Sadogo crouched beside. I saw Sogolon and went down. She wore white this morning, not the brown leather dress she was always in. The griot was at her feet, limbs twisted like a burned spider's, broken in too many places, dead. Her back was to me, and her robes flapped.

"Everybody still sleep?" she said.

"Except the Ogo."

"He said he just walk past him and off the roof like he go down the road."

"Maybe he walked on that road to the gods."

"This look like a time for mockery to you?"

"No."

"What he sing to you? In the day now gone, what he sing?"

"Truth? Love. That was all of his singing. Love looking. Love losing. Love like how poets from where Mossi come from talk about love. Love he did lose. That is all he was singing, love he did lose."

Sogolon looked up, past the house up into the sky.

"He spirit still walking on wind."

"Of course."

"I don't care if you agree or no, you hear m—"

"We agree, woman."

"No good for the others to know. Not even the buffalo; let him eat grass otherwhere."

"You want to drag the old man out into deep bush? You want him to be food for hyena and crow?"

"And then the worm and the beetle. It don't matter now. He with the ancestors. Trust the gods."

The Ogo came out to join us, his eyes still red. Poor Ogo, it was not that he was gentle. But something about someone else bringing his own self such violence shook him.

"We take him out to the bush, Sadogo."

This was still savannah. Not many trees, but yellow grass reaching my nose. Sadogo had picked him up and was cradling him like a baby, despite his bloody head. The two of us went out to taller grass.

"Death remains king over us, does he not? He still wants to choose when to take us. Sometimes even before our ancestors have made a place. Maybe he was a man in defiance of the final King, Ogo. Maybe he just said, Fuck the gods, I choose when to be with my own ancestors."

"Maybe," he said.

"I wish I had better words, words like he used to sing. But he must have thought that whatever was his purpose, he fulfilled it. After that there was nothing to—"

"You believe in purpose?" Sadogo asked.

"I believe people when they say they believe in it."

"Ogo has no use for gods of sky or place of the dead. When he is dead he is meat for crows."

"I like how the Ogo think. And if—"

It flew past my face so fast I thought it was a trick. Then another flew right past my head. The third came straight at my face and as if coming for my eyes, but I blocked it and its claws scratched my hand. One came for the Ogo's shoulder and he swatted it so quick and hard that it exploded in a cloud of blood. Birds. Two went for his face and he dropped the griot. He swatted away one and grabbed the other, crushing it whole. One scraped the back of my neck. I grabbed it from behind and tried to snap its neck but it was stiff, it flapped and clawed and snapped at my finger. I let go and it flew around and came right back at me. Sadogo jumped in my way and swatted it. On the ground I saw what they were, hornbills, white head with a black streak of feather on top, a long gray tail, and a huge red beak that curved down, bigger than his head, for the red meant male. Another landed on the griot and flapped his wings. The Ogo moved in to grab him when I looked up.

"Sadogo, look."

Right above us, swirling, screeching, a black cloud of hornbills. Three dived after us, then four, then more and more.

"Run!"

The Ogo stood and fought, punching and swatting and crushing in his knuckles and tearing wings, but they kept coming. Two heading for my head crashed into each other and fought on my scalp. I ran, my hand blocking my face, them scratching my fingers. The Ogo, tired of fighting, ran as well. Near the door of the house, they stopped following. Sogolon came back out and we turned around to see the swarm of birds—hundreds, if not more—clasp the griot with their claws, lifting him up slow and low above the ground, and flying him away. We said nothing.

We gathered our things, with Sogolon telling the others that the man is gone into deep wilderness to speak to spirits, which was not exactly a lie, and said we should take as much as we could carry. I said, Why would we need to, if we are less than a day to Dolingo citadel? She frowned and told the girl to grab more food. The girl hissed and said, If you want more food, go get it yourself. I wondered if Mossi was thinking as I did, and that this was not something I wanted to ask about right now. He grabbed a cloth and wrapped it around my neck for the scratch. Sogolon took one horse, the girl climbed up Sadogo's back and sat on his right shoulder. Mossi climbed on the buffalo and they both turned and looked at me when I started walking.

"Don't be foolish, Tracker, you will slow us down," Mossi said.

He held out his hand and pulled me up.

Day reddened, then blackened, and we were no-where near the Dolingo citadel. I nodded off, fell asleep on Mossi's shoulder, jumped back in horror, and fell asleep again, this time not caring, only to wake up finding that we were still not there. Dolingo must have been one of those lands that seemed small but took two lifetimes to travel. The first time I woke up I was hard. Truth, that is why I jumped back. It must have been a dream that vanished as soon as I woke. As dreams always do. Yes, as they always do. I shifted as far away from him as I could, for to tell truth, I could smell him. Yes, I could smell everyone, but everyone wasn't breathing much slower than everyone else. And with me cursing myself for sleeping on Mossi's shoulder, hoping I didn't drool or poke his back, though I shoot up when hard, not out. Of course hoping that I wasn't hard when I was asleep only made me grow hard awake, and I thought of hornbills, and night skies, and foul water, anything.

"Good buffalo, if you tire of us, we can walk," Mossi said.

The buffalo grunted, which Mossi took to mean stay as you are, though I wanted to climb off. But I also wished I wore thick, heavy robes this once. Not that robes hid any man's desire. But it was not desire, it was my body holding on to a dream that my head had long let go. We were climbing slightly, into cooler night air, and passing small hills and great rocks.

"Sogolon, you said we are in Dolingo. Then where is it?" I asked.

"Silly, stupid, tracking idiot. Do you think we pass mountains? Look up."

Dolingo. Not much had passed since we left the

griot's house, but as the bush grew thick with trees, I thought we were swerving around great rocks to avoid climbing them. I would have fallen off the buffalo, had Mossi not grabbed my hand.

Dolingo. These were not great rocks, even though they were as wide as mountains—a thousand, six thousand, maybe even ten thousand paces all around—but the trunks of trees with little branches sprouting low. Trees as tall as the world itself. At first, looking up, all I could see were lights and ropes, something reaching taller than the clouds. We came upon a clearing wide as a battlefield, enough for me to see two of them. The first spread as far as the field; the second, smaller. Both trunks rose through clouds and beyond. Mossi grabbed my knee, I am sure without thinking. The first had an edifice, maybe of wood or mortar or both that wrapped around the base of the trunk, and rising five floors, each floor maybe eighty to a hundred paces high. Light flickered from some windows and blazed bold from others. The trunk rose dark, and continued even higher, past more clouds, where it split like a fork. On the left, what looked like a massive fort, huge plain walls with high windows and doors, another floor on top, and another floor on top of that, going on and on for six floors, with a deck on the fifth and a platform hanging off, held by four ropes that must have been as thick as a horse's neck. At the very top, a compound with the magnificent towers and roofs of a grand hall. On the right, the branch went unadorned as high as the forts, with a one palace on top, but even that palace had many floors, planks, decks, and roofs of gold. Clouds shifted, the moon shone brighter, and I noticed that the fork had three necks, not two. A third branch, thick as the other two, and dressed with buildings finished and buildings being built. And a deck that stretched longer than all others, so far that I thought it would soon break off. From the deck hung several platforms, pulled up and down by ropes. What number of slaves did it take to pull them? And what kind of now was this, what kind of future, where people built high and not wide? On top of, but not beside each other? Where were the farms and where were the cattle, and without them what did such people eat? Farther out in the great expanse, seven more towering trees stood high, including one with massive shiny planks that looked like wings, and a tower shaped like a dhow sail. The other, the trunk pointed slightly west, but the structures shifted slightly east, as if all the buildings were sliding off the base. From branch to branch, building to building, ropes and pulleys, platforms, and suspended wagons moving to and from, above and below.

"What is this place?" Mossi said.

"Dolingo."

"I have never seen such magnificence. Do gods live here? Is this home of gods?"

"No. It is the home of people."

"I don't know if I want to meet such people," Mossi said.

"The women might like your myrrh musk."

Metal crunched, gears locked. Iron hit iron, and the platform lowered. The ropes all around tightened, and pulleys began to spin. The platform, above and coming down, blocked the moon and covered us in shadow. It was as long and wide as a ship, and when it landed it shook the ground.

Mossi's hand still grabbed my knee. Sogolon and the girl galloped ahead, expecting us to follow. The platform was already rising and the buffalo leapt up on it, sliding a little. Mossi's hand left my knee. He hopped off and wobbled a little, with the rising platform. From a tower on high, someone turned a giant glass or silver circle, perhaps a dish, that caught the moonlight, and shone it down on the platform. We could hear cogs, and gears, and wheels. We rose higher, and as we moved closer, I could see patterns along the walls, diamond after diamond, up, down, and crossways, and balls in the same pattern, and ancient glyphs and stripes and wild lines that looked as if they still moved, as if an art master had painted with wind. We rose higher, past the trunk, taller than any bridge or road, to the three branches. On the side of the right branch, someone had painted the black head of a woman, so tall it rose higher than four floors, and on her head a wrap rose even higher.

The platform leveled with a plank and all movement stopped. Sogolon stepped off first and Venin followed, walking without looking right or left, or above, which had several orbs of light, but no string or source. So did Sadogo and the buffalo. They had been here before, but I had not. Mossi was still in shock. Sogolon and Venin left the horse standing to the side. This was the right-side branch, the branch of the palace, and on the nearest wall, a sign in a language like one I knew, with letters as tall as any man.

"This is Mkololo, the first tree and seat of the Queen," Sadogo said.

The moon moved in so close she eavesdropped on us. We walked on a wide stone bridge that curved over a river and met a road that had no bend. I wanted to ask what kind of science makes a river flow from so high, but the palace stood before us, as if it only now rose from the ground, as if we were mice beholding trees. The moon made all the walls white. On the lowest level, a high wall and a bridge to the left above a waterfall. On the next level, something I have only seen in lands of the sand sea. An aqueduct. Above that, the first floor, with lit windows and two towers. And above that still more chambers and rooms, and halls, and towers and grand roofs, some like the dome of a calabash, some like the pointed tip of an arrow. Rising to the right, a long platform with people, throwing shadow beneath us, as we came to a double door about three men high. And standing guard, two sentries in green armour, with neck gorgets that rose right below the nose, and long lances in one arm. They grabbed the handles and pulled the door open. We walked past them, but my hands were on my axes and Mossi grabbed his sword.

"Don't insult the Queen's hospitality," Sogolon said.

Twenty paces in flowed a moat, with a bridge no wider than three men aside, taking us over to the other side. Sogolon went first, then the Ogo, Venin, the buffalo, Mossi, then me. I watched Mossi look around him, jumping at the slightest splash, or gasping from a bird above, or the crank of gears from the platforms outside. I watched him more than I did where we were going, and besides, Sogolon clearly knew. Heat came off the water, but fish and fish-beasts swam in it. We crossed the bridge and walked towards steps, watching men, women, standing beasts, and creatures I have never seen, dressed in iron plates and chain mail, and robes, and capes, and headdresses with long feathers. The men and women had skin the darkest I have ever seen. On each step stood two guards. At the top step, the entrance rose taller than I could measure.

Here is truth. I have been to magnificent dominions across the lands and under the seas, but where would one start with this court? Mossi stood still, struck with wonder, as I too stood still. The halls reached so high I expected the women and men to be as tall. In the great hall stood guards at positions along the walls, twenty plus ten more, and other guards, six, who stood facing us. They all had two swords and one spear and showed their faces, which were all a dark black-blue. Their hands as well. And the people who moved about the great hall, even those covered in colourful robes, still had the darkest skin I have seen since the Leopard when he moved like a cat. Guards stood on our landing as well, two of them. I wanted to see the make of their swords. This hall had gold on every pillar, and running through the trim of every armour, but gold would have been a terrible metal for a sword. The hall floor sunk lower than our platform, but the throne floor rose the highest, a pyramid that was all imperial seat, with a ledge or step all around on which several women sat, and above them, the actual throne and the actual Queen.

Her skin, like her men, a black that came from the deepest blue. Her crown, like a gold bird had landed on her head and wrapped her wings around her face. Gold also lined her eyes and glimmered from a small spot on both lips. A vest of gold straps hung loose from her neck and her nipples peeked out when she leaned back.

"Listen to me now," she said. Her voice was deeper than the hum of monks. "Rumors I already hear them. Rumors of men the colour of sand, some even the colour of milk, but I am Queen and I believe what I wish. So I did not believe they lived. But look at the one before us." The Dolingon tongue sounded like Malakal's. Sharp sounds spoken in the quick, and long sounds that linger on purpose. Mossi already furrowed his brow.

He nudged me. "What does she say?"

"You don't speak the Dolingon tongue?"

"Certainly. A fat eunuch taught me at four. Of course I don't speak it. What does she say?"

"She talks of men she has never seen. You. I am almost sure of it."

"Should I call him sandman?" she said. "I shall call him sandman, for I find this a funny thing. . . . I did say I find this a funny thing."

The entire hall broke into laughter, clapping, whistling, and shouts to the gods. She flashed a hand and they quit in a blink. She waved Mossi over, but he did not understand.

"Tracker, they laugh. Why do they laugh?"

"She just called you sand boy or sand person."

"This amuses them?"

"Is he deaf? I had bid him come over," the Queen said.

"Mossi, she speaks of you."

"But she said nothing."

"She is Queen, if she said she spoke, she spoke."

"But she said nothing."

"Fuck the gods. Go!"

"No."

Two spears poked him in the back. The guards started walking and had Mossi not moved, their blades would have pierced his skin. They went down the steps of our platform, crossed the vast floor and the women, men, and beasts of the court, and stopped at the foot of the throne floor. She beckoned him to come up, and the two guards blocking the steps shifted away.

"Chancellor, you already go to more territories than they write in all the great books. Tell me, have you ever see such a man as this?"

A tall slender man with long and thin hair stepped out of the floor, to speak to the Queen. He bowed first.

"Most excellent Queen, many time and here is the thing. He—"

"How come you never purchase one for me?"

"Forgive me, my Queen."

"Are men even lighter than this?"

"Yes, Most Magnificent."

"How frightening, and how delicious." Then, to Mossi, "What is your name?"

Mossi stared at her blankly, like he truly was deaf. Sogolon said he did not know their tongue.

A guard came forward and gave the chancellor Mossi's sword. The chancellor looked at the blade, examined the handle, and said in Kongori tongue, "How come you by such a sword?"

"'Tis from a strange land," Mossi said.

"Which land?"

"Home."

"And that is not Kongor?"

The chancellor, facing the Queen, said to Mossi, "Clearly somebody did name you. What is it? The name, the name."

"Mossi."

"Hmm?"

"Mossi."

"Hmm?"

The chancellor nodded and a spear poked Mossi's side.

"Mossi, most excellent Queen," Mossi said.

The chancellor repeated to the queen.

"Mossi? Just Mossi. Men like you fall from sky and just pick up names? Where do you hail, master Mossi? What house?" the chancellor asked.

"Mossi from the house of Azar, from the lands of the eastern light."

Chancellor repeated in Dolingo tongue and the Queen bleated out a laugh.

"Why would a man east of the sea live in these lands? And what is this disease that burned all the colour from your skin? Tell me now, since nobody in this court likes when you annoy their Queen. . . . I said, nobody in this court like if you annoy the Queen."

The court erupted in nos and uh-uhs, and shouts to the gods.

"And yet his hair is black as coal. Lift that sleeve. . . . Yes, yes, yes, but how is this? Your shoulder is lighter than your arm? I can see it right there, did they sew arms onto you? My wise counsel had better start counseling."

I was looking at all this and wondering if only the South had mad kings and queens. Sogolon stood back when I expected her to say something. I tried to read her face but hers was not mine. If you disgusted me, you knew as soon as I bid you morning greetings. The Queen was playing and what was play to her? The Ogo stood still but his knuckles cracked from him squeezing too hard. I touched his arm. Mossi was no better at hiding his mind from his face. And Mossi standing there, looking at everything, understanding nothing.

He saw my face, and his fell into worry. What? he mouthed to me, but I did not know how to say anything to him.

"I will see more. Remove it," the Queen said.

"Remove your robes," said the chancellor to Mossi.

"What?" Mossi said. "No."

"No?" the Queen said. That she understood despite the Kongori tongue. "Shall a queen wait for consent from a man?"

She nodded and two of her guards grabbed Mossi. He punched one straight on the cheek but the other pushed a knife against his throat. He turned to me and I mouthed, Peace. Peace, prefect. The guard used the same knife, lodged between the garment and his shoulders, and cut it off. The other guard pulled his belt and everything dropped on the floor.

"No gasps? I hear no gasping?" the Queen said, and the room erupted in gasps, coughs, wheezes, and shouts to the gods.

Mossi, thinking, These are the things that must happen to me, straightened his back, raised his head, and stood. The women and men and eunuchs, who sat at the foot of the Queen, all crawled closer to look. What was the mystery, I did not know.

"Strange, strange thing. Chancellor, why is it darker than the rest of him? Lift it, I will see the sac."

He came for Mossi's balls and Mossi jumped. Meanwhile in all this Sogolon said nothing.

"Just as dark? Yes, it is strange, chancellor."

"It is strange, Most Excellent."

"Are you a man made up of other men? Your arms darker than your shoulders, your neck darker than your chest, your buttocks whiter than your legs, and your, your . . ." Then, to the chancellor, "What do your courtesans call it?"

Truth, I laughed.

"I am not one for the company of courtesans, Most Excellent," said the chancellor.

"Of course you are, they walk on four legs and cannot speak but they are yours. Enough of this talk. I will know why it is so darker than the rest of him. Is that how all men are in other lands? Is this what I would have seen had I married one of the Kalindar princes? East man, why is it the colour of that man standing with Sogolon?"

The chancellor said only that it was curious that a man with such light skin had such dark balls.

Mossi saw me covering a laugh and he frowned. "The gods had some play with me, my Queen," he said.

The chancellor told the Queen what Mossi said, almost as he said it.

"Which man were they playing with when they took it from him to give it to this man? I will know these things. Right now."

Mossi looked perplexed again, but watched the people watching him. Still he said nothing.

Sogolon cleared her throat. "Most excellent Queen, remember why we come to Dolingo."

"I am not one for forgetting, Sogolon. Especially when it was a favor. Especially the way you begged for it."

Mossi looked at them with the shock I hid.

"Look at your stunned lips. And why would I, the wisest of queens, not speak that savage North tongue—especially when I constantly have to deal with savages? A child could learn it in a day. . . . Why does my court not ooh and aah?"

The chancellor translated for the court, which erupted in oohs and aahs and shouts to the gods.

She waved her hand and the guards poked at Mossi with their spears. He grabbed his clothes and walked back to us. I looked at him the whole time but he only looked ahead.

"You share with me your cause because you think we are sisters. But I am Queen, and you are less than a flame's moth."

"Yes, Most Excellent," Sogolon said, and bowed.

"I did agree to help you because Lissisolo and I should be queens together. And because your King gives even demons pause. How he wishes Dolingo was there for the conquering. I know what he thinks at night. That one day he will forget that Dolingo remains neutral and take the citadel for himself. And one day he will try. But not today, and not while I am Queen. I am also very bored. Your patched-up

man come the closest to something worth my eye in
moons. At least since I cut one of those princes of Mitu
in half to see if he was as empty as he sounded. You,
the one with marks, did you see our sky caravans?"

She spoke to me.

"Only on the way up to you, most excellent
Queen," I said.

"Many still wonder what craft or spell keeps them
in the sky. It's neither spell nor craft, it is iron and
rope. I don't have magicians, I have masters of steel
and masters of glass and masters of wood. Because
in our palace of wisdom are people who are actually
wise. I hate men who accept things as they are and
never question, never fix, never make better, or do
better. Tell me, do I frighten you?"

"No, my Queen."

"I will. Guards, take these two to Mungunga. The
Ogo and the girl can head to their rooms. Leave us
women to talk heavy matters. And feed the buffalo
some elephant ear grass. Must have been moons since
anyone give him food worthy of him. Leave now, all
of you. Except this woman who thinks she is a sister."

You should teach me such words, prefect," I said,
laughing. Mossi had been cursing and cursing in
his home tongue, pacing up and down the caravan,
stomping so hard it swung a little. He distracted me
from the fact that we were hanging at a great height,
being pulled across the great trees by gears. The more

he cursed, the less I imagined a rope bursting and us falling to death. The more he cursed, the less I imagined that the Queen sent us up so high in the sky and so far from the ground to kill us.

"Any higher and we could kiss the moon," I said.

"Fuck the moon and all who worship her," he said.

He still paced. Up and down, to the window and back; at least by following him I could see this caravan. This high, the moon shone so bright that green was green and blue was blue and his skin was almost white, now that he had tied his torn clothes at the waist and left his chest bare. What a caravan was this; at first I thought they flipped a wagon upside down so that the wheels were on top and then had the wheels along tight bands of rope. Then looking at how the caravan swelled like the fat belly of a big fish, I thought it was a boat that sailed on sky. It had a bow and stern just like a boat, was fattest in the middle just like a boat, but with house windows going all around and a roof of trunks slatted together with tar. The floor, flat and smooth, and wet with dew, almost slippery. Also this, the air blew cold this high, and whoever traveled on this thing last was bleeding. Mossi kept pacing and cussing and as he passed me I grabbed his arm. He tried to move, tried to push away my hand, tried to push me off, but I held on until he stopped huffing and cussing.

"What?"

"Stop."

"She did not humiliate **you.**"

"You were without clothes only a few nights ago. You were not angry then."

"I knew where I was and who I was with. Just because I live with you all does not mean I am not still a man of the East."

"You all?"

He sighed, and went over to the side to look out the window. A cloud so silver and so thin it would break away into nothing, and another caravan passing us much farther away, theirs lit by firelight.

"Who do you think they are? Why would anyone have business traveling at night? Where do they go?"

"Thinking like a prefect?"

He smiled. "Their guards did not follow us."

"This Queen does not see men as much of a threat. Or they will cut this loose before we make it to the other side. And we will plunge to our deaths."

"Neither of those brings a smile to my face, Tracker. Maybe with us both up here alone, they think we will talk, and maybe they have discovered some form of magic to listen."

"Dolingon are advanced for this age, but no one is that advanced."

"Maybe we should make as if we are fucking like violent sharks, to give them something to listen to. Uncock me at once, with that battering ram of yours! My hole, a chasm now it is!"

"How learned you, the ways that sharks fuck?"

"God, he knows. Was the first beast I could think of. God's words, Tracker, do you never smile?"

"What is there to smile about?"

"The lightness of my company, to begin with. The magnificence of this place. I tell you, gods come to lie here."

"I thought you worship only one god."

"Does not mean I do not see the others. What are these lands known for?"

"Gold and silver, and glass rock loved by lands far away. I think the citadel is on high because they have ruined the ground."

"Do you think these great trees are alive?"

"I think everything here is alive, by whatever keeps them living."

"Why does that mean?"

"Where are the slaves? And what do they look like?"

"Wise question. I—"

The shouting came upon us before the caravan, passing so close this time that we could smell spirits and smoke, so close that the drumming beat right into our ears and chest, while some plucked kora and lute as if about to pull the strings apart. The caravan passed until we faced each other. The drumming was not just the drum but also the feet of men and women jumping and stomping like the Ku or Gangatom in mating dance. A man, his face painted red and shiny, held a torch to his mouth and blew out fire like a dragon, fire that burst right between us. I jumped out of the way,

Mossi stood still. The caravan, which had not stopped, kept on until the drumming felt like the memory of beat. We were going to the branch away from the palace. The third one.

"Someone's blood was in this caravan, someone young," I said.

"Men and women seem very loose here. Maybe they killed a child for sport."

"What is loose? I have heard from men like you before."

"Men like me?"

"Men with one sad god. You act like old women who forgot that they were young women. Your one god, who thinks pleasure is a lesser thing."

"Can we talk about something else? We are almost on the other side. Tracker, what is our plan?"

"I'm not the one declaring herself ruler over us."

"If I wanted to know from her, I would have asked her. Tell me this. Is there a plan?"

"I don't know of any."

"That is madness. So the plan, as I see it, is we wait until you smell this magic boy close and when bloodsuckers or whatever they are manifest, we do what? Fight? Grab the child? Spin like dancing men? Do we just wait? Is there no cunning to this?"

"You ask me things I do not know."

"How are we to save this child from whatever evil guards him? And if we do save him, what then?"

"Maybe we should make a plan now," I said.

"Maybe you should leave, proving you're smart tongued to Sogolon."

"Truth?"

"That would be the preferred thing, if you can manage it."

"There was never a plan, other than fight whoever has the child and take him back. Kill if you have to. But no craft, so strategy, no subterfuge, no plan, as you said it. But that's not full truth. I think there is a plan."

"What is it?"

"I don't know. But Sogolon knows."

"Then why does she need us? Especially since she acts as if she does not."

I looked around. We were being watched, listened to, or our lips read.

"Move with me to the dark," I said, and he stepped into shadow with me.

"I think Sogolon has a plan," I said. "I don't know it, nor does the Ogo, or anybody else who journeyed with us before. But that's the plan too."

"What do you mean?"

"There is no plan for us because there will be no us. Send us to fight the bloodsuckers, maybe even be killed by them, while she and the girl save the boy."

"Is that not the pact you bound yourself to?"

"Yes, but something changed with Sogolon when she knew we were to head to Dolingo. I don't know what, but I know I won't like it."

"You don't trust her," Mossi said.

"She sent two pigeons out when we left the old man's house. Pigeons to the Queen."

"Do you trust me?" he asked.

"I . . ."

"Your heart searches for an answer. Good."

He smiled, and I tried to not smile but show a warm face.

"Why not just put a blade to her neck and demand to know?" he said.

"That how one gets a woman to obey in the East? She will not be threatened, that Sogolon. You have seen it, she can just blow you away."

"What I see is that someone hunts her," Mossi said.

"Someone hunts all of us."

"But her hunter is only after her. And he or she is without cease."

"I thought you only believe in one god and one devil," I said.

"I think you repeat that to the point of annoyance. I have seen many a thing, Tracker. Her enemies have gathered mass. Maybe all of them with causes just. Other side."

The caravan bumped something and shook. It threw the prefect right at me and I caught him as his head hit my chest. He grasped my shoulder and pulled himself up. I wanted to say something about myrrh. Or his breath in my face. He stood straight, but the caravan swung again and he grabbed my arm.

Five guards met us at the platform and said you land in Mungunga, the second tree. They took us over a steep stone bridge, with lookouts on both sides of the road, first to my room where they left me, and then, I presumed, to Mossi's. Mine looked like it hung off the great tree itself, and was hanging by rope. I don't know where they took the prefect. This was another room with a bed, something I was beginning to get used to, though why anyone would want a soft bed I didn't know. The more your bed felt like clouds, the less you would be alert if trouble roused you from sleep. But what a grand thought, sleeping in a bed. There was water to wash, and a jug of milk to drink. I stepped to the door and it opened without my touch. That made me stop and look around, twice.

The balcony outside was a thin platform, maybe two footsteps wide, and loose, with rope as high as the chest to stop drunk men from falling to their ancestors. Behind this tree, two trees stood, and behind them several more. My head was scrambling for a bigger word than vast, something for a city as large as Juba or Fasisi, but with everything stacked on top and growing into the sky instead of beside each other and spreading wide. Did these trees still grow? Many windows flickered with firelight. Music came from some windows, and loose sounds running on wind: eating, a man and woman in quarrel, fucking, weeping, voices on top of voices creating noise, and nobody sleeping.

Also this, a closed tower with no windows, but where all the ropes carrying caravans came in and out. The Queen was right when she said Dolingo did not run on magic. But it ran on something. Night was going, leaving us, leaving people who would not sleep, leaving me wondering what Sogolon spoke of to the Queen, and where she was right now. Maybe that was why it took me longer than it should to smell it on me. Myrrh. I rubbed my chest, cupped my nose, and breathed in as one would drink in.

In the dream jungle monkeys swung on vines, but the trees grew so tall that I could not see sky. It was day and night like it always is in the Darklands. I heard sounds, laughter that sometimes sounded like tears. I was hoping to see the prefect, expecting to see him, but a monkey walking on two legs pulled at my right hand, let go, and jumped off, and I followed him, and I was on a road, and I walked, then ran, then walked, and it was so very cold. I feared hearing black wings but did not hear them. And then fire broke out in the west, and elephants, and lions, and many beasts, and beasts with forgotten names ran past me. And a warthog with his tail on fire squealed, Is the boy, is the boy, is the boy.

A smell woke me up.

"Welcome to Dolingo the magnificent, Dolingo the unconquerable, Dolingo that make the gods of sky come down on earth for nothing in the sky was anything like Dolingo."

He stood over me, short, fat, and blue in day as the Dolingons were in night, and I almost told him that had I slept the way I usually do, with my ax under my pillow, he would be a headless man right now. Instead

I rubbed my eyes and sat up. He leaned in so close that I almost bumped his head.

"First you wash, no? Yes? Then you eat the rise meal, no? Yes? But first you wash, no? Yes?"

He wore a metal helmet that lacked the nose guard of a warrior. But it was trimmed in gold, and he looked like a man who would soon tell me such.

"Magnificent helmet," I said to him.

"Do you love it? No? Yes? Gold mined from the southern mines made its way to my head. This is no bronze that you see, only gold and iron."

"Did you fight in any wars?"

"Wars? Nobody wars with the Dolingon, but yes, you should know that I am indeed a very brave man."

"I can see it from what you wear."

Indeed, he wore the thick quilted tunic of warriors, but his belly poked through like a pregnant woman. Two things. "Wash" meant him summoning two servants to the room. Two doors to the side opened without a hand, and the servant pulled out a wood-and-tar tub full of water and spices. That was the first I knew there were doors there. They scrubbed me with stones, my back, my face, even scrubbed my balls with the same roughness that they scrubbed the bottoms of my feet. "Eat" meant a flat plank of wood pushing itself out of the wall, where no slot was before, and the man pointing me to the stool already there, then feeding me with those things beloved of flighty men from Wakadishu, knives and spoons, and making me feel like a child. I asked if he was a slave, and he laughed. The plank pulled itself back into the wall.

"In our radiant Queen is all wisdom and all answers," he said.

They left me and after going outside and walking ten paces in the cold, I went back in and dressed in the robes they left out. If anything these rare moments in robes made me hate them all the more. At the door, I heard a scuffle in the room, scurrying feet and huff. Charge in or sneak in, I wasn't sure, and when I did choose to swing the door open, the room was empty. Spies, I expected. What they could be looking for, I didn't know. Over by the balcony the door opened before I reached it. I pulled back a few steps and it closed. I stepped forward a few steps and it opened.

I left again and walked down to a path running along the edge of this floor. Dirt and stone as if cut from a mountain. This is what happened. I walked until I came to a break in the boundary, and attached to the break and hanging off the edge was a platform of wood slats, held by rope at the four corners. Without my word, and with no sight of anyone, the platform lowered a long drop to the floor below. I left the platform and walked down this new path, which was a road, wide as two. Across I could see the palace and the first tree. At the lowest level of this one, a small house with three dark windows and a blue roof, which seemed cut off from everything else. Indeed, no steps or road led to it. It stood in the huge shadow of the lookout platform, a shelf as wide as a battlefield, on which guards marched. The floors looked patched together, the lowest with a drawbridge and the wall a red colour, like savannah earth. The next floor a retaining wall that went half around. The third, high with massive arches underneath and trees, wild and scattered, and still another floor with the tallest walls, taller than seven, maybe eight times taller than the door and windows. This floor boasted towers with gold roofs, and still two more floors climbed higher. Across on the right to yet another tree, and level with my eyes, were wide steps leading up to a great hall. On the steps men in twos, in fives, and in larger, wearing blue, gray, and black coats sweeping the floor; sitting, standing, and looking like they were talking of serious things.

"I thought my poor balls would bleed the way those fucking eunuchs went at it," Mossi said when I saw him. They had put him on this floor. It came to me: Why would they scatter us so?

"I said, Sirs, I am not the one who clipped you both, don't take your anger out on my poor little knight. So that's what makes you laugh, tales of my suffering," Mossi said.

I didn't notice that I had laughed. He broke into a wide grin. Then his face went grave.

"Let us walk, I must speak with you," he said.

I was curious how roads worked in a city that went up instead of wide. What did that waterfall fall into?

"How sorry I am for you, Tracker. In a crowd you would have been lost to me."

"What?"

He pointed at what I was wearing, the same as he, and as many of the men and boys who passed us, a long tunic and a cloak clasped only at the neck. But only in the colours I saw before: gray, black, and blue. Some men, all older, wore red or green caps over their bald heads, and red and green sashes at the waist. The few women passed by on carts and open caravans, some in white gowns with wide sleeves like wings, the tops split open to plump up breasts, and head wraps in several colours pointing to peaks like a high tower.

"I have never seen you so dressed," he said.

A cart pulled by two donkeys passed us, with an old man and a boy in it. They went to the edge as far as I could see, then vanished. At first I thought the man rode the cart off to his death.

"The road spirals around, sometimes in and sometimes out of the tree. But at some point, if they want to leave the citadel, one of those bridges that pulled us up must take them down," Mossi said.

"One night and you are guide to all things Dolingo."

"You learn much in one night when you miss sleep. Like this. The Dolingon build on high because of an ancient prophecy that the great flood will one day return, which many still believe. An old man told me this, though he might have gone mad from walking the streets and not sleeping. The great flood that consumed all lands, even the Hills of Enchantment and the unnamed mountains beyond Kongor. The great flood that killed the great beasts that roamed the land.

Know this, I have been to many lands and one thing they all seem to share is this great flood that came to pass and another that will one day come true."

"Seems what all lands do share are gods so petty and jealous that they would rather destroy all the worlds than have one that moves on without them. You said we must speak."

"Yes."

He took my arm and started walking faster. "I think we should assume we are being watched, if not followed," he said. We went over the bridge and under a wide tower, with a blue stone archway taller than ten men. We continued walking, his hand still grabbing my arm.

"No children," I said.

"What?"

"I have seen no children. None last night, but I thought that was because it was night. But so far into this day, none I have seen."

"And your complaint is?"

"Have you seen even one?"

"No, but there is something else I must tell you."

"And slaves. Dolingo is not Dolingo because of magic. Where are the slaves?"

"Tracker."

"First I think the servants who scrubbed me are the slaves, but they seem like masters of their craft, even if the craft was back scrubbing and balls scraping."

"Tracker, I—"

"But something is not ri—"

"Fuck the gods, Tracker!"

"What?"

"This night gone. I was in the Queen's chambers. When the guards took you to your room, they took me to mine only to wash me and take me back."

"Why did she call you back?"

"The Dolingon are a very direct people, Tracker. She is a very direct queen. Don't ask questions where you know the answer."

"But I do not know."

"They took me back to her chambers, on the same caravan that we came over. This time four guards went with me. I would draw a sword but then I remembered they took our weapons. The Queen would see me again. I mystified her, it seems. She still thought my skin was magic and my hair and my lips, which she said looked like an open wound. She had me lie with her."

"I did not ask."

"You should know."

"Why?"

"I don't know! I do not know why I feel you must know, since it means nothing to you. Curse this. And she was cold, Tracker. I do not mean she was distant, or that she showed no feeling, not even pleasure, but that she felt cold, her skin colder than northern wind."

"What did she have you do?"

"This is what you are asking me?"

"What do you expect me to ask, prefect, how did

it make you feel? There are many women I could ask that question."

"I am not a woman."

"Of course not. Woman is supposed to look at this as a natural course of events. Man, he falls on his knees and screams what a horror, what a debasing."

"How you have no friends mystifies me," Mossi said.

He walked away. I had to skip to catch him.

"You asked for my ears and I gave you a fist," I said.

He walked several steps before he stopped and turned around. "I accept your apology, such as it is."

"Tell me all," I said.

Mungunga was waking up. Men dressed like elders on their way to where elders go. Jugs held by no hands, at windows throwing out the slop of last night into gutters that ran inside the trunk of the tree. Men in robes and caps passing by on foot with books and scrolls, men in cloaks and pants, passing by on carts driven by donkeys and mules, without bridles. Women pushing carts overflowing with silk, fruits, and trinkets. People hanging off the retaining walls, with dyes, and sticks, and brushes, back to painting the mural of the Queen on the side of the right-hand branch. Everywhere and nowhere, the sweet reek of chicken fat popping over flame, and bread baking in ovens. Also this, so everywhere that the noise of it became a new quiet: gears running, ropes creaking, and the beat and boom of big wheels turning, though nothing for the eye to put such sounds to.

"They would not even let me wash myself, saying that the Queen has a nose for filth and sneezes like a storm at even a hint of it. I said, Then like many in these lands you must be nose-blind to the funk under your arms. Then they rubbed me in a fragrance they said would be most pleasing to the Queen, which made me wince for the smell was like shit at the feet of growing crops. In my hair, in my nose, do you not smell it still on me?"

"No."

"Morning bathers scraped it off with all my skin and most of my hair then. Sogolon was there, Tracker."

"Sogolon? Watching?"

"They were all watching. No queen fucks alone, nor king either. Her handmaidens, her witchmen, two men who looked like counselors, a man of medicine, Sogolon, and all the Queen's guards."

"Something ill is in this kingdom. Did you—how does one—"

"Yes, yes, curse it. I think the old bitch promised this Queen something from me, and didn't ask me."

"What did she have you do?"

"What?"

"No children anywhere and the Queen has you lie with her the first night you are here. Did you—"

"Yes, if that is what you wish to know. I left my seed in her. You act if as arousal means anything. It does not even mean consent."

"I didn't ask."

"Your eyes asked. And they judged."

"My eyes don't care."

"Fine. Then I shall not care either. Then her witch-men and night nurses said it was so, that my seed was in her. The witchman made sure."

"Why does a queen bed a foreigner she had only just met to have him leave his seed in her? And why is that a matter for the whole court? I tell you, Mossi, something is wrong about these lands."

"And the Queen was cold as a mountaintop. She said nothing, and they warned me not to look straight at her. She didn't look as if she was breathing. And everyone watched as if I was there to patch a hole in the floor."

"Who warned you?"

"The guards who washed me."

"Did they look like her? Skin so black it's blue?"

"Isn't that everyone we see?"

"We have seen neither slaves nor children."

"You said that. She had a cage, Tracker. A cage with two pigeons. Strange pet."

"Nobody keeps that disgusting animal as a pet. The Aesi uses pigeons. So does Sogolon. She said she was sending word to the Dolingon queen when I asked her."

"Twice they made me spill inside her."

"What did Sogolon say to you?"

"Nothing."

"We should find the others."

I grabbed his hand and pulled him quick into a doorway and held him.

"Tracker, what in all the fucks—"

"Men, two in number, following us."

"Oh, the two men a hundred paces behind me, one in a blue cape and white robes, the other, open vest and white trousers like a horseman? Trying to look as if not in league with each other, but clearly walking together? I think, Tracker, they are following me."

"We could lead them to that plank, and throw them off."

"Are all your forms of fun this quick?"

I pushed him away. We kept on walking, past a number of steps I could not count, but I did notice the path took us right around the trunk, covered in little roofs, towers, and great halls, twice. And at almost every turn there was a new tree in the distance. And at every turn I was getting angry with Mossi and couldn't explain why.

"A city with no children, and a queen hungry to get one, even from you. There is some honor in that, is there not?"

"No honor to such lowly customs."

"And yet you dropped your robes, and rose to meet it."

"What is burning you?" he said.

I looked at him. "I feel lost and I do not know what to do here."

"How could you be lost? I am following you, so I am lost too."

The men stopped waiting on us and were approaching.

"Maybe what you're looking for is not a reason to

fight, or to save the boy, but just a reason," Mossi said.

"Fuck the gods if I know what that means."

"I've spent my life on the chase for men. People are either running to, or running from, but you just seem to be cut loose. You have no stakes in this and why should you? But have you a stake in anything? In anyone?"

At this I wished for nothing more than to punch the next remark back into his mouth.

He looked at me, his eyes sharp, waiting for an answer. I said, "How shall we deal with these men? We have no weapons, but we do have fists. And feet."

"Are they—"

"Do not turn around, they are upon us."

The two men looked like monks, tall and very thin, one with the long hair and the cultivated face of a eunuch. The other, not as tall but still thin, looked at us for less than a blink before looking past us. Mossi clutched at his sword but there was no sword. They walked past us. Both smelled heavy of spices.

O n the way back to my room not even the thought of the gods at peace could stop me from cursing.

"I cannot believe you fucked her."

He spun around to me. "What?"

I stopped and turned back. Only one cart passed us. The street stayed empty, but you could hear buying, selling, and yelling down the bazaars in the lanes.

"You heard what I said. Thank the gods, I am just a low jungle boy," I said. "She must think you're an eastern prince."

"You think that's how it is, that you're too low to be used and killed," Mossi said.

"If she conceives you can thank the gods you are a father of multitudes. Like a rat."

"Listen, you bush-fucker. Don't judge me for something you would have done. Was there any choice? Do you think I even wanted to? What would you do, insult the Queen the night she gives you hospitality? What would have happened to us?"

"This is new waters for me. Never had I had a man fuck somebody else for my benefit. If she conceives they will come for you."

"If she conceives they will come for everyone," Mossi said.

"No, you."

"Then let them come. They will learn there is one man who is not a coward in Dolingo."

"I could strike you so hard right now."

"You, the hound on two legs, thinks he can strike a warrior? I wish you would."

I walked right up to him, my fists clenched tight, just as several men in the gowns of scholars came out of an alley and walked past us. Three turned around, walking with their group, but backward to look at us. I turned away and walked to my room. I didn't want or expect Mossi to follow me, but he did and as soon as he came through the door I pushed him hard against the wall. He tried to push me off but could not, so he kneed me in the ribs, and they shifted like he broke one. The pain hit my chest and ran up to my shoulder. He pushed me off hard. I staggered, tripped, and fell.

"Fuck the gods," he said, and sighed.

He offered a hand to pull me up, but I pulled him down, punching him in the stomach. He fell, yelling, and I jumped on him trying to punch him, but he grabbed my hands. I pulled, and we rolled and hit the wall, rolled to the terrace door, which opened and we almost fell out. I rolled on top again and grabbed his neck. He swung his two legs up from behind me, crossed them at my shoulder, and pushed me off, then jumped on me when I slammed into the floor. He punched but I dodged and he hit the wood and yelled. I jumped on him again, wrapping my arm around his neck, and he flipped backward, slamming hard into the floor with me underneath him, and the air pushed right out of my nose and mouth. I couldn't move or see. He flipped under me, choking me with one arm and locking down my legs with his legs. I swung my one free arm and he caught it.

"Stop," he said.

"Go fuck the prickle palm."

"Stop."

"I will kill—"

"Stop or I start breaking fingers. Are you going to stop? Tracker. Tracker."

"Yes, fucking whorseson."

"Apologize for calling my mother a whore."

"I call your mother and your fath—"

I screamed the rest of the word out. He had pulled my middle finger so far back I could feel the skin about to pop.

"I apologize. Get off me."

"I'm under you," he said.

"Let go."

"By the gods, Tracker. Flush this fury from you. We have bigger fusses than this. Will you stop? Please."

"Yes. Yes. Yes."

"Give me your word."

"You have my fucking word!"

He let go. I wanted to turn around and punch him, or slap him if I couldn't punch, or kick him if I couldn't slap, or head-butt him if I couldn't kick, or bite him if he caught my head. But I stood up and squeezed my finger.

"It is broken. You have broken it."

He sat on the floor, refusing to get up.

"Your finger is no more broken than your ribs. Fingers are spiteful, though. If it is sprained it will stay sprained for a year."

"I will not forget this."

"Yes you will. You picked this fight because another deceived you long before I even met you. Or because I fucked a woman."

"I am the biggest fool. You all look at me, the fool with the nose. I am just a hound, as you say."

"I spoke harsh. In the middle of a fight, Tracker."

"I am the hound from the river lands, where we build huts from shit, so I am nothing but the beast to all of you. And everybody had two plans, or three, or four, plans so they win, and everybody else lose. What is your second plan, prefect?"

"My second plan? My first plan was to find out who murdered an elder and his family, until I came across some people who would not leave their bodies alone. My second was not to follow a suspect to the library that got burned down. My second plan was not to kill my own prefects. My second plan was not to be on the run with a bunch of bastards who can't even cross a road together, all because my brothers would kill me on sight. My second plan, believe it or not, was not to be stuck with such a sorry bunch of fellows because I have nowhere else to go."

He stood up.

"Fuck yourself and your self-pity," I said.

"My second plan is to save this boy."

"You have no stake in this boy."

"You are wrong. One night. It took one night to lose everything. But maybe everything was nothing if it could be lost so fast. This boy is now the only thing that will make my life seem as if the past few days have any sense to them. If I am going to lose everything, then fuck the gods and the devils if my life will not mean something. This boy is the only thing I have left."

"Sogolon wants to save the boy herself. Maybe the girl and the buffalo as well to protect them on the way back to Mantha."

"A thousand fucks for what Sogolon wants. She still needs you to find the boy. Here is a simple thing, Tracker. Give her no news."

"I don't—"

He looked at me and put a finger to his lips. Then he nodded over his shoulder. He stepped to me quiet until his lips touched my ear and whispered, "What do you smell?"

"Everything, nothing. Wood, skin, arm funk, body smells. Why?"

"Both of us have been scrubbed clean."

"What do you smell that you don't know?"

I switched places with him, backing slow to the other end of the room. My calf hit the stool and I moved it out of the way. Following me slow, Mossi picked up the stool, by the leg. Right before the side wall, the same wall that a table came out of, I stopped and turned around. Porridge, wood oil, dried grass rope, and sweat, and again the stink of an unwashed body. Behind the wall? In the wall? I pointed to the planks of wood and the look on Mossi's face asked the same questions. I slapped the wood and something scurried like a rat.

"I think it's a rat," Mossi whispered.

I moved my fingers along the top of the wood, and stopped at a slot about the size of three fingers. My fingers gripped the wood and yanked. I yanked again and the wood broke from the wall. My hand gripped the space and tore out the plank.

"Mossi, by the gods."

He looked in, and sucked in his breath. We stood there, staring. We grabbed planks and ripped them away, planks as tall as us, and what would not move we kicked in, and kicked away. Mossi grabbed at the boards almost in a panic, as if we were running out of time. We yanked and tore and kicked out a hole in the wall as wide as the buffalo.

The boy was neither standing nor lying, but leaning against a bed of dry grass. His eyes were wide open, seeing terror. He was scared but could not speak, tried to scamper but couldn't. The boy couldn't scream because of something like the innards of an animal pushed through his mouth and down his throat. He couldn't move because of the ropes. Every limb—legs, feet, toes, arms, hands, neck, and each finger—was tied to, and pulled, a rope. His eyes, wide open and wet, looked river blind, the black circles as gray as moody sky. He looked blind but he could see us, so terrified at us moving in closer that he pulled and yelped and grabbed and tried to shield his face from a blow. It made the room go mad, with the table pushing out and in, the door swinging open and shut, the balcony ropes loosening and tightening, the shit bucket emptying. Rope wrapped around his waist to keep him there, but one of the planks had a hole wide enough for his eye, so yes, he could see.

"Boy, we will not hurt you," Mossi said. He reached

in with his hand to the boy's face and the boy banged his head against the grass over and over, turning away, expecting a blow, his eyes running tears. Mossi touched his cheek and he screamed into the innard.

"He does not know our tongue," I said.

"Look at us, we are no one blue. We are no one blue," he said, and stroked the boy's cheek long and slow. He was still pulling and kicking and the tables, windows, and doors were still opening and closing, pushing out and slamming in. Mossi kept stroking his cheek until he slowed and then stopped.

"They must have tied these ropes with magic," I said.

I could not untie the knots. Mossi stuck his finger in a slot on his right sandal and pulled out a small knife.

"Sentries are less likely to search when you step in shit," he said.

We cut every rope away from the boy, but he stood there, leaning against the dry grass, naked and covered in sweat, his eyes wide open as if he was never anything but shocked. Mossi grabbed the tube going down his mouth, looked at him with all sadness, and said, "I am so, so sorry."

And he pulled it out not fast, but vigorously, and did not stop until it was all out. The boy vomited. With all the ropes cut, the door and all the windows closed shut. The boy looked at us, his body skinned by rope burns, his mouth quivering, as if about to speak. I did not say to Mossi that they might have cut his tongue out. Mossi, a prefect for one of the most unruly cities in the North, had seen everything but cruelty such as this.

"Mossi, every house, every room, those caravans, they are all like this."

"I know. I know."

"Everywhere I go to find this boy, to save this boy, I run into something worse than what we are saving him from."

"Tracker."

"No. These monsters won't kill him. No harm has come to the boy. None. I smell him; he is alive, no decay or death on him. Look at this boy you are holding up, he cannot even stand. How many moons was he behind that wall? From birth? Look at this nasty dream of a place. How are bloodsuckers any worse?"

"Tracker."

"How? You and I are the same, Mossi. When people call on us, we know we are about to meet evil. Lying, cheating, beating, wounding, murdering. My stomach is strong. But we still think monsters are the ones with claws, and scales and skin."

The boy looked at him as Mossi rubbed his shoulders. He stopped trembling, but looked past the balcony doors as if outside was something he had never seen. Mossi placed him on the stool and turned to me.

"You are thinking what can you do," he said.

"If you say nothing."

"I would never tell you what to think. Only . . . Tracker, listen. We come here for the boy. We are two against a nation and even those who came with us might be against us."

"Every person I have met says to me, Tracker, you have nothing to live for or die for. You are a man who if he were to vanish this night, nobody's life would be any worse. Maybe this is the kind of thing to die for. . . . Say it."

"Say what?"

"Say that this is bigger than me and us, that this is not our fight, that is the way of the foolish and not the wise, this will make no difference. . . . Well, what are you going to say?"

"Which of these mangy sons of bitches do we kill first?"

My eyes popped wide open.

"Consider this, Tracker: The plan is to never let us leave. So then let us stay. These cowards have lived without an enemy so long they probably think swords are jewelry."

"They have men in the hundreds upon hundreds. And hundreds more."

"We need not care about hundreds. Just the few at court. Beginning with that hideous Queen. Follow for now, play the fool. They will summon us to court soon, tonight. Right now we should really feed this—"

"Mossi!"

The stool sat empty. The terrace door swung back and forth. The boy was not in the room. Mossi ran so fast to the balcony that I had to grab his cloak so he wouldn't fall. No sound came out of Mossi's mouth but he was screaming. I pulled him back into the room but still he pushed forward. I wrapped my arms around him tighter and tighter. He stopped fighting and let me.

We waited until dark to set out for the Ogo. That idiot who fed me came to the door to tell me of dinner at court, though not with the Queen. I should go to the docks and wait for the caravan when the drums begin to sound. No? Yes? Mossi held back behind the door with his knife. Someone must have seen the boy jump to his death, even if the poor child said nothing all the way down. Or maybe a slave falling to his death was not a new thing in Dolingo. This is what I was thinking while the man kept trying to stick his head in my door until I said, Sir, if you come in I shall fuck you too, and his blue skin went green. He said he would return for a glorious breakfast tomorrow, no? Yes.

I sensed Sadogo in MLuma, the third tree, the one more like a pole with massive wings to trap sunlight. Mossi worried that guards would be watching us, but such was the arrogance of Dolingo that nobody looked at two future seed pods as much of a threat. I said to him, How quaint our weapons must have seemed to them, not just our weapons, but all weapons. They were like those plants with no thorns that have never known an animal to eat them. When the men and women staring at us made Mossi reach for the knife hidden in his coat, I touched his shoulder and whispered, How many men with skin such as yours have they seen? He nodded and kept his peace.

At MLuma, the caravan stopped at the fifth floor. Sadogo was on the eighth.

"I do not know why she is so sour. Sour before we even got to this city," Sadogo said.

"Who, Venin?" I asked.

"Stop calling me that foul name. That is what she said. But it is her name, what else should I call her? You were there when she said, My name is Venin, were you not?"

"Well she was always sour to me, so I—"

"Sour, she never was. I was never sour to her when I let her sit on my shoulder."

"Sadogo, there are more crucial things, and we need to have words."

"Why did they put us away from the others, Venin? That is all I said and she says that is not her name, and yells to take my monster arms and my monster face away, you will never get anywhere near me, for I am a fearsome warrior who wants to burn the world. And then she called me shoga. She is different."

"Maybe she did not see things the way you saw things, Sadogo," Mossi said. "Who knows the ways of women?"

"No, she is different and—"

"Do not say Sogolon. Her scrawny hand is in far too many bowls for us to talk about them all. There is a plot, Sadogo. And the girl might be in league with Sogolon."

"But she spat when I said her name."

"Who knows why they bicker? We have more serious issues, Ogo."

"All these ropes, coming from nowhere and pulling everything. Foul magic."

"Slaves, Ogo," Mossi said.

"I do not understand."

"Let that rest for another day, Sadogo. The witch had other plans."

"She does not want the boy?"

"That is still her plan. We are just not a part of it. She intends to get the boy herself after I find him, and with this Queen's help. I think the Queen and her struck a bargain. Maybe when Sogolon rescues the boy the Queen will give safe passage to the Mweru."

"But that is what we do. Why the deceit?"

"I don't know. This Queen gets to have us for their wicked science, maybe."

"Is that why everybody is blue? Wicked science?"

"I don't know."

"Venin, she pushed me out the door with one hand. How I must disgust her."

"She pushed you out? With one hand?" I asked.

"That is what I said."

"I have seen an enraged woman turn over a wagon full of metal and spices. It might have been my wagon, or I might have enraged her," Mossi said.

"Sadogo," I said, louder, to shut Mossi up. "We need to be on guard, we need weapons, we need to get off this citadel. How do you feel about the boy? Should we rescue him as well?"

He looked at both of us, then out the door, furrowing his brow. "We should save the boy. No blame is on him."

"Then that is what we shall do," Mossi said. "We wait for them to arrive in Dolingo. We take them on ourselves, not telling the witch."

"We need weapons," I said.

"I know where they keep them," said Sadogo. "No man could lift my gloves, so I took them to the swords keeper."

"Where?"

"On this tree, the lowest level."

"And Sogolon?" Mossi said.

"There," he said, and pointed behind us. The palace.

"Good. We go when the bloodsuckers come. Till then—"

"Tracker, what is that?" Mossi said.

"What is what?"

"Do you have a nose or no? That sweet scent on the air."

As he said so, I smelled it. The smell grew sweeter and stronger. In the red room nobody saw the orange mist coming from the floor. Mossi fell first. I staggered, fell to my knees, and saw Sadogo run to the door, punching the wall out of anger, fall back on his bottom, then full on his back, and shaking the room, before everything in the room went white.

NINETEEN

knew it was seven days since we left Kongor. And forty and three days since we set off on this journey. And in one whole moon. I knew because counting numbers was all that kept my feet on the ground. I knew we were in the trunk of one of the trees. One big shackle around my neck, attached to a long, heavy chain. My arms chained behind my back. My clothes gone. I had to turn to see the ball the chain was bolted to. Both were stone. Someone told them of me and metals. Sogolon.

"I say, tell us where is the boy," he said.

The chancellor. The Queen must be upstairs waiting for the news. No, not the Queen.

"If Sogolon wants news of the boy, tell the witch to come for it herself," I said.

"Boy, boy, boy it will be good to tell me of your nose. If I go other men will come with instruments, yes."

The last time I was in a dark room, shape-shifting

women came at me out of the dark. The memory made me wince, which this fool thought was because of his threat of torture.

"Do you yet sniff the boy?"

"I will talk to the witch."

"No, no, no, that is a no. Do you—"

"I smell something. I smell goat, the liver of a goat."

"How good you are, man of the Ku. Breakfast was indeed breakfast of liver, and sorghum from my own fields, and coffee from the merchants of the North, very exquisite, yes."

"But the goat liver I smell is raw, and why does the reek come from your crotch, chancellor? Your Queen knows that you practice white science?"

"Our glorious Queen allows all craft."

"As long as it is not in your glorious Queen's court. See now, you will have to torture me, chancellor, or at least kill me. You know this is true, nothing will stop me from telling anyone who should hear."

"Not if I cut out that tongue."

"Like you do your slaves? Does your Queen not want us, traveling men sound and whole?"

"Our Queen only needs one part of you, sound and whole."

I squeezed my legs together, without thinking, and he laughed loud.

"Where the boy is?"

"The boy is nowhere. He still travels from Wakadishu and does that not take days? You can meet him in Wakadishu."

"You are here to meet him in Dolingo."

"And he is not in Dolingo. Where is the witch? Does she listen? Does she have your ear, or are you just the fat echo of more important voices?"

He hissed.

"Yes it is said I have a nose, but nobody told you I also have a mouth," I said.

"If I go, I will return with—"

"With your instruments. Your words scared me more the first time."

I stood up. Even with the chain on my neck, and me having nowhere to go, the chancellor jumped a little.

"I will speak to neither you nor your Queen. Only the witch."

"I have the authority—"

"Only the witch, or start your torture."

He hiked his agbada off his feet and left me alone.

Though I smelled her coming, she still took me by surprise. The door across from my cell opened and she came through. Two guards followed, several paces behind. The one with keys, he opened the gate and gave her wide space. Guards trying to not show fear for the Moon Witch. She sat in the dark.

"I know you wonder it," she said. "You wonder why you never see a single child in Dolingo."

"I wonder why I never killed you when I had the chance."

"Some cities rear cattle, other cities grow wheat. Dolingo grow men, and not in no natural way. You do not need an explanation and it would take years to tell you. This is what you should know, for moon after moon, year after year, a cluster of years after cluster of years, the seed and the wombs of the Dolingon become useless. What is not barren breeds monsters unspeakable in look. Bad seed going into bad wombs, the same families, over and over, and the Dolingon go from the most wise of children to the most foolish. It take them fifty years to say to one another, Look at us, we need new seed and new wombs."

"Tell me there will be monsters in this boring tale."

"It greater than magic. If she conceive, they snatch him, take him into the trunk. He is the tap and they drain the tap. Drain him until he is dead. But that is only for who will be in the royal line. Other men they catch, and drain and kill for the rest of the people. Even your Ogo, whose seed useless, their scientist and witchman can make it sow and breed."

"So the citadel should be infested with children, then. They're hiding them?"

"Then they take the child before it born and store them in the great womb, and feed them and grow them, until they as big as you. Only then, they born. But they healthy and they live long."

"A man as old as me saying babababa and shitting himself twice a day. This is the great Dolingo."

"It be two days now. Where the boy?"

"No children, no slaves, no travelers either. You knew this. You knew this ever since the map showed that the next door led to Dolingo."

"Nobody get safe passage in Dolingo," she said. "You see how their head full of nothing but thinking. It take many beggings, papers, and a treaty just to pass through the main street. Look at the magnificence of the citadel. You think they get that by allowing anybody to pass through and steal their secrets? No, fool. They use anyone who come down their streets for breeding, and kill whoever they can't put to use."

"You sent those pigeons to tell her you were coming. With gifts."

"Why they so long in Wakadishu?"

"Me and the prefect and the Ogo."

"Why they don't come?" she asked.

"Maybe Wakadishu women have more meat and more blood. Are you not a southern woman?"

"The Aesi is already on caravan to Dolingo."

"Somebody betrayed you? What say you to that, Sogolon?"

"You do nothing but joke."

"And you do nothing but betray."

"Two Dolingos there was. Just as there was a Malakal before Malakal. Old Dolingo, they never have queen, or king, they have a grand counsel, all of them men. Why put the whole realm in the hand of just one man, they say the people tell them, which was a lie, for they never ask people nothing. These men, they say, Why put our future in the palm of one man? Come soon, or come late, if you put power in a man's hand, he going make a fist. Forget king and queen, build a counsel of our smartest men. Soon the smartest men listen to only the smartest men and soon they turn fool. Soon everything from where to collect shit, and who to fight war, take them men so long that shit run down the streets and they nearly lose in war with the four sisters of the South. Ten and two man and when they agree, nobody can see beyond their arrogance. When they don't have accord they fight and fight and people starve and die, and always they so arrogant, thinking that mean they wise. And the people of Dolingo realize a true thing. A beast with ten and two head not ten and two times the wiser. He a monster shouting down himself. So Dolingo kill ten and one and make the last one King."

"They're still frightened over a great flood that never set loose," I said.

"Now they the envy of the nine worlds. Every king want to ally with them, every king want to conquer them. But the first wise decree from the King? Dolingo will fight no war and have no enemy, no matter who. They sell to the good and the wicked."

"This story was neither good nor short."

"I tell Amadu he need none of you. Any five or six warriors and a hound. You is the only one I need, but even you is a fool. Every single one of you a fool. Spend so much time growl, and scowl like hungry hyena, none of you have time to find your own shit, much less a boy. You want to know what Kongor is to me? Kongor is where man teach me him true use. And even the last thing he good for a candlestick do it better."

"Yet you help to find a boy who will be a man," I said.

"But you know what I do? You know what I do? I take the greatest revenge. I bury every single one of you. Every single one. I was at every deathbed. Every mishap. Every plague of bad spirits. Every death turn. And I laugh. And if the knife was only halfway in, I push it deeper. Or I travel in the air and infect your mind. And I still living. I bury you and your son and your son's son. And will I live. I . . . I . . ." She stopped and looked around the cell as if it were the first time she was seeing it.

"Wherever you just went to, maybe go back," I said.

"What a day wh—"

"When a man tells you what to do. Don't you have enough spirits in your head doing that already?"

"We talking about you."

"You talking about everyone **but** me. Look at what all you do. Fellowship tear apart before it even come together in the valley. Three of you go off in the Darklands and one have to follow because you is man and man never listen. Delay we by one whole moon."

"So you sold us off."

"So I get you out of the way."

"And yet look at me, and look at you. One of us has a nose and the other one still needs it," I said.

"One of we in chains and one of we not."

"You never learned how to ask a favor."

"The Queen will treat you and the prefect and the Ogo better than concubines."

"Will she give us each a palace that she never visits?"

"All my life men telling me this would be the life above all lives. Well here come the Queen of Dolingo saying, That is all you have to be for however long you live. From how man talk, this should be the greatest gift."

"Would be much greater if the man get to choose it."

"So now you is like a woman in all things. How it feel?"

"Have the griots sing you a song about your victory over man."

"Man? You just a nose."

"A nose for which you still find use."

"Yes, a nose that may still to come to use. The rest of you just in the way. And when I get the boy, know that you help bring back the natural order to the North. Let that feed you as you settle the rest of your living days here."

"Here where everything is unnatural. A devil's fuck for the North."

"You look at me good, boy. Because you never see me before. You never in Kongor? You never see the Seven Wings amass? What you think in the heart of this King? The King in South too busy confusing his throne for his shithole to start a war, so why they amassing? And is not just mercenaries in Kongor. The infantry at the border of Malakal and Wakadishu get call back a moon ago. Fasisi horsemen all call to camp.

The South King one kind of mad. The North King another, much worse. First he going violate the treaty and go after Wakadishu, watch my word. And that won't be enough, for it never enough for anybody in this poison line. Then he going come conquering everywhere he can point on the map. Dolingo."

"He can burn Dolingo to the ground."

She stepped closer to me, still out of the reach of my chains when I stood up.

"Ha. You think he going stop at Dolingo and all the free states? What you think he going do with Ku and Gangatom and Luala Luala? A bigger kingdom will need more slaves. Where you think he going get them from? He won't care if they have legs like a giraffe or have no legs at all."

"Shit-cursed witch."

"A shit-curse witch who know the only future for your children is for Fasisi to return to being the true North. He already taking men and every healthy boy from Luala Luala. The world spinning off for too long, and everything off it balance. And this shriveled bitch here you looking at? She will take anything and take anyone, especially a boy lesser than a shit mark on convict's wall if that bring the true line of the sister back on the throne. True North. The future of the North is in the eye of the boy. And maybe then the gods will come back. The future bigger than me, it bigger than you, it even bigger than Fasisi. I don't expect you to understand, you still sleeping, and from that sleep man like you can never wake."

"Then look for my help in dreams, bitch."

"The Queen like her new seeder whole, this is a true thing. But she already pick her seeder, and is not you. The pretty prefect fuck her good, I was there to see it. So good even she don't see that is man he like. He going live nice until he seed done, or go bad, or he get old, or she get bored and then send him off to the fire chamber for other use. But you? They don't care which part of you they crush, break, or cut off, as long as is not that one. Listen to me, fool. You never have no stake in this, you already know that. You losing nothing, and all you was going to gain was little money. Money less than what I give to beggars on the street. Now you have plenty to lose. You see these people, they live their whole life keeping slave under control. You think they don't know what to do to you?"

"One thing, Moon Witch? Is that what they call you?"

"People always giving woman name when they already have one."

"You're using words like a woman, as if you speak for any. As if you come from some sisterhood. And yet how many sisters you betray?"

"The future of Fasisi bigger than anything you say."

"I still have one thing."

"What is your thing?"

"When I finally die, at the hand of the Dolingon, how many runes will you have to write each night to stop me coming for you?"

She stepped away from me, stepping into the dark before I could see her face. But both hands fell to her side.

"You in the Melelek. Do as they tell you and you live long."

"You know me enough to know I'll never do as they tell me. By the time I kill ten guards, they will have to kill me. And then you and me, we will have a dance in your head forever."

She went over to the gate, tired of looking at me.

"The future of Fasisi bigger than anything you say."

"Twice you said that. Really, Sogolon, you should take your shrivel s—"

Sogolon stepped out of the line of dark, but not close enough for me to grab her. She looked around, then back at me, and smiled. "The boy. He is here."

"Talking a wish does not make a wish true."

"But he in your nose. Your head swing right so hard you soon crick your neck. So he in the East. Tell me where he is, tell me now and you will never know pain."

"Pain is a sister to me."

"Tell me where he is and you will be in your own room, with all the food you want. Dolingo is not a place for you and men like you, but they might even find you a boy. Or a eunuch."

"I am going to kill you. You think I need to swear to the gods? Fuck the gods. Fuck the witches, and fuck the witchmen. I swear to myself. I will find you, and will kill you in this life or the next."

"Then I die. But I living three hundred, ten and five years, and not even death kill me yet. Before you die I hope you understand. True North above anything else. Everything else," she said.

She raised her hand and wind rattled the door across from us. The two guards ran in, and stood by the bars. The girl Venin followed them in. She looked straight at me.

"Your King, even after banishing he sister to Mantha, and telling her that is where she will live the rest of her life, still send an assassin every other moon to kill her. The last one we let Bunshi go into him through the mouth and boil him from the inside. Four of them I kill myself. One almost cut my throat, and one make the mistake to think he going to rape me first. I fuck him with a dagger and cut a koo all the way up to him neck. And when the King don't send assassins, he send poison. Fruits that kill the cow we feed it to. Rice that burn a goat tongue off. Wine that kill a serving girl who was just making sure it didn't get too warm."

She pointed at the guards and said, "You in the Melelek. The location of the boy before sunrise, or your body will be put to different use."

She left but the girl stayed. I wanted to ask if this is what she came to see. But she looked at me not in contempt—for I've seen many a contemptuous face—but curiosity. I stared at her and she stared at me and I was not about to look away, even with the guards opening the gate.

"They need you clean," one of them said.

"And what—"

The bucket, I did not see until the water came straight at my face. Both of the guards laughed, but the girl stood still.

"He clean now," one of them said.

Venin turned to leave.

"You go? Great sport is about to happen, is it not so, men? She goes, men, she goes. She leaves us alone. What shall we do?"

One of the guards approached, then walked behind me. I didn't bother to turn.

"Noble gentlemen, we are in the Melelek? What is the Melelek?" I asked.

The guard kicked the back of my knee hard and I dropped to the floor and howled. He kneed me in the back, pushed me to the ground to twist me over. The other guard ran towards me to grab my legs but he ran too fast. I swung my leg and kicked him straight in the balls. He crumbled into himself, and the guard at my neck jumped back, having probably never seen one fight back before. He hesitated, jerked again, his eyes wide, then he swung his stick.

I don't how long it was before I opened my eyes. The door opened and two men came through, both in black robes with hoods to hide their faces. One carried a bag, gripping it with hands light as powder. As they came to the gate, the guards stepped back until they were against the wall. The two men came in and the guards stepped out, trying not to run. The men came over to me and stooped down.

White scientists.

Some say they got their name because of working magics, and crafts, and potions, and burning vapors for so long they burned the brown away from their skin. I always thought the name came because they made wretched things out of nothing, and nothingness is white. People look at them and mistake them for albinos and albinos for them. But the albino's skin is the desire of the gods. In the white scientist is everything godless. Both uncovered their heads and locks like a bunch of tails spilled out. Locks as white as their skin, their eyes black, their beards patchy with locks as well. Thin faces with high cheekbones, thick pink lips. The one to the right had one eye. He grabbed my cheeks and squeezed my mouth open. Every word I tried to say came out my head as a wave that died as it reached my mouth. The one-eyed man stuck his fingers in one nostril, then the other, then looked at his finger and showed it to the other, who nodded. The other rubbed his hand along my ears, his fingers rough like animal skin. They looked at each other and nodded.

"I have one more hole so far unchecked. Will you check it?" I asked.

The one-eyed one brought his sack over.

"The pain you shall feel, it will not be small," he said.

Before I could say anything the other gagged my mouth with a stone ball. I wanted to say what fools they were, but not the first fool in Dolingo. How could I confess anything with my mouth gagged? And the boy's smell came to my nose again, so strong, almost as if he was right outside this cell, but now moving away. The one-eyed scientist pulled a knot at his neck and removed his hood.

Bad Ibeji. I heard of one found at the foot of the Hills of Enchantment, which the Sangoma burned, even though it was already dead. Even in death it shook the unshakable woman, for it was the one mingi she would kill on sight. Bad Ibeji was never to be born but is not the unborn Douada, who roams the spirit world, wiggling on air like a tadpole and sometimes slipping into this world through a newborn. Bad Ibeji was the twin that the womb squeezed and crushed, tried to melt, but could not melt away. Bad Ibeji grows on its malcontent like that devil of the body's own flesh, that bursts through the breasts of woman, killing her by poisoning her blood and bone. Bad Ibeji knows it will never be the favored one, so it attacks the other twin in the womb. Bad Ibeji sometimes dies at birth when the mind did not grow. When the mind did grow, all it knows to do is survive. It burrows into the twin's skin, sucking food and water from his flesh. It leaves the womb with the twin, and sticks so tight to his skin that the mother thinks this too is the baby's flesh, unformed, ugly like a burn and not handsome, and sometimes throws away them both to the open lands to die. It is wrinkled and puffy flesh, and skin and hair, and one eye big and a mouth that drools without stop, and one hand with claws and another stuck on the belly as if sewn, and useless legs that flap like fins, a thin penis, stiff like a finger, and hole that bursts shit like lava. It hates the twin for it will never be the twin, but it needs the twin for it cannot eat food, or drink water as it has no throat, and teeth grow anywhere, even above the eye. Parasite. Fat, and lumpy, like cow entrails tied together, and leaving slime where it crawls.

The Bad Ibeji's one hand splayed itself on the one-eyed scientist's neck and chest. He unhooked each claw and a little blood ran out of each hole. The second hand unwrapped itself from the scientist's waist, leaving a welt. I shook and screamed into the gag and kicked against the shackles but the only thing free was my nose to huff. The Bad Ibeji pulled his head off the twin's shoulder and one eye popped open. The head, a lump upon a lump, upon a lump, with warts, and veins, and huge swellings on the right cheek with a little thing flapping like a finger. His mouth, squeezed at the corners, flopped open, and his body jerked and sagged like kneaded flour being slapped. From the mouth came a gurgle like from a baby. The Bad Ibeji left the scientist's shoulder and slithered on my belly and up to my chest, smelling of arm funk and shit of the sick. The other scientist grabbed my head with both sides and held it stiff. I struggled and struggled, shaking, trying to nod, trying to kick, trying to scream, but all I could do was blink and breathe. The Bad Ibeji crawled up my chest, his body swelling like a ball and squeezing out breath like a puffer fish. He extended two long, bony fingers that walked past my lips and stopped at my nostrils. The Bad Ibeji's eye blinked sorrow, then he shoved two fingers up my nose and I screamed and screamed again, and tears sprung from my eyes. The fingers, the claws scraped the flesh, pushed up the hole, pushed through bone, cut through more flesh, moved past my nose, and between my eyes started to burn. His fingers passed my eyes, pushed through my forehead, my temples pumped and throbbed, and my mind went black, came back, and went black again. My forehead burned. I could hear his claws, cutting, scurrying in me like mice. The fire spread from my head down my back, along my legs to the tips of my feet, and I shook like a man whose head was taken over by devils. And dark came over my eyes and in my head and then a flicker.

And Sogolon came through the door and walked to the cell and the guards opened the gate and she walked in and bent to look and straightened herself and walked backward away from me, and nodded, and walked backward out the cell and backward on the steps, and the guard walked backward to the cell gate and locked it and Sogolon backed out the door that closed. And she stepped out and she stepped in again and Venin stood at the cell watching me and she stepped away backward and I yelled, and the bound boy jumped up from his fall and back to the balcony and sat in the chair and looked away from the balcony, and we retied him and pushed him back on the dried bush and the wall healed itself, sucking back up each broken chunk and Mossi and I unrolled on the floor, and I swung my one free arm and he caught it and he unlocked his legs from my legs and stopped choking me with one arm, then flipped me under him, choking me with one arm and locking down my legs with his legs and he yelled and pulled his punch from the wood as I dodged out of his arm and stood up, then I pulled back from punching him and fell back on the floor, and he withdrew his offering hand, but I pulled him down, punching him in the stomach, and in the house my grandfather is fucking my mother on the blue sheet that she bought to make mourning clothes and the climax goes back in his mouth and he is fucking up, not down, and he pulls out and slaps his hard penis until it gets soft and drops into the white bush of his hair, and my mother stops looking away and looks at him and spirits are in the tree that is not ours but the spirit is my father and he is mad at me, and my grandfather and every living thing sounds as if sucking the air back in, reverse breath, and the lighting jumps back from outside back inside and runs backways past me and the Leopard and that boy whose name I never remember and the Leopard is attacking a boy in the forest who wears white dust who I know but I can't remember his name, and then the Leopard is attacking me and then we go through a fire door to Kongor and another to Dolingo and the old man gathers up his flesh and juice and jumps back from the ground but I don't see where he goes and in Basu Fumanguru's yard it is night and the bodies in urns and the wife is nothing but clothes and bone and she is cut in two and in another urn is a boy clutching a cloth from a doll and the doll comes up to my nose, and the boy bursts in my face, and his feet smell of swamp moss and shit and his smell walks away and it is gone and it appears east of the Hills of Enchantment and the smell goes over hills and down in valleys to the west hill and it is gone and it appears in the ports of Lish and the smell of the boy crossed the sea and I try to stop the trail in my head for I know this Bad Ibeji is searching it and I bring up my mother and I bring up river goddesses who kill with disease, and two nomads who dared me to take them both at once in their tent and one sat on me and the other spread himself on the floor and I fucked him with my big toe but the Bad Ibeji burns it out and my forehead is afire and I scream into the gag and blink and my nose is on the boy and the boy crosses the bay from Lish to Omororo and they walk days and quartermoons and moons past lands I did not know and over the Hills of Enchantment to Luala Luala and his smell vanishes and appears south beyond the map and the smell of the boy walks or rides I do not know and the smell vanishes and appears in Nigiki walking running or riding and it stops in the city I can smell him go straight, then bend, then go around then in one corner and stay for long, maybe till nightfall and in the morning his smell leaves and goes down south to caves or somewhere and then it's night and his smell goes deep in the city and stops in the West, and stays there till night and then leaves again in morning, and several days have passed, and then the smell of the boy sets out far west, and keeps going west, he is leaving for Wakadishu he is leaving Wakadishu for Dolingo and I will think of Father, no, Grandfather, and the Leopard, and the colours gold and black, and rivers and seas and lakes and more rivers and the blue girl, and Giraffe Boy stay with me stay in my head grow now you must be growing you must have grown is that you running down the river say something, say that you hate how I never came but you can't remember me so you hate nothing you hate air you hate memory that you can't place like a smell you can't place but you know it because it takes you to a place where you were someone else don't leave children but the Bad Ibeji burns it out of my head my head boils and the memory is gone for good I can feel it I know it he wants to follow the boy but I will not follow the boy but his claws go up farther and I can't feel the cut but I hear it and my toes burn, they rot, they will fall off, he wants to find the boy, he is on the road with me I can only smell but he can see and now I can see, a road with people in robes and they are talking all men in Dolingo do is talk and we go over a bridge because his smell is getting stronger and stronger and the smell turns right and now

Bad Ibeji is seeing it and I am seeing it and it is a small alley like the alley with the bazaar and the alley with the bar but it is an alley that is just the back of a house and the smell goes to the caravan and I am in the caravan and it takes me over to the seventh tree, which they call Melelek, and down five levels almost to the trunk but not the trunk and everything is alley and tunnel and nobody sees the sun very much and the smell of the boy walks this wide road and he turns and he turns and he goes over a bridge and turns right and then right and then left and straight and then down, and he stays somewhere and the Bad Ibeji brings sight and I can see the boy and my head is burning and a white hand touches the boy's shoulder and points a long-nailed finger and the boy goes to the door of that house and he knocks hard and he's crying and he is saying something that I can't hear and I smell him like he is right here he is yelling he is afraid and an old woman opens the door and he does not run in, he steps back like he is afraid of her too and she tries to stoop but he touches her, and he looks behind suddenly, like somebody follows, and runs past her, and she wraps her pagne tighter over her shoulder, looks around then closes the door and my mind is gone. And when I open my eyes they still feel shut. They close and open again without my will. The Bad Ibeji scampers off me like a crab and climbs up to the one-eyed one's shoulder. The two white scientists are both over me looking on, the one-eyed one furrowing his brow, the other one raising his. Then they are by the cell bars. Then they are over my head again. Then they are going out the door. They will tell Sogolon. She will search and find the boy. I can still see him and the house he ran into, the Bad Ibeji's infection still in me. My lips went wet from blood dripping down my nose. This Queen will betray her. My head was too heavy to take that thought any further and inside my head still burned, and I thought it wasn't blood pouring from my nose but the inside of my head, melted to juice. My elbows gave out and I fell back, but when my head hit the floor it felt like I landed in water and I sunk.

And I sunk, and I sunk, and the fire was cooling in my head, and people kept coming in and out, and whispering to me and shouting at me, like they were all ancestors come to gather on the branches of the great tree in the front yard. But my head wouldn't settle. Something boomed, boomed again and then a memory or a daydream screamed, and then shouted, and slammed against my skull. The slam woke me up to see that I was not asleep. Something slammed against the door and fell to the ground. And then the boom hit like a bam and pushed a knuckle mark in the door as if somebody had punched dough. Another punch and the door flew off and hit the cell bars. I jumped up and fell down. Sadogo stomped in, wearing his gloves and holding up one of the guards by the neck. He threw him out of the way. Behind him came Venin, and Mossi with shiny things that hurt my head. Everything they said bounced around my head and left before I understood. The Ogo grabbed my cell lock and ripped it off. Venin walked with a club almost half her height and in my madness she picked it up as if it were a twig and swung it at the cell beside mine, whacking off the lock. The cell was so dark that I didn't know they kept other prisoners here, but why wouldn't they? Thinking on top of thinking made my head throb and I lowered it back down into hands cradling me. Mossi. I think he said, Can you walk? I shook my head no and could not stop shaking until he held my forehead and stilled it.

"The slaves are rebelling," he said. "MLuma, where we were, Mupongoro and others."

"How long was I here? I can't—"

"Three nights," he said.

Two guards rushed in with swords. One swung wide at Venin, who ducked and then swung around with her club and took his face off. My shock got lost in the sweep of Sadogo picking me up and throwing me over his left shoulder. Everything moved so slow. Three more guards ran in, maybe four or five, but this time they ran into the prisoners, men and women not from Dolingo, skin not blue, bodies not slim and withered. They picked up weapons, pieces of weapons, and bars that Sadogo pulled out, all scattered on the floor. My head bounced off Sadogo's back, making it swirl worse. Then he swung around and I saw the prisoners run over the guards like a wave over sand. They shouted, and rallied, and ran past us in the cell, all of them squeezing through the small door, sand through the time glass.

"The boy, I know where he is. I know where . . ." I said.

I couldn't tell where we were going until we passed through it. Then the sun touched my back and we stopped. I was flying through the air, I was on grass and the buffalo's snout was on my forehead. Mossi crouched beside me.

"The boy, I know where he is."

"We must forget the boy, Tracker. Dolingo is bleeding. Slaves have cut their ropes and attacked guards in the third and fourth trees. It will only spread."

"The boy is in the fifth tree," I said.

"Mwaliganza," Sadogo said.

"The boy is nothing to us," Mossi said.

"The boy is everything."

Noise ran in and out of me. Booms and bams and crackles and shouts and screams.

"You say that after what Sogolon did to you. To us."

"Is the boy blameless or not, Mossi?"

He looked away.

"Mossi, I would kill her for what she did, but this, this takes nothing from why she did it."

"Fucking nonsense about divine children. Who shall rise, who shall rule. I come from lands reeking with prophecies of child saviors, and nothing ever came out of them but war. We are not knights. We are not dukes. We are hunters, killers, and mercenaries. Why should we care about the fate of kings? Let them take care of their own."

"When kings fall they fall on top of us."

Mossi grabbed my chin. I knocked his hand away.

"Who is this that now lives in your head? Are you like her?" he said, pointing to Venin.

"Him."

"As you like. The Tracker helping the witch—"

"We are not helping her. I tell you true, if I see one of them taking her for the kill, I will watch it. Then I will kill him. And I . . . I . . . and even if I didn't care about rightful kings and queens, or what is wicked in the North, and what is just, I will take a son back to his mother," I said.

The sun mocked me. Smoke rose from a tower in the second tree and drums sounded as a warning. None of the caravans moved, for the slaves stopped moving them. Some swung midway with people inside them shouting and screaming. Every sound startled Sadogo; he darted left, right, and left again, squeezing his knuckles so hard the joints popped. A crash roused the buffalo, who snorted, telling us we had to leave. As I sat up, pushing away Mossi's help, Venin approached me, still gripping the club like a toy.

"I will go. I have unfinished business with Sogolon."

"Venin?" Mossi said.

"Who is that?" Venin said.

"What? You are who. Venin is what you go by since I met you. Who else would you be if not her?"

"It is not her," I said.

The him in her looked at me.

"You been thinking so a long time," they said.

"Yes but I could not be sure. You are one of the spirits Sogolon write runes to bind, but you broke from her."

"My name is Jakwu, white guard for the King Batuta who sits in Omororo."

"Batuta? He died over a hundred years ago. You are . . . no matter. Leave the old woman to the bloodsuckers. She is like them in company," Mossi said.

"Do all the spirits want what you want?" I asked.

"Revenge against the Moon Witch? Yes. Some want more. Not all of us died by her hand, but in all our deaths she is responsible. She drove me out of my body to appease an angry spirit, and now she thinks she has appeased me."

His voice was still Venin's but I have seen this in possession. The voice remains, but the tone, the pitch, the words he chooses are all so different that it sounds like another voice. Venin's voice went hoarse. It came out like a rumble, like the voice of a man long gone in years.

"Where is Venin?"

"Venin. She the girl. She gone. She will never be back in this body. Call her dead. It is not what she is, but it will do. Now she is doing what I did, roam the underworld until she remembers how she came by that place. And then she will seek out Sogolon, like all of us."

"She could barely ride a horse and now he wields a club. And you? You can barely stand," Mossi said.

At the end of the road, round the bend came yells. Noblemen and noblewomen of Dolingo walking swift, thinking that was enough. Looking back, walking faster, the men and women at the front not yet seeing the people behind them, then running, and the running crowd, maybe twenty, maybe more, pushing some out of the way, knocking down some, trampling some, as they ran this way. Behind them came the rumble. Mossi and Sadogo and Venin took places all around me and we readied our weapons. The screaming nobles ran around us like two rivers. Behind them, with bats, sticks, and clubs, and swords and spears, slaves, who ran and staggered like the zombi but were gaining. Eighty or more, chasing the nobles. A spearhead went through a noblewoman's back and out her belly, and she fell to the ground. The rebels stayed clear of us as they ran around us, save for one who ran too close and was kicked in two by Sadogo's boot, and one that ran into Mossi's sword, and two whose heads met Venin's swinging club. The rest ran past us, and soon swarmed the nobles. Flesh flew. Sadogo in front, we ran back the way they had all come, and one battle cry from Sadogo kept trailing rebels out of our way.

The caravans had all been stopped, many with people trapped inside, but the platforms took us down, those slaves not infected with freedom yet. On the ground, as we scrambled off the platform with me still swaying and tripping and Mossi still holding me up with his hand, Mungunga broke out in explosion and fire. Fire bit into some of the ropes and ran across to one of the caravans and coated it in flame. The people inside, some already on fire, jumped. At the foot of Mungunga a door the height of three men and ten strides wide broke at the hinges and fell down, shooting up dust. Naked slaves running out slowed to a stagger, some with sticks and rods and metals, all hobbling at first, blinking and holding up their arms to block the light. Cut ropes around necks and limbs, and carrying whatever they could hold. I could not tell men from women. The guards and the masters, so used to no resistance, forgot how to fight. They ran through us and past us, so many of them, some dragging whole bodies of masters, others carrying hands, feet, and heads.

Slaves still ran when from above fell elegant bodies. From terraces above ropes fell, and slaves pushed masters off. Noble bodies fell on slave bodies. Both killed. And more fell on top of them.

At Mwaliganza, the platform took us to the eighth floor. Quiet all around, it seemed, as if nothing had spread this far. I rode the buffalo, though I was lying on him, holding on to his horns so I did not fall off.

"This is the floor," I said.

"How are you sure?" Mossi asked.

"This is where my nose is taking us."

But I did not say my eyes, and that when the Bad Ibeji pushed his claws up through my nose, I could see the unit where the old woman lived, the gray walls wearing away to show orange underneath, and the small windows near the top of her roof. They followed me and the buffalo, as nobles and slaves jumped out of the way. We turned left and ran over a bridge to a dry road. The boy was in my nose. But also a living dead smell that I knew, well enough for me to jump in horror and such total disgust that I thought I was sick. But I could not name it. Smell sometimes did not open memory, only that I should remember it.

A small swarm of slaves and prisoners ran by, pulling the bodies of noblemen, naked and blue and dead. They paused at a door I had never seen and yet already knew. The old woman's door hung open and loose. In the doorway were two dead Dolingo guards, necks at an angle that necks do not bend. Right at the doorway, steps that climbed up past one floor to another, and from up there screams, crashes, metal on metal, metal on mortar, metal on skin. I made it to the door and fell back into Mossi's hands. He didn't ask and I didn't protest when he carried me over to the side, near a window, and sat me on the floor.

Then he, Sadogo, and Venin-Jakwu ran past me up the stairs, as two more men landed on the floor, dead before their bones broke. Men shouted orders, and I looked up and saw how wide the floor was. The torch above me flickered. Thunder broke in the room and everything shook. It broke again, as if a storm was a breath away. The ceiling cracked and dust came down. I was on the kitchen floor. Food already cooked was also on the floor, with fat thickening in a pot and palm oil in jars near the wall. I pulled myself up and reached for the torch. Dead guards spotted the entire floor, many of them husks, drained of all juice and coarse like a tree trunk. A balcony hung over the floor and dead men hung from it. Blood dripped down. A boy, hands to his side and still, flew over the balcony and rode the air. He hung there, eyes open but seeing nothing, flies swarming, and movement all over him. I raised the torch as all over his face, all over his hands, his belly, his legs, all his skin popped open holes big as seeds. The boy's skin looked like a wasp's nest, and red bugs covered in blood burrowed in and crawled out. Flies flew out his mouth and ears and fat larvae popped out all over his skin and plopped on the ground, flipped out wings, and flew back to the boy. Soon it was a swarm of flies in the shape of a boy. The swarm gathered into a ball and the boy fell, landing on the floor like dough. The swarm circled tighter and tighter, dropping lower and lower until it rested right above the floor, six paces from me. The bugs and the larvae and the pods squeezed and squashed into each other, shaping into something with two limbs, then three, then four with a head.

The Adze, bright eyes like fire, black skin that vanished in the dark room, a hunchback with long hands and fingers with claws that scraped the floor. He stomped his hooves and approached me, and I dodged back and waved the torch at him, which made him wheeze a laugh. He kept coming, and I stepped back and kicked over an oil jar. The oil started spreading on the floor and he yelled, skipped, and jumped back, broke up into bugs, and flew back upstairs. I heard the Ogo yell, and something crashed and broke wood. Mossi jumped up to the balcony, swinging one sword, spun and chopped off the head of a guard infected with lightning. He leapt back onto the floor and ran back into the fight.

Still holding the torch, I grabbed another jar full of palm oil and started upstairs. Five steps up my head pounded, the floor started to shift, and I leaned into the wall. I passed a man with a hole in his chest that went straight through his back. At the top of the stairs, I put down the jar, shook my head to clear it, and looked straight into yellow eyes and a long, thin face, red skin and white stripes up the forehead. Ears pointing up, hair green like grass on his arms and shoulders, white streaks all the way down his chest. He stood half a man above me, and smiled, his teeth pointed and sharp, like a great fish's. In his right hand a leg bone that he filed down to the shape of a dagger. He cackled something over and over, then lunged at me, but two flashes of light made his belly explode black blood. Mossi, jumping down, his two sword arms spread wide. He swung his hands across his chest, left sword slicing through the devil's back, his right sword slicing through half his neck. The devil fell, and rolled down the steps.

"Eloko, Eloko, he kept saying. I think his name is Eloko. Was," Mossi said. "Tracker, stay down."

"They come down."

He ran back into the fight. The room was a school. That was why they chose it and why it would have been so easy for the boy to fool whoever came to the door. Yet there was no sign of children. Across the room, near the window, Venin-Jakwu smiled as two Eloko charged, one from the floor and one from the ceiling. From a hanging plant the Eloko swung off to jump them, but they ran into him with the butt of their club, ramming him in the chest. He swiped with a long bone knife but Venin-Jakwu dodged and rammed the club handle straight into his nose. Another, behind, swung his knife, and cut across the back of their thigh. Venin-Jakwu yelled and dropped, but dropped into a dodge, swooping low and swinging the club from low right up into his face. The third Eloko snuck up from behind. I shouted, but I said Jakwu! And they swung left, though he was coming from the right. Just a breath behind them, Venin-Jakwu stopped the hard swing of the club, sent it down so that it swung right up, past their right side and right up between the Eloko's legs. He shrieked and fell to his knees. Venin-Jakwu bashed his head again and again until there was no more head. Thunder cracked again and mortar broke from the ceiling.

"Your leg," I said, pointing to the blood running down.

"Who you plan to kill with those?"

I looked at my torch and oil. Venin-Jakwu ran off. I followed, stronger, my mind less stormy, but still I wobbled. The Adze swung from a rafter in the ceiling as a hunchback, but dived after Sadogo as a swarm. He attacked Sadogo's left arm and shoulder. Sadogo swatted away many and crushed many, but Adze was too many. Some started burrowing in his shoulder and near his elbow and Sadogo yelled. I threw the jar and it shattered on his chest, splashing palm oil all over. He looked at me, enraged.

"Rub on your arm . . . the oil . . . rub it."

The flies dug into his skin. Sadogo scooped oil running down his belly and rubbed on his chest, arm, and neck. The bugs, they popped up in the quick, slipping out of larger holes like wounds, all falling to the floor. The rest of the swarm flew into madness, popping into each other, squeezing tight into one form, the form dropping lower and lower until on the floor and changing back into an Adze with one foot and half of a head, and in the head, bugs and larvae wiggling like maggots. Quicker than a blink, Venin-Jakwu smashed the rest of its head into a red, pulpy pool on the floor.

"Where is Sogolon? The boy?"

Sadogo pointed with his good arm to another room. Venin-Jakwu ran towards it, clubbing guards with lightning coursing through them. She ran to the door, right into a thunderclap that knocked her away from the archway and shook me off my balance. Inside, Mossi pulled himself out of a pile of tumbled shelves and clay pots.

His back was to me, and his feet were off the ground: Ipundulu. White streaks in his hair, long feathers at the back of his head sticking out like knives and going all the way down his back. White wings, black feathers at the tips and wide as the room. Body white and featherless, thin but muscular. Black bird's feet floating above the clay floor. Ipundulu. His right arm raised, claws around Sogolon's neck. I couldn't tell if she was alive, but blood spattered on the floor below her. Lightning crackled and jumped all over his skin. Ipundulu pulled a knife out of his shoulder and threw it at Mossi, who jumped out of the way, raised his swords, and glared at him. Sogolon, her lips white, opened one eye halfway and looked at me. Behind me, Venin-Jakwu rolled on the floor, trying to get up. Lightning jumped from Ipundulu's skin to Sogolon's face and she groaned through clenched teeth. Mossi was unsure how to strike. Maybe somebody told me, maybe I guessed, but I threw the torch straight for the lightning bird. It hit him in the center of his back and his whole body exploded in flames. He dropped Sogolon and shrieked like a crow, rolled and jerked, and tried to fly as the flames burned away feathers and skin so quick, so hungrily. Ipundulu ran into the wall and kept running, flaying and shrieking, a ball of bursting flame feeding on feathers, feeding on skin, feeding on fat. The room stank of smoke and charred flesh.

Ipundulu fell to the floor. Mossi ran over to Sogolon.

The lightning bird did not die. I could hear him wheeze, his body back in the shape of a man, his skin blackened where it had charred and red where the flesh was ripped open underneath.

"She lives," Mossi said. He stomped over to the Ipundulu, on the floor jerking and wheezing.

"He lives also," he said, and pushed the blade right under Ipundulu's chin.

Something drew me to look over at the toppled shelves—the plates, pots, and bowls of drying fish—and under a chair. Under the chair looked right back at me. Eyes wide and bright in the dim, staring at me staring at him. A voice in me said, There he is. There is the boy. His hair, wild and natty, for what else would a boy's hair be without a mother to groom and cut it? He jumped, frightened, and first I thought it was because of them who had him, for which child is not frightened by monsters? But he must have been in dozens of houses and seen dozens of kills, so much that the killing of a woman, and the eating of her, and the killing of a child and the eating of him was child's play. If you lived all your life with monsters, what was monstrous? He stared at me, and I stared at him.

"Mossi."

"Maybe you should have skipped Dolingo," he said to the Ipundulu.

"Mossi."

"Tracker."

"The boy."

He turned to look. Ipundulu tried to push himself up on his elbows, but Mossi pressed his sword into his neck.

"What is his name?" Mossi asked.

"He has none."

"Then what do we call him? Boy?"

Venin-Jakwu and Sadogo came up behind me. Sogolon was still on the floor.

"If she does not wake soon, all her spirits will know she is weak," I said.

"What should we do with this one?" Mossi said.

"Kill him," Venin said behind me. "Kill him, get the witch, and get the b—"

He burst through the window, blasting off a chunk of the wall that shattered into rocks, hitting Sadogo in the head and neck. Right behind me, his long black wing slammed Venin-Jakwu, sending them flying into the wall.

The smell, I knew the smell. I spun around and his wing knocked me off my feet, swung back and hit me square in the face. He stepped into the room, and Mossi charged him with both swords. Mossi's sword struck his wing and got stuck. He slapped the other sword out of Mossi's hands and charged him.

Flapping his black bat wings to lift his body, he

swung both feet up and kicked him in the chest. Mossi slammed into the wall, and he slammed into him. Then he dug his clawed finger into Mossi's head, cutting from the top of his forehead down, slicing through the brow and still moving down.

"Sasabonsam!" I said. He smelled like his brother.

He slapped Mossi away and faced me.

My head still moved slower than my feet. He came after me just as Sogolon stirred and whipped a wind that knocked him off his feet and pushed me to the ground. He fought against the wind, and Sogolon was losing strength. He staggered, but got close enough to cut into her raised hands with his claws. I tried to get up but fell to one knee. Mossi was still on the ground. I did not know where Venin-Jakwu was. And by the time Sadogo rose and remembered his rage enough to stomp to the room, Sasabonsam grabbed Ipundulu's leg with his iron claw hand wrapping around the leg like a snake, scooped the boy with the other hand, after the boy crawled out from under the chair, and ran straight to the window, blasting out the frame, the glass, and chunks of the wall. One of the guards, lightning coursing through him, ran after his new master and fell where Sasabonsam flew. I staggered in after Sadogo and saw Sasabonsam in the sky with his bat wings, dipping twice from Ipundulu's weight, then flapping harder, louder, and climbing high.

So. Sadogo, Venin-Jakwu, Mossi, and I stood in the room, surrounding Sogolon. She tried to stand up, darting at all of us. Outside, overturned carts, slaughtered bodies, and broken sticks and clubs littered the streets. Smoke from the two rebellious trees streaked the sky. Farther off, not far away, the rumble of a fight. And what fight? Dolingon guards were not made for any fight, much less a war. Over in the Queen's tree, the palace stood still. All ropes to and from appeared to be cut off. I saw the Queen in my mind-eye, crouched in her throne like a child, ordering her court to believe when she said that the rebellion would be smashed and smote in a blink, and them hollering, screaming, and shouting to the gods.

We stepped towards her, and Sogolon, not sure what to do, shifted back and forth, then skipped clear of us. She raised her left hand but stopped when it made her chest bleed. She kept darting at each of us, her eyes wide one blink, hazy the next, almost asleep, then stunned awake. She turned to Mossi.

"Consort, she was going treat you like. Keep her womb full and she wouldn't care."

"Until she turned tired and sent him to the trunk," I said.

"She treat the pretty ones better than a king be treating he concubines. That is truth."

"Not the truth you told me. Not in words, not in meaning, not even in rhyme."

We moved in closer. Sadogo squeezed his left knuckles, his right hand bloody and loose. Venin-Jakwu pulled a wrap around their leg wound and grabbed a dagger, Mossi, half his face covered in blood, pointed his two swords. Sogolon turned to me, the one without a weapon.

"From me could come a tempest to blow everybody out that window."

"Then you would be too weak to stop the blood leaking out of you, and the others coming after you. Just like the one in Venin," I said.

She backed into the wall. "All of you too fool. None of you ready. You think I was going leave the true fate of the North to all of you? No skill, no brain, no plan, all of you here for the coin, nobody here care about the fate of the very land you shit on. What a bliss, what a gift to be so ignorant or foolish."

"Nobody here was lacking skill, Sogolon. Or brain. You just had other plans," Mossi said.

"I tell you, I tell all of you, don't go through the Darklands. Stop walking in the room crotch first, and walk headfirst. Or step back and be led. You think I goin' trust the boy to people like you?"

"And where is your boy, Sogolon? Do you nest him so tight to your bosom we can't see him?" Mossi said.

"No skill, no brain, no plan, yet were it not for us, you would be dead," I said.

"Goddess of flow and overflow, listen to your daughter. Goddess of flow and overflow."

"Sogolon," I said.

"Goddess of flow and overflow."

"You still call to that slithering bitch?" Venin-Jakwu said.

"Bunshi. You calling for your goddess?"

"Don't speak of Bunshi," Sogolon said.

"Still there thinking you get to give orders," said Venin-Jakwu. "She don't change in a hundred years, this Moon Witch. I tell you true. Woman in Mantha still calling you prophet, or they finally see you just a thief."

"We need to save the boy, you know where they heading," she said to me.

Venin-Jakwu, the wrap around their leg almost full red, started circling her slow, like a lion, and began to talk.

"So what this Moon Witch be telling you about herself? For the only one who tell tales about Sogolon is Sogolon. She tell you she come from the Watangi warriors south of Mitu? Or that she was river priestess in Wakadishu? That she was the bodyguard and adviser to the sister of the King when she was just a water maid, who step over many heads to get to her chamber? Look at her, on a mission again. Save the royal sister's boy. She tell you that nobody ask her? She set off on mission to find boy, so that she no longer the joke of Mantha. And what a joke. The Moon Witch with one hundred runes but only one spell, finally get to show her quality. Maybe she going tell you later. Listen to me, I tell you this. The moon witch sure be three hundred, ten and five, I tell you true. I meet her when she was just two hundred. She tell you how she live that long? No? That one she keep close to her lanky bosom. Two hundred years ago I was still a knight and have only one hole, not two. You know who me be? Me be the one who knock her off her horse when she forget to write a rune strong enough to bind me."

Sogolon kept looking at me.

"And her little goddess, you meet it? It come sliming down the wall as of late? If she is a goddess then me is the divine elephant snake. That little river jengu, claiming she fight Omoluzu, when you could kill her with just seawater. Her goddess is an imp."

"None of you deserved to live, not a single one of you," Sogolon said, still looking at me.

"That is between we and the gods, not you, body thief," Venin-Jakwu said.

"You was always an ungrateful, stinking piece of dog shit, Jakwu. Killer and raper of women. Why you think I give you that body? One day all of that you do will happen to you."

"The body had an owner," I said.

"Every day before sun come, she running out to go back to the bush so Zogbanu can eat her. No matter where me take her and how me train her. Far better use of she body than she ever go use it," Sogolon said.

"You just wanted me to stop knocking you off your horse," Venin-Jakwu said. "Just like you been knocking people out of they body for a long, long time."

"How?" Mossi said.

"Don't ask me, ask she."

"Time running and passing, and they still have the boy. You know where they going, Tracker."

Sogolon looked around, at all of us, speaking to everybody, convincing no one.

"She didn't try to kill us," Sadogo said.

"Speak for yourself," Venin-Jakwu said.

"We agreed to save the boy," Mossi said, and walked over to me.

"You don't know her. I know her two hundred years, what she do more than anything else is plot how a person can be of use. She never ask you what is your use? I didn't agree to nothing with none of you," Venin-Jakwu said.

"Maybe not. But we go to save the boy, and we might need the deceiving Moon Witch."

"A dead Moon Witch not going to be any use to you."

"Nor a dead girl who tried to go through three of us to kill her."

Now Venin-Jakwu darted from face to face. They pushed a foot under the sword of a fallen guard and kicked it up in hand. They gripped it, liking the feel, and smiled.

"I am a man!" he said. "My name is—"

"Jakwu. I know your name. I know you must be a fearsome warrior with many kills. Help us save this child and there will be coin in it for you," I said.

"Coin can help me grow a cock?"

"Such an overpraised thing, a cock," Mossi said. I don't know if he was trying to make the room smile. Sogolon's chest right above the heart was red. Ipun-dulu had tried to cut her chest open and rip out the heart, but she would have us watch her collapse on the ground before telling anyone that.

"See to your heart," I said to her.

"My heart clear," she said.

"It's almost falling out of your chest."

"It never cut deep."

"Nothing seems to," Mossi said.

At the foot of the tree, the buffalo waited with two horses. Everything I wanted to ask with my mouth I seemed to ask with my eye, for he nodded, snorted, and pointed to the horses. Jakwu mounted the first.

"Sogolon rides with you," I said.

"I ride with no one," he said, and galloped off.

Mossi came up behind me. "How far shall he ride?" he said.

"Before he sees he does not know the way? Not very far."

"Sogolon."

"She can ride on the buffalo's back."

"As you wish," Mossi said.

I grabbed a piece of Mossi's tunic and wiped his face. The blood had stopped running.

"It is but a scratch," he said.

"A scratch from a monster with iron claws."

"You called it something."

"Give me this," I said, and took one of his swords. I cut a hole at the fringe of his tunic and tore off a long strip of cloth. This cloth I wrapped around his head, tying it at the back.

"Sasabonsam."

"That is not one of the names I remember from the old man's house."

"No. The Sasabonsam lived with his brother. They kill men from high up in the trees. His brother the flesh eater, him the bloodsucker."

"World's not short on trees. Why does he travel with this pack?"

"I killed his brother," I said.

Two things. The Sasabonsam took a sword to his wing. He was carrying both the boy and Ipundulu, who must have been as heavy as him.

On the ground the two burning trees seemed hundreds upon hundreds of paces away, which they were. We were about to ride off when several of the Queen's guard, ten and nine, maybe more, all on foot but in front of us, bid us to stop.

"Her Radiant Excellency said she never gave anyone leave."

"Her Radiance has worse things to worry about than who takes leave of her radiant ass," Mossi said, and rode right through them. They jumped out of the way when the buffalo brushed his front hoof in the dust.

"Such a shame to leave. This is a rebellion that brings me joy to see," Mossi said.

"Until the slaves see they would rather the bondage they know than the freedom they do not," I said.

"Remind me to pick this fight with you another time," he said.

We rode all night. We passed where the old man

lived but all that was left of his house was the smell of it. Nothing remained, not even the rubble of cracked mud and smashed bricks. Truly this made me worry that there had been no house and no man, but a dream of both. Since I alone noticed, I said nothing and we rode past the nothing in a blur. Jakwu tried to follow while being ahead, but pulled back three times. Even I had no memory of the way, unlike Mossi, who charged through the night. I just held on to his sides. Sogolon tried to sit upright on the buffalo as he ran almost as fast as the horses, but she almost fell off twice. We moved through the patch of the Mawana witches but only one broke through the ground to see us, and when she did, dove back down as if it were water.

Before sun chased night away, the boy left my nose. I jumped up. Sasabonsam had flown all the way to the gate and gone through. I knew. Mossi said something about my forehead punching the back of his neck, which made me pull back. He slowed the horse to a trot when we reached the dirt road. The door crackled, shifted the air around it, and gave off a hum, but was getting smaller. I could see the road to Kongor in yellow daylight.

"When they come—"

"The doors don't open themselves, Sogolon. They have already gone through it. We are too late," I said.

Sogolon rolled off the buffalo and fell. She tried to scream, but it came out a cough.

"You do this," she said, pointing at me. "You was

never fit, never ready, nothing in the face of them. None of you care. None of you see what the whole world going lose. First time in two years and you make them get away."

"How, old woman?" Mossi said. "By being sold into slavery? That was your doing. We could have taken on all of Dolingo and saved the boy. Instead we wasted time saving you. Safe passage my sore ass. You put the whole fate of your mission on a queen more concerned with breeding with me than listening to you. That was all your doing."

The gate was shrinking, large enough for a man, but not for the Ogo or the buffalo.

"Is going be days till one get to Kongor," she said.

"Then you'd better cut a stick and walk," Mossi said. "This is as far as we go."

"The slaver will double the money. I promise it."

"The slaver or the King sister? Or maybe the river jengu you pretend is a goddess?" I asked.

"It is only about the boy. You so fool you don't see? It was only for the boy."

"I have a feeling, witch, it was only for you. You keep saying we were useless when use is exactly what you put us to. And the girl, poor Venin, you rid of her own body because Jakwu, or whatever his name is, was of greater use. This whole failure is on you," Mossi said.

Jakwu jumped off his horse and stepped to the gate. I don't think he had ever seen one.

"What do I see through this hole?"

"The way to Mitu," Sadogo said.

"I shall take it."

"All might not be fine with you," I said. "Jakwu has never seen the ten and nine doors, but Venin has."

"What do you mean?"

"He means, though your soul is new, your body might burn," Mossi said.

"I shall take it," Jakwu said.

Sogolon looked at the gate the whole time. She staggered right up to it. I knew she thought of it. That she had made it to three hundred, ten and five years, mayhaps surviving worse, and besides, who had time for old woman tales that nobody could ever prove?

"Well you all seem like the gods smile on you, but nothing here for me," Jakwu said. "Maybe I go to the North and have those Kampara perverts make me one of their wooden cocks."

"May good fortune come to you," Mossi said, and Jakwu nodded.

He headed to the door. Sogolon stepped out of the way.

Mossi grabbed my shoulder and said, "Where now?" I didn't know what to say to him, or how to say that wherever it was I hoped it would be in his company.

"I have no stake in this boy, but I will go where you go," he said.

"Even if that means Kongor?"

"Well, I am one for amusements."

"People trying to kill you is an amusement?"

"I have laughed at worse."

I turned to Sadogo. "Great Ogo, where go you now?"

"Who care about the cursed giant?" Sogolon said. "All of you whining like all of you is little bitch, because the old woman outsmart you. This not what you all make for? And you can't smell it, touch it, drink it, or fuck it, so it mean nothing to you. Nothing bigger than yourself."

"Sogolon, you keep mourning this death of morals you never had," I said.

"Me telling you all. Whatever coin you want. Your own weight in silver. When the boy on the throne in Fasisi, you will have gold dust just to give your servants. You say you would do it for the boy if not for me. For the boy to see his mother. You like seeing a woman go down on her knees? You want my breasts in the dirt?"

"Don't disgrace yourself, woman."

"Me beyond honor or disgrace. Words, they just words. The boy is everything. The future of the kingdom is . . . the boy, he going—"

The door had shrunk to about half my height and hung above the ground. Jakwu's hand pushed through it, catching fire, grabbed the neck of Sogolon's dress, and pulled her right in. Her feet burst into flames before Jakwu dragged all of her through, but it was quick, quicker than a god's blink. Mossi and I rushed to the door but the opening was now smaller than our heads. Sogolon screamed from here to there, screamed at what we could only imagine was happening to her until the door closed on itself.

TWENTY

Strong winds blew into the sails and pushed the dhow. This was the fastest I ever see it go, save for a storm, the captain said, but claimed it was sake of neither river nor wind goddess. He wasn't sure which, even though the answer showed itself clear to anybody who went belowdecks. We boarded the dhow to Kongor a day ago, and here is why it made sense. We could not go through Dolingo, for no one had word on whether the rebellion had spread or if the Queen's men doused it. Dolingo's mountains rose higher than Malakal and would have taken five nights to cross, followed by four through Mitu, before we reached Kongor. But a boat on the river took three nights and half a day. The last I sailed on a dhow, the boat was less than ten and six paces long, not even seven paces wide, and carried five of us. This boat was half the walk of a sorghum field and wider than twenty paces, and had two sails, one as wide as the ship and just as high, the other half that size, both cut like shark fins.

Three floors belowdecks, all empty, made the ship sail faster, but also made it easier to capsize. A slave ship.

"That ship, have you ever seen the like?" Mossi said when I pointed it out docked by the river.

A half day's walk led us to a clearing and the river, which ran from far south of Dolingo, snuck past it on the left, snaked around Mitu, and split to surround Kongor. On the other side of the river, the giant trees and thick mists hid the Mweru.

"I have seen the like," I said to him about the ship.

We were all tired, even the buffalo and the Ogo. We were all sore, and the first night the Ogo's fingers were so stiff he swatted three mugs of beer away trying to pick them up. I couldn't remember what hit me in my back for it to smart so, and when I dipped in the river, every wound, scratch, and sore screamed. Mossi was sore as well and he tried to hide his limp, but winced when he stepped with his left foot. The night before, the cut above his forehead opened again, and blood streaked down the middle of his face. I cut another piece of his tunic, pounded wild bush into a paste, and rubbed it in his wound. He grabbed my hand and cursed at the sting, then eased his grip and dropped his hands to my waist. I wrapped his forehead.

"Then you know why it would dock here, on the outskirts of Dolingo."

"Mossi, Dolingo buys slaves, not sells them."

"What does that mean, that the ship is empty? Not after what's coming to pass in the citadel."

I turned to him, looking over at the buffalo, who snorted at the sight of the river.

"Look how it floats above the water. It's empty."

"I don't trust slavers. We could turn from guest to cargo in the course of one night."

"And how would a slaver do that with the likes of us? We need passage to Kongor, and this ship is going to either Kongor or Mitu, which is still closer than where we are now."

I hailed the captain, a fat slaver with a bald head he painted blue, and asked if he minded some fellow travelers. They all stood from the port, looking down on us, ragged and covered in bruises and dust, but with all the weapons we took from the Dolingons. Mossi was right, the captain looked us over, and so did his thirty-man crew. But Sadogo never took off his gloves, and one look from him made the captain charge us nothing. But you take that cow to the shed with the rest of the dumb beasts, he said, and the Ogo had to grab the buffalo's horn to stop him from charging. The buffalo took an empty stall beside two pigs who should have been fatter.

The second level had windows, and the Ogo took that one, and frowned when it looked like we would join him. He has nightmares and wishes that nobody knows, I said to Mossi when he complained. The captain said to me that he sold his cargo that night to a thin blue noble who pointed with his chin the whole time, only two nights before the god of anarchy let loose in Dolingo.

The ship would dock in Kongor. None of the crew slept below. One, whose face I didn't see, said something about slave ghosts, furious about dying on the ship for they were still chained to it and could not enter the underworld. Ghosts, masters of malice and longing, spent all their days and nights thinking of the men who wronged them, and sharpening those thoughts into a knife. So they would have no quarrel with us. And if they wanted ears to hear of their injustice, I have heard worse from the dead.

I went down the stairs to the first deck, the stairway so steep that by the time I reached the bottom, the steps behind me vanished into the dark. I couldn't see much in the dark but my nose took me over to where Mossi lay, the myrrh on his skin gone to everyone but me. He rolled rags from an old sail into a pillow and put it right against the bulkhead, so that he could hear the river. I went to sleep beside him, except I couldn't sleep. I turned on my side, facing him, watching him for such a long time that I jumped when I saw that he was looking at me, eye-to-eye. He reached over and touched my face before I could move. It seemed as if he wasn't even blinking, and his eyes were too bright in the dark, almost silver. And his hand had not left my face. He rubbed my cheek and moved up to my forehead, traced one brow, then the other, and went back down to my cheek like a blind woman reading my face. Then he put his thumb on my lip, then my chin, while his fingers caressed my neck. And lying there, I already forgot when I closed my eyes. Then I felt him on my lips. There is no such kiss among the Ku, and none with the Gangatom either. And nobody in Kongor or Malakal would do such gentle tongue play. His kiss made me want another. And then he pushed his tongue in my mouth and my eyes went wide open. But he did it again, and my tongue did it back to him. When his hand gripped me I was already hard. It made me jump again and my palm brushed his forehead. He winced, then grinned. Night vision made him out in the dark, gray and silver. He sat up, pulled his tunic over his head. I just looked at him, his bruised chest purple in spots. I wanted to touch him but was afraid he would wince again. He straddled my lap and grabbed my arms, to which I hissed. Sore. He said something about us being poor old injured men who have no business doing . . . I did not hear the rest, for he then bent down and sucked my right nipple. I moaned so loud, I waited for some sailor upstairs to cuss or whisper that something is afoot with those two. His knees against my own bruised ribs made me breathe heavy. I rubbed his chest and he sucked in air and moaned it back out. I was frightened that I hurt him, but he took my hand away and placed it on the floor. He blew on my navel, then moved lower between my legs and did precious art. I begged him to stop in the most feeble whisper. He climbed back on me. The floorboards, looser than they should have been, creaked with each jerk. I let everything out through gnashed teeth and grabbed his ass. I went on top. He grabbed my left ass cheek right on a raw bruise and I shouted. He laughed, pulling me deeper into him, my lips down on his. Both of us failing to not make a sound, then both thinking fuck the gods for we will have sound.

In the morning, when I woke, a boy looked down on me. Not surprised at all, I was waiting for him, and for more like him. He raised his eyebrows, curious, and scratched at the shackle around his neck. Mossi grunted, frightening him, and the boy faded into the wood.

"You have saved children before," Mossi said.

"I didn't see you were awake."

"You are different when you think no one watches you. I always thought that what made one a man was that he takes up so much space. I sit here, my sword is there, my water pouch there, tunic there, chair over there, and legs spread wide because, well, I love it so. But you, you make yourself smaller. I wondered if it was because of your eye."

"Which one?"

"Fool," he said.

He sat across from me, leaning against the wood planks. I rubbed his hairy legs.

"That would be the one I speak of," he said. "My father had two different eyes. Both were gray, until his enemy from childhood punched one brown."

"What did your father do to his enemy?"

"He calls him Sultan, Your Great Eminence, now." I laughed.

"There are children of great importance to you.

I have thought of such things, of children, but . . . well. Why think of flight when one can never be the bird? We are of strange passions in the East. My father—well my father is my father and just like the one before him. It was not that I . . . for I was not the first . . . not even the first carrying his name . . . and besides, my wife was chosen from a noble house before I was born, and so it would have gone, for such is the way of things. The thing is not what I did, the thing is the prophet allowed men to discover us and he was poor so he . . . I . . . they sent me away and told me never to sail back to their shores or it would be death."

"A wife? And a child?"

"Four. My father took them and gave them to my sister to raise. Better to keep my filth away from their memory."

Fuck the gods, I thought. Fuck the gods.

"Then I sailed off course. Maybe it was the gods. There are children you think of."

"Don't you?"

"A night never passes."

"This must be why loose wives dismiss us as soon as we burst. Sad talk of children."

He smiled.

"Do you know of mingi?" I asked.

"No."

"Some of the river tribes and even some places in great cities like Kongor kill newborns who are un-worthy. Children born weak, or limbless, or with top teeth before bottom, or with gifts or forms strange. Five of those children strange in form we saved, but they return to me in dreams—"

"We?"

"Does not matter now. These five return to me in dreams and I have tried to see them, but they live with a tribe that is my tribe's enemy."

"How?"

"I gave them to my tribe's enemy."

"Nothing you ever say ends the way I think you would end it, Tracker."

"After my tribe tried to kill me for saving mingi children."

"Oh. You and these people, none of your rivers run straight. Take us finding this boy. There is no straight line between us and this boy, only streams leading to streams, leading to streams, and sometimes—and tell me if I lie—you get so lost in the stream that the boy fades, and with him the reason you search for him. Fades like that boy who just vanished in the ship."

"You saw him?"

"Truth does not depend on me believing it, does it?"

"This is truth, there are times I forget who we are after. I don't even think of the coin."

"What compels you, then? Not reunite mother with child? You said that only a few days ago."

He crawled over to me and shafts of light marked stripes on his skin. He rested his head in my lap.

"This is what you ask?"

"Yes, this is what I ask."

"Why?"

"You know why."

I looked at him.

"The further I go—"

"Yes?"

"The more I feel that I have nothing to go back to," I said.

"This comes to you after how many moons?"

"Prefect, news such as this comes only one way: too late."

"Tell me about your eye."

"It is from a wolf."

"Those jackals you call wolves? Maybe you lost a bet with a jackal. This is not jest, is it? Which question do you desire first: how or why?"

"A shape-shifting hyena bitch in her woman form sucked the eye out of my skull, then bit it off."

"I should have asked why first. And after last night," he said.

"What of last night?"

"You . . . nothing."

"Last night was not a deposit on something else," I said.

"No, that it was not."

"Can we talk of something else?"

"We talk of nothing now. Except your eye."

"A gang ripped my eye out."

"A gang of hyenas, you said."

"Truth does not depend on you believing it, prefect. I wandered that wilderness between the sand sea and Juba for several moons, I can't remember how many, but I do remember wanting to die. But not before I killed the man responsible."

Here is a short tale about the wolf eye. After this man betrayed me to the pack of hyenas, I couldn't find him. After that I went roaming, and roaming, full and brimming with hate but with nowhere to let all this malcontent out. I went back to the sand sea, to the lands of beetles big as birds, and scorpions who stung the life out, and sat in a sand hole while vultures landed and circled. And then the Sangoma came to me, her red dress blowing though no wind blew, and her head circled by bees. I heard the buzz before I saw her, and when I saw her I said, This must be a fever dream, sun madness, for she was long dead.

"I expect the boy with the nose to not have the nose but did not think the boy with the mouth would no longer have a mouth," she said. It came trotting beside her.

"You brought a jackal?" I asked.

"Do not insult the wolf."

She grabbed my face, firm but not hard, and said words I did not understand. She grabbed some sand in her hand, spat in it, and kneaded it until the sand stuck together. Then she ripped off my patch and I jumped. Then she said, Close your good eye. She put the sand on my eye hole and the wolf came in closer. The wolf growled, and she whimpered, and she whimpered some more. I heard something like a stab and more growls from the wolf. Then nothing. Sangoma said, Count to ten and one before you open them. I started counting and she interrupted me.

"She will come back for it, when you are near gone. Look out for her," she said.

So she lent me a wolf's eye. I thought I would see far and long and make people out in the dark. And I can. But lose colour when I close my other eye. This wolf will one day come back and claim it. I couldn't even laugh.

"I could," Mossi said.

"A thousand fucks for you."

"A few more before we dock will be fine enough. You might even turn into something of a lover."

Even if he was joking, he annoyed me. Especially if he was joking, he annoyed me.

"Tell me more about witches. Why you hate them so," he said.

"Who said I hate witches?"

"Your own mouth."

"I fell sick in the Purple City many years ago. Sick near death—a curse some husband paid a fetish priest to put on me. A witch found me and promised me a healing spell if I did something for her."

"But you hate witches."

"Quiet. She was not a witch, she said, just a woman who had a child without a man, and this city can be wicked in its judgment of such things. They took her child, she said, and gave it to a rich but barren woman. Will you make me well, I asked, and she said,

I will give you freedom from want, which did not sound like the same thing. But I followed my nose and found her child, took her away from that woman in the night, disturbing no one. Then I don't know what happened, except I woke up the next morning, well, with a pool of black vomit on the floor."

"Then why—"

"Quiet. It really was her child. But she had a smell about her. Tracked her down two days later in Fasisi. She was expecting someone else. Somebody to buy the two baby hands and one liver she left out on the table. Witches cannot work spells against me, though she tried. I chopped her in the forehead before she could chant, then hacked her head off."

"And you have hated witches ever since."

"Oh I've hated them from long before that. I hate myself for trusting one, is more the like. People always go back to their nature in the end. It's like that gum from the tree, that no matter how far you pull it, snaps itself back."

"Maybe you bear hatred for women."

"Why would you say that?"

"I've never heard you speak good of a single one. They all seem to be witches in your world."

"You don't know my world."

"I know enough. Perhaps you hate none, not even your mother. But tell me I lie when I say you always expected the worst of Sogolon. And every other woman you have met."

"When have you seen me say any of this? Why do you say this to me now?"

"I don't know. You can't go inside me and not expect me to go inside you. Will you think on it?"

"I have nothing to think—"

"Fuck the gods, Tracker."

"Fine, I shall think on why Mossi thinks I hate women. Anything more before I go on deck?"

"I have one thing more."

We docked a day and a half later at noon. His forehead wound looked sealed, and none of us were sore, though we were all covered in scabs, even the buffalo. Most of that day I passed in the slave cabin, me fucking Mossi, Mossi fucking me, me loving Mossi, Mossi loving me, and me going above deck to check faces to see if anyone would start words with me. They either didn't know or care—sailors are sailors everywhere—not even when Mossi stopped grabbing my hand to cover his shouts. The rest of the time Mossi gave me too many things to think about and it all came back to my mother, who I never, ever wanted to think about. Or the Leopard, who I had not thought of in moons, or what Mossi said that inside me is a hate for all women. It was a harsh thought and a lie, as I could not help that I have run into witches.

"Maybe you draw the worst to you."

"Are you the worst?" I asked, annoyed.

"I hope not. But I think of your mother, or rather the mother you told me about who might not even be real, or if she is real, not as you say. You sound like fathers where I am from who blame the daughter for rape, saying, Had you not legs to run away? Had you not lips to scream? You think as they do that suffering from cruelty or escaping it is a matter of choice or means, when it is a matter of power."

"You say I should understand power?"

"I say you should understand your mother."

The night before we docked he said, Tracker, you are at all times a vigorous lover, but I do not think that was praise, and he kept asking me about long gone things, dead things, afterward. So much so that yes, I was getting a little tired of the prefect and his questions. In the morning the crew repaired a hole the Ogo punched through the bulkhead, without asking any questions. He said it was a nightmare.

Kongori deserted their streets at noon, a perfect time to slip into the city and vanish down an alley. Take away the streets where the Tarobe, or the Nyembe, or the Gallunkobe/Matyube lived, and people made house anywhere they could buy, cheat, inherit, or claim, which meant that if most of the people stayed indoors then the entire city would look as if it hid behind walls. Not even the sentries, usually on guard around the city limits, stood by the shore. Mossi and I took two of the ship crewmen's clothes in exchange for cowrie shells, and one, stunned, said, I have killed men for less. We wore the sea-worn robes of sailors, robes with hoods, and trousers like men from the East.

More than seven nights had gone since we saw the city last. Maybe more but I could not remember. No loud music and nothing left of Bingingun masquerade but bits of straw, cloths, sticks, and staffs in red and green, all scattered on the street, with no master to claim them.

I looked for the Ogo to look at me and the prefect with different eyes, but saw nothing. If anything, the Ogo talked more than he had in almost a moon, on everything from the agreeable sky to this most agreeable buffalo, that I almost told him that a chatter-loving Ogo would bring attention to us. I wondered if Mossi thought the same and that was why he kept behind us, until I caught his eye sweeping up and down and behind and beside, past each crossroad, his hand never leaving his sword. I pulled back, walking beside him.

"Chieftain army?"

"Down a merchant's street? They paid us well to never come to these parts."

"Then who?"

"Anyone."

"Which enemy is expecting us, Mossi?"

"Not enemies on the ground. It's pigeons in the sky that worry me."

"I know. And I have no friends here. I—"

I had to stop right there, right on that road as we walked. I clutched my nose and backed against the wall. So many at once that an older me would have gone a little mad, but now they slapped my mind around, pushing me forward, and back, and all around at once; my nose making me dizzy.

"Tracker?"

I can walk in a land of a hundred smells I do not know. I can walk into a place with many smells I know if I know this is the place where they will be, and decide what scent my mind will follow. But six or even four ambushing me unawares and I go almost mad. So many years have gone since this has happened to me. I remembered the boy who trained me to cluster on one, the boy I had to kill. There, all of them came at me, all I remember, not all I remember being in Kongor.

"You smell the boy," Mossi said, grabbing my arm.

"I'm not going to fall."

"But you smell the boy."

"More than this boy."

"Is that good or not so?"

"Only the gods know. This nose is a curse, it is no blessing. Much afoot in this city, more than when I was last here."

"Speak plain, Tracker."

"Fuck the gods, do I sound mad?"

"Peace. Peace."

"That's what that fucking cat used to say."

He grabbed me and pulled me into his face.

"Your temper is making it worse," he said.

The Ogo and buffalo had walked on, not noticing we had stopped. He touched my cheek and I flinched.

"No one sees us," he said. "Besides, it gives you something else to worry about." He smiled.

"I think someone tracks us. How far are the Nyembe streets?" I asked.

"Not far, north and west of here. But there's no masking these two," he said, pointing at the buffalo and the Ogo.

"We should stay along the coast. Do we go to the boy?" Mossi asked.

"It's only three of them now, and the Ipundulu is wounded. No witch-mother to quicken his healing."

"You say wait?"

"No."

"Then what are you saying?"

"Mossi."

"Tracker."

"Quiet. I say while we hunt people, people hunt us. The Aesi might still be in Kongor. And I have this feeling he watches us, just waiting for us to fall into his lap. And others, others who track us."

"My sword is ready when they find us."

"No. We shall find them."

Dusk came before we snuck through deserted alleys to get west. We passed a lane narrow enough for only one to pass through that Mossi dashed in and came back with blood on his sword. He did not say, I did not ask. We continued north and east, lane to lane, until we reached the Nyembe quarter and that snake street that led to the old lord's house.

"Last I was on this street it was infested with Seven Wings," I said.

He pointed to the flag of the black sparrow hawk, still flying from that tower three hundred paces away. "That still flies, though. And the Fasisi King's mark is everywhere."

We came to the doorway, suspiciously open.

"There's a mark right here on this wall that I know," I said.

"I thought you would give word about the piss first."

Mossi jumped, but I did not move, though I wished I had an ax. He came from somewhere deep in this house, running down the narrow hallway leading outside, and leapt straight at me, knocking me down flat on the ground. The buffalo snorted, the Ogo ran to my side, and Mossi drew his two swords.

"No," I said. "He's a—"

The Leopard licked my forehead. He rubbed his head against my right cheek, dipped under my chin, and rubbed against the left. He rubbed his nose against my nose and rested his forehead on mine. He hummed and purred as I sat up. Then he shifted shape.

"Picked that up from lions, you poor excuse of a leopard," I said.

"Shall we go into the foul things you've picked up, wolf? Because foul they are. Soon I shall hear that you kiss with tongue."

The snort came from me, not the buffalo.

"You, with your eye of a dog, me with my eyes of a cat. We are quite the pair, are we not, Tracker?"

Leopard jumped to his feet and pulled me up. Mossi still had both swords drawn, but the Ogo went right up to the Leopard and picked him up.

"I like you more than most cats," he said.

"How many cats do you know, Sadogo?"

"Only one."

Leopard touched his face.

"Ay, buffalo, even now you have been no man's meal?"

The buffalo stomped in the dirt and the Leopard laughed. Sadogo put him down.

"Who is this, with swords drawn? A foe?"

"To tell true, Leopard, I half thought to draw my knife as well."

"Why?"

"Why? Leop . . . Is that boy with you?"

"Of course he is. . . . Oh, wait. Yes, yes, yes. I would have drawn a knife on me too, this is a true thing. There is a story I must tell you. An ass is fucked, so you shall love it. And how many you must have to tell me? First who is this good man who still won't withdraw his sword?"

"Mossi. He used to be chieftain army."

"I am Mossi."

"So he just said. I've been through a few chieftains, not so chieflike, they were. How do you come to be with these . . . what do I call you, call us?"

"The story is long. But now I also search for the boy. With him," Mossi said.

"So you told him about the boy," Leopard said, looking at me.

"He knows everything."

"Not everything," Mossi said.

"Fuck the gods, prefect."

Leopard looked at him, then me, and broke into a wicked grin. A thousand fucks for him doing that.

"Where is Sogolon?"

"This is a very long story. Longer than yours. I will have words with the lord of this house. He has a man who looks just like him in Dolingo."

"What took you to Dolingo? Alas, the only thing to meet us when we came were spiders, empty it was. Every room, every window, not even a plant left. Go in, good Ogo and prefect, whatever your name is."

"Mossi."

"Yes, that was it. Buffalo, our vegetables inside are better than anything on this foul ground. Go around the back and let them give you through the window."

That was the first in a long time I heard the buffalo make that sound that I still swear was a laugh.

"Mossi, you look like a swordsman," Leopard said.

"Yes, and what of it?"

"Nothing, but I have two swords that are no use to a beast on four legs. Fine blades made in the South. Belonged to a man whose neck I chopped off."

"Do you or this one ever leave a man whole?"

The Leopard looked at me, then at Mossi, and laughed. Then he slapped Mossi hard on the back and pushed him off with a "They are in there." I can't imagine Mossi liked it, not as much as I liked seeing it.

"Tracker, she is here also."

"Who?"

He nodded for me to follow.

"We get the boy tomorrow night," he said.

As we entered, Fumeli, whom I had not seen for so long, ran up to us, but slowed quick when the Leopard snarled.

"I will be asking about that later," I said.

"We shall do as we always do, Tracker. Contest story against story. I believe I will again win."

"You have not heard my story."

He faced me. His whiskers stuck out under his nose, and his hair looked longer, wilder. I missed this man so much that my heart still jumped at the slightest movement from him. At him turning around with a wicked grin. At him scratching his crotch against the robe, hating clothes as much as me.

"It will not match mine, I can promise you," he said.

The Leopard led me up six flights. We approached a room I had not seen before when the smell of the river came to me. Not from outside, but one of the five or six smells I knew but did not welcome. One was in the room, the rest were close but not here.

"I smell the boy," I said, "not far from here. We should go get him now, before they can move again."

"A man of the same mind as me. I said the same thing three times now. But they say too many are they that hunt them, and an entire army hunts me, so we must move at night."

I did not know that voice.

"The Tracker is here. He can tell you what happens when plan is thrown to whim."

That voice I knew. I stepped in and looked for the new voice first. She lay on cushions and rugs, a mug in her hand, strong drink of the Fasisi coffee bean. A hat on her head, wide at the top like a crown, but of red fabric, not gold. A veil, silk maybe, rolled up to reveal her face. Two large disks at her ears, the pattern a circle of red, then white, then red, then white again. Her gown also red, her sleeves baring her shoulders but hiding her arms. A large blue pattern in the front, shaped like two arrowheads pointing at each other. I almost said, I know no nun who ever dressed so, but my mouth had gotten me into enough trouble. Two women servants stood behind her in the same leather dress that Sogolon loved to wear.

"You are the one they call Tracker," the King sister said.

"That is what they call me, Your Excellence."

"I am nothing close to excellent and everything far from perfect for years now. My brother saw to that. And Sogolon is no longer with you. Has she perished?"

"She had what was coming to her," I said.

"She was one for plans, Sogolon. Give us tidings."

"She went through a door she should not have, which probably burned her to death."

"A horrible one from what I know of deaths. Strength through your sorrow, this I wish for you."

"I have no sorrow for her. She sold us as slaves in exchange for safe passage through Dolingo. She also took the body of a girl and gave it to the soul of a man whose body she stole long ago."

"You don't know any of that!" Bunshi said. I wondered when she would speak. She rose from a puddle on the floor to the right of the King sister.

"Who knows, water witch? Perhaps he took revenge by dragging her with him through one of the ten and nine doors. I heard that you cannot return to a door until you have been through all ten and nine. This she proved true, if you were one of those that wonder," I said.

"And you let him."

"It happened so quick, Bunshi. Quicker than one could care."

"I should drown you."

"When did you learn that she changed the plan? Did she not tell you? You a liar or a fool?" I said.

"With your permission," Bunshi said to the King sister, but she shook her head.

"At some point, she decided we were all unfit to save your precious boy. Even as we, the unfit, freed ourselves and saved her from the one called Ipundulu," I said.

"She—"

"Made a mistake that cost her the child? Yes, that would be what she did," I said.

"Sogolon only tried to serve her mistress," Bunshi said to the King sister, but she was already facing me.

"Tracker? What is your real name?" the King sister said.

"Tracker."

"Tracker. I understand you. This child carries no stakes for you."

"I hear he is the future of the kingdom."

She rose.

"What else did you hear?"

"Too much and not nearly enough."

She laughed and said, "Strength, guile, courage, where were men of such quality when we needed them? Where is the woman that you have hurt and abandoned?"

"She hurt herself."

"Then she must be a woman of more power and means than me. Every scar I have, it is somebody else who put it there. Which woman is this?"

"His mother," said the Leopard. I could have killed him in that moment.

"His mother. She and I have much in common."

"You've both abandoned your own children?"

"Maybe we've both had our lives ruined by men only to have our children grow up blaming us for it. Pray forgive that remark; I have also been living in a nunnery across from a whorehouse. Think of it, I, the

King sister, in hiding with old women because he has sent assassins to the same fortress he imprisoned me. Seven Wings, they left to join the King's armies in Fasisi. From there they will invade Luala Luala first, and the Gangatom and the Ku, and force every man, woman, and child into slavery. Not will, has. Luala Luala is already under control. War weapons do not build themselves."

"Respect of the kings to you. But you stand there and try to make ordinary men and women care about the fates of princes and kings, as if what happens to you changes anything that happens to us," I said.

"The Leopard tells me you have children among the Gangatom."

"Don't think I have been in any koo long enough to seed a child," I said.

"Is this the mouth you warned me of?" she said, looking at both Bunshi and the Leopard. The Leopard nodded. She sat back down on a stool.

"How lovely a family you must have had, so that the loss of a son means nothing to you."

"Not my—"

"Tracker," Leopard said, shaking his head.

"The view is different when you are the child lost, Your Excellence. Then all you think of is the disappointment that is parents," I said.

She laughed.

"Do I look calm to you, Tracker? Do you think here is one possessed with Itutu? How is the King sister so calm when monsters and men have taken her son? Maybe it is only the latest violation. Maybe I am tired. Maybe I take a bath every night so that I scream underwater and wash away tears. Or maybe a thousand fucks for you, thinking any of this is your business. Word has already reached several of the elders that not only do I have a child, but a child of a legal union with a prince. They know I will go to Fasisi and I will bring my claim of succession to the elders, the court, the ancestors, and the gods. My brother even thinks he has killed all the southern griots, but I have four. Four with account of the true history, four whose account will not be questioned by any man."

"Why do all this to put another man on the throne? A boy."

"A boy trained by his mother. Not by men who can only raise a boy to become another just like him. My brother's army marched north to the river lands two days ago. Do you not have blood there?"

"No."

"Gangatom is just across the river. And what he will do with the children too young to be slaves? You ever heard word of the white scientists?"

It took everything in me to answer quickly, and I still spoke too late.

"No."

"Thank your gods that you never cross them," she said, but she looked at me with one raised eyebrow, and slowed her words.

"White because even their skin rebel against their evil, for there is only so much vileness that your own skin can agree to. White like only the purest evil. The children, they take and bind to beasts, and devils. Two attacked me myself, one had wings of a bat as big as that flag. When my men killed it with arrows, it was just a boy, and the wings were part of his skin and bones now, even blood ran through it. And they do other things, turning three girls into one girl, sewing tongue to tongue to the boy so that he hunts like a crocodile and giving him bird eyes. You know why they take them young? Think, Tracker. Turn a man into a killer and he can turn back, or he can kill you. Raise a little one to be a killer and killing is all he does. He lives for blood, with no remorse. They take the children and turn them like they are plants, with every wicked art of the white science, worse if the children already come with gifts. Now they work for my brother and the bitch of Dolingo."

"Sogolon said you were allies. Sisters together."

"I was never sisters with that woman. Sogolon is who she knows. Knew."

"Then I go to Gangatom."

"You know some, don't you? Children with gifts."

"I go to Gangatom," I said again.

"What? Nobody here told me you came with your own army. Your own mercenaries, maybe? Maybe two spies? A witchman to mask your approach? How shall you save them? And why would you care what happens to any child? The Leopard tells me they are even mingi. Tell me true. Is one blue with no skin, one with legs like an ostrich, and still one with no legs at all? Many men who march believe in the old ways. They will be in a white science house if not killed first. Worthless and useless."

"They are worth more than a useless shit of a king on a useless shithole of a throne. And I will kill whoever takes them."

"But you are not with them, and you do not have them. How does such fathering work? Yet you think you can judge me."

I had nothing to say to her. She came over to me, but walked to the window.

"Sogolon burned to her death, you say?"

"Yes. She was haunted by many spirits."

"She was. Some of them her own children. Dead children. I grow tired of dead children, Tracker, children who do not need to die. You talk of stakes. I do not know how to give you any. But right now, two have my child, because of a mistake this one made that Sogolon went desperate trying to redeem. I don't need a man on a mission and I don't need a man who believes in kings or gods any more than I need a man who thinks he will shit a gold nugget. I just want someone who when he says, I will bring you your son, brings him to me."

"I am still doing this for coin."

"I expect no less."

"Why did you not tell us from the beginning? The truth."

"What is truth?"

"That is your answer? I would have cared more had your river demon told us everything."

"You needed more than what you heard to care?"

"What I heard and what I saw were two different things."

"I thought it was your nose you trusted. You and your company look like you still have wounds to tend to."

"Me and my company are fine."

"Nevertheless. Go get my boy tomorrow night."

I have something for you," the Leopard said.

I took one of the rooms on the top floor, but facing the snake street. Rugs on the floor, spilled civet musk, and a head plate for sleeping, which I had not seen since my father's house. Grandfather's. He threw one of the axes at me and I caught it in the spin. He nodded, impressed. The second was in a harness, which I put over my shoulder.

"I brought something else," he said, and gave me a jar that smelled like tree gum.

"Black ochre in shea butter, perfect for you. You can blend in dark and shadow without wearing all those rags that makes your nipples and asshole itch. Walk with me."

Outside, we walked down to the river and along the bank.

"Things have changed between you and this Fumeli," I said.

"Yes?"

"Or maybe me. You snap at him more but I care less."

He turned to face me, walking backward again.

"Tracker, you must tell me. How evil was I?"

"Like a mangy dog robbed of his last meal. You were odd, Leopard, one day the man of mirth that made me laugh like no other. The next you're not just wishing me harm, you bit me in the neck."

"That is impossible, Tracker. Even at my worst I could never—"

"Look at my scar," I said, and pointed. "Those were your teeth. Your malcontent was fierce."

"Fine, fine. Dear Tracker, now I have such sorrow. I was not myself."

"Then who were you?"

"I promised you a tale strange. Fumeli, how I laugh when I think about it. But this, this boy, fuck the gods. Hear me now."

We kept walking along the shore, both of us wearing hoods, and the clothing of those devoted to the gods. The old lord's clothes.

"Fumeli, he thought that he should have me and no one else shall. Especially you, Tracker. Somehow you as friend frightened him more than any other man as lover. But he was frightened by that as well. So he put me under strange enchantment. Something that would make me think myself his all the time. Babacoop."

"Devil's whisper? Potion's so foul no wine can mask it. No beer either. How did he get it past your mouth, Leopard?"

"He did not get it past my mouth."

"Even as vapor, it burns the nose."

"Not my nose either. Tracker, how do I tell you this? Fumeli, he would dip his finger in devil's whisper, and then he would . . . after that, before the time glass is even flipped he could tell me to do anything and I would do it, tell me to believe anything and I would believe it, tell me to hate anything, and I would hate it. It would be several days, I will remember nothing and whenever we fucked again he would stick more devil's whisper up my hole."

"When did you discover his ways?"

"He added another finger."

I burst out laughing.

"I grabbed him. I saw his hands and said what is this? I tell you true, Tracker, I beat him to near death until he told me, and then I beat him to near death again when he told me."

I laughed so hard I fell to the sand in a fit. And I could not stop. I would look at his face and laugh, look at his leg and laugh, look at him scratch his ass and laugh. Laugh until I heard my laugh come back to me from the river. He laughed as well, but not as loud. He even said, "Come now, Tracker, surely this could not be so funny."

"Yes it is, Leopard, yes it is," I said, and started

laughing again. I laughed until I hiccupped. "You know what they say, **Hunum hagu ba bakon tsuliya bane.**"

"I don't know that tongue."

"The left hand is not a new thing to the anus."

I collapsed in laughter again.

"Hold. Why is he still with you?" I asked.

"A Leopard still cannot carry his own bow, Tracker. And here is truth, he is far better with it than I ever was, and I was very good. Soon as I remembered myself, I whipped his buttocks until he told me where you were all heading to. So we rode back to Kongor, where I have been waiting in this house. Bunshi found us when we crossed into Nimbe and took us here. I might have left had you not come, though."

"Your poisoned asshole could give me laughs for a whole moon."

"Laugh. Spare me not. Now all that stops me from killing him is who will carry my bow? Tracker, there is more that I must show you, though you might not want to see it."

We left the shore and went down an alley that I did not know. Still not many people on the street, even though noon had long passed.

"I still have questions about your Queen," I said.

"My Queen? Bunshi smuggled her into town in an oil urn. And don't think that just because she is here in secret she is not giving orders. I thought that water witch answered to no one."

I stopped. "I have missed you, Leopard."

He took my hand at the wrist. "Much has happened to you," he said.

"Much."

"Did you search for the boy?" he asked.

"Not with Fumeli having me do his bidding I did not. He couldn't care less for the boy. We were living on the top floor of an abandoned house right in Kongor when I discovered his poison. He was always ready to stick me as soon as I got confused. It went like this, me saying, By the gods, where are we? He says, Don't you remember? Fuck me some more."

"Let that be a lesson to all guided by their cocks."

"Or the other man's finger."

We laughed loud enough for people to look at us.

"And the King sister?"

"What of her?"

"She told me you were on your way back to Kongor and not with good news. But the boy was here. This was only a few days ago, Tracker."

This I take you to, you will not like. But we must go before we get the boy."

I gave him a nod that said, I trust you. Also this, when scents come together, even those I know, I lose track of who gives what, worse when the smells are so far apart. But down this narrow street, past houses not joined together, until we came to one facing the end of the road, one smell rose above all others.

Khat.

I reached for my ax but the Leopard touched my arm and shook his head. He knocked on the door three times. Five locks someone unlocked. The door opened slow, as if the wood was suspicious. We went inside before I saw her. Nsaka Ne Vampi. She nodded when she saw me. I stood there, waiting for her smart mouth, but she had nothing on her face but weariness. Her hair matted and dirty, the long black dress streaked with dirt and ash, her lips dry and chapped. Nsaka Ne Vampi looked like she had not eaten and did not care. She started walking down a corridor and we followed.

"We go this night?" she asked.

"One night hence," the Leopard said.

She opened the door and blue light flashed upon the wall and my face. Lightning first, crackling through his fingers up to his brain, and down to his legs, toes, and the tip of his penis. All around him the bones of dogs and rats, gourds of food untouched and rotting, blood, and shit. And on him skin flaking off still, which had become his mark.

Nyka.

Rags lay in a pile to one corner. He saw Nsaka Ne Vampi and spat. Nyka leapt to his feet and dashed at her, the chain at his feet clanging until he ran as far as it would go. It stopped him, just a finger's reach away from her.

"I can smell your bitch koo from here," he said.

"Eat your food. The rats know you going to eat them and won't come out anymore."

"You know what I going to eat? I going to chew around my own ankle, rip off the skin, rip out the flesh, rip out the bone, until this shackle falls off, and then I going come for you, and cut you deep in your chest, so that he will smell you and come for me, and I will say, Master, look what I prepared for you. And here is what he will do. He will drink from you, and I will watch. Then I will drink from him."

"You have claws like him? Teeth? All you have is dirty fingernails to shame your mother," she said.

"Fingernails going to claw into your pox face and dig out your witch eyes. And then I . . . I . . . please, please unshackle me. It cuts and it itches, please, by all that is of the gods, please. Please, sweetness. I am nothing, I have nothing . . . I yes, yes, yes yes yes yes yesyesyes!"

He turned to the wall behind him and ran straight into the corner. I heard his head hit the wall. He fell back on the ground. Nsaka Ne Vampi looked away. Was she crying, I wanted to know. Lightning coursed through him again and he trembled, in a fit. We watched until it passed, and he stopped banging his head on the floor. He stopped panting and breathed slow. Only then, still lying on the floor, did he look at the Leopard and me.

"I know you. I have kissed your face," he said.

I said nothing. I wondered why Leopard brought me here. If this came from his head or hers. That to see him there, hate left me. That is not full truth. Hate there was, but the hate before was of him and for him, like love. This hate was at a pathetic, wretched thing that I still wanted to kill, the way you come across a near-dead animal eating shit, or a raper of women beaten near to death. He was still looking at me, looking for something in my face. I stepped to him, and Nsaka Ne Vampi drew a knife. I stopped.

"Do you not hear? Do you not hear him calling? His sweet voice, so much pain he is in. So much pain. Agony. Oh he suffers so," Nyka said.

Nsaka Ne Vampi looked at the Leopard and said, "He has been saying that for nights."

"The vampire is wounded," I said.

"Tracker?" Leopard said.

"I threw flame on him and he caught fire. Burst into flames, Nyka."

"You tried to kill him, yes you did, but my lord, he will not die. No one shall kill him, you shall see, and he will kill you, all of you, even you, woman, you shall all see it. He will—"

Lightning crackled through him again.

"Khat is the only thing that calms him," she said.

"You should kill him," I said, and walked out.

"I remember your lips!" he shouted as I walked out.

I almost got to the door when a hand grabbed my wrist and pulled me back. Nsaka Ne Vampi, with the Leopard coming up behind her.

"Nobody is killing him," she said.

"He is already dead."

"No. No. What you are doing is lying. You lie because there is great hate between you."

"There is no hatred between us. There is only the hatred I had for him. But now I don't even have hate, I have sadness."

"He can't put pity to use."

"Not for him, I have disgust for him. I have pity for me. Now that he is dead I cannot kill him."

"He is not dead!"

"He is dead in every way that dead is dead. The lightning in him is all that stops him from stinking."

"You think you can tell me how he is."

"Of course. There was a woman. The one you all followed in your glorious chariot? Give us tidings, woman. Did she lead you all into a trap? Here is a weird thing. From what I hear Ipundulu turns mostly children and women, so why did he change Nyka instead of killing him?"

"He has turned soldiers and sentries," she said.

"And Nyka is neither."

Nsaka Ne Vampi sat down by the door. It irritated me that she thought I would stay and hear her story.

"Yes, how easy it looked. How we rode, how proud we were when we left behind you and the fools with you. Such fools, especially that old woman. Going to Kongor, why? Why when his lightning slave runs north? I was glad when we left, glad to get him away from you."

"Is that what he is? A lightning slave? Why did you take me here, Leopard?"

Leopard looked at me, blank, saying nothing.

"Here is truth," I said. "Years I have thought about

this. Years. His ruin. I hated him so much that I would kill the man who ruined him before me. Now I have nothing."

"He said you led him to a pack of hyenas, but he escaped."

"He said much, this Nyka. What did he say of my eye? That I plucked it from a dead dog, and shoved it in my face? Poor Nyka, he could have been a griot, but would cheat history."

"You hate him so."

"Hate? This is what I did when I could not find him. I hunted down his sister and his mother. I would kill them both. Found both of them. Do you hear me, Nyka, I found them. Even had words with the mother. I should have killed them, but I did not, do you know why? Not because the mother told me all the ways she failed him."

"I will have him back," Nsaka Ne Vampi said.

"Ipundulu's witch is dead. There is no back."

"What if we kill him, the Ipundulu? You said he was injured and weak. If we kill him, Nyka will come back to me."

"Nobody has ever killed an Ipundulu, so how in a thousand fucks would any soul know?"

"What if we killed him?"

"What if I don't care? What if I lose no sleep over your man dead? What if I feel deep sorrow, such deep sorrow for not killing him myself? What if I didn't give a thousand fucks for your 'we'?"

"Tracker."

"No, Leopard."

"This is a tickle for you. This gives you joy."

"What gives me joy?"

"Seeing him so low."

"You would think so, would you not? I despise him and even a deaf god hears I have no love for you. But no, this does not tickle me. As I said, it disgusts me. He is not even worth my ax."

"I will have him back."

"Then get him back, so I can kill an actual man, instead of what you have in there."

"Tracker, she comes with us. She will go for the lightning bird, while we get the child," the Leopard said.

"You know who he is, Leopard. The other one who travels with the boy. We killed his brother. You and I. Remember the flesh eater in the bush, the forest of enchantment when we stayed with the Sangoma, do you yet remember? The one who strung me in that tree with all those bodies? We were but boys then."

"Bosam."

"Asanbosam."

"I remember. The stench of that thing. Of that place. We never found his brother."

"We never looked."

"I'll bet he dies from the arrow, just like his brother."

"Four of us and we couldn't kill him."

"Maybe you four—"

"Don't assume what you don't know, cat."

"Listen to both of you. Talking like I vanished from

the room," Nsaka Ne Vampi said. "I will join you to get the boy and I will kill this Ipundulu. And I will have my Nyka back. Whatever he is to you, he is not to me and that is all I have to say."

"How many times has he broken your heart? Four? Six?"

"I am sorry for all he is to you. But he is none of those things to me."

"So you've said. But those things he is to you, he was to me once as well."

She looked at me as I looked at her. Us understanding each other.

"If you still want him after all this, if you want us, we will be waiting," she said.

Then we heard the thump of Nyka running into the wall again and Nsaka Ne Vampi sighed.

"Wait outside for me," I said to the Leopard. She shut her eyes and sighed when he bumped into the wall again. I wondered how would she fight with Nyka making her tired.

"He also made me love him once, this is what he does," I said. "Nobody works harder at getting you to love him, and nobody works harder to fail you once you do."

"I am my own woman and feel for myself," she said.

"Nobody needs Nyka. Not what he is."

"He is this because of me."

"Then his debt is paid."

"You said he betrayed you. He was the first man to not betray me."

"How do you know?"

"Because he's still alive, unlike all the other men who betrayed me. One used to farm me out as his slave every night for men to do as they wished. I was ten and four. When he and his sons weren't raping me himself. They sold me to Nyka one night. He put a knife in my hand and put the hand to his throat, and said do as you wish this night. I thought he was speaking a foreign tongue. So I went to the master's room and slit his throat, then I went to his sons' room and killed them all. What a terrible thing to lose a father and all your stepbrothers, the town people said. He let the town think he murdered them and fled in the night."

"Sogolon had a story like yours."

"What do you think makes the sisters of Mantha, sisters?"

"You were—"

"Yes."

"You're not showing him love. You're repaying a debt."

"I find girls who are about to become me, and save them from the men doing the coming. Then I take them to Mantha. They are who I owe. Nyka I always said I owed him nothing."

———

Why did you not kill her?" Leopard asked outside.

"Who?"

"Nyka's mother. Why didn't you?"

"Instead of killing her, I would tell her of his death. Slowly. In every detail, right down to how it sounds to hack off his neck in three chops."

"Leave, both of you," she said.

Walking back to the lord's house, Leopard said, "Your eyes still don't know when your lips lie."

"What?"

"Just now. All that show about Nyka's mother. That's not why you didn't kill her."

"Really, Leopard, tell me."

"She was a mother."

"And!"

"You still wish for the like."

"I had the like."

"No, you didn't."

"Now you speak for me?"

"You are the one who just said 'had.'"

"Why did you take me there?"

"Nsaka Ne Vampi asked the King sister. Tracker, I think she was hoping for your pity."

"She didn't ask for it."

"Did you think she would?"

"She wants the fruit to stay on the branch and be in her mouth at the same time."

"Forgiveness, Tracker."

"I don't care. I don't care about Nsaka Ne Vampi, or this queen, and no matter how many moons pass, I still don't care for this boy."

"Fuck the gods, Tracker, of what **do** you care?"

"When do we leave for Gangatom?"

"We will."

"Our children are as bound to you as to me. How can you let them sit there?"

"Our children? Oh, so now you think you can judge me. Before the King sister told you about white scientists, when last you saw them? Said a word? Even thought of them?"

"I think of them more than you know."

"You said nothing like this last time we spoke. Anyway, what good is your thinking? Your thinking brings no child close."

"So what now?"

We turned down the same road as before, walked the streets. Two men looking like guards passed by on horseback. We jumped into a doorway. The old woman in the doorway looked at me and frowned, as if I was exactly who she was expecting. The Leopard looked his least Leopard, even the whiskers were gone. He nodded for us to go.

"Tomorrow night, we get this boy once and for all. The day after, we go to the river lands and get our children. The day after that, who in all the fucking gods knows?" Leopard said.

"I have seen these white scientists, Leopard. I have seen how they work. They do not care about the pain of others. It's not even a wickedness; they are just blind to it. They just glut on the conceit of their wicked craft. Not what it means, only how new it will look. I have seen them in Dolingo."

"The King sister still has men, she still has people who believe in her cause. Let her help us."

I stopped. "We forget someone. The Aesi. His men must have followed us to Kongor. The doors, he knows of them even if he doesn't use them."

"Of course, the door. I have no memory."

"Doors. Ten and nine doors and the bloodsuckers have been using them for years. That is why the boy's smell can be in front of me one blink, half a year away the next."

"Did he follow you through this door, the Aesi?"

"I just said no."

"Why?"

"I don't know."

"Then the son of a hyena bitch either hunts you in Mitu or Dolingo, or maybe the poor fool and his troops got what he was looking for by whatever the gods shat out in the Mweru. Nobody from the King is in Kongor, Tracker—no royal caravan, no battalion. The town crier announced the King's leaving the day we came."

"You forgave the boy?" I asked.

"Weather changed quick on this conversation."

"You wish I go back to white scientists cutting up and sewing our children?"

"No."

"So is Fumeli not with us?"

"Would he dare go someplace else?" He laughed.

"We should have chosen a different road," I said.

"You're as suspicious as Bunshi."

"I am nothing like Bunshi."

"Let us not talk of her. I want to know what happened in Dolingo. And of this prefect who has your eyes bewitched."

"You want to know if I have relations with this prefect."

"**'Relations'?** Mark you and your words. The man has knocked all coarseness out of you. A most magnificent fuck—or is he more?"

"This is talk you enjoy, Leopard, not me."

"Fuck the gods, Tracker. **'This is talk you enjoy.'** You enjoyed it much when it was I talking about men's journeys to and from my ass. I have told you everything and you have told me nothing. This prefect, I better watch him. He's taken up some space in you. You didn't even see it until I said so."

"Stop talking about this, or I shall leave."

"Now all we need is a woman for the Ogo who will not burst from just looking at his—"

"Leopard, watch me as I walk away."

"Did this not make you think less of the children? Talk true."

"Leaving I am."

"Have no guilt, Tracker."

"Now you accuse me."

"No, I confess. I feel it too. Remember, they were

my children before they ever smelled you coming. I was saving them from the bush from before you even knew you were Ku. I want to show you one more thing."

"Fuck all the living and dead gods, what?"

"The boy."

The Leopard took me down to near the end of the Gallunkobe/Matyube quarter, where the houses and inns thinned to a few. Past the slave shacks and the freemen quarters, to where the people worked as artisans of a different nature. Nobody came down this part of the street unless sending something to a grave of secrets or buying something that could only be bought in the Malangika. I smell necromancy on this street, I told him. We took a street that had sunk underwater halfway. These were the large houses of noblemen before flooding sent them north to the Tarobe quarter. Most of the houses had long been looted, or collapsed into soggy mud. But one house still stood, a third of it under the water, the turrets on the roof broken off, the windows gouged out and black, the side wall caving in, and the trees all around it dead. The front had no door, as if begging to be raided, until Leopard said that was exactly how they wanted it. Any beggar foolish enough to seek shelter because of an open doorway would never be heard from again. We stood behind some dead trees a hundred paces away. In one of the dark windows blue light flashed for a blink. "This is what we will do," said the Leopard.

"But first, tell me of Dolingo."

The next night came quick, but wind on the river rippled slow. I wondered what was this black skin butter the Leopard gave me that did not wash off in the water. No moon, and no fire, light in homes hundreds of paces away. Behind me the wide river; in front, the house. I slipped under the water, feeling myself in the dark. My hand ran into the back wall, soaked enough that I could scoop chunks of mud out. I felt down until my hands went through what the water ate away, a hole as wide as my span. Only the gods knew why this building still stood. The water was colder, smellier, more thick with rotten things that I was glad I could not see, but I held my hands out, since it was far better for my hands to touch something wretched than my face. On the inside I stopped paddling and rose slow to the surface, first just my forehead and then just the ridge of my nose. Planks of woods floated past me, and other things that I could tell by smell that made me shut my lips tighter. It came straight for me, almost hitting the side of my face before I saw that it was the body of a boy, everything below the waist missing. I shifted out of the way and something below scraped across my right thigh. I clamped so hard on my teeth I nearly bit my tongue. The house kept silence thick. Above me, the roof that I knew was there but couldn't see was thatch. The stairs to my right led to the floor above, but made as it was from mud and clay, steps had washed away. Above, blue light flickered. The Ipundulu. Blue lit up the three windows almost halfway from the roof, two small, one large enough to fit through. I could stand now on solid floor, but I crouched, not rising above my neck. Bobbing by the wall, not far from me, were the legs and buttocks of a man, and nothing else. The bodies in the tree came back to me, the stink and rot of them. Sasabonsam was not finished feeding on them, floating in the water in front of me. He was supposed to be the blood drinker, not the flesh eater. I retched and clapped my mouth. The Leopard was outside, climbing down from the roof, where he would enter through the middle window. I listened for him but he truly was a cat.

Somebody whimpered by the doorway. I dipped back down in the water. She whimpered again and waded into the water, carrying a torch that lit the water and the walls but threw too much shadow. The water not as high in the doorway as it was in the rest of the room, which slanted as if about to slide into the river. This was a merchant's house I guessed, and this room a dining hall perhaps, wider than any room I have ever lived in. The Sasabonsam ran across my nose, also the Ipundulu, but the boy's smell vanished. Wings flapped once above me, up in the ceiling. Ipundulu lit the room again, and I saw Sasabonsam, his wide wings slowing his jump down, his legs stretched out to grab the woman, which would probably kill her if his claws dug deep. He flapped his wings again, and the woman turned to the door, looking as if she heard the sound but thinking maybe it came from outside. She raised the torch, but did not look up. I saw him as he flapped again, lowering himself clumsily, thinking he moved with stealth.

He flapped down, his back to the window as the Leopard locked his ankles around one of the turrets sticking out of the wall and swung upside down until he and his bow and arrow were in the window frame. He fired the first and drew the second, and fired the second and drew the third, and fired the third, all **zup zup zup** in Sasabonsam's back. He squawked like a crow, flapped, crashed into the wall, then fell into the water. He jumped up as I jumped up and I hurled one of my axes into his back. He flipped around, not wounded, not pained, just annoyed. The woman, Nsaka Ne Vampi, held the torch close to her mouth and blew a storm of flame that jumped on his hair. Sasabonsam squawked and screamed and swung both his wings open, the right knocking out part of the steps, the left cracking the wall. Leopard jumped through the window with his bow firing into the water, and I almost shouted that I'm down here. He landed on his toes at the top of the steps, and jumped right off, right into the swat of Sasabonsam's wing, which sent him into a pile that sounded like dead branches breaking. I swam to the stairs, and jumped up on a step that crumbled under me. I jumped up again as Nsaka swam towards me. Sasabonsam, trying to pull arrows out of his back, grabbed her by the hair and pulled her across the water. Nsaka Ne Vampi, daggers in both hands, stabbed him in the right thigh, but he caught her left hand and pulled it back, determined to break it off. She screamed. I pulled my second ax to jump over the stairs at him when Sadogo ran in and punched Sasabonsam straight in the temple. He fell back, letting go of Nsaka Ne Vampi. Sasabonsam howled, but ducked Sadogo's second punch. His brother was the cunning one; he was the fighter. He tried to swing his huge wing around to swat Sadogo, but Sadogo punched a hole through it and tore his hand free. Sasabonsam screamed. He seemed to fall back, but jumped up and kicked Sadogo right in the chest with both feet. Sadogo went barreling, stumbling and falling in the water. Sasabonsam leapt after him. Mossi jumped in, from where I do not know, bracing a spear in the water and setting it slant for Sasabonsam to land on it, the spear going right through his side. Sadogo jumped back up and began punching into the water.

"The boy!" Mossi said.

He waded over to the steps and I pulled him up. Nsaka Ne Vampi walked past me, but I knew she wasn't trying to save the boy. Mossi drew his two swords and followed me. At the top of the stairs were two rooms. Nsaka Ne Vampi stood in the entry to one of the rooms, feeling the knives in her hands, until blue light flashed from the right. I got to the door first. Ipundulu was on the floor, charred, black, half-changed into a man but all along his arms stalks jutted out, all that was left of his wings. He jumped when he saw me, opened his arms, and there was the boy lying on his chest. He pushed the boy off hard and he stumbled away, cowering in a corner. Both Nsaka Ne Vampi and Mossi stepped past me. They looked at him, Nsaka already screaming that she will kill him for infecting Nyka with his demon sickness. Mossi held out both swords, but also looked behind us, hearing Sadogo still fighting Sasabonsam with the King sister's men, who must have been down there by now. I looked at the boy. I would have sworn to any god that before Ipundulu pushed him away, the boy was sucking the lightning bird's nipple, drinking from it like he was suckling a mother. Maybe a boy torn too early from his mother still yearned for the breast, or maybe this Ipundulu was doing indecent acts with the boy, or maybe my eyes worked lies in the dark.

The Ipundulu, he lay there on the floor, sputtering from his mouth, blabbering, and groaning and trembling as if fever made him shake. Watching him, and watching Mossi and Nsaka Ne Vampi close in on him, I felt something. Not pity, but something. Outside, Sasabonsam screeched, and all of us turned around. The Ipundulu jumped and ran for the window. He limped, but was still much stronger than I thought from all the trembling and sputtering. Before Mossi turned to chase him Nsaka Ne Vampi's first dagger burst right through the back of his neck. Ipundulu fell to his knees but not flat on the ground. Mossi ran up, swung his sword, and chopped his head off.

In the corner, the boy cried. I walked over, thinking of what to say to him, something warm, like Young one, it is over, your torment, or Behold, we take you to your mother, or Come now, you are so young but I will give you dolo so that you sleep and will awake in your own bed for the first time in your still short life. But I said nothing. He cried, gentle sobs, and stared at the rugs Ipundulu had slept on. Here is what I saw. From his mouth came a child's sorrow, a cry that turned into a cough and back into a cry. From his eyes, nothing. From his cheeks and his brow, nothing. Even his mouth barely moved more than a mumble. He looked at me with the same hollow face. Nsaka Ne Vampi grabbed him under his arms, and scooped him up. She held him over her shoulder and walked out.

Mossi came over and asked if I was well, but I didn't answer him. I did nothing until he grabbed my shoulder and said, We go.

Sadogo and Sasabonsam still struggled. I ran down the steps, shouted to the Leopard, and threw him my ax. Sasabonsam looked straight up at me.

"I know the smell," he said.

Leopard grabbed Sadogo's belt, pulled himself up on his back, flipped over on his shoulder, and leapt after the beast's head. Sasabonsam turned to me when Leopard jumped straight for his head, swung the ax, and slashed across his cheek, slicing into the face, cutting right across, as blood and spit splashed into the air. Sasabonsam yelled and clutched his face. Sadogo kicked him down in the water, grabbed his left foot before he could resist, swung, and flung him against the wall. Sasabonsam burst through it and fell outside. Before he fell into the water, two arrows, shot from Fumeli, hit him in the leg. His good wing swept up water, a huge torrent that knocked Fumeli down. Sasabonsam turned to lift himself and turned right into the buffalo, who hooked him with his horns and flung him a hundred paces into the river. He stayed under, as if drowned, or a strong current dragged him away. But then Sasabonsam leapt from the water, flapped his wings, bawling at the damaged one, and lifted himself out of the river. He flapped again and again, yelling each time, and finally flew away, dropping once, falling into the river once, flying low, but still flying away. We left this place quietly, with care, though it did not fall. The boy's scent vanished again, but I looked over at Nsaka Ne Vampi's shoulder and there he was.

Back at the house, climbing the stairs all the way up to the sixth floor, with Nsaka Ne Vampi and the child and Mossi ahead of me, the Leopard asked me a question about Sogolon.

"I have no good words for her," I said. But before I entered the room, somebody said, "Save those good words for me."

In the center of the sixth floor the King sister, struggling to get up, as if someone kept kicking her down. Bunshi, her eyes shut tight, a dagger, green and almost glowing, stroking her neck and another arm across her chest, pulling her against him.

The Aesi.

TWENTY-ONE

Some truth now, I hope you take it. When you crossed the Mawana witches, I would have gambled on your death. But look. You live. In one way or another," the Aesi said.

Outside a black flurry turned into birds. One hundred, two hundred, three hundred and one. Birds looking like pigeons, looking like vultures, looking like crows landing on the windowsill and peeking through the window. Black wings flew past the window as well, and I could hear them landing on the roof, the turrets, the ledges, and the ground. Outside marching feet moved closer, but no soldier or mercenary was supposed to be in the city. The King sister sat up, but would not look at me.

"Did you know they came before the world? Even the gods came and saw them and even the gods didn't dare. All children come from the mother's will, not from mating with a father. When the world was just a gourd, the witches six were one, and she circled the world until her mouth reached her tail."

"A spy I knew called you a god, once," I said.

"I shall bless him, though I am not much of a god."

"He was not much of a spy."

Bunshi would not change to water and slip out of his hands. She could not change in the hands of Sadogo either, but there was no scent of enchantment about him. He was behind me, Sadogo, his metal knuckles clenching tight, iron grating on iron, itching for another fight. Mossi tried to draw his swords but the Aesi pressed the knife closer to Bunshi's neck.

"You overestimate her value to us," I said.

"Perhaps. But mine is not the estimation she fears. So if you will not beg me for her life, I will let her beg you."

The boy, his head on Nsaka Ne Vampi's shoulder, looked like he was asleep, but when she turned around, his eyes were open, and staring.

"Popele," Aesi said, whispering to Bunshi in the way of people who want to be overheard. "Your life for the child. I think you are the one who should beg for it. For these brave men and women plus one fool are war-eager and will not listen to me. Popele, you of a thousand years and more, shall we let them see that you too can die? Their ears go deaf at my voice, goddess, and this dagger is so hungry."

Aesi looked at me.

"Such was a time when I could have used a tracker.

Many a time, many a place. Especially one so good at killing."

"I am not a killer."

"Yet your road from Malakal to Dolingo to Kongor is paved with corpses. Who am I, do you know?"

"You tried to kill me in a dream once," I said.

"Are you sure it was me you met in dreams? You still live."

"You are the extra four limbs of the Spider King."

He laughed. "Yes, I have heard that is the way you call your King behind his eye. The King is his own, entire. I have no stake."

"Never met a king who does his own thinking," Mossi said.

"You do not hail from these lands."

"I do not."

"Of course, eastern light. The people who believe in one god, and everything else is either a slave to the god or an evil spirit. Every belief comes in two, which leads to a god two-sided. Vengeful and mad in his ways and takes his fury out on womenfolk. Yours is the silliest of all the gods. No art to his thoughts, no craft to his deeds. I've heard that you think men in the constant visitation of ancestors to be mad."

"Or possessed."

"What a land. Possession you call bad, spirits you call evil, and love? Love, as your heart calls it, makes men force you to leave. I sniff you and get a whiff of Tracker. More than a whiff, indeed a funk. What shall your father think?"

"I go by my own thoughts," Mossi said.

"You must be a king. As for him, this little fly, your little king, the one who drools at this woman's neck, even though he is six years gone in age. Tracker, it has been said you have a nose. Is the shit we smell not his?"

"There is a big piece of black shit in this room, no doubt of that," I said.

"If you're going to tell them who you are, tell them who you are," the King sister said.

She still sat on the floor, still looking weak, as if drained. She finally looked at us.

"This, this Aesi, these four limbs of the Spider King. Tell them about your prophecy. Tell them about how you just appeared in our hearts and minds as someone who was there all along, but no woman or man can remember when you first came," the King sister said.

"I want what is best for the King," Aesi said.

"You want what is best for you. For now that is the same as what the King wants. Meanwhile nobody notices that you the same today as you was twenty years ago, and even before that. Call yourself by your name, necromancer. Man of sorcery and wicked art. You are what you are. You build nothing, disrupt everything, destroy everything. You know what he does? He waits until all are asleep, then he jumps through the air or runs under the ground. He goes to covens in caves and rapes babies offered up by mothers. Breeds children with sister upon sister and brother, but they all die. Eater of human flesh. I saw you, Aesi. I saw you as the wild boar, and the crocodile, and the pigeon, and the vulture, and the crow. Your evil will soon eat itself."

Just out of her reach lay a bag made of rags, tied at the neck with a carving sticking out. A phuungu. A charm, like a nkisi, to protect against witchcraft. She tried to grab it, but her head slammed into the ground and the charm rolled away.

"I want what goes best for the King," the Aesi said.

"You should want what goes best for the kingdom. Not the same thing," I said.

"Look at you, noble men and women, and one fool. None of you bear any stake in this room. Some of you have been wounded, some of you have died, but this boy means nothing more than coin to you. Truly, I wondered how women and men could risk limb for a child not their own, but such is money in this age. But now I am bidding you all farewell, for this is a family argument."

The King sister laughed. "Family? You dare to call yourself family? Did you marry one of my slow cousins in some cave? Will you not tell them your grand plan, king kisser? God butcher. Oh, that one moves you. God butcher. Butcher of gods. Sogolon knew. She told my servant. She said, I go to the temple of Wakadishu. I go to the steps of Mantha. I go north, and east, and west, and I have not felt the presence of the gods. Not one. But that is another of your tricks, is it not, God butcher? Nobody knows what they lost because nobody remembers what they have had. Is this the night where you stop the King just as you have stopped the gods? Is it? Is it?"

A flap of huge wings, we heard it.

"Leave the child and go. Don't hesitate and set him down gently. Just drop him and go," the Aesi said.

He locked his eyes on Nsaka Ne Vampi.

"He is your King," the King sister said.

They saw nothing. But the nothing grabbed the King sister and slapped her left and right. Leopard ran to her, but the nothing kicked him away. He rolled and caught himself right beside me. He crouched again to pounce, but I bent down and touched the back of his neck. The nothing pulled up the King sister and shoved her down on a stool.

"King? This is the King. Have you seen his face? Do you know the taste in his mouth? It is fouler than the swordsman's shit. This is your King? Shall we call him Khosi, our lion? Get him a kaphoonda for his royal head. Three brass rings for his ankle. We should call players of moondu and matuumba, and all drums. Shall we call xylophone? Shall we call all earth chiefs to come and bow down in red dirt? Shall I pluck a hair from my head and stick it in his? And what is your stake in this, river nymph? Did the false queen seek you? Did you seek the false queen? Did she tell you of how glorious it will be when the King returns to the glorious line of mothers? Oh Mama, I beat my slit drum so that he will tell a secret to my big vagina **nkooku maama, kangwaana phenya mbuta.** You believed in a bad oracle, King sister. Your **ngaanga ngoombu** lied to you. Filled your head with wicked gold. You should have called a diviner. Instead you surrounded yourself with women even women have forgotten. Look at him, who you would have as King. He is lower than an it."

The Aesi pointed the green knife at me.

"My boy will be king," the King sister said.

"The North already has a King. Have you looked upon your son? How could you, you have never even known your son. Put your gaze on him now. If a demon beast bared a nipple, he would grab it and suck it. You, Tracker, and the pale one, you promised to deliver the boy and you have delivered. What do you wish? Coin? Cowrie shells the weight of your body? This woman and her little river nymph deceived you, how many times? Even now, tell the room true. Do you believe any of their stories? No. Or you would have at least tried to throw that ax. The knife at her neck—if I were to kill her right now you would not even look me in the eye. Sogolon knew not to trust men who had nothing to lose. A pity how she died. I wish I had seen it."

I heard marching outside, marching that knocked down the doors and came in the house. Mossi could hear it too. He looked up at me and I nodded, hoping it said what I did not know.

"Leave the child here, then go, and I promise when I meet you next, it will be over some dolo, some good soup, and there shall be mirth," the Aesi said.

"I scarce think there is any mirth in you," Mossi said.

"I would have loved to talk to you about your belief in your one god some more. I have met so many gods."

"Met and killed them, God butcher," the King sister said.

The Aesi laughed. "Your friend the Tracker, he said he did not believe in belief; I saw that too. You think he believes in a butcher of the gods? He would have to believe in gods first. Did you notice, Tracker, that nobody worships anymore? I know you do not believe in gods but you know many who do. Have you not noticed that more and more, the men of the lands are like you, and the women too? You have been around witchmen and fetish priests, but when have you last seen an offering? A sacrifice? A shrine? Women gathered in praise? Fuck the gods, you say. I have heard you. And yes fuck them, this is the age of kings. You don't believe in belief. I butcher belief. We are the same."

"I will tell my mother she has one more son. She will laugh," I said.

"Not with your grandfather's cock in her mouth she will not."

My head went red. I grabbed my ax from the Leopard, who growled.

"You must be sad, then, with Sogolon dead and nobody to see through you," I said.

"Sogolon? What good are the eyes of an old moon witch when the eyes of a hundred angry spirits are upon her? You did not sleep the night you rode from Kongor, so someone must have told you that I visit dreams."

"I did not sleep."

"I know. But you, behind him, you slept deeper than a deaf child."

He pointed his finger at the Ogo. Sadogo looked at us, at his hands, out the window, back at himself, as if he heard something but not words.

"An Ogo's dream jungle is so wide, so rich, so open to possibility. Sometimes he was blind to me traveling in his head, opening one eye when he slept. Sometimes he fought me in dream. Did he not punch a hole in that ship? Sometimes from his mouth came what I said in his sleep, and sometimes people heard. Is that not so, dear Ogo? Pity your friends here did not share as much with you as I would have liked, or I would have known your plans in Dolingo. Maybe they did not trust the giant?"

Sadogo growled, looking around for the somebody the Aesi might be speaking of.

"And what I saw through your eyes. What I heard through your ears. Your friends, this might give them laughter. Was even a moon gone when I spoke through your mouth? You will not remember. I spoke and you spoke and that man, that old man was on the roof and he heard you. Me. I am who he heard, but you, dear Ogo, you are the one who grabbed the man, crushed his throat so he could not scream, and with your dear hands you threw him off the roof."

I knew Sadogo would look to see who watched him. I did not look. Sadogo squeezed his knuckles so tight I heard the iron bend. The Leopard did not turn around. Mossi did.

"He is the father of lies, Sadogo," Mossi said.

"Lies? What is one more death to the Ogo? At least he didn't kill that Zogbanu slave girl by letting her sit on his little ogo. But she sat on it many times in his daytime dreaming. What a noise she was making in your dream jungle. Made me shoot seed twice myself. But this Ogo here, his cum almost burst through the roof. But which was the wilder dream, you inside her or you calling her wife? You thinking you will make a half Ogo? I was there. I was there when—"

"Do not listen, Sadogo," Mossi said.

"Do not interrupt. Wondering if she could ever love an Ogo, are you the first who is more than beast?"

"He's trying to provoke you, Sadogo. He would not make you angry if he didn't have a plan," Mossi said.

Sadogo growled. I turned to face him, but my gaze landed on the boy on Nsaka Ne Vampi's shoulder, his mouth open wide as if he was going to bite her, but he closed his mouth when he saw me looking. His eyes, wide open and blank, so black, almost blue.

"Provoke? If I wanted to provoke him would I not have said half giant?" the Aesi said.

Sadogo bellowed. I spun around to see him punch the wall. He squeezed his knuckles and stamped after the Aesi but right then the dark turned on him, jumped out from the shadows, grabbed his limbs as he yelled, and pulled him out of the room. Leopard jumped right for the King sister and bit into the nothing that still rested on her shoulder. Red spurted in his mouth. The nothing screamed.

"Fuck the gods indeed," the Aesi said, and slashed Bunshi's throat. She fell.

Mossi pulled both swords and ran towards him. I threw my ax. A wind whipped up, blew Mossi hard against the wall, and sent the ax flying back to my face, but the iron could not touch me and the ax flew by. Nsaka Ne Vampi ran out with the child, and the King sister wailed. The Aesi turned to chase Nsaka Ne Vampi, but stopped quick and caught an arrow with his left hand, stopping it from his face. With his right he caught another. His hands full, the third and fourth shot straight into his forehead. I saw Fumeli, his bow still pulled, two arrows between his fingers. The Aesi fell back and crashed into the floor, the arrows flag-posts in his forehead. The nothing lost his spell and died a Tokoloshe. The birds, flapping and squawking, flew away from the window.

"We must go," Leopard said to the King sister.

He grabbed her hand and yanked her away. I could hear Sadogo fighting the invisible monsters and crashing through one wall and then another. I stared at the Aesi lying there and thought not of him, but of

Omoluzu, who always attacked from above, not behind. I ran to Sadogo. Killing the Aesi dropped his
invisible enchantment. All black and tarlike, but not
Omoluzu. Red eyes, but not like Sasabonsam. Shadow
creatures who could still break, like the neck that Sadogo just snapped. I ran into the dark, swinging my
ax through shadow, but it felt like chopping flesh and
chunking bone. Two of the shadowings jumped me,
one kicking me in the chest and one trying to stomp
me down. I pulled my knife and rammed it right up
where his balls would be. He squealed. Or she. On
the floor I swung the ax and chopped off toe after
toe, then jumped back up. The shadowings ran up
and down the Ogo, enraging him so much that he
grabbed at the dark, crushing a head with his right
hand, breaking a neck with his left, and stomping
two so hard into the floor that he kicked a hole right
through it. I rolled out of the shadows and a hand
grabbed my ankle. I chopped it off.

"Sadogo!"

They crawled all over him. As he pulled off one,
another came. They climbed and crawled all over him
so that all but his head vanished. He looked over at
me, his eyebrows raised, his eyes lost. I stared at him,
trying to hold him with just a look. I rose and gripped
my ax, but he closed his eyes slow, opened them and
looked at me again. I couldn't read his eyes. Then a
shadow creature crawled over his face.

"Sadogo," I said.

He stomped, stomped, and stomped until he cracked

the floor wider open and, with the shadow creatures grabbing him, fell through. I heard one crash the floor, then another, and another, and another and another. Then nothing. I went to the hole and looked down, but saw hole after hole after hole, then darkness. At the foot of the final steps, the door ahead, I looked over to the pile of dirt, bricks, dust, and black shadow, and something that glimmered just a little. His iron glove. Sadogo. He could never face such a life of knowing he killed the old man with such wickedness, even if it was not him. Not truly. I stood there, looking, waiting, not hoping, but waiting all the same, but nothing moved. I knew if anything moved it would be something from the black. And soon.

Mossi ran in shouting something about people and birds. I didn't hear him. I looked over into the dark, waiting.

Mossi touched my cheek and turned my head to his face.

"We must go," he said.

Outside people from the city stood about two hundred paces away and watched us. Nsaka Ne Vampi and the King sister mounted horses, the Leopard and Fumeli shared one. The King sister placed the boy in front of her and held him with one hand, the reins in the other. The people stood back. Birds bunched, thick in the sky, then flew apart, then came together again.

"Leopard, look up. Are they possessed?" I asked.

"I don't know. The Aesi is dead."

"I do not see any weapons," Mossi said.

"We also stole these horses," the Leopard said.

Mossi mounted his horse and pulled me up. The crowd made a noise and charged after us. The King sister galloped off, not waiting. Nsaka Ne Vampi turned to us and, riding off, shouted, "Ride! Fools."

We took off as the crowd starting flinging rocks. I lost the boy's smell, even though I could still see the King sister.

"Where are we going?" he said.

"The Mweru," I said.

The crowd kept chasing us even as we rode away, down to the border road and then west, then south, along the Gallunkube/Matyube, which took us west again until we saw the docks and the shore. We continued south and did not stop until the horses crossed the canal and took us out of the city. Above, a flock of birds followed us. They followed us even as we rode through forest and grassland, and as the sky started changing colour of day. Until we could no longer see Kongor. Right above us some dove for our heads. Pigeons. Nsaka Ne Vampi yelled and the King sister shouted, Move! Nsaka Ne Vampi led her through a patch of trees, which blocked the birds, but they started diving again as soon as we were out of the patch.

Ahead of us was something white and moving, either clouds or dust. The King sister rode straight for it and we followed. The birds dove at us one more time. One flew straight into Mossi's head. He yelled for me to get it out so I yanked it and threw it away. Fumeli slapped away birds with his bow, as the Leopard rode hot after the two women. The buffalo charged on past us. We rode so hard that it was not until we were in the mist—for it was a mist—that I noticed the birds did not follow. I had no name for the smell. Not a stench, but not a fragrance either. Maybe something like when clouds are fat with rain and lightning has scorched them. We rode to a stop beside the King sister—a good thing too, for she stopped at the steep drop of a cliff. Mossi nudged me to dismount. Below us, but still a distance away, lay those lands, waiting on any fool to enter it.

"Sogolon said take him to the Mweru," the King sister said. "He would be safe from all magic and white science in the Mweru. In that, at least, we can trust her."

She said it in a way that I could not tell if she was telling or asking. I turned to her and saw her looking at me.

"Trust the gods," I said.

She pointed to the trail leading down, laughed, and rode off without saying anything of gratitude. I could not smell the boy even when I looked at him. As they rode off his smell finally came to me, then it vanished again. Did not fade, but vanished. Nsaka Ne Vampi turned to me, nodded, then rode off back to Kongor.

"Leopard," I said.

"I know."

"What will she be riding back to, with the Ipundulu dead?"

"I don't know, Tracker. Whatever it is, it will not be what she wants. . . . So, Tracker."

"Yes?"

"The ten and nine doors. Was there a map? Did you see one?"

"We both saw one," Mossi said.

"From here to Gangatom we would have to cross a river to Mitu, ride around the Darklands, cut through the long rain forest, and follow two sisters river west. That is at least ten and eight days and that's not counting pirates, Ku warriors, and this King's army and mercenaries already plundering the river folk," I said.

"What about the doors?" Leopard said.

"We would have to sail against current to Nigiki."

"You wish us go back past Dolingo?" Mossi said, loud enough but clearly to only me.

"Six days to Nigiki if we go by river. Take the door at Nigiki and we are in the Hills of Enchantment, three days from Gangatom."

"That's nine days," the Leopard said. "But Nigiki is South Kingdom, Tracker. Catch us they will, and kill us as spies before we even get to that door."

"Not if we move with a hush."

"Quiet? Us four?"

"Darklands to Kongor, Kongor to Dolingo. We can only go one way," I said.

He nodded.

"Take care," I said to everyone. "Slip in like thieves, slip out before anyone, even the night, knows."

"To the river," the Leopard said.

Fumeli kicked the horse and they galloped off. I turned back to look at the Mweru. In the dark, with the sky a rich blue, all I could see were shadows. Hills rising upward, too smooth and precise. Or towers, or things left behind by giants who practiced wicked arts before man.

"Sadogo," I said to Mossi. "I loved that giant, even if he went mad when one called him so. If I had fallen asleep, had you let me, I would have been the one to throw that old man from the roof. Do you know how much it pained him to kill? He told me of all his killings one night. Every single one, for his memory was a curse. It took us right into the break of morning. Most of the killings were no fault of his—an executioner's job is still but a job, no worse than the man who increases taxes by the year."

They came, the tears. I could hear myself bawl and was shocked at it. What kind of dawn was this? Mossi stood by me, silent, waiting. He put his hands on my shoulder until I stopped.

"Poor Ogo. He was the only—"

"Only?"

I tried to smile. Mossi squeezed my neck with a soft hand, and I leaned into it. He wiped my cheek and brought my forehead to his. He kissed me on the lips, and I searched for his tongue with mine.

"All your cuts are open again," I said.

"You'll be saying I'm ugly next."

"These children will not want me."

"Maybe, maybe not."

"Fuck the gods, Mossi."

"But they will never need you more," he said, mounting the horse and pulling me up behind him. The horse broke into a trot, then a full gallop. I wanted to look back, but did not. I didn't want to look ahead either, so I rested my head on Mossi's back. Behind us, light shone ahead as if it came from the Mweru, but it was just the break of daylight.

5

HERE
IS ONE
ORIKI

O nifs osupa. Idi ti o n
bikita nipa awsn iraws.

TWENTY-TWO

And that is all and all is truth, great inquisitor. You wanted a tale, did you not? From the dawn of it to the dusk of it, and such is the tale I have given you. What you wanted was testimony, but what you really wanted was story, is it not true? Now you sound like men I have heard of, men coming from the West for they heard of slave flesh, men who ask, Is this true? When we find this, shall we seek no more? It is truth as you call it, truth in entire? What is truth when it always expands and shrinks? Truth is just another story. And now you will ask me again of Mitu. I don't know who you hope to find there. Who are you, how dare you say what I had was not family? You, who try to make one with a ten-year-old.

Oh, you have nothing to say. You will push me no further.

Yes, it is as you say, I was in Mitu for four years and five moons. Four years from when we left the boy in the Mweru. I was there when this rumor of war turned into a real war. What happened there is something you can ask the gods. Ask them why your South has not been winning this war, but neither the North.

The child is dead. There is nothing else to know. Otherwise, ask the child.

Oh you have nothing left to ask? Is this where we part?

What is this? Who comes in this room?

No, I do not know this man. I have never seen his back or his face.

Don't ask me if I recognize you. I do not know you.

And you, inquisitor, you give him a seat. Yes, I can see he is a griot. Do you think he brought the kora to sell it? Why would this be the time for praise song?

It is a griot with a song about me.

There are no songs about me.

Yes, I know what I said before, I was the one who said it. That was a boast—who am I that I would be in any song? Which griot makes a song before you pay them? Fine, let him sing; it is nothing to me. Nothing he sings I will know. So sing.

Thunder god mystic brother
blessed with tongue, and the gift of kora.
It is I, Ikede, son of Akede,
I was the griot that lived in the
  monkeybread tree.

I been walking many days and many nights,
  when across it I come,

the tree near a river
I climb up and hear the parrot, and the
  crow, and the baboon
I hear children
laughing, screaming, fighting, making gods
  hush
and there up top lie a man on a rug.
What kind of man is this?
not like any man in Weme Witu, Omororo,
  or even Mitu.

And he said,
are you looking for beauty?
I said I think I found it
And hark, the man laugh and he say
the women of Mitu find me so ugly,
when I take the children to the markets they
  say
Look at that ugly family, look at those
  wretched beasts,
but that one khita, ngoombu, haamba he
  have hair like a horse.
But I say, beautiful wise bountiful women
plump in bosom and wide in smile
I am not a zombi, I am pretty like kaolin
  clay
and they laugh so hard, they give me doro
  beer and play in my hair
and I tell you, in none of these things I find
  any offense.

And I say to him
This tree, do you live in it?
He say, There is no you, only we and we are
   a strange house.
Stay with us as long as you wish.

When I climb through a hole and sit in the
   spot
I see he coming, bringing back meat
I say, Who is the man so sour with the eye of
   a wolf?
Who curse him so?
But children little, children big, children
   who is but air
run down the tree and stampede him
and don't care that he cursing would scare
   the owl.
And they jump up on him and sit on his
   head, and rest under his arm
And I thinking these children have big
   feelings for this man,
and the sour face gone.
And the Wolf Eye climb up the top and stop
   when he see me,
and keep climbing.
And when he reach the top, he see the other
   man,
and they put lips together, and open their
   mouths,
I know.

The one with the wolf eye, he is the one
who says, The night is getting old, why are
  you not sleeping?
The sun is in the sky, why are you not
  waking?
Food is ready
when are you going to eat it?
Did the gods curse me and make me a
  mother?
No he blessed me and made you my wife,
the one called Mossi say,
and the children laugh, and the Wolf Eye
  scowl
And scowl, and scowl, and scowl into a
  laugh.
I was there, I see it.

And I see it when they chase all the children
  out and say go,
go to the river now,
and stay 'til the sun start to shift
And when they all gone, they think I gone
  too
For Mossi speak the Wolf Eye own tongue
Se ge yi ye do bo, he say
Se ge yi ye do bo
Let us love each other
For they two, they grab each other and kiss
  lip
then kiss tongue,

then kiss neck and nipple
and lower.
And one was the woman, and one was the
   man,
and both was the woman, and both was the
   man,
and neither was neither.
And the Wolf Eye, he rest his head in Mossi
   lap.
Mossi, he be rubbing the Wolf Eye's chest.
They just stay there looking at each other,
eye studying eye.
Face at rest
maybe they sharing a dream.

One day Wolf Eye call them all together.
Children, he say, come out from the river
and present yourselves
you not raised by the jackal or the hyena.
And each child present me his name,
but their names I have all forgotten.

This is what Wolf Eye say.
He say, Mossi I am Ku,
and a Ku man can only be one kind of man
and Mossi said to him, How are you not a
   man
what do I grab between the legs
Mossi make joke

Wolf Eye not making joke.
He say
I been running, I been hiding, I been
  looking for
something that I don't know, but I know I
  looking for it
And I don't know, but every Ku find it
but there is blood between me and the Ku
and I could never go back.

So he call the Gangatom
And the Gangatom chief say, Nobody ever
  wait so long,
I've been waiting all my life, Wolf Eye say.
And Wolf Eye pull his tunic and say,
Look at me, look where there is woman,
And when I cut it off I will be a man
and Mossi he catch a fright, for he think if
  this is what make him love him,
But Wolf Eye say, Everything between me
  and you,
eastern man, is not down there, but up here,
he say and point to his heart.
And the chief say,
What you asking for not old,
what you asking for new.
You is Ku
and you have no father.
In this way you enrage the gods.

Says the Wolf Eye:
The ceremony to become a man
is in praise of the gods, and so
how could any god be mad.

So Wolf Eye,
The Gangatom prick the cow and spill the
　　blood
in a bowl
Wolf Eye drink one then two
he drink and wipe his mouth.

The next day come,
For him to jump the bulls.
They line them up, twenty strong
plus ten more for he take too late to be a man
You have to run on the backs of bulls and
　　you cannot fall,
For if you fall, the gods laugh
So Wolf Eye,
He naked in oil and shea butter.
Then praise the gods, he run
bull back to bull back, one two three four
five six seven more.
And the people cheer and rejoice
The elder say all these moons you in the
　　in-between place
and there is no shame,
but middle is nowhere.

But some of the elders, they say
he not coming from the enki paata.
He not been wandering for four moons
as a boy supposed to do before he become
    man
where on him be the mark that he kill the
    great lion?
And the chief, he say, Look on him
and you see the mark of him killing lion and
    everything else.
So the elders, they sit quiet, though some
    still grumble,
and the chief, he say to Wolf Eye
You never wander for four moons
So stay for four nights
in the open and with the cows, sleep in
    grass, stand on dirt.
And on the five morning
they come for him
and they bathe him from the bucket, with
    an ax head in it
to cool the water

And now as be the custom, the men say,
big man fitting in boy skin
to become a man, but look he is a fool.
As be the custom, the men say,
look at him little boy kehkeh, it not ready to
    be a man yet.

He can't work a woman koo, better he dig
    an anthole.
As be the custom, the men say.
Is that why you have husband and not a
    wife?
Is you the wife?
Strength now, Wolf Eye. Anger is weakness.

So in come the cutter ready for the event
sharp with one knife
the Wolf Eye, he have no mother,
so the chief wife, she be the mother.
She send ox hide for him to sit on
and that way not shame the gods.
They lead him, yes they lead him
past the cattle kraal
past the houses of great elder
up to a little hill where on top is a hut
and he say
Kick the knife, and we will kill you.
Run from the knife
And we disown you
The grand cutter, he take chalk and mark a
    line
from forehead to nose.
The grand cutter, he take milk and pour all
    over the Wolf Eye.
The grand cutter, he grab the slain and pull,
    and pull
he say, One cut!

Kick the knife and we will kill you.
Run from the knife and we will disown you.
He say, One cut!
And the Wolf Eye, he grab the cutter arm

and he say, No.
Listen to me, he say No.
The man in the mountain and the women in
  the river
hear a whisper that drop like thunder
and everybody quiet.
The Wolf Eye say, The sum of my days
is all about cutting the woman out
Cut her out of me
cut her out of my mother
cut her out of all who walk and carry the
  world
And he look down at him maleness
crowned at the top by femaleness
and say
What in this make wrong,
how is this not the will of the gods
and if it's not the will of the gods
then it is the will of me
he look at Mossi and say
You tell me I cut all woman out
from my mother to whoever pass the house
when it is I who leave my mother
and I who would now cut away my own
  self

and with this he get up
and with this he leave the knife
and he walk away
and the people silent for he still a fierce
     man

But Mossi trouble him more
Soon as they come back to the tree
this he say,
Stop thinking you have peace
you know what I mean
and Wolf Eye say he don't know. So stop
and Mossi say, Why tell me stop if you don't
     know
And in this way Mossi nag Tracker
And nag and nag and boy he nag
and Tracker raise his hand to strike Mossi
and Mossi say, Nobody has ever loved you
     finer
but lay that hand on me and you will see it
     cut off
and shoved in your mouth.
Fine, Tracker say, I will go
just to stop you from being the cockatoo.

And the day come when he turn to go
And he stagger, and he fall, and he say
Come with me or I will fall in the bush
And Mossi go, and the children go

and even me go for Tracker say, Don't act as
  if you
don't belong to this house
And in this way
Tracker and his kin set off for his mother
What a sight we must be in Juba!
But that is not the story
For Tracker stagger ten times before we get
  to the gate.
And Mossi hold him up ten times strong
So they get to the door
and a girl open the door who look like
  him
that is what me and Mossi think
And she don't say nothing, but she let
  them in
and jump out of the way when the Ball
  Boy
roll through, and the Giraffe Boy had to
  duck
and in a blue room
she sit
looking old and weak but her eyes look
  young
When did he die? Tracker ask.
When a grandfather was supposed to die,
  she say.
And he look at her like he have something
  to say

And his mouth quiver like he have
    something to say
And Mossi start to move we out of the
    room
like he have something to say
But Tracker stagger again and this time he
    fall
And she stoop down and touch his cheek
One of your eyes didn't come from me,
    she say
and what come out his mouth was a wail
And he wail for his mother
And he wail for his mother
And night come for day
And day come for night
And still he wail.

Hear me now,
I stay in the monkeybread tree ten and nine
    moons.
The day I was leaving the children cry,
and Mossi hang his head down low
and even the Wolf Eye said, But why do you
    leave your home?
But a man like me, we are like the beast,
we must roam,
or we die.
Listen to me now.
The day before I leave,
A black Leopard come to the tree.

Stop him.

Stop him now. Stop him or I will find a way to end everything this very night. And then you will know nothing about how anything ended.

I will tell you what happened next.

I will tell you everything.

6

DEATH
WOLF

Mun be kini wuyi a lo bwa.

TWENTY-THREE

I want it known that you made me do this. I want to see it written in a tongue that I recognize. Show me. I will not speak until you show me. How will you write it? Will you note what I said, or just say, The prisoner said this? Stop talking about truth—I fed you truth all along, but as I said before, what you want is story. I have given you many, but I will give you a final one. Then you can talk to her and send us to burn.

In this story I see her. She walked like somebody was following her.

Why do you stop me?

Did you not hear the griot?

The Leopard came to visit me and seduced me with talk of adventure. Of course he was all cunning—he is a leopard. And I went with him to find a fat and stupid man who sold gold and salt and smelled of chicken shit, who had vanished. But he had not vanished. Fuck the gods, inquisitor, which story do

BLACK LEOPARD, RED WOLF

you wish to hear? No I will not tell you both. Look at me.

I will not tell you both.

So.

She walked as people who think they are followed walk. Looking ahead when she reached the mouth of each lane, looking behind when she reached the foot of it. Slipping from shadow to shadow, as she moved down a still street. Floating overhead the raw burn of opium, and flowing on the ground, the overspill of shit water. She tripped and grabbed her cargo tight, ready to brace for the fall rather than let it go. The sky had a ceiling in this place, a hundred paces high in some parts, with holes burrowed through to let in the white light of the sun and the silver light of the moon. She stooped below a torch beside a door, shifted underneath, stood up again, and scraped her back along the wall like a crab, to the corner.

The Malangika. The tunnel city, somewhere west of the Blood Swamp but east of Wakadishu, about three hundred paces below the ground and as big as a third of Fasisi. Hundreds of years ago, before people wrote accounts, the first people from above had a quarrel with the gods of sky over rain, and the gods of earth gave them this place to hide from sky wrath. They dug wide and deep, and the caverns rose high to hold buildings of three, four, and even five floors. Columns from chopped-down trees and stone to brace the tunnels so that they never collapsed, though two sections collapsed twice. Throughout the tunnels, builders carved out holes above to let the sun and moon light the street, like the lamps of Juba. People in the Malangika were the true first ones to unlock the secret of metals, some say. But they were selfish and greedy, and became the first blacksmith kings. They died holding on to their iron and silver. And some working other kinds of art and craft dug even deeper. But the people of this city soon died out, and the city itself was forgotten. And only in a place forgotten could a new city arise, a city with no notice, a city that was a market. A place that sold what could not be sold aboveground, not even at night. The secret witches market.

The market cleared out. Somebody had woven powerful magic to make everyone forget the street. Most lanes showed the backside of inns where nobody stayed, taverns where nobody left, and sellers of things of all kinds of uses. But in this lane darkness hung low. She walked many steps before stopping, looking around as two spirits pulled themselves from a wall and came at her. Another rose out of the ground, stumbling as if drunk. In the quick, she pulled the amulet from between her breasts. The spirits squealed and backed away; the ground spirit went back under. All the way down the lane, she held out the amulet, and voices squawked, muttered, and hissed. Their hunger was huge, but not bigger than the fear of the nkisi around her neck. Through the mist, at the end of the lane, she pressed herself against a fresh mud wall on the right, then turned around the corner right into my blade.

She jumped. I grabbed her hand, yanked it behind her back, pressing my knife to her neck. She tried to scream but I pressed the knife harder. Then she started to utter a whisper I knew. I whispered something back and she stopped.

"I am protected by a Sangoma," I said.

"You pick here to rob a poor woman? You pick this place?"

"What is it you carry, girl?" I asked.

For she was a girl and thin, her cheeks hungry. Her hand, which I still held, was near down to bone, something I could break with just a twist.

"Curse you if you make me drop it," she said.

"What shall you drop?"

"Take your eyes out of my bosom, or take my purse and go."

"Money is not what I look for. Tell me what you carry or I will stab it."

She flinched, but I knew what it was before the dried milk vomit smell came to me, and before it gurgled.

"How many cowries buys a baby in the Malangika?"

"You think I selling my baby? What kind of witch sell her own baby?"

"I don't know. What kind of witch buys one, that I know."

"Let me go or I going scream."

"A woman's scream in these tunnels? That is every street. Tell me how you come by the baby."

"You deaf? I say—"

I twisted her arm behind her back, right up almost to her neck, and she screamed, and screamed again, trying to not drop the child. I released her hand a little.

"Go slip back in your mother cunt," she said.

"Whose baby?"

"What?"

"Who is the mother of the baby?"

She stared at me, frowning, thinking of something to say that would make a lie out of the sound of this baby waking up and hating the rough cloth he was wrapped in.

"Mine. Is mine. Is my own baby."

"Not even a whore would take her child to the Malangika unless she goes to sell it. To a—"

"I not no whore."

I let her go. She turned away from me as if to run, and I pulled one of the axes from my back.

"Try to run and this will split the back of your head before you reach fifty paces. Test me if you wish."

She looked at me and rubbed her arm.

"I look for a man. A special man, special even in the Malangika," I said.

"I don't mess with no man."

"And yet you just said this is your baby, so messed with a man, you did. He is hungry."

"He not no concern for you."

"But hungry he is. So feed him."

She pulled the cloth from the baby's head. I smelled baby vomit and dried piss. No shea butter, no oil, no silks, nothing that graces a baby's precious buttocks. I nodded and pointed my ax at her breasts. She pulled her robe and the right breast slipped out, thin and lanky above the baby's face. She shoved the breast into the baby's mouth and it started sucking, pulling so hard she winced. The baby spat out her breast, and cried into a scream.

"You have no milk," I said.

"He not hungry. What you know about raising a child?"

"I raised six," I said. "How were you going to feed him?"

"If you didn't interfere, we would reach home long time now."

"Home? The nearest village is three days away on foot. Can you fly? The child would starve by then."

She dug into her dress for the pouch, and tried to pull it open with both hands while still holding the child.

"Look here, dog-fucker or whatever you be. Take the coin and go buy yourself a girl so you can kill and eat her liver. Leave me be, me and my child."

"Hark those words. I would say raise your child around better folks, but it is not your child."

"Leave me be!" she shouted, and pulled the pouch open. "Here, see it here. Take it all."

She held it out, but then dashed it. I swung my ax to knock it out of the way and it hit the wall and fell to the ground. Little vipers came out and grew big. She ran but I chased her, gained on her, grabbed her hair and she screamed. She dropped the baby. I pushed her hard, and picked up the child as she staggered to a fall. She shook her head and wobbled as I pulled the boy out of the nasty cloth. His body, dark as tea, she had marked with white clay. A line around the neck. A line at each joint in the arms and legs. A cross at his navel, and circles around his nipples and his knees.

"What a night you were planning for yourself. You are no witch, not yet, but this would have made you one, maybe even a powerful one, instead of someone's apprentice."

"Get you cock sting by a scorpion," she said, sitting up.

"On the art of cutting up a child, you have no expertise, so he drew where to cut. The man who sold you the baby."

"All coming out of your mouth is wind."

The boy wiggled in my arms.

"Men in the Malangika, they sell wretched things, unspeakable things. Women do this too. But a baby, alive, untouched, is no easy thing to find. This is not bastard or foundling. Only the purest child could give you the most powerful magic, so you bought yourself the purest child. Stolen from a noblewoman. And no easy thing to buy, three days from the nearest city. So you must have given him something of great value. Not gold, or cowries. You gave him another life. And since merchants can only appreciate things of value, that life must have been valuable to you. A son? No, a daughter. Child brides go for even more than the newborn here."

"A thousand fucks—"

"I have long passed a thousand fucks. Where is the master who sold you this baby?"

Still on the ground, she scowled at me, even as she rubbed her forehead with her right hand. I stepped on her left hand and she yelled.

"If I ask again, it will be after I chop this hand off."

"You bastard son of a whoring North wolf bitch. Cut the hand off a defenseless woman."

"You just defended yourself with a spell of vipers. Which of his feet was for the amulet, left or right?"

"What plenty you know about witch and witch-men. You must be the real witch."

"Or maybe I kill witches. For money, yes. One can always use money. But really for sport. The merchant, where is he?"

"Fool, he shift whereabouts every night. No elephant remember the way there, no crow can find him."

"But you bought the child this night."

I stomped harder on her hand and she yelled again.

"The midnight street! Go to the end, and turn right past the dead tree, then down the three sets of steps, deep in the dark. So dark that you can't see, only feel. He in the house of a witchman with the heart of an antelope rotting on the door."

I stepped off her hand and she grabbed it, cursing me under her breath.

"No good going come to you. Before you meet him, you going meet two."

"What charity, giving me warning."

"Warning not going save you. Me telling you not going mean a thing."

I rubbed the baby's belly. He was hungry. One of these merchants—sellers, witchmen, or witches—must have had some goat's milk. I would kick down the next door, ask for goat's or cow's milk, and chop off hands until a hand brought me some.

"Say, hunter," she said. Still on the ground, the witch started hiking up her skirt.

"What use the baby be to you? What use he be to the mother? You never going find them, and them never going find you. Put the baby to use. Think, good hunter, what I can give you when I come into my power. You want coin? You want the finest merchants to just look at you and give you fine silks and their plumpest daughter? I can do that. Give me the little baby. He so sweet. I can smell the good he going to do. I can smell it."

She stood up and held out her hands for the child.

"Here is what I shall give you. I will give you a count to ten before I throw this ax and split the back of your head open like a nut."

The young witch cursed and screwed her face, like the man whose opium you took away. She turned to go, then spun back and shouted for her baby.

"One," I said.

"Two."

She ran off.

"Three."

I flung my ax, sending it spinning after her. She ran past four doors before she heard the whir coming. The witch turned around and it struck her in the face. She landed flat on her back. I went over and pulled the ax out of her head.

I passed two lanes and went down a third that carried fragrance. The fragrance was not real and neither was the lane. A street for the wicked but foolish, a street to lure people through doors from which they would never return. So I knocked on the third door I passed, the one the fragrance came from. An old woman opened the door, and I said, I smell milk here and I will have it. She pulled out a breast, squeezed it hard, and said, Any milk you get drink it, ash boy. Ten paces down, a fat man in a white agbada opened his door to my ax. Milk, I said. Inside was not inside and his house had no roof. Goats and sheep ran around bleating, eating, and shitting and I did not ask what he used them for. I placed the child on a table.

"I will be back for the child," I said.

"Which voice in this house say you can leave him?"

"Feed him milk of the goat."

"You leave a boy child with me? Many a witch come and many a witch go looking for baby skin. What to stop me from fatting up me purse?"

The fat man reached for the child. I chopped his hand off. He screamed and cussed and wailed and bawled in a tongue I didn't know. I took the hand.

"I will return your hand in three flips of the time glass. If the child is gone I will use your own hand to find you and cut you to pieces, one piece a day."

Midnight street was called so because at the mouth of it was a sign marked MIDNIGHT. This is how anyone coming would see me. Wearing nothing but white clay, from neck to ankles, my hands and feet. Straps for axes and sheaths for knives. Around my eyes, dark so the weak would see a man of bones coming for them. I was nothing.

Ten and five paces, the air grew colder, and heavier. Out of this strange air I stepped, then walked forward again until sour dew touched my face. The enchantment left my mouth a whisper, and after that I waited. And waited. Something scurried behind me and I pulled my knives quick, then turned around to see rats running away. So I waited longer. I was about to start walking when above me the air crackled and sparked, then burst in a flame that raced in a circle the span of my arms, and went out. The air was less heavy and sour, but the road looked the same. Not one of the ten and nine doors, but just a door. Seven steps in, the floor vanished. I tried to jump back but fell in, spun, and stabbed the knives into the dirt around me. Below my feet, only air. The drop could have been to the center of the world, or into a pit of spikes or snakes. I pulled myself up, ran back, dashed to the edge, leapt into the air, missed the landing, and slammed into the side, stabbing the dirt to not fall in again.

The path ended in a bank of bush. I turned right past the dead tree the witch spoke of, and came to a cliff with a drop, this time with steps cut into the dirt going down three flights. At the bottom, another path leading to the door of a hut cut into the rock, with two windows above, yellow with flickering light. My nose was searching for sour air, and each hand still gripped a knife. I sheathed them and pulled out an ax. Nobody had locked the door. Nobody was supposed to get this far. I stepped inside a house at least five times larger than it looked from outside, like the great halls I have seen men make on the inside of a baobab tree. Around the room books showed their backs on shelves, and scrolls and papers sat on tables. In glass jars everything that could come out of the body was kept in liquid. In a bigger jar with the water all yellow, a baby with his mother rope floating like a snake. At the right, cages one atop the other with birds of every colour. Not all of them were birds; some looked like lizards with wings, and one had the head of a meerkat.

In the middle of the room stood a man as small as a boy, but old, with a thick plank of glass strapped to his eyes, which made each eye look as large as a hand. I crept in, my feet kicking away papers covered in shit, some of it fresh. Something laughed from above me and I looked up to see swinging from a rope in the ceiling and hanging by the tail two mad monkeys.

Face like a man, but green like rot. Two eyes white and popping, the right small, the left bigger. Not in clothes, but ripped cloth flapped all over them. Their noses punched in like an ape's, and long jagged teeth when they smiled. One was smaller than the other.

The small monkey jumped down before I could pull my second ax. He leapt onto my chest. I pushed him away from my face as he tried to bite my nose off. Both of them EEEEEEEEEEEEEE'd. The man ran into the other room. The small one whipped his tail around, trying to slash me, but I grabbed his neck with one hand and held the ax for him to slash his tail right into the blade. He shrieked and fell back, bawling. I pulled my second ax and hammered both at his body, but the larger monkey yanked him away with his tail. The bigger monkey threw a jar at me, I ducked and it smashed into the wall. He slapped the smaller monkey to shut him up. I ran over to a shelf as glass jars kept shattering around me. Then silence.

Near my foot, a wet hand lay. I grabbed it and threw it to my right. Jar after jar smashed against the wall. I grabbed my axes, jumped up, threw the first one. The large monkey dodged the first but ran into the second, which chopped his forehead. He fell against a shelf, pulling it down with him. The smaller one picked up his tail and ran off through a dark crevice between two shelves. I pulled away books and scrolls until I saw the stem of my ax. I hammered into the mad monkey's head with both axes until his flesh hit my face.

In the room but behind me it was, the door where from the rotting heart of an antelope hung a cracked Ifa bowl.

Inside the room, the man sat with a woman, and child sat at the table. Both woman and boy styled their hair stranger than in any land I have been to, branches sticking out of their heads as with the deer, and dried dung holding hair and branches together. The woman looked at me with glowing eyes, and the child, a boy, perhaps, smiled as a flower popped open from one of the branches. The man looked up.

"You wearing nothing but white. Who do you mourn?" he said.

He saw me looking at the wife.

"She good with the fucky-fucky, but gods alive, she can't cook. Can't cook a shit. Me no know if me can offer none of this to you. Cook it too long, I tell you. You hear me, woman, you can't cook it too long. Blink three time and peppered afterbirth is ready. You want a piece, my friend? It just come out of a woman from the Buju-Buju. She don't care that she make the ancestors mad for not burying it."

"Did the afterbirth come with a baby?" I asked.

He frowned, then smiled. "Strangers, they be coming to the doctor with jokes and jokes. No so, wife?"

The wife looked at him, then at me, but said nothing. The boy cut a piece of the afterbirth with his knife and shoved it in his mouth.

"So, you are here," he said. "Who you is?"

"You sent two of yours to welcome me."

"They welcome everybody. And since you is standing there, they—"

"Gone."

I put away my axes and pulled the knives. They continued eating, trying to pretend I was gone, but kept looking in my direction, the woman especially.

"You the baby seller?"

"I transact many a thing, always with a honest man heart."

"An honest man's heart must be why you are in the Malangika."

"What you want?"

"When did your skin return to you?"

"You still talking nothing but foolishness."

"I seek someone who does business in the Malangika."

"Everybody do business in the Malangika."

"But what he buys, you're of a few who sell it."

"So go check the few."

"I have. Four before you, one after you. Four so far dead."

The man paused, but just for a blink. The woman and child kept on eating. His face was to his wife but his eyes followed me.

"Not before my wife and child," he said.

"Wife and child? This wife and this child?"

"Yes, don't do—"

I threw both knives; one struck the woman in the neck, the other struck the boy in the temple. Both shook and jerked, shook and jerked, then their heads crashed on the table. The old man screamed. He jumped up, ran to the boy, and grabbed his head. The flower on his head wilted, and something black and thick oozed slow from his mouth. The old man wailed and screamed, and bawled.

"I seek someone who does business in the Malangika."

"Oh gods, look!"

"You kill children now," a voice I knew said.

"What he buys, you have been known to sell," I said to the old man. **"Sakut vuwong fa'at ba,"** I said to the thought.

"Oh gods, my sorrow. My sorrow," he cried.

"Merchant, if any god were to look, what would he say about you and your obscene family?"

"There were voices, you heard them say that we were an obscene family," the voice I knew said.

"They were my one. They were my one."

"They were white science. Both of them. Grow another one. Or two. You might even get a pair who can talk next time. Like a grass parrot."

"I call black heart men. I tell them hunt you and kill you!"

"Mun be kini wuyi a lo bwa, old man. I brought weeping to the house of death. Do you know what I wish for?"

I came nearer. The woman's face was rougher up close, as was the boy's. Not smooth, but run through with lines and ridges, like vines intertwined.

"Neither is of flesh," I said.

"They were my only one."

I pulled my ax.

"You sound as if you wish to be with them. Shall I make this happen? Right—"

"Stop," he said.

He cried to his gods. He may have really loved this woman. This boy. But not enough to join them.

"Not every man is fine in face such as yourself. Not every man can find love and devotion. Not every man can say the gods have blessed them. Some men even the gods find ugly, even the gods have said there shall be no hope for your blood. She smiled at me! The boy smiled at me! How dare you judge a man for refusing to die of loneliness. Gods of sky, judge this man. Judge what he done."

"There is no sky. Mayhaps call gods under the earth," I said.

He took his son in his arms and held him, shushing him as if the boy was crying.

"Poor merchant, you have never had the kiss of a beautiful woman, you say." He looked up at me, his eyes wet, his lips quivering, everything about him saying sorrow. "Is this because you keep killing them?" I said.

The sorrow left his face and he went back to his seat.

"And the men too. You hunt them down. No, there is no blood on your hands. You are too much a coward to fetch your own kill, so you send men out. They put people under spells with potions, for you wish them whole, with no poison in them, for that taints the heart. Then you kill some, and sell them for all sorts of secret magicks and white science. Some you keep alive because the foot of a living man, or the liver of a living woman is worth five times more on the market. Maybe even ten. And what of the baby that you just bartered with a young witch?"

"What you want?"

"I seek a man who comes to you for hearts. Hearts of women. You sometimes give him hearts of men, thinking he will never know. He knows."

"What your business with him?"

"No business of yours."

"I sell gold dust, crafts from the river lands, and fruits from the North. I do not sell such things."

"I believe you. You live in the Malangika because the rent you find agreeable. Is it one heart every nine nights or two?"

"Go let ten demons fuck you."

"Every soul in Malangika has a wish for my asshole."

He sat back down at the head of the table. "Leave me to bury my wife and child."

"In the dirt? Do you not mean sow them?"

I stood beside him.

"You know the man I speak of. You know he is not a man. Skin white like kaolin, just like his cape with black trim. You have seen him once; you thought, Hark, his cloak looks like feather. You thought he was beautiful. They are all beautiful. Tell me where he lives."

"I say get out and go—"

I pressed his hand with mine and chopped his finger. He screamed. Tears ran rivers down his face. I grabbed his neck.

"Understand something, little man. Inside you there is fear, I know. And you should be scared of the lightning bird. He is a beast of great misery and will come for your heart, or turn you into a thing that will never know peace."

I stood up and pulled him up until his eyes were almost level with mine.

"But know this. I will chop off your fingers, arms, legs, and feet, piece by piece, until you have no fingers, arms, legs, or feet. Then I will slice right around the top of your head and peel the scalp off. Then I will slice your cock into little strands so that it looks like a bush skirt. I will go over there, grab the torch, and seal each wound so you live. Then I will set fire to your tree-son and your vine-wife so that you can never grow them back. And that will be just the beginning. Do you understand, little man? Shall we play another game?"

"I . . . I never touch the living, never touch them, never, never, only the just dead," he said.

I grabbed his hand, bleeding at the finger stumps.

"The road of blind jackals!" he shouted. "The road of blind jackals. Down where the tunnels all fall down and all sort of thing live in the rubble. West of here."

"Any enchantments in the road, like the pit you wanted me to fall into?"

"No."

"A witchman told me no man needs his right middle finger."

"No!" he shouted, still bawling out his words. "There is no enchantment on that road, none from my craft. Why would it need it? No man go down that road unless he choosing to lose his life. Not even the witch, not even the ghost dog. Not even memory live there."

"Then that is where I will find him and . . ."

Standing in this room and in the outer chamber as long as I did, the smells all became known to me. But I turned to leave and a new smell brushed my nose. As it always is, I did not know what it was other than it was not the others. An odor, a scent of the living. I dropped the merchant's hand and walked over to a wall on the left, kicking away bottles with candles melting on top. The merchant said there was nothing there but the wall, and I turned to see him scoop his fingers into his hands. The smell was stronger at the wall. Piss, but fresh, the freshness of now. Things in it I knew from smell, wicked minerals, mild poisons. I whispered at the wall.

"Nothing there but the earth this hut cut out of. Nothing there, I say."

Flame sparked at the top of the wall and split to both edges, came down the sides, joining at the bottom and burning a rectangle that disappeared to reveal a room. A room as large the one we were in, with five lamps hanging on the walls. On the floor, four mats. On the mats four bodies, one with no arms or legs, one cut open from neck to penis, his ribs poking out, one full in body but not moving, and another, his eyes open, his hands and legs bound by rope, and a cross mark across his chest in kaolin clay. The boy had pissed on his belly and chest.

"Them sick. You try find a medicine woman in the Malangika, you try."

"You are harvesting them."

"Not true! I—"

"Merchant, you bawl to the gods, scream and wail like a priestess secretly fingering herself, and yet there is a broken Ifa bowl on your door. Not only are the gods gone, you wish they never come back."

"That is madness! Ma—"

My ax chopped his neck, blood splashed the wall, and his head fell and swung from a strip of skin. He fell onto his back.

"You have killed children," the voice that knew me said.

"Begging does not stop killing if one has decided to kill," I said.

Nothing walked this road of blind jackals but the fear to walk it. Two spirits did come to me screaming, looking for their bodies, but nothing struck fear in me anymore. Nothing was struck in me, not even sadness. Not even indifference. The two spirits both ran through me and shivered. They looked at me, screamed, and vanished. They were right to scream. I would kill the dead.

The entrance was so small that I crawled inside until I was again in a wide space, as high as before, but all around was dust, and bricks, cracked walls, broken wood, rotting flesh, old blood, and dried shit. Carved out of this was a seat like a throne. And there he was, sprawled on it, looking at the two rays of light that hit his legs and his face. The white wings, black at the tips, spread out and hanging lazy, his eyes barely open. A little bolt jumped off his chest and vanished. The Ipundulu, the lightning bird, looking as if he could not bother with this business of being Ipundulu. I stepped into something brittle that broke at my feet. Shed skin.

"Greetings, Nyka," I said.

TWENTY-FOUR

Y ou are the last of your kind, Nyka. One the Ipundulu chose to change rather than kill. Such honor he saves for those he enslaves and those he has fucked, so which are you?"

"Ipundulu can only be a man, no woman can be Ipundulu."

"And only a body possessed by his lightning blood can be Ipundulu."

"I told you. Ipundulu can only be a man. No woman can be Ipundulu."

"That is not the part I asked you."

"The last man he bit but did not kill, that man becomes the next Ipundulu, unless crossed by a mother witch, and he has no mother."

"That part I know. Your dodge is neither skillful nor artful, Nyka."

"He would rape and kill my woman. He had her by the neck, his claw already in her chest. I told him to take me instead. I told him to take me."

He looked away.

"The Nyka I know would have fed him bits of his own woman himself," I said.

"That Nyka you know. I don't know this Nyka. And I do not know you."

"I am—"

"Tracker. Yes, I know your name. Even witchmen and devils know it. They even whisper, Watch the Tracker. He has turned from red to black. Do you know what they mean? There is trouble all around you. I look at you and see a man darker than me."

"All men are darker than you."

"I see death as well."

"What a deep thinker you have become, Nyka, now that you eat women's hearts."

He laughed, looking at me as if just seeing me. Then he laughed again, the cackle of the mad, or the cackle of one who had seen all the madness of the world.

"And yet I'm the one in this room with a heart," he said.

His words did not upset me, but I thought right then of the me that it would have once struck. I asked him how he came to be this way, and this is what he told me.

That he and Nsaka Ne Vampi set off, not because of me, for he would have dealt with me, for such violent hate could exist only where there was still violent love beneath it. He and she set off, for he did not trust the fish woman and despised the Moon Witch, who was the one who made her sisters drive Nsaka Ne Vampi from the King sister guard.

"Have you ever seen a compass, Tracker?" Nyka asked. "Men from the eastern light carry them, some as large as a stool, some so small they disappear in the pocket. She would run, the lightning woman, run to the end of the rope and get pulled back so hard that her neck would soon break. So Nsaka shot her with a poison arrow, which did not kill her, only made her slow. These are the things that happened to us. The lightning woman kept running northwest, so we went northwest. We came upon a hut. Is this not how all stories of fright go, that we come upon a house where no one lives? Being who I am, I ran up and kicked down the door. First thing I saw, the child. Second thing I saw, a bolt of lightning ramming me in the chest and burning through every hole in my skin, and knocking me right out of the hut. Nsaka, she jumped over me and fired two arrows into the hut, one hitting a red one with grass for hair. Another came at her from the side and grabbed her bow, but she kicked him in the balls and he dropped to the ground and wailed. But the bug one, he is all flies, this bug one, he became a cloud of flies, and he surrounded her and stung all over her back through her tunic, and I could see it, the flies burrowing into her back as if they were coming home, and how my Nsaka did scream and fall to the ground on her back, to get them out for they bit and stung and sucked blood from her, and I rose and the Ipundulu struck lightning again but it hit her, not me, and the blast sent fire through her, but it also sent fire to the bug one, who shrieked and burned and drew all the flies back to his form. The bug one ran into the hut and went after the bird and they fought, knocking each other over, and the little boy watched. And the Ipundulu turned into a full bird. And he swatted the bug man away and threw lightning at him again, and the bug man flew away. I heard others coming and I ran in when the Ipundulu was looking at his bug man, and ran my sword through his back, and ducked when he swung his wing around. He laughed, would you believe this? He pulled out the sword and fought me with it. I pulled Nsaka's sword quick, in time to block his blow, and swung it up to chop him but he blocked mine. I dropped to a squat and swung for his legs but he jumped and flapped his wings and his head burst through the hut roof. He jumped back down and threw mud chunks at my head and knocked me in the fore-head, and I fell to one knee. And upon me, he was, but I grabbed a stool and blocked his blow and thrust from underneath and stabbed him in the side. That made him stagger. I pulled back and charged in straight for the heart but he blocked and kicked me in the chest, and I rolled and landed flat on my face and did not move and he said, You, I expected more game in you. He turned his back to me and I grabbed a knife—do you remember how good I was with knives, Tracker? Was it not I that taught you how to wield them? And the lightning woman, she ran to his side and he caressed her head and truly she purred and hunched herself under his touch like a cat, and then he took both his hands and broke her neck. I was on my knees, and I pulled two knives and this, this I will never forget, Tracker. The boy shouted at him. Not words, but he alerted him. Tell you truth, I remember nothing but lightning.

I woke again to see two of the grass-haired devils. They ripped off Nsaka's robes and spread her legs, and the Ipundulu was hard. I don't know why he listened to me when I begged him to ravage me instead. Maybe he saw me as more beautiful. I was too weak and they were upon me. How he mounted me, Tracker—no wet, no spit, he rammed into me until I cut and bled and hark, he used my own blood to ease his fuck into me. Then he bit me until he supped blood, and he drank and he drank and the others drank too, and then he kissed the cut right in my neck and lightning left him and went right into my blood rivers. All this made her watch. They didn't have to make the boy.

"You ever feel fire burn you from the inside out? And then everything was white and blank like highest noon. Tell you truth, I had no memory from then until I woke up as the Ipundulu in Kongor. Some things come, like the eating of rats, and the sound of loose chains. I looked at my hands and saw white, and at my feet I saw a bird and my back itched and itched until I saw I sat on wings. And my Nsaka. Dear gods, my Nsaka. She was in the room with me, maybe she saw me when I was changing. Such is the wicked way of the gods. And how she must have loved me to just . . . to just . . . without fight. . . . Dear wicked gods. When I remembered I was me, I saw her on the floor, her neck broken, and a big bloody hole where used to be her heart. Dear wicked, wicked, gods. I think of her every day, Tracker. I have caused the death of many souls. Many souls. But how deep my heart troubles over this one."

"Indeed."

"I have killed my—"

"Only one."

"How did you—"

"Those words are popular this night."

"I have no heart for killing," he said.

He brought his feet up to his chest and wrapped his arms around them. I clapped. I had sat down on the floor while he spoke, but rose and clapped.

"Instead you have others do the killing for you. You forget what led me to you. Save the heart pull for the next sad girl whose own heart you rip out, Ipundulu. You are still a murderer and a coward. And a liar."

The sour look came back to his handsome face.

"Hmm. Had you come to kill me, that torch you would have thrown already. What is your desire?"

"Was there one with him, with bat wings?"

"Bat wings?"

"Like a bat. His feet the same as his hands, with iron claws. Huge."

"No, there was no one such. I am telling the truth."

"I know. If he was among them he would never have let you live."

"What do you want, old friend? We are old friends, no?"

"The creature with bat wings, people call him Sasabonsam. That boy you speak of, we reunited him with his mother five years ago. Sasabonsam and the child are together again."

"He stole the boy."

"That is what his mother says."

"You do not."

"No, and you just said why."

"Indeed. The boy was strange. I thought he would have even tried to run to those who came to save him."

"Instead he warned those who took him. He is like no boy of this age."

"That was pompous, Tracker. Not like you."

"How would you know what I am like if you have forgotten, as you say?"

I went up to his shamble throne and sat down close, facing him.

"Where you could not save him, we did. And even with all of us, we could only hurt Sasabonsam, not stop him. There was something wrong with that boy. His smell would be strong, and then it would fade as if he was running hundreds of days away, and then he would be right in front of me.

"Here is a story. We tracked them to Dolingo. When I found them, I caught the Ipundulu pushing

the boy from his chest. The little boy, he was sucking his nipple. Would you believe what I thought?
I thought of a boy child and his mother, some boy
child who never stopped longing for the mother's
milk. Except this mother had no koo. And then I
thought, what kind of wickedness was this, how foul
was this that he had been raping the boy so long that
he thought this was the natural way of things. And
then I saw it for what it was. No rape. Vampire blood.
His opium."

"There are women and boys who come to me as if
I am their opium. Some have run from so far, for so
long, they have no feet. But none has found me in the
Malangika. He will want it more than the embrace of
his own mother."

"Sasabonsam went for him in the Mweru."

"No man leaves the Mweru. Why would anyone
even enter?"

"He is not a man. It does not matter. I think the
boy went of his own will."

"Maybe he was offering something more than toys
or breasts." Nyka laughed. "Tracker, I remember you.
You still lie by only saying half the truth. So a stupid
boy that you found was stolen again by a demon with
wings like a bat. Nobody tasked you to find him. No
one is paying you. And the sun is the sun and the
moon is the moon whether you find him or not."

"You just said you did not know me."

"He is nothing to you, and neither is the bat man."

"He took something from me."

"Who? And will you take something from him?"

"No. I will kill him. And all like him. And all who help him. And all who have helped him. And all who stand in the way between me and him. Even this boy."

"Still smells like a game. You want me to help you find him."

"No I want to help him find you."

So I went back for the child and the three of us left the Malangika. We went above, following a tunnel at the end of the road of blind jackals. Aboveground was no more at war than before I went under. The Ipundulu took nothing, just wrapped his wings tight around his body so that he looked like a strange lord, a lower god wearing a thick agbada. By then the sun had dropped and flamed the sky orange, but everything else was dark.

"Would you like me to take the child who you carry with you?" he asked.

"Touch him and I will throw this torch in your face."

"Helpful is all I am trying to be."

"Your eyes will pop out of your skull from the effort."

The tunnel led out to a small town, where I left the child with a goat skin full of milk at the door of a known midwife. Just outside the town, north of the Blood Swamp, were wildlands. I started walking, but Nyka stood still.

"Once out of the Malangika, the boy will sense you and come running," I said.

"So will every lightning woman and blood slave," he said.

He wished he was the man who loved such devotion, but they were not devoted to him. "They are devoted to the taste of my blood," he said.

"To tell truth, I thought more of you would be waiting above. The giant, I expected. The Moon Witch, perhaps. Most certainly the Leopard. Where is he?"

"I am no keeper of the Leopard," I said.

"But where is he? You have great love for that cat. Wouldn't you know where he is?"

"No."

"You two do not speak?"

"My mother or my grandmother, which are you?"

"No question was ever simpler."

"You wish to know about the Leopard, go and ask the Leopard."

"Will your heart not grow fond when you see him next?"

"When I see him next, I shall kill him."

"Fuck the gods, Tracker. Do you plan to kill everybody?"

"I will murder the world."

"That is a big task. Bigger than killing the elephant or the buffalo."

"Do you miss being a man?"

"Do I miss warm blood running through me,

and skin not the colour of all wickedness? No, good Tracker. I love waking up thanking gods I'm a demon now. If I could ever sleep."

"Now that I see you, I think for a man like you, this was the only future for your form. What do you think the boy has been feeding on all these years, if not your blood?"

"The blood is his opium or his physic, not his food."

"Now that you are aboveground, he will seek you."

"What if he is a year away?"

"He has wings."

"Why do you not smell him?"

We kept walking alongside dying sunrays, which meant north. Night would come down before we got to the Blood Swamp.

"Why do you not smell him?"

"We head north. Unlike the Ipundulu . . . you . . . the former you. Sasabonsam hates cities, and towns, and would never rest in one. He could never hide his form like the Ipun . . . like you. He would much rather hide where travelers pass and pick them off one by one. Him and his brother. Before I killed the brother. The Leopard killed the brother. The Leopard killed the brother, but he smelled my scent on him, so he thinks it was me."

"How did the Leopard kill him?"

"Saving me."

"Then why do you blame the Leopard?"

"This is not what I blame him for."

"Then what—"

"Quiet, Nyka."

"Your words—"

"Fuck your thoughts on my words. This is what you do, what you always do. Ask, and ask, so that you will know and know. And when you finally know all there is to know of someone, you use that knowledge to betray them. Help yourself, you cannot, for it is your nature, as eating her young is crocodile's nature."

"Where is the giant?"

"Dead. And he was not a giant, he was an Ogo."

We came to the edge of the Blood Swamp. I have heard of monstrous things in these wet lands, insects as big as crows, snakes wider than the trunks of trees, and plants hungry for flesh, blood, and bone. Even the heat took shape, like a mad nymph out to poison. But no beast came near us, sensing two creatures worse. Not even when swamp water reached us at our waists. We walked until the water fell to our knees, then our ankles, until we stepped on mud and rough grass. All around us, thick vines and thin trunks twisted and bent and wrapped into each other, making a wall as dense as a Gangatom hut.

The smell came to me before we came to it. An open savannah, with few trees, little grass, but reeking of death stink. Old death stink; whatever rotted started rotting seven days ago. I stepped on it before I saw it, and it gave way under my foot. An arm. Two paces from it a helmet with a head still in it. Ten or so paces away, vultures flapped their wings, pulling entrails out, while above a flock of the same, fat with food, flew away. A battlefield. All that was left of war. I looked up and the birds went as far as I could see, circling bodies, landing for more, picking meat off men, men baking in metal armour, men so bloated they bubbled, heads of men looking like they were buried up to their necks in the ground, their eyes pecked away by the birds. There were too many to smell any one. I kept walking, looking for North or South colours. Ahead of us, spear shafts and swords were the only things that stood. Nyka followed me, also looking.

"You think a soldier willed himself to live for eight days so you could pluck his heart?" I asked.

Nyka said nothing. We kept walking until the savannah ran out of bodies, and parts of bodies, and the birds were behind us. Soon we ran out of trees and were standing at the edge of the Ikosha, the salt plains, two and half days' ride across, and nothing but dirt cracked like dried mud and silver like the moon. He walked towards us as if he just appeared from nothing and started walking. Nyka's wings opened but he saw that I did nothing and closed them.

"Tracker. I remind you this is your idea to take me with you."

"It's not my idea."

"I am indeed the owner of this idea," he said as he approached.

That is what he said, in the very way I knew he would say it. We had been hunting for two moons and nine days. He looked at us with arms akimbo, like a mother about to scold us.

The Aesi.

Nyka struck some dry branches with lightning. Fire woke up quick, and he jumped back. I came back from deeper in the swamp with a young warthog. The body I cut open to stick on a spit, the heart I cut out and threw to Nyka. He would not have shame this hour. He would not eat it with both me and the Aesi looking, but neither of us would turn away. He hissed, sat on the ground, and bit into it. Blood exploded over his mouth and nose.

I looked at the two of them, both I had once tried to kill, both known to have wings—one white, the other black. The me who once would have pulled axes to kill both of them on sight, I wondered where he went.

"Perilous thing it is, being in the South. Enemy territory in the middle of war—are all your plans this mad?" the Aesi said.

"You did not have to come," I said.

"What is his plan?" Nyka said, red all around his mouth.

I cut off pieces of the hog and handed some to both. Both shook their heads. Nyka said something about the taste of burned flesh is now foul to him, which made me think of the Leopard and I did not want to think of the Leopard.

"We are seeking the boy and his monster," the Aesi said.

"He already told me this," Nyka said.

"I am seeking the boy. He is seeking the monster. The monster attacked a caravan north of here; one man said he ripped a cow in half with his feet, then flew away with both halves. The boy was on his shoulders like a child with his father. They flew off into the rain forest between here and the Red Lake," the Aesi said.

"Are you not still with the North King? My memory, sometimes she comes and more times she goes, but I remember that once we were supposed to find this boy and save him from you. Now you both search for the boy to kill him?"

"Things change," I said, before the Aesi opened his mouth and bit into a piece of hog. I glared at him.

"They did save him. Did you not, Tracker?" asked the Aesi. "Saved the boy from his band of undead and led him and his mother to the Mweru. Three years later you . . . Shall I tell this story?"

"I control no man's mouth," I said.

The Aesi laughed. He wrapped his black robe around himself and sat down on a mound made by dead branches and moss.

"Do you remember when you hid from me, Tracker? Hide from me you did, in the dream jungle. I found the Ogo instead. Poor man. Mighty, but simple."

"Do not ever speak of him."

The Aesi bowed his head. "Forgive me." Then, to Nyka, "The Tracker knew to stay awake, for I roamed the dream jungle, looking for him. But many years later—shall we count the years?—he found me one night. The boy, I will give him to you if you help me find him who I seek, he said before even saying peace be with you. And if you help me kill him, he said. What was strange, and I thought so at the time, was that Tracker's dream was coming from the Mweru."

"No man leaves the Mweru," Nyka said.

"But a boy can. It is in the prophecies that a boy who will come from those lands will be the dark cloud above the King. But who has time for prophecy?" the Aesi said.

"Who has time for any of this?" I said, and cut off two pieces of hog and wrapped them in leaf. "Sasabonsam attacked a caravan heading north. We too should go north, on the Bakanga trail, and stop telling tall tales by a fucking fire, as if we are boys."

"Sasabonsam is not a wanderer, Tracker. He heads to the rain forest. He will make home—"

"We travel together, so how is your news always different from mine? He will choose a trail so that he can kill any fool who takes it. The winged one is not like his brother. He doesn't wait for food to come to him, he seeks it. He will go where he sees men go, and he will go where they are not protected."

"He is still on his way to the forest."

"Both of you are fools," Nyka said. "You are saying two parts of the same thing. He will head to the rain forest with the boy. But he will feed and gather bodies along the way."

"The Aesi is forgetting to tell you that we are not the only ones looking for the boy," I said. "Nobody here is lacking rest, so we leave."

"Where is North, Tracker?"

"It's on the other side of my shit-filled ass," I said.

"The night has had enough of you," the Aesi said.

"I wish the night would try and—"

"Enough."

Monsoon is the real enemy when it comes to war," the Aesi said.

The sun bounced through the knotty branches and hurt my eyes. I closed them and rubbed until they itched.

"Our King wants this war to end before the rains. Rain season comes with flood, comes with disease. He needs victory and he needs it soon."

"He's not my king," Nyka said.

I sat up and heard the rush of the river. They must have dragged me to the edge of the salt plains, for I rolled over and saw open grasslands. Grass tall and yellow, hungry for the rain season he was talking about. The bobbing and swaying heads of giraffes far off gobbling leaves from tall trees. Rustling through the bush, guinea fowl, cat, and fox. Above, a flock of sand grouse calling family to water. I smelled lion and

cattle and gazelle shit. My calf rubbed against something hard that would cut it.

"Obsidian. There is no obsidian in these lands,"
I said.

"A man before you must have left it there. Or
maybe you think you were first."

"What did you do to me?"

Aesi turned to me. "Your brain was all fire. You
would burn yourself out."

"Do that to me again and I will kill you."

"You could try. Do you remember many moons
ago once in Kongor, when I chased you down that
market street? Every mind on the street was mine but
yours and the . . . him . . . your—"

"I remember."

"Your mind was closed to me because of the Sangoma. You have felt it, haven't you? Her enchantment
is leaving you. You lost it when you left the Mweru."

"I can still unlock doors."

"There are doors and there are doors."

"I have faced swords since then."

"Because you are the goat looking for the butcher."

"Why didn't you possess Mossi?"

"Sport. But last night you needed to cool yourself
before you lose use."

Truth be told, I felt sore in every muscle, in every
joint. I felt no pain the night before, when anger ran
through my blood. But now, even kneeling made my
legs hurt.

"But you are right, Tracker. We lose time. And I

have only seven more days with you, before I have to save this King from himself."

The Bakanga trail. Not a road or even a path, just a stretch trod by wagon and horse and feet so much that plants stopped growing. On both sides, a forest of whistling thorns giving off ghost music, swaying trunks with branches thinner than my arm. The trail turned to dirt, cracked mud, and rocks, but it reached the horizon and then went beyond it. On both sides, yellow grass with patches of green, and small trees round like the moon, and taller trees where the leaves spread wide and the tops were flat. I heard Nyka say the biggest and the fattest of gods squatted on them too long, which is why the tops sat so flat. I turned and looked behind me, saw him talking to the Aesi and realized that he had said nothing. I was remembering him from another time. This trail was at times full and noisy with animals, but none stirred. None of the giraffes from near the swamp, no zebra, no antelope, no lion hunting the zebra or antelope. No rumble of elephant. Not even the hiss warning of the viper.

"There are no beasts in this place," I said.

"Something has scared them away," the Aesi said.

"We agree he is a thing, then."

We kept walking.

"I have seen him like this before," Nyka said to the Aesi, speaking only to him but wanting me to hear. "Strangest of things that I remember."

The Aesi said nothing, and Nyka always took silence as a sign to continue. He told him that Tracker cares about nothing and loves no one, but when he has been wronged deeply, his whole self, and the self beyond the self, seek only destruction. "I have seen him this way once. And not even seen but heard. His need for vengeance was like life fire."

"Who was the man that made him seek revenge?" the Aesi asked.

I know Nyka. I know he stopped and turned to face him, eye-to-eye, when he said, Me. He sounded almost proud. But then even the most wretched things Nyka ever said or did were always followed by a voice that sounded like he would kiss you many times and softly.

"He will kill this Sasabonsam, is that how you call it? He will kill him on just malcontent alone. What did this beast do?"

I waited for the Aesi to answer, but he said nothing. Sunlight left us, but it was still day, at least near evening.

Clouds gathered in the sky, gray and thick, even though rain season was a moon away. Before deep dusk, we came upon a village, a tribe none of us knew. A fence on both sides of the trail made of tree branches thatched together that ran for three hundred paces. Ten and eight huts, then two more that I did not see at first glance. Most on the left of the trail, only five on the right, but no different. Huts built of mud and branches with one window to look out, some with two. Thick thatch roof held down by vine. Three were twice the size of the others, but most were the same. The tribe gathered their huts in clusters of five or six. Outside some of the huts lay scattered gourds, and fresh footsteps, and the thin smoke of fire put out in a rush.

"Where are the people?" Nyka said.

"Maybe they saw your wings," the Aesi said.

"Or your hair," Nyka said.

"Would you like a pause in the bush to fuck each other?" I asked. The Aesi made some remark about me forgetting my place in this meet, and that as the adviser of kings and lords, he could leave me and resume his real business, and not to forget, ungrateful wolf, that it was I that saved you from the Mweru, since no man who enters the Mweru ever leaves.

"They are here," I said.

"Who?" Nyka said.

"The people. No man flees a village without his cow."

In the center of one cluster, cows lay lazy and goats hopped on tree stumps and loose wood. I went to the first hut on my left and pushed in the door. Dark inside and nothing moved. I went to the next, which was empty as well. Inside the third was nothing but rugs and dried grass on the ground, clay jars with water, and fresh cow dung on the east wall, not yet dry. Outside Nyka was about to speak when I raised my hand and stepped back in. I grabbed the large rug and yanked it away. The little girls screamed into a slap on the mouth from their mother. On the floor, her children curling into her like not-born babies. One girl crying, the mother her eyes wet but not weeping, and the other daughter frowning straight at me, angry. So little and already the brave one ready to fight. Do not fear us, I said in eight tongues until the mother heard enough words to sit up. Her daughter broke from her, ran straight up to me, and kicked my shin. Another me would have held her back and laughed, and played in her hair, but this me let her kick my shin and calf until I grabbed her hair and pushed her back. She staggered into her mother.

I go outside, I said, but the mother followed me.

The Aesi gave Nyka his cloak. This village must have heard of Ipundulu, or he guessed they would have terror for any man with wings. More men and women came out from their huts. An old man said something I barely understood, something about he that comes at night. But they heard strange men were coming down the road, including a man white like kaolin, so they hid. They had been hiding for a long time now. Terror, the old ones say, used to come at noon, but now it comes at night, the old man said. He looked like an elder, almost like the Aesi, but taller, and much thinner, wearing earrings made of beads, and a clay skull plate at the back of his head. A brave man with many killings who now lived in fear. His eyes, two cuts in a face full of wrinkles.

He approached us three, and sat down on a stool by a hut. The rest of the village stepped to us slow and afraid, as if at the slightest move, they would scream. They all came out of their huts now. Some men, more women, more children, the men bare in chest and wearing short cloths around the waist, the women wearing leather-skin covered in beads from neck to knee, with their nipples popping out from both sides, and the children wearing beads around the waist, or nothing. You saw it on the women and children most, eyes staring blank, exhausted from fear, except that angry little girl from the hut who still looked at me like she would kill me if she could.

More and more came out of their huts, still looking around, still slow, still eyeing us from head to foot, but not looking at Nyka as any different from the rest of us. The Aesi spoke to the old man, then spoke to us.

"He says they leave the cows open and he take a cow, sometimes a goat. Sometimes he eat them there and leave the rest for the vulture. One time a boy, he never listen to his mother. This boy who think he is man because he soon go into the bush, he run outside, why only the gods know. Sasabonsam take the boy but he leave the boy left foot. But two nights ago . . ."

"Two nights ago, what?" I asked. The Aesi spoke to him again. I could understand some of what the old man spoke, enough before the Aesi looked at me and said, "That is the night he knocked down the wall of that house over there on the other side, and he go in and he take the two boys of a woman who scream, I do nothing but miscarry. Them is the only boys the gods give me, and he try to take the boys away, and the men, who weak before, find some power in their arms and legs and they rush out and throw stones and rocks at him, and hit him in the head, and he try to bat away the rocks, and dirt, and shit with his wings, and still fly and still carry two boys, and could not, so he let go of one."

"Ask if any of these men fought off the beast."

The Aesi regarded me for a few blinks, not liking how strange it is, a man telling him what to do.

Two men came forward, one with beads around his head, the other with a clay skull plate painted yellow.

"He stunk like a corpse," the beaded one said. "Like the thick stink of rotten meat."

"Black hair, like the ape but he not the ape. Black wings, like the bat, but he not the bat. And ears like a horse."

"And he feet like he hands, and they grab like hands, but big like his head, and he come from sky and try to go back to it."

"There are many flying beasts on this trail," I said.

"Maybe they fly over the White Lake from the Darklands," Nyka whispered to me.

I wanted to tell him that one would have to go to a dark street where men fuck holes in walls and call them sister to find a remark less stupid.

"Sun queen just gone back home," said the one with the skull cap. "Sun queen just gone when he first come, ten nights ago. He fly down, we hear the wing first, and then a shadow that block out the last light. Somebody look up and she scream and he try to grab her and she drop to the ground, and everybody running and yelling, and bawling, and we run to we huts, but an old man, he was too slow and his hunchback hurt, and the beast grab him with leg hands and bite his face off, but then spit him out, like the blood was poison, and he chase after a woman who was the last to reach her hut, I see it myself in the bush I hide myself, he catch her foot before she run in her hut, and he fly off with her, and we don't see her no more. And since then he come every two night."

"Some of we, we try to leave, but the cows slow, and we slow, and he find we on the trail and kill everybody and drink out the blood. Every man and woman and beast rip in two. Sometimes he eat the head."

"Ask him when he came around last," I said.

"Two night ago," the old man says.

"We need to locate the boy," the Aesi said.

"We've found the boy. I was waiting for him to find Nyka. But we have found him."

"No one here mentioned anything of a boy," the Aesi said.

"Good men speak of me as if I am not here. You wish to leave me out in the open so that your boy will find me?" Nyka asked.

"We will not have to. When Sasabonsam comes tonight, he will bring the boy. The boy will demand it until there is no quieting him," I said.

"I do not like this plan," the Aesi said.

"There is no plan," I said.

"That is what I do not like."

"It took six of us to beat him last time and we still could not kill him. Ask what weapons they have."

"I say we let what happen, happen and follow him to where he hides," the Aesi said.

"Where he hides could be two days' walk."

"He is too smart to risk the boy."

"I will kill this thing tonight or fuck the gods."

"Shall I say something?" Nyka said.

"No," we both said.

"Ask them what weapons they have."

Four axes, ten torches, two knives, one whip, five spears, and a pile of stones. I tell truth, these people, who left the hunt for the field, were foolish to forget that this was still a land full with wicked beasts. The men brought the weapons, threw them at our feet, then scrambled to their huts like mad ants. This did not surprise me—all men are cowards, and men together only added fear to fear to fear. Darkness snatched the sky, and the crocodile had eaten half of the moon. We hid by the fence near the north of the village. The Aesi crouched low, holding a stick I did not see him with before, his eyes closed.

"Do you think he calls on spirits?" Nyka said.

"Speak louder, vampire. I do not think he heard you."

"Vampire? How harsh, your words. I am not like who we hunt."

"You have witchmen hunt them for you. We will not have this argument again."

"It would please the night if you were both quiet," the Aesi said.

But Nyka wanted to talk. He was always like this, needing endless chatter. He used chat to mask what he was plotting at the same time.

"I have not killed a man today," I said.

"You said many times, over many years I have known you, I am a hunter, not a killer."

"If not Sasabonsam, then I will kill every man here for being so weak and pathetic."

"Careful, Tracker. You're in the presence of a vampire and . . . whatever this Aesi is, and yet you burn with the most ill will. And even if you do joke, you were funnier back then," Nyka said.

"Which then? Before or after you betrayed me?"

"I have no memory of that."

"Memory has much of you. You never asked about my eye."

"Did I too cause that?"

I stared at him, but turned away when seeing him only made me see myself. I told him how I got the wolf eye.

"I thought a man punched you in the eye and left it so," he said. "But I see I am responsible for that too."

He looked away. I could think of nothing more

to do with Nyka's remorse than punch him in the face with it. How I wished I had Sadogo's knuckles to punch his head clean off. Sadogo. I had not thought of him in many long moons. Nyka opened his mouth again, and the Aesi covered it.

"Listen," he whispered.

The sound cut through the dark, shuffling, jumping, running, falling over the fence, and cracking branches. And coming at us. No flapping of wings. None of the giggle, gurgle, and hiss of a child failing to mask himself. One rammed me in the chest and knocked me over. Then another. His knee in my chest, he looked up, sniffed quick, and turned to see others piling themselves all over Nyka, and the Aesi, screaming, grunting, shrieking, and grabbing. Lightning men and women. More than I could count, some with one hand, some with one leg, some with no feet, some with nothing below the waist. All of them rushing at Nyka. Two larger ones, both men, kicked the Aesi out of the way. Nyka yelled. The lightning women and men search and seek the Ipundulu; he is their only desire and purpose and they yearn for him forever. I have seen them run towards their master, desperate and hungry, but I had never seen what happens when they finally find him.

"They devour me!" Nyka shouted.

He flapped his wings and blasted lightning, which hit several of them, but they sucked it in, fed on it, grew more mad. I pulled both axes. The Aesi kept touching his temple and sweeping his hands over them, but nothing happened. The lightning people were an anthill on Nyka. I backed up, ran, leapt up, landed on the back of one, and rained his back with hacks. Left, right, left, right, left. I kicked one and chopped the side of his head. One wrapped her hand around Nyka's neck and I chopped at her shoulder until her arm fell off. They would not let go and I would not stop.

A foot coming from nowhere kicked me in the chest. I flew in the air and landed on my belly. Two jumped to charge me. I had one ax and pulled my knife. One jumped at me, I rolled out of his way, and he landed on the ground. Knife in hand, I rolled back to him and plunged it in his chest. The second ran at me but I spun on the ground and chopped her leg. She fell and I hacked half her head off. They were still on Nyka. The Aesi pulled two, throwing them away like they were small rocks. Nyka kept pushing them off but would not attack them. I ran back to the pile, pulled one out by the foot, and stabbed him in the neck. Another I pulled and he punched me in the belly, and I fell to the ground, howling in pain. Now I was mad. The Aesi grabbed another. I pulled myself up with an ax and found another. One that crouched on Nyka's chest to suck his neck, I chopped straight in the back of the neck. Lightning flashed through all of them, but they would not even turn from him. I rained chops down on his head and kicked off a woman beside him. She rolled off and came running back. I crouched, swung my ax, and hacked her right above the heart when she ran into me, and I swung the other down on her forehead. I chopped them all away, until there was Nyka, covered in bites and bleeding black blood. The last one, a child, jumped on Nyka's head and gnashed his teeth at me. Lightning lit his eyes. I jammed my knife straight in his throat and he dropped in Nyka's lap.

"He was a boy."

"He was nothing," I said.

"Something here is not right," the Aesi said.

I jumped right before a woman from the village screamed.

"At the back!"

The Aesi ran off first, and I chased after him, jumping over these bodies, some of which still sparked lightning. We ran past huts hiding in the dark. Nyka tried to fly but could only hop. We got to the outer boundary to see Sasabonsam, his foot claws around a woman and flying away. The woman still screamed. I hurled an ax and hit his wing but it cut shallow. He did not turn.

"Nyka!" I said.

Nyka flapped his wings and thunder shook and lightning burst from him, but it shot west and south of him, not straight at the beast. Sasabonsam flapped and flew away, the woman still fighting. She struggled, until he kicked her in the head with his other foot. But there was no thicket to hide him in this savannah. My ax glinted in the dirt.

"He is flying north," the Aesi said.

A flock of birds that I did not see far off changed course and flew straight to Sasabonsam. They charged him two and three at a time and he tried to swat them away with his hand and wings. I could not see all, but one flew in his face, and it looked like he bit into it. More came after him. The Aesi's eyes were closed. The birds dived for Sasabonsam's face and arms, and he started to swing his arms wildly. He dropped the woman, but from so high that when she hit the ground she did not move. Sasabonsam swatted away so many birds that they shot through the sky. The Aesi opened his eyes and the remaining birds flew away.

"We will never catch him," Nyka said.

"But we know where he is going," said the Aesi.

I kept running, jumping over shrubs and chopping through bush, following him in the sky, and when I couldn't see him, I followed the smell. This was when I wondered why this all-powerful Aesi did not supply us horses. He wasn't even running. I could turn my fury at him but that would be a waste. I kept running. The river came upon me. Sasabonsam flew over it to the other side. It was fifty paces, sixty paces wide, I could not guess, and the moonlight danced wild on it, meaning rough and perhaps deep. This part of the river was unknown to me. Sasabonsam was flying away. He had not even seen me, not even heard me.

"Sasabonsam!"

He did not even turn. I gripped both axes as if it was them that I hated. He made me think dark thoughts, that he held no joy for what he did, or even pride, but nothing. Nothing at all. That my enemy did not even know that I sought him, and even in the presence of my smell and my face I was no different from any other fool throwing an ax. Nothing, nothing at all. I shouted at him. I sheathed my axes and ran right into the river. My toe hit a sharp rock but I did not care. I tripped on stones but did not care. Then the ground fell from under my feet and I sank, inhaled water, and coughed. I pushed my head out of the water but my feet could not find ground. And then something like a spirit pulled me, but it was the water, cold and pulling me hard to the middle of the river, and then drawing me under, mocking my strength to swim, spinning me head over foot, yanking me beyond where the moon could shine, and the more I fought the more it pulled, and I did not think to stop fighting, and I did not think, I'm tired, and I did not think the water was colder and blacker. And I stretched my hand out and thought it would reach into air, but I was so far down and sinking, sinking, sinking.

And then a hand grabbed mine and pulled me up. Nyka, trying to fly and stumbling, bouncing, then falling into the water. Then he tried to fly again while drawing me out, but could only pull me up to my shoulder and fight the current. In this way he dragged me to the riverbank, where the Aesi waited.

"The river nearly had you," the Aesi said.

"The monster flees," I said, gasping for air.

"Maybe it was offended by your sourness."

"The monster flees," I said.

I caught my breath, pulled my axes, and started walking.

"No gratitude for the Ip—"

"He is getting away."

I ran off.

The river had washed off all the ash and my skin was black as sky. The land was still savannah, still dry with shrubs and whistling thorn that sat close together, but I did not know this place. Sasabonsam flapped his wings twice and it sounded far away, as if it wasn't the flutter but the echo. Tall trees rose, three hundred paces ahead. Nyka shouted something I did not hear. A flutter again; it sounded like it came from the trees, so there is where I ran. I hit a stone, tripped, and fell, but rage fought pain and I got up and kept running. The ground went wet. I ran through a drying pond, through grass scratching my knee, past thorny shrubs scattered like warts on skin that I jumped over and stepped in. No sound of flutter came but my ears were on him; I would hear him closer soon. I did not even need my nose. The trees did what trees do, stood in the way. No valley path, only giant thorns and wild bush, and as I went around I ran right into them.

Men on horseback, I would guess a hundred. I studied the horses for their mark. A ridge of armour over the head coming down the long face. Body draped in warm cloth, but not long like the Juba horses. Tails kept long. A saddle on top of layers of thick cloth and at the corners of the cloth, northern marks I had not seen in years. Maybe half of the horses black, the rest brown and white. I should have studied the warriors. Thick garments to stop a spear, and spears with two prongs. Men, all of them, except one.

"Announce yourself," she said when she saw me. I said nothing.

Seven of them surrounded me, lowering their spears. I usually thought nothing of swords or spears but something was different. The air around them and me.

"Announce yourself," she said again. I did nothing.

In the moonlight they were all plume and shine. Their armour silver in the dark light, the feathers in their headdresses ruffling like a meeting of birds. Their dark arms pointed spears at me. They couldn't tell who I was in the night. But I could tell who they were.

"Tracker," I said.

"He does not speak our language," another warrior said.

"Nothing special about the language of Fasisi," I said.

"Then what is your name?"

"I am Tracker," I said.

"I will not ask again."

"Then don't. I said my name is Tracker. Is your name Deaf One?"

She stepped to the front, and poked me with her

spear. I staggered back. I could not see her face, only her shiny war helmet. She laughed. She poked me again. I gripped my ax. Panic felt a day away, then it was right behind me, then it was in my head, and I squeezed my eyes shut.

"Maybe your name is Deathless, since you seem to have no fear of me killing you."

"Do what you must. If I take just one of you with me, that is a good death."

"Nobody here would hate to die, hunter."

"Do any of you hate to talk?"

"For a man who looks like river folk, you have quite the mouth."

"Pity I know no rebel Fasisi verse."

"Rebel?"

"No Fasisi army has made it to the south border of Wakadishu, or you would have been corpses on a battlefield. No women walk in Fasisi ranks. And no Fasisi guard could have ever landed this far south, not with war here. You are Fasisi born but not loyal to Kwash Dara. King sister guards."

"You know much about us."

"I know that this is all there is to know."

The spears moved in closer.

"I am not the one being rude in the face of seventy and one spears," she said.

She pointed at me.

"Men and their cursed arrogance. You curse, you shit, you wail, you beat women. But all you really do is take up space. As men always do, they cannot help themselves. It's why they must spread their legs when they sit," she said.

The men laughed, all who heard whatever kind of joke this was.

"How great your brotherhood of men must be that all they think about is men spreading their legs."

She scowled, I could see it, even in the dark. The men grumbled.

"Our Queen—"

"She is not a queen. She is the King sister."

The warrior chief laughed again. She said something about how I must either seek death or think I cannot die.

"Did he teach you that as well, the one who rides with you? You would do good to keep him up front with you, for his kind prefers to kill from behind," I said.

He rode his horse right up to the front until he was beside the warrior chief. Dressed as they were with the feather helmet taming his wild hair, he seemed not only odd on the horse but that he knew it. The way a dog would look riding a cow.

"How it goes, Tracker?"

"Never seems to go away, Leopard."

"It's been said you have a nose."

"Under your armour, you stink worse than them."

He gripped the bridle harder than he needed to, and the horse jerked her head. His whiskers, which rarely showed when he was a man, shone in the night. He took his helmet off. Nobody moved their spears. There were things I wanted to ask him. How a man never interested in long-term hire found long-term hire. How they got him to wear such armour, and robes that must drag, and tear, and chafe, and itch. And if part of the bargain was that he never changed to his true nature again. But I asked none of that.

"How different you look," he said.

I said nothing.

"Hair wilder than mine, like a seer nobody listens to. Thin as witch stick. No Ku marks?"

"They washed in the river. Much has happened to me, Leopard."

"I know, Tracker."

"You look the same. Perhaps because nothing ever happens to you. Not even what you cause."

"Where do you head, Tracker?"

"We go where you come from. Where we come from you go."

The Leopard stared at me. He would have known who I searched for. Or he was a fool. Or he thought me to be one.

"Tell them that you are headed home, Tracker, for your sake."

"I have a home? Tell me where, Leopard. Point me where to go."

Leopard stared at me. The warrior chief cleared her throat.

"Let me state it clear that I tried to help you," he said.

"'Let me state it clear'? From where did you get this tongue? Your help is worse than a curse," I said.

"Enough. You two fight like people who have fucked. You came upon us, traveler. Be on with you and . . . Who are those two?"

Behind me Nyka and the Aesi were at least a hundred paces away. The Aesi covered his hair with a hood. Nyka wrapped his wings tight around himself.

She continued, "You and your kind go. You already delay us."

She reined her horse.

"No," the Leopard said. "I know him. You cannot let him go."

"He is not the one we look for."

"But if the Tracker is here then he's already found him."

"This man. He is just some man you know. You seem to know many," she said.

I hoped she smiled in the dark. I really hope she did.

"Fool, how do you not know who this is? Even after he said his name. He is the one who insulted your Queen. The one who came to kill her son, but he was already gone. The one who—"

"I know who he is." Then, to me, "You, Tracker, you come with us."

"I go nowhere with any of you."

"You're the second man to think I am offering choices. Take him."

Three warriors dismounted and stepped towards me. I held both axes in hand and gripped them tight. I had just cut a child's throat and split a woman's head in two, so I would kill anyone here. But I looked straight at the Leopard when I thought it. The three stepped to me and stopped. They lowered their spears and approached. Before, I could not smell it anymore, the fear metals had for me. I could stand tall like the person in the storm who never got hit by hail. Now I looked left and right, thinking who I should dodge first. I looked up and saw Leopard watching me.

"Tracker?" he said.

"Have all my men gone deaf in the night? Take him!"

The warriors would not move. They shook and strained, forcing their lips to speak, their hips to turn, to say that they wanted to do as she wished, but could not.

Nyka and the Aesi came up behind me.

"And who are these two?"

"I am sure they have mouths. Ask them," I said.

Every man holding spears lifted them away. The chief looked around in shock, and spooked her horse. She rubbed his cheek hard, trying to calm him.

"Who is . . ." Leopard said, but his words vanished.

The Aesi came to stand by me. With both hands he pulled back his hood.

"Kill him! Kill him!" Leopard shouted.

The warrior chief yelled, "Who is he?" The Aesi's eyes went white. Every single horse jumped and kicked, throwing themselves up in the air, throwing off the riders, and kicking whoever they could strike. A warrior got struck in the head. Those who held on to their horses yelled in fright as the horses ran into each other and attacked those on foot. Three horses ran, trampling two men underfoot.

"This is his will! This is his will!" Leopard shouted to the chief.

She grabbed Leopard by his arm and both fell off their horses. Most of the horses ran away. Some of the men ran after them but stopped, then turned around, pulled their swords, and attacked each other. Soon everyone fought someone. One killed another by driving a sword into his chest. A warrior fell from a sword in his back. Leopard punched the chief and knocked her out. He rose and snarled at the Aesi. The Aesi stared at him as he approached. He touched his temple. He tried to work his mind on the cat, but Leopard changed into beast and charged. He leapt at the Aesi but horses ran straight into him, cutting him off and knocking him down. Nyka spread his wings, walked through the fighting men, and stopped at one on the ground bleeding from a mortal wound. I know he told him that he was sorrowful. And that he was quick. He punched straight into the man's chest and pulled out his heart. He did it to two more wounded soldiers before all the men, alive and near-dead, fell asleep. All except the chief, who had a stab wound in the shoulder. The Aesi stooped down beside her. She flinched, tried to hit him, but her hand stood up in the air.

"When your brothers awake in the morning, they will see what was done here. They will know that brother raised sword against brother in madness, and killed many," the Aesi said.

"You are the living evil. I have heard of you. You set yourself against women and men. The wicked half of the Spider King."

"Do you not know, brave warrior? Both halves are wicked. Sleep now."

"I will kill—"

"Sleep."

She fell back on the ground.

"And have a sweet voyage to the dream jungle. It will be the last pleasant dream you shall ever have."

He stood up. Behold, I call three horses, he said to me.

There was a door in the Blood Swamp, but it would have taken us to Luala Luala, too far north. At first I thought the Aesi knew nothing of the ten and nine doors, but he only chose not to use them. This is what I suspected: that going through a door weakened him, just as it weakened the Moon Witch. The massive number of wronged spirits and devils that waited for him in the doorway of each door, snatching him at the one point when he was just like them, all spirit and no body, and could be grabbed, or taken, or fought, or even killed. This is what I thought: that there were things we could not see, many hands perhaps, grabbing for any part of him, vengeance lust coursing through them where blood used to run.

"Tracker! Are you lost? I called you three times," Nyka said.

He had already mounted his horse. It looked like it was fidgeting, disturbed by the unnatural thing on its back. It reared, trying to throw him off, but Nyka grabbed its neck. The Aesi turned to the horse and it calmed.

We rode off in the dark, on what would be a night's journey north, then west, along grasslands, until we got to the rain forest. It had no name, this forest, and I did not remember it from the map. The Aesi rode in front, at a quick gallop several paces ahead of us, and I don't know why I thought so, but it looked as if he was trying to get away. Or get to them first. When he came for me in the Mweru I told him that he could have the boy, do as he pleased, take a circumcision knife and slice his whole body in two for all I cared, just help me kill the winged devil. But I would kill this boy. Or I would kill the world. People passing me keep saying we are at war. We are in war. Then let there be killing and let there be death. Let us all go down to the underworld and let the gods of death talk about true justice. The gold grass turned silver in the night.

Their hooves hitting the ground, the horses struck up a thunder. Deeper dark lay ahead of us, dense dark like mountains. We could see it across the flat land, but it would still be dawn before we reached it. Riding through the black, and thinking wickedness, and smelling him without thinking about him, I didn't see the Leopard until he was a length away and pushing his horse hard, trying to catch me. I leaned into my horse harder, pushing him to a full gallop. Now that my nose remembered his smell, I could sense him getting closer and closer. He snarled at his horse, frightening her, until we were riding tail-to-head, head-to-trunk, neck-to-neck. He jumped from his horse right onto me and knocked me off. I spun around in the fall so I landed on top of him. We still hit the grass hard and rolled, and rolled, and rolled several paces, him grabbing on to me. A dead anthill finally stopped us, and he flew off me. The Leopard landed on his back and jumped up, right into my knife pressed at his throat. He jerked backward and I pressed deeper into his neck. He raised his hand and I pressed and drew blood. His face was bright in the moon dark, his eyes wide open; in shock yes, in regret perhaps, blinking very little, as if begging me to do something. Or none of those things, which made me mad. I had not seen him in moons, for my mind burned with what I would do to him should we again cross paths. Should I be on top in him, should I overpower him, should I have an ax or a knife. Like the knife at his throat. No god could count how many times I had thought of this. I could have cut my hate out of him, as deep and as wide as my knife would go.

Say something, Leopard, I thought. Say, Tracker, is this how we will now find sport, you and me—so I would cut you and shut you up. But he just stared at me.

"Do it," said Nyka the Ipundulu. "Do it, dark wolf. Do it. Whatever peace you seek you will never find.

And it will never find you, so do it. Forget peace. Seek vengeance. Tear a hole a hundred years wide. Do it, Tracker. Do it. Is he not the reason you suffer?"

Leopard looked at me, his eyes wet. He tried to say something but it came out as just sounds, like a whimper, though he was too brave to whimper. I wanted to cut a hole in something so badly. And then a rumble rose under him in the quick. The dirt broke up into dust and pulled him under the earth. I jumped back and shouted his name. He forced his hand through the ground and kicked and kicked, but the ground swallowed him. I looked up as the Aesi draped his hood over his head.

TWENTY-FIVE

You killed him!"

"I pulled my ax.

"Child of a fucking whore, you killed him," I said.

"Tracker, how tiresome you are. For moons you have thought of killing this beast. You have slit his throat in the dream jungle. You have tied him to a tree and burned him. You have shoved all sorts of things up in every part of his body. You had a knife to his neck. You name him as the cause of all your misery. And yet now you scream when finally you get what you wish."

"I never wished for that."

"You didn't have to."

"Go into my head again and you will—"

"I will what?"

"Free him."

"No."

"You know I will kill you."

"You know you cannot."

"You know I will try."

We stood there. I ran back to where the Leopard was. The ground was the mound of a new grave. I was about to dig him out with my hands when a whistle came from behind me, a cold wind that looked like smoke. It dove into the mound and made a hole as wide as my fist.

"Now he breathes," the Aesi said. "He will not die."

"Pull him out."

"You would best think about what you want in these last days, Tracker. Love or revenge. You cannot have both. Let him dig himself out. It will take him days, but he will have enough strength to do so. And enough rage. Come, Tracker, Sasabonsam sleeps by day."

He and Nyka mounted their horses. The mound was too still. I stepped away but still watched it. I thought I heard him, but it was creatures of dawn. We rode away.

Gods of morning broke daylight. The forest was in sight but still not close. The horses grew tired, I could feel it. I did not shout to Aesi to stop, though he slowed to a trot. Sasabonsam would have gone to sleep. I rode up to him.

"The horses will have rest," I said.

"We won't need them when we reach the forest."

"That was not a question."

I halted my horse and climbed off. Nyka and the Aesi looked at each other. Nyka nodded.

I slept, I do not know for how long, but warm sun woke me up. Not noon, but after. None of us spoke as we mounted our horses and rode off. We would reach the forest before evening if the horses ran steady. The afternoon was still hot and wet in the air, and we came across another battlefield, from a long-fought battle, with skulls and bones, and parts of armour not salvaged scattered about. The skulls and bones led up to a hill as high as a house with two floors, maybe two hundred paces to the right of us. A hill of spear shafts, other broken weapons, and shields, dented and cracked, and bones scraped clean of flesh and sinew. The Aesi stopped and reined his horse.

He watched the hill. I asked him nothing, and neither did Nyka. From behind the hill of spears appeared a headdress, then a head. Someone walked to the top. The face, in a mask of white clay covering all but eyes, nose, and lips, her headdress dried fruits, or seeds, along with bones, tusks, and long feathers hanging down and brushing her shoulders. White clay on her bare breasts, down to her belly, with stripes that looked like the zebra's, and a ripped leather skirt on her hips.

"I shall meet you by the mouth of the forest," the Aesi said, and rode towards her. Nyka hissed the curse that could not come out of my mouth. The woman turned and went back where she came from. I rode off and after a while heard Nyka riding behind me.

We were some time in the forest before either of us noticed. The bush was too thick with grass and fallen trees for the horses, so we went on foot.

"Should we wait for the Aesi?" Nyka said, but I ignored him and kept walking.

Something about this forest reminded me of the Darklands. Not the trees pushing their way up into sky or plants, tufts, and ferns spreading out of the trunks like flowers. Or the mist so thick it felt like light rain. The silence is what took me back to that forest. The quiet is what bothered me. Some vines reached down right in front of us like rope. Some swung back up and around branches like snakes. Some vines were snakes. Dark had not yet come, but no sunlight came through these leaves. But this was not the Darklands, for the Darklands had many ghost beasts. Things cooed, and cawed, and screeched, and bawled. Nothing growled, nothing roared.

"This shit," Nyka said. I turned around and saw him scraping worms off his foot. "Worms know decay when it steps on them," he said.

I climbed over a fallen tree, the trunk as wide as I was high, and kept walking. The tree was far behind me when I noticed that Nyka did not follow.

"Nyka."

He was not on the other side of the tree either.

"Nyka!"

His smell was everywhere, but no trail opened up to me. He became air—everywhere but nothing. I turned around only to see two gray legs spread wide, and before I could see between them something white and wet shot into my face.

He tore it from my head, my face, my eyes, something that also went in my mouth that felt like silk and had no taste. The silk off my eyes, I could see it wrapped around me, tight and shiny, though I could see my skin through it. A butterfly wrapped in a cocoon. My hands, my feet, none could move no matter how I tried to kick, stomp, tear, or roll. I was stuck to the trunk of a weak branch bending with me. This made me think of Asanbosam, Sasabonsam's brother with no wings, hopping up and down on his tree branches full of rotting women and men. Except nothing rotted here. I thought this good until I heard him above me and saw that he preferred his meat fresh. He bit off a little monkey's head and the tail dropped limp. He saw me looking up at him only when all was gone but the tail, which he sucked into his mouth with a wet, slithering sound.

"Honk honk honk, that be all they do. Me, me not even was hungry. Know this pretty ape, when mami kipunji come looking for baby kipunji I going be eating her too. Make a mess, such a mess these kipunji, make a mess, they swing over looking for fruit and make such a mess in me house, yes they be making it and making it, and shit all over the leaves, shitting it, yes they shitting it and my mami-mami she going say, she would say, not going say for mami-

mami, she be dead—oh, but she say keep a clean house or the wrong woman going want you, that be what she say kippi-lo-lo that be what she say."

He started to climb down the tree trunk, crouching like a spider, so low that his belly rubbed the bark. First I thought no ghommid was ever this big. Shoulders like a thin man with all muscle, but his upper arm was as long as a tree branch and his forearm stretched longer, so that his whole arm was longer than all of me. And legs as long as his arms. This is how he came down to me, stretching his right hand out straight and digging into the bark with his claws, lifting his right leg and bending it over his back, over his shoulder and head, and grabbing the trunk. Then his left hand and his left foot, his belly rubbing the trunk. He crawled down, right above my head, crawled backways, lifted himself up to the waist, and twisted his body around, almost a full twist, and reached for the last branch sticking out, first left hand, then right, and then left foot and right, still twisted at the waist so that right below his waist was his buttocks, not his crotch. He swung one arm over as if it would break and scratched his back. He crouched on the branch in front of me and his knees went past his head and his arms almost touched the ground. And between his legs, a hairy sheath like that of a dog, and from it came the juice he shot in my face. The juice hit the tree trunk across and turned to silk. He crawled over to that trunk and shot another silk line back to the branch. Then, crawling on both lines, he weaved a pattern with his hands and toes until he built something strong enough to sit on, which he did. Skin gray and covered in scars and marks like river folk, so light you could see the blood rivers along his limbs. Bald head with a sprout of hair on top, white eyes with no black, teeth yellow, and sharp, and poking out of his mouth.

"Take a story and give me, yes? Take a story and give me."

"I know no monster of your sort."

He belched and laughed like a hiss. He looked at me and wiped off his laugh.

"Take a story and—"

He swung both legs behind his shoulders and his sheath shot wet silk high up in the trees. He grabbed the web with his arms and pulled her down, the mother monkey. She honked and honked and he held her right above his face. Face-to-face, the mother monkey whimpering in fear. She was smaller than my arm. He split his mouth open and bit her head off. Then he chewed up the rest of her and sucked in the tail. He looked at me again as he licked his lips.

"Take a story and give me, yes? Take a story and give me."

"I had heard that those like you, you are the ones who give stories. And lies. And tricks."

"Those like me. Like me? Nobody like me. No no no no. I will have story. I have no more of my own. Take a story and give me to feed, yes? Or I going feed on something else."

"You are the trickster and storyteller. Are you not one of Nan Si? And this is one of your tricks?"

He jumped over on me, his toes digging into the tree, his arms grabbing branches, his crotch right in front of my face. He bent his head so low that I thought he was about to lick himself, but stared right at me.

"This is what you wish, I can see it. Killing or dying, either death the same. You welcome either, you want both. I can give it to you. But who is Nan Si?"

"What are you?"

"Tell me you see my pale tone, hunter. I am like the one you came in with."

"Did you kill him?"

"He leave you."

"Not for the first time."

"He don't know that you gone. This forest has plenty enchantments."

"So has every forest."

"Know that I am not of the forest, I am not of the Nan Si. Not one, no, not one. I was a man of great breadth with knowledge of science and mathematics."

"White science and black math. You were a white scientist. Now you are a was."

He nodded, too hard and too long.

"What did you push?"

"What was already in the mind. Beyond the fetish priest, and beyond the prophet. Beyond the seer. Even beyond the gods! True wisdom is never without, it is within, was always within. Within always."

"And now you are a beast, eating monkeys and their mothers, and making webs out of your cum."

"There was fear in you. It is gone, gone, gone. I so hunger for a tale. None of these beasts speak. None have magic."

"I seek a flying beast and his boy."

"A flying beast? Will you kill him? Will you do it slow? What shall you do with them?"

"He came past you."

"No beast come past here."

"This is a forest, and Sasabonsam rests in forest."

"This is a forest of life, and he is among the dead things of the world."

"So you know him."

"Never said I didn't."

He grabbed something above my head and put it in his mouth.

"I will meet them. In the field or the swamp. Or the sand sea. Or here."

I tried to pull my hands but the silk squeezed tighter. I yelled at the white scientist. I jerked forward, trying to pop my cocoon off the tree, but it would not budge. He smiled, watching my struggle. He even grinned when I jerked. I cursed him again.

"Let me kill him, him and the boy, and I will return for you to kill me. Smash my head open and suck the brain out. Cut me open and show me what first you will eat. Do what you wish. I swear it."

He went back to the branch.

"Kamikwayo is what some called me."

"Where did you practice white science?"

"Practice? Practice is for the student."

"The white scientists of Dolingo enter men's heads so they desire unnatural things."

"Dolingon are butchers. A meat shop with all of them. Meat shop! I was neither scientist nor witch-man. I was an artist. The greatest student to leave the University of Wakadishu—not even the wisest seers, and teachers, and masters could teach me, for I was wiser than them all. They said, You, Kamikwayo, must devote the rest of your days to the life of the mind. That is what they said, I was there when they said it. Go to the Wakadishu palace of wisdom. I studied the spider to get the secret of his delicious web. You are a small mind, perhaps Gangatom, so you cannot think as the scientist, but think of the web, think of how far it stretches before it breaks. Think it, think it, think it now. I said to all of them, Think of rope that can stick to the man the way web sticks to the fly. Think of armour soft as cotton but can block the spear, and even the arrow. Think of a bridge across the river, the lake, the swamp. Think of all these things and more things if we could make the web just like the spider. Hear this, river man. This scientist could not make the web. I mixed so many spiders, I squeezed their bellies, I taste the thing in my mouth to tell the ingredients apart, but still it slipped away from me like a slimy thing. Slip away! But I worked day and night, and night into day, until I make a potion, I make a glue like the sap from the tree and I take a stick and stretched it like a long line of spit, and it dried, and it cooled and it was solid. And I called my brothers and said, Lo! I made the web. And they were amazed. And they said we have not seen anything of the like in all science and mathematics, brother. And then it cracked, and then it broke, and they laughed, how they laughed, and one said it broke on the floor just as I am broke in the mind, and they laughed even more, and they shamed me and went away to their quarters to sleep and talk of potions to make a woman forget they raped her.

"I tell you a true thing. I was beyond sad, beyond grief. This science was poisoning me, so I grabbed my bottles and drank the poison. I would sleep and never wake up. And then I did. I woke up with a fever in me that did not cool. I woke up and saw that I slept on the ceiling, not the bed on the floor. I rubbed my eyes and saw long gray monster's hands come at my face. I cried, but my cry came out a shriek, and I fell to the floor. My arms so long, my legs so long, my face, oh my face, for I tell you more truth, I was the prettiest of the scientists, yes I was, men came at me with grosser propositions than they did concubines, saying, Pretty one, offer your hole, your mind is of no use. I cried, and I screamed and I wailed until I felt nothing. And nothing, nothing was the best. I liked nothing. By noon I loved my nothing. I crawled on the ceiling. I ate food while sitting on the wall and

I did not fall. I thought I was going to piss, or cum, but it was a sweet and sticky thing that came out, and I could hang from the wall!

"My brothers, they did not understand. My brothers all, they all have the failure of the nerves, they achieve nothing because they risk nothing. One shouted, Demon! and threw bottles at me, and even I did not know that I could duck so low that only my elbows and knees were in the air. I spurt web around his face until he could breathe no more. Now listen to this, for I not going to say it again. I killed the first one before he make alarm. The rest, they up in another room doing science on village girls, so I go up to the inner room, one hand carrying precious oil, the other carrying a torch. And I walked on the ceiling and kicked down the door, and one of them inside said, Kamikwayo, what is this madness? Get off the ceiling. And I thought something smart and final to say, something to follow with a wicked laugh. But I had no words, so I shattered the jug of oil, then I threw down the torch, and then I closed the door. Yes I did. How they howled, oh how they howled. The sound was pleasing to me. I ran to the bush, the great forest where I am free to ponder on big things and small things, but who is there to tell me great tales?"

He pointed at me and grinned.

"Good hunter, you pulled a story out of me. Now you shall tell me a tale. I go sick from the company of people, and yet I am so very lonely. Even that tells you how much I am alone for no lonely person says so. I know this is true, I know it. Take a story and give me, yes? Take a story and give me."

I looked at him, rubbing his legs together, his eyes wide and his hollow cheeks packed from a grin. He would have been an albino or a grown mingi had his white skin not taken on the pale gray of the white scientists.

"Will you give me freedom if I tell you a story?"

"Only if it gives me great mirth. Or great sadness."

"Oh, you must be moved. Otherwise you bite my head off and eat me in five bites," I said.

He looked at me, stunned. I think he said something about not knowing the monkey was my kin, but his web hole dripped silk.

"No. I am a man and a brother. I am a man!"

He hopped over to me and grabbed my neck. He snarled and growled, ripped the silk around me, tore my clothes, and scraped one of his claws against my neck.

"Am I not a man? I ask you. Am I not a man?"

His eyes went red and his breath was foul.

"What kind of man eats other men? Am I not a man? Am I not a brother? Am I not man?"

His voice rose louder and louder, like a shriek.

"You are a brother. You are my brother."

"Then what is my name?"

"Kami . . . Kami . . . Kami . . . Kola."

This is where he was most a man. I could not read his face. Monsters can never hide a face behind a face, but men can.

"Take a story and give me."

"You wish for a story? I shall give you a story. There was a queen, and she had men and women who bowed to her like a queen. But she was no queen, only the sister of Kwash Dara, the North King. He exiled her to Mantha, the hidden fortress on the mountain west of Fasisi, breaking his father's wish that she stay at court. But that father had broken with his father before that, for each generation has sent the eldest sister to Mantha before she could claim the rightful line to the throne. But that is not the story."

This King sister who thinks she is a queen, Lissisolo was her name. She plotted against the King with several men, and Kwash Dara, he punished her. He killed her consort and her children. He could not kill her, for great a curse it is for family blood to kill family blood, even bad blood. So he banished her to the hidden fortress, where she was to be a nun the rest of her life, but this King sister, she schemed. This King sister, she plotted. This King sister, she schemed more. She found one of the hundreds of princes with no kingdoms in Kalindar and took him as a husband in secret so that when she gave birth to a child he would be no bastard. She hid the child to save him from the anger of the King, for he was angry indeed when his spy told him of the marriage and the birth. And he set out to kill the child. But that is not the story.

This King sister, she lost the child, or men stole him, and she hired me and others to find the child.

And we found him, captive to bloodsuckers, and a man with hands like his feet and wings like a bat, and breath like the stench of long-dead men, which gave his brother joy to eat, for he prefers the blood. And even as we returned the child, for there were several of us, there was something about this child, a smell that was there and not there. But men of the King were after the child and the King sister so we rode with them to the Mweru, where the prophecy said they would be safe, though another prophecy says no man can ever leave the Mweru. But that is not the story.

I tell you true. Something about that boy would trouble the gods, or anyone who desires his heart always to be at peace. I was the only one who saw, but I said nothing. So he stayed in the Mweru with his mother, and with the personal guards of women and the rebel infantry of men who stood guard outside the lands, for no man who enters the Mweru leaves. And it so happened that the one demon we did not kill, the one with bat wings, the one they call Sasabonsam, he came for the boy and he snatched him, or so they said and will still say. And he flew away with the boy, who never screamed, though he could scream, never shouted, though he shouted at many things, never, ever raised alarm, though his mother was always expecting an intruder. You cannot push the person who jumped. And the bat man and the boy, they did much terrible sport. Much that is vile and disgusting, much that would outrage the lowest god and the wickedest witch. And one day they came upon a tree where . . .

they came upon a place where love lived. The boy was with him, someone wrote in blood on sand. A beautiful hand wrote on the sand in blood. But that is not the story.

For the man who lived in the house of love, he came upon the message written in blood, by one who was dead. And he was beyond words, but filled himself with grief and rage, for they were dead. They were all dead. Some of them only half was left. Some of them half-eaten, some of them drained of blood, and drained empty. And this man he cried, and this man he wailed, and this man he cursed the silence of the gods, then cursed them too. And this man, he buried them, but could not bury the one made of spirits, for though they could not kill her, the killing ground made her go mad and she roams all the way to the sand sea, groaning a spirit song. And this man fell to his knees nine times in great grief, and profound dismay, and magnificent sorrow. And this man, after season upon season of grief, let that grief sink, and harden, and turn into rage, which sunk, and hardened, and turned into purpose. For he knew who the boy came with, or who came with the boy. He knew it was the beast whose brother the Leopard killed, though the beast came and took his revenge on him. He said to his friend, All these deaths are on your hands. And he sharpened his axes and dipped his knives in viper spit, and he set out for the Mweru, for that is where the boy came from and that is where he would go back to. Here is truth, the man did not think on this very long, for he was still beyond thought. Here is deeper truth. He would kill the boy and whoever protected him, and the bat and whoever stood in his way. He knew nothing of the ways of bats, but knew the ways of boys, and all boys make their way home to their mothers.

This man rode one horse into the dirt, another one into the sand, one into bush, and one right into the Mweru. The night was open in all the lands, and outside the lands was the infantry. Who knows how many were lazy from food, or asleep? He came upon them, rode through them with a torch in his hand, kicking over pots and trampling one soldier, and they hurled spears and missed, and searched for arrows but were too tired or too drunk and shot at each other, and when a few roused themselves enough to grab spear, and bow, and clubs, they saw where he was headed, and stopped. For if death seems so sweet to him, who are we to stop him, one of them must have said.

And what did this man wear other than rage and sadness? He rode the horse through the harsh soil of the Mweru, lighter than sand and thicker than mud, past springs that would boil off man flesh and stank of sulfur. Past fields where nothing grew and underfoot old bones of men cracked and broke. One of those lands where the sun never rose. He came upon a lake of black, brown, and gray that ate away at the shore and he rode around it, for who knew what creature lived in there? He wanted to shout at the lake that he would take any monster that came out for delaying him, but rode around.

The ten nameless tunnels of the Mweru. Like ten overturned urns of the gods. His horse stood outside one, as high as four hundred paces upon four hundred, or higher, taller than a battlefield, taller than a lake was wide, so high that the roof vanished in shadow and fog. And wide as a field as well. At the mouth of the tunnels, his horse was an ant and he was less. The farthest tunnel had the widest mouth, beside it a tunnel that was the tallest, but the entrance smaller than a man standing on another's shoulder. Beside it, a tunnel just as tall, the entrance sunken in to the earth so he could ride the horse straight in. Beside that, a tunnel not much higher than the horse. And so on. But each tunnel rose much higher than their openings, and more than toppled urns, they looked like giant worms asleep or felled. On the walls at the base of the tunnels, copper or rust, fashioned by divine blacksmiths, or someone else. Or iron, or brass, burned together in some craft only the gods know. On the outside walls of the tunnels, sheets of metal, in rust and in shine, from ground to sky.

A screech. Birds with tails, and thick feet, and thick-skin wings. Moss and brown grass overrun the ceiling of every tunnel, joining them together. Bad growth hiding what they were. Everything becoming brown. He and horse rode down the middle tunnel to the light at the end, which was not a light, for the Mweru had no light, only things that glow.

And at the end of the tunnel, wide flatlands pock-marked with perfect holes, with pools of water that smelled like sulfur, and at the foot of the wilderness, a palace that looked like a big fish. Up close it looked like a grounded ship made of nothing but sails, fifty and a hundred, even more. Sail upon sails, white and dirty, brown and red, looking like blood spatter. Two stairways, two loose tongues rolled out of two doors. No sentries, no guards, no sign of magic or science.

At the doorway, he threw away the torch and pulled both axes. In the hallway, tall as five men standing on shoulders, but wide as one man with his arms spread, orbs floated free, blue, yellow, and green and burning light like fireflies. Two men, blue like the Dolingon, came at him from both sides, saying, How can we help you, friend? At the same time, both drawing their swords slow. He leapt and swung both hands down on the left guard, hacking him again and again in the face. Then he chopped him once in the neck. The right guard charged, and he jumped out of the way of his first strike, spun on the ground, and hacked him in the knee. The guard dropped on that same knee and howled and the man chopped him in the temple, the neck, the left eye, then kicked him over. He kept walking, then running. More men came, and he jumped, leapt, dropped, chopped, hacked, cutting them all down. He dodged out of one sword and elbowed the swordsman in the face, grabbed his neck, and slammed him into the wall twice. He kept running. A guard in no armour but with a sword screamed and ran straight for him. He blocked the sword with one ax, dropped to his knees, and chopped the guard's shin. The guard dropped the sword, which he grabbed and stabbed him with.

An arrow shot past his head. He grabbed the near-headless guard and swung him around to catch the second arrow. As he ran, he felt each arrow pierce the guard until he was close enough to throw the first ax, which hit the bowman right between the nose and the forehead. He took the bowman's sword and belt. He ran until he came out of the corridor into a great hall, with nothing but orbs of light. A giant came at him and he thought of an Ogo, who was his great friend, who was a man, not a giant, a man of always present sorrow, and he howled in rage, and ran and jumped on the giant's back and hacked and hacked at his head and neck until there was no head and neck, and the giant fell.

"King sister!"

No sound in the room but his echo, bouncing mad on the walls and ceiling, then disappearing.

"Will you kill everyone?" she said.

"I will kill the world," he said.

"The giant was a dancer and nurse of children. He had never done any in this world a bad thing."

"He was in this world. That is enough. Where is he?"

"Where is who?"

He grabbed a spear and threw it where he thought

the voice was coming from. It struck wood. The orbs shone brighter. She sat on a black throne ringed with cowries, and several hands above it lodged the spear. Two guards, women, stood by her side with swords, two beside them crouched with spears. Two elephant tusks at her feet and carved columns tall as trees behind her. Her headdress, thick cloth wrapped around and around to look like a flaming flower. Flowing robes from chest to feet, gold breastplate on her chest, as if she was one of the warrior queens.

"How hard it is, exile to this place of no life," he said.

She stared at him, then laughed, which made him furious. He was not speaking wit.

"I remember you being so red, even in the dark. Red ochre, like a river woman," she said.

"Where is your son?"

"And how skillful you were with an ax. And a Leopard who traveled with you."

"Where is your boy?"

"Bunshi, she was the one who said, They will find your boy, especially the one called Tracker. It has been said he has a nose."

"It's been said you have a cunt. Where is your fucking boy?"

"What is my boy to you?"

"I have business with your son."

"My son has no business with men I don't know."

He smelled him coming in the dark, trying to move in the shadow, to move quiet. Coming from the right.

The man did not even turn, just threw his ax and it hit the guard in the dark. He yelped and fell.

"Call them. Send for every guard. I will build a mountain of corpses right here."

"What do you want with my boy?"

"Call them. Call your guards, call your assassins, call your great men, call your best women, call your beasts. Watch me build a lake of blood right before your throne."

"What do you wish with my boy?"

"I will have justice."

"You will have revenge."

"I will have whatever I choose to name it."

He stepped towards the throne and two women guards swung down at him from ropes. The first, carrying a sword, missed him, but the second, with a club, knocked him over. He fell and slid on the smooth ground. He ran to the dead guard's sword and grabbed it right before the second guard swung her club at him again. She swung hard but could not stop his swing quick enough. He kicked her in the back and she fell. He charged but she swung the club up and struck him in the chest. He fell on his back and she jumped up. He tried to swing his sword but she stomped on his hand. He kicked her in the koo, and she fell hard on her knees into his chest, which knocked his air out. The guard, her knuckles hard leather, punched him in the face, and punched him and punched him again and knocked him out.

———

Hear this. He woke in a cell like a cage hanging off the floor. It was a cage. The room, dark and red, not the throne room.

"He would have me give suckle. What mockery they would have sung had a griot lived in these lands. You will say what must there be in a land with no griot. Mark it, even though he was past six in years, and was a boy soon a man. He came to my breasts before he even looked at my face."

The man turned to where the voice was coming from. Five torches lined a wall to his right, but lit nothing. Below it, dark and shadow, a throne maybe, but he could not see anything above two thin pillars, carved like birds.

"Give a man a free hand, he rub it all over you. Give a boy . . . Well, he would not be denied it. And what would the gods say, about a woman who denied her child food? Her boy? Yes, they have been blind and deaf, but which god will still not judge a mother for how she raised the future King? Look at me, what milk could be in these breasts?"

She paused as if waiting for an answer.

"And yet even full men, you all must suck the breast. And my precious boy. Come to the breast like he come to war. Should I tell you this, that he almost bit my nipples off? The left, then the right? Tore the skin, cut the flesh, and still he kept sucking. Well, I am a woman. I shouted at him and he would not stop, his eyes closed like how you men close when you cum. My boy, I had to grab his neck and strangle him until he stopped. My boy, he looked at me and he smiled. Smiled. His teeth red from my blood. From then I gave him a servant girl. She was not stupid in the head. She cut herself every night so that he could suck. Is there strangeness in this? Are we strange? You are Ku. You cut the cow's throat to drink the blood, is there strangeness in such?"

The man said nothing. He grabbed the bars of the cage.

"What you think is all over your face. You look at me, with your disgust and your judgment. But do you know what it is to have child? What you would do for it?"

"I do not know. Perhaps abandon him to be killed. No, sold. No, stolen, and raised by vampires. And maybe always have someone to ask someone to ask someone find the little one, with lie after lie so that no one would even know that you had a son. Is that what it is like to have a child?"

"Quiet."

"Finest of mothers you must be."

"I will not let you near him."

"Did you let him go or did you lose him again, fine mother?"

"You seem to think my son has done wickedness."

"Your son **is** wickedness. A devil—"

"You know nothing. Devils are born. All the griots sing of this."

"You have no griot. And devils are made. You make them. You make them by leaving them to anyone who fancies a—"

"You dare to know what goes on in my head? You judge me, a queen? Who are you to tell me what to do with my child? You have none. Not a single one."

"Not a single one."

"What?"

"Not a single one."

And the man told her a story:

"They did not have names, for Gangatom never gave them names, for they were all so strange to them. Which is not to say that the Gangatom made much fuss over the strange. But if one were to say Giraffe Boy, all in the village would know who it is they call. I was not like you, none of them were my blood. But I was like you, I let others raise them, and said it was for their own sake when it was for mine. Someone said the North King was making slaves of the river tribes to serve his war, so we went for them, for war is like fever, everybody gets infected. We took them from the Gangatom, but some of them did not want to go. I said to the children, Let us go, and two of them said no, then three, then four, for why should they go with a man they do not know and another they do not like? And he who was partner to me, he said look at this, and he showed them a coin and then closed his hands, then opened them again, and the coin vanished, and closed his hands again, and he asked in which hand is the coin, and Giraffe

Boy pointed to his left, so he opened his left and a butterfly flew away. Tell you truth, they followed him, not me. So we all followed him to the land of Mitu, and there we lived in a baobab tree. And we said to the children, You need names, for Giraffe Boy and Smoke Girl are not names, they are what people call you. One by one they lost their anger for me, Smoke Girl last. Of course, the albino, who was no boy, but tall like a man, we named him Kamangu. Giraffe Boy, who was always tall, we named him Niguli, for he was not even like the giraffe. He had no spots and it was his legs, not his neck, that was long. Kosu is what we called the boy with no legs. He rolled everywhere like a ball, but always picked up dirt, or shit, or grass, or when he yelled, a thorn. First we gave the joined twins names that joined and they cursed us like old widows. You and him share everything and yet you have different names, they said to me and Mossi. So the noisy one, we called him Loembe, and the more quiet but still loud one we called Nkanga. And Smoke Girl. He who was mine said, One of them must have a name from where I come from. One must remind me of me. So he named Smoke Girl Khamseen, for the wind that blows fifty days. You talk to me of children—what was the name of your boy, but boy? Did you ever name him?"

"Shut your mouth."

"You queen among mothers."

"Quiet!"

She shifted in her seat but remained in the dark.

"I will not sit here in judgment by a man. Making all sorts of claims about my boy. Did rage bring you here? For it was not wisdom. How shall we play? Shall I bring my son out, right now, and give you a knife? Love is blindness, is it not? I ache for your loss. But you might as well have told me about the death of stars. My son is not here. How quickly you refuse to see that he is a victim as well. That I woke up to hear my son gone. Kidnapped. That my son has spent so many years and moons not living according to his will or mine. How could he know anything else?"

"A devil the size of three men, with wings as wide as a canoe, slipped into your palace unnoticed."

"Take him out," she said to the guards.

A cloth fell on the cage and left him in black. The cage fell to the ground and the man slammed against the bars. They kept him in the dark for the longest time—who knows how many nights? When they lifted the cloth from his cage, he was in another room, with an opening in the roof and red smoke rushing through the sky. The King sister was standing by another chair, not like her throne, but with a tall back.

"My birthing chair shows me my past. Do you know what I see? He was born feet first. I would take it as an omen, had I believed in omens. What did Sogolon say about you? It has been said you have a nose. Maybe she was not the one who told me. You want to find my son. I would like that too, but not for your reasons. My son is a victim too, even if he walked out into the Mweru on his own, why can you not see?"

He did not say to her, Because I have seen your boy. I have seen how he looks when he thinks no one watches him.

"My yeruwolo said I should trust you to find my boy. Maybe even save him from the bat. I think she is a fool, but then . . . I have no ending for what I was about to say."

She nodded to the Tracker, and one of her water women came to him with a piece of cloth, green and white. Torn from what, who knew.

"It is said you have a nose," she said.

She pointed at him and the water woman ran to the cage, threw the cloth, then ran away from it. He picked it up.

"Will this tell you where he goes?" she said.

He squeezed the cloth but did not smell it, held it away from his nose and caught the King sister, her eyes wide, waiting. He threw the cloth away. They covered the cage again. When he woke in the throne room, he knew sleep had taken him for days. That they must have put him under wicked vapors or sleeping magic. The room had more light than before but still it was dark. She sat on her throne, the same women behind her, guards at both walls, and an old woman, her face white, walking towards him. They had left his hands free, but put a copper collar that felt like tree bark around his neck. Two guards stood behind him, moving nearer as he tried to walk.

"I make you an offer again, Tracker. Find my boy. Do you not see that he needs to be saved? Do you not see that he is blameless?"

"Only days ago you said, I shall not let you near him," he said.

"Yes, near. Seems the Tracker is the only man who knows how to get near my son."

"That is no answer."

"Maybe I appeal to the very heart that seeks revenge. An appeal is of the heart too."

"No. You've run out of men. Now you ask the man sworn to kill him."

"When did you swear? To whom? This must be one of those things that men say, like when he says this is the best, but this is my favorite. I have never believed in oaths or in men who swear by them. I want your word that should I release you, you will find my son and bring him back to me. Kill the monster if you must."

"You have an infantry. Why not send them?"

"I have. Hence my asking you. I could have ordered you. I am your queen."

"You are no Queen."

"I am Queen here. And when the wind in these lands turns I will be the mother of a king."

"A king you have lost twice."

"So find him for me. How can I mend your sorrow? I cannot. But I have known loss."

"Have you?"

"Of course."

"Then it pleases my heart to know. Tell me now that I am not the only one to come home to find his son with half of his head missing. Or just the hand of another son. Or him most dear with a hole where his chest and belly used to be. Or maybe hanging from—"

"Are we to compare loves murdered and children butchered? This is where you will judge to see if you are better than me?"

"Your child was just hurt."

"My other children were murdered by my brother."

"Shall we compare so you can come out victorious?"

"I never said this was a contest."

"Then stop trying to win."

He said nothing.

"Will you find your King?"

He paused. Waited. Knew she expected him to wait, to pause, to think, to even struggle within the head, then come to a decision.

"Yes," he said.

The old woman looked up at him and tilted her head as if that was the way to know a person true.

"He lies. There is no question he will kill him," she said.

He elbowed the guard behind him in the nose, pushed him away, grabbed and pulled out the guard's sword, and stabbed it deep in its master's belly. He ducked without looking, knowing the other guard would go for the neck. The guard's sword cut through air above his head. He swung from below and chopped him in the calf. The guard fell and he shoved the sword in his chest, then took his sword too. More guards all stepped out as if they had popped out of the wall. Two came at him first and he became Mossi, he of the two swords, from the East, who never visited him in mind or spirit since he wrote in his own blood in the dirt. Mossi did not visit him now; Tracker just thought of him standing on rocks, practicing with swords. He kicked the first guard in the balls, jumped on him when he fell, leapt at two other guards, knocked away their spears with his left sword, and sliced one in the belly with the right sword and chopped the other in the shoulder. But hark, his back burst with blood and the guard who slashed him charged. He rolled out of the guard's second strike. The guard swung again, but he hesitated—on orders not to kill, this was clear. The guard paused too long; Tracker's sword went right through him.

Men surrounded him. He lunged at them, they stepped back. The collar clamped around his neck squeezed in tight, like a hand pulling a noose tighter. From his hands, both swords fell. He coughed and couldn't cough, growled and couldn't growl. Tighter, tighter, his face swelled, his head about to burst. And his eyes. Fright. Not fright. Shock. **You look like you didn't know. Bad man, you must did know. The Sangoma's enchantment is fading from you. You will have no mastery of metals.** No wind came in the nose, no wind left. He fell to one knee. The guards stepped away. He looked up, tears blinding him, and the old woman held out her right hand and made a fist. She did not smile, but looked like a woman thinking a happy thought. He tried to cough again; he could barely see her. He pawed the floor and found the sword. Scooping up the grip, he held it up like a spear and threw it hard and quick. The spear struck the old woman right in the heart. Her eyes popped. She opened her mouth and black blood came out. She fell and the collar broke from his neck. A guard struck him in the back of his head.

S mell it," the King sister said to Tracker when he woke up. Who knew which room this was, but he was back in the cage and the same strip of cloth was at his feet.

"It is from him. His favorite bedding. He would have the servants wash it every quartermoon, indeed it was many colours once. I can make you a new bargain. Find him and bring him back, and do whatever you wish to the other one. If you can leave the Mweru. Many men enter, but no man can ever leave."

"Witchcraft?"

"Which witch would want a man to stay? But you can try to leave. Smell the rag."

He grabbed the piece of cloth, brought it to his nose, and breathed in deep. The smell filled his head, and he knew what it was before his nose took flight, followed the source; he jumped on it as it took him right between her legs.

"Look at you. You wanted to know where he was going and I gave you where he came from."

She laughed loud and long and the laugh bounced over the empty hall.

"You. You will be the one to murder the world?" she said, and left him.

That night Tracker was awake in the dream jungle. Past trees as small as shrubs and shrubs as tall as elephants, the Tracker went and looked for him. He came upon a still pond where nothing seemed to live. First he saw himself. Then he saw the clouds, then mountains, then a path and elephants running away, then antelopes, then cheetahs, and past them another road that led to a city wall, and up the wall a tower, and in the tower looking out, then straight at him, eye-to-eye, the one he searched for. This man was he ever surprised to hear the Tracker's call, but he knew why before asking.

"You know I can kill you in your sleep," he said.

"But you wonder why I would have called you, the worst of enemies," Tracker said. "Tell no lie. No man can leave the Mweru, but you are no man."

He smiled and said, "True, you cannot leave the Mweru without either dying or going mad, a goddess with revenge towards me made it so, unless there is one beyond magic to lead you out. But what shall I get for it?"

"You want this boy's head. I am the only one who can find him," Tracker said.

It was a lie, for he had lost all track of the boy's smell, and he would learn after that the boy no longer had a smell, truly none at all, but a bargain they struck, him and the Aesi.

"Tell me where in the palace you are when you find out," the Aesi said.

This man who was not a man came for him; indeed it took him one and a half moons to do so, and the North had long thrown first spears at the South. Wakadishu and Kalindar.

This is what happened. The Tracker woke to the sound of bodies falling. A guard entered his cell and nodded for him to follow, saying nothing. They both stepped over the dead guards and kept walking. Down a corridor, past a hall, down steps, up steps, and down more. Down another corridor, past many dead guards and sleeping guards and felled guards. This guard who said nothing pointed to a horse waiting at the foot of the massive steps leading out, and Tracker turned to say what, he did not know, only to see that the guard's eyes were wide open but saw nothing. Then he fell. Tracker ran down the steps, stopped midway to grab a dead guard's sword, then mounted the horse and rode away, past the smoking lakes, through the tunnel, and right to the edge of the Mweru. The horse dug into his hooves and threw him, but he grabbed the reins even as he flew off the horse. The horse turned and galloped away.

Tracker kept walking and after a while saw a figure in the dark wearing a hood. He sat cross-legged and wrote in the air the way Sogolon had, and was off the ground, floating on air. Tracker approached and the man stretched his hand out to say stop. He pointed right and Tracker walked right, and when he had stepped ten and five paces, fire shot out of the earth before him. He jumped back. The man beckoned Tracker forward ten steps and gestured to stop. The earth below him cracked and split and moved apart in a loud rumble, shaking the ground like an earthquake. The man put both feet down, rubbing something sticky in his right hand. He threw it— a heart—into the chasm and the chasm hissed and coughed, and closed itself. Then he waved at Tracker to come. He threw something else and it sparked the air like lightning. Spark spread to spark, which spread to spark, and then a boom that knocked Tracker down.

"Get up and run," the man said. "I no longer have a hold on any of them."

Tracker turned around and saw a cloud of dust coming. Riders.

"Run!" the man shouted.

Tracker ran, with the riders coming up behind him, to where the man was, and both stood, Tracker trembling as the riders rode straight at them. He saw the calm in the man and borrowed it even as everything in him wanted to scream, We will be trampled, fuck the gods, why do we not run? A horseman came within a breath of his face before he rode into the wall that was not there. Man and horse slammed into it one after the other, and many at once, some horses breaking their necks and legs, some riders flying into the sky and slamming into the wall, some horses stopping quick and throwing their riders off.

Tracker caught the Aesi as he passed out, and pulled him away.

"And that is the story I have taken and given to you," I said.

"But, but . . . but . . . but . . . that is no story. That is not even half of one. Your story is only half-delicious. Shall I only kill half of you? And who is this man who is not a man? Who is he? I will have a name, I will have it!"

"Do you not know? They call him the Aesi."

The white man went all blue. His jaw dropped and he grabbed his shoulders, as if cold.

"The god butcher?"

I did not wake from sleep. And yet right there I was in another forest that felt different from the one I was in before. I blinked several times, but this was a different forest. Nothing lived and nothing moved. None of the smells of life, no new flower, no recent rain, no fresh dung, the spider, gone like an afterthought. At my foot was a pile of something pale gray and white and thin enough to see through, like shed skin. Beside it, hiding in the grass, my two axes and the back harness to hold them. I wedged my finger in one of the slits I had made in the leather and pulled it out, Nyka's feather. His whole path opened up to me as soon as I brushed the feather past my nose.

Behind me, maybe thirty paces, then right, then a bend, then down, maybe downhill and then across, then up again, a small hill perhaps, but still under forest cover, then into someplace that he had not left. Or this could still be a dream jungle of some kind. I once overheard a drunk man in a bar in Malakal say that if you are ever lost in a dream and cannot tell if you are asleep or awake, take a look at your hands, for in a dream you always have four fingers. My hands showed five.

I grabbed my things and ran. Forty paces through wet grass and mud, and ferns that stung my calves, then right, almost into a tree, and dodging them left and right and left, over the corpse of a beast, then slowing down because the forest was too thick to run and every step was a shrub or tree, then to a bend like a river, then downhill until I smelled the river first and then heard it, a waterfall rushing down on rocks. And I skipped over the rocks, climbed slow but still tripped, and hit my calf against a sharp rock edge that drew blood. But who could stop to look at blood? I climbed down to the river and walked in the water to wash away the blood, and after much time I ran up a bank that rose higher and higher, and then

I pulled my ax and cut through even thicker bush and all the time Nyka's smell came on stronger and stronger. And I cut and pushed my way through thick, wet leaves and branches slapping my back, until I came upon not a clearing, just a gathering of trees taller than towers, with much space in between. He was near, so near that I looked above me, expecting Sasabonsam to have him hanging high. Or that he and Sasabonsam would meet as one, vampire to vampire, and both were already conspiring to pull me up into one of these trees and tear me in half. Deep in whatever was there for his heart, I expected it of Nyka.

I was walking. I heard my own footsteps in the bush. A man walked before me, several paces ahead, and I wondered how I had not seen him before. Slow he walked, with no purpose in step, just wandering. His hair long, and curly, and when he pulled his cloak tighter, arms light as sand itself. Something jumped into my heart. I ran up close to him and stopped, I didn't know why. Up close the wet hair, the sharp turn from jaw to chin, the beard red, the cheekbones high, all were enough for me to think it was him and not enough for me to say, No, it could not be. The cape hid his legs, but I knew the wide stride, the balls of his feet hitting the ground before the heel, even in boots. I waited for his smell, but none came. The cape fell off and rolled into the bush. His feet I saw first, green from grass and brown from dirt. Then his calves, always so thick and strong, so unlike any man from these lands. And the back of his knee, and his buttocks, always so smooth and white, as if he never liked lying naked in the sun at the top of the baobab tree like one of the monkeys. Above his buttocks, trees and sky. Below his shoulders, trees and sky. Above his buttocks a hole, a nothing, everything eaten out from his belly to his back, leaving a gap big as the world. Dripping blood and flesh, and still he walked.

But I could not. My legs had never been this weak, and I fell to my knees and breathed heavy and slow, waiting for Itutu to come to my heart. It did not. All in my head was my crawling on top of him, cradling his head, for there were flies everywhere else, and weeping, and bawling, and screaming, and screaming, and screaming into the trees and sky. And reading what he wrote in his own blood in the sand:

The boy, the boy was with him.

I cried, Beautiful man, I should not have been late. I should have come before you left this world and coaxed your soul into a nkisi, and wrapped it around my neck, so I could rub it and feel you. A mystic with a nkisi shaped like a dog said, There is a tormented spirit that would have words with you, Wolf Eye, but I wanted no words. I called his name and it came out a whimper.

This Mossi kept walking into the deep bush. This I know. A time surely comes when grief is nothing but a sickness, and I had grown sick of sickness. I raged and howled and the smell of that monster and of that vampire bird both came upon me, and I rose

and pulled both my axes and ran shouting at nothing, chopping at nothing. I ran from a new thing, it
must have been a head witch trying to drive a needle
through deaths upon deaths and sew them together.
My father whom I did not know, and my unavenged
brother. And Mossi, and so many more. Not a head
witch, but the god of the underworld telling me of
the wronged dead that I must make right, as if I am
why they are dead. How must the Tracker who lives
for no one have so many dead on his watch? Must
he be blamed for them all? My head argued with
my head, making me stumble. The Leopard should
have been right here, right now, so I could stab him
in the heart. My foot hit a downed tree and I fell.

When I looked up I saw feet. Hanging high above
me even when I stood up. Legs white like kaolin dust
with his black feet loose and dangling. Ribs pressed
out of his thin chest and black blood streaks dried
up from running down his belly. Two black spots
where his nipples used to be and dried blood that
had flowed from them. Bite marks all over his chest,
and neck, and his left cheek. Somebody was looking
for a tender spot to bite. His chin resting on his chest,
his arms spread out and tied off with vines. His wings
spread wider and trapped in branches and leaves.

"Nyka," I whispered.

Nyka did not move. I said his name louder. A giggle came out of the bushes below. I looked into the
bush and into the bush looked at me. He stared as he
did before, eyes wide for no reason, not delight, not

malice, not care, not even curiosity. Just wide. Older. Taller. I could tell from just the eyes and his thin, bony cheek. I would rather he laughed. I would rather he said, Look at me, I am your villain. Or whimper and plead, Look at me, your real victim. Instead he just looked. I looked at his eyes and saw Mossi's dead eyes, looking forever and seeing nothing. He dashed out of that grass patch right before my ax came for his face. I charged straight into the bush, thinking the beast growl came from another mouth but mine. I surged through branches and ripped through leaves into darker bush. Nothing. Bloodsucker-tit-biting ghoul, still giggling like a baby. Gone.

Above me Nyka groaned. I stepped out of the bush and walked right into Sasabonsam's hand-foot kicking me in the face.

My head and back hit the ground. I rolled up to my knees, and jumped back to my feet. He flapped his wing but it kept hitting trees, so he landed on his feet and looked at me. Sasabonsam. I had never stopped to look at his face. His big white eyes, jackal ears, and sharp bottom teeth sticking out from his lips like a warthog's. His whole body overrun with black hair except for his pale chest and pink nipples, an ivory necklace, and a loincloth that made me laugh. He growled.

"Your smell, I remember it. I follow it," he said.

"Quiet."

"Come round looking for it."

"Silence."

"You not there. So I eat. The little ones, they taste strange."

I charged at him, ducking before he swung his wing. Then I rolled to his left foot and chopped it with both axes. He jumped and shrieked like a crow. **You always aim for the toes,** said a voice that sounded like me. The ax barely touched him. He tried to swat me with his hand but I ducked, jumped to his knee, and swung my ax at his face as I leapt off. The blunt side hit his cheekbone and he snarled, then swatted at me. His hand missed me but his claws slashed four lines across my chest. I fell to one knee and he kicked me away. My back slammed into a tree trunk and my breath rushed out.

And my eyes rolled. And there was nothing. My chin grazed my chest, and I saw my nipples and belly. My head grew heavy, and my eyes did not work well. Nyka groaned and pulled at his hands. My chin hit my chest again. I looked up straight into Sasabonsam's knuckles.

"Six of them for one of you. Look at your quality," he said.

He said more but blood trickled from my right ear and I could not hear. He punched at my face, but I nodded and his hand struck the tree. He howled and slapped me. I spat blood on my legs, and my legs did not work.

"Where are my askis, the little one say."

He grabbed my throat.

"The little ball, the little one he tried to roll away.

You want know how far he get? He the one that say, My father going come back and kill you. He going chop you with he two askis."

"Kosu."

"Father, he call you. Father? You don't roll like a ball. You don't have no askis now. Look at your quality."

"Kosu. Ko—"

He punched me again. I spat out two teeth. He wrapped his long fingers around my head and pulled me up.

Axes, he was saying that Father was going to chop him with axes.

"He never scream. And I have him in many bites."

"Kosu."

I could only see bits of light through his thick and stinking fingers. His claws scratched my neck.

"When I reach the bone in his back, still he did not cry. Then he die. And I bite the back of the head and suck—"

"Fuck the gods."

He threw me and a peace came over me in flight that cut when I landed in branches and leaves. He grabbed at my ankle and I kicked him away. He giggled and grabbed my leg again and kept giggling as he pulled me out of the branches. My back and head hit the ground and then I was moving; he was pulling me.

"You the fool and she the fool. She the one in gold and red and all she do, she sit. I see her through the window. Only I know the boy. I come for him in the weird place and he follow me. He even call me, for the white one teach him how to call. Me never want the boy for he don't want me, he want the lightning one, but he call me and I come take him, and the night did quick and I fly away with him and he say I hear my mother talk about the wolf and he cubs and how she try to make him her soldier and they live in the monkeybread tree and I say that is the one who kill my brother, I hear, he says so and the boy say fly with me on your back and I can take you, and he take me."

I said, Quiet, but it died before it fell out of my mouth. I don't know where he was dragging me, and my back scraped against grass and dirt and stones in water, and then my head sunk underwater as he pulled me through a river, and the back of my head hit a rock, and I went dark. I woke up and I was still under the water and coughing and choking until he pulled me out into grass and under trees again.

"The white one, the pretty one, the one who when I squeeze him until I see the blood flow under the skin, delicious, he a fighter, he better fighter than you. He get teach by the one with the two sword. The two of them, I break down the door and the two of them swing down from the tree saying they going fight me. And they jump up on me and strike and the one with two sword throw one sword to the white-skin and he come at me, this boy, he jump, and the boy he strike me in the head and it hurt and

the man jab me in the side right here, right here
and the sword go in but stop at my chest cage right
here, I thump him with me knuckle and he fall back
and the white-skin run at me and duck before I swat
him with my wing and he grab my wing and stab
right through it, see right there how it still a hole,
that the white-skin do and I grab him with this foot
and grab him with my other foot and fling his up
into the tree and a branch knock him quiet. Yes yes.
And the one that is a ball, he roll up behind me and
knock me off me two foot. And I fall and he laugh
but I grab him before he run away and I bite him and
pull the flesh out, sweet flesh, sweet, sweet flesh, and I
take another bite and another bite and the man with
hair scream. He put some of them on horse and
slap the horse. And they ride off and he come for
me and he angry, and I like angry and he fight and
fight and fight, and stab and cut and go for my eye
and I catch the sword and the white-skin stab me
right up me shithole and now I is fury, yes I was."

He pulled me out of light grass into dark and above
me was also dark. I kicked at his hand again and
he swung me up and slammed me back down on the
grass. Blood poured out of my ear again.

"I grab white-skin and I smash him, and smash
him, and smash him, and smash him, and smash him
until all he juice run out. And the long hair one he
bawl and bawl and make like a dog, but he fight like
a warrior man, he and two swords, better than you
with one ax. Stay still and make me smash you too,

I say to him, but he do this and this like a fly and he cut me across my back—he cut the skin! Nobody cut the skin and is many moon me see me own blood, then he flip around, better than you, and stab me in the belly and he look at me, and I stop and make him look at me, because many man think something down there, but nothing down there but flesh. I beat him away with this hand."

He dropped me to show me his hand.

"And pull out the sword with this hand. I don't use sword good but he reaching for he knife and I push it right through he chest just like I push my finger through mud. I swing the sword and cut he throat. And then I jump on him and eat the nice part first. Oh, the belly, then the red part, oh the fat, like a hog. They think my brother like the flesh and I like the blood, but I eat anything."

I wished I had a voice to beg him to stop, and I wished he had ears to hear.

"Then I go after the others, the runners, yes I did. How they going flee far when I faster than a horse? The two-head one."

"They were two, you son of a bitch. Two."

"The other head he start cry for his brother. You know what I tell the ostrich one?"

"Niguli. His name is Niguli."

"A strange taste. You feed him strange? He cried. I say, Cry, boy, cry. You not the one I come for, he should get eat instead of you."

"No."

"Lie. Lie. Lie. I lie. Me would eat you first then them. They call you Father?"

"I was—"

"You didn't breed none. And you don't after watch none. You open the pen and let in the wolf."

"The Leopard. The Leopard killed your brother."

He grabbed my throat again.

"The ghost one, I couldn't grab her. She be a dust in wind," Sasabonsam said.

He tossed me to the ground. Dark came on me in the day. Wanting to kill, wanting to die, in your head they are the same colour, and the door to one leads to the other. I wanted to say he would get no joy out of killing me, that I had walked from north to south of these lands and walked through the two kingdoms in war, and walked through arrows and fire and the killing plans of people and did not care, so kill me now, kill me hence, kill me quick, or kill me from toe to finger to knee and up, and I still would not care. But instead I said:

"You know no griot."

Sasabonsam's ears flattened, and he squeezed his brows. He stomped towards me. He stood over me, and I was between his legs. He spread his wings. He bent down until his face was right in front of my face, his eye on my eye. Rotten flesh settled between his teeth.

"I know how a little boy taste," he said.

I took my two knives and stabbed his two eyes.

Blood from his almost blinded mine. He roared

like ten lions, fell back on his own right wing, and snapped it at the bone. He roared louder and flailed around until he grabbed both knives and pulled them out, screaming with each pull. He ran straight into a tree, fell on his back, jumped up, and ran again, right into another. I grabbed a stick and threw it behind him. He jumped, swung around, and ran into another tree. Sasabonsam tried to flap his wing but only the left flapped. The right swung but it was broken and limp. I searched around for the knives as he ran into trees. He roared again and stomped the ground, and scraped the grass and ground with his hands looking for me, coming up with clumps of dirt and leaves and grass and panting, and roaring, and shrieking. Then he would touch his eyes and howl.

I found one knife. I looked at his neck. And his pale chest and pink nipples. At his fright at everything. At him backing into his right wing and cracking it again.

He fell on his back.

I stood up and almost fell to one knee. I rose again and limped away.

Back through the bushes and down the hill and across the river, Sasabonsam was still howling, squealing, and bawling. Then he went quiet.

The me of many moons ago would search for why neither fate made a difference to me. I did not care. Nyka was still up in the tree, still trying to free himself. I had found one ax in the bush under his tree, and the other several paces away. I heard him before

I saw him, crawling down the tree on hands and legs like the white spider before, crawling to get to Nyka, to a sweet spot to drink blood. The boy. I threw my ax, but the pain in my leg made me miss, just a hand's length from the boy's face. He scurried back up the tree. I threw the second ax to Nyka's right and cut through the vines gripping his hand. He pulled it free. I thought he would say something. I thought how there could be nothing that he would say that I would care to hear. I fell to one knee. Then he shouted my name and I heard a wing flap.

I spun around and saw Sasabonsam swinging hands in the air and scraping the ground, sniffing. Smelling me out the way I smell everyone. I lurched backward and tripped over a fallen branch.

And then it was all thunder and then lightning, one bolt, then three, all striking Sasabonsam, but with no end, just blasting and striking and spreading all over him and running into his mouth and ears and coming out of his eyes and mouth, as fire and juice and smoke and something came out of his mouth, not a scream, or a shriek, or a yell. A wail. Hair and skin caught flame and he staggered and dropped to one knee as lightning still struck him and thunder still dropped heavy on him, and fell Sasabonsam did, his body burning in a huge flame, then going out just as quick.

Nyka fell from the tree.

He was saying something to me, but I did not listen. I grabbed my ax and went over to the charred carcass of Sasabonsam and swung it down at the neck. I yanked out and chopped, yanked out and chopped until the ax hacked through skin, through bone, straight to the ground. I fell on my knees and didn't know I was shouting until Nyka touched my shoulder. I pushed him away, almost swinging my ax at him.

"Take your disgusting hands off me," I said. He backed away, his hands in the air.

"I saved your life," Nyka said.

"You also took it. Not much it was, but you took it."

Not far from the Sasabonsam, I dug a hole in the earth with my hands, placed the necklace of my children's teeth in it, then covered the hole back up. I patted the earth slow until it was smooth, and still I would not leave, would not stop patting and smoothing it until it felt like I was making a beautiful thing.

"I never buried Nsaka. When I woke and saw her dead, I knew I had to flee. Because I was changed, you see. Because I was changed."

"No. Because you were a coward," I said.

"Because I went to sleep for a long time, and when I woke up my skin was white and I had wings."

"Because you are a coward with no bones, who can only deceive. She was the one who did all the fighting, I will guess. How did you rid yourself of it?"

"My memory?"

"Your guilt," I said.

He laughed. "You wish to hear of my remorse for betraying you."

"I do not wish to hear anything."

"You just asked the question."

"You answered it. You had no remorse to get rid of. You're not a man, I knew that before I came across your shed skin. You act as if it makes you itch, but losing skin is nothing new for you."

"True, even when I was a man I was closer to the snake, or the lizard, even the bird."

"Why did you betray me?"

"So you **are** looking for remorse."

"Fuck the gods with your remorse. I want the tale."

"The tale? The tale is when it came to you, my friend, I was bewitched by the very conceit of it. You wish for something more? A reason? A way that I told myself it was just? Perhaps coin, or cowrie? The truth was I just fed my fill on the conceit of it. You think of the time I betrayed you? Think of the many times I did not betray you. The Bultungi hounded me for ten and three moons. That was ten and three moons of me thinking not of myself but of you."

"Now you wish praise?"

"I wish for nothing."

He started walking out of the bush, now all blue from night light. As it fell dark, his skin and feathers began to glow. I didn't know where he was going and listened for the sound of the river, but I heard nothing.

"When the Aesi freed me, he told me of the new

age," I said. "Of how a bigger war was coming as sure as this war was here, a war to destroy everything. And at the heart of this war this boy. This abominable, perverted thing."

"And you let him live," Nyka said.

"It was only a guess. A heart twitch, not my head. Something amiss; I saw it as I saw him. He was already mad from it. Mad for it. Ipundulu blood. I saw it, I saw it then."

"And you let him live."

"I did not know."

"The boy who led Sasabonsam to your house to kill—"

"I said I did not know."

We kept walking for several paces.

"I cannot help rid you of it," he said.

"Of what?"

"Your guilt."

"Call the boy so I can kill him," I said.

"What is his name? I know not."

"Just call him boy, or crackle a lightning from your nipples or asshole or whichever place."

Nyka laughed loud. He said he didn't have to call him, for he knew where he was. We walked through bush and under trees until we came upon a clearing leading to a lake. I thought it was the White Lake, but was not sure. It looked like the White Lake, which had a pool at the end, not very wide, but very deep. They looked at us as if waiting for us to appear. The Leopard, the boy, and, holding a torch, with her face and breast hidden under kaolin clay, and with her headdress of feathers and stones, the woman on the mound before. Sogolon.

Seeing her on the other side of the lake did not shock me. Nor did my not recognizing her before, perhaps because when women age in these lands, they become the same woman. Perhaps she wore kaolin to hide what must have been horrible burn scars, but from where we stood, I saw nose, lips, even ears. I wondered how she survived, while not being surprised that she did. Meanwhile the Leopard, white from dust, stood a few paces behind her, with the boy between them. The boy looked at them, and at me. He saw Nyka and turned to run but Sogolon grabbed his thick hair and pulled him back.

"Red wolf," she said. "No, not red no more. Wolf."

I said nothing. I looked at the Leopard. Back in his armour like a man bound to a cause not his own. Not even a mercenary, just a soldier. I told myself I did not want to know what had gone inside his heart and grabbed it, what made this man who lived for no one and nobody turn to fight for the whims of kings. And their mothers. Look at you who we once called reckless and said it with love and envy. How low you have become, lower than shame, your neck hanging off your shoulder, as if the armour made you hunch. The boy was still struggling, trying to pull himself away from Sogolon, when she slapped him. He did what I saw before: shriek, then whimper, but with no feeling in his face. He was bigger now, almost as tall as Sogolon, but not much else showed in the dimness. He looked thin, like boys who grew but were not becoming men. Smooth, in just a loincloth, his legs and arms thin and long. Looking like no king or future king. He stared at Nyka, his tongue hanging out. I gripped my ax.

"**Edjirim ebib ekuum eching otamangang na ane-iban,**" she said. "When darkness falls, one embraces one's enemy."

"Did you translate for me or him?"

"You betray what you fight so long for?" Sogolon said.

"Look at you, Moon Witch. You don't even look three hundred years old. But then, **gunnugun ki ku lewe.** How did you survive going back through that door?"

"You betraying that what you long fight for," she said again.

"You talking to me or the Leopard?" I asked.

He looked straight at me. Sogolon and the boy were at the edge of the water and even in the dimness I saw their reflections. The boy looked like the boy, the torch rounding out his large head. Sogolon looked like a shadow. No kaolin clay, and blacker than dark everywhere, even her head, which had neither feathers nor hair.

"Ay, Leopard, is there no one left? No one for you to fail?" I asked.

He said nothing, but pulled his sword. I kept looking at the black figure in the water, the torch in her hand. The water was still and calm and dark blue as coming night. In the reflection I saw the Leopard run for the child. I looked up just as he swung the sword for the little boy's head. Sogolon did not even turn, but whipped up a hard wind in a blink, which knocked over the Leopard, threw him up in the air, and slammed him against a tree. And right behind him, his sword, kicked up in the air by the wind, went straight like a bolt into his chest and pinned him to the trunk. His head slumped.

I yelled at the Leopard and threw my ax at the Moon Witch. It cut through the wind and she ducked, missing the blade, but the handle knocked her in the face and her whole body blinked. The kaolin vanished, then appeared, then vanished, then appeared again, then vanished. Nyka and I ran around this large pond. Sogolon was a burned-up husk, all black skin and fingers fused together, holes for eyes and mouth, before the kaolin appeared, and her skin and her feather headdress, her spell again strong. She still held on to the boy. The Leopard was still.

The boy began to laugh, a small giggle, then a loud cackle so loud it bounced across the water. Sogolon slapped him, but he kept laughing. She slapped him again, but he caught her hand with his teeth and bit hard. She pushed him, but he would not let go. She slapped him again and still he would not let go. He bit hard enough that Sogolon could no longer see to the wind, and her little storm weakened to a breeze, then nothing.

The ground shook, rumbling as if about to crack. A wave rose out of the lake and crashed on the banks, knocking over Sogolon and the boy. Sogolon began waving her hands to whip up the wind again, but the ground split open and sucked her in right up to the neck, then closed around her. She yelled and cursed and tried to move but could not.

And there was the Aesi, right on the banks, as if he was never not there. The Aesi stood in front of the boy, viewing him as one would a white giraffe or a red lion. Curious more than anything. The boy looked at him the same way.

"How did anyone think you could become King?" he said.

The boy hissed. He cowered from the Aesi like a shunned snake, writhing and curling, as if he would roll on the ground.

"I destroyed you," Sogolon said to the Aesi.

"You delayed me," the Aesi said, walking past her and grabbing the boy by the ear.

"Stop! You know that he is the true King," she said.

"True? You wish to bring back the matriarchy, is it? The line of kings descended from the King sister and not the King? You, the Moon Witch, who claim to be three hundred years old, and you know nothing of this line you've sworn to protect, this great wrong in all the lands, and all the worlds that you will make right?"

"All you have is pretty talk and lies."

"A lie is thinking this abomination can be a king. He can barely speak."

"He told Sasabonsam where I lived," I said, picking up my ax.

"Yelp and whimper, like a bush dog. Sucking blood from his mother's breast, he is not even a vampire but an imitation of one. And yet I feel remorse for this child. None of this was his choice," the Aesi said.

"Then neither shall death be his choice," I said.

"No!" Sogolon screamed.

The Aesi said, "You have one task. And you have done it well, Sogolon. There is disgrace. Look at your sacrifice. Look at your charred face, your burned skin, your fingers have all become one fin. All for this boy. All for the myth of the sister's line. Did the King sister tell you the history of our ways? That these sisters beget kings by fucking their fathers? That each king's mother was also his sister? That this is why the mad kings of the South are always mad? The same bad blood coursing through them for year upon year, and age upon age. Not even the wildest of beasts do such a thing. This is the order the woman called Sogolon wishes to restore. You of the three hundred years."

"You is nothing but evil."

"And you are nothing but simple. This latest mad king, Sogolon, we say he is the maddest for starting a war he couldn't win because he wanted to rule all kingdoms. He may be mad, but he is no fool. A threat is coming, witch, and not from the South, or North, or even East, but the West. A threat of fire and disease and death and rot coming from across the sea—all the great elders, fetish priests, and yerewolos have seen it. I have seen them in the third eye, men red like blood and white like sand. And only one kingdom, a united kingdom, can withstand them and the moons, years, and ages of assault. And only one strong king, not a mad one, and not a malformed blood addict with a mother mad for power, for neither could conquer, nor rule, nor a whole kingdom keep. This Mweru queen, does she not know why the house of Akum ended that line of succession? He said it all night. A threat was coming, an ill wind. And that boy, that little abomination, he must be destroyed. You are nothing but a life lived in a lie."

"A lie, a lie, a lie," the boy said, and giggled. We all looked at him. Up to now I had never heard him speak. He still writhed and bent himself, touching his toes, curling on the ground, the Aesi having let go of his ear.

"He dies tonight," the Aesi said.

"He dies from my ax," I said.

"No," Sogolon said.

"A lie, a lie, a lie ha ha ha," the boy said again.

"A lie, a lie, a lie ha ha ha," Nyka said. I had forgotten about him. He approached the child, both of them saying it over and over until they were one voice. Nyka stopped right in front of the child.

The child ran towards him and leapt into an embrace. Nyka grabbed him, wrapped him in a hug. The boy leaned in on his chest, resting, nuzzling like a baby lamb. Then Nyka flinched and I knew the boy had bitten into him. The boy was sucking blood like mother's milk. Nyka wrapped his arms around him. He flapped his wings until his feet were off the ground. He rose higher, and higher, this time not sinking, not collapsing, not dipping from the weight or from his weakness. Nyka flapped his wings again and a lightning bolt, white and brighter than the sun, sliced through the sky and struck them both. The ground shook from the boom, which was too loud for anyone to hear the boy scream. The lightning struck and stayed, blasting them both as Nyka held tight against the boy kicking and scream-ing, until the long bolt sparked a flame that spread over them and blew out quick, leaving nothing but little light embers that vanished in the black.

"Oh cursed kings, oh cursed kings!" Sogolon wailed.

She wailed for so long that when it finally weak-ened, it became a whimper. I smelled burned flesh, and waited for something to come over me—not peace, not satisfaction, not the sense of balance from revenge, but something I did not know. But I knew I waited for it, and I knew it would not come. The Leopard coughed.

"Leopard!"

I ran over to him, and he nodded his head like a drunkard. I knew his blood was gone. I pulled the sword from his chest and he gasped. He fell from the tree and I caught him and we both fell to the ground. I pressed my hand to his chest. He had always wanted to die as a leopard, but I couldn't imagine him changing now. He grabbed my hand and pulled it to his face.

"Your problem is that you were never any better than a bad archer. This is why we have had such bad fates, you and I," he said.

I held his head and stroked the back of his neck as I would a cat, hoping it brought relief. He was still trying to change, I could feel it under his skin. His forehead thickened, and his whiskers and teeth grew, his eyes shone in the dark, but he could change no further.

"Let us switch bodies in the next of our lives," I said.

"You hate raw meat and could never bear even a finger up your ass," he said, and laughed, but it turned into a cough. The cough shook him and blood from his wound oozed between my fingers.

"Should never have come for you. Should never have taken you out of your tree," he said, coughing.

"You came for me because you knew I would go. Here is truth. I was in love and I was in boredom, both at the same time, two rulers in the same house. I was going mad."

"I made you leave. Remember what I said? **Nkita ghara igbo uja a guo ya aha ozo.**"

"If a wolf refuses to howl, people will give it another name."

"I lied. It was if a dog refuses to bark."

I laughed while he tried to.

"I left because I wanted to."

"But I knew you would. In Fasisi when they asked, How will you find this man? He . . . has been dead twenty moons. I said . . . I said—" He coughed. "I said, I know a tracker, he could never resist good sport. He says he works for the coin, but the work is his pay though he will never admit it."

"I should not have left," I said.

"No, you should not have. What lives we lead. Remorse for what we should not have done, regret for what we should. I miss being a leopard, Tracker. I miss never knowing should."

"And now you are dying."

"Leopards do not know of death. They never think of it, because it is nothing to think of. Why do we do this, Tracker? Why do we think of nothing?"

"I don't know. Because we have to believe in something."

"A man I knew said he didn't believe in belief." He laughed and coughed.

"A man I knew said nobody loves no one."

"Both of them only fools. Only f . . ."

His head fell back in my arms.

Give them no peace, cat. Find sport in the underworld and shame its lords, I thought but did not say. He was the first man I could say I loved, though he was not the first man I would say it to.

I wondered if I would ever stop to think of these years, and I knew I would not, for I would try to find sense, or story, or even a reason for everything, the way I hear them in great stories. Tales about ambition and missions, when we did nothing but try to find a boy, for a reason that turned false, for people who turned false.

Maybe this was how all stories end, the ones with true women and men, true bodies falling into wounding and death, and with real blood spilled. And maybe this is why the great stories we told are so different. Because we tell stories to live, and that sort of story needs a purpose, so that sort of story must be a lie. Because at the end of a true story, there is nothing but waste.

Sogolon spat in the dirt.

"I wish my eyes had never seen your face," I said.

"I wish my eye never see me too."

I picked up Leopard's sword. I could bring it down on her head right there, slice the skull in two like cutting a melon open.

"You wish to kill me. Better hurry up and do it. For me live a good—"

"Fuck the gods and your mouth, Sogolon. Your queen couldn't even remember your name when I told her you were dead. Besides, if I kill you, who will send news to the King sister that her little snake is dead? How goes our fellowship now, witch? The Leopard should see the one who killed him, right behind him in the underworld. The gods would laugh, wouldn't they?"

"There are no gods. This Aesi didn't tell you? Even

now you head so hard you don't see what truly taking place."

"Truth and you never lived in the same house. We are at the end of this tale, you and I."

"He is the god butcher!"

"A new thing? But we are at the end of this story, Moon Witch. Take up this new thing with whatever hungry beast comes for your face."

Sogolon gulped.

"Survival has always been your only skill," I said.

"Wolf boy, give me drink. Give me drink!"

I looked at her head, like a black stone on the ground, swinging around, trying to move out of the ground. I searched for my ax and could not find it. And my knives were long gone. Losing them made me think of losing everything else. Cutting everything loose. I took the holster off my back, pulled my belt, and stepped out of my tunic and loincloth. I started walking north, following that star to the right of the moon. He came and went quick, like an afterthought, he did. The Aesi. He appeared in that way, as if he was always here, and left in that way, as if he never was. The hyenas would make use of the Leopard. It was the way of the bush, and it would have been what he wanted.

Maybe this was the part where men with smarter heads and bigger hearts than mine looked at how the crocodile ate the moon, and how the world spins around the gods of sky, especially the gone sun god, regardless of what men and women do in their lands. And maybe from that came some wisdom, or something that sounded like it. But all I wanted to do was walk, not to anything, not from anything, just away. From behind me I heard, "Give me drink! Give me drink!"

Sogolon kept shouting.

I kept walking.

I walked the lands for days, and across wetlands and dryland until I was in Omororo, the seat of your mad King. Where men detained me as a beggar, took me for a thief, tortured me as a traitor, and when the King sister heard of her child dead, arrested me as a murderer.

And now look at me and you, in Nigiki city-state, where neither of us wants to be, but neither of us has anywhere to go.

I know you've heard her testimony. So, what does mighty Sogolon say?

Does she say, Do not trust one word coming from Tracker's mouth? Not about the boy, not about the search, not about Kongor, not about Dolingo, not about who died and who was saved, not about the ten and nine doors, not about his so-called friend, the Leopard, or his so-called lover from the East, called Mossi, and was that even his name, and were they even lovers? Or his precious mingi children that he did not spawn? Did she say, Trust no word coming from the lips of that Wolf Eye?

Tell me.

ACKNOWLEDGMENTS

Writers never create great stories. We find them. So thanks to everyone who allowed me to listen in and find worlds beyond words.

For immense support, guidance, generosity, and sometimes blind faith, I would like to thank Ellen Levine, my wonderful agent; Jake Morrissey, my just as wonderful editor; Jeff Bennett, writer, researcher, assistant, great friend, and fine human being; Jynne Dilling Martin, Claire McGinnis, Geoffrey Kloske, and all the folks at Riverhead; Martha Kanya-Forstner, Kiara Kent, and everybody else at Doubleday Canada; Simon Prosser at Hamish Hamilton; Macalester College English Department; Robert McLean; all the researchers and scholars doing the tireless, sometimes thankless investigative and archival work on African history and mythology, including those badass librarians from Timbuktu; Fab 5 Freddy for putting up that Facebook post that sparked a million ideas; and Pablo Camacho for that absolutely stunning cover. My mother is allowed to read all but two pages of this book.